PS, I LOVE YOU

Before embarking on her writing career, Cecelia Ahern completed a degree in journalism and media studies. Her first novel, *PS, I Love You* was one of the biggest-selling debut novels of 2004 and a number one bestseller. Her successive bestselling novels are *Where Rainbows End*, *If You Could See Me Now* and *A Place Called Here*. *PS, I Love You*, starring Hilary Swank, is now a major motion picture.

Cecelia lives in County Dublin where she is currently working on her next novel. For more information on Cecelia Ahern, please visit www.cecelia-ahern.com.

Visit www.AuthorTracker.co.uk for exclusive updates on Cecelia Ahern.

Praise for Cecelia Ahern:

'There's more than a touch of fairytale about Cecelia Ahern's novels.'
Glamour

'A sensational debut novel that proves true love never dies.'
Cosmopolitan

'A wonderfully life-affirming debut.'
Company

'Like an Irish *Sleepless in Seattle* and almost certainly the chick-lit bestseller of the year.'
In Style

By the same author

Where Rainbows End
A Place Called Here

CECELIA AHERN

PS, I Love You

If You Could See
Me Now

HARPER

Harper
An imprint of HarperCollins*Publishers*
77–85 Fulham Palace Road,
Hammersmith, London W6 8JB

www.harpercollins.co.uk

This omnibus edition 2008
1

Set in Sabon by Palimpsest Book Production Limited,
Polmont, Stirlingshire

Printed and bound in Great Britain by
Clays Ltd, St Ives plc

Mixed Sources
Product group from well-managed
forests and other controlled sources
www.fsc.org Cert no. SW-COC-1806
© 1996 Forest Stewardship Council
FSC

FSC is a non-profit international organisation established to promote the
responsible management of the world's forests. Products carrying the FSC
label are independently certified to assure consumers that they come from
forests that are managed to meet the social, economic and
ecological needs of present and future generations.

Find out more about HarperCollins and the environment at
www.harpercollins.co.uk/green

PS, I Love You

Writing this book was a labour of love and there are so many people I owe thanks to for allowing me to share it with the world.

I owe huge gratitude to my family for their love and support, without which this book would most definitely never have been born. The ever patient and encouraging clan, the big engine that is such a motivation to this little train; Mimmie, Dad, Georgina, Nicky and David. Welcome to the world Rocco and Jay.

Thank you to my agent Marianne Gunn O'Connor who goes far beyond the call of duty to encourage, inspire and help make the magic happen. Thanks also to Vicki Satlow and Pat Lynch for such hard work and belief in my work.

Thank you to the HarperCollins team for their endless support. Thanks to Lynne Drew, Maxine Hitchcock, Amanda Ridout, Moira Reilly (who was there before it even started), Fiona Mcintosh, Claire Bord and the many many other people involved.

Thank you to all the readers and booksellers for getting behind this book in such an overwhelming way. I am eternally grateful.

But most importantly, thank you to Holly and Gerry for visiting my imagination that night with their story. You made an impact and have never left my mind.

For David

Chapter One

Holly held the blue cotton sweater to her face and the familiar smell immediately struck her, an overwhelming grief knotting her stomach and pulling at her heart. Pins and needles ran up the back of her neck and a lump in her throat threatened to choke her. Panic took over. Apart from the low hum of the fridge and the occasional moaning of the pipes, the house was quiet. She was alone. Bile rose in her throat and she ran to the bathroom, where she collapsed to her knees before the toilet.

Gerry was gone and he would never be back. That was the reality. She would never again run her fingers through his soft hair, never share a secret joke across the table at a dinner party, never cry to him when she got home from a hard day at work and just needed a hug, she would never share a bed with him again, never be woken up by his fits of sneezes each morning, never laugh with him so much her stomach would ache, never fight with him about whose turn it was to get up and turn the bedroom light off. All that was left was a bundle of memories, and an image of his face that became more and more vague each day.

1

Their plan had been very simple: to stay together for the rest of their lives. A plan that anyone within their circle would agree was accomplishable. They were best friends, lovers and soul mates, destined to be together, everyone thought. But as it happened, one day destiny greedily changed its mind.

The end had come all too soon. After complaining of a migraine for a few days, Gerry had agreed to Holly's advice to see his doctor. This was done one Wednesday on a lunch break from work. They thought the migraine was due to stress or tiredness, and agreed that at the very worst he might need glasses. Gerry had been upset that he might need glasses. He needn't have worried, since it turned out it wasn't his eyes that were the problem. It was the tumour growing inside his brain.

Holly flushed the toilet and, shivering from the coldness of the tiled floor, she shakily steadied herself to her feet. He was thirty years old. By no means was he the healthiest man on the earth, but he was healthy enough to . . . well, to live a normal life. When he became very sick he would bravely joke about how he shouldn't have lived life so safely. Should have taken drugs, should have drunk more, should have travelled more, should have jumped out of aeroplanes while waxing his legs . . . his list went on. Even as he laughed about it Holly could see the regret in his eyes. Regret for the things he'd never made time to do, places he'd never seen and sorrow for the loss of future experiences. Did he regret the life he had had with her? Holly never doubted that he loved her, but feared he felt he had wasted precious time.

Growing older became something he wanted desperately to accomplish rather than merely a dreaded inevitability. How presumptuous they both were never to consider growing old as an achievement and a challenge. Ageing was something they wanted so much to avoid.

Holly drifted from room to room while she sobbed far, salty tears. Her eyes were red and sore, and there seemed to be no end to this night. None of the rooms in the house provided her with any solace, just unwelcoming silences as she stared around at the furniture. She longed for the couch to hold out its arms to her but even it ignored her.

Gerry would not be happy with this, she thought. She took a deep breath, dried her eyes and tried to shake some sense into herself. No, Gerry would not be pleased at all.

Holly's eyes were tender and puffy from crying all through the night. Just as she had every other night for the past few weeks, she had fallen into fitful sleep in the early hours of the morning. Each day she woke to find herself sprawled uncomfortably across some piece of furniture – today it was the couch. Once again it was the phone call from a concerned friend or family member that roused her. They probably thought that all she did was sleep. Where were their phone calls when she listlessly roamed the house like a zombie, searching the rooms for . . . for what? What was she expecting to find?

'Hello,' she answered groggily. Her voice was hoarse from all the tears but she had long stopped

3

caring about maintaining a brave face. Her best friend was gone and nobody understood that no amount of make-up, fresh air or shopping was going to fill the hole in her heart.

'Oh, sorry, love, did I wake you?' the concerned voice of Holly's mother came across the line. Every morning her mother called to see if she had survived the night alone, always afraid of waking her, yet always relieved to hear her speak; safe in the knowledge her daughter had braved the ghosts of the night.

'No, I was just dozing, it's OK.' Always the same answer.

'Your dad and Declan have gone out and I was thinking of you, pet.'

Why did that soothing sympathetic voice always send tears to Holly's eyes? She could picture her mother's face, eyebrows furrowed, forehead wrinkled with worry. But it didn't soothe Holly. It made her remember why they were worried and that they shouldn't have to be. Everything should be normal. Gerry should be here beside her, rolling his eyes up to heaven and trying to make her laugh while her mother yapped on. So many times Holly would have to hand the phone over to Gerry as her fit of giggles took over. Then he would chat away, ignoring Holly as she jumped around the bed, pulling her silliest faces and doing her funniest dances just to get back at him. It seldom worked.

She 'ummed' and 'aahed' throughout the conversation, listening but not hearing a word.

'It's a lovely day, Holly. It would do you the world of good to go out for a walk. Get some fresh air.'

4

'Um, I suppose.' There it was again – fresh air, the alleged answer to all her problems.

'Maybe I'll call round later and we can have a chat.'

'No thanks, Mum. I'm OK.'

Silence.

'Well, all right . . . give me a ring if you change your mind. I'm free all day.'

'OK.' Another silence. 'Thanks, though.'

'Right then . . . take care, love.'

'I will.' Holly was about to replace the phone when she heard her mother's voice again.

'Oh, Holly, I almost forgot. That envelope is still here for you – you know, the one I told you about. It's on the kitchen table. You might want to collect it. It's been here for weeks now and it might be important.'

'I doubt it. It's probably just another card.'

'No, I don't think it is, love. It's addressed to you and above your name it says . . . oh, hold on while I get it . . .'

The phone was put down, the sound of heels on the tiles toward the table, chairs screeched against the floor, footsteps getting louder, phone being picked up . . .

'You still there?'

'Yeah.'

'OK, it says at the top "The List". Maybe it's from work or something, love. It's worth just taking a . . .'

Holly dropped the phone.

Chapter Two

'Gerry, turn off the light!' Holly giggled as she watched her husband undress before her. He danced around the room performing a striptease, slowly unbuttoning his white cotton shirt with his long slender fingers. He raised his left eyebrow towards Holly and allowed the shirt to slide from his shoulders, caught it in his right hand and swung it around over his head.

Holly giggled again.

'Turn off the light? What, and miss all this?' he grinned cheekily while flexing his muscles. He wasn't a vain man but had much to be vain about, thought Holly. His body was strong and perfectly toned. His long legs were muscular from hours spent working out in the gym. At almost six foot he was tall enough to make Holly feel safe when he stood protectively beside her five foot five. Most of all she loved that when she hugged him her head would rest neatly just below his chin, where she could feel his breath lightly blowing her hair and tickling her head.

Her heart leaped as he lowered his boxers, caught them on the tip of his toes and flung them at her where they landed on her head.

'Well, at least it's darker under here, anyway,' she laughed. He always managed to make her laugh. When she came home tired and angry after work he was invariably sympathetic and listened to her complaining. They seldom fought, and when they did it was over stupid things that amused them after, like who had left the porch light on all day or who had forgotten to set the alarm at night.

Gerry finished his striptease and dived into the bed. He snuggled up beside her tucking his freezing cold feet underneath her legs to warm himself.

'Aaaagh! Gerry, your feet are like ice cubes!' Holly knew that this position meant he had no intention of budging an inch. 'Gerry,' Holly's voice warned.

'Holly,' he mimicked.

'Didn't you forget something?'

'No, not that I know of,' he answered.

'The light?'

'Ah yes, the light,' he said sleepily, and pretended to snore loudly.

'Gerry!'

'I had to get out of bed and do it last night, as I remember.'

'Yeah, but you were just standing right beside the switch a second ago!'

'Yes . . . just a second ago,' he repeated.

Holly sighed. She hated having to get back out of bed when she was nice and snug, step onto the cold wooden floor, and then fumble around in the darkness on the way back to the bed. She tutted.

'I can't do it all the time, you know, Hol. Someday I might not be here and then what will you do?'

'Get my new husband to do it,' Holly huffed, trying her best to kick his cold feet away from hers.

'Ha!'

'Or just remember to do it myself before I get into bed.'

Gerry snorted. 'Fat chance of that happening, my dear. I'll have to leave a message on the light switch for you before I go, just so you'll remember.'

'How thoughtful of you but I would rather you just leave me your money.'

'And a note on the immersion,' he continued on.

'Ha-ha.'

'And on the milk carton.'

'You're a very funny man, Gerry.'

'Oh, and on the windows so you don't open them and set the alarm off in the mornings.'

'Hey, why don't you just leave me a list of things for me to do in your will if you think I'll be so incompetent without you?'

'Not a bad idea,' he laughed.

'Fine then, I'll turn off the bloody light.' Holly grudgingly got out of bed, grimaced as she stepped onto the ice-cold floor and switched off the light. She held out her arms in the darkness and slowly began to find her way back to the bed.

'Hello? Holly, did you get lost? Is there anybody out there, there, there, there?' Gerry shouted out to the black room.

'Yes, I'm hhhhowwwwwwcch!' she yelped as she stubbed her toe against the bedpost. 'Shit, shit, shit, fuck, bastard, shit, crap!'

Gerry snorted and sniggered underneath the duvet.

8

'Number two on my list: watch out for bedpost . . .'

'Oh, shut up, Gerry, and stop being so morbid,' Holly snapped back at him, cradling her poor foot in her hand.

'Want me to kiss it better?' he asked.

'No, it's OK,' Holly replied sadly, 'if I could just put them here so I can warm . . .'

'Aaaaah! Jesus Christ, they're freezing!!'

Which made her laugh again.

So that was how the joke about the list came about. It was a silly and simple idea that was soon shared with their closest friends, Sharon and John McCarthy.

It was John who had approached Holly in the school corridor when they were just fourteen and muttered the famous words, 'Me mate wants to know if you'll go out with him.' After days of endless discussion and emergency meetings with her friends, Holly eventually agreed.

'Aah, go on, Holly,' Sharon had urged. 'He's such a ride, and at least he doesn't have spots all over his face like John.'

How Holly envied Sharon right now. Sharon and John had married the same year as Holly and Gerry. Holly was the baby of the bunch at twenty-three, the others were twenty-four. Some said she was too young and lectured her about how, at her age, she should be travelling the world and enjoying herself. Instead, Gerry and Holly travelled the world together. It made far more sense that way because when they weren't together . . . well, Holly just felt as though she was missing a vital organ from her body.

Her wedding day was far from the best day of her life. Like most little girls, she had dreamed of a fairy-tale wedding with a princess dress and beautiful, sunny weather, in a romantic location surrounded by all who were near and dear to her. She imagined the reception would be the best night of her life, pictured herself dancing with all of her friends, being admired by everyone and feeling special. The reality was quite different.

She woke up in her family home to screams of, 'I can't find my tie!' (her father), or, 'My hair looks shite' (her mother), and the best one of all was, 'I look like a bloody whale! There's no way I'm going to this bleeding wedding looking like this. I'll be scarlet! Mum, look at the state of me! Holly can find another bridesmaid 'cos I'm not bleedin goin. Oi! Jack, give me back that feckin hair dryer, I'm not finished!' That unforgettable statement was made by her younger sister, Ciara, who very regularly threw tantrums and refused to leave the house on the basis of having nothing to wear, regardless of her bursting wardrobe. She was currently living somewhere in Australia with strangers, and the only communication the family had with her was an email from her every few weeks. Holly's family spent the rest of the morning trying to convince Ciara how she was the most beautiful woman in the world. All the while Holly silently dressed herself feeling like shite. Ciara eventually agreed to leave the house when Holly's usually calm dad screamed at the top of his voice, and to everyone's amazement, 'Ciara, this is Holly's bloody day, NOT YOURS! And you WILL go to the wedding and enjoy yourself AND when Holly walks downstairs you WILL tell her how beautiful she looks and I don't wanna hear a peep out of you FOR THE REST OF THE DAY!'

So when Holly walked downstairs everyone oohed and aahed while Ciara, looking like a ten-year-old who had just been spanked, tearfully gazed at her with a trembling lip and said, 'You look beautiful, Holly.' All seven of them squashed into the limo – Holly, her parents, three brothers and Ciara, and sat in terrified silence all the way to the church.

The whole day just seemed a blur to her now. She barely had time to speak to Gerry, as they were both being pulled in opposite directions to meet Great-aunt Betty from the back arse of nowhere, whom Holly hadn't seen since she was born, and Grand-uncle Toby from America, who had never been mentioned before but was suddenly a very important member of the family.

And nobody told her it would be so tiring either. By the end of the night Holly's jaw was sore from smiling for photographs, and her feet were killing her from running around all day in very silly little shoes. She desperately wanted to join the large table of her friends who had been howling with laughter all night, obviously enjoying themselves. Well for some, she thought. But as soon as Holly stepped into the honeymoon suite with Gerry her worries of the day faded and the point of it all became clear.

Tears once again rolled down Holly's face and she realised she had been daydreaming again. She sat frozen on the couch with the phone still off the hook

11

beside her. The hours just seemed to pass her by these days without her knowing what time or even what day it was. She seemed to be living outside of her body, numb to everything but the pain in her heart, in her bones, in her head. She was just so tired . . . Her stomach grumbled and she realised she couldn't remember the last time she had eaten. Had it been yesterday?

She shuffled into the kitchen, dressed in Gerry's dressing gown and her favourite pink 'disco diva' slippers that Gerry had bought her the previous Christmas. She was his disco diva, he used to say. Always the first on the dance floor, always the last out of the club. Huh, where was that girl now? She opened the fridge and stared in at the empty shelves. Just vegetables and yogurt long past its sell-by date leaving a horrible stench in the fridge. She smiled weakly as she shook the milk carton. Empty. Third on his list . . .

Christmas two years ago Holly had gone shopping with Sharon for a dress for the annual ball they attended at the Burlington Hotel. Shopping with Sharon was always a dangerous outing, and John and Gerry had joked about how they would once again suffer through Christmas without any presents as a result of the girls' sprees. They weren't far wrong. Poor neglected husbands, the girls always called them.

Holly had spent a disgraceful amount of money in Brown Thomas on the most beautiful white dress she had ever seen.

'Shit, Sharon, this will burn a huge hole in my

pocket,' she said guiltily, biting her lip and running her fingers over the soft material.

'Aah, don't worry, Gerry can stitch it up for you,' Sharon replied with her infamous cackle. 'And stop calling me "shit Sharon". Every time we go shopping you address me as that. If you're not careful I might start taking offence. Buy the damn thing, Holly. It's Christmas, after all, the season of giving and all that.'

'God, you are so evil, Sharon. I'm never shopping with you again. This is like half my month's wages. What am I going to do for the rest of the month?'

'Holly, would you rather eat or look fab?'

'I'll take it,' Holly said excitedly to the sales assistant.

The dress was low cut, which showed off Holly's neat little chest perfectly, and it was split to the thigh, displaying her slim legs. Gerry hadn't been able to take his eyes off her. It wasn't because she looked so beautiful, however. He just couldn't understand how on earth such a little slip of material had cost that much. Once at the ball, Ms Disco Diva once again overindulged in the alcoholic beverages and succeeded in destroying her dress by spilling red wine down her front. Holly tried but failed to hold back her tears while the men at the table drunkenly informed their partners that number fifty-four on the list prevented you from drinking red wine while wearing an expensive white dress. It was then decided that milk was the preferred beverage, as it wouldn't be visible if spilt on expensive white dresses.

Later, when Gerry knocked his pint over causing it to dribble off the edge of the table into Holly's lap, she tearfully yet seriously announced to the table (and some of the surrounding tables), 'Rule fitty-fife ov the list: NEFFER EFFER buy a spensive white dress.' So it was agreed, and Sharon awoke from her coma from somewhere underneath the table to applaud and offer moral support. A toast was made (after a startled waiter had delivered a tray full of glasses of milk) to Holly and to her profound addition to the list.

'I'm sorry bout your spensive white dress, Holly,' John had hiccuped to Holly, before falling out of the taxi and dragging Sharon alongside him into their house.

Was it possible that Gerry had kept his word and had written a list for her before he died? She had spent every minute of every day with him up until his death and he had never even mentioned it, nor had she noticed any signs of him writing it. No, Holly, pull yourself together and don't be stupid, she told herself. She so desperately wanted him back that she was imagining all kinds of crazy things. He wouldn't have. Would he?

Chapter Three

Holly was walking through an entire field of pretty tiger lilies; the wind was blowing gently, causing the silky petals to tickle the tips of her fingers as she pushed through long strands of bright green grass. The ground was soft and bouncy beneath her bare feet and her body felt so light she was almost floating just above the spongy earth. All around her, birds whistled their happy tune as they went about their business. The sun was so bright in the cloudless sky she had to shield her eyes, and with each brush of wind that passed her face the sweet scent of the tiger lilies filled her nostrils. She felt so . . . happy, so free.

Suddenly the sky darkened as the Caribbean sun disappeared behind a looming grey cloud. The wind picked up and the air chilled. Around her all the petals of the tiger lilies were racing through the air wildly, blurring her vision. The once spongy ground was replaced with sharp stones that cut and scraped her feet with every step. The birds had stopped singing and instead perched on their branches and stared. Something was wrong, and she felt afraid. Ahead of her in the distance a grey stone was visible amidst the tall grass. She wanted to run back to her pretty flowers, but she needed to find out what was ahead.

As she crept closer she heard BANG! BANG! BANG! She quickened her pace and raced over the sharp stones and jagged-edged grass that tore at her arms and legs. She collapsed to her knees in front of the grey slab and let out a scream of pain as she realised what it was. Gerry's grave. BANG! BANG! BANG!

He was trying to get out. He was calling her name; she could hear him!

Holly jumped from her sleep to a loud banging on the front door.

'Holly! Holly! I know you're there! Please let me in!' BANG! BANG! BANG!

Confused and half asleep, she made her way to the door to a frantic-looking Sharon.

'Christ! What were you doing? I've been banging on the door for ages!'

Holly looked around outside, still not fully alert. It was bright and slightly chilly – must be morning.

'Well, aren't you going to let me in?'

'Yeah, Sharon, sorry. I was just dozing on the couch.'

'God, you look terrible, Hol.' Sharon studied her face before giving her a big hug.

'Wow, thanks.' Holly rolled her eyes and turned to shut the door. Sharon was never one to beat about the bush, but that's why she loved her so much. That's also why Holly hadn't been around to see Sharon for the past month. She didn't want to hear the truth. She didn't want to hear how she had to get on with

16

her life; she just wanted . . . oh, she didn't know what she wanted. She was content to be miserable. It somehow felt right.

'God, it's so stuffy in here. When's the last time you opened a window?' Sharon marched around the house, opening windows and picking up empty cups and plates. She brought them into the kitchen where she placed them in the dishwasher and then proceeded to tidy up.

'Oh, you don't have to do it, Sharon,' Holly protested weakly. 'I'll do it . . .'

'When? Next year? I don't want you slumming it while the rest of us pretend not to notice. Why don't you go upstairs and shower, and we'll have a cup of tea when you come down?'

A shower. When was the last time she had even washed? Sharon was right, she must have looked disgusting, with her greasy hair, her dark roots and dirty robe. Gerry's robe. But that was something she never intended to wash. She wanted it exactly as Gerry had left it. Unfortunately, his smell was beginning to fade, replaced by the unmistakable stink of her own skin.

'OK, but there's no milk. I haven't got around to . . .' Holly felt embarrassed by her lack of care for the house and for herself. There was no way she was letting Sharon look inside that fridge or she would definitely have her committed.

'Ta-da!' Sharon sang, holding up a bag Holly hadn't noticed her carry in. 'Don't worry, I took care of that. By the looks of it you haven't eaten in weeks.'

'Thanks, Sharon.' A lump formed in Holly's throat

17

and tears welled in her eyes. She was being so good to her.

'Hold it! There will be no tears today! Just fun and laughter and general happiness, my dear friend. Now shower, quick!'

Holly felt almost human when she came back downstairs. She was dressed in a blue tracksuit and allowed her long blonde (and brown at the roots) hair to fall down on her shoulders. All the windows downstairs were wide open and the cool breeze rushed through Holly's head. It felt as though it was eliminating all her bad thoughts and fears. She laughed at the possibility of her mother being right after all. Holly snapped out of her trance and gasped as she looked around the house. She can't have been any longer than a half an hour but Sharon had tidied and polished, vacuumed and plumped, washed, and sprayed air freshener in every room. She followed the humming noise she could hear to the kitchen where Sharon was scrubbing the hobs. The counters were gleaming; the chrome taps and draining board sparkling.

'Sharon, you absolute angel! I can't believe you did all this. And in such a short time!'

'Ha! You were gone for over an hour. I was beginning to think you'd fallen down the plughole. You would and all, the size of you.' She looked Holly up and down.

An hour? Once again Holly's daydreaming had taken over her mind.

'OK, so I just bought some vegetables and fruit, there's cheese and yogurts in there, and milk, of

18

course. I don't know where you keep the pasta and tinned foods so I just put them over there. Oh, and there's a few microwave dinners in the freezer. That should do you for a while, but by the looks of you it'll last you the year. How much weight have you lost?'

Holly looked down at her body. Her tracksuit was sagging at the bum and the waist tie was pulled to its tightest, yet still drooped to her hips. She hadn't noticed the weight loss at all.

She was brought back to reality by Sharon's voice again: 'There's a few biscuits there to go with your tea. Jammie Dodgers, your favourite.'

That did it. This was all too much for Holly. The Jammie Dodgers were the icing on the cake. She felt the tears run down her face. 'Oh, Sharon,' she wailed, 'thank you so much. You've been so good to me and I've been such a horrible, horrible bitch of a friend.' She sat at the table and grabbed Sharon's hand. 'I don't know what I'd do without you.' Sharon sat opposite her in silence, allowing her to continue. This is what Holly had been dreading, breaking down in front of people at every possible occasion. But she didn't feel embarrassed. Sharon was just patiently sipping her tea and holding her hand like it was normal. Eventually the tears stopped falling.

'Thanks.'

'I'm your best friend, Hol; if I don't help you then who will?' Sharon said, squeezing her hand and giving her an encouraging smile.

'Suppose I should be helping myself.'

'Pah!' Sharon spat, waving her hand dismissively.

'When-ever you're ready. Don't mind all those people who say that you should be back to normal in a month. Grieving is all part of helping yourself, anyway.'

She always said the right things.

'Yeah, well, I've been doing a lot of that. I'm all grieved out.'

'You can't be!' said Sharon, mock disgusted. 'And only a month after your husband is cold in his grave.'

'Oh, stop! There'll be plenty of that from people, though, won't there?'

'Probably, but screw them. There are worse sins in the world than learning to be happy again.'

'Suppose.'

'Promise me you'll eat.'

'Promise.'

'Thanks for coming round, Sharon. I really enjoyed the chat,' Holly said, gratefully hugging her friend. 'I feel a lot better already.'

'You know it's good to be around people, Hol. Friends and family can help you. Well, actually, on second thoughts, maybe not your family,' she joked, 'but at least the rest of us can.'

'Oh, I realise that now. I just thought I could handle it on my own at first.'

'Promise me you'll call round. Or at least get out of the house once in a while.'

'Promise.' Holly rolled her eyes. 'You're beginning to sound like my mum.'

'We're all just looking out for you. OK, see you soon,' Sharon said, kissing her on the cheek, 'and EAT!' she added, poking her in the ribs.

Holly waved to Sharon as she pulled away in her car. It was nearly dark. They had spent the day laughing and joking about old times, then crying, followed by some more laughing, then more crying again. Sharon had given her perspective too. Holly hadn't even thought about the fact that Sharon and John had lost their best friend, that her parents had lost their son-in-law and Gerry's parents had lost their only son. She had just been so busy thinking about herself. It had been good being with the living again, instead of moping around with the ghosts of her past. Tomorrow was a new day and she intended on beginning it by collecting that envelope.

Chapter Four

Holly started her Friday morning well by getting up early. However, although she had gone to bed full of optimism, and excited about the prospects that lay ahead of her, she was struck afresh by the harsh reality of how difficult every moment would be. Once again she awoke in an empty bed to a silent house, but there was one small breakthrough. For the first time in over a month, she had woken up without the aid of a telephone call. She adjusted her mind, as she did every morning, to the fact that the dreams of her and Gerry being together, which had lived in her mind for the past ten hours, were just that: dreams.

She showered and dressed comfortably in her favourite blue jeans, trainers and a baby-pink T-shirt. Sharon had been right about her weight: her once-tight jeans were just about staying up with the aid of a belt. She made a face at her reflection in the mirror. She looked ugly. She had black circles under her eyes, her lips were chapped and chewed and her hair was a disaster. First thing to do was to go down to her local hairdressers and pray they could squeeze her in.

'Jaysus, Holly!' her stylist, Leo, exclaimed. 'Would ya look at the state of ya! People, make way! Make way! I have a woman here in a critical condition!' He winked at her and proceeded to push people from his path. He pulled out the chair for her and pushed her into it.

'Thanks, Leo. I feel really attractive now,' Holly muttered, trying to hide her beetroot-coloured face.

'Well, don't, 'cos you're in bits. Sandra, mix me up the usual, Colin get the foil, Tania get me my little bag of tricks from upstairs – oh, and tell Will not to bother getting his lunch, he's doing my twelve o'clock.' Leo ordered everyone around, his hands flailing wildly as though he was about to perform emergency surgery. Perhaps he was.

'Oh sorry, Leo, I didn't mean to mess up your day.'

'Of course you did, love. Why else would you come rushing in here at lunchtime on a Friday without an appointment? To help world peace?'

Holly guiltily bit her lip.

'Ah, but I wouldn't do it for anyone else but you, love.'

'Thanks.'

'How have you been?' He rested his skinny little behind on the counter facing Holly. Leo must have been fifty years old yet he didn't look a day over thirty. His honey-coloured hair matched his honey-coloured skin, and he always dressed so perfectly. He was enough to make any woman feel like crap.

'Terrible.'

'Yeah, you look it.'

'Thanks.'

23

'Ah well, at least by the time you walk out of here you'll have one thing sorted. I do hair, not hearts.'

Holly smiled gratefully at his odd little way of showing he understood.

'But, Jaysus, Holly, when you were coming in the door did you see the word "magician" or "hairdresser" on the front of the salon? You should have seen the state of the woman who came in here today. Mutton dressed as lamb. Not far off sixty, I'd say. Handed me a magazine with Jennifer Aniston on the cover. "I want to look like that," she says.'

Holly laughed at his impression. He had the facial expression and the hand movements all going at the same time.

'"Jaysus," I says, "I'm a hairdresser, not a plastic surgeon. The only way you'll look like that is if you cut out the picture and staple it to your head."'

'No! Leo, you didn't tell her that?' Holly's jaw dropped in surprise.

'Of course I did! The woman needed to be told – sure, wasn't I helping her? Swanning in here dressed like a teenager. The state of her!'

'But what did she say?' Holly wiped the tears of laughter from her eyes. She hadn't laughed like this for months.

'I flicked the pages of the mag for her and came across a lovely picture of Joan Collins. Told her it was right up her street. She seemed happy enough with that.'

'Leo, she was probably too terrified to tell you she hated it.'

'Ah, who cares? I have enough friends.'

'Don't know why,' Holly laughed.

'Don't move,' Leo ordered. Suddenly he had become awfully serious and his lips were pursed together in concentration as he separated Holly's hair ready for colouring. That was enough to send Holly into stitches again.

'Ah, come on, Holly,' Leo said in exasperation.

'I can't help it, Leo. You got me started and now I can't stop . . .'

Leo paused in what he was doing and watched her with amusement. 'I always thought you were for the madhouse. No one ever listens to me.'

She laughed even harder. 'Oh, I'm sorry, Leo. I don't know what's wrong with me, I just can't stop.' Holly's stomach ached from laughing so hard and she was aware of all the curious glances she was attracting but she just couldn't help it. It was as if all the missed mirth from the past couple of months were tumbling out at once.

Leo propped himself back on the counter and watched her. 'You don't need to apologise, Holly. Laugh all you like. You know they say it's good for the heart.'

'Oh, I haven't laughed like this for ages,' she chortled.

'Well, you haven't had much to laugh about, I suppose,' he smiled sadly. Leo had loved Gerry too. They'd teased each other whenever they'd met, but they'd both known it was all in fun. Leo snapped himself out of his thoughts, tousled Holly's hair playfully and planted a kiss on the top of her head. 'But you'll be all right, Holly Kennedy,' he assured her.

'Thanks, Leo,' she said, calming herself down,

25

touched by his concern. He went back to work on her hair, putting on his funny little concentrating face, which started Holly off again.

'Oh, you laugh now, Holly, but wait till I accidentally give you a stripy head of colour. We'll see who's laughing then.'

'How's Joe?' Holly asked, keen to change the subject before she embarrassed herself again.

'He dumped me,' Leo said, pushing aggressively with his foot on the chair's pump, sending Holly higher into the air and causing her to jerk wildly in her chair.

'O-oh, Le-eo, I-I-I-'m soooo sor-reeee. Yo-ooou twooo we-eerree soooo gree-aat togeeeeth-eeer.'

'Yeah, well, we're not so gree-aat together now, missy. I think he's seeing someone else. Right. I'm going to put two shades of blonde in: a golden colour and the blonde you had before. Otherwise it'll go that brassy colour that's reserved for my prostitute clientele only.'

'Oh, Leo, I'm sorry. If he has any sense at all he'll realise what he's missing.'

'He mustn't have any sense so. We split up two months ago and he hasn't realised it yet. Or else he has and he's delighted. I'm fed up; I've had enough of men. I'm just going to turn straight.'

'Now *that's* the stupidest thing I've ever heard . . .'

Holly bounced out of the salon with delight. Without Gerry beside her, a few men looked her way, something that was alien to her and made her feel uncomfortable, so she ran to the safety of her car and

26

prepared herself for her parents' house. So far, today was going well. It had been a good move to visit Leo. Even in his heartbreak he worked hard to make her laugh. Holly took note of it.

She pulled up to the kerb outside her parents' house in Portmarnock and took a deep breath. To her mother's surprise Holly had called her first thing in the morning to arrange a time to meet up. It was three thirty now, and Holly sat outside in the car with butterflies in her tummy. Apart from the visits her parents had paid to her over the past month Holly had barely spent any proper time with her family. She didn't want all the attention directed at her, the intrusive questions about how she was feeling and what she was going to do next being fired at her all day. However, it was time to put that fear aside. They were her family.

Her parents' house was situated directly across the road from Portmarnock beach, the blue flag baring testament to its cleanliness. She parked the car and stared across the road to the sea. She had lived here from the day she was born till the day she moved out to live with Gerry. She had loved waking up to the sound of the sea lapping against the rocks, and the excited call of the seagulls. It was wonderful having the beach as your front garden, especially during the summer. Sharon had lived around the corner, and on the hottest days of the year the girls would venture across the road in their summer best and keep an eye out for the best-looking boys. Holly and Sharon were the complete opposite of each other: Sharon with her brown hair, fair skin, and huge bosom; Holly with her blonde hair, sallow skin, and small chest. Sharon would be loud, shouting to the boys and calling them over. Holly would just stay quiet and flirt with her eyes, fixing them on her favourite boy and not moving them till he noticed. Holly and Sharon really hadn't changed all that much since.

She didn't intend staying long, just have a little chat and collect the envelope. She was determined to end her silent self-torture about what could be inside. She took a deep breath, rang the doorbell and placed a smile on her face for all to see.

'Hi, love! Come in, come in!' said her mother with her usual welcoming, loving face that Holly just wanted to kiss every time she saw her.

'Hi, Mum. How are you?' Holly stepped into the house and was comforted by the familiar smell of home. 'You on your own?'

'Yes, your father's out with Declan, buying paint for his room.'

'Don't tell me you and Dad are still paying for everything for him?'

'Well, your father might be, but I'm certainly not. He's working at nights now so at least he has a bit of pocket money these days. Although we don't see a penny of it being spent on anything for here,' she chuckled, and brought Holly to the kitchen where she put the kettle on.

Declan was Holly's youngest brother and the baby of the family, so her mum and dad still felt they had to spoil him. But their 'baby' was now a twenty-two-year-old, studying film production at college and he constantly had a video camera in his hand.

'What job has he got now?'

Her mother rolled her eyes to heaven. 'He's joined some band. The Orgasmic Fish, I think they call themselves, or something like that. I'm sick to death of hearing about it, Holly. If he goes on one more time about who was there at the gigs promising to sign them up and how famous they're going to be I'll go mad.'

'Ah, poor Deco. Don't worry, he'll find something eventually.'

'I know, and it's funny because, of all you darling children, he's the least I worry about. He'll find his way.'

They brought their mugs into the sitting room and settled down in front of the television. 'You look great, pet. I love the hair. Do you think Leo would ever do mine for me, or am I too old for his styles?'

'Well, as long as you don't want Jennifer Aniston's hairstyle, you'll have no problems.' Holly explained about the woman in the salon and they both rolled around laughing.

'I don't want the Joan Collins look, so I'll just stay clear of him.'

'That might be wise.'

'Any luck with a job yet?' Her mother's voice was casual but Holly knew she was just dying to find out.

'No, not yet, Mum. To be honest, I haven't even started looking. I don't quite know what I want to do.'

'You're right,' her mother nodded. 'Take your time and think about what you like or else you'll end up rushing into a job you hate, like the last time.' Holly was surprised to hear this. In fact, everyone was

29

surprising her these days. Perhaps it was herself with the problem and not the rest of the world after all.

The last job Holly had was working as a secretary for an unforgiving little slimeball in a solicitor's office. She had been forced to leave her job when the creep failed to understand that she needed time off work to be with her dying husband. Now she had to go looking for a new one. For a new job that was. But at the moment it seemed unimaginable to go to work in the morning.

Holly and her mother sat in a relaxed atmosphere, falling in and out of conversation for a few hours until Holly finally built up the courage to ask for the envelope.

'Oh, of course, love, I completely forgot about it. I hope it's nothing important. It's been there for a long time.'

'I'll find out soon enough.'

They said their goodbyes and Holly couldn't get out of the house quickly enough.

Perching herself on the grass overlooking the golden sand, Holly ran the envelope over her hands. Her mother hadn't described it very well, for it was not an envelope at all but a thick brown package. The address had been typed onto a plain sticker so she couldn't even guess the origin. But most importantly, above the address were two words, thick and bold: 'THE LIST'.

Her stomach did a little dance. If it wasn't from Gerry, then Holly finally had to accept the fact that he was gone completely from her life and she had to start thinking about existing without him. But if it *was* from him, though she would be faced with the same future, at least she could hold on to some fresh memory. A memory that would have to last her a lifetime.

Her trembling fingers gently tore at the seal of the package. She turned it upside down and shook the contents out. Out fell ten separate tiny envelopes of the kind you would expect to find on a bouquet of flowers, each with a different month written on them. Her heart missed a few beats as she saw the familiar handwriting on a loose page underneath the pile of envelopes.

It was from Gerry.

Chapter Five

Holly held her breath and with tears in her eyes and a pounding heart, she read the words, aware all the time that the person who had sat down to write to her would never be able to do so again. She ran her fingers over Gerry's handwriting, knowing that the last person to have touched the page was him.

My darling Holly,

I don't know where you are or when exactly you are reading this. I just hope that my letter has found you safe and healthy. You whispered to me not long ago that you couldn't go on alone. You can, Holly.

You are strong and brave and you can get through this. We shared some beautiful times together and you made my life . . . you made my life. I have no regrets.

But I am just a chapter in your life – there will be many more. Remember our wonderful memories, but please don't be afraid to make some more.

Thank you for doing me the honour of

*being my wife. For everything, I am eternally
grateful.*

*Whenever you need me, know that I am
with you.*

*Love for ever,
Your husband and best friend,
Gerry.*

*PS. I promised a list, so here it is. The
following envelopes must be opened exactly
when labelled and <u>must be obeyed</u>. And
remember, I'm looking out for you, so I will
know . . .*

Holly broke down, sadness sweeping over her. Yet she
felt relief at the same time; relief that Gerry would
somehow continue to be with her for another little
while. She leafed through the small white envelopes and
searched through the months. It was April now. She
had missed March so she delicately picked out the envelope. She opened it slowly, wanting to savour every
moment. Inside was a small card with Gerry's handwriting on it. It read:

*Save yourself the bruises and buy a bedside
lamp!*

PS. I love you . . .

Her tears turned to laughter as she realised her Gerry
was back!

Holly read and reread his letter over and over again
in an attempt to summon him back to life. Eventually,

33

when she could no longer see the words through her tears, she looked out to sea. She had always found the sea so calming, and even as a child she would run across the road to the beach if she was upset and needed to think. Her parents knew that when she went missing from the house they would find her here by the sea.

She closed her eyes and breathed in and out along with the gentle sighing of the waves. It was as though the sea was taking big deep breaths; pulling the water in while it inhaled and pushing it all back up onto the sand as it exhaled. She continued to breathe along with it and felt her pulse rate slow down as she became calmer. She thought about how she used to lie by Gerry's side during his final days and listen to the sound of his breathing. She had been terrified to leave him, even to answer the door, to fix him some food or to go to the toilet, just in case that was the time he chose to leave her. When she would return to his bedside she would sit frozen in a terrified silence while she listened for his breathing and watched his chest for any movement.

But he'd always managed to hang on. He had baffled the doctors with his strength and determination to live; Gerry wasn't prepared to go without a fight. He kept his good humour right up until the end. He was so weak and his voice so quiet, but Holly had learned to understand his new language as a mother does her babbling child just learning to talk. They would giggle together late into the night and other nights they would hold each other and cry. Holly remained strong for him. Throughout, her new job was to be there for him whenever he needed her.

Looking back on it, she knew that she really needed him more than he needed her. She needed to be needed so she could feel that she wasn't just standing idly by, utterly helpless.

On the second of February at four o'clock in the morning, Holly held Gerry's hand tightly and smiled at him encouragingly as he took his last breath and closed his eyes. She didn't want him to be afraid, and she didn't want him to feel that she was afraid, because at that moment she wasn't. She felt relief – relief that his pain was gone, and relief that she had been there with him to witness the peace of his passing. She felt relieved to have known him, to have loved him and to be loved by him, and relief that the last thing he saw was her face smiling down on him, encouraging him and assuring him it was OK to let go.

The days after that were a blur to her now. She had occupied herself by making the funeral arrangements and by meeting and greeting Gerry's relatives and old school friends that she hadn't seen for years. She remained so solid and calm through it all. She was just thankful that, after months, his suffering was over. It didn't occur to her to feel the anger or bitterness that she felt now for the life that was taken away from her. That feeling didn't arrive until she went to collect her husband's death certificate.

And then that feeling made a grand appearance.

As she sat in the crowded waiting room of her local health clinic, waiting for her number to be called, she wondered why on earth Gerry's number had been called so early in his life. She was sandwiched between a young couple and an elderly one – the picture of what she and Gerry had once been, and a glimpse of the future they could have had. And it all just seemed unfair. While the noise of screaming children was amplified in the room, Holly felt squashed between the shoulders of her past and her lost future, and she felt suffocated. She shouldn't have to be there.

None of her friends had to be there.

None of her family had to be there.

In fact the majority of the population of the world didn't have to be in the position she was in right then.

It didn't seem fair.

Because it just wasn't fair.

After presenting the official proof of her husband's death to bank managers and insurance companies, as if the look on her face wasn't proof enough, Holly returned home to her nest and locked herself away from the rest of the world that contained hundreds of memories of the life she had once had. The life she had been very happy with. So why had she been given another one, and a far worse one at that?

That was two months ago, and she hadn't left the house until today. And what a welcome she had been given, she thought, smiling down at the envelopes. Gerry was back.

Holly could hardly contain her excitement as she furiously dialled Sharon's number with trembling hands. After reaching a few wrong numbers she eventually calmed herself and concentrated on dialling correctly.

'Sharon!' she squealed as soon as the phone was picked up. 'You'll never guess what. Oh my God, I can't believe it!'

'Eh, no . . . it's John, but I'll get her for you now.'
A worried John rushed off to get Sharon.

'What, what, what?' panted a very out-of-breath
Sharon. 'What's wrong? Are you OK?'

'Yes, I'm fine!' Holly started giggling hysterically,
not knowing whether to laugh or cry and suddenly
forgetting how to structure a sentence.

John watched as Sharon sat down at her kitchen
table, looking very confused while she tried with all
her strength to make sense of the rambling Holly. It
was something about Mrs Kennedy giving Holly a
brown envelope with a bedside lamp in it. It was all
very worrying.

'STOP!' shouted Sharon, much to Holly and John's
surprise. 'I cannot understand a word you are saying,
so please,' Sharon spoke very slowly, 'slow down, take
a deep breath and start from the very beginning,
preferably using words from the English language.'

Suddenly she heard quiet sobs from the other end.

'Oh, Sharon,' Holly's words were quiet and broken,
'he wrote me a list. Gerry wrote me a list.'

Sharon froze in her chair while she digested this
information.

John watched his wife's eyes widen and he quickly
pulled out a chair and sat next to her, shoving his
head towards the telephone so he could hear what
was going on.

'OK, Holly, I want you to get over here as quickly
but as *safely* as you can.' Sharon paused again and
swatted John's head away as if he was a fly so she
could concentrate on what she had just heard. 'This
is . . . great news?'

John stood up from the table, insulted, and began to pace the kitchen floor, trying to guess what the news could be.

'Oh, it is, Sharon,' sobbed Holly, 'it really is.'

'OK, make your way over here now and we can talk about it.'

'OK.'

Sharon hung up the phone and sat in silence.

'What? What is it?' demanded John.

'Oh, sorry, love. Holly's on the way over. She . . . em . . . she said that eh . . .'

'WHAT, for Christsake?'

'She said that Gerry wrote her a list.'

John studied her face and tried to decide if she was serious. Sharon's worried blue eyes stared back at him and he realised she was. He joined her at the table and they both sat in silence and stared at the wall, lost in thought.

Chapter Six

'Wow,' was all Sharon and John could say as the three of them sat around the kitchen table in silence, staring at the contents of the package that Holly had emptied as evidence. Conversation between them had been minimal for the last few minutes as they all tried to decide how they felt. It had gone something like this:

'But how did he manage to . . . ?'

'But how didn't we notice him . . . well . . . ? God.'

'When do you think he . . . ? Well, I suppose he was on his own sometimes . . .'

Holly and Sharon just sat looking at each other while John stuttered and stammered his way through trying to figure out just when, where and how his terminally ill friend had managed to carry out this idea all alone without anyone finding out.

'Wow,' he eventually repeated after coming to the conclusion that Gerry had done just that. He had carried it out alone.

'I know,' Holly agreed. 'So the two of you had absolutely no idea then?'

'Well, I don't know about you, Holly, but it's pretty

clear to me that John was the mastermind behind all of this,' Sharon said sarcastically.

'Ha-ha,' John replied drily. 'He kept his word, anyway, didn't he?' John looked to both of the girls with a smile on his face.

'He sure did,' Holly said quietly.

'Are you OK, Holly? I mean, how do you feel about all this? It must be . . . weird,' asked Sharon again, clearly concerned.

'I feel fine.' Holly was thoughtful. 'Actually, I think it's the best thing that could have happened right now! It's funny, though, how amazed we all are, considering how much we went on about this list. I mean, I should have been expecting it.'

'Yeah, but we never expected any of us to ever do it!' said John.

'But why not?' questioned Holly. 'This was the whole reason for it in the first place! To be able to help your loved ones after you go.'

'I think Gerry was the only one who took it really seriously.'

'Sharon, Gerry is the only one of us who is gone. Who knows how seriously anyone else would have taken it?'

There was a silence.

'Well, let's study this more closely then,' perked up John, suddenly starting to enjoy himself. 'There's how many envelopes?'

'Em . . . there's ten,' counted Sharon, joining in with the spirit of their new task.

'OK, so what months are there?' John asked. Holly sorted through the pile.

'There's March, which is the lamp one I've already opened, April, May, June, July, August, September, October, November and December.'

'So there's a message for every month left in the year,' Sharon said slowly, lost in thought. They sat in silence, thinking the same thing: Gerry had known he wouldn't live past February.

Holly looked happily at her friends. Whatever Gerry had in store for her was going to be interesting, but he had already succeeded in making her feel almost normal again, laughing with John and Sharon while they guessed what the envelopes contained. It was as though he was still with them.

'Hold on!' John exclaimed very seriously.

'What?'

His blue eyes twinkled. 'It's April now and you haven't opened this month's envelope yet.'

'Oh, of course! Should I do it now?'

'Go on,' encouraged Sharon.

Holly picked up the envelope and slowly opened it. There were only eight more to open after this and she wanted to treasure every second before it became another memory. She pulled out the little card.

A disco diva must always look her best. Go shopping for an outfit as you'll need it for next month!
    PS. I love you . . .

'Ooooh,' John and Sharon squealed with excitement, 'he's getting cryptic!'

Chapter Seven

Holly lay on her bed, switching the lamp on and off, with a smile on her face like a demented woman. She and Sharon had gone shopping in Bed Knobs and Broomsticks in Malahide, and both girls had eventually agreed on the beautifully carved wooden stand and the cream shade that matched the cream and wooden furnishings of the master bedroom (of course they had chosen the most ridiculously expensive one, it would have been wrong to spoil tradition). And although Gerry hadn't physically been there with her as she bought it, she felt as though they had made the purchase together.

She had drawn the curtains of her bedroom in order to test her new merchandise. The bedside lamp had a softening effect on the room, making it appear warmer. How easily this could have ended their nightly arguments, but perhaps neither of them wanted to end them. It had become a routine, something familiar that made them feel closer. How she would give anything to have one of those little arguments now. And she would gladly get out of her cosy bed for him, she would gladly walk on the cold floor for him, and she would gladly bruise herself on the bedpost whilst fumbling in the dark for the bed. But that time was gone.

The sound of Gloria Gaynor's 'I Will Survive' snapped her back to the present as she realised her mobile phone was ringing.

'Hello?'

'G'day, mate, I'm hooooome!' shrieked a familiar voice.

'Oh my God, Ciara! I didn't know you were coming home!'

'Well, neither did I, actually, but I ran out of money and decided to surprise you all!'

'Wow, I bet Mum and Dad were surprised all right.'

'Well, Dad did drop the towel with fright when he stepped out of the shower.'

Holly covered her face with her hands, 'Oh, Ciara, he didn't!'

'No hugs for Daddy when I saw him!' Ciara laughed.

'Oh, yuck, yuck, yuck. Change the subject, I'm having horrible visions,' Holly laughed.

'OK, well, I was calling to tell you that I was home, obviously, and that Mum's organising dinner tonight to celebrate.'

'Celebrate what?'

'Me being alive.'

'Oh, OK. I thought you might have an announcement or something.'

'That I'm alive.'

'O . . . K. So who'll be there?'

'The whole family.'

'Did I mention that I'm going to the dentist to have all my teeth pulled out? Sorry I can't make it.'

'I know, I know, I said the same thing to Mum, but we haven't all been together for ages. Sure, when's the last time you've even seen Richard and Meredith?'

'Oh, good ol' Dick – he was in flying form at the funeral. Had lots of wise and comforting things to say to me like, "Did you not consider donating his brain to medical science?" Yes, he's a fantastic brother all right.'

'Oh gosh, Holly, I'm sorry, I forgot about the funeral.' Her sister's voice changed. 'I'm sorry I couldn't make it.'

'Ciara, don't be silly. We both decided it was best you stay,' Holly said briskly. 'It's far too expensive to be flying back and forth from Australia so let's not bring it back up, OK?'

'OK.'

Holly quickly changed the subject. 'So when you say the whole family, do you mean . . . ?'

'Yes, Richard and Meredith are bringing our adorable little niece and nephew. And Jack and Abbey are coming, you'll be pleased to know. Declan will be there in body but probably not in mind, Mum, Dad and me, of course, and you WILL be there.'

Holly groaned. As much as Holly moaned about her family she had a great relationship with her brother Jack. He was only two years older than she, so they had been close when growing up, and he had always been very protective of her. Their mother had called them her 'two little elves', because they were always getting up to mischief around the house, usually aimed at their eldest brother, Richard. Jack was similar to Holly in both looks and personality, and she considered him to be the most normal of her siblings. It also helped that she got along with his partner of seven years, Abbey, and when Gerry was alive the four of them often met up for dinner and drinks. When Gerry was alive . . . God, that didn't sound right.

Ciara was a different kettle of fish altogether. Jack and Holly were convinced she was from the planet Ciara, population: one. Ciara had the look of their father – long legs and dark hair. She also had various tattoos and piercings on her body as a result of her travels around the world. A tattoo for every country, her dad used to joke. A tattoo for every man, Holly and Jack were convinced.

Of course, this carry-on was all frowned upon by the eldest sibling, Richard (or Dick, as he was known to Jack and Holly). Richard was born with the serious affliction of being an eternal old man. His life revolved around rules and regulations and obedience. When he was younger he had one friend and they had a fight when they were ten, and after that Holly could never remember him bringing anyone home, having any girlfriends or ever going out to socialise. She and Jack thought it was a wonder he even met his equally joyless wife, Meredith – probably at an anti-happiness convention.

It wasn't as though Holly had the *worst* family in the world, it was just that they were such a strange mix of people. The huge clashes of personalities usually led to arguments at the most inappropriate times or, as Holly's parents preferred to call them, 'heavy discussions'. They *could* get along, but that was with everyone really trying and being on their best behaviour.

Holly and Jack often met up for lunch or for drinks, just to catch up on each other's lives. She enjoyed his company and considered him to be not only a brother but a real friend. Lately they hadn't seen much of each other. Jack understood Holly well and knew when she needed her space.

The only time Holly caught up on her younger brother, Declan's, life was when she called at the house looking for her parents and he would answer. Declan wasn't a great conversationalist. He was an overgrown 'boy' who didn't yet quite feel comfortable in the company of adults so Holly never really knew that much about him. Although she was aware of his unbreakable loyalty to his band, The Orgasmic Fish (whom she had yet to see perform), and if it wasn't a guitar that he had in his hand, it was a video camera. A nice guy, he just had his head up in the clouds a bit.

Ciara, her twenty-four-year-old little sister, had been away for the entire year and Holly had missed her. They were never the kind of sisters to swap clothes and giggle about boys – their tastes differed so much – though as the only two girls in a family of brothers, they formed a bond. But Ciara was closer to Declan; both of them were dreamers. With Jack and Holly inseparable as children and friends as adults, that left Richard. He was out on his own in the family but Holly suspected he liked that feeling of being separated from those he couldn't quite understand. Holly was dreading his lectures on all-things-boring, his insensitive questioning of her life and just the whole feeling of being frustrated by comment after comment at the dinner table. But it was a welcome-home dinner for Ciara, and Jack would be there; Holly could count on him.

But was Holly looking forward to tonight? Absolutely not.

Holly reluctantly knocked on the door and immediately heard the pounding of tiny feet flying towards the door, followed by a voice so loud that should not have belonged to a child.

'Mummy! Daddy! It's Aunty Holly, it's Aunty Holly!' It was nephew Timothy, nephew Timothy.

His happiness was suddenly crushed by a stern voice (although it was unusual for her nephew to be happy about Holly's arrival. Things must be even more boring in there than usual). 'Timothy! What did I tell you about running in the house? You could fall and hurt yourself. Now go stand in the corner and think about what I said. Do I make myself clear?'

'Yes, Mummy.'

'Ah, come on, Meredith, will he hurt himself on the carpet or on the comfy padded couch?'

Holly laughed to herself; Ciara was definitely home. Just as Holly was contemplating escape, the door swung open and there stood Meredith. She looked even more sour-faced and unwelcoming than usual.

'Holly.' She nodded her head in acknowledgement.

'Meredith,' Holly imitated.

Once in the living room Holly looked around for Jack, but to her disappointment he was nowhere to be seen. Richard stood in front of the fireplace, dressed in a surprisingly colourful sweater; perhaps he was letting his hair down tonight. He had his hands in his pockets and was rocking back and forth from his heels to the balls of his toes like a man mid-lecture. His lecture was aimed at their father, Frank, who sat uncomfortably in his favourite armchair, looking like a chastised schoolboy. Richard was so lost in his story he didn't see Holly. She blew her poor father a kiss from across the room, not wanting to be brought into their conversation. He smiled at her and pretended to catch her kiss.

Declan was slumped on the couch wearing his ripped jeans and South Park T-shirt, puffing furiously on a cigarette while Meredith warned him of the dangers of smoking. 'Really? I didn't know that,' he said, sounding worryingly interested while stabbing out his cigarette. Meredith's face looked satisfied until Declan winked at Holly, reached for the box and immediately lit up another one. 'Tell me some more, please, I'm just dying to know.' Meredith stared back at him in disgust.

Ciara was hiding behind the couch, throwing pieces of popcorn at the back of Timothy's head. He stood facing the wall in the corner of the room, too afraid to turn round. Abbey was pinned to the floor and being bossed around by little five-year-old Emily and an evil-looking doll. She caught Holly's eye and mouthed 'Help' to her.

'Hi, Ciara.' Holly approached her sister, who jumped up and gave her a big hug, squeezing Holly a bit tighter than usual. 'Nice hair.'

'You like it?'

'Yeah, pink is really your colour.'

Ciara looked satisfied. 'That's what I tried to tell them,' she said, squinting at Richard and Meredith. 'So how's my big sis?' Ciara asked softly, rubbing Holly's arm affectionately.

'Oh, you know,' Holly smiled weakly. 'I'm hanging in there.'

'Jack is in the kitchen helping your mum with the dinner, if you're looking for him, Holly,' Abbey announced, then widening her eyes and mouthing 'Help me' again.

Holly raised her eyebrows at Abbey. 'Really? Well, isn't he great, helping out Mum?'

'Oh, Holly, you know how much Jack just *loves* cooking. Can't get enough of it,' she said sarcastically.

Holly's dad chuckled to himself, which stopped Richard in his tracks.

'What's so funny, Father?'

Frank shifted in his seat nervously. 'I just find it remarkable that all this happens in one tiny little test tube.'

Richard let out a disapproving sigh at his father's stupidity. 'Yes, but you have to understand these are so minuscule, Father, it's rather fascinating. The organisms combine with the . . .' And away he went again while his father settled back down in his chair and tried to avoid eye contact with Holly.

Holly tiptoed quietly into the kitchen where she found her brother at the table with his feet up on a chair, munching on some food. 'Ah, here he is, the Naked Chef himself.'

Jack smiled and stood up. 'There's my favourite sister.' He scrunched up his nose. 'I see you got roped into coming to this thing as well.' He walked towards her and held out his arms to offer her one of his big bear hugs. 'How are you?' he said quietly into her ear.

'I'm OK, thanks.' Holly smiled sadly and kissed him on the cheek before turning to her mother. 'Darling Mother, I am here to offer my services at this extremely stressful and busy time of your life,' Holly said, planting a kiss on her mother's flushed cheek.

'Oh, aren't I just the luckiest woman in the world, having such caring children like you?' Elizabeth said sarcastically. 'Tell you what, you can just drain the water from the potatoes there.'

'Mum, tell us about the time when you were a little girl during the famine and the spuds were gone,' Jack said, putting on an exaggerated Irish accent.

Elizabeth hit him across the head playfully with the tea towel. 'Ah sure, 'tis years before my time, son.'

'Sure, 'tis true,' said Jack.

'No, you t'aren't at all,' joined in Holly.

They both stopped and stared at her. 'Since when is there such a word as "t'aren't"?' laughed her mum.

'Ah, shut up, the both of you.' Holly joined her brother at the table.

'I hope you two won't be getting up to any mischief tonight. I would like this to be an argument-free zone for a change.'

'Mother, I am shocked the thought even crossed your mind.' Jack winked across to Holly.

'All right,' she said, not believing a word of it. 'Well, sorry, my babies, but there's nothing else to be done here. Dinner will be ready in a few minutes.'

'Oh.' Holly was disappointed.

Elizabeth joined her children at the table and the three of them stared at the kitchen door, all thinking the same thing.

'No, Abbey,' squealed Emily loudly, 'you're not doing what I tell you,' and she burst into tears. This was shortly followed by a loud guffaw from Richard; he must have cracked a joke because he was the only one laughing.

'But I suppose it's important that we all stay here and keep an eye on the dinner,' Elizabeth added.

'OK, everyone, dinner is served,' announced Elizabeth, and the family made their way to the dining room. There was an awkward moment like at a children's birthday party while everyone scuffled to sit beside their best friend. Eventually Holly was satisfied with her position at the table and settled down with her mother on her left at the end of the table and Jack to her right. Abbey sat with a scowl on her face as she had been placed between Jack and Richard. Jack would have some making up to do when he got home. Declan sat opposite Holly and wedged in between him was an empty seat where Timothy should be sitting, then Emily and Meredith, then Ciara. Holly's father got a raw deal, sitting at the head of the table between Richard and Ciara, but he was such a calm man he was the best one for the job.

Everyone oohed and aahed as Elizabeth brought out the food and its aroma filled the room. Holly had always loved her mother's cooking; she was never afraid to experiment with new flavours and recipes, a trait that had not been passed down to her daughter.

51

'Hey, poor little Timmy must be starving out there,' Ciara exclaimed to Richard. 'He must have done his time by now.'

She knew she was skating on thin ice but she loved the danger of it and, more importantly, she loved to wind up Richard. After all, she had to make up for lost time – she had been away for a year.

'Ciara, it's important that Timothy knows when he has done something wrong,' explained Richard.

'Yeah, but couldn't you just tell him?'

The rest of the family tried hard not to laugh.

'He needs to know that his actions will lead to serious consequences so he will not repeat it.'

'Ah well,' she said, raising her voice a few decibels, 'he's missing all this yummy food. Mmm mmm mmm,' she said, licking her lips.

'Stop it, Ciara,' Elizabeth snapped.

'Or you'll have to stand in the corner,' Jack added sternly.

The table erupted with laughter – bar Meredith and Richard, of course.

'So, Ciara, tell us about your adventures in Australia,' Frank moved swiftly on.

Her eyes lit up. 'Oh, I had the most amazing time, Dad. I would definitely recommend going there to anyone.'

'Awful long flight, though,' Richard said.

'Yeah, it is but it's so worth it.'

'Did you get any more tattoos?' Holly asked.

'Yeah, look.' With that, Ciara stood up at the table and pulled down her trousers, revealing a butterfly on her behind.

Mum, Dad, Richard and Meredith protested in outrage while the others sat in convulsions of laughter. Finally, when Ciara had apologised and Meredith had removed her hands from Emily's eyes, the table settled down.

'They are revolting things,' Richard said in disgust.

'I think butterflies are pretty, Daddy,' said Emily with big innocent eyes.

'Yes, some butterflies are pretty, Emily, but I'm talking about tattoos. They can give you all sorts of diseases and problems.' Emily's smile faded.

'Hey, I didn't exactly get this done in a dodgy place sharing needles with drug users, you know. The place was perfectly clean.'

'Well, that's an oxymoron if ever I heard one,' sniffed Meredith.

'Been in one recently, Meredith?' Ciara asked a bit too forcefully.

'Well, em . . . n-n-n-no,' she stuttered, 'I have never been in one, thank you very much, but I am sure they are.' Then she turned to Emily. 'They are dirty, horrible places, Emily, where only dangerous people go.'

'Is Aunt Ciara dangerous, Mummy?'

'Only to five-year-old little girls with red hair,' Ciara said, stuffing her face with potatoes.

Emily froze.

'Richard dear, do you think that Timmy might want to come in now for some food?' Elizabeth asked politely.

'It's Timothy,' Meredith interrupted.

'Yes, Mother, I think that would be OK.'

A very sorry little Timothy walked slowly into the room with his head down, and took his place silently beside Declan. Holly's heart leaped out to him. How cruel to treat a child like that, how cruel to stop him from being a child . . . Her sympathy diminished immediately as she felt his foot kick her shin underneath the table. They should have left him out there.

'So, Ciara, come on, give us the gossip. Do anything wild and wonderful out there?' Holly pushed for more information.

'Oh yeah, I did a bungee jump, actually – well, I did a few. I have the photo here.' She reached into her back pocket and everyone looked away just in case she was planning on revealing any more bits of her anatomy. Thankfully she took out only her wallet and passed the photo from it around the table.

'The first one I did was off a bridge and my head hit the water when I fell . . .'

'Oh, Ciara, that sounds dangerous,' her mother said with her hands across her face.

'Oh no, it wasn't dangerous at all,' she reassured her.

The photograph was passed to Holly, and she and Jack burst out laughing. Ciara dangled upside down from a rope with her face contorted in the middle of a scream of pure terror. Her hair (it was blue at that time) was shooting out in all directions as though she had been electrocuted.

'Attractive photo, Ciara. Mum, you must get that framed for over the fireplace,' Holly joked.

'Yeah!' Ciara's eyes lit up. 'That would be a cool idea.'

'Sure, darling, I'll just take down the one of you making your Holy Communion and replace it with that,' Elizabeth said sarcastically.

'Well, I don't know which one would be scarier,' said Declan.

'Holly, what are you doing for your birthday?' asked Abbey, leaning across towards her. She was clearly dying to get out of the conversation she was having with Richard.

'Oh, that's right!' shouted Ciara. 'You're gonna be thirty next week!'

'I'm not doing anything big at all,' she warned everyone. 'I don't want any surprise party or anything, PLEASE.'

'Oh, you have to—' said Ciara.

'No, she doesn't have to if she doesn't want to,' her father interrupted, and winked supportively at Holly.

'Thank you, Dad. I'm just going to have a girly night out clubbing or something. Nothing mad, nothing wild.'

Richard tutted as the photograph reached him and passed it on to his father, who chuckled to himself over the sight of Ciara.

'Yes, I agree with you, Holly,' said Richard, 'those birthday celebrations are always a bit embarrassing. Grown adults acting like children, doing "Rock the boat" on the floor and drinking far too much. You're quite right.'

'Well, I actually quite enjoy those parties, Richard,' Holly shot back, 'but I just don't feel in the celebratory mood this year, that's all.'

There was a silence for a moment before Ciara piped up, 'A girly night it is then.'

'Can I tag along with the camera?' asked Declan.

'For what?'

'Just for some footage of clubs and stuff for college.'

'Well, if it'll help . . . but as long as you know I won't be going to all the trendy places that you like.'

'No, I don't mind where you g— OW!' he shouted, and stared menacingly at Timothy.

Timmy stuck his tongue out at him and the conversation continued. After the main course was finished Ciara disappeared out of the room, returned with a bulging bag in her hand and announced, 'Presents!'

Timmy and Emily cheered. Holly hoped that Ciara had remembered to get them something.

Her father received a colourfully painted boomerang that he pretended to throw down to his wife; Richard was given a T-shirt with the map of Australia on it, which he immediately began to teach to Timmy and Emily at the table; Meredith quite comically wasn't given anything; Jack and Declan were given T-shirts with perverted pictures and a caption saying, 'I've been to the bush', and Elizabeth received a collection of old aboriginal recipes. Holly was touched by her dream catcher made from brightly coloured feathers and sticks.

'So all your dreams come true,' Ciara whispered in her ear before kissing her on the cheek.

Thankfully Ciara had bought sweets for Timmy and Emily, which looked strangely like the sweets they could buy from the local shop. These were briskly taken away by Richard and Meredith, who claimed they would rot their teeth.

'Well, give them back then so I can rot my own,' Ciara demanded.

Timmy and Emily looked around sadly at everyone's presents and were immediately chastised by Richard for not concentrating on the map of Australia. Timmy made a face at Holly and a warm feeling returned to her heart. As long as the kids kept acting as if they deserved their treatment, that was OK with her.

'Right, we better hit the road, Richard, or the children will fall asleep where they sit,' announced Meredith. The children were wide awake and were kicking Holly and Declan repeatedly under the table.

'Well, before everybody goes disappearing –' Holly's father announced loudly over the chatter. The table grew silent – 'I would like to propose a toast to our beautiful daughter Ciara.' He smiled at her and Ciara lapped up all the attention. 'We missed you, love, and we're glad you're home safely,' Frank finished. He lifted his glass into the air. 'To Ciara!'

'To Ciara!' everyone repeated.

As soon as the door closed behind Richard and Meredith everyone else began to leave one by one. Holly stepped into the chilly air and walked to her car alone. Her mum and dad stood at the door waving her off but she still felt so lonely. Usually she left dinner parties with Gerry, or if not *with* him then she was returning home *to* him. But not tonight or the next night or the night after that.

Chapter Eight

On her birthday, Holly stood in front of the full-length mirror and inspected herself. She had carried out Gerry's orders and had purchased a new outfit. What for, she didn't know but several times a day she had to drag herself away from the temptation of opening the envelope for May. There were only two days left until she could and the anticipation left her no room to think of anything else.

She had settled on wearing an all-black outfit to suit her current mood. Black fitted trousers slimmed her legs and were tailored perfectly to sit over her black boots. A black corset that made her look like she had a bigger chest finished the outfit off perfectly. Leo had done a wonderful job on her hair, tying it up and allowing strands to fall in loose waves around her shoulders. Holly ran her fingers through her hair and smiled at the memory of her time at the hairdressers . . .

She had arrived at the salon with her face flushed, and out of breath. 'Oh, I'm so sorry, Leo. I got caught on the phone and didn't realise the time.'

'Don't worry, love. Whenever you make an appointment I have the staff trained to pencil it in for half an hour later. COLIN!' he yelled, clicking his fingers in the air.

Colin dropped everything and ran.

'God, are you taking horse tranquillisers or something? The length of your hair already, and I just cut it a few weeks ago.'

He pumped vigorously on the chair, raising Holly higher. 'Anything special tonight?' he asked.

'The big three-0,' she said, biting her lip.

'What's that, your local bus route?'

'No! I'm the big three-0!'

'Of course I knew that, love. COLIN!' he yelled again, snapping his fingers in the air once more.

Colin appeared from the staff room behind Holly with a cake in his hand, followed by a row of hairdressers joining Leo in a chorus of 'Happy Birthday'. Holly was dumbfounded. She battled the tears that were welling in her eyes and failed miserably. By this stage the entire salon had joined in and Holly was so overwhelmed by their show of love. When it was over everyone applauded and normal business resumed.

Holly couldn't speak.

'Christ Almighty, Holly, one week you're in here laughing so hard you practically fall off your chair and the next visit you're crying!'

'Oh, but that was just so special, Leo, thank you,' she said, drying her eyes and giving him a huge hug and a kiss.

'Well, I had to get you back after you mortified me,' he said, shrugging her off, uncomfortable with the sentimentality.

Holly laughed, remembering Leo's surprise fiftieth

birthday party. The theme had been 'feathers and lace'. Holly had worn a beautiful tight-fitting lace dress, and Gerry, who was always game for a laugh, had worn a pink feather boa to match his pink shirt and tie. Leo claimed to have been excruciatingly embarrassed but everyone knew he was secretly delighted with all the attention. The next day, Leo had rung every guest who had attended the party and left a threatening message on their machine. Holly had been terrified to make an appointment with him for weeks after that in case he butchered her hair. Word had it that business was very slow for Leo that week.

'Well, you enjoyed the stripper that night, anyway,' Holly teased.

'Enjoyed? I went out with him for a month after that. The bastard.'

A slice of cake arrived in front of each customer and everyone turned to thank her.

'Don't know why they're thanking you,' Leo muttered under his breath. 'I'm the one who bloody bought it.'

'Don't worry, Leo, I'll make sure your tip covers the cost.'

'Are you mad? Your tip wouldn't cover the cost of my bus fare home.'

'Leo, you live next door.'

'Exactly!'

Holly pouted her lip and pretended to sulk.

Leo laughed. 'Thirty years old and you're still acting like a baby. Where are you off to tonight?'

'Oh, nowhere mad. I just want a low-key, nice quiet night out with the girls.'

'That's what I said at my fiftieth. Who's going?'

'Sharon, Ciara, Abbey, and Denise – haven't seen her for ages.'

'Ciara home?'

'Yeah, her and her pink hair.'

'Merciful hour! She'll stay away from me if she knows what's good for her. Right, missus, you look fab, you'll be the belle of the ball – have fun!'

Holly stopped daydreaming and gazed at her reflection in the mirror. She didn't look thirty or feel thirty. But then again what was being thirty supposed to feel like? When she was younger, thirty seemed so far away, she'd thought that a woman of that age would be wise and knowledgeable, settled in her life with a husband and children and a career. She had none of those things. She still felt as clueless as when she was twenty, only with a few grey hairs, and crow's feet around her eyes. She sat down on the edge of the bed and continued to stare at herself. There was nothing about being thirty worth celebrating.

The doorbell rang and Holly could hear the excited chatter of the girls outside. She tried to perk herself up, took a deep breath and plastered a smile on her face.

'Happy birthday!' they all yelled in unison.

She stared back at their smiling faces and was immediately cheered by their enthusiasm. She ushered them into the living room and waved hello to the camera being brandished by Declan.

'No, Holly, you're supposed to ignore him!' hissed Denise, and dragged her by the arm onto the couch where they all surrounded her and immediately started thrusting presents in her face.

61

'Open mine first!' squealed Ciara, knocking Sharon out of the way so hard that she toppled off the couch. Sharon froze in horror, unsure of how to react, then burst into giggles.

'OK, calm down, everyone,' said the voice of reason (Abbey), struggling to help up a hysterical Sharon. 'I think we should pop open the bubbly first and *then* open the pressies.'

'OK, but as long as she opens mine first,' pouted Ciara.

'Ciara, I promise to open yours first.' Holly spoke as though addressing a child.

Abbey raced into the kitchen and returned with a tray full of champagne flutes.

'Anyone for champers, sweetie darlings?'

The flutes had been a wedding gift and one of the glasses had Gerry and Holly's name inscribed on it, which Abbey had tactfully removed from the set. 'OK, Holly, you can do the honours,' Abbey said, handing her the bottle.

Everyone ran for cover and ducked as Holly began to remove the cork. 'Hey, I'm not that bad, everyone!'

'Yeah, she's an old pro at this by now,' said Sharon, appearing from behind the couch with a cushion on her head.

The girls all cheered as they heard the pop and crawled out from their hiding places.

'The sound of heaven,' Denise said dramatically, holding her hand up to her heart.

'OK, now open my present,' Ciara screamed again.

'Ciara!' they all shouted.

'After the toast,' added Sharon.

Everyone held up her glass.

'OK, here's to my bestest friend in the whole world who has had such a difficult year, but throughout all has been the bravest and the strongest person I've ever met. She's an inspiration to us all. Here's to her finding happiness for the next thirty years of her life! To Holly!'

'To Holly,' they all chorused. Everyone's eyes were sparkling with tears as they all took sips of their drinks, except of course for Ciara, who had already knocked back her glass of champagne and was scrambling to give her present to Holly.

'OK, first you have to wear this tiara because you are our princess for the night, and secondly here's my present from me to you!'

The girls helped Holly put on the sparkling tiara that luckily went perfectly with her glittery corset. At that moment, surrounded by her friends, she really did feel like a princess.

Holly carefully removed the sellotape from the neatly wrapped parcel.

'Oh, just rip it open,' said Abbey to everyone's surprise.

Holly looked at the box inside, confused. 'What is it?'

'Read it!' Ciara said excitedly.

Holly began to read aloud from the box, 'It's a battery operated . . . oh my God! Ciara! You naughty girl!' Holly and the girls laughed hysterically.

'Well, I'll definitely need this,' Holly laughed, holding the box up to the camera.

Declan looked as if he was about to throw up.

'Do you like it?' Ciara asked, searching for approval. 'I wanted to give it to you at dinner last week but I didn't think it would be appropriate.'

'Gosh! Well, I'm glad you saved it till now!' Holly laughed, giving her sister a hug.

'OK, me next,' Abbey said, putting her parcel on Holly's lap. 'It's from me and Jack so don't expect anything like Ciara's.'

'Well, I would worry if Jack gave me something like that,' Holly said, opening it. 'Oh, Abbey, it's beautiful!' Holly said, holding up the sterling silver-covered photo album.

'For your new memories,' Abbey said softly.

'Oh, it's perfect,' Holly said, wrapping her arms round her and squeezing her. 'Thank you.'

'OK, well, mine is less sentimental but as a fellow female I'm sure you will appreciate it,' said Denise, handing her an envelope.

'Oh, brilliant! I've always wanted to go here,' Holly exclaimed as she opened it. 'A weekend of pampering at Haven's health and beauty clinic!'

'God, you sound like you're on *Blind Date*,' teased Sharon.

'Let us know when you want to make an appointment, it's valid for a year, and the rest of us can book the same time. Make a holiday out of it!'

'Oh, that's a great idea, Denise. Thank you!'

'OK, last but not least!' Holly winked at Sharon. Sharon fidgeted with her hands nervously while she watched Holly's face.

The present was a large silver photo frame with a photograph of Sharon, Denise and Holly at the

Christmas Ball two years ago. 'Oh, I'm wearing my spensive white dress!' sobbed Holly playfully.

'*Before* it was ruined,' pointed out Sharon.

'God, I don't even remember that being taken!'

'I don't even remember being there,' mumbled Denise.

Holly continued to stare at the photo sadly while she walked over to the fireplace. That had been the last ball that she and Gerry had been to, as he had been too ill to attend last year's.

'Well, this will take pride of place,' Holly announced, walking over to the mantelpiece and placing it beside her wedding photo.

'OK, girls, let's get some serious drinking done!' screamed Ciara, and everyone dived to safety as another bottle of champagne was popped open.

Two bottles of champagne and several of red wine later the girls stumbled out of the house and piled into a taxi. Through the hilarity and shouting, someone managed to explain to the taxi driver where they were going. Holly insisted on sitting in the passenger seat and having a heart-to-heart with Nick, the driver, who probably wanted to kill her by the time they reached town.

'Bye, Nick!' they all shouted to their new best friend before falling out onto the kerb, where they watched him drive off at high speed. They had decided (while drinking their third bottle of wine) to chance their luck at Dublin's most stylish club, Boudoir. The club was reserved for the rich and famous only, and it was a well-known fact that if you weren't either, you then had to have a membership card to be granted access.

Denise walked up to the door coolly waving her video store membership card in the bouncer's faces. Amazingly, they stopped her.

The only famous faces the girls saw overtaking them to enter the club, as they fought with the bouncers to get in, were some newsreaders from the national TV station, whom Denise smiled at and hilariously kept repeating, 'Good evening,' very seriously to their faces. Unfortunately, after that Holly remembered no more.

Holly awoke with her head pounding. Her mouth was as dry as Gandhi's sandal and her vision was impaired. She leaned up on one elbow and tried to open her eyes, which were somehow glued together. She squinted around. It was bright, very bright, and the room seemed to be spinning. Something very odd was going on. Holly caught sight of herself in the mirror ahead and startled herself. Had she been in an accident last night? She ran out of energy and collapsed flat on her back again. Suddenly the house alarm began wailing and she lifted her head slightly from the pillow and opened one eye. Oh, take whatever you want, she thought, just as long as you bring me a glass of water before you go. After a while she realised it wasn't the alarm but the phone ringing beside her bed.

'Hello?' she croaked.

'Oh good, I'm not the only one,' said a desperately ill-sounding voice on the other end.

'Who are you?' croaked Holly again.

'My name is Sharon, I think,' came the reply, 'although don't ask me who Sharon is because I don't know. The man beside me in bed seems to think I know him.'

Holly heard John laughing loudly in the background.

'Sharon, what happened last night? Please enlighten me.'

'Alcohol happened,' said Sharon drowsily, 'lots and lots of alcohol.'

'Any other information?'

'Nope.'

'Know what time it is?'

'Two o'clock.'

'Why are you ringing me at this hour of the morning?'

'It's the afternoon, Holly.'

'Oh. How did that happen?'

'Gravity or something. I was out that day from school.'

'Oh God, I think I'm dying.'

'Me too.'

'I think I'll just go back to sleep. Maybe when I wake up the ground will have stopped moving.'

'Good idea. Oh, and, Holly, welcome to the thirties club.'

Holly groaned. 'I have not started as I mean to go on. From now on I will be a sensible, mature thirty-year-old woman.'

'Yeah, that's what I said too. Good night.'

'Night.' Seconds later Holly was asleep. She awoke at various stages during the day to answer the phone, the conversations all seeming part of her dreams. And she made many trips to the kitchen for water to re-hydrate herself.

Eventually, at nine o'clock that night, Holly succumbed to her stomach's screaming demands for food. As usual there was nothing in the fridge so she decided to treat herself to a Chinese takeaway. She sat snuggled up on the couch in her pyjamas watching the very best of Saturday night TV while stuffing her face. After the trauma of being without Gerry for her birthday the previous day, Holly was surprised to notice that she felt very content with herself. It was the first time since Gerry died that she was comfortable with her own company. There was a slight chance she could make it without him.

Later that night Jack called her on her mobile. 'Hey, sis, what are you doing?'

'Watching TV, having Chinese,' she said.

'Well, you sound in good form. Unlike my poor girlfriend, who's suffering here beside me.'

'I'm never going out with you again, Holly,' she heard Abbey scream weakly in the background.

'You and your friends perverted her mind,' he joked.

'Don't blame me. She was doing just fine all by herself as far as I remember.'

'She says she can't remember anything.'

'Neither can I. Maybe it's something that happens as soon as you hit thirty. I was never like this before.'

'Or maybe it's just an evil plan you all hatched so you wouldn't have to tell us what you got up to.'

'I wish it was . . . Oh, thanks for the pressie by the way, it's beautiful.'

'Glad you like it. It took me ages to find the right one.'

'Liar.'

He laughed. 'Anyway, I was ringing to ask you if you're going to Declan's gig tomorrow night.'

'Where is it?'

'Hogan's pub.'

'No way. There is no way I'm ever setting foot in a pub again, especially to listen to some loud rock band with screeching guitars and noisy drums,' Holly told him.

'Oh, it's the old, "I'm never drinking again" excuse, is it? Well, don't drink then. Please come, Holly. Declan's really excited about it and no one else will come.'

'Ha! So I'm the last resort, am I? Nice to know you think so highly of me.'

'No, you're not. Declan would love to see you there and we hardly got a chance to talk at dinner. We haven't gone out for ages,' he pleaded.

'Well, we're hardly going to have a heart-to-heart with the Orgasmic Fish banging out their tunes,' she said sarcastically.

'They're actually called Black Strawberries now, which has a much sweeter ring to it, I think,' he laughed.

Holly held her head in her hands and groaned, 'Oh, please don't make me go, Jack.'

'You're going.'

'OK, but I'm not staying for the whole thing.'

'We can discuss that when we get there. Declan will be chuffed when I tell him; the family never usually goes to these things.'

'OK then, about eight-ish?'

69

'Perfect.'

Holly hung up and sat stuck to the couch for another few hours. She felt so full, she couldn't move. Maybe that Chinese hadn't been such a good idea after all.

Chapter Nine

Holly arrived in Hogan's pub feeling a lot fresher than the day before, but her reactions were still a little slower than usual. Her hangovers seemed to be getting worse as she got older, and yesterday took the gold medal for the hangover of all hangovers. She had gone for a long walk along the coast from Malahide to Portmarnock earlier that day, and the crisp fresh breeze had helped to clear her fuzzy head. She had called in to her parents for Sunday dinner, when they presented her with a beautiful Waterford Crystal vase for her birthday. It had been a wonderful relaxing day and she almost had to drag herself off the comfortable couch to go to Hogan's.

Hogan's was a popular three-storey building situated in the centre of town, and even on a Sunday the place was jammed. The first floor was a trendy nightclub that played all the latest music from the charts. It was where the young beautiful people went to show off their latest fashions. The ground floor was a traditional Irish pub for the older crowd (usually containing old men perched up on their bar stools, bent over their pints, contemplating life). A few nights a week there was a traditional Irish music band that played all the old favourites, which was popular with the young and old. The basement, where bands usually played, was dark and dingy, and the clientele was purely students. Holly seemed to be the oldest person in there. The bar consisted of a tiny counter in the corner of the long hall and was surrounded by a huge crowd of young students dressed in scruffy jeans and ripped T-shirts, pushing each other violently in order to be served. The bar staff also looked as if they should be in school, and were rushing around at a hundred miles per hour with sweat dripping from their faces.

The basement was stuffy, with no ventilation or air conditioning at all, and Holly was finding it difficult to breathe in the smoky air. Practically everyone around her seemed to be smoking and her eyes were already stinging. She dreaded to think what it might be like in an hour's time.

She waved at Declan to let him know she was there but decided not to make her way over as he was surrounded by a crowd of girls. She didn't want to cramp his style. Holly had missed out on the whole student scene when she was younger. She had decided not to go to college after school and instead begun working as a secretary, moving from job to job every few months, ending with the awful job she had left so she could spend time with Gerry while he was sick. She doubted she would have stayed in it that much longer anyway. Gerry had studied Marketing at Dublin City University but he never socialised much with his college friends. Instead he chose to go out with Holly, Sharon and John, Denise and whoever she was with at the time. Looking around at everyone, Holly didn't feel that she had missed anything special.

Finally Declan managed to tear himself away from his female fans and made his way over to Holly.

'Well, hello, Mr Popular. I feel privileged you chose me to speak to next.' All the girls stared Holly up and down and wondered what the hell Declan saw in this older woman.

Declan laughed and rubbed his hands together cheekily. 'I know! This band business is great. Looks like I'll be getting a bit of action tonight,' he said cockily.

'As your sister it's always a pleasure to be informed of that,' Holly replied sarcastically. She was finding it impossible to maintain a conversation with Declan as he refused eye contact with her and instead was scouring the crowds.

'OK, Declan, just go, why don't you, and flirt with these beauties instead of being stuck here with your old sister?'

'Oh no, it's not that,' he said defensively. 'It's just that we were told there might be a record company guy coming to see us play tonight.'

'Oh, cool!' Holly's eyes widened with excitement. This obviously meant a lot to her brother and she felt guilty for never taking an interest in it before. She glanced around and tried to spot someone who might be a record company person. What would they look like? It's not as if they would be sitting in the corner with a notebook scribbling furiously. Finally her eyes fell upon a man who seemed much older than the rest of the crowd, more her own age. He was dressed in a black leather jacket, black slacks and a black T-shirt, and stood with his hands on his hips staring at the stage. Yes, he was definitely a record company guy. He had stubble all around his jaw and looked like he hadn't been to bed for days. He probably smelled bad as well. Or else he was just a weirdo who liked to go to student nights and ogle all the young girls. Also a possibility.

'Over there, Deco!' Holly raised her voice over the noise and pointed at the man.

Declan looked excited and his eyes followed to where her finger pointed. His smile faded as he obviously recognised the man. 'No, it's just DANNY!' he yelled, and wolf-whistled to grab the guy's attention.

Danny twirled round, trying to find his caller, nodded his head in recognition and made his way over.

'Hey, man,' Declan said, shaking his hand.

'Hi, Declan, how are you set?' The man looked stressed.

'Yeah, OK,' Declan nodded unenthusiastically. Somebody must have told Declan that acting like you didn't care was cool.

'Sound check go OK?'

'There were a few problems but we sorted them out.'

'So everything's OK?'

'Sure.'

'Good.' His face relaxed and he turned to face Holly. 'Sorry for ignoring you there. I'm Daniel.'

'Nice to meet you. I'm Holly.'

'Oh, sorry,' Declan interrupted. 'Holly, this is the owner; Daniel, this is my sister.'

'Sister? Wow you look nothing alike.'

'Thank God,' Holly mouthed to Daniel so Declan couldn't see, and he laughed.

'Hey, Deco, we're on!' yelled a blue-haired boy at him.

'See you two later,' and Declan ran off.

'Good luck!' yelled Holly after him. 'So you're a Hogan,' she said, turning to face Daniel.

'Well, no, actually I'm a Connolly,' he smiled. 'I just took over the place a few weeks ago.'

'Oh.' Holly was surprised. 'I didn't know they'd sold it. So are you going to change it to Connolly's then?'

'Can't afford all the lettering on the front. It's a bit long.'

Holly laughed. 'Well, everyone knows the name Hogan's at this stage; it would probably be stupid to change it.'

Daniel nodded in agreement. 'That was the main reason, actually.'

Suddenly Jack appeared at the main entrance and Holly waved him over. 'I'm so sorry I'm late. Did I miss anything?' he said, giving her a hug and a kiss.

'Nope, he's just about to go on now. Jack, this is Daniel, the owner.'

'Nice to meet you,' Daniel said, shaking his hand.

'Are they any good?' Jack asked him, nodding his head in the direction of the stage.

'To tell you the truth, I've never even heard them play,' Daniel said worriedly.

'That was brave of you!' laughed Jack.

'I hope not too brave,' he said, turning to face the front as the boys took to the stage.

'I recognise a few faces here,' Jack said, scanning the crowd. 'Most of them are under eighteen as well.'

A young girl dressed in ripped jeans and a belly top walked slowly by Jack with an unsure smile on her face. She placed her finger over her lip. Jack smiled and nodded back.

Holly looked at Jack questioningly. 'What was that about?'

'Oh, I teach her English. She's only sixteen or seventeen. She's a good girl, though.' Jack stared after her as she walked by, then added, 'But she'd better not be late for class tomorrow.'

Holly watched the girl down a pint with her friends, wishing she had had a teacher at school like Jack; all the students seemed to love him. And it was easy to see why: he was a lovable kind of person. 'Well, don't tell *him* they're under eighteen,' Holly said under her breath, nodding in the direction of Daniel.

The crowd cheered and Declan took on his moody persona as he lifted his guitar strap over his shoulder. The music started and after that there was no chance of carrying on any kind of conversation. The crowd began to jump up and down, and once too often Holly's foot was stomped on. Jack just looked at her and laughed, amused at her obvious discomfort.

'CAN I GET YOU TWO A DRINK?' Daniel yelled, making a drinking motion with his hand. Jack asked for a pint of Budweiser while Holly settled for a 7-Up. They watched Daniel battle through the moshing crowd and climb behind the bar to fix the drinks. He returned minutes later with their glasses and a stool for Holly. She and Jack turned their attention back to the stage and watched their brother perform. The music really wasn't Holly's type of thing, and it was so loud and noisy it was difficult for her to tell if they were actually any good. It was a far cry from the soothing sounds of her favourite Westlife CD.

After four songs Holly had had enough, and gave Jack a hug and a kiss goodbye. 'TELL DECLAN I STAYED TILL THE END!' she yelled. 'NICE MEETING YOU, DANIEL! THANKS FOR THE DRINK!' she screamed, and made her way back to civilisation and cool fresh air.

Her ears continued to ring all the way home in the car. It was ten o'clock by the time she got there. Only two more hours till May. And that meant she could open another envelope.

Holly sat at her kitchen table nervously drumming her fingers on the wood. She gulped back her third cup of coffee and uncrossed her legs. Staying awake for just two more hours had proved more difficult than she'd anticipated; she was obviously still tired from overindulging at her party the night before last. She tapped her feet under the table with no particular rhythm, and then crossed her legs again. It was eleven thirty. She had the envelope on the table in front of her and she could almost see it sticking its tongue out and singing 'Nah nah na-nah nah.'

She picked it up and ran her hands over it. Who would know if she opened it early? Sharon and John had probably forgotten there was even an envelope for May, and Denise was no doubt conked out after the stress of her two-day hangover. Holly could just as easily lie if they ever asked her, but then again they probably wouldn't even care. No one would know and no one would care.

But that wasn't true.

Gerry would know.

Each time Holly held the envelopes in her hand she felt a connection with Gerry. The last two times she'd opened them she'd felt as though Gerry were sitting right beside her and laughing at her reactions. She felt as if they were playing a game together, even though they were in two different worlds. But she could *feel* him, and he would know if she cheated, he would know if she disobeyed the rules of their game.

After another cup of coffee Holly was bouncing off the walls. The small hand of the clock seemed to be auditioning for a part in *Baywatch* with its slow-motion run around the dial, but eventually it struck midnight. Once again she slowly turned the envelope over and treasured every moment of the process. Gerry sat opposite her at the table. 'Go on: open it!'

She carefully tore open the seal and ran her fingers along it, knowing the last thing that touched this was Gerry's tongue. She slid the card out of its pouch and opened it.

Go on, disco diva! Face your fear of karaoke at Club Diva this month, and you never know, you might be rewarded . . .
PS. I love you . . .

She felt Gerry watching her and the corners of her lips lifted into a smile. She began to laugh, repeating,

'NO WAY!' whenever she caught her breath. Finally she calmed down and announced to the room, 'Gerry! You bastard! There is absolutely no way I am going through with this!'

Gerry laughed louder.

'This is *not* funny. You know how I feel about karaoke, and I refuse to do it. Nope. No way. Not doing it.'

'You have to do it, you know,' laughed Gerry.

'I do not have to do this!'

'Do it for me.'

'I am not doing it for you, for me or for world peace. I hate karaoke!'

'Do it for me,' he repeated.

The sound of the phone caused Holly to jump in her seat.

It was Sharon. 'OK, it's five past twelve, what did it say? John and I are dying to know!'

'What makes you think I opened it?'

'Ha!' Sharon snorted. 'Twenty years of friendship qualifies me as an expert; now come on, tell us what it says.'

'I'm not doing it,' Holly stated bluntly.

'What? You're not telling us?'

'No, I'm not doing what he wants me to do.'

'Why, what is it?'

'Oh, just Gerry's *pathetic* attempt at being *humorous*,' she snapped at the ceiling.

'I'm intrigued now,' Sharon said. 'Tell us.'

'Holly, spill the beans, what is it?' John was on the downstairs phone.

'OK . . . Gerry wants me . . . to . . . singatakaraoke,' she rushed out.

'Huh? Holly, we didn't understand a word you said,' Sharon gave out.

'No, I did,' interrupted John. 'I think I heard something about karaoke. Am I right?'

'Yes,' Holly replied.

'And do you have to sing?' enquired Sharon.

'Ye-eess,' she replied slowly. Maybe if she didn't say it, it wouldn't have to happen.

The others burst out laughing so loud, Holly had to remove the phone from her ear. 'Phone me back when the two of you shut up,' she said angrily, hanging up.

A few minutes later they called back.

'Yes?'

She heard Sharon snort down the phone, relapse into a fit of the giggles and then the line went dead.

Ten minutes later she phoned back.

'Yes?'

'OK.' Sharon had an overly serious 'let's get down to business' tone in her voice. 'I'm sorry about that, I'm fine now. Don't look at me, John,' she said away from the phone. 'I'm sorry, Holly, but I just kept thinking about the last time you—'

'Yeah, yeah, yeah,' Holly interrupted, 'you don't need to bring it back up. It was *the most embarrassing day of my life* so I just happen to remember it. That's why I'm not doing it.'

'Oh, Holly, you can't let a stupid thing like that put you off!'

'Well, if that wouldn't put a person off, then they're clinically insane!'

'Holly, it was only a little fall . . .'

'Yes, thank you! I remember it just fine! Anyway, I can't even sing, Sharon; I think I established that fact marvellously the last time!'

Sharon was very quiet.

'Sharon?'

More silence.

'Sharon, you still there?'

There was no answer.

'Sharon, are you laughing?' Holly gave out.

Holly heard a little squeak and the line went dead.

'What wonderfully supportive friends I have,' she muttered under her breath.

'Oh, Gerry!' she yelled. 'I thought you were supposed to be helping me, not turning me into a nervous wreck!'

She got very little sleep that night.

Chapter Ten

'Happy birthday, Holly! Or should I say Happy belated birthday?' Richard laughed nervously. Holly's mouth dropped open in shock at the sight of her older brother standing on her doorstep. This was a rare occurrence; in fact it may even have been a first. She opened and closed her mouth like a goldfish, completely unsure what to say.

'I brought you a potted mini phalaenopsis orchid,' he said, handing her a plant. 'They have been shipped fresh, budding and are ready to bloom.' He sounded like an advertisement.

Holly was even more stunned. She fingered the tiny pink buds. 'Gosh, Richard, orchids are my favourite!'

'Well, you have a nice big garden here anyway, nice and . . .' he cleared his throat, 'green. Bit overgrown, though . . .' he trailed off and began that annoying rocking thing he did with his feet.

'Would you like to come in or are you just passing through?' Please say no, please say no. Despite the thoughtful gift, Holly was in no mood for Richard's company.

'Well, yes, I'll come in for a little while so.' He

wiped his feet for a good two minutes at the door before stepping into the house. He reminded Holly of her old maths teacher at school, dressed in a brown knitted cardigan with brown trousers that stopped just at the top of his neat little brown loafers. He hadn't a hair on his head out of place and his fingernails were clean and perfectly manicured. Holly could imagine him measuring them with a little ruler every night to see that they didn't outgrow the required European standard length for fingernails, if such a thing existed.

Richard never seemed comfortable in his own skin. He looked as if he was being choked to death by his tightly knotted (brown) tie, and he always walked as if he had a barge pole shoved up his backside. On the rare occasions that he smiled, the smile never quite managed to reach his eyes. He was the drill sergeant of his own body, screaming at it and punishing himself every time he lapsed into human mode. The sad thing was that he thought he was better off than everyone else for it. Holly led him into the living room and placed the ceramic pot on top of the TV for the time being.

'No, no, Holly,' Richard said, wagging a finger at her as though she was a naughty child, 'you shouldn't put it there. It needs to be in a cool, draught-free location away from harsh sunlight and heat vents.'

'Oh, of course.' Holly picked the pot back up and searched around the room in panic for a suitable place. What had he said? A draught-free, warm location? How did he always manage to make her feel like an incompetent little girl?

'How about that little table in the centre? It should be safe there.'

Holly did as she was told and placed the pot on the table, half expecting him to say 'good girl'. Thankfully he didn't.

Richard took his favourite position at the fireplace and surveyed the room. 'Your house is very clean,' he commented.

'Thank you. I just, eh . . . cleaned it.'

He nodded as if he already knew.

'Can I get you a tea or a coffee?' she asked, expecting him to say no.

'Yes, great,' he said, clapping his hands together. 'Tea would be splendid. Just milk no sugar.'

Holly returned from the kitchen with two mugs of tea and placed them down on the coffee table. She hoped the steam rising from the mugs wouldn't murder the poor plant. It being a heat vent and all.

'You just need to water it regularly and feed it during the spring months.' He was still talking about the plant. Holly nodded, knowing full well she would not do either of those things.

'I didn't know you had green fingers, Richard,' she said, trying to lighten the atmosphere.

'Only when I'm painting with the children,' he laughed, cracking a rare joke.

'Do you do much work in your garden?' Holly was anxious to keep the conversation flowing; as the house was so quiet every silence was amplified.

'Oh, yes, I love to work in the garden.' His eyes lit up. 'Saturdays are my garden days,' he said, smiling into his mug of tea.

Holly felt as though a complete stranger was sitting beside her. She realised she knew very little about her brother and he equally knew very little about her. But that was the way Richard had always liked to keep things. He had distanced himself from the family even when they were younger. He never shared exciting news with them or even told them how his day went. He was just full of facts, facts and more facts. The first time the family had even heard of Meredith was the day they both came over for dinner to announce their engagement. Unfortunately, by that stage it was too late to convince him not to marry the flame-haired, green-eyed dragon. Not that he would have listened, anyway.

'So,' she announced far too loudly for the echoing room, 'anything strange or startling?' Like why are you here?

'No, no, nothing strange. Everything is ticking over as normal.' He took a sip of tea, then a while later added, 'Nothing startling either, for that matter. I just thought I would pop in and say hello while I was in the area.'

'Ah, right. It's unusual for you to be over this side of the city,' Holly laughed. 'What brings you to the dark and dangerous world of the north side?'

'Oh, you know, just a little business,' he mumbled to himself. 'But my car's parked on the other side of the river, of course!'

Holly forced a smile.

'Just joking,' he added. 'It's just outside the house . . . It will be safe won't it?' he asked seriously.

'I think it should be OK,' Holly said. 'There doesn't seem to be anyone suspicious hanging around the cul-de-sac in broad daylight today.' Her humour was lost on him. 'How's Emily and Timmy – sorry, I mean Timothy?' An honest mistake for once.

Richard's eyes lit up, 'Oh, they're good, Holly, very good. Worrying, though.' He looked away and surveyed her living room.

'What do you mean?' Holly asked, thinking that perhaps Richard may open up to her.

'Oh, there isn't one thing in particular, Holly. Children are a worry in general.' He pushed the rim of his glasses up his nose and looked her in the eye. 'But I suppose you're glad you will never have to worry about all this children nonsense,' he said, laughing.

There was a silence.

Holly felt as if she had been kicked in the stomach.

'So have you found a job yet?' he continued on.

Holly sat frozen on her chair in shock. She couldn't believe he had had the audacity to say that to her. She was insulted and hurt and she wanted him out of her house. She really wasn't in the mood to be polite to him any more, and certainly couldn't be bothered explaining to his narrow little mind that she hadn't even begun looking for a job yet as she was still grieving the death of her spouse – 'nonsense' that he wouldn't have to experience for another fifty years or so.

'No,' she spat out.

'So what are you doing for money? Have you signed on the dole?'

'No, Richard,' she said, trying not to lose her temper. 'I haven't signed on the dole. I get *widow's* allowance.'

'Ah, that's a great, handy thing, isn't it?'

'Handy is not quite the word I would use. Devastatingly depressing is more like it.'

The atmosphere was tense. Suddenly he slapped his leg with his hand, signalling the end of the conversation. 'I better motor on so and get back to work,' he announced, standing up and exaggerating a stretch as though he had been sitting down for hours.

'OK then,' Holly was relieved. 'You better leave while your car is still there.'

Once again her humour was lost on him as he was peering out the window to check.

'You're right; it's still there, thank God. Anyway, nice to see you and thank you for the tea.'

'You're welcome, and thank you for the orchid,' Holly said through gritted teeth.

He marched down the garden path and stopped midway to look at the garden. He nodded his head disapprovingly and shouted to her, 'You really must get someone to sort this mess out,' and drove off in his brown family car.

Holly fumed as she watched him drive away, and banged the door shut. That man made her blood boil so much she felt like knocking him out. He just hadn't a clue . . . about anything.

Chapter Eleven

'Oh, Sharon, I just *hate* him,' Holly moaned to her friend on the phone later that night.

'Just ignore him, Holly. He can't help himself, he's an idiot,' she replied angrily.

'But that's what annoys me even more. Everyone says he can't help himself or it's not his fault, but he's a grown man, Sharon. He's thirty-six years old. He should bloody well know when to keep his mouth shut. He says those things deliberately,' Holly fumed.

'I really don't think he does, Holly,' Sharon said soothingly. 'I genuinely think he called round to wish you a happy birthday . . .'

'Yeah! And what's that about?' Holly ranted. 'Since *when* has he ever called round to my house to give me a birthday present? NEVER! That's when!'

'Well, thirty is more of a big deal than any other—'

'Not in his eyes it's not! He even said so at dinner the other day. If I recall, his exact words were,' she mimicked his voice, 'I don't agree with silly celebrations blah blah blah I'm a sap blah blah blah. He really is a Dick.'

Sharon laughed at her friend sounding like a ten-year-old. 'OK, so he's an evil monster of a being who deserves to burn in hell!'

Holly paused. 'Well, I wouldn't go that far, Sharon . . .'

Sharon laughed. 'Oh, I just can't please you at all, can I?'

Holly smiled weakly. Gerry would know exactly how she was feeling, he would know exactly what to say and exactly what to do. He would give her one of his famous hugs and all her problems would melt away. She grabbed a pillow from her bed and hugged it tight. She couldn't remember the last time she had hugged someone, *really* hugged someone. And the depressing thing was that she couldn't imagine ever embracing anyone the same way again.

'Helloooo? Earth to Holly? You still there or am I talking to myself again?

'Oh, sorry, Sharon, what did you say?'

'I said have you given any more thought to this karaoke business?'

'Sharon!' Holly yelped. 'No more thought is required on that subject.'

'OK, calm down, woman! I was just thinking that we could hire a karaoke machine and set it up in your living room. That way, you'll be doing what he wants minus the embarrassment! What do you think?'

'No, Sharon, it's a great idea but it won't work; he wants me to do it in Club Diva, wherever that is.'

'Ah! So sweet! Because you're his disco diva?'

'I think that was the general idea,' Holly said miserably.

'Ah! That's a lovely idea, although Club Diva? Never heard of it.'

'Well, that's that settled then. If no one knows where it is, then I just can't do it, can I?' Holly said, satisfied she had found a way out.

They both said their goodbyes but as soon as Holly had hung up, the phone rang again.

'Hi, sweetheart.'

'Mum!' Holly said accusingly.

'Oh God, what have I done now?'

'I received a little visit from your evil son today and I'm not very happy.'

'Oh, I'm sorry, dear, I tried to call you earlier to tell you he was on his way over but I kept getting that bloody answering machine. Do you ever turn your phone on?'

'That is not the point, Mum.'

'I know, I'm sorry. Why, what did he do?'

'He opened his mouth. There lies the problem in itself.'

'Oh no, and he was so excited about giving you that present.'

'Well, I'm not denying the fact that the present was very nice and thoughtful but he said some of the most insulting things without batting an eyelid!'

'Do you want me to talk to him for you?'

'No, it's OK; we're big boys and girls now. But thanks, anyway. So what are you up to?' Holly was anxious to change the subject.

'Ciara and I are watching a Denzel Washington film. Ciara thinks she's going to marry him someday,' Elizabeth laughed.

'I am too!' Ciara shouted in the background.

'Well, sorry to burst her little bubble but tell her he's already married.'

'He's married, honey,' Elizabeth passed on the message.

'Hollywood marriages . . .' Ciara mumbled.

'Are the two of you on your own?' Holly asked.

'Frank is down the pub and Declan is at college.'

'College? But it's ten o'clock at night!' Holly laughed. Declan was probably out somewhere doing something illegal and using college as an excuse. She didn't think her mum would be so gullible to believe that line, especially after having four other children.

'Oh, he's a very hard worker when he puts his mind to it, Holly. He's working on some project. I don't know what it is; I don't listen half the time.'

'Mmm,' Holly replied, not believing a word of it.

'Anyway, my future son-in-law is back on television so I must be off,' Elizabeth laughed. 'Would you like to come round and join us?'

'Thanks but no, I'm OK here.'

'All right, love, but if you change your mind you know where we are. Bye, dear.'

Back to her empty, silent house.

Holly woke up the next morning still fully dressed and lying on her bed. She could feel herself slipping into her old habits again. All her positive thoughts of the past few weeks were melting away bit by bit every day. It was so bloody tiring trying to be happy all the time and she just didn't have the energy any more. Who cared if the house was a mess? Nobody but she was going to see it, and she certainly didn't care one way or the other. Who cared if she didn't wear make-up or wash for a week? She had no intention of impressing anyone. The only guy she was seeing regularly was the pizza delivery boy, and she even had to tip him to make him smile. *Who bloody cared?*

Her phone vibrated beside her, signalling a text message. It was from Sharon.

Club Diva no 36700700
Think bout it. Wud b fun.
Do it 4 Gerry?

Gerry's bloody dead, she felt like texting back. But ever since she had begun opening the envelopes he didn't feel dead to her. It was as though he was just away on holiday and he was writing her letters so he wasn't *really* gone. Well, the very least she could do was ring the club and suss out the situation. That didn't mean she had to go through with it.

She dialled the number and a man answered. She couldn't think of anything to say and quickly hung up again. Oh, come on, Holly, she told herself, it's really not that difficult. Just say a friend is interested in singing.

Holly braced herself and pressed redial.

The same voice answered, 'Club Diva.'

'Hi, I was wondering if you do karaoke nights there?'

'Yes, we do. They are on a . . .' she heard him leafing through some pages, 'yeah, sorry, they're on a Thursday.'

'Thursday?'

'No, sorry, sorry, hold on . . .' He leafed through some pages again. 'No, they're on a Tuesday night.'

'Are you sure?'

'Yes, they are definitely on a Tuesday.'

'OK, em, well, I was wondering if, em . . .' Holly took a deep breath and began the sentence again. 'My friend might be interested in singing and she was wondering what she would have to do?'

There was a long pause on the other end.

'Hello?' Was this person stupid?

'Yeah, sorry, I don't actually organise the karaoke nights so . . .'

'OK.' Holly was losing her temper. It had taken a lot to summon up the courage to actually make the call and some underqualified unhelpful little twit wasn't going to ruin it for her. 'Well, is there anyone there who might have a clue?'

'Eh, no, there isn't. The club isn't actually open yet. It's very early in the morning still,' came the sarcastic response.

'Well, thank you very much. You've been a terrific help,' she matched his sarcasm.

'Excuse me, if you can just bear with me for a moment, I'll try and find out for you.' Holly was put on hold and was forced to listen to 'Greensleeves' for the next five minutes.

'Hello? Are you still there?'

'Barely,' she said angrily.

'OK, I'm very sorry about the delay but I just made a phone call there. What's your friend's name?'

Holly froze; she hadn't planned on this. Well, maybe

93

she could just give her name and then get 'her friend' to call back and cancel if she changed her mind.

'Em, her name is Holly Kennedy.'

'OK, well, it's actually a karaoke competition on Tuesday nights. It goes on for a month and every week two people out of ten are chosen till the last week of the month, where the six people sing again in the final.'

Holly gulped and felt butterflies in her tummy. She didn't want to do this.

'But unfortunately,' he continued, 'the names have all been entered a few months in advance so you can tell your friend that maybe she could try again at Christmas. That's when the next competition is on.'

'Oh, OK.'

'By the way, the name Holly Kennedy rings a bell. Would that be Declan Kennedy's sister?'

'Eh, yeah. Why, do you know her?' asked a shocked Holly.

'I wouldn't say I know her I just met her briefly here the other night with her brother.'

Was Declan going around introducing girls as his sister? The sick and twisted little . . . No, that couldn't be right.

'Declan played a gig in Club Diva?'

'No, no,' the man laughed, 'he played with his band downstairs in the basement.'

Holly quickly digested the information until the facts finally clicked in place.

'Is Club Diva in Hogan's?'

He laughed again. 'Yeah, it's on the top floor. Maybe I should advertise a bit more!'

'Is that Daniel?' Holly blurted out and then kicked herself for being so stupid.

'Eh, yeah, do I know you?'

'Em, no! No, you don't! Holly just mentioned you in conversation, that's all.' Then she realised how that sounded. 'Very briefly in conversation,' she added. 'She said you gave her a stool.' Holly began hitting her head softly against the wall.

Daniel laughed again. 'Oh, OK, well, tell her if she wants to sing in the karaoke at Christmas I can put her name down now for it. You wouldn't believe the amount of people that want to sign up.'

'Really?' Holly said weakly. She felt like a fool.

'Oh, by the way, who am I speaking to?'

Holly paced her bedroom floor. 'Em, Sharon. You're speaking to Sharon.'

'OK, Sharon, well, I have your number on caller ID so I'll call you if anyone backs out.'

'OK, thanks a lot.'

And he hung up.

Holly leaped into bed, throwing the duvet over her head as she felt her face burn with embarrassment. She hid under the covers, cursing herself for being such a bimbo. Ignoring the phone ringing, she tried to convince herself she hadn't been a complete idiot. Eventually, after she had persuaded herself she could show her face in public again (it took a long time) she crawled out of bed and hit the button on her answering machine. The electronic voice announced she had one message.

'Hi, Sharon, I must have just missed you. It's Daniel here from Club Diva,' he paused and then, laughing, added, 'in Hogan's. Em, I was just looking through the list of names in the book and it seems somebody already entered Holly's name a few months back. In fact it's one of the first entries. Unless it's another Holly Kennedy . . .' he trailed off. 'Anyway, call me back when you get a chance so we can sort it out. Thanks.'

Holly sat shocked on the edge of her bed, unable to move.

Chapter Twelve

Sharon, Denise and Holly sat by the window in Bewley's café overlooking Grafton Street. They often met up there to watch the world go by. Sharon always said it was the best window shopping she could ever do as she had a bird's-eye view of all her favourite stores.

'I can't believe Gerry organised all this!' gasped Denise when she heard the news.

'It'll be a bit of fun, won't it?' Sharon said excitedly.

'Oh God.' Holly had butterflies in her stomach just at the thought of it. 'I still really, really, *really* don't want to do it but I feel I have to finish off what Gerry started.'

'That's the spirit, Hol!' cheered Denise. 'And we'll all be there to cheer you on!'

'Now hold on a minute, Denise,' Holly said, dampening the celebratory tone, 'I just want you and Sharon there, no one else. I don't want to make a big deal out of this at all. Let's keep it between us.'

'But, Holly!' Sharon protested. 'It is a big deal! No one ever thought you'd do karaoke again after last time . . .'

'Sharon!' warned Holly. 'One must not speak of such things. One is still scarred from that experience.'

'Well, I think one is a daft cow for not getting over it,' mumbled Sharon.

'So when's the big night?' Denise changed the subject, sensing bad vibes.

'Next Tuesday,' Holly groaned, bending forward and banging her head playfully on the table repeatedly. The surrounding tables of customers stared at her curiously.

'She's just out for the day,' Sharon announced to the room, pointing at Holly.

'Don't worry, Holly; that gives you seven days exactly to transform yourself into Mariah Carey. No problem at all,' Denise said, smiling at Sharon.

'Oh, please, we would have a better chance teaching Lennox Lewis how to do ballet,' said Sharon.

Holly looked up from banging her head, 'Well, thanks for the encouragement, Sharon.'

'Ooh, but imagine Lennox Lewis in a pair of tights, that tight little arse dancing around . . .' Denise said dreamily.

Holly and Sharon stopped growling at each other to stare at their friend.

'You've lost the plot, Denise.'

'What?' Denise said defensively, snapping out of her fantasy. 'Just imagine those big muscular thighs . . .'

'That would snap your neck in two if you went near him,' Sharon finished for her.

'Now *there's* a thought,' Denise said, widening her eyes.

'I can see it all now,' Holly joined in, staring off

into space. 'The deaths column would read: "Denise Hennessey, tragically died after being crushed to death by the most tremendous thunder thighs after briefly catching a glimpse of heaven . . ."'

'I like that,' she agreed. 'Ooh, and what a way to die! Give me a slice of that heaven!'

'OK, you,' Sharon interrupted, pointing her finger at Denise, 'keep your sordid little fantasies to yourself, please. And you,' she pointed at Holly, 'stop trying to change the subject.'

'Oh, you're just jealous, Sharon, because your husband couldn't snap a matchstick between his skinny little thighs,' teased Denise.

'Excuse me, but John's thighs are perfectly fine. I just wish mine could be more like his,' Sharon finished.

'Now you,' Denise pointed at Sharon, 'keep your sordid little fantasies to yourself.'

'Girls, girls!' Holly snapped her fingers in the air. 'Let's focus on me now, focus on me,' she gracefully motioned with her hands, bringing them towards her chest.

'OK, Ms Selfish, what are you planning on singing?'

'I have no idea, that's why I called this emergency meeting.'

'No, it's not, you told me you wanted to go shopping,' Sharon said.

'Oh, really?' Denise looked at Sharon and raised an eyebrow. 'I thought you were both coming to visit me on my lunch break.'

'You are both correct,' Holly asserted. 'I am shopping for ideas and I need you both.'

'OK, OK!' Sharon exclaimed excitedly. 'I think I've

got an idea. What was that song we sang for the whole two weeks in Spain and we couldn't get it out of our heads? It used to bug the hell out of us?'

Holly shrugged her shoulders. If it bugged the hell out of them it was hardly a very good choice.

'I don't know, I wasn't invited on that holiday,' muttered Denise.

'Oh, you know the one, Holly!'

'I can't remember.'

'Oh, you have to!'

'Sharon, I don't think she can remember,' Denise said frustratedly to Sharon.

'Oh, what was it?' Sharon put her face in her hands, irritated. Holly shrugged her shoulders at Denise again. 'OK, I've got it!!' she announced happily, and began to sing loudly in the café. '"Sun, sea, sex, sand, come on boy, give me your hand!".'

Holly's eyes widened and her cheeks flushed with embarrassment as the surrounding tables turned to stare. She turned to Denise for support in silencing Sharon.

'"Ooh ooh ooh *so sexy, so sexy!*"' Denise joined in with Sharon. Some people stared with amusement but most with loathing while Denise and Sharon warbled their way through the tacky European dance song that was a hit a few summers previously. Just as they were about to sing the chorus for the fourth time (neither of them could remember the verses) Holly silenced them.

'Girls, I can't sing that song! Besides, the verses are rapped by a guy!'

'Well, at least you wouldn't have to sing too much,' chuckled Denise.

'No way! I am not rapping at a karaoke competition!'

'OK, well, what CD are you listening to at the moment?' Denise got serious again.

'Westlife?' She looked at them hopefully.

'Then sing a Westlife song,' Sharon encouraged. 'That way, at least you'll know all the words.'

Sharon and Denise began to laugh uncontrollably. 'You might not get the tune right,' Sharon forced out between hacking laughs.

'But at least you'll know the words!' Denise managed to finish for her before the two of them doubled over at the table.

First Holly was angry but looking at both of them crouched over holding their stomachs in hysterics, she had to chuckle. They were right, Holly was completely tone deaf and hadn't a note in her head. Finding a song she could actually sing was going to prove impossible.

Finally, after the girls had settled down again, Denise looked at her watch and moaned about having to get back to work. They left Bewley's, much to the other customers' delight. 'The miserable sods will probably throw a party now,' Sharon had mumbled, passing their tables.

The three girls linked arms and walked down Grafton Street, heading towards the clothes store where Denise was manager. The day was sunny with just a light chill in the air; Grafton Street was busy as usual with people running around on their lunch breaks while shoppers slowly meandered up the street taking full advantage of the lack of rain. At every stretch of the road there was a busker fighting for

101

attention from the crowds, and Denise and Sharon embarrassingly did a quick Irish dance as they passed a man playing the fiddle. He winked at them and they threw some money into his tweed cap on the ground.

'Right, you ladies of leisure, I'd better head back to work,' Denise said, pushing the door to her shop open. As soon as her staff saw her they scarpered from gossiping at the counter and immediately began to tidy the clothes rails. Holly and Sharon tried not to laugh. They said their goodbyes and both headed up to Stephen's Green to collect their cars.

'"Sun, sea, sex, sand,"' Holly quietly sang to herself. 'Oh shit, Sharon, you've got that stupid song in my head now,' she complained.

'You see, there you go with that "shit Sharon" thing again. So negative, Holly.' Sharon began humming the song.

'Oh, shut up!' Holly laughed, hitting her on the arm.

Chapter Thirteen

It was four o'clock by the time Holly eventually got out of town and started heading home to Swords. Evil Sharon had convinced Holly to go shopping after all, which resulted in her splashing out on a ridiculous top she was far too old to wear. She really needed to watch her spending from now on. Her funds were running low and without regular income she could sense tense times ahead. She needed to start thinking about getting a job, but she was finding it hard enough to get out of bed in the morning as it was – another depressing nine-to-five job wasn't going to help matters. But it would pay the bills. Holly sighed loudly. All these things she had to handle by herself. She spent too much time on her own thinking about them. She needed people around her, like today with Denise and Sharon, as they always took her mind off things.

She phoned her mum and checked if it was all right for her to call round.

'Of course you can, love, you're always welcome.' Then Elizabeth lowered her voice to a whisper. 'Just as long as you know that Richard is here.' Christ!

What was with all the little visits all of a sudden?

Holly contemplated heading straight home when she heard that, but convinced herself she was being silly. He was her brother and, as annoying as he was, she couldn't go on avoiding him forever.

She arrived to an extremely loud and crowded house, and it felt like old times again, hearing screams and shouts in every room. Her mum was setting an extra place at the table just as Holly walked in.

'Oh, Mum, you should have told me you were having dinner,' Holly said, giving her a hug and a kiss.

'Why, have you eaten already?'

'No, actually I'm starving but I hope you didn't go to too much trouble.'

'No trouble at all, dear. It just means that poor Declan will have to go without food for the day, that's all,' she said, teasing her son, who was taking his seat. He made a face at her.

The atmosphere was so much more relaxed this time around – or maybe it had just been Holly who was uptight last time they met up.

'So, Mr Hard Worker, why aren't you in college today?' she said sarcastically.

'I've been in college all morning,' Declan replied, making a face. 'And I'm going back in at eight o'clock, actually.'

'That's very late,' said his father, pouring gravy all over his plate. Frank always ended up with more gravy than food.

'Yeah, but it was the only time I could get the editing suite.'

'Is there only one editing suite, Declan?' piped up Richard.

'Yeah.' Ever the conversationalist.

'And how many students are there?'

'It's only a small class so there are twelve of us.'

'Don't they have the funds for any more?'

'For what, students?' Declan teased.

'No, for another editing suite.'

'No, it's only a small college, Richard.'

'I suppose the bigger universities would be better equipped for things like that. They're better all round.'

And there was the dig they were all waiting for.

'No, I wouldn't say that. The facilities are top of the range, there's just fewer people so less equipment. And the lecturers aren't inferior to university lecturers. They're a bonus because they work in the industry as well as lecturing. In other words, they practise what they preach. It's not just textbook stuff.'

Good for you, Declan, Holly thought, and winked across the table at him.

'I wouldn't imagine they get paid well doing that, so they probably have no choice but to lecture too.'

'Richard, working in film is a very good job; you're talking about people who have spent years in college studying for degrees and masters . . .'

'Oh, you get a degree for that, do you?' Richard was amazed. 'I thought it was just a little course you were doing.'

Declan stopped eating and looked at Holly in shock. Funny how Richard's ignorance still amazed everyone.

'Who do you think makes all those gardening

programmes you watch, Richard?' Holly interfered. 'They're not just a crowd of people who are doing a little course.'

The thought that there was a skill involved had never even crossed his mind. 'Great little programmes they are,' he agreed.

'What's your project on, Declan?' Frank asked.

Declan finished chewing his food before he spoke. 'Oh, it's too messy to go into but basically it's on club life in Dublin.'

'Ooh, will we be in it?' Ciara broke her unusual silence.

'Yeah, I might just show the back of your head or something,' he joked.

'Well, I can't wait to see it,' Holly said encouragingly.

'Thanks.' Declan put his knife and fork down and started laughing, 'Hey, what's this I hear about you singing in a karaoke competition next week?'

'What?' Ciara yelled, her eyes nearly popping out of her head.

Holly pretended not to know what he was talking about.

'Ah, come on, Holly!' he persisted. 'Danny told me!' He turned to the rest of the table and explained, 'Danny is the owner of the place where I did the gig the other night and he told me Holly has entered a karaoke competition in the club upstairs.'

Everyone oohed and aahed and talked about how great it was.

Holly refused to give in. 'Declan, Daniel's just playing games with you. Sure, everyone knows I can't sing! Now, come on,' she addressed the rest of the table.

'Honestly, if I was singing in a karaoke competition I *think* I would tell you all.' She laughed as if the thought was so ridiculous. In fact the thought *was* so ridiculous.

'Holly,' Declan chuckled, 'I saw your name on the list. Don't lie.'

Holly put her knife and fork down. She suddenly wasn't hungry any more.

'Holly, why didn't you tell us you're going to sing in a competition?' her mother asked.

'Because I can't sing!'

'Then why are you doing it?' Ciara burst out laughing.

She may as well tell them, otherwise Declan would beat it out of her and she didn't like lying to her parents.

'OK, it's a really complicated story, but basically Gerry entered my name in months ago because he really wanted me to do it and as much as I *don't* want to do it, I feel I have to go through with it. It's stupid, I know.'

Ciara stopped laughing abruptly.

Holly felt paranoid by her family staring at her, and she nervously tucked her hair behind her ears.

'Well, I think that's a wonderful idea,' her dad suddenly announced.

'Yes,' added her mum, 'and we'll all be there to support you.'

'No, Mum, you really don't have to. It's no big deal.'

'There's no way my sister is singing in a competition without me being there,' declared Ciara.

107

'Here, here,' said Richard. 'We'll all go so. I've never been to a karaoke before. It should be . . .' he searched his brain for the right word, '. . . fun.'

Holly groaned and closed her eyes, wishing she had gone straight home from town.

Declan was laughing hysterically, 'Yes, Holly, it'll be . . . hmmm . . .' he said, scratching his chin, '. . . fun!'

'When is it on?' Richard said, taking out his diary.

'Eh . . . Saturday,' Holly lied, and Richard began writing it down.

'It is not!' Declan burst out. 'It's next Tuesday, you liar!'

'Shit!' cursed Richard, much to everyone's surprise. 'Has anyone got any Tippex?'

Holly could not stop going to the toilet. She was nervous and had had practically no sleep the night before. And she looked how she felt. There were huge bags around her bloodshot eyes and her lips were bitten.

The big day had arrived, her worst nightmare – singing in public.

Holly wasn't even the kind of person who sang in the shower for fear of cracking all the mirrors. But man, was she spending time in the toilet today. There was no better laxative than fear, and Holly felt as if she had lost a stone in just one day. Her friends and family had been as supportive as ever, sending her good luck cards. Sharon and John had even sent her a bouquet of flowers, which she placed on the draught-free, heat-vent-free coffee table beside her half-dead orchid. Denise had 'hilariously' sent her a sympathy card.

Holly dressed in the outfit Gerry had told her to buy last month and cursed him throughout. There were far more important things to worry about right now than irrelevant little details like how she looked. She left her hair down so it covered her face as much as possible and piled on the waterproof mascara as though it was going to prevent her from crying. She could foresee the night ending in tears. She tended to have psychic powers when it came to facing the shittiest days of her life.

John and Sharon collected Holly in a taxi and she refused to talk to them, cursing everyone for forcing her to do this. She felt physically sick and she couldn't sit still. Every time the taxi stopped at a red light she contemplated jumping out and running for dear life but by the time she would build up the courage the lights would go green again. Her hands fidgeted nervously and she kept opening and closing her bag, pretending to Sharon she was searching for something just to keep herself occupied.

'Relax, Holly,' Sharon said soothingly, 'everything will be fine.'

'Fuck off,' she snapped.

They continued on in silence for the rest of the journey: even the taxi driver didn't speak. After a tense journey they finally reached Hogan's, and John and Sharon had a hell of a time trying to stop Holly ranting (something about preferring to jump in the Liffey) and persuading her to go inside. Much to Holly's horror, the club was absolutely jammed and she had to squeeze by everyone to make her way to her family, who had saved a table (right beside the toilet as requested).

Richard was sitting awkwardly on a stool, looking out of place in a suit. 'So tell me about these rules, Father. What will Holly have to do?'

Holly's dad explained the 'rules' of karaoke to Richard and her nerves began to build even more.

'Gosh, that's terrific, isn't it?' Richard said, staring around the club in awe. Holly didn't think he had ever been in a nightclub before.

The sight of the stage terrified Holly. It was much bigger than she had expected and there was a huge screen on the wall for the crowd to see the words of the songs. Jack was sitting with his arm draped around Abbey's shoulders; they both gave her supportive smiles. Holly scowled at them and looked away.

'Holly the funniest thing happened earlier on,' Jack said laughing. 'Remember that guy Daniel we met last week?'

Holly just stared at him, watching his lips moving but not giving a damn about what he said. 'Well, me and Abbey got here first to keep the table and we were having a kiss and your man came over and whispered in my ear that you were gonna be here tonight. He thought we were going out and that I was doing the dirt!' Jack and Abbey laughed hysterically.

'Well, I think that's disgusting,' Holly said, and turned away.

'No,' Jack tried to explain, 'he didn't know that we were brother and sister. I had to explain . . .' Jack trailed off as Sharon shot him a warning look and silenced him.

'Hi, Holly,' Daniel said, approaching her with a clipboard in his hand. 'OK, here's the order of tonight:

first up is a girl called Margaret, then a guy called Keith and then you're up after him. Is that OK?'

'So I'm third.'

'Yeah, after—'

'That's all I need to know,' Holly snapped rudely. She just wanted to get out of this stupid club and wished that everyone would stop annoying her and leave her alone to wish evil thoughts on them all. She wished the ground would swallow her up, that a natural disaster would occur and everyone would have to evacuate the building. In fact, that was a good idea. She searched around frantically for a button to raise the fire alarm, but Daniel was still talking away to her.

'Look, Holly, I'm really sorry to disturb you again, but could you tell me which of your friends is Sharon?' He looked as if he was afraid she was going to bite his head off. So he should be, she thought, narrowing her eyes.

'Her over there.' Holly pointed to Sharon. 'Hold on, why?'

'Oh, I just wanted to apologise for the last time we spoke.' He started to walk towards Sharon.

'Why?' Holly said, the panic in her voice making him turn around again.

'We just had a minor disagreement on the phone last week.' He looked at her confused.

'You know you really don't need to do that. She's probably forgotten about it completely by now,' she stammered. This was the last thing she needed.

'Yeah, but I would still like to apologise,' and he headed over to Sharon. Holly leaped from her stool.

'Sharon, hi, I'm Daniel. I just wanted to apologise about the confusion on the phone last week.'

Sharon looked at him as though he had ten heads. 'Confusion?'

'You know, on the phone?'

John placed his arm protectively around Sharon's waist.

'On the phone?'

'Eh . . . yes, on the phone,' he nodded.

'What's your name again?'

'Em, it's Daniel.'

'And we spoke on the phone?' Sharon said with a smile appearing on her face.

Holly gestured wildly to her behind Daniel's back.

Daniel cleared his throat nervously. 'Yes, you called the club last week and I answered – does that ring a bell?'

'No, sweetie, you've got the wrong girl,' Sharon said politely.

John threw Sharon a dirty look for calling him sweetie; if it was up to him he would have told him where to go.

Daniel brushed his hand through his hair and appeared to be more confused than everyone else. He began to turn round to face Holly.

Holly nodded her head frantically to Sharon.

'Oh . . .' Sharon said, looking as though she finally remembered. 'Oh – Daniel!' she yelled a bit over enthusiastically. 'God, I am so sorry, my brain cells seem to be going a bit dead.' She laughed like a mad woman. 'Must be too much of this,' she chortled, picking up her drink.

Relief washed over Daniel's face. 'Good, I thought it was me going mad there for a minute! OK, so you remember us having that conversation on the phone?'

'Oh, *that* conversation we had on the phone. Listen, don't worry about it,' she said, waving her hand dismissively.

'It's just that I only took over the place a few weeks ago and I wasn't too sure of the exact arrangements for tonight.'

'Don't worry . . . we all need our time . . . to adjust . . . to things . . . you know?' Sharon looked at Holly to see if she had said the right thing or not.

'OK then. Well, it's nice to finally meet you in person,' Daniel laughed. 'Can I get you a stool or anything?' he joked.

Sharon and John sat on their stools and stared back at him in silence, not knowing what to say to this strange man.

John watched with suspicion as Daniel walked away.

'What was that all about?' Sharon screamed at Holly as soon as he was out of earshot.

'Oh, I'll explain it to you later,' said Holly. She turned to face the stage as their karaoke host stepped on stage.

'Good evening, ladies and gentlemen!' he announced.

'Good evening!' shouted Richard, looking excited. Holly rolled her eyes to heaven.

'We have an exciting night ahead of us . . .' he went on and on and on in his DJ voice while Holly danced nervously from foot to foot. She desperately needed the toilet again.

'So first up tonight we have Margaret from Tallaght who is going to sing the theme to *Titanic*, "My Heart Will Go On" by Celine Dion. Please put your hands together for the wonderful Margaret!' The crowd went wild. Holly's heart raced. The hardest song in the world to sing – typical.

When Margaret started to sing, the room became so quiet you could almost hear a pin drop. Holly watched everyone's faces. They were all staring at Margaret in amazement, including Holly's family, the traitors. Margaret's eyes were closed and she sang with such passion, as though she had lived every line of the song. Holly hated her and contemplated tripping her up on her way back to her seat.

'Wasn't that incredible?' the DJ announced. The crowd cheered again; Holly prepared herself not to hear that sound after she sang. 'Next up we have Keith. You may remember him as last year's winner and he's singing "America" by Neil Diamond. Give it up for Keith!' Holly didn't need to hear any more and rushed to the toilet.

She paced up and down and tried to calm herself, but her knees were knocking, her stomach was twisted in knots and she felt the beginnings of vomit rising to her mouth. She looked at herself in the mirror and tried to take big deep breaths. It didn't work, as it only made her feel dizzy. The crowd applauded outside and Holly froze. She was next.

'Wasn't Keith terrific, ladies and gentlemen?'

Lots of cheers again.

'Perhaps Keith is going for the record of winning two years in a row. Well, it doesn't get any better than that!'

It was about to get a lot worse.

'Next we have a newcomer to the competition and her name is Holly and she's singing . . .'

Holly ran to the toilet and locked herself in. There was no way in this world they were getting her out of there.

'So, ladies and gentlemen, please put your hands together for Holly!'

There was a huge applause.

Chapter Fourteen

It was three years ago that Holly had taken to the stage for her debut karaoke performance.

Not coincidentally, it was three years *since* Holly had taken to the stage to do karaoke.

A huge crowd of her friends had gone to their local pub in Swords to celebrate one of the lad's thirtieth birthdays. Holly had been extremely tired as she had been working overtime for the past two weeks and she really wasn't in the mood to go out partying. All she wanted was to go home, have a nice long bath, put on the most unsexy pair of pyjamas she owned, eats lots of chocolate and snuggle up on the couch in front of the TV with Gerry.

After standing on an overcrowded Dart all the way from Blackrock to Sutton Station, Holly was definitely not in the mood to stand all night in a packed stuffy pub. On the train, half her face had been squashed up against the window and the other half lodged underneath the sweaty armpit of a very unhygienic man. Right behind her a man was breathing alcoholic fumes rather loudly down her neck. It didn't help matters that every time the train swayed he 'accidentally' pressed his big beer belly up against her back. She had suffered through this ordeal everyday going to work and coming home for two weeks and she could take it no longer. She wanted her pyjamas.

Finally she arrived at Sutton Station and the very clever people there thought it was a great idea to all get *on* the train while passengers tried to get off. It took her so long to fight her way through the crowd to get *off* the train that by the time she reached the platform she saw her feeder bus drive off, packed with happy little people smiling out the window at her. And because it was after six o'clock, the coffee shop had closed and she was left standing in the freezing cold waiting for another half-hour till the next bus arrived. On top of everything else, this strengthened her desire to cuddle up in front of the fire.

But a good evening at home was not to be. Her beloved husband had other plans. She arrived home tired and extremely pissed off to a crowded house and thumping music. People she didn't even know were wandering around her living room with cans of beer in their hands and slumping themselves on the couch she had intended to inhabit for the next few hours. Gerry stood at the CD player acting DJ and trying to look cool. At that moment in time she had never seen him look so uncool in her life.

'What is wrong with you?' Gerry asked her after seeing her storming upstairs to the bedroom.

'Gerry, I am tired, I am pissed off, I am not in the mood to go out tonight and you didn't even ask me if it was all right to invite all these people over. And, by the way, WHO ARE THEY?' she yelled.

117

'They're friends of Conor's and, by the way, THIS IS MY HOUSE TOO!' he yelled back.

Holly placed her fingers on her temples and began to gently massage her head, she had such a headache and the music was driving her crazy.

'Gerry,' she said quietly, trying to stay calm, 'I'm not saying that you can't invite people over. It would be fine if you had planned it in advance and told me. *Then* I wouldn't care, but today of all days when I am so so tired . . .' her voice became weaker and weaker with every word, 'I just wanted to relax in my own house.'

'Oh, everyday's the same with you,' he snapped. 'You never want to do anything any more anyway. Every single night, you come home in your cranky moods and bitch at me about everything!'

Holly's jaw dropped. 'Excuse me! I have been working hard!'

'And so have I, but you don't see me biting your head off every time I don't get my own way.'

'Gerry this isn't about me getting my own way, this is about you inviting the whole street into our h—'

'IT'S FRIDAY,' he yelled, silencing her, 'IT'S THE WEEKEND! When is the last time you went out? Leave your work behind and let your hair down, for a change. Stop acting like such a GRANNY!' And he stormed out of the bedroom and slammed the door.

After spending a long time in the bedroom hating Gerry and dreaming of a divorce she managed to calm down and think rationally about what he had said. And he was right. OK, he wasn't right in the way he had phrased it but she *had* been cranky and bitchy all month and she knew it.

Holly was the type of person who finished work at 5 p.m. and had her computer switched off, lights off, desk tidied and was running for her train by 5.01 p.m. whether her employers liked it or not. She never took her work home, never stressed about the future of the business because, quite frankly, she didn't care, and phoned in sick as many Monday mornings as possible without running the risk of being fired. But due to a momentary lapse of concentration when looking for new employment, she had found herself accepting an office job that forced her to take paperwork home, agree to work late and worry about the business, which she was not happy with *at all*. How she even managed to stay there for an entire month was anybody's guess but, nevertheless, Gerry had been right. Ouch, it even hurt to think it. She hadn't gone out with him or her friends for weeks and fell asleep the minute her head hit the pillow every night. Come to think of it, that was probably Gerry's main problem, never mind the bitchiness.

But tonight would be different. She intended showing her neglected friends and husband that she was still the fun and frivolous Holly who could drink them all under the table and still manage to walk the white line all the way home. This show of antics began by preparing home-made cocktails. God only knows what was in them, but they worked their magic, and at eleven o'clock they were all dancing down the road to the pub where karaoke was taking place. Holly demanded to be first up and heckled the karaoke host until she got her way. The pub was jammed and that night there was a very rowdy crowd who were out on a stag night. It was as though a film crew had arrived in the pub hours earlier and worked away, setting the scene for disaster. They couldn't have done a better job.

The DJ gave Holly a huge build-up after believing her lies of being a professional singer. Gerry lost all power of speech and sight from laughing so hard but she was determined to show him that she could still let her hair down. He needn't plan that divorce just yet. Holly decided to sing 'Like a Virgin' and dedicated it to the man who was getting married the next day. As soon as she started singing, Holly had never heard so many boos in her whole life and at such a loud volume. But she was so drunk she didn't care and continued on singing to her husband, who seemed to be the only one without a moody face.

Eventually, when people began to throw things at the stage, and when the karaoke host himself encouraged them to boo even louder, Holly felt that her work there had been done. When she handed him back the microphone there was a cheer so loud that people from the pub next door came running in. There were all the more people to see Holly trip down the steps in her stilettos and fall flat on her face. They all watched as her skirt went flying over her head to reveal the old underwear, which had once been white and which she hadn't bothered to change when she got home from work.

Holly was taken to hospital to see to her broken nose.

Gerry lost his voice from laughing so loudly and Denise and Sharon helped matters by taking photographs of the scene of the crime, which Denise then chose as the cover for the invitations to her Christmas party with the heading, 'Let's get legless!'

Holly vowed *never* to do karaoke again.

Chapter Fifteen

'Holly Kennedy? Are you here?' the karaoke host's voice boomed. The crowd's applause died down into a loud chatter as everyone looked around in search of Holly. Well, they would be a long time looking, she thought as she lowered the toilet seat lid and sat down to wait for the excitement to settle so they could move on to their next victim. She closed her eyes, rested her head on her hands, and prayed for this moment to pass. She wanted to open her eyes and be at home safely, a week from now. She counted to ten, praying for a miracle and then slowly opened them again.

She was still in the toilet.

Why couldn't she, at least just this once, suddenly find magical powers?

Holly knew this would happen. From the moment she opened that envelope and read Gerry's third letter, she foresaw tears and humiliation. Her nightmare had come true.

Outside, the club sounded very quiet and a sense of calm engulfed her as she realised they were moving on to the next singer. Her shoulders relaxed and she unclenched her fists, her jaw relaxed and air flowed more easily into her lungs. The panic was over but she decided to wait until the next singer began before she made a run for it. She couldn't even climb out the window – well, not unless she wanted to plummet to her death.

Outside the cubicle Holly heard the toilet door open and slam. Uh-oh, they were coming to get her, whoever *they* were.

'Holly?'

It was Sharon.

'Holly, I know you're in there so just listen to me, OK?'

Holly sniffed back the tears that were beginning to well.

'OK, I know that this is an absolute nightmare for you and I know you have a major phobia about this kind of thing but you need to relax, OK?'

Sharon's voice was so soothing, Holly's shoulders once again relaxed.

'Holly, I hate mice, you know that.'

Holly frowned, wondering where this little pep talk was going.

'And my worst nightmare would be to walk out of here to a room full of mice. Now could you imagine me?'

Holly smiled at the thought and remembered the time when Sharon moved in with Gerry and Holly for two weeks after she had caught a mouse in her house. John, of course, had been granted conjugal visits.

'Yeah, well, I would be right here where you are now and nothing in the whole world would bring me out.' She paused.

123

'What?' the DJ's voice said into the microphone, and then started laughing, 'Ladies and gentlemen, it appears that our singer is currently in the toilets.' The entire room erupted in laughter.

'Sharon!' Holly's voice trembled in fear. She felt as though the angry mob were about to break down the door; strip her of her clothes and carry her over their heads to the stage for her execution. Panic took over for the third time.

Sharon rushed her next sentence. 'Anyway, Holly, all I'm saying is that you don't have to do this if you don't want to. Nobody here is forcing you . . .'

'Ladies and gentlemen, let's let Holly know that she's up next!' yelled the DJ. 'Come on!'

Everybody began to stamp their feet and chant her name.

'OK, well, at least nobody who cares about you is forcing you to do this,' stammered Sharon, now under pressure from the approaching mob. 'But if you don't do this, I know you will never be able to forgive yourself. Gerry wanted you to do this for a reason.'

'HOLLY! HOLLY! HOLLY!'

'Oh, Sharon!' Holly repeated, panicking. Suddenly the walls of the cubicle felt like they were closing in on her, beads of sweat formed on her forehead. She had to get out of there. She burst through the door. Sharon's eyes widened at the sight of her distraught friend, who looked like she had just seen a ghost. Her eyes were red and puffy with black lines of mascara streaming down her face (that waterproof stuff never works) and her tears had washed the rest of her make-up away.

'Don't mind them, Holly,' Sharon said coolly. 'They can't make you do anything you don't want to do.'

Holly's lower lip began to tremble.

'Don't!' Sharon said, gripping her by the shoulders and looking her in the eye. 'Don't even think about it!'

Her lip stopped trembling but the rest of her didn't. Finally, Holly broke her silence. 'I can't sing, Sharon,' she whispered, her eyes wide with terror.

'I know that,' Sharon said, laughing, 'and your family knows that! Screw the rest of them! You are never gonna see any of their ugly mugs EVER AGAIN! Who cares what they think? I don't, do you?'

Holly thought about it for a minute. 'No,' she whispered.

'I didn't hear you – what did you say? Do you care what they think?'

'No,' Holly said, a little stronger.

'Louder!' Sharon shook her by the shoulders.

'No!' Holly yelled.

'Louder!'

'NOOOOOOOOOO! I DON'T CARE WHAT THEY THINK!' Holly screamed so loud the crowd began to quieten down outside. The two of them smiled at each other and then began to giggle at their stupidity.

'Just let this be another silly Holly day so we can laugh about it a few months from now,' Sharon pleaded with her.

Holly cast one last look at her reflection in the mirror, took a deep breath and charged towards the door like a woman on a mission. She opened the door to her adoring fans, who were all still chanting her name. They all began to cheer when they saw her and she took an extremely theatrical bow and headed towards the stage to the sound of claps and laughter, and a yell from Sharon saying, 'Screw them!'

Holly had everybody's attention now, whether she liked it or not. If she hadn't run into the toilet the people who were chatting down the back of the club probably wouldn't even have noticed her singing, but now she had attracted even more interest.

She stood with her arms folded and stared at the audience in shock. The music had started without her even noticing, and she missed the first few lines of the song. The DJ stopped the track and put it back to the start.

There was complete silence. Holly cleared her throat and the sound echoed around the room. Holly stared down at Denise and Sharon for help and her whole table gave her the thumbs-up. Ordinarily Holly would have laughed at how corny they all looked but right then it was strangely comforting. Finally the music began again and Holly held the microphone tightly in her two hands and prepared to sing. With an extremely shaky and timid voice she sang: '"What would you do if I sang out of tune? Would you stand up and walk out on me?"'

Denise and Sharon howled with laughter at the wonderful choice of song and gave her a big cheer. Holly struggled on, singing dreadfully and looking as if she was about to burst into tears. Just when she felt she was about to hear boos again, her family and friends joined in with the chorus. '"Ooh, I'll get by with a little help from my friends; yes I'll get by with a little help from my friends."'

The crowd turned to her table of family and friends and laughed, and the atmosphere warmed a little more. Holly prepared herself for the high note coming up and yelled at the top of her lungs, '"Do you *neeeed* anybody?"' She even managed to give herself a fright with the volume and a few people helped her out to sing, '"I need somebody to love."'

'"Do you *neeeed* anybody?"' she repeated, and held the microphone out to the crowd to encourage them to sing and they all sang, '"I need somebody to love,"' and gave themselves a round of applause. Holly felt less nervous now and battled her way through the rest of the song. The people down the back resumed chatting, the bar staff carried on serving drinks and smashing glasses until Holly felt that she was the only one listening to herself.

When she had finally finished singing, a few polite tables up the front and her own table to the right were the only people to acknowledge her. The DJ took the microphone from her hand and managed to say between laughs, 'Please give it up for the incredibly brave Holly Kennedy!'

This time her family and friends were the only people to cheer. Denise and Sharon approached her with cheeks wet from tears of laughter.

'I'm so proud of you!' Sharon said, throwing her arms around Holly's neck. 'It was awful!'

'Thanks for helping me, Sharon.' Holly hugged her friend.

Jack and Abbey cheered, and Jack shouted, 'Terrible! Absolutely terrible!'

Holly's mother smiled encouragingly at her, knowing

she had passed her special singing talent down to her daughter, and Holly's father could barely look her in the eye he was laughing so much. All Ciara could manage was to repeat over and over again, 'I never knew anyone could be so bad.'

Declan waved at her across the room with a camera in his hand and gave her the thumbs-down. Holly hid in the corner at the table and sipped on her water while she listened to everyone congratulating her on being so desperately awful. Holly couldn't remember the last time she had felt so proud.

John shuffled over to Holly and leaned against the wall beside her where he watched the next act on stage in silence. Eventually he plucked up the courage to speak and said, 'Gerry's probably here, you know,' and looked at her with watery eyes.

Poor John, he missed his best friend too. She gave him an encouraging smile and looked around the room. He was right. Holly *could* feel Gerry's presence. She could feel him wrapping his arms around her and giving her one of his hugs she missed so much.

After an hour the singers had finally finished and Daniel and the DJ headed off to tot up the votes. Everyone had been handed a voting slip as they paid at the door and Holly couldn't bring herself to write her own name down so she gave her slip to Sharon. It was pretty obvious that Holly wasn't going to win but that had never been her intention. And on the off chance that she did win she shuddered at the thought of having to return in two weeks' time to repeat the whole experience. She hadn't learned a thing from it, only that she hated karaoke even more. Last year's winner, Keith, had brought along at least thirty of his friends, which meant that he was a sure winner, and Holly doubted very much that her 'adoring fans' in the crowd would vote for her.

The DJ played a pathetic CD of a drum roll as the winners were about to be announced. Daniel took to the stage once again in his black leather jacket and black slacks uniform and was greeted by wolf-whistles and screams from the girls. Worryingly, the loudest of these girls was Ciara. Richard looked excited and crossed his fingers at Holly, a very sweet but incredibly naïve gesture, she thought. He obviously didn't understand the 'rules' properly.

There was a bit of embarrassment as the drum-roll began to skip and the DJ rushed over to his equipment to shut it down. The winners were announced undramatically, in dead silence. 'OK, I'd like to thank everyone for taking part in tonight's competition. You provided us all with some terrific entertainment.' That last part was directed at Holly and she slithered down her seat in embarrassment. 'So the two people that will be going through to the final are – ' Daniel paused for dramatic effect – 'Keith and Samantha!'

Holly jumped up with excitement and danced around in a huddle with Denise and Sharon. She had never felt such relief in her life. Richard looked on very confused while the rest of Holly's family congratulated her on her victorious losing.

'I voted for the blonde one,' Declan announced with disappointment.

'That's just because she had big tits,' Holly laughed.

129

'Well, we all have our own individual talents,' Declan agreed.

Holly wondered what hers were as she sat back down. It must be a wonderful feeling to win something, to know that you have a gift. Holly had never won anything in her life. She didn't do any sports, couldn't play an instrument – now that she thought about it she didn't have *any* hobbies or special interests. What would she put down on her CV when she eventually got around to applying for a job? 'I like to drink and shop' wouldn't go down very well. She sipped her drink thoughtfully. Holly had lived her life being interested in Gerry – in fact, everything she did revolved around him. In a way, being his wife was all she was good at; being his partner was all she knew. Now what did she have? No job, no husband and she couldn't even sing in a karaoke competition properly, never mind win it.

Sharon and John seemed engrossed in a heated discussion, Abbey and Jack were gazing into each other's eyes like love-struck teenagers, as usual, Ciara was intent on getting to know Daniel better and Denise was . . . Actually, where was Denise?

Holly looked around the club and spotted her sitting on the stage swinging her legs and striking a very provocative pose for the karaoke host. Holly's parents had left hand in hand just after her name wasn't announced as a winner, which left . . . Richard.

Richard sat squashed beside Ciara and Daniel, looking around the room like a lost puppy and taking a sip from his drink every few seconds out of paranoia. Holly realised she must have looked like him –

a complete loser. But at least this loser had a wife and two children to go home to, unlike Holly, who had a date with a microwave dinner.

Holly moved over and sat on the high stool opposite Richard, and struck up a conversation.

'You enjoying yourself?'

He looked up from his drink, startled that someone had spoken to him. 'Yes, thank you, I'm having fun, Holly.'

If that was him having fun Holly dreaded to think what he looked like when he wasn't.

'I'm surprised you came, actually. I didn't think this would be your scene.'

'Oh, you know . . . you have to support the family.' He stirred his drink.

'So where's Meredith tonight?'

'Emily and Timothy,' he said, as if that explained it all.

'You working tomorrow?'

'Yes,' he said, suddenly knocking back his drink, 'so I best be off. You were a great sport tonight, Holly.' He looked around awkwardly at his family, deciding whether to interrupt them and say goodbye but eventually deciding against it. He nodded to Holly and off he went, manoeuvring his way through the dense crowd.

Holly was once again alone. As much as she wanted to grab her bag and run home she knew she should sit this one out. There would be plenty of times in the future when she would be alone like this, the only singleton in the company of couples, and she needed to adapt. She felt awful though, and also angry with the others who didn't even notice her. Then she cursed herself for being so childish. She couldn't have asked for more supportive friends and family. Holly wondered whether this had been Gerry's intention. Did he think that this situation was what she needed? Did he think that this would help her? Perhaps he was right because she was certainly being tested. It was forcing her to become braver in more ways than one. She had stood on a stage and sang to hundreds of people and now she was stuck in a situation where she was surrounded by couples. Whatever his plan was, she was being forced to become braver without him. Just sit it out, she told herself.

Holly smiled as she watched her sister nattering away to Daniel. Ciara was nothing like her at all; she was so carefree and confident, and didn't seem to worry about anything. For as long as Holly could remember, Ciara had never managed to hold down a job or a boyfriend. Her brain was always somewhere else, lost in the dream of visiting another far-off country. Holly wished she could be more like her. She had been to far-flung places too, but always with Gerry by her side, and never for more than a few weeks. Unlike Ciara, Holly was a home-bird and could never imagine herself moving away from her family and friends and leaving the life she had made for herself here. At least, she could never have left the life she had once had.

She turned her attention to Jack, who was still lost in a world with Abbey. She even wished she could be more like him; he absolutely loved his job as a secondary school teacher. He was the cool English teacher that all the teenagers respected, and whenever Holly and Jack passed one of his students on the street they always greeted him with a big smile and a 'Hiya, sir!' All the girls fancied him and all the boys wanted to be like him when they got older. Holly sighed loudly and drained her drink. Now she was bored.

Daniel looked over. 'Holly, can I get you a drink?'

'Ah no, it's OK, thanks, Daniel. I'm heading home soon anyway.'

'Ah, Hol!' protested Ciara. 'You can't go home so early! It's your night!'

Holly didn't feel as though it was her night. She felt rather as if she had gate-crashed a party and didn't know anyone there.

'No, I'm all right, thanks,' she assured Daniel again.

'No, you're staying,' Ciara insisted. 'Get her a vodka and Coke, and I'll have the same again,' she ordered Daniel.

'Ciara!' Holly exclaimed, embarrassed at her sister's rudeness.

'No, it's OK!' Daniel assured her. 'I asked.' And he headed off to the bar.

'Ciara, that was so rude,' Holly gave out to her sister.

'What? It's not like he has to pay for it; he owns the bloody place,' she said defensively.

'That still doesn't mean you can go around demanding free drinks—'

'Where's Richard?' Ciara interrupted.

'Gone home.'

'Shit! How long ago?' She jumped down from her seat in a panic.

'I dunno, about five or ten minutes. Why?'

'He's supposed to be driving me home!' She threw everyone's coats into a pile on the floor while she rooted around for her bag.

'Ciara, you'll never catch him now, he's been gone far too long.'

'No, I will. He's parked ages away and he'll have to drive back down this road to get home. I'll get him while he's passing.' She finally found her bag and legged it out the door yelling, 'Bye, Holly! Well done, you were shite!' before disappearing.

Holly was once again alone. Great, she thought, watching Daniel carrying the drinks back to the table. Now she was stuck talking to him all by herself.

'Where's Ciara gone?' Daniel said, placing the drinks on the table and sitting down opposite Holly.

'Oh, she said to say she's really sorry but she had to chase my brother for a lift.' Holly bit her lip guiltily, knowing full well that Ciara hadn't even given Daniel a second thought as she raced out the door. 'Sorry for being so rude to you earlier as well.' Then she started laughing, 'God, you must think we're the rudest family in the world. Ciara's a bit of a motor mouth; she doesn't mean what she says half the time.'

'And you did?' he smiled.

'At the time, yes.' She laughed again.

'Hey, it's fine, just means there's more drink for you,' he said, sliding a shot glass across the table to her.

'Ugh, what is this?' Holly wrinkled her nose up at the smell.

Daniel looked away awkwardly and cleared his throat. 'I can't remember.'

134

'Oh, come on!' Holly laughed. 'You just ordered it! It's a woman's right to know what she's drinking, you know!'

Daniel looked at her with a smile on his face. 'It's called a BJ. You should have seen the barman's face when I asked for one. I don't think he knew it was a shot!'

'Oh God,' Holly laughed, 'what's Ciara doing drinking this? It smells awful!'

'She said she found it easy to swallow.' He started laughing again.

'Oh, I'm sorry, Daniel. She really is ridiculous sometimes.' Holly shook her head over her sister.

Daniel stared past Holly's shoulder with amusement. 'Well, it looks like your friend is having a good night, anyway.'

Holly turned and saw Denise and the DJ wrapped around each other beside the stage. Her provocative poses had obviously worked.

'Oh no, not the horrible DJ who forced me to come out of the toilet,' Holly groaned.

'That's Tom O'Connor from Dublin FM.' Daniel laughed. 'He's a friend of mine.'

Holly covered her face in embarrassment.

'He's working here tonight because the karaoke went out live on the radio,' he said seriously.

'WHAT?' Holly nearly had a heart attack for the twentieth time that night.

Daniel's face broke out into a smile, 'Only joking; just wanted to see the look on your face.'

'Oh my God, don't do that to me,' Holly said, putting her hand on her heart. 'Having the people in

135

here listening to me was bad enough, never mind the entire city as well.' She waited for her heart to stop pounding while Daniel stared at her with an amused look in his eye.

'If you don't mind me asking, if you hate it so much why did you enter?' he asked carefully.

'Oh, my hilarious husband thought it would be funny to enter his tone-deaf wife into a singing competition.'

Daniel laughed. 'You weren't *that* bad! Is your husband here?' he asked. 'I don't want him thinking I'm trying to poison his wife with that awful concoction.' He nodded towards the shot glass.

Holly looked around the club and smiled. 'Yeah, he's definitely here . . . somewhere.'

Chapter Sixteen

Holly secured her bed sheet onto the washing line with a peg and thought about how she had bumbled around for the remainder of May trying to get her life into some sort of order. Days went by when she felt so happy and content, and *confident* that her life would be OK, and then as quickly as the feeling came it would disappear and she would feel sadness setting in again. She tried to find a routine she could fall into so that she felt as though she belonged in her body and her body belonged in this life, instead of wandering around like a zombie, watching everybody else live theirs while she waited for hers to end.

Unfortunately the routine hadn't turned out exactly as she hoped it would. She found herself immobile for hours in the sitting room, reliving every single memory that she and Gerry had shared. She spent most of that time thinking about every argument they'd had, wishing she could take them back, wishing she could take back every horrible word she had ever said to him. She prayed that Gerry had known her words had only been spoken in anger and that they had not reflected her true feelings. She tortured herself for the times she

137

had acted selfishly, going out with her friends for the night when she was mad at him instead of staying home with him. She chastised herself for walking away from him when she should have hugged him, when she held grudges for days instead of forgiving him, when she went straight to sleep some nights instead of making love to him. She wanted to take back every moment she knew he had been so angry with her and hated her. She wished all her memories were of the good times but the bad times kept coming back to haunt her. They had all been such a waste.

And nobody had told them that they were short on time.

There were her happy days, when she would walk around in a daydream with nothing but a smile on her face, catching herself giggling as she walked down the street when a joke of theirs would suddenly pop into her head.

Then she would fall into days of deep dark depression; then finally build up the strength to be positive and to snap out of it for another few days. But the tiniest and simplest thing would trigger off her tears again. That was her routine. It was a tiring process and most of the time she couldn't be bothered battling with her mind. It was far stronger than her body.

Friends and family came and went; sometimes helping her with her tears, other times making her laugh. But even in her laughter there was something missing. She never seemed to be truly happy; she just seemed to be passing time till she waited for something else. She was tired of just existing; she wanted to live. But what was the point in living when there was no *life* in it. These questions went through her mind over and over again till she reached the point of not wanting to wake up from her dreams that felt so real.

Deep down, she knew it was normal to feel like this. She didn't particularly think she was losing her mind. She knew that people said that one day she would be happy again and that this feeling would just be a distant memory. It was getting to that feeling that was the hard part.

She read and reread Gerry's letter over and over again, analysing each word and each sentence, and each day coming up with a new meaning. But she could sit there till the cows came home trying to read between the lines and guess the hidden message. The fact was that she would never *really* know *exactly* what he meant because she would never speak to him *ever again*. It was this that she had the most difficulty trying to come to terms with.

Now May had gone and June had arrived, bringing bright long evenings and beautiful mornings. And along with these sunny days June also brought clarity. There was no hiding indoors as soon as it got dark, no lie-ins until the afternoon. It seemed as though the whole of Ireland had come out of hibernation, taken a big stretch and a yawn, and suddenly started living again. It was time to open all the windows and air the house, to free it of the ghosts of the winter and dark days, to get up early with the songbirds and go for a walk and look people in the eye and smile and say hello instead of hiding under layers of clothes with eyes to the ground while running from destination to destination, ignoring the world. It was time to stop

139

hiding in the dark and to hold your head up high and come face to face with the truth.

June also brought another letter from Gerry.

Holly had sat out in the sun, revelling in the new brightness of life and nervously yet excitedly read the fourth letter. She loved the feel of the card and the bumps of Gerry's handwriting under her finger as it ran over the dried ink. Inside, his neat script had listed the items that belonged to him that remained in the house, and beside each of his possessions he explained what he wanted Holly to do with them and where he wished for them to be sent. At the bottom it read:

> PS. I love you, Holly, and I _know_ you love me. You don't need my belongings to remember me by, you don't need to keep them as proof that I existed or still exist in your mind. You don't need to wear my sweater to feel me around you; I'm already here . . . _always_ wrapping my arms around you.

That had been difficult for Holly to come to terms with. She almost wished he would ask her to do karaoke again. She would have jumped from an aeroplane for him; run a thousand miles, _anything_ except empty out his wardrobes and rid herself of his presence in the house. But he was right and she knew it. She couldn't hang on to his things for ever. She couldn't pretend to herself that he was coming back to collect them. The physical Gerry was gone; he didn't need his clothes.

It was an emotionally draining experience. It took her days to complete. She relived a million memories with every garment and piece of paper she bagged. She held each item near to her before saying goodbye. Every time it left her fingers it was like saying goodbye to a part of Gerry all over again. It was difficult; so difficult – and at times too difficult.

She informed her family and friends of what she was about to do and although they all offered their assistance and support time and again, Holly knew she had to do this alone. She needed to take her time; say a proper goodbye because she wouldn't be getting anything back. Just like Gerry, his things couldn't return.

Despite Holly's wishes of wanting to be alone, Jack had called round a few times to offer some brotherly support and Holly had appreciated it. Every item had a history and they would talk and laugh about the memories surrounding it. He was there for her when she cried and he was there when she finally clapped her hands together, ridding her skin of the dust that remained. It was a difficult job, but one that needed to be done. And one, that was made easier by Gerry's help. Holly didn't need to worry about making all the big decisions, Gerry had already made them for her. Gerry was helping her and, for once, Holly felt as though she was helping him too.

She laughed as she bagged the old, dusty cassettes of his favourite rock band from his schooldays. At least once a year Gerry came across the old shoebox during his efforts to control the mess that grew inside his closet. He would blast the heavy metal music from every loudspeaker in the house just to torment Holly with its screeching guitars and badly produced sound quality. She always told him she couldn't wait to see the end of the tapes, but now the relief didn't wash over her as she once hoped it would.

Lying in a crumpled ball in the back corner of the wardrobe her eyes rested upon Gerry's lucky football jersey. It was still covered in grass and mud stains, fresh from its last victorious day on the pitch. She held it close to her and inhaled deeply, the smell of beer and sweat faint, but still there. She put it aside to be washed and passed on to John.

So many objects, so many memories. Each were being labelled and packed away in bags just as they were in her mind. To be stored in an area that would sometimes be called upon to teach and help in the future. Objects that were once so full of life and importance but that now lay limp on the floor. Without him they were just *things*.

Gerry's wedding tuxedo, his suits, shirts and ties that he would moan about having to wear every morning before going to work. The fashions of the years gone by, the eighties shiny suits and shell tracksuits bundled away. A snorkel from their first time scuba-diving, a shell that he had picked up off the ocean floor ten years ago, his collection of beer mats from every country they had visited. Letters and birthday cards from friends and family sent over the years. Valentine's Day cards from Holly. Childhood teddies and dolls put aside to be sent back to his parents. Records of bills, his golf clubs for John, books for Sharon, memories, tears and laughter for Holly.

His entire life bundled into twenty refuse sacks.

His and her memories bundled away into Holly's mind.

Each item unearthed dust, tears, laughter and memories. She bagged the items, cleared the dust, wiped her eyes and filed away the memories for safe-keeping.

Holly's mobile began to ring, disrupting her thoughts, and she dropped the laundry basket onto the grass under the washing line and ran through the patio doors into the kitchen to answer the phone.

'Hello?'

'I'm gonna make you a star!' Declan's voice screeched hysterically on the other end, and he broke into uncontrollable laughter.

Holly waited for him to calm down while she tried to figure out what he could be talking about. 'Declan, are you drunk?'

'Maybe jus a lil bit, but that's completely irrevelant,' he hiccuped.

'Declan, it's ten o'clock in the morning!' Holly laughed. 'Have you been to bed yet?'

'Nope,' he hiccuped again. 'I'm on the train home now and will be in bed in proximately three hours.'

'Three hours! Where are you?' Holly laughed. She was enjoying this as it reminded her of when she used to call Jack at all hours of the morning from all sorts of locations after misbehaving on a night out.

'I'm in Galway. The wards were on last night,' he said, as if she should know.

'Oh, sorry for my ignorance but what awards were you at?'

'I told you!'

'No, you didn't.'

'I told Jack to tell you, the bastard . . .' he stumbled over his words.

'Well, he didn't,' she interrupted, 'so now you can tell me.'

'The student media wards were on last night and I won!' he yelled, and Holly heard what sounded like the entire carriage celebrating with him. She was delighted.

'And the prize is that my film is gonna be aired on Channel Four next week! Can you blieve it!' There were more cheers this time, and Holly could barely hear what he was saying. 'You're gonna be famous, sis!' was the last thing she heard before the line went dead.

She rang round her family to share the good news but learned that they had all received similar phone calls. Ciara had stayed on the phone for ages chattering like an excited schoolgirl about how they were going to be on TV, and eventually her story ended with her marrying Denzel Washington.

It was decided that the family would gather in Hogan's pub next Wednesday to watch the documentary being aired. Daniel had kindly offered Club Diva to Declan as the venue so they could watch it on the big wall screen. Holly was so excited for her brother, and rang Sharon and Denise to let them know the good news.

'Oh, this is brill, Holly!' Sharon whispered excitedly.

'Why are you whispering?' Holly whispered back.

'Oh, old wrinkly face here decided it would be a great idea to ban us from accepting personal calls,' moaned Sharon referring to her boss. 'She says we spend more time chatting on the phone to friends than doing business so she's been patrolling our desks all morning. I swear I feel like I'm back at school again with the old hag keeping her eye on us.' Suddenly she spoke up and became businesslike. 'May I take your details, please?'

Holly laughed. 'Is she there?'

'Yes, absolutely,' Sharon continued.

'OK, well, I won't keep you very long then. The details are that we're all meeting up in Hogan's on Wednesday night to watch it so you're welcome to come.'

'That's great . . . OK.' Sharon pretended to take her details.

'Brilliant, we'll have fun. Sharon what will I wear?'

'Hmm . . . brand new or second-hand?'

'No, I really can't afford anything new. Even though you forced me to buy that top a few weeks ago I'm refusing to wear it on the grounds that I am no longer eighteen. So probably something old.'

'OK . . . red.'

'The red top I wore to your birthday?'

'Yes, exactly.'

'Yeah, maybe.'

'What's your current state of employment?'

'To be honest I haven't even started looking yet.' Holly chewed the inside of her mouth and frowned.

'And date of birth?'

'Ha-ha, shut up, you bitch,' Holly laughed.

'I'm sorry, we only give motor insurance to ages twenty-four and older. You're too young, I'm afraid.'

'I wish. OK I'll speak to you later.'

'Thank you for calling.'

Holly sat at the kitchen table wondering what she should wear next week; she wanted something new. She wanted to look sexy and gorgeous, for a change, and she was sick of all her old clothes. Maybe Denise had something in her shop. She was about to call when she received a text message from Sharon.

Hag rite bhind me
Tlk 2 u l8r xxx

Holly picked up the phone and called Denise at work.

'Hello, Casuals,' answered a very polite Denise.

'Hello, Casuals, Holly here. I know I'm not supposed to call you at work but I just wanted to tell you that Declan's documentary won some student award thingy and it's gonna be aired on Wednesday night.'

'Oh, that's so cool, Holly! Are we gonna be in it?' she asked excitedly.

'Yeah, I think so. So we're all meeting up in Hogan's to watch it that night. You up for that?'

'Of course! I can bring my new boyfriend too,' she giggled.

'What new boyfriend?'

'Tom!'

'The karaoke guy?' Holly asked in shock.

'Yeah, of course! Oh, Holly, I'm so in love!' she giggled childishly again.

'In love? But you only met him a few weeks ago!'

'I don't care; it only takes a minute . . . as the saying goes.'

'Wow, Denise . . . I don't know what to say!'

'Tell me how great it is!'

'Yeah . . . wow . . . I mean . . . of course . . . It's really great news.'

'Oh, try not to sound too enthusiastic, Holly,' she said sarcastically. 'Anyway I can't wait for you to meet him. You'll absolutely love him. Well, not as much as I do but you'll certainly really *really* like him . . .' she rambled on about how great he was.

'Denise, aren't you forgetting that I've met him already?' Holly interrupted her in the middle of a story about how Tom had saved a child from drowning.

'Yeah, I know you have, but I would rather you meet him when you're not acting like a demented woman hiding in toilets and shouting into microphones.'

'Look forward to it then . . .'

'Yeah, cool, it's gonna be great! I've never been to my own premiere before!' she said excitedly.

Holly rolled her eyes at her dramatics and they said their goodbyes.

Holly barely got any housework done that morning as she spent most of the time talking on the phone. Her mobile was burning and it was giving her a headache. She shuddered at the thought. Every time she had a headache it reminded her of Gerry. She hated to hear her loved ones complaining of headaches and migraines, and would immediately launch herself at them, telling them how they should take it more seriously and go see their doctors. She ended up petrifying everyone with her stories and they eventually stopped telling her whenever they felt ill.

She sighed loudly. She was turning into such a hypochondriac even her doctor was sick of the sight of her. She went running to her in a panic over the tiniest little things: if she had a pain in her leg or a cramp in her stomach. Last week she was convinced there was something wrong with her feet; her toes just didn't look quite right. Her doctor had examined them seriously and then had immediately started to scribble her prescription down on a slip of paper while Holly watched in terror. Eventually she handed her the piece of paper, and scrawled messily in that handwriting only doctors can perfect was: 'Buy bigger shoes.'

It may have been funny but it cost her forty euro.

Holly had spent the last few minutes on the phone listening to Jack ranting and raving about Richard. Richard had paid him a little visit too. Holly wondered whether he was just trying to bond with his siblings after years of hiding from them. Well, it was too little too late for most of them, it seemed. It was certainly very difficult trying to hold a conversation with someone who hadn't yet mastered the art of politeness.

Oh, stop, stop, stop! she silently screamed to herself. She needed to stop worrying, stop thinking, stop making her brain go into overdrive, and she certainly needed to stop talking to herself. She was driving herself crazy.

She finally finished hanging out the washing more than two hours later and piled another load into the machine. She switched the radio on in the kitchen, had the television blaring from the living room and went about her housework. Perhaps that would drown out the whinging little voice from her head.

Chapter Seventeen

Holly arrived at Hogan's and pushed her way through the old men in the pub to the stairs to Club Diva. The traditional band was in full swing and the crowd was joining in with all their favourite Irish songs. It was only seven thirty so Club Diva wasn't officially open yet, and the empty space looked like a completely different venue from the one where she had been so terrified in a few weeks ago. She was the first to arrive and settled herself at a table right in front of the big screen so she would have a perfect view of her brother's documentary.

A glass smashing over by the bar made her jump, and she looked up to see who had joined her in the room. Daniel's head emerged from behind the bar with a dustpan and brush in his hand.

'Oh, hiya, Holly. I didn't realise anyone had come in.'

'I came early, for a change.' She walked over to the bar to greet him. He looked different tonight, she thought, inspecting him.

'God, you're really early,' he said. 'The others probably won't be here for another hour or so.'

Holly looked confused and glanced at her watch. 'But it's seven thirty – the show starts at eight, doesn't it?'

Now Daniel looked confused. 'No, I was told nine o'clock but I could be wrong . . .' he reached for that day's paper and looked at the TV page. 'Yep, nine o'clock, Channel Four.'

Holly rolled her eyes. 'Oh, no, I'm sorry, I'll wander around town for a bit and come back later so,' she said hopping off her stool.

'Hey, don't be silly.' Daniel flashed his pearly whites. 'The shops are all closed by now and you can keep me company – that's if you don't mind . . .'

'Well, I don't mind if you don't mind.'

'I don't mind,' he said firmly.

'Then I'll stay so,' she said happily, hopping back on to her stool.

Daniel leaned his hands against the taps in a typical barman pose. 'So now that that's settled, what can I get you?' he said smiling.

'Well, this is great, no queuing or shouting my order across the bar or anything,' she joked. 'I'll have a sparkling water, please.'

'Nothing stronger?' He raised his eyebrows. His smile was infectious; it seemed to reach from ear to ear.

'No, I'd better not or I'll be drunk by the time everyone gets here.'

'Good thinking,' he agreed, and reached behind him to the fridge to retrieve the bottled water.

Holly realised what it was that made him look so different: he wasn't in his trademark black. He was wearing faded blue jeans and an open light blue shirt, with a white T-shirt underneath, that complemented his blue eyes so that they seemed to twinkle even more than usual. The sleeves of his shirt were rolled up to just below his elbows, and Holly could see his muscles through the light fabric. She quickly averted her eyes as he slid the glass towards her.

'Can I get you anything?' she asked him.

'No, thanks, I'll take care of this one.'

'No, please,' Holly insisted. 'You've bought me plenty of drinks. It's my turn.'

'OK, I'll have a Budweiser then, thanks.' He leaned against the bar and continued to stare at her.

'What? Do you want me to get it?' Holly laughed, jumping off her stool and walking round the bar. Daniel stood back and watched her with amusement.

'I always wanted to work behind a bar when I was a kid,' she said, grabbing a pint glass and pulling down on the tap. She was enjoying herself.

'There's a spare job if you're looking for one,' Daniel said, closely watching her work.

'No, thanks, I think I do a better job on the other side of the bar,' she laughed, filling the pint glass.

'Mmm . . . well, if you're ever looking for work you know where to come,' Daniel said, after taking a gulp of his pint. 'You did a good job.'

'It's not exactly brain surgery,' she smiled, bouncing across to the other side of the bar. She took out her purse and handed him money. 'Keep the change.'

'Thanks,' he smiled, turning to open the cash register and she scorned herself for checking out his bum. It was nice, though – firm, but not as nice as Gerry's, she decided.

'Has your husband deserted you again tonight?' he teased, walking round the bar to join her.

Holly bit her lip and wondered how to answer him. Now wasn't really the time to talk about something so depressing to someone who was only making chitchat, but she didn't want the poor man to keep asking her every time he saw her. He would soon realise the truth, which would cause him even more embarrassment.

'Daniel,' she said softly, 'I don't mean to make you uncomfortable but my husband passed away.'

Daniel stopped in his tracks and his cheeks blushed slightly, 'Oh, Holly, I'm sorry, I didn't know,' he said sincerely.

'It's OK, I know you didn't.' She smiled to show him she wasn't upset by his mistake.

'Well, I didn't meet him the other night but if someone had told me, I would have gone to the funeral to pay my respects.' He sat beside her at the bar.

'Oh no, Gerry died in February, Daniel. He wasn't here the other night.'

Daniel looked confused. 'But I thought you told me he was here . . .' he trailed off, thinking he had misheard.

'Oh, yeah,' Holly looked down at her feet with embarrassment. 'He wasn't here,' she said, looking around the club, 'but he was here.' She put her hand on her heart.

'Ah, I see.' He finally understood, 'Then you were even braver the other night than I thought, considering the circumstances,' he said gently.

Holly was surprised at how at ease he seemed.

Usually people stuttered and stammered their way through a sentence and either wandered off or changed the subject. She felt relaxed in his presence, though, as if she could talk openly without fear of crying. Holly smiled and briefly explained the story of the list.

'So that's why I ran off after Declan's gig that time,' Holly laughed.

'It wasn't because they were so terrible, by any chance?' Daniel joked, then he looked lost in thought. 'Ah yes, that's right, that was the thirtieth of April.'

'Yeah, I couldn't wait any longer to open the note,' Holly explained.

'Hmm . . . when's the next one?'

'July,' she said excitedly.

'So I won't be seeing you on the thirtieth of June then,' he said drily.

'Now you're getting the gist,' she laughed.

'I have arrived!' announced Denise to the empty room as she swanned in, dolled up to the nines in the dress she had worn to the ball last year. Tom strolled in behind her, laughing and refusing to take his eyes off her.

'God, *you're* dressed up,' Holly remarked, staring her friend up and down. In the end Holly had decided to wear a pair of jeans, black boots and a very simple black top. She hadn't been in the mood to get all dressed up after all, especially as they were only sitting in an empty club, but Denise hadn't quite grasped that concept.

Tom and Daniel greeted each other with hugs. 'Baby, this is Daniel, my best friend,' Tom said, introducing Daniel to Denise. Daniel and Holly raised their

153

eyebrows at each other and smiled, both registering the use of the word 'baby'.

'Hi, Tom.' Holly shook his hand after Denise had introduced her and he kissed her on the cheek. 'I'm sorry about the last time I met you. I wasn't feeling very sane that night.' Holly blushed at the memory of the karaoke.

'That's no problem,' Tom smiled kindly. 'If you hadn't entered then I wouldn't have met Denise, so I'm glad you did.'

After a while Holly discovered she was enjoying herself; she wasn't just pretending to laugh or finding things mildly amusing, she was genuinely happy. The thought of that made her even happier, as did the knowledge that Denise had finally found someone she really loved.

Minutes later the rest of the Kennedy family arrived, along with Sharon and John. Holly ran down to greet her friends.

'Hiya, hon,' Sharon said, giving her a hug. 'You here long?'

Holly started laughing. 'I thought it was on at eight o'clock so I came at half seven.'

'Oh no.' Sharon looked anxious.

'Don't worry, it was fine. Daniel kept me company,' Holly said, pointing him out.

'Him?' John said angrily. 'Watch yourself with him, Holly. He's a bit of an oddball. You should have heard the stuff he was saying to Sharon the other night.'

Holly guessed she'd caused this confusion, and quickly excused herself from their company to join her family.

'Meredith not with you tonight?' she asked Richard.

'No she's not,' he snapped back rudely, and headed over to the bar.

'Why does he bother coming to these things at all?' she moaned to Jack as he held her head to his chest and rubbed her hair, playfully consoling her.

'OK everyone!' Declan was standing on a stool to address the gathering. 'Because Ciara couldn't decide what to wear tonight, we're all late and *my* documentary is about to start any minute,' he said proudly, 'so if you can just all shut up and sit down, that would be great.'

'Oh, Declan . . .' His mother admonished him for his rudeness.

Holly searched the room for Ciara and spotted her glued to Daniel's side at the bar. She laughed to herself and settled down to watch the documentary. As soon as the announcer introduced it everybody cheered but were quickly hushed by an angry Declan, who didn't want them to miss a thing.

The title *Girls and the City* appeared over a beautiful night-time shot of Dublin, and Holly became nervous. The words 'The Girls' appeared over a black screen, followed by footage of Sharon, Denise, Abbey and Ciara all squashed up beside each other in the back of a taxi.

Sharon was speaking: 'Hello! I'm Sharon and this is Abbey, Denise and Ciara.'

Each of the girls posed for her close-up as she was introduced.

'And we're heading to our best friend Holly's house because it's her birthday . . .'

155

The scene changed to the girls surprising Holly with shouts of 'Happy Birthday' at her front door. Then the camera returned to Sharon in the taxi. 'Tonight it's gonna be just us girls and NO men . . .'

The scene switched to Holly opening the presents and holding the vibrator up to the camera and saying, 'Well, I'll definitely need this,' before returning to Sharon in the taxi saying: 'We are gonna do lots and *lots* of drinking . . .'

Now Holly was popping open the champagne, then the girls were knocking back shots in Boudoir, and eventually there was Holly with her crooked tiara on her head and drinking out of a champagne bottle with a straw.

'We are gonna go clubbing . . .'

There was a shot of the girls in Boudoir, doing some very embarrassing moves on the dance floor.

'But nothing too mad! We're gonna be good girls tonight!' said Sharon sincerely.

The next scene showed the girls, protesting wildly, being escorted out of the club by three bouncers.

Holly's jaw dropped and she stared in shock at Sharon, who was equally surprised. The men laughed their hearts out and slapped Declan on the back, congratulating him for exposing their partners. Holly, Sharon, Denise, Abbey and even Ciara slithered down in their seats with humiliation.

What on earth had Declan done?

Chapter Eighteen

There was complete silence in the club as everyone stared at the screen in anticipation. Holly held her breath; she was nervous now about what was going to appear. Perhaps the girls would be reminded of what exactly they had all conveniently succeeded in forgetting about that night. The truth terrified her. After all, how drunk must they all have been to forget completely the events of that night? Unless, somebody was lying, in which case, they should be even more nervous right now. Holly looked around at the girls. They were all chewing on their fingernails. Holly crossed her fingers.

A new title appeared on the screen: 'The Gifts'.

'Open mine first,' shrieked Ciara from the television, thrusting her present towards Holly and shoving Sharon off the couch and on to the floor. Everyone in the club laughed while they watched Abbey dragging a horrified Sharon to her feet. Ciara left Daniel's side and tiptoed over to the rest of the girls for security. Everyone oohed and aahed, as one by one Holly's birthday presents were unveiled. A lump formed in Holly's throat as Declan zoomed in on the two photographs on the mantelpiece while Sharon's toast was made.

Once again a new title took over the screen, 'Journey to the City', and showed the girls scrambling over one another to get into the taxi. It was obvious they were pretty pissed by now. Holly was shocked; she had actually thought she was quite sober at that stage.

'Oh, Nick,' Holly moaned drunkenly to the taxi driver from the passenger seat, 'I'm thirty today, can you believe it?'

Nick the taxi driver, who couldn't give a flying flute what age she was, glanced over at her and laughed, 'Sure, you're only a young one still, Holly,' his voice low and gravelly. The camera zoomed in on Holly's face and she cringed at the sight of herself. She looked so drunk, so *sad*.

'But what am I gonna do, Nick?' she whinged. 'I'm thirty! I have no job, no husband, no children and I'm thirty! Did I tell you that?' she asked him, leaning towards him.

Beside her in the club, Sharon giggled. Holly thumped her.

In the background the girls were all chattering excitedly to one another. It sounded as if they were talking over one another; it was hard to see how any type of conversation was going on.

'Ah, enjoy yourself tonight, Holly. Don't get caught up in silly emotions on your birthday. Worry about all that shite tomorrow, love.' Nick sounded so caring, and Holly made a mental note to call him and thank him.

The camera stayed with Holly as she leaned her head against the window and remained silent, lost in thought for the rest of the journey. Holly couldn't get over how lonely she looked. She didn't like it. She looked around the room in embarrassment and caught Daniel's eye. He winked at her in encouragement. She smiled weakly and turned back to face the screen in time to see herself screaming to the girls on O'Connell Street.

'OK, girls. We are going to Boudoir tonight and *no one* is going to stop us from getting in, *especially* not any *silly bouncers* who *think* they own the place.' And she marched off in what she'd thought at the time was a straight line. All the girls cheered and followed after her.

The scene immediately jumped to the two bouncers outside Boudoir shaking their heads. 'Not tonight, girls, sorry.'

Holly's family howled with laughter.

'But you don't understand,' Denise said calmly to the bouncers. 'Do you not know who we are?'

'No,' they both said, and stared over their heads, ignoring them.

'Huh!' Denise put her hands on her hips and pointed to Holly. 'But this is the very, very extremely famous . . . em . . . Princess Holly from the royal family of . . . Finland.'

On camera Holly frowned at Denise.

Her family once again howled with laughter. 'You couldn't write a script better than this,' Declan laughed.

'Oh, she's royalty, is she?' the bouncer with a moustache smirked.

'Indeed she is,' Denise said seriously.

'Finland got a royal family, Paul?' moustache man turned to his colleague.

'Don't think so, boss.'

Holly fixed the crooked tiara on her head and gave them both a royal wave.

'You see?' Denise said, satisfied. 'You men will be very embarrassed if you don't let her in.'

'Supposing we let her in, then you'll have to stay outside,' moustache man said, and motioned for the people behind them in the queue to pass them and enter the club. Holly gave them a royal wave as they passed.

'Oh, no, no, no, no,' Denise protested. 'You don't understand. I am her . . . lady-in-waiting so I need to be with her at all times.'

'Well then, you won't mind waiting till she comes out at closing time,' Paul smirked.

Tom, Jack and John all started laughing, and Denise slithered down even further in her seat.

Finally Holly spoke, 'Oh, one *must* have a drink. One is *dreadfully* thirsty.'

Paul and moustache man snorted and tried to keep straight faces while still staring over the girl's heads.

'No, honestly, girls, not tonight. You need to be a member.'

'But I am a member, of the royal family!' Holly said sternly. 'Off with your heads!' she commanded, pointing at the both of them.

Denise quickly forced Holly's arm down. 'Honestly, the princess and I will be no trouble at all. Just let us in for a few drinks,' she pleaded.

Moustache man stared down at the two of them, then raised his eyes to the sky. 'All right then, go on in,' he said, stepping aside.

'God bless you,' Holly said, making the sign of the cross at them as she passed.

'What is she, a princess or a priest?' laughed Paul as she entered the club.

'She's out of her mind,' laughed moustache man, 'but it's the best excuse I've heard while I've been on the job,' and the two of them sniggered. They regained their composure as Ciara and her entourage approached the door.

'Is it OK if my film crew follow me in?' Ciara said confidently in a brilliant Australian accent.

'Hold on while I check with the manager.' Paul turned his back and spoke into a walkie-talkie. 'Yeah, that's no problem, go ahead,' he said, holding the door open for her.

'That's that Australian singer, isn't it?' moustache man said to Paul.

'Yeah. Good song, that.'

'Tell the boys inside to keep an eye on the princess and her lady,' said moustache man. 'We don't want them bothering that singer with the pink hair.'

Holly's father choked on his drink from laughing, and Elizabeth rubbed his back for him while chortling herself.

As Holly watched the image of the inside of Boudoir on the screen she remembered being disappointed by the club. There had always been a mystery as to what Boudoir looked like. The girls had read in a magazine that there was a water feature into which

161

Madonna had apparently jumped one night. Holly had imagined a huge waterfall cascading down the wall of the club that continued to flow in little bubbling streams while all the glamorous people sat around it and occasionally dipped their glasses into it to fill them with more champagne. Holly had imagined a champagne waterfall. What she got was an oversized fish bowl in the centre of the circular bar. What that had to do with anything she didn't know. Her dreams were shattered. The room wasn't as big as she thought it would be, and was decorated in rich reds and gold. On the far side of the room there was a huge gold curtain acting as a partition, which was blocked by another menacing-looking bouncer.

At the top of the room the main attraction was the massive king-size bed, which was tilted on a platform towards the rest of the club. On top of the gold silk sheets were two skinny models dressed in no more than gold body paint and tiny gold thongs. It was all a bit too tacky.

'Look at the size of those thongs!' gasped Denise in disgust. 'I have a plaster on my baby finger bigger than those.'

Beside her in Club Diva, Tom chuckled and began to nibble on Denise's baby finger. Holly looked away and returned her gaze to the screen.

'Good evening and welcome to the twelve o'clock news. I'm Sharon McCarthy.' Sharon stood in front of the camera with a bottle in her hand serving as a microphone. Declan had angled the camera so that she could get Ireland's famous newsreaders in the shot.

'Today is the thirtieth birthday of Princess Holly

162

of Finland. Her royal self and her lady-in-waiting finally succeeded in being granted access to the famous celebrity hang-out Boudoir. Also present is Australian rock chick Ciara and her film crew and . . .' She held her finger to her ear as though she were receiving more information. 'News just in. It appears that Ireland's favourite newsreader, Tony Walsh, was seen smiling just moments ago. Here beside me I have a witness to the fact. Welcome, Denise.' Denise posed seductively at the camera. 'Denise, tell me, where were you when this event was taking place?'

'Well, I was just over there beside his table when I saw it happening.' Denise sucked in her cheekbones and smiled at the camera.

'Can you explain to us what happened?'

'I was just standing there minding my own business when Mr Walsh took a sip of his drink and then shortly afterwards he smiled.'

'Gosh, Denise, this is fascinating news. And are you sure it was a smile?'

'Well, it could have been trapped wind causing him to make a face but others around me also thought it was a smile.'

'So there were others who witnessed this?'

'Yes, Princess Holly beside me here, saw the whole thing.'

The camera panned across to Holly where she stood drinking from a champagne bottle with a straw. 'So, Holly, can you tell us, was it wind or a smile?'

Holly looked confused, then rolled her eyes, 'Oh, wind. Sorry, I think it's this champagne that's doing it to me.'

163

Club Diva erupted in laughter. Jack as usual laughed the loudest. Holly hid her face in shame.

'OK then . . .' Sharon said, trying not to laugh, 'so you heard it here first. The night when Ireland's grimmest presenter was seen smiling. Back to you at the studio.' Sharon's smile faded as she looked up and saw Tony Walsh standing beside her, not surprisingly without a smile on his face.

Sharon gulped and said, 'Good evening,' and the camera was switched off. Everyone in the club was laughing at this stage, including the girls. Holly was finding the whole thing just so ridiculous that she had to laugh.

The camera was switched back on and this time it was focused on the mirror in the ladies' toilet. Declan was filming from outside through a slit in the doorway and Denise and Sharon's reflections were clearly visible.

'I was only having a laugh,' Sharon huffed, fixing her lipstick.

'Don't mind the miserable sod, Sharon. He just doesn't want the camera in his face all night, especially on his night off. I can understand that.'

'Oh, you're on his side, I suppose,' Sharon said grumpily.

'Ah, shut up, you moany old whore,' Denise snapped.

'Where's Holly?' Sharon asked, changing the subject.

'Don't know. Last time I saw her she was doing a few funky moves on the dance floor,' said Denise. The two of them looked at each other and laughed.

'Ah . . . our poor little disco diva,' said Sharon sadly. 'I hope she finds someone gorgeous out there tonight and snogs the face off him.'

'Yeah,' agreed Denise. 'Come on then, let's go find her a man,' she added, putting her make-up back in her bag.

Just after the girls left, a toilet flushed, the cubicle door opened and out stepped Holly.

In Club Diva, Holly's big smile faded quickly when she saw her face on the screen.

Through the crack in the door Holly's reflection was visible in the mirror; her eyes were red from crying. She blew her nose and stared miserably at herself for a while. She took a deep breath, opened the door and carried on downstairs to her friends.

Holly hadn't remembered crying that night – in fact, she thought she had got through it very well. She rubbed her face while she worried about what else was coming up that she couldn't remember.

Finally the scene changed and the words 'Operation Gold Curtain' came up.

Denise screamed, 'Oh my God, Declan, you bastard!' very loudly, and rushed to hide in the toilet.

She had obviously remembered something.

Declan chuckled and lit himself another cigarette.

'OK, girls,' Denise was announcing, 'it is now time for Operation Gold Curtain.'

'Huh?' Sharon and Holly announced groggily from the couch where they had collapsed in a drunken stupor.

'Operation Gold Curtain!' Denise exclaimed excitedly, trying to drag them to their feet. 'It's time to infiltrate the VIP bar!'

'You mean this isn't it?' Sharon said sarcastically, looking around the club.

'No! That's where the real celebs go!' Denise pointed at the gold curtain, which was blocked by possibly the biggest and tallest man on the planet.

'I don't really care where the celebs are, to be honest, Denise,' piped up Holly. 'I'm fine here where I am,' and she snuggled into the cosy couch.

Denise groaned and rolled her eyes, 'Girls! Abbey and Ciara are in there, why aren't we?'

Jack looked curiously across at his girlfriend. Abbey shrugged her shoulders weakly and held her face in her hand. None of this was jogging anybody's memory except Denise's, and she had fled the room. Jack's smile suddenly faded and he slid down in his chair and crossed his arms. It was obviously all right for his sisters to act the fool but his girlfriend was a different matter. Jack placed his feet up on the chair in front of him and quietened down for the rest of the documentary.

Once Sharon and Holly had heard that Abbey and Ciara were in the room they sat up attentively and listened to Denise's plan.

'OK, girlies, here's what we're gonna do . . .'

Holly turned away from the screen and nudged Sharon. Holly couldn't remember doing or saying any of these things at all; she was beginning to think Declan had hired lookalike actors as a horrible practical joke. Sharon turned to face her with wide worried eyes and shrugged. Nope, she wasn't there that night either.

The camera followed the three girls as they very

suspiciously approached the gold curtain and loitered around like idiots. Sharon finally built up the courage to tap the giant on the shoulder, causing him to turn round and provide Denise with enough time to escape under the curtain. She got down on her hands and knees and stuck her head through to the VIP bar while her bum and legs stuck out from the other side of the curtain.

Holly kicked her in the bum to hurry her along.

'I can see them!' Denise hissed loudly. 'Oh my God! They're speaking to that Hollywood actor guy!' She took her head back out from under the curtain and looked at Holly with excitement. Unfortunately Sharon was running out of things to say to the giant bouncer and he turned his head just in time to catch Denise.

'No, no, no, no, no!' Denise said calmly again. 'You don't understand! This is Princess Holly of Sweden!'

'Finland,' Sharon corrected her.

'Sorry, Finland,' Denise said, remaining on her knees. 'I am bowing to her. Join me!'

Sharon quickly got on her knees and the two of them began to worship her feet. Holly looked around awkwardly as everyone in the club began to stare and she once again gave them the royal wave. Nobody seemed very impressed.

'Oh, Holly!' her mother said, trying to catch her breath after laughing so hard.

Big burly bouncer turned his back and spoke into his walkie-talkie. 'Boys, got a situation with the princess and the lady.'

Denise looked at both the girls in panic and mouthed,

'Hide!' The girls jumped to their feet and fled. The camera searched through the crowds for them but couldn't find them.

From her seat in Club Diva, Holly groaned loudly and held her head in her hands as it clicked with her what was about to happen.

Chapter Nineteen

Paul and moustache man rushed upstairs to the club and met the very big man at the gold curtain.

'What's going on?' moustache man asked him.

'Those girls you told me to keep my eye on tried to crawl through to the other side,' big man said seriously. You could tell by looking at him that his previous job involved killing people. He was taking this breach of security very seriously.

'Where are they?' moustache man asked.

Big man cleared his throat and looked away, 'They're hiding, boss.'

Moustache man rolled his eyes.'They're hiding?'

'Yes, boss.'

'Where? In the club?'

'I think so, boss.'

'You think so?'

'Well, they didn't pass us on our way in so they must still be here,' Paul piped up.

'OK,' moustache man sighed. 'Well, let's start looking, then. Get someone to keep an eye on the curtain.'

The camera followed the three bouncers as they patrolled the club, looking behind couches, under tables, behind curtains and they even got someone to check the toilets. Holly's family laughed hysterically at the scene unfolding before their eyes.

There was a bit of commotion at the top of the club and the bouncers headed towards the noise to sort it out. A crowd was beginning to gather, and the two skinny dancers dressed in gold body paint had stopped dancing and were staring with horrified expressions at the bed. The camera panned across. Underneath the gold silk sheets there appeared to be three pigs fighting under a blanket. Sharon, Denise and Holly rolled around screaming at each other, trying to make themselves as flat as possible so they wouldn't be noticed. The crowd thickened and soon enough the music was shut down. The three big lumps under the bed stopped squirming and suddenly froze, not knowing what was going on outside.

The bouncers counted to three and pulled the covers off the bed. Three very startled-looking girls, like deer caught in headlights, stared back at them, lying there as flat as they could with their arms stiffly by their sides.

'*One* just had to get forty winks before *one* left,' Holly said in her royal accent, and the other girls burst out laughing.

'Come on, princess, the fun's over,' said Paul. The three men accompanied the girls outside, assuring them that they would never be allowed back into the club ever again.

'Can I just tell my friends that we're gone?' Sharon asked.

The men tutted and looked away.

'Excuse me? Am I talking to myself? I asked you if it was OK if I go in and tell my friends that we had to leave?'

'Look, stop playing around, girls,' moustache man said angrily. 'Your friends aren't in there. Now off you go, back to your beds.'

'Excuse me,' Sharon repeated angrily, 'I have two friends in the VIP bar; one of them has pink hair and the other one—'

'Girls!' the bouncer raised his voice. 'She does not want anyone bothering her. She is no more your friend than the man on the moon. Now clear off before you get yourselves into more trouble.'

Everyone in the club howled with laughter.

The scene changed to 'The Long Journey Home', and all the girls were in the taxi. Abbey sat like a dog, with her head hanging out of the open window by order of the taxi driver. 'You're not throwing up in my cab. You either stick your head out the window or you walk home.' Abbey's face was almost purple and her teeth were chattering but she wasn't going to trek all the way home. Ciara sat with her arms crossed, in a huff, angry with the girls for forcing her to leave the club so early but, more embarrassingly, for blowing her cover as a famous rock singer. Sharon and Denise had fallen asleep with their heads resting on one another.

The camera turned round to focus on Holly, who was sitting in the passenger seat once again. But this time she wasn't talking the ear off the taxi driver; she rested her head on the back of the seat and stared straight ahead out into the dark night. Holly knew what she was thinking as she watched herself. Time to go home to that big empty house all alone again.

'Happy birthday, Holly,' a very cold Abbey's tiny little voice trembled.

Holly turned round to smile at her and came face to face with the camera. 'Are you *still* filming with that thing? Turn it off!' and she knocked the camera out of Declan's hand.

The End.

As Daniel went to turn the lights up in the club, Holly slipped quickly away from the gang and escaped through the nearest door. She needed to collect her thoughts before everyone started talking. She found herself in a tiny storeroom surrounded by mops and buckets and empty kegs. What a stupid place to hide, she thought. She sat down on a barrel and thought about what she had just seen. She was in shock. She felt confused and angry at Declan; he had told her that he was making a documentary about club life. She distinctly remembered him not mentioning anything about making a show of her and her friends. And he had literally made a show of them. If he had asked her politely whether he could do it that would have been a different matter. Although she still wouldn't have agreed to it.

But the last thing she wanted to do right now was to scream at Declan in front of everyone. Apart from the fact that it had completely humiliated her, Declan had actually filmed it and edited it very well. If it was anyone else but her on the TV, Holly would have thought it most deserving of the award. But it *was* her so therefore it *didn't* deserve to win . . . Parts of

172

it had been funny, she agreed, and she didn't mind so much the bits of her and her friends being so silly; it was more the sneaky shots of her unhappiness that bothered her.

Thick salty tears trickled down her face and she wrapped her arms around her body to comfort herself. She had seen on television how she truly felt. Lost and alone. She cried for Gerry, she cried for herself with big heaving sobs that hurt her ribs whenever she tried to catch her breath. She didn't want to be alone any more and she didn't want her family seeing the loneliness she tried so hard to hide from them. She just wanted Gerry back and didn't care about anything else. She didn't care if he came back and they fought every day, she didn't care if they were broke and had no house and no money. She just wanted him. She heard the door open behind her and felt big strong arms wrapping themselves round her frail body. She cried as though months of built-up anguish were all tumbling out at once.

'What's wrong with her? Didn't she like it?' she heard Declan ask worriedly.

'Just leave her be, son,' her mum said softly, and the door was closed behind them again as Daniel stroked Holly's hair and rocked her softly.

Finally, after crying what felt like all the tears in the world, Holly stopped and let go of Daniel. 'Sorry,' she sniffed, drying her face with the sleeves of her top.

'There's no need to be sorry,' he said, gently removing her hand from her face and handing her a tissue.

She sat in silence while trying to compose herself.

'If you're upset about the documentary, then there's

no need,' he said, sitting down on a crate of glasses opposite her.

'Yeah, right,' she said sarcastically, wiping her tears again.

'No, really,' he insisted. 'I thought it was really funny. You all looked like you were having a great time.'

'Pity that's not how I felt,' she said sadly.

'Maybe that's not how you felt but the camera doesn't pick up on feelings, Holly.'

'You don't have to try to make me feel better.' Holly was embarrassed at being consoled by a stranger.

'I'm not *trying* to make you feel better, I'm just saying it like it is. Nobody but you noticed whatever it is that's upsetting you. I didn't see anything so why should anyone else?'

Holly felt mildly better. 'Are you sure?'

'I'm sure I'm sure,' Daniel said, smiling. 'Now you really have to stop hiding in all the rooms in my club. I might take it personally,' he laughed.

'Are the girls OK?' Holly asked, hoping it was just her being stupid after all.

There was loud laughter from outside.

'They're fine, as you can hear.' He nodded towards the door. 'Ciara's delighted everyone will think she's a star, Denise has finally come out of the toilet and Sharon just can't stop laughing. Although Jack's giving Abbey a hard time about throwing up on the way home.'

Holly chuckled.

'So you see, nobody even noticed what you saw.'

'Thanks, Daniel.' She took a deep breath and smiled at him.

'You ready to go face your public?'

174

'Think so.' Holly stepped outside to the sounds of laughter. The lights were up and everyone was sitting around the table and happily sharing jokes and stories. Holly sat beside her mum. Elizabeth wrapped her arm round her daughter and gave her a kiss on the cheek.

'Well, I thought it was great,' announced Jack enthusiastically. 'If only we could get Declan to go out with the girls all the time, then we'd know what they get up to, eh, John?' he winked at Sharon's husband.

'Well, I can assure you,' Abbey spoke up, 'that what you saw is not a regular girls' night out.'

The boys weren't having any of it.

'So is it OK?' Declan asked Holly, afraid he had upset her.

Holly threw him a look.

'I thought you would like it, Hol,' he said worriedly.

'I might have liked it if I had *known* what you were doing,' she snapped back.

'But I wanted it to be a surprise,' he said genuinely.

'I hate surprises.' She rubbed her stinging eyes.

'Let that be a lesson to you, son,' Frank warned Declan. 'You shouldn't go around filming people without them knowing what you're doing. It's illegal.'

'I bet they didn't know that when they chose him for the award,' Elizabeth agreed.

'You're not gonna tell them, are you, Holly?' Declan asked worriedly.

'Not if you're nice to me for the next few months,' Holly said slyly, twisting her hair around her finger.

Declan made a face. He was stuck and he knew it. 'Yeah, whatever,' he said, waving her away.

'To tell you the truth, Holly, I have to admit I

thought it was quite funny,' giggled Sharon. 'You and your Operation Gold Curtain.' She thumped Denise playfully on the leg.

Denise rolled her eyes. 'I can tell you all something – I am *never* drinking again.'

Everyone laughed and Tom put his arm round her shoulders.

'What?' she said innocently. 'I really mean it.'

'Speaking of drink, would anyone like one?' Daniel stood up from his chair. 'Jack?'

'Yeah, a Budweiser, thanks.'

'Abbey?'

'Em . . . a white wine, please,' she said politely.

'Frank?'

'A Guinness, thanks, Daniel.'

'I'll have the same,' said John.

'Sharon?'

'Vodka and Coke, please. Holly you want the same?'

Holly nodded.

'Tom?'

'JD and Coke, please, Dan.'

'Me too,' said Declan.

'Denise?' Daniel tried to hide his smile.

'Em . . . I'll have a . . . gin and tonic please.'

'Ha!' everyone jeered her.

'What?' She shrugged her shoulders as though she didn't care. 'One drink is hardly going to kill me . . .'

Holly was standing over the sink with her sleeves rolled up to her elbows, scrubbing the pots, when she heard the familiar voice.

'Hi, honey.'

She looked up and saw him standing at the open patio doors. 'Hello, you,' she smiled.

'Miss me?'

'Of course.'

'Have you found that new husband yet?'

'Of course I have. He's upstairs in bed asleep,' she laughed, drying her hands.

Gerry shook his head and tutted. 'Shall I go up and suffocate him for sleeping in our bed?'

'Ah, give him another hour or so,' she joked, looking at her watch. 'He needs his rest.'

He looked happy, she thought, fresh-faced and still as beautiful as she remembered. He was wearing her favourite blue top she had bought him one Christmas. He stared at her from under his long eyelashes with his big brown puppy eyes.

'Are you coming in?' she asked, smiling.

'No, I just popped by to see how you are. Everything going OK?' he leaned against the door jamb with his hands in his pockets.

'So, so,' she said, weighing her hands in the air. 'Could be better.'

'I hear you're a TV star now,' he grinned.

'A very reluctant one,' she laughed.

'You'll have men falling all around you,' he assured her.

'Falling all around me is right,' she joked. 'The problem is they keep missing the target.' She pointed to herself. He laughed. 'I miss you, Gerry.'

'I haven't gone far,' he said softly.

'You leaving me again?'

177

'For the time being.'

'See you soon,' she smiled.

He winked at her and disappeared.

Holly woke up with a smile on her face and felt as if she had slept for days. 'Good morning, Gerry,' she said happily, staring up at the ceiling.

The phone rang beside her. 'Hello?'

'Oh my God, Holly, just take a look at the weekend papers,' Sharon said in a panic.

Chapter Twenty

Holly immediately leaped out of bed, threw on a track-suit and drove to her nearest newsagent. She reached the newspaper stand and began to leaf through the pages in search of what Sharon had been raving about. The man behind the counter coughed loudly and Holly looked up at him.

'This is not a library, young lady. You'll have to buy that,' he said, nodding at the newspaper in her hand.

'I know that,' she said, irritated by his rudeness. Honestly, how on earth was anyone supposed to know which paper they wanted to buy if they didn't even know which paper had what they were looking for? She ended up picking up every single newspaper from the stand and slammed them down on the counter, smiling sweetly at him.

The man looked startled and started to scan them into the register one by one. A queue began to form behind her.

Holly stared longingly at the selection of chocolate bars displayed in front of her and looked around to see if anyone was looking at her. *Everyone* was staring. She quickly turned back to face the counter.

Finally her arm jumped up and grabbed the two king-size chocolate bars nearest to her on the shelf from the bottom of the pile. One by one the rest of the chocolate began to slide on to the floor. The teenager behind her snorted and looked away, laughing, as Holly bent down with a red face and began to pick them up. So many had fallen she had to make several trips up and down. The shop was silent apart from a few coughs from the impatient queue behind her. She sneakily added another few packets of sweets to her pile, 'For the kids,' she said loudly to the newsagent, hoping everyone behind her would also hear.

He just grunted at her and continued scanning the items. Then she remembered she needed to get milk so she rushed from the queue to the end of the shop to retrieve a pint of milk from the fridge. A few women tutted loudly as she made her way back to the top of the queue where she added the milk to her pile. The newsagent stopped scanning to stare at her, she stared back blankly at him.

'Mark,' he yelled.

A spotty young teenager appeared from one of the shopping aisles with a pricing gun in his hand. 'Yeah?' he said grumpily.

'Open the other till, will ya, son? We might be here for a while.' The newsagent glared at Holly.

She made a face at him.

Mark dragged his body over to the second till, all the time staring at Holly. What? she thought defensively. Don't blame me for you having to do your job. He took over the till and the entire queue behind her rushed over to the other side.

Satisfied that no one was staring at her any more she grabbed a few packets of crisps from below the counter and added them to her purchases. 'Birthday party,' she mumbled.

In the queue beside her, the teenager quietly asked for a packet of cigarettes.

'Got any ID?' Mark asked loudly.

The teenager looked around in embarrassment with a red face. Holly snorted at him and looked away.

'Anything else?' the newsagent asked sarcastically.

'No, thank you, that will be all,' she said through gritted teeth. She paid her money and fumbled with her purse, trying to put all the change back in.

'Next,' the newsagent nodded to the customer behind her.

'Hiya, can I have twenty Benson and—'

'Excuse me,' Holly interrupted the man, 'could I have a bag please?' She stared at the huge pile of groceries in front of her.

'Just a moment,' he said rudely, 'I'll deal with this gentleman first. Yes, sir, cigarettes, is it?'

'Please,' the customer said, looking at Holly apologetically.

'Now,' the newsagent said, returning to Holly, 'what can I get you?'

'A bag.' She clenched her jaw.

'That'll be twenty cents please.'

Holly sighed loudly and reached into her handbag, searching through the mess to find her purse again. Another queue formed behind her.

'Mark, take over the till again, will you?' the man said arrogantly.

Holly took the coin out of her purse, slammed it down on the counter and began to fill the bag with her items.

'Next,' the newsagent said again, looking over her shoulder to the next customer. Holly felt under pressure to get out of the way and began stuffing the bag full in panic.

'I'll wait till the lady here is ready,' the customer said politely.

Holly smiled at him appreciatively and turned to leave the shop. She was walking away grumbling to herself when Mark, the boy behind the counter, startled her by yelling, 'Hey, I know you! You're the girl from the telly!'

Holly swirled round in surprise and the plastic handle broke from the weight of all the newspapers. Everything fell onto the floor and her chocolate, sweets and crisps went rolling in all directions.

The friendly customer got down on his knees to help her gather her belongings while the rest of the shop watched in amusement, wondering who the girl from the telly was.

'It is you, isn't it?' the boy laughed.

Holly smiled up weakly at him from the floor.

'I knew it!' He clapped his hands together with excitement. 'You're cool!'

Yeah, she really felt cool, on her knees on the floor of a shop, searching for bars of chocolate. Holly's face went red and she nervously cleared her throat, 'Em . . . excuse me, could I have another bag, please?'

'Yeah, that'll be—'

'There you go,' the friendly customer interrupted

him, placing a twenty-cent coin down on the counter. The newsagent looked perplexed and continued serving the customers.

'I'm Rob,' the man said, helping Holly put all her chocolate back into the bag, then holding his hand out.

'I'm Holly,' she said, a little embarrassed by his over-friendliness, and took his hand. 'And I'm a chocoholic.'

He laughed.

'Thanks for the help,' she said gratefully, getting to her feet.

'No problem.' He held the door open for her. He was good-looking, she thought, a few years older than she, and he had the oddest coloured eyes, a kind of a grey-green colour. She squinted at him and took a closer look.

He cleared his throat.

She blushed, suddenly realising she had been staring at him like a fool. She walked out to her car and placed the bulging bag on the back seat. Rob followed her over. Her heart did a little flip.

'Hi again,' he laughed. 'Em . . . I was wondering if you would like to go for a drink?' Then he laughed, glancing at his watch. 'Actually, it's a bit too early for that. How about a coffee?'

He was a very confident man and he rested himself coolly against the car opposite Holly, his hands in the pockets of his jeans with his thumbs resting outside and those weird eyes just staring back at her. However, he didn't make her feel uncomfortable, he was just very relaxed, as though asking a stranger out for coffee was the most natural thing in the world. Was this what people did these days?

'Em . . .' Holly thought about it. What harm could it do to go for a coffee with a man who had been so polite to her? The fact that he was absolutely gorgeous also helped. But regardless of his looks, Holly really craved company, and he seemed like a nice decent man to talk to. Sharon was out and Denise was at work and Holly couldn't keep calling over to her mother's house; Elizabeth had work to do too. Holly really needed to start meeting new people. Many of Gerry and Holly's other friends had been people with whom Gerry worked, but once he had died all those 'friends' of theirs hadn't been too much of a familiar feature around her house. At least she knew who her true friends were.

She was just about to say yes to Rob when he glanced down at her hand and his smile faded. 'Oh, sorry, I didn't realise . . .' He backed away from her awkwardly as though she had some kind of disease. 'I have to rush off anyway.' He smiled quickly at her and scarpered off down the road.

Holly stared after him, confused. Had she said something wrong? Had she taken too long to decide? Had she broken one of the silent rules of this new meeting-people game? She looked down at the hand that had caused him to run away from her and saw her wedding ring sparkle back at her. She sighed loudly and rubbed her face tiredly.

Just then the teenager from the shop walked by with a gang of friends and a cigarette in his mouth and snorted at her.

She just couldn't win.

Holly slammed the door of her car and looked

184

around. She wasn't in the mood to go home, she was sick of staring at the walls all day every day and talking to herself. It was still only ten o'clock in the morning and beautifully sunny and warm outside. Across the road her local café, The Greasy Spoon, was setting up tables and chairs outside. Her stomach grumbled. A nice big Irish breakfast was exactly what she needed. She took her sunglasses from the glove compartment of her car, carried her newspapers with both hands and wandered across the road.

A plump lady was cleaning the tables. Her hair was tied back tightly in a large bun, and a bright red and white checked apron covered her flowery dress. Holly felt like she had walked straight into a country kitchen.

'Been a while since these tables have seen sunlight,' the woman said happily to Holly as she approached the café.

'Yeah, it's a beautiful day, isn't it?' Holly said, and the two of them stared up at the clear blue sky. It was funny how good weather in Ireland always seemed to be the conversation of the day with everyone. It was such a rare sight that everyone felt blessed when it finally arrived.

'You want to sit out here, love?'

'Yes, I will. Might as well make the most out of it. It'll probably be gone in an hour,' Holly laughed, taking a seat.

'You need to think positively, love.' The waitress busied herself around Holly. 'Right, I'll get you the menu,' she said, turning to leave.

'No, it's OK,' Holly called after her, 'I know what I want. I'll have the Irish breakfast.'

'No problem, love,' the woman smiled, and her eyes widened when she saw the pile of newspapers on the table, 'You thinking of starting your own newsagents?' she chuckled.

Holly looked down at the pile and laughed at the sight of the *Arab Leader* lying on the top. She had grabbed every single paper and hadn't even thought to check what they were. She doubted very much the *Arab Leader* contained any articles about the documentary.

'Well, to tell you the truth, love,' the woman said, cleaning the table beside her, 'you'd be doing us all a favour if you put that miserable ol' bastard out of business.' She glared across the road to the newsagent. Holly laughed as the woman waddled back into the café.

Holly just sat there for a while, watching the world go by. She loved catching snippets of people's conversations as they walked past; it gave her a sneaky peak into the lives of others. She loved to guess what people did for a living, where they were heading as they rushed by, where they lived, if they were married or single . . . Sharon and Holly always used to sit in Bewley's overlooking Grafton Street and they would do their people spotting. They would create little scenarios in their heads to pass the time, although Holly seemed to be doing this very regularly these days – just another demonstration of how her mind was caught up in other people's lives instead of focusing on her own.

For example, the new little scenario she was creating involved the man walking down the path holding hands with his wife. Holly decided that he was secretly gay and the man headed toward them was his lover.

186

Holly watched their faces as they approached each other, wondering if they would make eye contact. They went one better than that, and Holly tried not to giggle as the three of them stopped just in front of her table.

'Excuse me? Have you got the time?' lover asked secretly gay man and wife.

'Yes, it's a quarter past ten,' secretly gay man answered him, looking at his watch.

'Thanks a lot,' lover said, touching his arm, and walked on.

Now it was as clear as day to Holly that that had been secret code for a rendezvous later. She continued her people spotting for a little while longer until she eventually got bored and decided to live her own life for a change.

Holly flicked through the pages of the tabloids and came to a small article in the review section that caught her eye.

Girls and the City a Hit in the Ratings
by Tricia Coleman

For any of you unfortunate people who missed out on the outrageously funny TV documentary *Girls and the City* last Wednesday, do not despair because it will be back on our screens soon.

The hilarious fly-on-the-wall documentary, directed by Irishman Declan Kennedy, follows five Dublin girls out for a night on the town. They lift the lid on the mysterious world of celebrity life in trendy club Boudoir and provide us with thirty minutes of stomach-aching laughter.

The show proved to be a success when first aired on Channel 4, the latest TAM ratings revealing 4 million people tuned in in the UK. The show is to be repeated again Sunday night at 11p.m. on Channel 4. This is must-see TV, so don't miss it!

Holly tried to keep her cool as she read through the article. It was obviously great news for Declan but disastrous for her. Having that documentary aired once was bad enough, never mind a second time. She really needed to have a serious talk with him about this. She had let him off lightly the other night because he had been so excited and she didn't want to make a scene, but at this stage she had enough problems on her plate without having to worry about this too.

She flicked through the rest of the papers and saw what it was Sharon was ranting about. Every single tabloid had an article about the documentary and one had even printed a photograph of Denise, Sharon and Holly from a few years ago. How they got their hands on it she did not know. Thank God the broadsheets contained some real news or Holly would have really worried about the world. She wasn't too happy with the use of the words, 'mad girls', 'drunken girls', and the description from one of the papers that they were 'well up for it'. What did that even mean?

Holly's food finally arrived and she stared at it in shock, wondering how on earth she was going to get through it all.

'That'll fatten you up, love,' the plump lady said, placing it on the table. 'You need a bit of meat on your bones; you're far too skinny,' she warned her, waddling off again. Holly felt pleased at the compliment.

The plate was piled high with sausages, bacon, eggs, hash browns, black and white pudding, baked beans, fried potatoes, mushrooms, tomatoes and five slices of toast. Holly looked around her with embarrassment, hoping no one would think she was a complete pig. She saw that annoying teenager heading towards her with his gang of friends again and she picked up her plate and ran inside. She hadn't much of an appetite lately; but she finally felt ready to eat and she wasn't going to let some stupid spotty teenager ruin her breakfast for her.

Holly must have stayed in The Greasy Spoon much longer than she thought, because by the time she reached her parents' house in Portmarnock it was almost two o'clock. Against her prediction, the sun was still sitting high in the cloudless blue sky. She looked across at the crowded beach in front of the house and found it difficult to tell where the sky ended and the sea began. Busfuls of people where continuously being unloaded across the road, and there was a lovely smell of sun-tan lotion in the air. There were gangs of teenagers hanging around the grassy area with CD players blaring out the latest tunes. The sound and the smell brought back every happy childhood memory for Holly.

Holly rang the doorbell for the fourth time and still no one answered. She knew somebody had to be home because the bedroom windows were wide open upstairs. Her mum and dad would never leave them open if they weren't home, especially with throngs of strangers wandering around the area. Holly walked across the grass and pressed her face against the living-room window to see if there was any sign of life. She was just about to give up and wander over to the beach when she heard the screaming match between Declan and Ciara.

'CIARA, GET THE DAMN DOOR!'

'NO, I SAID! I . . . AM . . . BUSY!'

'WELL, SO AM I!'

Holly rang the doorbell again, just to add fuel to the fire.

'DECLAN!' Ouch, that was a bloodcurdling scream.

'GET IT YOURSELF, YOU LAZY COW!'

'HA! *I'M* LAZY?'

Holly took out her mobile phone and rang the house.

'CIARA, ANSWER THE PHONE!'

'NO!'

'Oh, for Christsake,' Holly snapped loudly, and hung up the phone. She dialled Declan's mobile number.

'Yeah?'

'Declan, open the goddamn fucking door now or I'll kick it in,' Holly growled.

'Oh sorry, Holly, I thought Ciara had answered it,' he lied.

He opened the door in his boxer shorts and Holly stormed in. 'Jesus Christ! I hope you two don't carry on like that *every* time the doorbell rings.'

He shrugged his shoulders noncommittally, 'Mum and Dad are out,' he said lazily, and headed up the stairs.

'Hey, where are you going?'

'Back to bed.'

'No you are not,' Holly said calmly, 'you are going to sit down here with me,' she patted the couch, 'and we're gonna have a nice long chat about *Girls and the City*.'

'No,' Declan moaned. 'Do we have to do this now? I'm really, really tired.' He rubbed his eyes with his fists.

Holly had no sympathy for him, 'Declan, it's two o'clock in the afternoon, how can you still be tired?'

'Because I only got home a few hours ago,' he said, cheekily winking at her. Now she definitely had no sympathy for him; she was just plain jealous.

'Sit!' she ordered him.

He moaned again and dragged his weary body over to the couch where he collapsed and stretched out along the entire thing, leaving no room for Holly. She rolled her eyes and dragged her dad's armchair closer to Declan.

'I feel like I'm with a shrink,' he laughed, crossing his arms behind his head and staring up at her.

'Good, because I'm really going to pick your brains.'

Declan whinged again, 'Oh, Holly, do we have to? We just talked about this the other night.'

'Did you honestly think that was all I was going to say? "Oh, I'm sorry, Declan, but I didn't like the way you publicly humiliated me and my friends. See you next week"?'

'Obviously not.'

'Come on, Declan,' she said, softening her tone, 'I just want to understand why you thought it would be such a great idea not to tell me you were filming me and my friends?'

'You *knew* I was filming,' he said defensively.

'For a documentary about *club life*!' Holly raised her voice in frustration at her younger brother.

'And it *was* about club life,' Declan laughed.

'Oh, you think you're so bloody clever,' she snapped at him, and he stopped laughing. She counted to ten and breathed slowly to prevent herself from attacking him.

'Come on, Declan,' she said quietly. 'Do you not think that I am going through enough right now without having to worry about this as well? And without even asking me? I cannot for the life of me understand why you would do it!'

Declan sat up on the couch and became serious for a change, 'I know, Holly, I know you've been through hell but I thought this would cheer you up. I wasn't lying when I said I was going to film the club because that's what I had planned on doing. But when I brought it back to college to begin the edit everyone thought that it was just so funny that I couldn't *not* show it to people.'

'Yeah, but you put it on TV, Declan.'

'I didn't know that was the prize, honestly,' he said, wide-eyed. 'Nobody knew, not even my lecturers! How could I say no to it when I won?'

Holly gave up and ran her fingers through her hair.

'I honestly thought you would like it,' he smiled. 'I checked with Ciara and *even she* said you'd like it. I'm sorry if I upset you,' he mumbled.

Holly continued nodding her head through his explanation, realising he genuinely had good intentions, however misguided. Suddenly she stopped.

What had he just said? She sat up, alert in her seat. 'Declan, did you just say that Ciara knew about the tape?'

Declan froze in his seat and tried to think of a way to back himself out of the corner he found himself in. Coming up with nothing, he threw himself back onto the couch and covered his head with a cushion, knowing he had just started World War Three.

'Oh, Holly, don't say anything to her. She'll kill me!' came his muffled reply.

Holly bounded out of her seat and stormed upstairs, thumping her feet on every stair to show Ciara she was *really* mad. She yelled threats at Ciara all the way up and pounded on her bedroom door.

'Don't come in!' yelled Ciara from inside.

'You are in so much trouble, Ciara!' Holly screamed. She burst her way inside, putting on her most terrifying face.

'I told you not to come in!' wailed Ciara.

Holly was about to start screaming all sorts of insulting things at her sister but stopped herself when she saw Ciara sitting on the floor with what looked like a photo album on her lap and tears streaming down her face.

Chapter Twenty-One

'Oh, Ciara, what's wrong?' Holly said soothingly. She was worried; she couldn't remember the last time she had seen Ciara cry. In fact, she didn't even know Ciara knew *how* to cry. Whatever had reduced her to tears must be something serious.

'Nothing's wrong,' Ciara said, snapping the photo album shut and sliding it under her bed. She seemed embarrassed to be caught crying and she wiped her face roughly, trying to look as if she didn't care.

Downstairs on the couch, Declan peeped his head out from under the cushion. It was eerily quiet up there; he hoped they hadn't done anything stupid to one another. He tiptoed upstairs and listened outside the door.

'Something *is* wrong,' Holly said, crossing the room to join her sister on the floor. She wasn't sure how to deal with Ciara like this. This was a complete role reversal; ever since they were kids it had always been Holly who had done all the crying. Ciara was supposed to be the strong one.

'I'm fine,' Ciara snapped.

'OK,' Holly said looking around, 'but if there's

something on your mind that's upsetting you, you know you can talk to me about it, don't you?'

Ciara refused to look at her and just nodded her head. Holly began to stand up to leave her sister in peace when all of a sudden Ciara burst into tears again. Holly quickly sat back down and wrapped her arms protectively round her younger sister. Holly stroked Ciara's silky pink hair while she cried quietly.

'Do you want to tell me what's wrong?' she asked softly.

Ciara gurgled some sort of reply and sat up to slide the photo album back out from under the bed. She opened it with trembling hands and flicked a few pages.

'Him,' she said, sadly pointing to a photograph of her and some guy Holly didn't recognise. In fact, Holly barely recognised her sister. She looked so different and so much younger. The photograph was taken on a beautiful sunny day on a boat overlooking the Sydney Opera House. Ciara was sitting happily on his knee with her arms wrapped round his neck and he was staring at her with a huge smile on his face. Holly couldn't get over how pretty Ciara looked. She had blonde hair, which Holly had never seen on her sister before, and a great big smile on her face. Her features looked much softer – she didn't look as if she was going to bite someone's head off for a change.

'Is that your boyfriend?' Holly asked gently.

'Was,' Ciara sniffed, and a tear landed on the page.

'Is that why you came home?' she asked softly, wiping a tear from her sister's face.

Ciara nodded.

'Do you want to tell me what happened?'

Ciara gasped for breath. 'We had a fight.'

'Did he . . .' Holly chose her words carefully, 'he didn't hurt you or anything did he?'

Ciara shook her head. 'No,' she spluttered, 'it was just over something really stupid and I said I was leaving and he said he was glad . . .' She trailed off as she started sobbing again.

Holly held her in her arms and waited till Ciara was ready to talk again.

'He didn't even come to the airport to say goodbye to me.'

Holly rubbed Ciara's back soothingly as though she was a baby who had just drunk her bottle. She hoped Ciara wouldn't throw up on her. 'Has he called you since?'

'No, and I've been home for two months, Holly,' she wailed. She looked up at her older sister with such sad eyes Holly felt like crying too. She didn't like the sound of this guy at all for hurting her sister. Holly smiled at her encouragingly. 'Then do you think that maybe he's not the right kind of person for you?'

Ciara started crying again. 'But I love Mathew, Holly, and it was just a stupid fight. I only booked the flight because I was angry. I didn't think he would let me go . . .' She stared for a long time at the photograph.

Ciara's bedroom windows were wide open and Holly listened to the familiar sound of the waves and the laughter coming from the beach. Holly and Ciara had shared this room together as they grew up, and a weird sense of comfort now embraced her as she smelled the same smells and listened to the familiar noises.

Ciara began to calm down. 'Sorry, Hol.'

'Hey, you don't need to be sorry at all,' she said, squeezing her hand. 'You should have told me all this when you came home instead of keeping it all inside.'

'But this is only minor compared to what's happened to you. I feel stupid even crying about it.' She wiped her tears, angry with herself.

Holly was shocked, 'Ciara, this *is* a big deal. Losing someone you love is always hard, no matter if they're alive or . . .' She couldn't finish the sentence. 'Of course you can tell me anything.'

'It's just that you've been so brave, Holly. I don't know how you do it. And here I am crying over a stupid boyfriend I went out with for only a few months.'

'Me? Brave?' Holly laughed. 'I wish.'

'Yes, you are,' Ciara insisted. 'Everyone says so. You've been so strong through everything. If I were you I'd be lying in a ditch somewhere.'

'Don't go giving me ideas, Ciara,' Holly smiled at her, wondering who on earth had called her brave.

'You're OK, though, aren't you?' Ciara said, worriedly studying her face.

Holly looked down at her hands and slid her wedding ring up and down her finger. She thought about that question for a while and the two girls became lost in their own thoughts. Ciara, suddenly calmer than Holly had ever seen her, sat by her side patiently awaiting Holly's reply.

'Am I OK?' Holly repeated the question to herself. She looked ahead at their collection of teddy bears and dolls that their parents had refused to throw out. 'I'm lots of things Ciara,' Holly explained, continuing to roll her ring around on her fingers. 'I'm lonely, I'm tired, I'm sad, I'm happy, I'm lucky, I'm unlucky; I'm a million different things everyday of the week. But I suppose OK is one of them.' She looked to her sister and smiled sadly.

'And you're brave,' Ciara assured her. 'And calm and in control. And organised.'

Holly shook her head slowly, 'No, Ciara, I'm not brave. You're the brave one. You were always the brave one. As for being in control, I don't know what I'm doing from one day to the next.'

Ciara's forehead creased and she shook her head wildly. 'No, I am far from being brave, Holly.'

'Yes you are,' Holly insisted. 'All those things that you do like jumping out of aeroplanes and snow boarding off cliffs . . .' Holly trailed off as she tried to think of more crazy things her little sister did.

Ciara shook her head in protest. 'Oh no, my dear sister. That's not brave, that's *foolish*. Anybody can bungee jump off a bridge. You could do it,' Ciara nudged her.

Holly's eyes widened, terrified at the thought and she shook her head.

Ciara's voice softened. 'Oh, you would *if you had to,* Holly. Trust me, there's nothing brave about it.'

Holly looked at her sister and matched her tone, 'Yes, and if your husband died you would cope *if you had to*. There's nothing brave about it. There's no choice involved.'

Ciara and Holly stared at each other, aware of the other's battle.

Ciara was the first to speak. 'Well, I guess you and

I are more alike than we thought.' She smiled at her big sister and Holly wrapped her arms round her small frame and hugged her tightly, 'Who would have thought?'

Holly thought her sister looked like such a child, with her big innocent blue eyes. She felt as though they were both children again, sitting on the floor where they used to play together during their childhood, and where they would gossip when they were teenagers.

They sat in silence, listening to the sounds outside.

'Was there something you were going to scream at me about earlier on?' Ciara asked quietly in a childish voice. Holly had to laugh at her sister for trying to take advantage.

'No, forget about it, it was nothing,' Holly replied, staring out at the blue sky.

From outside the door, Declan wiped his brow and breathed a sigh of relief; he was in the clear. He tiptoed silently back into his bedroom and hopped back into bed. Whoever this Mathew was he owed him big time. His phone beeped, signalling a message, and he frowned as he read the text. Who the hell was Suzanne? Then a grin crept across his face as he remembered last night.

Chapter Twenty-Two

It was eight o'clock when Holly finally drove up her driveway, and it was still bright. She smiled; the world never felt quite so depressing when it was bright. She had spent the day with Ciara, chatting about her adventures in Australia. Ciara had changed her mind at least twenty times in the space of a few hours about whether or not she should call Mathew in Australia. By the time Holly left, Ciara was adamant she would never speak to him again, which probably meant she had already called him by now.

She walked up the path to the front door and stared at the garden curiously. Was it her imagination or did it look a little tidier? It was still a complete mess, with weeds and overgrown shrubs sprouting up everywhere, but something about it looked different.

The sound of a lawnmower started and Holly spun round to face her neighbour, who was out working in his garden. She waved over to thank him, presuming it was he who had helped her, and he held his hand up in response.

It had always been Gerry's job to do the garden. He wasn't necessarily a keen gardener, it was just that Holly was an incredibly unkeen one and somebody had to do the dirty work. It had been agreed between them that there was no way in the world Holly was going to waste her day off toiling in the soil. As a result, their garden was simple; just a small patch of grass surrounded by a few shrubs and flowers. As Gerry knew very little about gardening he often planted flowers in the wrong season, or put them in the wrong place so they ended up dying. Now the garden just looked like an overgrown field. When Gerry died, the garden had died along with him.

Which reminded her of the orchid in her house. She rushed inside, filled a jug with water and poured it over the extremely thirsty-looking plant. It didn't look very healthy at all and she promised herself she wouldn't let it die under her care. She threw a chicken curry into the microwave and sat down to wait at the kitchen table. Outside on the road she could still hear the kids playing happily. She always used to love when the bright evenings came, it meant Mum and Dad would let them all play outside longer, which meant she wouldn't have to go to bed till later than usual and that had always been a treat. Holly thought back over her day and decided it had been a good one, apart from one incident . . .

She looked down at the rings on her wedding finger and she immediately felt guilty. When that man Rob had walked away from her Holly had felt so awful. He had given her that look as if she was about to initiate an affair when that was the last thing in the world she would ever do. She had felt guilty for even

201

considering accepting his invitation to go for a coffee.

If Holly had left her husband because she absolutely couldn't stand him any more she could understand being able eventually to be attracted to someone else. But her husband had died when they were both still very much in love and she couldn't just fall out of love all of a sudden just because he wasn't around any more. She still *felt* married, and going for coffee today would have seemed as if she was betraying Gerry. The very thought disgusted her. Her heart, soul and mind still belonged with him.

Holly twisted her ring around on her finger, lost in thought. At what point should she take her wedding ring off? Gerry was gone almost six months now. Where was the rulebook for widows that explained when exactly the ring should be taken off? And when it finally did come off, where would she put it, where *should* she put it? In the bin? Beside her bed so she could be reminded of him every single day? She continued to twist the ring around her finger and plagued herself with question after question. No, she wasn't quite ready to give up her Gerry yet. As far as she was concerned he was still living.

The microwave beeped. She took the dish out and threw it straight into the bin. She had suddenly lost her appetite.

Later that night Denise rang her in a tizzy. 'Switch Dublin FM on, quick!'

Holly raced to the radio and flicked the switch, 'I'm Tom O'Connor and you're listening to Dublin FM. If you've just joined us we are talking about bouncers. In light of the amount of persuasion it took

202

the *Girls and the City* girls to blag their way into Boudoir, we wanna know what your thoughts on bouncers are. Do you like them? Do you not? Do you agree or understand why they are the way they are? Or are they too strict? The number to call is . . .'

Holly picked the phone back up, having forgotten for a moment that Denise was still on the other end.

'Well?' Denise said, giggling.

'What the hell have we started, Denise?'

'I know,' she chuckled. It was obvious she was loving every minute of it. 'Did you see the papers today?'

'Yeah, it's all a bit silly really. I agree it was a good documentary but the stuff they were writing was just stupid.'

'Oh, honey, I love it! And I love it even more because I'm in it!'

'I bet you do,' Holly laughed.

They both remained quiet while they listened to the radio. Some guy was giving out about bouncers and Tom was trying to calm him down.

'Oh, listen to my baby,' Denise said. 'Doesn't he sound so sexy?'

'Em . . . yeah,' Holly mumbled. 'I take it you two are still together?'

'Of course.' Denise sounded insulted by the question. 'Why wouldn't we be?'

'Well, it's been quite a while now, Denise, that's all,' Holly quickly tried to explain so she wouldn't hurt her friend's feelings. 'And you always said you couldn't be with a man for over a month, that you hate being tied down to one person.'

'Yes, well, I said I *couldn't* be with a man for over

a period of a month but I never said I *wouldn't*. Tom is different, Holly,' Denise added breathily.

Holly was surprised to hear this from Denise, the girl who wanted to remain single for the rest of her life. 'Oh, so what's so different with Tom then?' Holly rested the phone between her ear and her shoulder and she settled down in the chair to examine her nails.

'Oh, there's just this *connection* between us. It's like he's my soul mate. He's so thoughtful, always surprising me with little gifts and taking me out for dinner and spoiling me. He makes me laugh *all the time* and I just love being with him. I haven't got sick of him like all the other guys. *Plus* he's good-looking.'

Holly stifled a yawn. Denise tended to say this after the first week of going out with all her new boyfriends and then she would quickly change her mind. But then again, perhaps Denise meant what she said this time; after all they had been together for several weeks now.

'I'm very happy for you,' Holly replied genuinely.

The two girls began listening to a bouncer speaking on the radio.

'Well, first of all I just want to tell you that for the past few nights we have had I don't know how many princesses and ladies queuing up at our door. Since that bloody programme was aired people seem to think we're going to let them in if they're royalty! And I just want to say, girls, it's not going to work again so don't bother!'

Tom kept laughing and tried to hold himself together. Holly flicked the switch off on the radio.

'Denise,' Holly said seriously, 'the world is going mad.'

The next day Holly dragged herself out of bed to go for a stroll in the park. She needed to start doing some exercise before she turned into a complete slob and she also needed to start thinking seriously about job-hunting. Everywhere she went she tried to picture herself working in that environment. She had definitely ruled out clothes stores (the possibility of having a boss like Denise had talked her out of that one), restaurants, hotels, pubs and she certainly didn't want another nine-to-five office job, which left . . . nothing. Holly decided she wanted to be like the woman in the film she had seen last night; she wanted to work in the FBI so she could run around solving crimes and interrogating people and then eventually fall in love with her partner, whom she hated when they first met. However, seeing as she neither lived in America nor had any police training, the chances of that happening didn't seem too hopeful. Maybe there was a circus she could join somewhere . . .

She sat down on a park bench opposite the playground and listened to the children's screams of delight. She wished she could go in and play on the slide and be pushed on the swings instead of sitting here and watching. Why did people have to grow up? Holly realised she had been dreaming of going back to her youth all weekend.

She wanted to be irresponsible, she wanted to be looked after, to be told that she didn't have to worry about a thing and that someone else would take care of everything. How easy life would be without having grown-up problems to worry about. And then she could grow up all over again and meet Gerry all over again and force him to go to the doctor months earlier and then she would be sitting beside Gerry here on the bench watching their children playing. What if, what if, what if . . .

She thought about the stinging remark Richard had made about never having to bother with all that children nonsense. It angered her just thinking about it. She wished so much that she could be worrying about all that children nonsense right now. She wished she could have a little Gerry running around the playground while she shouted at him to be careful and did other mummy things, like spit on a tissue and wipe his pudgy little dirty face.

Holly and Gerry had only started talking about having children a few months before he was diagnosed. They had been so excited about it and used to lie in bed for hours trying to decide names, creating scenarios in their heads of what it would be like to be parents. Holly smiled at the thought of Gerry being a father; he would have been terrific. She could imagine him being so patient while he sat helping the kids with their homework at the kitchen table. She could imagine him being so overprotective if his daughter ever brought a boy home. Imagine if, imagine if, imagine if . . .

But Holly needed to stop living her life in her head, remembering old memories and dreaming of impossible dreams. It would never get her anywhere.

Well, talk of the devil, Holly thought to herself,

seeing Richard leaving the playground with Emily and Timmy. He looked so relaxed, she thought, watching him in surprise as he chased the children around the park. They looked as though they were having fun, not a very familiar sight. She sat up on the bench and zipped up her extra layer of thick skin in preparation for their conversation.

'Hello, Holly!' Richard said happily, spotting her and walking across the grass to her.

'Hello!' Holly said, greeting the kids as they ran over to her and gave her a big hug. That made a nice change. 'You're far from home,' she said to Richard. 'What brings you all the way over here?'

'I brought the children to see Grandma and Granddad, didn't I?' he said, ruffling Timmy's head.

'*And* we had McDonald's,' Timmy said excitedly, and Emily cheered.

'Oh, yummy!' Holly said, licking her lips. 'You lucky things. Isn't your daddy the best?'

Richard looked pleased.

'Junk food?' Holly questioned her brother.

'Ah,' he waved his hand dismissively and sat down beside her, 'everything in moderation, isn't that right, Emily?'

Five-year-old Emily nodded her head as though she had completely understood her father. Her big green eyes were wide and innocent and her nodding head was sending her red ringlets bouncing. She was eerily like her mother and Holly had to look away. Then she felt guilty and looked back and smiled . . . then had to look away again. There was something about those eyes and that hair that scared her.

207

'Well, one McDonald's meal isn't going to kill them,' Holly agreed with her brother.

Timmy grabbed at his throat and pretended to choke. His face went red as he made gagging noises and he collapsed on the grass and lay very still. Richard and Holly laughed. Emily looked as if she was going to cry.

'Oh dear,' Richard joked, 'looks like we were wrong, Holly. The McDonald's did kill Timmy.'

Holly looked at her brother in shock for calling his son Timmy, but she decided not to mention it. It was obviously just a slip of the tongue.

Richard got up and threw Timmy over his shoulder. 'Well, we better go bury him now and have a funeral.' Timmy giggled as he dangled upside down on his father's shoulder.

'Oh, he's alive!' Richard laughed.

'No, I'm not,' giggled Timmy.

Holly watched in amusement at the family scene before her. It had been a while since she had witnessed anything like this. None of her friends had children and Holly was very rarely around any. There was obviously something seriously wrong with her if she was doting on Richard's children. And it wasn't the wisest decision to become broody when there was no man in your life.

'OK, we best be off,' laughed Richard. 'Bye, Holly.'

'Bye, Holly,' the children cheered, and Holly watched Richard walk off with Timmy slung over his right shoulder, as little Emily hopped, skipped and danced along beside him while gripping his hand.

Holly stared in amusement at the stranger walking

off with two children. Who was this man who claimed to be her brother? Holly certainly had never met *that* man before.

Chapter Twenty-Three

Barbara finished serving her customers and as soon as they left the building she ran into the staffroom and lit up a cigarette. The travel agent's had been so busy all day and she had to work all through her lunch break. Melissa, her colleague, had called in sick that morning although Barbara knew very well she had partied too hard the night before and any sickness she might have was self-inflicted. So she was stuck in this boring job all by herself today. And, of course, it was the busiest day they'd had in ages. As soon as November came, with those horrible depressing dark nights and dark mornings and piercing wind and sheets of rain . . . everyone came running in the door, booking holidays to beautiful hot sunny countries. Barbara shuddered as she heard the wind rattle the windows and made a note to herself to check for any special holiday deals.

Her boss had finally gone out to run some errands and she had flown into the staffroom as quickly as she could to light up a cigarette. The bell over the door sounded and Barbara cursed the customer entering the shop for disturbing her precious break. She puffed on the cigarette furiously, almost making herself dizzy, reapplied her glossy red lipstick, made sure her name badge was still pinned on and sprayed her perfume all around the room, so her boss wouldn't notice the smoke. She left the staff room expecting to see a customer sitting behind the counter but instead the old man was still slowly making his way over. Barbara tried not to stare and began pressing random buttons on her keypad.

'Excuse me?' the man's weak voice called to her.

'Hello, sir, how can I help you?' she said for the hundredth time that day. She didn't mean to be rude by staring at him but she was surprised at how young the man actually was. From far away his slumped figure looked like that of a pensioner. His body was hunched and the walking stick in his hand seemed to be the only thing preventing him from collapsing to the floor in front of her. His skin was very white and pasty, as though he hadn't seen the sun for years, but he had big brown puppy eyes that seemed to smile at her from under his long lashes. She couldn't help but smile back at him.

'I was hoping to book a holiday,' he said quietly, 'but I was wondering if you could help me choose a place.'

Usually Barbara would have silently screamed at the customer for making her do this unbelievably impossible task. Most of her customers were so fussy that she could be sitting there for hours with them flicking through brochures and trying to persuade them where to go when the truth is she really couldn't give a toss where they went. But this man seemed pleasant so she was glad to help. She surprised herself.

'No problem, sir. Why don't you take a seat there and we'll search through the brochures.' She pointed to the chair in front of her and looked away again so she didn't have to watch his struggle to sit down.

'Now,' she said, full of smiles, 'is there any country in particular that you would like to go to?'

'Em . . . Spain . . . Lanzarote, I think.'

Barbara was glad; this was going to be a lot easier than she'd thought.

'And is it a summer holiday you're looking for?'

He nodded slowly.

They worked their way through the brochure and finally the man found a place that he liked. Barbara was happy that he took her advice into account, unlike some of her other customers, who just ignored every single bit of her knowledge.

'OK, any month in particular?' she said, looking at the prices.

'August?' he asked, and those big brown eyes looked so deep into Barbara's soul she just wanted to jump over the counter and give him a big hug.

'August is a good month,' she agreed with him. 'Would you like a sea view or a pool view? The sea view is an extra thirty euro,' she added quickly.

He stared into space with a smile on his face as though he was already there. 'A sea view, please.'

'Good choice. Can I take your name and address, please?'

'Oh . . . this isn't actually for me . . . it's a surprise for my wife and her friends.'

Those brown eyes looked sad. Barbara cleared her throat nervously, 'Well, that's very thoughtful of you, sir,' she felt she had to add. 'Could I have their names then, please?'

She finished taking his details and he settled the bill. She began to print the arrangements from the computer to give to him.

'Oh, do you mind if I leave the details here with you? I want to surprise my wife and I would be afraid of leaving papers around the house in case she finds them.'

Barbara smiled; what a lucky wife he had.

'I won't be telling her till July so do you think it could be kept quiet till then?'

'That's no problem at all, sir. Usually the flight times aren't confirmed till a few weeks before anyway, so we would have no reason to call her. I'll give the other staff strict instructions not to call the house.'

'Thank you for your help, Barbara,' he said, smiling sadly with those puppy eyes.

'It's been a pleasure Mr—?'

'It's Gerry,' he smiled again.

'Well, it's been a pleasure, Gerry. I'm sure your wife will have a wonderful time. My friend went there last year and she loved it.' Barbara felt the need to re-assure him his wife would be fine.

'Well, I'd better head back home before they think I've been kidnapped. I'm not even supposed to be out of bed, you know.' He smiled again and a lump formed in Barbara's throat.

She jumped to her feet and ran round the other side of the counter to hold the door open for him. He smiled appreciatively as he walked past her and she watched as he slowly climbed into the taxi that had been waiting outside for him. Just as Barbara was about to close the door her boss walked in and it banged against his head. She looked over at Gerry, who was still waiting in the taxi to move out onto the road and he laughed and gave her the thumbs-up.

Her boss threw her a look for leaving the counter unattended and marched into the staffroom. 'Barbara,' he yelled, 'have you been smoking in here again?'

She rolled her eyes and turned to face him.

'God, what's wrong with you? You look like you're about to burst into tears!'

It was the first of July and Barbara sat grumpily behind the counter of Swords travel agents. Everyday she had worked this summer had been beautiful and sunny, but the last two days she'd had off it had pissed down with rain. Today was typically the complete opposite. It was the hottest day of the year, all her customers kept on bragging as they strolled in in their little shorts and skimpy tops, filling the room with the smell of coconut sun cream. Barbara squirmed in her chair in her uncomfortable and incredibly itchy uniform. She felt as if she was back at school again. She banged on the fan once again as it stalled.

'Oh, leave it, Barbara,' Melissa moaned. 'That'll only make it worse.'

'As if that could be possible,' Barbara grumbled, and spun round in her chair to face the computer where she pounded on the keypad.

'What is it with you today?' Melissa asked.

'Oh, nothing much,' Barbara said through gritted teeth. 'It's just the hottest day of the year and we're stuck in this *crappy* job in this *stuffy* room with *no air conditioning* in these horrible *itchy uniforms*.' She shouted each word towards her boss's office, hoping he would hear. 'That's all.'

Melissa sniggered. 'Look, why don't you go outside for a few minutes to get some air and I'll deal with this next customer,' she said, nodding to the woman making her way in.

'Thanks, Mel,' Barbara said, relieved at finally being able to escape. She grabbed her cigarettes. 'Right, I'm going to get some fresh air.'

Melissa looked down at her hand and rolled her eyes. 'Hello, can I help you?' she smiled at the woman.

'Yes, I was wondering if Barbara still works here?'

Barbara froze just as she was reaching the door and contemplated whether to run outside or to go back to work. She groaned and headed back to her seat. She looked at the woman behind the counter. She was pretty, she decided, but her eyes looked tired and drawn as she stared frantically from one girl to the other.

'Yes, I'm Barbara.'

'Oh, good!' The lady looked relieved and she dived on to the stool in front of her. 'I was afraid you might not work here any more.'

'She wishes,' Melissa muttered under her breath.

'Can I help you?'

'Oh God, I really hope you can,' the lady said a bit hysterically, and rooted through her bag. Barbara raised her eyebrows over at Melissa and the two of them tried to hold in their laughs.

'OK,' she said eventually, pulling a crumpled

envelope out of her bag. 'I received this today from my husband and I was wondering if you could explain it to me.'

Barbara frowned as she stared at the dog-eared piece of paper on the counter. A page had been torn out of a holiday brochure and written on it were the words: 'Swords Travel Agent. Attn: Barbara.'

Barbara frowned again and looked at the page more closely. 'My friend went there two years ago on holiday but other than that it means nothing to me. Did you not get any more information?'

The lady shook her head vigorously.

'Well, can't you ask your husband for more information?' Barbara was confused.

'No, he's not here any more,' she said sadly, and tears welled in her eyes. Barbara panicked. If her boss saw her making someone cry she really would be given her marching orders. She was on her last warning as it was.

'OK then, can I take your name, and maybe it will come up on the computer?'

'It's Holly Kennedy.' Her voice shook.

'Holly Kennedy, Holly Kennedy . . .' Melissa was listening in on their conversation. 'That name rings a bell. Oh, hold on, I was about to call you this week! That's weird! I was under strict instructions by Barbara not to ring you until July for some reason—'

'Oh!' Barbara interrupted her friend, finally realising what was going on. 'You're Gerry's wife?' she asked hopefully.

'Yes!' Holly threw her hands to her face in shock. 'He was in here?'

'Yes, he was,' Barbara smiled encouragingly. 'He was a lovely man,' she said, reaching out to Holly's hand on the counter.

Melissa stared at the two of them, not knowing what was going on.

Barbara's heart went out to the lady across the counter: she was so young and it must be so hard for her right now. But Barbara was delighted to be the bearer of good news.

'Melissa, can you get Holly some tissues, please, while I explain to her exactly why her husband was here.' She beamed across the counter at Holly, then let go of Holly's hand to tap away at the computer while Melissa returned with a box of tissues.

'OK, Holly,' Barbara said softly, 'Gerry has arranged a holiday for you and a Sharon McCarthy and a Denise Hennessey to go to Lanzarote for one week, arriving on the thirtieth of July to return home on the fifth of August.'

Holly's hands flew to her face again in shock, and tears poured from her eyes.

'He was adamant that he found the perfect place for you,' Barbara continued, delighted at her new role. She felt like one of those television hosts who sprang surprises on their guests. 'That's the place you're going to,' she said, tapping the crumpled page in front of her. 'You'll have a fab time, believe me. When my friend was there she just loved it. There are loads of restaurants and bars around and . . .' She trailed off, realising Holly probably didn't give a damn about whether she had a good time or not.

'When did he come in?' Holly asked, still in shock.

Barbara tapped away on the computer. 'The booking was made on the twenty-eighth of November.'

'November?' Holly gasped. 'He shouldn't even have been out of bed then! Was he on his own?'

'Yes, but there was a taxi waiting outside for him the whole time.'

'What time was this at?' Holly asked quickly.

'I'm sorry but I really can't remember. It was quite a long time ago—'

'Yes, of course, I'm sorry,' Holly interrupted.

Barbara completely understood. If that was her husband – well, if she ever met someone worthy of ever becoming her husband – she would also want to know every single detail. Barbara told her as much as she could remember until Holly could think of no more questions to ask.

'Oh, thank you, Barbara, thank you so much.' Holly reached over the counter and gave her a big hug.

'No problem at all,' Barbara hugged her back, feeling satisfied with her good deed for the day. 'Come back and let us know how you get on,' she smiled. 'Here's your details.' She handed Holly a thick envelope and watched her walk away. She sighed, thinking her crappy job might not be so crappy after all.

'What on earth was that all about?' Melissa was dying to find out. Barbara began to explain the story.

'OK, girls, I'm taking my break now. Barbara, no smoking in the staffroom.' Their boss closed and locked his door and then turned to face them. 'Christ Almighty, what *are* you two crying about now?'

Chapter Twenty-Four

Holly eventually arrived at her house and waved to Sharon and Denise, who were sitting on her garden wall sunbathing. They jumped up as soon as they saw her and rushed over to greet her.

'God, you both got here quick,' she said, trying to inject energy into her voice. She felt completely and utterly drained, and she really wasn't in the mood to have to explain everything to the girls right now. But she would have to.

'Sharon left work as soon as you called and she collected me from town,' Denise explained, studying Holly's face and trying to assess how bad the situation was.

'Oh, you didn't have to do that,' Holly said lifelessly, as she tried to put the key in the door.

'Hey, have you been working in your garden?' Sharon asked, looking around and trying to lighten the atmosphere.

'No, my neighbour's been doing it, I think.' Holly pulled the key from the door and searched through the bunch for the correct one.

'You think?' Denise tried to keep the conversation

going while Holly battled with yet another key in the lock.

'Well, it's either my neighbour or a little leprechaun lives down the end of my garden,' she snapped, getting frustrated with the keys. Denise and Sharon looked at each other and tried to figure out what to do. They motioned to one another to stay quiet as Holly was obviously stressed.

'Oh, fuck it!' Holly yelled, and threw her keys on the ground. Denise jumped back, just managing to avoid the heavy bunch from slamming into her ankles.

Sharon picked them up. 'Hey, hon, don't worry about it,' she said light-heartedly. 'This happens to me all the time. I swear the bloody things jump around on the keyring deliberately just to piss us off.'

Holly smiled wearily, thankful that somebody else could take control for a while. Sharon slowly worked her way through the keys, talking calmly to her in a singsong voice as though Holly was a child. The door finally opened and Holly rushed in to turn the alarm off. Thankfully she remembered the number: the year Gerry and she had met and the year they got married. As if she could ever forget those numbers.

'OK, why don't you two make yourselves comfortable in the living room and I'll follow you in a minute?' Sharon and Denise did as they were told while Holly headed into the toilet to splash cold water on her face. She needed to snap out of this daze, take control and be as excited about this holiday as Gerry had intended. When she felt a little more alive she joined the girls in the living room.

She pulled the footrest over to the couch and sat opposite the girls.

'OK, I'm not going to drag this one out. I opened the envelope for July today and this is what it said.' She rooted in her bag for the small card, which had been attached to the brochure that she'd shown to the girl at the travel agent and handed it to them. It read:

> *Have a good Holly day!*
> *PS. I love you . . .*

'Is that it?' Denise wrinkled up her nose, unimpressed. Sharon nudged her in the ribs. 'Ow!'

'Well, Holly, I think it's a lovely note,' Sharon lied. 'It's so thoughtful and it's . . . a lovely play on words.'

Holly had to giggle. She knew Sharon was lying because she always flared her nostrils when she wasn't telling the truth. 'No, you fool!' she said, hitting Sharon over the head with a cushion.

Sharon began to laugh. 'Oh good, because I was beginning to worry there for a second.'

'Sharon, you are always so supportive you make me sick sometimes!' Holly grinned. 'Now this is what else was inside.' She handed them the crumpled page that was torn from the brochure.

She watched with amusement as the girls tried to figure out Gerry's writing and Denise finally held her hand up to her mouth. 'Oh my God!' she gasped, sitting forward on her seat.

'What what what?' Sharon demanded, and leaned forward with excitement. 'Did Gerry buy you a holiday?'

'No.' Holly shook her head seriously.

'Oh.' Sharon and Denise both sat back in their seats with disappointment.

Holly allowed an uncomfortable silence to lapse between them until she spoke again.

'Girls,' she said with a smile beginning to spread across her face, 'he bought *us* a holiday!'

The girls opened a bottle of wine and squealed with excitement.

'Oh, this is incredible,' Denise said after the news had sunk in. 'Gerry's such a sweetie.'

Holly nodded, feeling proud of her husband, who had once again managed to surprise them all.

'So you went down to see this Barbara person?' Sharon asked.

'Yes, and she was the sweetest girl,' Holly smiled. 'She sat with me for ages telling me about the conversation they had that day. He went in at the end of November.'

'November?' Sharon looked thoughtful. 'That was after the second operation.'

Holly nodded. 'The girl said he was pretty weak when he went in.'

'Isn't it funny that none of us had any idea at all?' Sharon said.

They all nodded silently.

'Well, it looks like we're all off to Lanzarote!' Denise cheered, and she held her glass up. 'To Gerry!'

'To Gerry!' Holly and Sharon joined in.

'Are you sure Tom and John won't mind?' Holly asked, suddenly aware that the girls had partners to think of.

'Of course John won't mind!' Sharon laughed. 'He'll probably be delighted to be rid of me for a week!'

'Yeah, and me and Tom can go away for a week another time, which actually suits me fine,' agreed Denise, 'because that way we're not stuck together for two weeks on our first holiday together!' she laughed.

'Sure, you two practically live together anyway!' Sharon laughed, nudging her.

Denise gave a quick smile but didn't answer and the two of them dropped the subject. That annoyed Holly because they were always doing that. She wanted to hear how her friends were getting on in their relationships but nobody seemed to tell her any of the juicy gossip any more out of fear of hurting her. People seemed to be afraid to tell her about how happy they were or about the good news in their lives. Then again they also refused to moan about the bad things. So instead of being informed of what was really going on in her friends' lives she was stuck with this mediocre chitchat about . . . nothing really, and it was starting to bother her. She couldn't be shielded from other people's happiness for ever – what good would that do her?

'I have to say that leprechaun really is doing a great job on your garden, Holly,' Denise cut into her thoughts as she looked out the window.

Holly blushed. 'Oh, I know. I'm sorry for being a bitch earlier, Denise,' she apologised. 'I suppose I should really go next door and thank him properly.'

After Denise and Sharon had headed off home Holly grabbed a bottle of wine from the stash under the stairs and carried it next door to her neighbour. She rang the bell and waited.

'Hi, Holly,' Derek said, opening the door, 'come in, come in.'

Holly looked past him and into the kitchen, and saw the family sitting around the table eating dinner. She backed away from the door slightly.

'No, I won't disturb you. I just came by to give you this,' she handed him the bottle of wine, 'as a token of my thanks.'

'Well, Holly, this is really thoughtful of you,' he said, reading the label. Then he looked up with a confused expression on his face. 'But thanks for what, if you don't mind me asking?'

'For tidying up my garden,' she said, blushing. 'I'm sure the entire estate was cursing me for ruining the appearance of the street,' she laughed.

'Holly, your garden certainly isn't a worry to anyone – we all understand – but I haven't been tidying it for you, I'm sorry to say.'

'Oh.' Holly cleared her throat, feeling very embarrassed. 'I thought you had been.'

'No, no . . .'

'Well, you wouldn't by any chance know who has been?'

'I have no idea,' he said, puzzled. 'I thought it was you, to be honest,' he laughed. 'How odd.'

Holly wasn't quite sure what to say next.

'So perhaps you would like to take this back,' he said awkwardly, thrusting the wine bottle towards her.

'Oh no, that's OK,' she laughed again, 'you can keep that as thanks for . . . not being neighbours from hell. Anyway, I'll let you get back to dinner.' She ran off down the driveway with her face burning with embarrassment. What kind of fool wouldn't know who was tidying her own garden?

She knocked on a few more doors around the estate and to her embarrassment nobody seemed to know what she was talking about. Everyone seemed to have jobs and lives and, remarkably enough, they didn't spend their days monitoring her garden. She returned to her house even more confused. As she walked in the door the phone was ringing and she ran to answer it.

'Hello?' she panted.

'What were you doing, running a marathon?'

'No I was chasing leprechauns,' Holly explained.

'Oh, cool.'

The oddest thing was that Ciara didn't even question her.

'It's my birthday in two weeks.'

Holly had completely forgotten. 'Yeah, I know,' she said matter-of-factly.

'Well, Mum and Dad want us all to go out for a family dinner . . .'

Holly groaned loudly.

'Exactly.' And she screamed away from the phone, 'Dad, Holly said the same thing as me.'

Holly giggled as she heard her father cursing and grumbling in the background.

Ciara returned to the phone and spoke loudly so her father could hear. 'OK, so my idea is to go ahead with the family dinner but to invite friends as well so that it can actually be an enjoyable night. What do you think?'

'Sounds good,' Holly agreed.

Ciara screamed away from the phone, 'Dad, Holly agrees with my idea.'

'That's all very well,' Holly heard her dad yelling, 'but I'm not paying for all those people to eat.'

'He has a point,' Holly added. 'Tell you what, why don't we have a barbecue? That way Dad can be in his element and it won't be so expensive.'

'Hey, that's a cool idea!' Ciara screamed away from the phone once again, 'Dad, what about having a barbecue?'

There was a silence.

'He's loving that idea,' Ciara came back. 'Mr Super Chef will once again cook for the masses.'

Holly smirked at the thought. Her dad got so excited when they had barbecues; he took the whole thing incredibly seriously and stood by the grill constantly, watching over his wonderful creations. Gerry had been like that too. What was it with men and barbecues? Probably because it was the only way that the two of them could actually cook. Either that or they were closet pyromaniacs.

'So will you tell Sharon and John, Denise and her DJ bloke, and will you ask that Daniel guy to come too? He's yummy!' Ciara demanded.

'Ciara, I hardly know the guy. Ask Declan to ask him; he sees him all the time.'

'No, because I want you to subtly tell him that I love him and want to have his babies. Somehow I don't think Declan would feel very comfortable doing that.'

Holly groaned.

'Stop it!' Ciara gave out. 'He's *my* birthday treat!'

'OK,' Holly gave in, 'but why do you want all my friends there? What about your friends?'

'Holly, I've lost contact with all my friends, I've been away for so long. And all my other friends are in Australia and the stupid bastards haven't bothered to call me,' Ciara huffed.

Holly knew to whom she was specifically referring. 'But don't you think this would be a great opportunity to catch up with your old friends – you know, invite them to a barbecue? It's a nice relaxed atmosphere.'

'Yeah, right. What would I have to tell them when they start asking questions? Have you a job? Eh . . . no. Have you a boyfriend? Eh . . . no. Where do you live? Eh . . . actually I still live with my parents. How pathetic would I sound?'

Holly gave up. 'OK, whatever . . . Anyway I'll call the others and . . .'

Ciara had already hung up.

Holly decided to get the most awkward phone call out of the way first and she dialled the number to Hogan's.

'Hello, Hogan's.'

'Hi, can I speak to Daniel Connolly, please?'

'Yeah, hold on.' She was put on hold and 'Greensleeves' belted out into her ear.

'Hello?'

'Hi, Daniel?'

'Yeah, who's this?'

'It's Holly Kennedy.' She paced nervously around her bedroom, hoping he would recognise the name.

'Who?' he yelled as the noise in the background became louder.

Holly dived on to her bed in embarrassment. 'Holly Kennedy? Declan's sister?'

'Oh, Holly, hiya. Hold on a second while I go somewhere quieter.'

Holly was stuck listening to 'Greensleeves' again, and she danced around her bedroom and started singing along.

'Sorry, Holly,' Daniel said, picking up the phone again. He started laughing. 'You like "Greensleeves"?'

Holly's face went scarlet. 'Em, no, not really.' She couldn't think of what else to say, then she remembered why she was ringing.

'I was just ringing to invite you to a barbecue.'

'Oh great, yeah, I would love to go.'

'It's Ciara's birthday on Friday week – you know my sister, Ciara?'

'Eh . . . yes, the one with the pink hair.'

Holly laughed. 'Yeah, stupid question, everyone knows Ciara. Well, she wanted me to invite you to the barbecue and to subtly tell you that she wants to marry you and have your babies.'

Daniel started laughing. 'Yes . . . that was very subtle all right.'

Holly wondered whether he was interested in her sister, if she was his type.

'She'll be twenty-five,' Holly added for some unknown reason.

'Oh . . . right.'

'Em, well, Denise and your friend Tom are coming as well, and Declan will be there with his band, of course, so you'll know plenty of people.'

'Are you going?'

'Of course!'

'Good. I'll know even more people then, won't I?' he laughed.

'Oh great, she'll be delighted you're coming.'

'Well, I would feel rude for not accepting an invitation from a princess.'

At first Holly thought he was flirting and then she realised he was referring to the documentary so she mumbled some sort of incoherent answer.

He was just about to hang up the phone when a thought suddenly popped into her head. 'Oh, there's just one more thing.'

'Go for it,' he laughed.

'Is that position behind the bar still available?'

Chapter Twenty-Five

Thank God it was a beautiful day, Holly thought as she locked her car and walked round to the back of her parents' house. The weather had drastically changed this week and it had rained and rained continuously. Ciara was in hysterics about what would become of her barbecue, and she had been hell to be with all week. Luckily for everyone's sake the weather had returned to its former splendour. Holly already had a good tan from lying out in the sun all month, one of the perks of not having a job, and she felt like showing it off today by wearing a cute little denim skirt she had bought in the summer sales and a simple tight white T-shirt that made her look even browner.

Holly was proud of the present she had bought Ciara and she knew she would love it – a butterfly belly-button ring, which had a little pink crystal in each wing. She had chosen it to co-ordinate with Ciara's new butterfly tattoo, and her pink hair, of course. She followed the sounds of laughter and was glad to see that the garden was already full with family and friends. Denise had arrived with Tom and Daniel, and they had all flaked out on the grass. Sharon had turned up without John and she was sitting chatting to Holly's mum, no doubt discussing Holly's progress in life. Well, she was out of the house, wasn't she? Holly frowned as she noted Jack was once again not present. Ever since he had helped her carry out the task of cleaning Gerry's wardrobe, he had been unusually distant. Even as children Jack had always been great at understanding Holly's needs and feelings without her having to point it out to him, but when she had told him that she needed space after Gerry's death, she didn't mean she wanted to be *completely* ignored and isolated. It was so out of character for him not to be in contact for so long. Nerves fluttered through Holly's stomach and she prayed that he was all right.

Ciara was standing in the centre of the garden, screaming at everyone and loving being the centre of attention. She was dressed in a pink bikini top, to match her pink hair, and blue denim cut-offs.

Holly approached her with her present, which was immediately grabbed from her hand and ripped open. She needn't have bothered wrapping it so neatly.

'Oh, Holly, I love it!' Ciara exclaimed and threw her arms round her sister.

'I thought you would,' Holly said, glad she had chosen the right thing because no doubt her beloved sister would have let her know about it if she hadn't.

'I'm gonna wear it now, actually,' Ciara said, ripping out her current belly-button ring and piercing the butterfly through her skin.

'Ugh,' Holly shuddered, 'I could have lived without seeing that, thank you very much.'

There was a gorgeous smell of barbecued food in

the air and Holly's mouth began to water. She wasn't surprised to see all the men huddled around the barbecue, with her dad taking pride of place. Hunter men must provide food for women.

Holly spotted Richard and marched over. Ignoring the small talk she just charged right in. 'Richard, did you tidy my garden?'

Richard looked up from the barbecue with a confused expression on his face. 'Excuse me, did I what?' The rest of the men stopped their conversation and stared.

'Did you tidy my garden?' she repeated with her hands on her hips. She didn't know why she was acting so angry with him, just a force of habit probably, because if he had tidied it he had done her a huge favour. It was just annoying to keep returning home to see another section of her garden cleared and not to know who was doing it.

'When?' Richard looked around at the others frantically, as though he had been accused of murder.

'Oh, I don't know when,' she snapped. 'During the days for the past few weeks.'

'No, Holly,' he snapped back. 'Some of us have to work, you know.'

Holly glared at him and her father interjected, 'What's this, love? Is someone working on your garden?'

'Yes, but I don't know who,' she mumbled, rubbing her forehead and trying to think again. 'Is it you, Dad?'

Frank shook his head wildly, hoping his daughter hadn't finally lost the plot.

'Is it you, Declan?'

'Eh . . . think about it, Holly,' he said sarcastically.

She turned to the stranger standing next to her father. 'Is it you?'

'Um . . . no, I just flew into Dublin . . . um . . . for the . . . um weekend,' he replied nervously with an English accent.

Ciara started laughing. 'Let me help you, Holly. IS ANYBODY HERE WORKING ON HOLLY'S GARDEN?' she yelled.

The whole party stopped what they were doing and shook their heads, blank expressions on their faces.

'Now wasn't that much easier?' Ciara cackled.

Holly looked with disbelief at her sister and joined Denise, Tom and Daniel on the far side of the garden.

'Hello, Daniel,' Holly leaned over to greet Daniel with a kiss on the cheek.

'Hi, Holly. Long time no see.' He handed her a can from beside him.

'You still haven't found that leprechaun yet?' Denise laughed.

'No,' Holly said, stretching her legs out in front of her and resting back on her elbows, 'but it is just *so* odd!' She explained the story to Tom and Daniel.

'Do you think maybe your husband organised it?' Tom blurted out, and Daniel threw his friend a look.

'No,' Holly said, looking away, angry that a stranger knew her private business. 'It's not part of that.' She scowled at Denise for telling Tom her business.

Denise just held her hands up helplessly and shrugged.

Holly turned to Daniel, ignoring the other two. 'Thanks for coming, Daniel.'

233

'No problem at all. I was glad to come.'

It was weird, seeing him out of his usual wintery clothes; he was dressed in a navy vest and navy combat shorts that went just below his knees, with a pair of navy trainers. She watched his biceps as he took a slug of his beer. She had no idea he was that fit.

'You're very brown,' she commented, trying to think of an excuse for being caught staring at his biceps.

'And so are you,' he said, purposely staring at her legs.

Holly laughed and tucked them up underneath her. 'A result of unemployment. What's your excuse?'

'I was in Miami for a while last month.'

'Ooh, lucky you. Did you enjoy it?'

'Had a great time,' he nodded, smiling. 'Have you ever been?'

She shook her head, 'But at least us girls are heading off to Spain shortly. Can't wait.' She rubbed her hands together excitedly.

'Yes, I heard that. I'd say that was a nice surprise for you.' He gave her a smile, his eyes crinkling at the corners.

'You're telling me.' Holly shook her head, still not quite believing it.

They chatted together for a while about his holiday and their lives in general and Holly gave up eating her burger in front of him, as she could find no easy way of consuming it without tomato ketchup and mayonnaise dribbling down her mouth.

'I hope you didn't go to Miami with another woman or poor Ciara will be devastated,' she joked, and then kicked herself for being so nosy.

'No, I didn't,' Daniel said seriously. 'We broke up a few months ago.'

'Oh, I'm sorry to hear that,' she said genuinely. 'Were you together long?'

'Seven years.'

'Wow, that is a long time.'

'Yeah.' He looked away and Holly could tell he didn't feel comfortable talking about it so she quickly changed the subject.

'By the way, Daniel,' she lowered her voice to a hushed tone and he moved his head closer, 'I just wanted to thank you so much for looking out for me the way you did after the documentary. Most men run a mile when they see a girl cry; you didn't, so thank you.' Holly smiled gratefully.

'No problem at all, Holly. I don't like to see you upset.' Daniel returned the smile.

'You're a good friend,' Holly said, thinking aloud.

Daniel looked pleased. 'Why don't we go out for drinks or something before you go away?'

'Maybe I can get to know as much about you as you know about me.' Holly laughed. 'I think you know my whole life story by this stage.'

'Yeah, I'd like that,' Daniel agreed, and they arranged a time to meet.

'Oh, by the way, did you give Ciara that birthday present?' Holly asked excitedly.

'No,' he laughed. 'She's been kind of . . . busy.'

Holly turned round to look at her sister and spotted her flirting with one of Declan's friends, much to Declan's disgust. Holly laughed at her sister. So much for wanting Daniel's babies.

'I'll call her over, will I?'

'Go on,' Daniel laughed.

'Ciara!' Holly called. 'Got another pressie for you!'

'Ooh!' Ciara screamed with delight and abandoned a very disappointed-looking young man.

'What is it?' She collapsed on the grass beside them.

Holly nodded over at Daniel. 'It's from him.'

Ciara excitedly turned to face him.

'I was wondering if you would like a job working behind the bar in Club Diva?'

Ciara's hands flew to her mouth. 'Oh, Daniel, that would be brill!'

'Have you ever worked behind a bar?'

'Yeah, loads of times.' She waved her hand dismissively.

Daniel raised his eyebrows.

'Oh, I've done bar work in practically every country I've been to, honestly!' she said excitedly.

Daniel smiled. 'So do you think you'll be able for it?'

'Ooh, would I ever?' she squealed, and threw her arms around him.

Any excuse, Holly thought as she watched her sister practically strangling Daniel. His face started to turn red and he made 'rescue me' faces towards Holly.

'OK, OK, that's enough, Ciara,' she laughed, dragging her off Daniel. 'You don't want to kill your new boss.'

'Oh, sorry,' Ciara said backing off. 'This is *so* cool! I have a *job*, Holly!' she squealed again.

'Yes, I heard,' Holly laughed.

Suddenly the garden became very quiet and Holly

looked round to see what was happening. Everyone was facing the conservatory as Holly's parents appeared at the door with a large birthday cake in their hands singing 'Happy Birthday'. Every one else joined in and Ciara lapped up all the attention. As her parents stepped outside Holly spotted someone following behind them carrying a huge bouquet of flowers. Her parents walked towards Ciara and placed the birthday cake on the table before her and the stranger behind slowly removed the bouquet from in front of his face.

'Mathew!' Ciara gasped.

Holly grabbed Ciara's hand as her face went white.

'I'm sorry for being such a fool, Ciara,' Mathew's Australian accent echoed around the garden. Some of Declan's friends smirked loudly, obviously feeling uncomfortable at this open show of emotion. He actually looked as if he was acting out a scene from an Australian soap, but then again drama always seemed to work for Ciara. 'I love you! Please take me back!' he announced, and everyone turned to stare at Ciara to see what she would say.

Her lower lip started to tremble and she leaped up from the grass, ran over to Mathew and jumped on him, wrapping her legs round his waist and her arms round his neck.

Holly was overcome with emotion, and tears welled in her eyes at the sight of her sister being reunited with the man she loved. Declan grabbed his camera and began filming.

Daniel put his arm round Holly's shoulders and gave her an encouraging squeeze.

'I'm sorry, Daniel,' Holly said, wiping her eyes, 'but I think you've just been dumped.'

'Not to worry,' he laughed. 'I shouldn't mix business with pleasure anyway.' He seemed relieved.

Holly continued to watch as Mathew spun Ciara round in his arms.

'Oh, get a room!' Declan yelled with disgust, and everyone laughed.

Holly smiled at the jazz band as she passed and looked around the bar for Denise. They had arranged to meet up in the girls' favourite bar, Juicy, favoured for its extensive cocktail menu and relaxing music. Holly had no intention of getting drunk tonight as she wanted to be able to enjoy her holiday as much as she could, starting the next day. She intended to be bright-eyed and bushy-tailed for her week of relaxation from Gerry. She spotted Denise snuggling up to Tom on a comfortable large black leather couch in a conservatory area that overlooked the River Liffey. Dublin was lit up for the night and all its colours were reflected in the water. Daniel sat opposite Denise and Tom, sucking fiercely on a strawberry daiquiri, eyes surveying the room. Nice to see Tom and Denise were ostracising everyone again.

'Sorry I'm late,' Holly apologised, approaching her friends. 'I just wanted to finish packing before I came out.'

'You're not forgiven,' Daniel said quietly into her ear as he gave her a welcoming hug and kiss.

Denise looked up at Holly and smiled, Tom waved slightly and they returned their attention to each other.

'I don't know why they even bother inviting other people out. They just sit there staring into each other's eyes, ignoring everyone else. They don't even talk to each other! And then they make you feel like you've interrupted them if you strike up a conversation. I think they've got some weird telepathic conversation going on there,' Daniel said, sitting down again and taking another sip from his glass. He made a face at the sweet taste. 'And I really need a beer.'

Holly laughed. 'Oh, so all round it sounds like you've been having a fantastic night.'

'Sorry,' Daniel apologised. 'It's just been so long since I've spoken to another human being, I've forgotten my manners.'

Holly grinned. 'Well, I've come to rescue you.' She picked up the menu and surveyed the choice of drinks before her. She chose a drink with the lowest alcohol content and settled down in the cosy chair. 'I could fall asleep here,' she remarked, snuggling further down.

Daniel raised his eyebrows. 'Then I would *really* take it personally.'

'Don't worry, I won't,' she assured him. 'So, Mr Connolly, you know absolutely *everything* about me. Tonight I am on a mission to find out about you, so be prepared for my interrogation.'

Daniel smiled. 'OK, I'm ready.'

Holly thought about her first question. 'Where are you from?'

'Born and reared in Dublin.' He took a sip of the red cocktail and winced again. 'And if any of the people I grew up with saw me drinking this stuff and listening to jazz, I'd be in trouble.'

Holly giggled.

'After I finished school I joined the army,' he continued.

Holly raised her eyes, impressed. 'Why did you decide to do that?'

He didn't even think about it. 'Because I hadn't a clue what I wanted to do with my life, and the money was good.'

'So much for saving innocent lives.'

'I only stayed with the army for a few years.'

'Why did you leave?' Holly sipped on her lime-flavoured drink.

'Because I realised I had urges to drink cocktails and listen to jazz music and they wouldn't permit it in the army barracks,' he explained.

'Really, Daniel,' Holly laughed.

He smiled. 'Sorry, it just wasn't for me. My parents had gone down to Galway to run a pub and the idea of that appealed to me. So I moved to Galway to work there and eventually my parents retired, I took over the pub, decided a few years ago that I wanted to own one of my own, worked really hard, saved my money, took out the biggest mortgage ever and moved back to Dublin and bought Hogan's. And here I am, talking to you.'

'Well, that's a wonderful life story, Daniel.'

'Nothing special, but a life all the same.' He returned her smile.

'So where does the ex come into all this?' Holly asked.

'Laura's right in between running the pub in Galway and leaving to come to Dublin.'

'Ah . . . I see.' Holly nodded, understanding. She drained her glass and picked up the menu again. 'I think I'll have Sex on the Beach.'

'When? On your holidays?' Daniel teased.

Holly thumped him playfully on the arm. Not in a million years.

Chapter Twenty-Six

'We're all going on our summer Holly days!' the girls sang in the car all the way to the airport. John had offered to drive them there but he was fast regretting it. They were acting as though they had never left the country before. Holly couldn't remember the last time she had felt so truly excited. She felt as if she was back at school and was off on a trip. Her bag was packed with sweets, chocolate and magazines, and the girls couldn't stop singing cheesy songs in the back of the car. Their flight wasn't until 9 p.m. so they wouldn't arrive at their accommodation until the early hours of the morning.

They arrived at the airport and piled out of the car while John lifted their suitcases from the boot. Denise ran across the road and into the departure lounge as if doing so would get her to Lanzarote any faster but Holly stood back from the car and waited for Sharon, who was saying her goodbyes to her husband.

'You'll be careful now, won't you?' he asked her worriedly. 'Don't be doing anything stupid over there.'

'John, of course I'll be careful.'

John wasn't listening to a word she said. 'Because

it's one thing messing around over here but you can't act like that in another country, you know.'

'John,' Sharon said, wrapping her arms around his neck, 'I'm just going for a nice relaxing holiday; you don't need to worry about me.'

He whispered something in her ear and she nodded. 'I know, I know.'

They gave each other a long goodbye kiss and Holly watched her life-long friends embrace. She felt around in the front pocket of her bag for the August letter from Gerry. She would be able to open it in a few days, lying on the beach. What luxury. The sun, sand, sea *and* Gerry all in one day.

'Holly, take care of my wonderful wife for me, will you?' John asked, breaking into Holly's thoughts.

'I will, John. We're only going for a week, you know,' Holly laughed, and gave him a hug.

'I know but after seeing what you girls get up to on your nights out, I'm just a little worried,' he smiled. 'You enjoy yourself, Holly. You deserve the rest.'

John watched them as they dragged their luggage across the road and into the airport.

Holly paused as she entered and took in a deep breath. She loved airports. She loved the smell, the noise, the whole atmosphere as people walked around happily tugging their luggage, looking forward to going on their holidays or heading back home. She loved to see people arriving and being greeted with a big cheer by their families, and she loved to watch them all giving each other emotional hugs. It was a perfect place for people spotting. The airport always gave her a feeling of anticipation in the pit of her stomach as though she was about

243

to do something amazing. Queuing at the boarding gate felt like waiting to go on a roller coaster ride at a theme park, like an excited little child.

Holly followed Sharon and they joined Denise halfway down the extremely long check-in queue.

'I told you we should have come earlier,' Denise moaned.

'Well, then we would be waiting at the boarding gate for just the same amount of time,' reasoned Holly.

'Yeah, but at least there's a bar there,' explained Denise, 'and it's the only place in this entire stupid building that us smoker freaks can smoke in,' she mumbled.

'Good point,' Holly said.

'Now can I just point out something to you two before we even leave – I'm not going to be doing any crazy drinking or having any wild nights. I just want to be able to relax by the pool or on the beach with my book, enjoy a few meals out and go to bed early,' Sharon said seriously.

Denise looked at Holly in shock. 'Is it too late to invite someone else, Hol? What do you reckon? Sharon's bags are still packed and John can't be too far down the road.'

Holly laughed. 'No, I have to agree with Sharon on this one. I just want to go and relax and not do anything too stressful.'

Denise pouted like a child.

'Oh, don't worry, pet,' Sharon said softly, 'I'm sure there will be other kids your age who you can play with.'

Denise threw her the finger. 'Well, if they ask me

if I have anything to declare when we get there I'm telling everyone my two friends are dry shites.'

Sharon and Holly sniggered.

After thirty minutes of queuing they finally checked in and Denise ran around the shop like a mad woman, buying a lifetime's supply of cigarettes.

'Why is that girl staring at me?' Denise said through gritted teeth, eyeing up the woman at the end of the bar.

'Probably because you're staring at her,' Sharon responded, checking her watch. 'Only fifteen more minutes.'

'No, honestly, girls,' Denise turned back round to face them, 'I'm not being paranoid here. She is definitely staring at us.'

'Well then, why don't you go over to her and ask her if she wants to take it outside,' Holly joked, and Sharon smirked.

'Oh, here she comes,' Denise said, and turned her back to her.

Holly looked up and saw a skinny blonde-haired girl with big fake tits heading towards them. 'You better get those knuckle-dusters out, Denise. She looks like a dangerous one,' Holly teased, and Sharon almost choked on her drink.

'Hi, there!' the girl squeaked.

'Hello,' Sharon said, trying not to laugh.

'I didn't mean to be rude by staring but I just had to come over and see if it was really you!'

'It's me all right,' Sharon said, 'in the flesh.'

'Oh, I just *knew* it!' the girl squealed, and jumped up and down with excitement. Unsurprisingly her chest stayed still. 'My friends kept telling me I was wrong but I *knew* it was you! That's them over there.' She turned round and pointed to the end of the bar, and the other four spice girls twinkled their fingers back. 'My name's Cindy . . .'

Sharon nearly choked on her water again.

'. . . and I'm just the biggest fan of all of you,' she squealed excitedly. 'I just love that show that you're all in. I've watched it dozens and dozens of times! You play Princess Holly, don't you?' she said, pointing a manicured nail in Holly's face.

Holly opened her mouth to speak but Cindy kept on talking.

'And you play her lady!' she pointed at Denise. 'And *you,*' she squealed even louder, pointing at Sharon, 'you were friends with that Australian rock star!'

The girls looked at each other worriedly as she pulled out a chair and sat down at their table.

'You see, I'm an actress myself . . .'

Denise rolled her eyes.

'. . . and I would just love to work on a show like yours. When are you making the next one?'

Holly opened her mouth to explain that they weren't actually actresses but Denise beat her to it.

'Oh, we're in discussions right now about our next project,' she lied.

'How fantastic!' Cindy clapped her hands. 'What's it about?'

'Well, we can't really say right now but we have to go to Hollywood for filming.'

Cindy looked as if she was going to have a heart attack. 'Oh my God! Who's your agent?'

'Frankie,' Sharon interrupted Denise, 'so Frankie and us are all going to Hollywood.'

Holly couldn't hold her laugh in.

'Oh, don't mind her, Cindy, she's just excited,' explained Denise.

'Wow, and so you should be!' Cindy looked down at Denise's boarding pass on the table and nearly had heart failure. 'Wow, you girls are going to Lanzarote too!'

Denise grabbed her boarding pass and shoved it in her bag, as if that would make a difference.

'I'm going there with my friends. They're just over there.' She turned round *again* and waved at them *again* and they waved back *again*. 'We're staying in a place called Costa Palma Palace. Where are you guys staying?'

Holly's heart sunk. 'Oh I can't quite remember the name, girls, can you?' She looked to Sharon and Denise with wide eyes.

They shook their heads vigorously.

'Oh well, not to worry.' Cindy shrugged her shoulders happily. 'I'll see you when we land anyway! I better go now and board. I wouldn't want the plane to fly off without me!' she squeaked so loudly that the surrounding tables turned to stare. She gave each of the girls a big hug and tottered off back to her friends.

'Looks like we needed those knuckle-dusters after all,' Holly said miserably.

'Oh, it doesn't matter,' perked up Sharon, always the optimist. 'We can just ignore her.'

They all stood up and headed over to the boarding gate. As they made their way to their seats on the plane Holly's heart sunk once again and she immediately dived onto the seat on the far side of the aisle. Sharon sat down beside her and Denise's face was a picture when she realised who she had to sit next to.

'Oh, fab! You get to sit beside me!' Cindy squeaked at Denise.

Denise threw Sharon and Holly the nastiest look and plonked herself beside Cindy.

'See? I told you that you'd find yourself a little friend to play with,' Sharon whispered to Denise.

Sharon and Holly broke into fits of laughter.

Chapter Twenty-Seven

Four hours later the plane glided over the sea and landed at Lanzarote airport. Everyone cheered and applauded and no one on the plane was more relieved than Denise.

'Oh, I have the biggest headache,' she complained to the girls as they made their way to the luggage reclaim. 'That bloody girl just talks and talks and talks.' She massaged her temples and closed her eyes, relieved at the peace.

Sharon and Holly spotted Cindy and her crew making their way over to them and dashed off into the crowd, leaving Denise standing alone with her eyes closed.

They beat their way through the rabble so they had a good view of the luggage. Everybody thought it would be a great idea to stand right next to the conveyer belt and to lean forward so that nobody beside could see what was coming. They stood there for almost a half an hour before the conveyer belt even started moving and a further half an hour later they were still standing there waiting for their bags while the majority of the crowd had headed outside to their coaches.

'You bitches,' Denise said, angrily approaching them, dragging her suitcase behind her. 'You still waiting for your bags?'

'No I just find it strangely comforting standing here and watching the same leftover bags going around and around and around. Why don't you go on ahead to the coach and I'll just stay here and continue enjoying myself?' Sharon said.

'Well, I hope they lost your case,' Denise snapped, 'or even better, I hope your bag bursts open and all your big knickers and bras are spread all over the conveyer belt for everyone to see.'

Holly looked at Denise with amusement. 'You feel better now?'

'Not until I have a cigarette,' she replied, but she still managed to smile.

'Ooh, there's my bag!' Sharon said happily, and swung it off the conveyer belt, managing to whack Holly in the shins.

'OW!'

'Sorry, but must save clothes.'

'If they lost my clothes I'm going to sue them,' Holly said angrily. By now everyone had left and they were the only people still inside. 'Why am I always the last person waiting for my bags?' she asked her friends.

'Murphy's law,' Sharon explained. 'Ah, here it is.' She grabbed the suitcase and once again whacked it against Holly's already sore shins.

'OW! OW! OW!' Holly yelled, rubbing her legs, 'Could you at least swing the bloody thing the other way?'

'Sorry,' Sharon looked apologetic, 'I only swing one way, darling.'

The three of them headed off to meet their holiday rep.

'Stop, Gary! Get off me!' they heard a voice screeching as they rounded a corner. They followed the sound and spotted a young woman dressed in a red holiday rep uniform being attacked by a young man also dressed in a holiday rep uniform. The girls approached her and she straightened herself up.

'Kennedy, McCarthy and Hennessey?' she said in a thick London accent.

The girls nodded.

'Hi, I'm Victoria and I'm your holiday rep for the next week.' She plastered a smile on her face. 'So follow me and I'll show you to the coach.' She winked cheekily at Gary and led the girls outside.

It was two o'clock in the morning, and yet a warm breeze greeted them as they stepped outside. Holly smiled at the girls; now they were really on holiday.

When they stepped on the coach everybody cheered and Holly silently cursed them all, hoping this wasn't going to be a cheesy 'let's all make friends' holiday.

'Woo-hoo,' Cindy sang over to them. She was standing up and waving over at them. 'I kept you all a seat back here!'

Denise sighed loudly over Holly's shoulder and the girls trudged down to the back seat of the bus. Holly was fortunate enough to sit next to the window where she could ignore the rest of them. With luck Cindy would understand that she wanted to be left alone, the major hint being the fact that Holly had ignored her since the moment she had tottered over to their table.

Forty-five minutes later they reached Costa Palma Palace and the excitement once again returned to Holly's stomach. There was a long driveway in and tall palm trees lined the centre of the drive. A large fountain was lit up with blue lights outside the main entrance and, to her annoyance, everybody on the bus cheered once again when they pulled up outside. The girls were booked into a studio apartment that was a nice neat size, containing one bedroom with twin beds, a small kitchen and living area with a sofa bed, a bathroom and a balcony. Holly stepped on to the balcony and looked out to the sea. Although it was too dark to see anything Holly could hear the water gently lapping up against the sand. She closed her eyes and listened.

'Cigarette, cigarette, must have cigarette,' Denise joined her, ripping the cigarette packet open and inhaling deeply. 'Ah! That's much better; I no longer have the desire to kill people.'

Holly laughed; she was looking forward to spending time with her friends.

'Hol, do you mind if I sleep on the sofa bed? That way I can keep the door open and smoke . . .'

'Only if you do keep the door open, Denise,' Sharon yelled from inside. 'I'm not waking up in the morning to the stink of smoke.'

'Thanks,' Denise said happily.

At nine o'clock that morning Holly was woken up to the sound of Sharon stirring. Sharon whispered to her she was going down to the pool to save them some sun beds.

Fifteen minutes later she returned to the apartment. 'The Germans have nicked all the sun beds,' she said grumpily. 'I'll be down on the beach if you want me.' Holly sleepily mumbled a response and fell back asleep again.

At ten o'clock Denise jumped on her in bed and they decided to get up and join Sharon at the beach.

The sand was hot, and they had to keep moving so as not to burn the soles of their feet. As proud as Holly had been about her tan back in Ireland, it was obvious they had just arrived on the island. They were the whitest people there. They spotted Sharon sitting under the shade of an umbrella, reading her book.

'Oh, this is so beautiful, isn't it?' Denise smiled, looking around.

'Heaven,' Sharon agreed.

Holly gazed about, hoping Gerry had come to the same heaven. Nope, no sign of him. All around her there were couples: couples massaging sun cream onto each other's bodies, couples walking hand in hand along the beach, couples playing beach tennis and, directly in front of her sun bed, a couple snuggled up together sunbathing. But Holly didn't have time to be depressed as Denise had stepped out of her sundress and was hopping around on the hot sand in nothing but a skimpy leopardskin thong, demanding attention.

'Will one of you put sun cream on me?'

Sharon put her book down and stared at her over the rim of her reading glasses. 'I'll do it but you can put the cream on your tits and bum yourself.'

'Damn,' Denise joked. 'Don't worry about it, I'll go ask someone else then.' She sat at the end of Sharon's sun bed while she applied the cream. 'You know what, Sharon?'

'What?'

'You'll get an awful tan line if you keep that sarong on.'

Sharon looked down at herself and pulled the little skirt further down her legs. 'What tan? I never get a tan. Denise, didn't you know that the colour blue was the new brown.'

Holly and Denise laughed. As much as Sharon tried to tan over the years she just ended up getting sunburned and then it would peel. She had finally given up trying for a tan and accepted the fact that her skin was meant to be pale.

'Besides, I look like such a blob these days I wouldn't want to scare everyone off.'

Holly looked at her friend, annoyed at her for calling herself a blob. She had put a little bit of weight on but was by no means fat.

'Why don't you go up to the swimming pool then, and scare all those Germans away?' Denise joked.

'Yeah, girls, we really need to get up earlier tomorrow to get a place by the pool. The beach gets boring after a while,' Holly suggested.

'Don't vorry. Ve vill get ze Germans,' joked Sharon.

The girls relaxed by the beach for the rest of the day, occasionally dipping themselves into the sea to cool down. They ate lunch at the beach bar and generally had a lazy day just as they had planned. Holly gradually felt all the stress and tension working its way out of her muscles, and for a few hours she felt free.

254

That night they successfully managed to avoid the Barbie brigade and they enjoyed dinner in one of the many restaurants that lined the busy street not far from the apartment complex.

'I can't believe it's ten o'clock and we're heading back to the apartment already,' Denise said, staring longingly at the huge choice of bars around them.

People overflowed from the bars onto the streets, music, vibrating from every building, mixing together to form an unusual eclectic sound. Holly could almost feel the ground pulsing beneath her. Conversation between them stopped as they took in the sights, sounds and smells around them. There was loud laughter, clinking glasses and singing coming from every direction. Neon lights flashed and buzzed, each bar battling for custom. On the street, bar owners fought hard against each other to convince passers-by to enter, handing out leaflets, free drinks and concessions.

Tanned young bodies hung out in big groups around the outdoor tables and strolled confidently by them on the street, the smell of coconut sun cream rich in the air. Looking at the average age of the clientele, Holly felt old.

'Well, we can go to a bar for a few drinks if you want,' she said uncertainly, watching the younger ones dancing around on the street.

Denise stopped walking and assessed the bars.

'All right, beautiful.' A very attractive man stopped and flashed his pearly whites at Denise. He had an English accent. 'Are you coming in here with me?'

Denise stared at the young man for a while, lost in thought. Sharon and Holly smirked at each other, knowing that Denise wouldn't be going to bed early after all. In fact, Denise may not get to bed at all tonight, knowing her.

Finally Denise snapped out of her trance and straightened herself up. 'No, thank you. I have a boyfriend and I love him!' she announced proudly. 'Come on girls!' she said to Holly and Sharon, and walked off in the direction of the apartment.

The two girls remained on the street, mouths open in shock. They couldn't quite believe it. They had to run to catch up with her.

'What are you two gawking at?' Denise smiled.

'You,' Sharon said, still shocked. 'Who are you and what have you done with my man-eating friend?'

'OK,' Denise held her hands up in the air and grinned, 'maybe being single isn't all it's cracked up to be.'

Holly lowered her eyes and kicked a stone along the path as they made their way back to their resort. It sure wasn't.

'Well, good for you, Denise,' Sharon said happily, wrapping her arm round Denise's waist and giving her a little squeeze.

A silence fell between them and Holly listened as the music faded away slowly, leaving only a beat of the bass in the distance.

'That street made me feel so old,' Sharon said suddenly.

'Me too!' Denise's eyes widened. 'Since when did people start going out so young?'

Sharon began to laugh. 'Denise, the people aren't getting younger; *we* are getting older, I'm afraid.'

Denise thought about that for a while. 'Well, it's not like we're *old*, old for God's sake. I mean it's not exactly time for us to hang up our dancing shoes and grab our walking sticks. We could stay out all night if we wanted to, we just . . . are tired. We've had a long day . . . oh God, I do sound old.' Denise rambled on to herself as Sharon was too busy watching Holly, head down, still kicking a stone along the path.

'Holly, are you OK? You haven't said a word in a while.'

'Yeah, I was just thinking,' Holly said quietly, keeping her head down.

'Thinking about what?' Sharon asked softly.

Holly's head shot up. 'Gerry.' She looked at the girls. 'I was thinking about Gerry.'

'Let's go down to the beach,' Denise suggested and they slipped out of their shoes and allowed their feet to sink into the cooling sand.

The sky was clear black and a million little stars twinkled down on them, as if someone had thrown glitter up into a massive black net. The full moon rested itself low over the horizon, reflecting its beam and showing where the sea met the sky. The girls sat in its path along the shore. The musical water gently lapped before them, calming them, relaxing them. The air was warm but a slight breeze brushed past Holly, causing her hair to tickle her skin. She closed her eyes, took a deep breath and filled her lungs with fresh air.

'That's why he brought you here, you know,' Sharon said, watching her friend relaxing.

Holly's eyes remained closed and she smiled.

'You don't talk about him enough, Holly,' Denise

257

said, casually making designs with her finger in the sand.

Holly slowly opened her eyes. Her voice was quiet but warm and silky. 'I know.'

Denise looked up from drawing circles in the sand. 'Why not?'

Holly paused for a while and looked out to the black sea. 'I don't know how to talk about him.' She paused again. 'I don't know whether to say "Gerry was" or "Gerry is". I don't know whether to be sad or happy when I talk about him to other people. It's like if I'm happy when I talk about him, certain people judge and expect me to be crying my eyes out. When I'm upset when talking about him it makes people feel uncomfortable.' She stared out to the sparkling black sea and her voice was quieter when she spoke again. 'I can't tease about him in conversation like I used to because it feels *wrong*. I can't talk about things he told me in confidence because I don't want to give his secrets away, because they're *his* secrets. I just don't quite know *how* to remember him in conversation. It doesn't mean I don't remember him up here,' she tapped her temples.

The three girls continued to sit cross-legged on the soft sand.

'Me and John talk about Gerry all the time.' Sharon looked at Holly with glittering eyes. 'We talk about the times he made us laugh, which was *a lot*. We even talk about the times we fought. Things we loved about him, things he did that *really* annoyed us.'

Holly raised her eyebrows.

Sharon continued, 'Because to us, that's just how

Gerry was. He wasn't all nice. We remember *all* of him and there's absolutely *nothing* wrong with that.'

There was a long silence.

Denise was the first to speak. 'I wish my Tom had known Gerry.' Her voice trembled a little.

Holly looked at her in surprise.

'Gerry was my friend too,' Denise said, tears pricking in her eyes. 'And Tom doesn't even know him at all. So I try to tell him things about Gerry all the time, just so he knows that not long ago one of the nicest men on this earth was *my* friend and I think *everyone* should have known him.' Her lip wobbled and she bit down on it hard. 'But I can't believe that someone I now love so much, who knows everything else about me, doesn't know a friend who I loved for ten years.'

A tear ran down Holly's cheek and she reached out to hug her friend. 'Well then, Denise, we'll just have to keep telling Tom about him, won't we?'

They didn't bother meeting up with their holiday rep the next morning, as they had no intention of going on any tours or taking part in any silly sports tournaments. Instead, they got up early and took part in the sun bed dance, running around trying to throw their towels on the sun beds to reserve their positions for the day. Unfortunately, they still didn't manage to get up early enough. ('Don't those bloody Germans ever sleep?' Sharon gave out.) Finally, after Sharon had sneakily thrown a few towels away from some unattended beds, the girls managed to get three beds together.

Just as Holly found herself nodding off she heard

piercing screams and a crowd ran by her. For some reason, Gary, the holiday rep the girls had seen at the airport, thought it would be a really funny idea to dress in drag and be chased around the swimming pool by Victoria. Everyone around the pool cheered them on as the girls rolled their eyes. Eventually Victoria caught Gary and they both managed to fall on top of each other into the swimming pool.

Everyone applauded.

Minutes later, as Holly was taking a quiet swim, a woman announced into a microphone attached to her head that she was going to begin aqua aerobics in the pool in five minutes. Victoria and Gary, helped by the Barbie brigade, ran round all the sun beds, dragging everyone up and forcing them to take part.

'Ah, would you ever fuck off!' Holly heard Sharon screaming as someone tried to drag her into the pool. Holly was soon forced out of the pool by what looked like an approaching herd of hippopotami, who were about to dive in for their much-needed aqua aerobics session. They sat through an incredibly annoying half-hour session of aerobics with the instructor yelling out the movements into the headpiece. When it was finally over they announced a water polo tournament was about to take place, so the girls immediately jumped up and headed over to the beach for some peace and quiet.

'You ever hear from Gerry's parents, Holly?' Sharon asked as they lounged on their Lilos in the sea.

'Yeah, they send me postcards every few weeks, telling me where they are and how they're getting on.'

'So they're still on that cruise?'

'Yeah.'

'Do you miss them?'

'To be honest, their son's gone and they have no grandchildren so I don't really think they feel we have any connection any more.'

'That's bullshit, Holly. You were married to their son and that makes you their daughter-in-law. That's a very strong connection.'

'Oh, I don't know,' she sighed. 'I just don't think that's enough for them.'

'They're a bit backward, aren't they?'

'Yeah, *very*. They hated me and Gerry "living in sin", as they said. Couldn't wait for us to get married. And *then* they were even worse when we did! They couldn't understand why I wouldn't change my name.'

'Yeah, I remember that,' Sharon laughed. 'His mum gave me an earful at the wedding. She said it was the woman's duty to change her name as a sign of respect to her husband. Imagine that? The cheek of her!'

Holly laughed.

'Ah well, you're better off without them being around anyway,' Sharon assured her.

'Hello, girls.' Denise floated out to meet them.

'Hey, where have you been?' Holly asked.

'Oh, I was just chatting to some bloke from Miami. Really nice guy.'

'Miami? That's where Daniel went on holiday,' Holly replied, lightly running her fingers through the clear blue water.

'Hmm,' Sharon mused, 'nice guy, Daniel, isn't he?'

'Yeah, he's a really nice guy,' Holly agreed. 'Very easy to talk to.'

'Tom was telling me he's really been through the wars recently,' Denise said, turning to lie on her back.

Sharon's ears pricked up at the sound of gossip, 'Why's that?'

'Oh, he was engaged to be married to some chick and it turns out she was sleeping with someone else. That's why he moved to Dublin and bought the pub, to get away from her.'

'I know. It's awful, isn't it?' Holly said sadly.

'Where did he live before?' Sharon asked.

'Galway. He used to run a pub there,' Holly explained.

'Oh,' Sharon said, surprised, 'he doesn't have a Galway accent.'

'Well, he grew up in Dublin and joined the army, then he left and moved to Galway where his family own a pub, then he met Laura, they were together for seven years, were engaged to be married but she cheated on him so they broke up and he moved back to Dublin and bought Hogan's.' Holly caught her breath.

'Don't know much about him, do you?' Denise teased.

'Well, if you and Tom had paid the slightest bit of attention to us the other night in the pub, then maybe I wouldn't know so much about him.' Holly rolled her eyes at Sharon. 'Honestly, Sharon, they invite me and Daniel out and then they ignore us both.' She pretended to be insulted.

Denise sighed loudly. 'God, I really miss Tom.'

'Did you tell the guy from Miami that?' Sharon laughed.

'No I was just chatting to him,' Denise said defensively. 'To be honest, nobody else interests me. It's really weird – it's like I can't even *see* any other men, I don't even *notice* them. And as we are currently surrounded by hundreds of half-naked men I think that's saying a lot.'

'I think they call it love, Denise,' Sharon smiled.

'Well, whatever it is I've never felt like this before.'

'It's a nice feeling,' Holly said, more to herself.

They lay in silence for a while, lost in their own thoughts, allowing the gentle motion of the waves to soothe them.

'Holy shit!' Denise suddenly yelled, causing the other two to jump. 'Look how far out we are!'

Holly sat up immediately and looked around. They were out so far from the shore everybody on the beach looked like little ants.

'Oh, shit!' panicked Sharon, and as soon as Sharon panicked Holly knew they were in trouble.

'Start swimming quick!' Denise yelled, and they lay on their stomachs and started splashing around with all their might. After a few minutes of tirelessly going at it they gave up, out of breath. To their horror they were even further out than they had been when they started.

It was no use, the tide was moving out too quickly and the waves were just too strong.

Chapter Twenty-Eight

'Help!' Denise screamed at the top of her lungs and waved her arms wildly.

'I don't think they can hear us,' Holly said, tears welling in her eyes.

'Oh, could we be any more stupid?' Sharon gave out, and continued to rant on about the dangers of Lilos in the sea.

'Oh, forget about that, Sharon,' Denise snapped. 'We're here now so let's all scream together and maybe they'll hear us.'

They all cleared their throats and sat up on their Lilos as much as they possibly could without causing them to sink under their weight.

'OK one, two, three . . . HELP!' they all yelled, and waved their arms frantically.

Eventually they stopped screaming and stared in silence at the dots on the beach to see if it had made any impact. Everything remained as it was.

'Please tell me there aren't any sharks out here,' Denise whimpered.

'Oh, please, Denise,' Sharon snapped viciously, 'that is the last thing we need to be reminded of right now.'

Holly gulped and stared down into the water. The once-clear blue water had darkened. Holly hopped off her Lilo to see how deep it was and as her legs dangled her heart began to pound. This was bad.

Sharon and Holly tried to swim for it while dragging their Lilos behind them, while Denise continued her bloodcurdling screams.

'Jesus, Denise,' Sharon panted, 'the only thing that's gonna respond to that is a dolphin.'

'Look, why don't you two just stop swimming because you've been at it now for a few minutes and you're still right beside me?'

Holly stopped swimming and looked up, Denise stared back at her.

'Oh.' Holly tried to hold back her tears. 'Sharon, we might as well stop and save our energy.'

Sharon stopped swimming and the three of them huddled together on their Lilos and cried. There was really nothing more they could do, Holly thought, her panic increasing. They had tried shouting for help but the wind was carrying their voices in the other direction; they had tried swimming, which had been completely pointless, as the tide was too strong. It was beginning to get chilly and the sea was looking dark and ugly. What a stupid situation to get themselves into. Through all her fear and worry, Holly managed to surprise herself by feeling completely humiliated.

She wasn't sure whether to laugh or cry, but the unusual sound of both began to tumble out of her mouth, causing Sharon and Denise to stop crying and stare at her as though she had ten heads.

'At least one good thing came out of this,' Holly half-laughed and half-cried.

'There's a good thing?' Sharon said, wiping her eyes.

'Well, the three of us always talked about going to Africa,' she sniggered like a mad woman, 'and by the looks of things I would say we're probably halfway there.'

The girls looked out to sea, to their future destination.

'It's a cheaper mode of transport too,' Sharon joined in.

Denise stared at them as if they were mad, and just one look at her lying in the middle of the ocean, naked except for a leopardskin thong, and with blue lips, was enough to set the girls off laughing.

'What?' Denise looked at them wide-eyed.

'I'd say we're in deep, deep trouble here,' Sharon giggled.

'Yeah,' Holly agreed. 'We're in way over our heads.'

They lay there laughing and crying for a few minutes more till the sound of a speed boat approaching caused Denise to sit up and start waving frantically again. Holly and Sharon laughed even harder at the sight of Denise's chest bouncing up and down as she waved at the approaching lifeguards.

'It's just like a regular night out with the girls,' Sharon laughed, watching Denise being dragged half-naked into the boat by a muscular lifeguard.

'I think they're in shock,' one lifeguard said to the other as they dragged the remaining hysterical girls onto the boat.

'Quick, save the Lilos!' Holly just about managed to blurt out through her laughter.

'Lilo overboard!' Sharon screamed.

The lifeguards looked at each other worriedly, as they wrapped warm blankets around the girls and sped off back to the shore.

As they approached the beach there appeared to be a large crowd gathering. The girls looked at each other and laughed even harder. As they were lifted off the boat there was a huge applause; Denise turned and curtsied to them all.

'They clap now, but where were they when we needed them?' Sharon grumbled.

'Traitors,' Holly agreed.

'There they are!' They heard a familiar squeal and saw Cindy and the Barbie brigade pushing their way through the crowd. 'Oh my God!' she squeaked. 'I saw the whole thing through my binoculars and called the lifeguards. Are you OK?' She looked to each of them frantically.

'Oh, we're fine,' Sharon said rather seriously. 'We were the lucky ones. The poor Lilos never even had a chance.' With that Sharon and Holly cracked up laughing and they were ushered away to be looked at by a doctor.

That night the girls realised the seriousness of what had happened to them and their moods drastically changed. They sat almost in silence throughout dinner, all thinking about how lucky they were to be rescued and kicking themselves for being so careless. Denise squirmed uncomfortably in her chair and Holly noticed she had barely touched her food.

'What's wrong with you?' Sharon said, sucking in a piece of spaghetti and causing the sauce to splash all over her face.

'Nothing,' Denise said quietly, refilling her glass with water.

They sat in silence for a while longer.

'Excuse me, I'm going to the toilet.' Denise stood up and walked awkwardly to the ladies.

Sharon and Holly frowned at each other.

'What do you think is wrong with her?' Holly asked.

Sharon shrugged. 'Well, she's drunk about ten litres of water through dinner so no wonder she keeps going to the toilet,' she exaggerated.

'I wonder if she's mad at us for going a bit funny out there today.'

Sharon shrugged again and they continued to eat in silence. Holly had reacted unusually out there in the water and it bothered her to think about why she had. After the initial panic of thinking she was going to die, she'd become feverishly giddy as she'd realised that if she did she would be with Gerry, that she didn't care whether she lived or died. Those were selfish thoughts. She needed to change her perspective on her life.

Denise winced as she sat down.

'Denise, what is wrong with you?' Holly asked.

'I'm not telling either of you or you'll laugh,' she said childishly.

'Oh, come on, we're your friends. We won't laugh,' Holly said, trying to keep the smile off her face.

'I said no.' She filled her glass with more water.

'Ah, come on, Denise, you know you can tell us

268

anything. We promise not to laugh.' Sharon said it so seriously that Holly felt bad for smiling.

Denise studied both their faces trying to decide whether they could be trusted.

'Oh, OK,' she sighed loudly, and mumbled something very quietly.

'What?' Holly said, moving in closer.

'Honey, we didn't hear you, you were too quiet,' Sharon said, pulling her chair in as well.

Denise looked around the restaurant to make sure nobody was listening and she moved her head into the centre of the table. 'I said, from lying out in the sea for so long, my bum is sunburned.'

'Oh,' Sharon said, sitting back in her chair abruptly.

Holly looked away to avoid eye contact with Sharon and she counted the bread rolls in the basket to take her mind off what Denise had just said.

There was a long silence.

'See, I told you you would both laugh,' Denise huffed.

'Hey, we're not laughing,' Sharon said shakily.

There was another silence.

Holly couldn't help herself. 'Just make sure you put plenty of sun cream on it so that it doesn't peel.' The two of them broke down.

Denise just nodded her head and waited for them to stop laughing. She had to wait a long time. In fact, hours later, as she lay on the sofa bed trying to sleep, she was still waiting.

The last thing she heard before she went to sleep was a smart remark from Holly. 'Make sure you lie on your front, Denise.'

'Hey, Holly,' Sharon whispered after they had finally calmed down, 'are you excited about tomorrow?'

'What do you mean?' Holly asked yawning.

'The letter!' Sharon replied, surprised that Holly didn't remember immediately. 'Don't tell me that you forgot.'

Holly reached her hand under her pillow and felt around for the letter. In one hour she would be able to open Gerry's sixth letter. Of course she hadn't forgotten.

The next morning Holly awoke to the sound of Sharon throwing up in the toilet. She followed her in and gently rubbed her back and held her hair back.

'You OK?' she asked worriedly after Sharon had eventually stopped.

'Yeah, it's just those bloody dreams I had all night. I dreamed I was on a boat and on a Lilo, I think it made me seasick.'

'I had those dreams too. It was scary yesterday, wasn't it?'

Sharon nodded. 'I'm never going on a Lilo again,' she smiled weakly.

Denise arrived at the bathroom door, already dressed in her bikini. She had borrowed one of Sharon's sarongs to cover up her burned behind and Holly had to bite her tongue to stop herself from teasing her, as she was clearly in a great deal of pain.

When they arrived at the swimming pool, Denise and Sharon joined the Barbie brigade. Well, it was the least they could do, seeing as they were the ones who had called for help. Holly couldn't believe that she had fallen asleep before midnight the previous night. She had planned to get up quietly without waking the girls, sneak out to the balcony and read the letter. How she fell asleep in all her excitement was beyond her, but she couldn't listen to the Barbie brigade any longer. Before Holly was dragged into any conversation she signalled to Sharon that she was leaving and Sharon gave her an encouraging wink, knowing why she was disappearing. Holly wrapped her sarong around her hips and carried her small beach bag containing the all-important letter.

She positioned herself away from all the excited shouts of children and adults playing and ghetto blasters blaring out the latest chart songs. She found a quiet corner and made herself comfortable on her beach towel to avoid more contact with the burning sand. The waves crashed and fell. The seagulls called out to one another in the clear blue sky, flew down, dipped themselves into the cool, crystal water to catch their breakfasts. It was morning and already the sun was hot.

Holly carefully pulled the letter out of her bag as though it was the most delicate thing in the world and she ran her fingers along the neatly written word 'August'. Taking in all the sounds and smells of the world around her she gently tore open the seal and read Gerry's sixth message.

Hi, Holly,
I hope you're having a wonderful holiday. You're looking beautiful in that bikini, by the way! I hope I picked the right place for you.

271

*It's where you and I almost went for our
honeymoon, remember? Well, I'm glad you
got to see it in the end . . .*

*Apparently if you stand at the very end of
the beach near the rocks across from your
apartment, and look round the corner to the
left, you'll see a lighthouse. I'm told that's
where the dolphins gather . . . not many
people know that. I know you love dolphins
. . . tell them I said hi . . .*

PS. I love you, Holly . . .

With shaking hands Holly put the card back into the
envelope and secured it safely in a pocket of her bag.
She would guard it with her life until she returned
home to Dublin where it would take pride of place
with the other envelopes in the top drawer of her
bedside cabinet. She felt Gerry's eyes on her as she
stood up and quickly rolled up the beach towel. She
felt as though he was here with her. She quickly ran
to the end of the beach that suddenly stopped at a
cliff. She put her trainers on and began to climb the
rocks so she could see around the corner.

And there it was.

Exactly where Gerry had described it, the lighthouse sat high on the cliff, bright white, as though it
was some sort of torch to heaven. Holly carefully
climbed over the rocks and made her way round the
little cove. She was on her own now. It was completely
private. And then she heard the noises: the playful
squeaks of dolphins playing near to the shore, away
from the view of all the tourists on the beach beside

it. Holly collapsed on the sand to watch them play and listen to them talk to one another.

Gerry sat beside her.

He may have even held her hand.

Holly felt happy enough to head back to Dublin, relaxed, destressed and brown. Just what the doctor ordered. That didn't stop her from groaning when the plane landed in Dublin airport to heavy rain. This time the passengers didn't applaud and cheer, and the airport seemed a very different place from the one she had left last week. Once again Holly was the last person to receive her luggage and an hour later they trudged gloomily out to John, who was waiting in the car.

'Well, it looks like the leprechaun didn't do any more work in your garden while you were away,' Denise said, looking at the garden as they arrived at Holly's home.

Holly gave her friends a big hug and a kiss and made her way into her quiet empty house. There was a horrible musty smell inside, and she made her way to the kitchen patio doors to let the fresh air circulate.

She froze just as she was turning the key in the door and stared outside.

Her entire back garden had been transformed.

The grass was cut. The weeds were gone. The garden furniture had been polished and varnished. A fresh coat of paint gleamed from her garden walls. New flowers had been planted and in the corner, underneath the shade of the great oak tree, sat a wooden bench. Holly was in shock. Who on earth was doing all this?

Chapter Twenty-Nine

In the days following her return from Lanzarote, Holly kept a low profile. Holly, Denise and Sharon were all keen to spend the next few days apart from each other. It wasn't something that they had talked about, but after living in each other's ears all day, every day for a whole week, Holly was sure they all agreed this would be healthy.

Ciara was impossible to get hold of, as she was either working hard at Daniel's club or spending time with Mathew. Jack was spending his last few precious weeks of freedom that the summer holidays brought down in Cork at Abbey's parents' house and Declan was . . . well, who knew where Declan was.

Now she was back, Holly wasn't exactly bored with her life, but she wasn't exactly overjoyed either. It just seemed so . . . nothing and so pointless. She'd had the holiday to look forward to, but now felt as though she had no real reason to get out of bed in the morning. And as she was taking time out from her friends, she really had nobody else to talk to. There was only so much conversation she could have with her parents. Compared to last week's sweltering heat in Lanzarote, Dublin was wet and ugly, which meant she couldn't even work at maintaining her beautiful tan or appreciate her new back garden.

Some days she never even got out of bed – she just watched television and waited . . . waited for next month's envelope from Gerry, wondering what journey he would take her on next. She knew her friends would disapprove after she'd been so positive on holiday, but when he was alive she had lived for him and now he was gone she lived for his messages. Everything was about him. She had truly believed that her purpose in life had been to meet Gerry and enjoy all their days together for the rest of their lives. What was her purpose now? Surely she had one, or perhaps there had been an error in the administration way up above.

Something that she did feel she should do was catch the leprechaun. After further interrogation of her neighbours she still knew nothing more of her mystery gardener. Eventually she had convinced herself that a gardener had made a mistake and that he was working on the wrong garden, so she checked the post every day for a bill that she was going to refuse to pay. But no bill arrived, of that variety anyway. Plenty of others did and she was running out of money fast. She had loans up to her eyeballs, electricity bills, phone bills, insurance bills. Everything that came through her door was a bloody bill and she hadn't a clue how she was going to continue paying them all. But she didn't even care; she had become numb to all those irrelevant problems in life. She just dreamed impossible dreams.

One day Holly realised why the leprechaun hadn't

returned. Her garden was only tidied when she wasn't home. So she got out of bed early one morning and drove her car round the corner from her house. She then walked back home and settled down on her bed and waited for her mystery gardener to appear.

After three days, the rain finally stopped and the sun began to shine again. Holly was about to give up hope of ever solving the mystery when she heard a van pull up outside and then someone approach her garden. She jumped out of bed in a panic, unprepared for what she should do, even though she had spent days planning. She peeped over her windowsill and spotted a young boy, about twelve years old, walking down her drive, tugging a lawnmower along behind him. She threw on Gerry's oversized dressing gown and raced down the stairs, not caring what she looked like.

She pulled open the front door, causing the young boy to jump. His arm froze mid-air and his finger hovered just over the doorbell. His mouth dropped open at the sight of the woman in front of him.

'A-HA!' Holly yelled happily. 'I think I've caught my little leprechaun!'

He opened and closed his mouth like a goldfish, unsure of what to say. After a few moments he scrunched up his face as though he was about to cry and screamed, 'Da!'

Holly looked up and down the road in search of his father and decided to squeeze as much information out of the boy before the adult reached them.

'So you're the one who's been working on my garden?' She folded her arms across her chest.

He shook his head wildly and gulped.

'You don't have to deny it,' she said gently. 'You've been caught now.' She nodded over at the lawnmower.

He turned round to stare at it and yelled again, 'Da!' His dad slammed the door of the van and made his way over to her house.

'What's wrong, son?' He wrapped his arm round the child's shoulders and looked at Holly for an explanation.

Holly wasn't going to fall for this little charade. 'I was just asking your son here about your little scam.'

'What scam?' The man looked angry.

'The one where you work on my garden without my permission and then you expect me to pay for it. I've heard about this kind of thing before.' She put her hands on her hips and tried to look as though she couldn't be messed with.

The man looked confused. 'Sorry, I don't know what you're talking about, missus. We've never worked on your garden before.' He stared at the state of her front garden, thinking the woman was insane.

'Not *this* garden, you landscaped my *back* garden.' She smiled and raised her eyebrows, thinking she had caught him.

He laughed back at her. 'Landscaped your garden? Lady, are you mad? We cut grass, that's all. See this? This is a lawnmower, nothing else. All it does is cut the bloody grass.'

Holly dropped her hands from her hips and slowly placed them in the pockets of her gown. Maybe they were telling the truth. 'Are you sure you haven't been in my garden?' she squinted her eyes.

'Lady, I have never even worked on this street before, never mind your garden, and I can guarantee I won't be working in your garden in the future.'

Holly's face fell. 'But I thought—'

'I don't care what you thought,' he interrupted. 'In future you try to get your facts straight before you start terrorising my kid.'

Holly looked at the young boy and saw his eyes fill with tears. Her hands flew to her mouth with embarrassment. 'Gosh, I'm so sorry. Just hold on there a minute.'

She rushed into the house to get her purse and returned to squeeze her last fiver into his chubby little hand. His face lit up.

'OK, let's go,' his dad said, turning his son round by the shoulders and leading him down the drive.

'Da, I don't wanna do this job any more,' the boy moaned as they carried on to the next house.

'Ah, don't worry, son, they won't all be as mad as her.'

Holly closed the door and studied her reflection in the mirror. He was right; she had turned into a mad woman; now all she needed was a house full of cats.

The phone rang.

'Hello?' Holly said.

'Hiya, how are you?' Denise asked happily.

'Oh, full of the joys of life,' Holly said.

'Me too!' Denise giggled in response.

'Really? What's got you so happy?'

'Nothing much. Just life in general.'

Of course, just life. Wonderful, wonderful, beautiful life. What a silly question.

'So what's happening?'

'I'm calling to invite you out for dinner tomorrow night. I know it's short notice so if you're too busy . . . cancel whatever it is you have planned!'

'Hold on and let me check my diary,' Holly said sarcastically.

'No problem,' Denise said seriously, and was silent while she waited.

Holly rolled her eyes. 'Oh, look at that, whaddaya know? I appear to be free tomorrow night.'

'Goody!' Denise said happily. 'We're all meeting in Chang's at eight.'

'Who's we?'

'Sharon and John are going, and some of Tom's friends too. We haven't been out together for ages so it'll be fun!'

'OK then, see you tomorrow.' Holly hung up, feeling angry. Had it completely slipped Denise's mind that Holly was still a grieving widow and that life just wasn't fun for her any more?

She stormed upstairs and opened her wardrobe. Now what piece of old and disgusting clothing could she wear tomorrow night and how on earth was she going to afford an expensive meal? She could barely even afford to keep her car on the road. She grabbed all her clothes from her wardrobe and flung them across the room, screaming her head off until she finally felt sane again. Perhaps tomorrow she would buy those cats.

Chapter Thirty

Holly arrived at the restaurant at eight twenty as she had spent hours trying on different outfits and ripping them off again. Eventually she settled with the outfit that she had been instructed to wear by Gerry for the karaoke just so she could feel closer to him. She hadn't been coping very well over the past few weeks; she had had more downs than ups and was finding it harder to pick herself back up again.

As she was walking towards the table in the restaurant her heart sank.

Couples-R-Us.

She paused halfway and quickly sidestepped, hiding behind a wall. She wasn't sure she could go through with this. She hadn't the strength to keep battling with her emotions. She looked around to find the easiest escape route; she certainly couldn't leave the way she had come in or they would definitely see her. She spotted the fire escape beside the kitchen door, which had been left open to clear some of the steam. The moment she stepped out into the cool fresh air she felt free again. She walked across the car park, trying to formulate an excuse to tell Denise and Sharon.

'Hi, Holly.'

She froze and slowly turned round, realising she had been caught. She spotted Daniel leaning against his car, smoking a cigarette.

'Hiya, Daniel.' She walked towards him. 'I didn't know you smoked.'

'Only when I'm stressed.'

'You're stressed?' They greeted each other with a hug.

'I was trying to figure out whether to join happy couples united in there.' He nodded towards the restaurant.

Holly smiled. 'You too?'

He laughed. 'Well, I won't tell them I saw you if that's what you want.'

'So you're going in?'

'Have to face the music sometime,' he said grimly, stabbing out his cigarette with his foot.

Holly thought about what he said. 'I suppose you're right.'

'You don't have to go in if you don't want to. I don't want to be the cause of you having a miserable night.'

'On the contrary, it would be nice to have another loner in my company. There are so very few of our kind in existence.'

Daniel laughed and held out his arm. 'Shall we?'

Holly linked his arm and they slowly made their way into the restaurant. It was comforting to know she wasn't alone in feeling alone.

'By the way, I'm getting out of here as soon as we finish the main course,' he smiled.

'Traitor.' She thumped him on the arm. 'Well, I have to leave early anyway to catch the last bus home.' She hadn't had the money to fill the tank in the car for the past few days.

'Then we have the perfect excuse. I'll say we have to leave early because I'm driving you home and you have to be home by . . . what time?'

'Half eleven?' At twelve she planned on opening the September envelope.

'Perfect,' he smiled, and they made their way into the restaurant, feeling slightly reinforced by each other's company.

'Here they are!' Denise announced as they made their way to the table.

Holly sat down beside Daniel, sticking to her alibi like glue. 'Sorry we're late,' she apologised.

'Holly, this is Catherine and Mick, Peter and Sue, Joanne and Conal, Tina and Bryan, John and Sharon you know, Geoffrey and Samantha, and last but not least this is Des and Simon.'

Holly smiled and nodded at all of them.

'Hi, we're Daniel and Holly,' Daniel said smartly, and Holly giggled beside him.

'We had to order already, if you don't mind,' Denise explained, 'but we just chose loads of different dishes so we can all share them. Is that OK?'

Holly and Daniel nodded.

The woman beside Holly, whose name she couldn't remember, turned to her and spoke loudly. 'So, Holly, what do you do?'

Daniel raised his eyebrows at Holly.

'Sorry, what do I do when?' Holly answered seriously.

She hated nosy people and conversations that revolved around what people did for a living, especially when she had just met those people less than a minute ago. She felt Daniel shaking with laughter beside her.

'What do you do for a living?' the woman asked again.

Holly had intended on giving her a funny but slightly rude answer but suddenly stopped herself as all the conversations around the table died down and everyone's attention was focused on her. She looked round with embarrassment and cleared her throat nervously. 'Em . . . well . . . I'm currently between jobs right now.' Her voice shook.

The woman's lips began to twitch and she scraped a piece of bread from between her teeth rudely.

'What is it that you do?' Daniel asked her loudly, breaking the silence.

'Oh, Geoffrey runs his own business,' she said proudly, turning to her husband.

'Oh right, but what is it that *you* do?' Daniel repeated to her.

The lady seemed flushed that her answer hadn't been good enough for him. 'Well, I keep myself busy all day every day doing various things. Honey, why don't you tell them about the company?' She turned to her husband again to divert the attention from herself.

Her husband leaned forward in his seat. 'It's just a small business.' He took a bite out of his bread roll, chewed it slowly and everyone waited while he swallowed so he could continue.

'Small but successful,' his wife added for him.

Geoffrey finally finished eating his bread. 'We make car windshields and sell them to the warehouses.'

'Wow, that's very interesting,' Daniel said drily.

'So what is it that you do, Dermot?' the woman said, turning to look at Daniel.

'Sorry, my name is Daniel, actually. I'm a publican.'

'Right,' she nodded and looked away. 'Awful weather we're having these days, isn't it?' she addressed the table.

Everyone fell into conversation and Daniel turned to Holly. 'Did you enjoy your holiday?'

'Oh, I had a fabulous time,' she smiled. 'We took it easy and relaxed, didn't do anything wild and weird.'

'Just what you needed,' he smiled. 'I heard about your near-death experience.'

Holly rolled her eyes. 'I bet Denise told you that.'

He nodded and laughed.

'Well, I'm sure she gave you the exaggerated version.'

'Not really, she just told me about how you were surrounded by sharks and had to be air-lifted from the sea by a helicopter.'

'She didn't!'

'No, not really,' he laughed. 'Still, that must have been some conversation you were having to not notice you were drifting out to sea!'

Holly's face blushed a little as she recalled that they had been talking about him.

'OK, everyone,' Denise called for attention. 'You're probably wondering why me and Tom invited you all here tonight.'

'Understatement of the year,' Daniel mumbled, and Holly giggled.

'Well, we have an announcement to make.' She looked around at everyone and smiled.

Holly's eyes widened.

'Myself and Tom are getting married!' she squealed, and Holly's hands flew up to her mouth in shock. She had *not* seen that one coming.

'Oh, Denise!' she gasped, and walked round the table to hug them. 'That's wonderful news! Congratulations!'

She looked at Daniel's face: it had gone white.

They popped open a bottle of champagne and everyone raised their glasses as Jemima and Jim or Samantha and Sam or whatever their names were made a toast.

'Hold on! Hold on!' Denise stopped them just before they started. 'Sharon, did you not get a glass?'

Everyone looked at Sharon, who was holding a glass of orange juice in her hand.

'Here you go,' Tom said, pouring her a glass.

'No no no! Not for me, thanks,' she said.

'Why not?' Denise huffed, upset that her friend wouldn't celebrate with her.

John and Sharon looked at each other and smiled. 'Well, I didn't want to say anything because it's Denise and Tom's special night . . .'

Everyone urged her to speak.

'Well . . . I'm pregnant! John and I are going to have a baby!'

John's eyes began to water and Holly just froze in shock in her seat. She had *not* seen that one coming either. Tears filled her eyes as she went over to congratulate Sharon and John. Then she sat down and took deep breaths. This was all too much.

'So let's make a toast to Tom and Denise's engagement and Sharon and John's baby!' Jemima and Jim or Sam and Samantha announced.

Everyone clinked glasses and Holly ate dinner in silence, not really tasting anything.

'You want to make that time eleven o'clock?' Daniel asked quietly, and she nodded in agreement.

After dinner Holly and Daniel made their excuses to leave and nobody really tried to persuade them to stay.

'How much should I leave towards the bill?' Holly asked Denise.

'Oh, don't worry about it.' She waved her hand at her dismissively.

'No, don't be silly. I couldn't let you pay for it. How much honestly?'

The woman beside her grabbed the menu and started adding up the price of all the meals they had bought. There had been so many, but Holly had only picked at her own and had even avoided eating a starter so she could afford it.

'Well, it works out at about fifty each, and that's including all the wine and bottles of champagne.'

Holly gulped and stared down at the thirty euro in her hand.

Daniel grabbed her hand and pulled her up. 'Come on, let's go, Holly.'

She opened her mouth to make the excuse of not bringing as much money as she thought but when she opened her palm and looked at the money, there appeared to be an extra twenty.

She smiled at Daniel gratefully and they both headed out to the car.

They sat in the car in silence, both thinking about what had happened that night. She wanted to feel happy for her friends, really she did, but she couldn't shake off the feeling of being left behind. Everyone else's life was moving on except hers.

Daniel pulled up outside her house. 'Do you want to come in for a tea or coffee or anything?' She was sure he would say no and was shocked when he undid his seat belt and accepted her offer. She really liked Daniel, he was very caring and fun to be with, but right now she just wanted to be alone.

'That was some night, wasn't it?' he said, sitting down on the couch and taking a sip of his coffee.

Holly just shook her head with disbelief. 'Daniel, I have known those girls practically all of my life and I did *not* see any of that coming.'

'Well, if it makes you feel any better I've known Tom for years too and he didn't mention a thing.'

'Although Sharon wasn't drinking when we were away,' she hadn't listened to a word Daniel had said, 'and she did throw up a few mornings, but she said it was seasickness . . .' She trailed off and her brain went into overdrive as things started to add up.

'Seasickness?' Daniel asked, confused.

'After our near-death experience.'

'Oh, right.'

This time neither of them laughed.

'It's funny,' he said, settling down into the couch.

Oh no, Holly thought, he's never going to leave now.

'The lads always said that myself and Laura would be the first to get married,' he continued. 'I just didn't think that Laura would be getting married before me.'

'She's getting married?' Holly asked gently.

He nodded and looked away. 'He used to be a friend of mine too.' He laughed bitterly.

'Obviously not any more.'

'Nope,' he shook his head, 'obviously not.'

'Sorry to hear that,' she said genuinely.

'Ah well, we all get our fair share of bad luck. You know that better than anyone.'

'Huh, fair share,' she repeated.

'I know, there's nothing fair about it but don't worry, we'll have our good luck too.'

'You think?'

'I hope.'

They sat in silence for another while and Holly watched the clock. It was five past twelve. She really needed to get Daniel out of the house so she could open the envelope.

He read her mind. 'So how's the messages from above going?'

Holly sat forward and placed her mug down on the table. 'Well, I've another one to open tonight, actually. So . . .' She looked at him.

'Oh right,' he said, jumping to attention. He sat up quickly in his chair and put his mug down on the table. 'I'd better leave you at it so.'

Holly bit her lip, feeling guilty at ushering him out so quickly, but she was also relieved he was finally going.

'Thanks a million for the lift, Daniel,' she said, following him to the door.

'No problem at all.' He grabbed his coat from the banister and headed out the door. They gave each other a quick hug.

'See you soon,' she said, feeling like a right bitch, and watched him walk to his car in the rain. She waved him off and her guilt immediately faded as soon as she closed the door.

'Right, Gerry,' she said as she headed towards the kitchen and picked up the envelope from the table, 'what have you got in store for me this month?'

Chapter Thirty-One

Holly held the tiny envelope tightly in her hands and glanced up at the clock on the wall over the kitchen table. It was twelve fifteen. Usually Sharon and Denise would have called her by now, all excited to hear about what was inside the envelope. But so far neither of them had called. It seemed news of an engagement and a pregnancy beat the news of a message from Gerry these days. Holly scorned herself for being so bitter. She wanted to be back in the restaurant right now celebrating their good news with them like the old Holly would have done. But she couldn't bring herself even to smile for them.

She was jealous of them and their good fortune. She was angry with them for moving on without her. Even in the company of friends she felt alone, in a room of a thousand people she would feel alone. But it was when she roamed the rooms of her quiet house that she felt most alone.

She couldn't remember the last time she had felt truly happy, when somebody or something caused her to laugh so hard her stomach pained her and her jaw ached. She missed going to bed at night with absolutely nothing on her mind; she missed enjoying eating food instead of it becoming something she had to endure in order to stay alive, she hated the butterflies she got in her tummy every time she remembered Gerry. She missed *enjoying* watching her favourite television programmes instead of it being something she would stare blankly at to pass the hours. She hated feeling that she had no reason to wake up; she hated the feelings she had when she *did* wake up. She hated the feeling of having no excitement to look forward to. She missed the feeling of being loved, of sensing Gerry's eyes on her as she entered a room; she missed his touches, his hugs, his words of advice; his words of love.

She hated counting down the days till she could read another one of his messages because they were all she had left of him, and after this one there would only be three more. And she hated to think of what her life might be like when there would be no more Gerry. Memories were fine but you couldn't touch them, smell them or hold them. They were never exactly as the moment was, and they faded with time.

So damn Sharon and Denise – they could go on with their happy lives but for the next few months all Holly had was Gerry. She wiped a tear from her face and she slowly opened her seventh envelope.

> *Shoot for the moon and if you miss you'll still be among the stars. Promise me you will find a job you love this time!*
> *PS. I love you . . .*

Holly read and reread the letter, trying to discover how it made her feel. She had been dreading going back to work for such a long time, had believed that she wasn't ready to move on, that it was too soon. But now she knew she had no choice. It was time. And if Gerry said it was to be, it would be.

Holly's face broke into a smile. 'I promise, Gerry,' she said happily. Well, it was no holiday to Lanzarote but at least it was one step further to getting her life back on track. She studied his writing for a long time after reading it as she always did, and when she was satisfied with the fact she had analysed every word she rushed over to the kitchen drawer, took out a notepad and pen and began to write her own list of possible jobs.

LIST OF POSSIBLE JOBS.

1. FBI agent – Am not American. Do not want to live in America. Have no police experience.
2. Lawyer – Hated school. Hated studying. Do not want go to college for ten million years.
3. Doctor – Uugghh.
4. Nurse – Unflattering uniforms.
5. Waitress – Would eat all the food.
6. Professional people spotter – Nice idea but no one would pay me.
7. Beautician – Bite my nails and wax as rarely as possible. Do not want to see areas of other people's bodies.

8. Hairdresser – Would not like boss like Leo.
9. Retail Assistant – would not like boss like Denise.
10. Secretary – NEVER AGAIN.
11. Journalist – Cont spill properly enuff. Ha ha, should be comedienne.
12. Comedienne – *Re* read last joke. Wasn't funny.
13. Actress – Could not possibly out-do my wonderful performance in the critically acclaimed *Girls in the City*.
14. Model – Too small, too fat, too old.
15. Singer – *Re* think idea of comedienne (number 12).
16. Hot-shot advertising businesswoman in control of life – Hmm . . . must do research tomorrow . . .

Holly finally collapsed onto her bed at three in the morning and dreamed of being a big hot-shot advertising woman, making a presentation in front of a huge conference table on the top floor of a skyscraper overlooking Grafton Street. Well, Gerry did say shoot for the moon . . .

She woke up early that morning, excited by her dreams of success, had a quick shower, beautified herself and walked down to her local library to look up jobs on the Internet.

Her heels made a loud noise on the wooden floor as she walked across the room to the librarian's desk, which caused several people to look up from their books and stare at her. She continued clattering across the huge room and her face blushed as she realised everyone was watching her. She slowed down immediately and started to tiptoe so as not to attract any more attention. She felt like one of those cartoon characters on TV who hugely exaggerated their tiptoeing, and her face flared up even more when she realised she looked like a complete idiot. A couple of school kids dressed in their uniforms, who were obviously playing truant for the day, sniggered together as she made her way past their table.

'Shush!' The librarian scowled at the school kids.

Holly decided to keep on walking and quickened her pace. Her heels clicked loudly on the floor and echoed around the room and the sound got faster and faster as she raced to the desk in order to end this humiliation.

The librarian looked up and smiled and tried to appear surprised to see someone standing at the counter. As if she hadn't heard Holly thudding across the room.

'Hi,' Holly whispered, 'I was wondering if I could use the Internet.'

'Excuse me?' the librarian spoke normally and moved her head closer to Holly so she could hear.

'Oh.' Holly cleared her throat, wondering what happened to having to whisper in libraries. 'I was wondering if I could use the Internet.'

'No problem, just over there,' she smiled, directing her over to the row of computers on the far side of the room. 'It's five euro for every twenty minutes online.'

Holly handed over her last ten euro. It was all she had managed to take out of her bank account that morning. She had kept a long line of people waiting behind her at the ATM as she worked her way down from one hundred euro to ten, the ATM beeping embarrassingly every time she entered a sum of money to let her know she had 'insufficient funds'. She couldn't believe that was all she had left, but it had given her even more reason to go job-hunting immediately.

'No, no,' the librarian said, handing back her money. 'You can pay when you finish.'

Holly stared across the floor to the computers. She would have to make another big noise just to get there. She took a deep breath and raced over, passing rows and rows of tables. Holly nearly laughed at the sight of everyone: They were almost like dominos as she passed, each head rising from a book to stare at her. Finally she reached the computers and realised that there was none free. She felt like she had just lost a game of musical chairs. This was getting ridiculous. She raised her hands angrily at the spectators as if to say, 'What are you all looking at?' and they quickly buried their heads in their books again.

Holly stood in the centre of the floor between the rows of tables and computers, drummed her fingers on her handbag and looked around. Her eyes nearly popped out of her head as she spotted Richard tapping away on one of the computers. She tiptoed over to him and tapped him on the shoulder. He jumped with fright and swirled round in his chair.

'Hiya,' she whispered.

'Oh, hello, Holly. What are you doing here?' he said uneasily, as though she had caught him doing something naughty.

'I'm just waiting for a computer,' she explained. 'I'm finally looking for a job,' she added proudly. Even saying the words made her feel like less of a vegetable.

'Oh right.' He turned to face his computer and shut down the screen. 'You can use this one so.'

'Oh no, you don't have to rush for me!' she said quickly.

'Not at all. I was just doing some research for work.' He stood up from his chair and made room for her to sit down.

'All the way over here?' she said surprised. 'Don't they have computers in Blackrock?' she joked. She wasn't quite sure what exactly it was that Richard did for a living, and it would seem rude to ask him after ten years of his working there. She knew it involved him wearing a white coat, wandering around a lab and dropping colourful substances into test tubes. Holly and Jack had always said he was making a secret potion to rid the world of happiness. She felt bad now for ever saying that.

'My work brings me everywhere,' he joked awkwardly.

'Shush!' the librarian said loudly in their direction. Holly's audience once again looked up from their books. Oh, so *now* she was supposed to whisper, Holly thought angrily.

Richard said a quick goodbye, made his way over to pay at the desk and slipped quietly out of the room.

Holly sat down at the computer and the man beside her smiled strangely at her. She smiled back and glimpsed nosily at his computer screen. She nearly gagged at the sight of the porn on his screen and looked away quickly. He continued to stare at her with a scary smile on his face while Holly ignored him and became engrossed in her job-hunting.

Forty minutes later she shut down the computer happily, made her way to the librarian and placed her ten euro on the desk. The woman tapped away on the computer and ignored the money on the counter. 'That's fifteen euro, please.'

Holly gulped as she looked down at her note. 'But I thought you said it was five for twenty minutes.'

'Yes, that's right,' the librarian smiled at her.

'But I was online for only forty minutes.'

'Actually, you were on for forty-four minutes, which cuts into the extra twenty minutes,' the woman said, consulting her computer.

Holly giggled. 'But that's only a few minutes more. It's hardly worth five euro.'

The librarian just continued to smile back at her.

'So you expect me to pay?' Holly asked, surprised.

'Yes, that's the rate.'

Holly lowered her voice and moved her head closer to the woman. 'Look, this is really embarrassing but I actually only have the ten on me now. Is there any way I can come back with the rest later on today?'

The librarian shook her head. 'I'm sorry but we can't allow that. You need to pay the entire amount.'

'But *I don't have* the entire amount,' Holly protested.

She stared back blankly.

'Fine,' Holly huffed, taking out her mobile.

'Sorry, but you can't use that in here.' The librarian pointed to the 'no mobile phones' sign on the counter.

Holly looked up slowly at her and counted to five

in her head. 'If you *won't* let me use my phone I *can't* phone somebody for help. If I *can't* phone somebody then they *can't* come down here to give me the money. If they *don't* come down here with the money then *I can't pay you.* So we have a little problem here, don't we?' She raised her voice.

The librarian shuffled nervously from foot to foot. 'Can I go outside to use the phone?'

The woman thought about the dilemma. 'Well, usually we don't allow people to leave the premises without paying but I suppose I can make an exception,' she smiled, and then added quickly, 'as long as you stand just in front of the entrance there.'

'Where you can see me?' Holly said sarcastically.

The woman nervously shuffled papers below the counter and pretended to go back to work.

Holly stood outside the door and thought about who to call. She couldn't call Denise and Sharon. Although they would probably rush home from work she didn't want them to know about her failures in life now that they were both so blissfully happy. She couldn't call Ciara because she was on a day shift at Hogan's, Jack was back teaching, Abbey was too, Declan was at college and Richard wasn't even an option.

Tears rolled down her face as she scrolled down through the list of names in her phone book. The majority of those people hadn't even called her since Gerry had died, which meant she had no other friends to call. She turned her back on the librarian so she wouldn't see that she was upset. What should she do? How embarrassing it was to actually have to call somebody to ask for five euro. The fact she had absolutely nobody to call was even more embarrassing. But she had to or the snotty librarian would probably call the police on her. She dialled the first number that came into her head.

'Hi, this is Gerry, please leave a message after the beep and I'll get back to you as soon as I can.'

'Gerry,' Holly said crying, 'I need you . . .'

Holly stood outside the door of the library and waited. The librarian kept a close watch on her just in case she ran off. Holly made a face at her and turned her back to her.

'Stupid bitch,' she growled.

Finally her mum's car pulled up outside and Holly tried to make herself appear as normal as she could. Watching her mother's happy face as she drove in and parked in the car park brought back memories. Her mum used to collect her from school every day when she was younger and she was always so relieved to see that familiar car come to rescue her after her hellish day. Holly felt like a child. She had always hated school – well, she had until she met Gerry. Then she would look forward to going to school each day so they could sit together and flirt at the back of the class.

Holly's eyes filled with tears again and Elizabeth rushed over to her and wrapped her arms around her. 'Oh, my poor poor Holly . . . What happened, love?' she said, stroking her hair and casting evil glances in at the librarian as Holly explained the story.

'OK, love, why don't you wait out in the car and I'll go in and deal with her?'

Holly did as she was told and sat in the car, flicking

through the radio stations as her mum confronted the school bully.

'Silly cow,' her mother grumbled as she climbed back into the car. She glanced over at her daughter who looked so lost. 'Why don't we go home and we can relax?'

Holly smiled gratefully and a tear trickled down her face. Home. She liked the sound of that.

Holly snuggled up on the couch with her mum. She felt like a teenager again. She and her mum always used to cuddle up on the couch and fill each other in on all the gossip in their lives. Holly wished she could have the same giggling conversations with her now.

Her mum broke into her thoughts. 'I rang you last night at home, were you out?'

Holly took a sip of her tea. Oh, the wonders of the magical tea, the answer to all of life's little problems. You have a gossip and you make a cup of tea, you get fired from your job and you have a cup of tea, your husband tells you he has a brain tumour and you have a cup of tea . . .

'Yeah, I went out to dinner with the girls and about a hundred other people I didn't know.' Holly rubbed her eyes tiredly.

'How are the girls?' Elizabeth asked fondly. She had always got along well with Holly's friends, unlike Ciara's, who terrified her.

Holly took a sip of her tea. 'Sharon's pregnant and Denise got engaged,' she replied, staring off into space.

'Oh,' Elizabeth squeaked, not sure how to react in front of her obviously distressed daughter. 'How do you feel about that?' she asked softly, brushing a hair away from Holly's face.

Holly stared down at her hands and tried to compose herself. She wasn't successful and her shoulders began to tremble and she tried to hide her face behind her hair.

'Oh, Holly,' Elizabeth said sadly, putting her cup down and moving closer to her daughter. 'It's perfectly normal to feel like this.'

Holly couldn't even manage to get any words out of her mouth.

The front door banged and Ciara announced to the house, 'We're hoooome!'

'Great,' Holly sniffed, resting her head on her mum's chest.

'WHERE IS EVERYONE?' Ciara shouted, banging doors.

'Just a minute, love,' Elizabeth called out, angry that her moment with Holly had been ruined. It had been a long time since Holly had confided in her; she had chosen to bottle everything up since the funeral and it seemed it had all become too much for her. She didn't want an overexcited Ciara to send her back into her shell again.

'I HAVE NEWS!' Ciara's voice got louder as she got nearer to the living room. Mathew burst open the door, carrying Ciara in his arms. 'Me and Mathew are moving back to Australia!' she yelled happily. She froze as she saw her upset sister in her mum's arms. She quietly jumped down from Mathew's arms, led him out of the room and closed the door silently behind them.

'Now Ciara's going too, Mum.' Holly cried even harder, and Elizabeth cried softly for her daughter.

Holly stayed up late that night talking to her mum about everything that had been bubbling up inside her for the past few months. And although her mother offered many words of kind reassurance, Holly still felt as trapped as before. She stayed in the guest bedroom that night and woke up to a mad house the following morning. Holly smiled at the familiarity of the sound of her brother and sister running around the house, screaming about how they were late for band rehearsals and for work, followed by their dad grumbling at them to get a move on, followed by her mum's gentle pleas for everyone to stay silent so as not to disturb Holly. The world went on, simple as that, and there was no bubble big enough to protect her.

At lunchtime Holly's dad dropped her home and squeezed a cheque for five thousand euro into her hand.

'Oh, Dad, I can't accept this,' Holly said, overcome with emotion.

'Take it,' he said gently, pushing her hand away. 'Let us help you, love.'

'I'll pay back every cent,' she said, hugging him tightly.

Holly stood at the door and waved her father off down the road. She looked at the cheque in her hand and immediately a weight was lifted from her shoulders. She could think of twenty things she could do with this cheque and for once buying clothes wasn't one of them. Walking into the kitchen she noticed the red light flashing on the answering machine on the table in the hall. She sat at the bottom of the stairs and hit the button.

She had five new messages.

One was from Sharon, ringing to see if she was OK because she hadn't heard from her all day. The second was from Denise ringing to see if she was OK because she hadn't heard from her all day. The two girls had obviously been talking to each other. The third was from Sharon, the fourth was from Denise and the fifth was just somebody hanging up. Holly pressed delete and ran upstairs to change her clothes. She wasn't quite ready to talk to Sharon and Denise yet; she needed to get her life in order first so she could be more supportive towards them.

She sat in the spare room in front of her computer and began to type up her CV. She had become an old pro at doing this, having changed jobs so often. It had been a while since she had to worry about going to interviews, though. And if she did get an interview, who would want to hire someone who hadn't been working for a whole year?

It took her two hours to print out something that she finally thought was half decent. In fact she was really proud of what she had done: she had somehow managed to make herself look intelligent and experienced. She laughed evilly loudly, hoping she would manage to fool her future employers into thinking she was a capable worker. Reading back over her CV she decided that even she would hire herself.

On Monday she dressed smartly and drove down

to the village in the car she had finally managed to fill with petrol. She parked outside the recruitment office and applied lip-gloss in the rear-view mirror. There was to be no more time-wasting. If Gerry said to find a job, she was going to find a job.

Chapter Thirty-Two

A few days later Holly sat out on her newly renovated garden furniture in her back garden, sipped on a glass of red wine and listened to the sound of wind chimes making music in the breeze. She looked around at the neat lines of her newly landscaped garden and decided that whoever was working on it had to be a professional. She breathed in and allowed the sweet scent of flowers to fill her nostrils. It was eight o'clock and already it was beginning to get dark. The bright evenings were gone, and everybody was once again preparing for hibernation.

She thought about the message she had received on her answering machine that day. It had been from the recruitment agency, and she'd been shocked to receive a reply from them so quickly. The woman on the phone had said that there had been a great response to her résumé, and already Holly had two job interviews lined up.

Butterflies fluttered around her stomach at the thought of them. She had never been particularly good at interviews, but then again she had never been particularly keen on any of the jobs she was being interviewed for. This time she felt different; she was excited to get back to work and to try something new. Her first interview was for a job selling advertising space for a magazine that circulated throughout Dublin. It was something she had absolutely no experience in, but she was willing to learn because the idea of it sounded far more interesting than any of her former jobs, which had mostly entailed answering the phone, taking messages and filing. Anything that involved not having to do any of those things all day was a step up.

The second interview was with a leading Irish advertising company, and she knew she had absolutely no hope of getting it. But Gerry had told her to shoot for the moon . . .

Holly also thought about the phone call she had just received from Denise. Denise had been so excited on the phone she didn't seem to be at all bothered by the fact that Holly hadn't talked to her since they went out for dinner last week. In fact, Holly didn't think she had even noticed. Denise had been all talk about her wedding arrangements, and rambled on for almost an hour about what kind of dress she should wear, which flowers she should choose, where she should hold the reception. She started sentences and then forgot to finish them as she jumped from topic to topic. All Holly had to do was make a few noises to let her know she was still listening . . . although she wasn't. The only piece of information she had taken in was that Denise was planning to marry on New Year's Eve, and by the sound of it Tom wouldn't be having a say in how Denise's special day should be run.

Holly was surprised to hear they had set a date so soon – she had just assumed it would be one of those long-winded, last-a-few-years kind of engagements, especially as Denise and Tom had only been an item for five months. But Holly didn't worry about that as much as she would have done when she was her old self. She was now a regular subscriber to the finding-love-and-holding-on-to-it-forever magazine. Denise and Tom were right not to waste time worrying about what people thought if they knew in their hearts it was the right decision.

Sharon hadn't called Holly since the day after she had announced her pregnancy, and Holly knew she would have to call her friend soon before the days passed her by and it was too late. This was an important time in Sharon's life and she knew she should be there for her, but she just couldn't bring herself to. She was being jealous, bitter and incredibly selfish, she knew that, but Holly needed to be selfish these days in order to survive. She was still trying to get her head round the fact that Sharon and John were managing to achieve everything that everyone had always assumed Holly and Gerry would do first. Sharon had always said she hated kids, Holly thought angrily.

It began to get chilly and Holly took her glass of wine inside to her warm house where she refilled it. All she could do for the next couple of days was attend her job interviews and pray for success. She went into the sitting room, put her and Gerry's favourite album of love songs on the CD player and snuggled up on the couch with her glass of wine where she closed her eyes and pictured them dancing around the room together.

The following day she was awoken by the sound of a car pulling into her driveway. She got out of bed and threw Gerry's dressing gown on, presuming it was her car being returned from the garage, where she'd left it for its annual service. She peeped out of the curtains and immediately jumped back as she saw Richard stepping out of his car. She hoped he hadn't seen her because she really wasn't in the mood for one of his visits. She paced the bedroom floor, feeling guilty as she ignored the doorbell ringing for the second time. She knew she was being horrible but she just couldn't bear sitting down with him for another awkward conversation. She really hadn't anything to talk about any more; nothing had changed in her life, she had no exciting news, not even any normal news to tell *anybody*, never mind Richard.

She breathed a sigh of relief as she heard him walk away and then his car door bang shut. She stepped into the shower and allowed the warm water to run over her face and she was once again lost in a world of her own. Twenty minutes later she padded downstairs in her disco diva slippers. A scraping noise from outside made her freeze in her step. She pricked her ears up and listened more closely, trying to identify the sound. There it was again: a scraping noise and a rustling, as if somebody were in her garden . . . Holly's eyes widened as she realised that her leprechaun was outside.

She crept into the living room, stupidly thinking

the person outside would hear her wandering around her house, and got down on her knees. Peering above the windowsill she gasped as she saw Richard's car still sitting in the driveway. What was even more surprising was the sight of Richard on his hands and knees with a small gardening implement in his hand, digging up the soil and planting new flowers. She crawled away from the window and sat on the carpet in shock, unsure what to do next. The sound of her car being parked outside the house snapped her back to attention and her brain went into overdrive as she tried to figure out whether to answer the door to her mechanic or not. For some reason Richard didn't want Holly to know that he was working on her garden and she decided she was going to respect that wish . . . for now.

She hid behind the couch as she saw the mechanic approach the door and she had to laugh at how ridiculous this all seemed. The doorbell rang and she scurried even further behind the couch as her mechanic walked over to the window and stared in. Her heart beat wildly and she felt as though she were doing something illegal. She covered her mouth and tried to smother her laughs. She felt like a child again. She had always been hopeless at playing hide-and-seek; whenever she felt her seeker coming near her she would always get an attack of the giggles and her hiding place would be found. Then, for the rest of the day, she would have to search for everybody else. She breathed a sigh of relief as she heard the mechanic drop the keys through the letterbox and walk away.

A few minutes later she stuck her head out from

behind the couch and checked if it was safe to come out. She stood up and brushed the dust off her clothes, telling herself she was too old to be playing silly games. She peeked out from behind the curtain again and saw Richard packing up his gardening equipment. Holly kicked off her slippers and shoved her feet into her trainers.

On second thought, these silly games were fun and she had nothing else to do. As soon as she saw Richard drive down the road she ran outside and hopped into her car. She was going to follow her leprechaun.

She managed to stay three cars behind him all the way, just like they did in the movies, and she slowed down as she saw him pulling over ahead of her. He parked his car and went into the newsagent and returned with a newspaper in his hand. Holly put her sunglasses on, adjusted her baseball cap and peered over the top of the *Arab Leader* that was covering her face. She laughed at herself as she caught sight of her reflection in the mirror. She looked like the most suspicious person in the world. She watched Richard cross the road and head into The Greasy Spoon. She was slightly disappointed; she was hoping for a far juicier adventure than this.

She sat in her car for a few minutes, trying to formulate a new plan, and jumped with fright when a traffic warden banged on her window.

'You can't park here,' he said, motioning towards the car park. Holly smiled back sweetly and rolled her eyes as she backed into a free space. Surely Cagney and Lacey never had this problem.

Eventually her inner child settled down to have a

nap and mature Holly took her cap and glasses off and tossed them onto the passenger seat, feeling foolish. Silly games over. Real life starting now.

She crossed the road and looked around inside the café for her brother. She spotted him sitting down with his back to her, hunched over his newspaper and drinking a cup of tea. She marched over happily with a smile on her face.

'God, Richard, do you ever go to work?' she joked loudly, causing him to jump. She was about to say more but stopped herself as he looked up at her with tears in his eyes and his shoulders began to shake.

Chapter Thirty-Three

Holly looked around to see if anyone else in the café had noticed, and she slowly pulled out a chair to sit down beside Richard. Had she said something wrong? She looked at Richard's face in shock, not knowing what to do or say. She could safely admit that she had *never* been in this situation before.

Tears rolled down his face and he tried with all his might to stop them.

'Richard, what's wrong?' she asked, confused, and placed her hand awkwardly on his arm and patted it.

Richard continued to shake with tears.

The plump lady, dressed in a canary-yellow apron this time, made her way round the counter and placed a box of tissues on the table beside Holly.

'Here you go,' she said, handing Richard a tissue. He wiped his eyes and blew his nose loudly, a big old man blow, and Holly tried to hide her smile.

'I'm sorry for crying,' Richard said, embarrassed, avoiding eye contact with her.

'Hey,' she said softly, placing her hand more easily on his arm this time, 'there's nothing wrong with crying. It's my new hobby these days so don't knock it.'

He smiled at her weakly. 'Everything just seems to be falling apart, Holly,' he said sadly, catching a tear with the tissue before it dropped from his chin.

'Like what?' she asked, concerned at her brother's transformation. She had seen so many sides to him over the past few months that he had her slightly baffled.

Richard took a deep breath and gulped back his tea. Holly looked up at the woman behind the counter and ordered another pot.

'Richard, I've recently learned that talking about things helps,' Holly said gently, 'and coming from me that's a huge tip, because I used to keep my mouth shut thinking I was Superwoman.' She smiled at him encouragingly. 'Why don't you tell me about it?'

He looked doubtful.

'I won't laugh, I won't say anything if you don't want me to. I won't tell a soul what you tell me, I'll just listen,' she assured him.

He looked away from her and focused on the salt and pepper shakers at the centre of the table, and then he spoke quietly. 'I lost my job.'

Holly remained silent and waited for him to say more. After a while Richard looked up to face her.

'That's not so bad, Richard,' she said softly then, giving him a smile. 'I know you loved your job but you can find another one. Hey, if it makes you feel any better I used to lose my jobs all the time—'

'I lost my job in April, Holly,' he interrupted her angrily. 'It is now September. There's nothing for me . . . not in my line of work . . .' He looked away.

'Oh . . .' Holly didn't know quite what to say. After a long silence she spoke again. 'But at least Meredith is still working, so you still have a regular income. Just take the time you need to find the right job . . . I know it doesn't feel like it right now but—'

'Meredith left me last month,' he interrupted her again, and this time his voice was weaker.

Holly's hands flew to her mouth. Oh, poor Richard. She had never liked the bitch, but Richard had adored her.

'The kids?' she asked carefully.

'They're living with her,' he said, and his voice cracked.

'Oh, Richard, I'm so sorry.' Holly fidgeted with her hands, not knowing where to put them. Should she hug him?

'I'm sorry too,' he said miserably, and continued to stare at the salt and pepper shakers.

'It wasn't your fault, Richard, so don't go telling yourself it was,' she protested strongly.

'Wasn't it?' he said, his voice beginning to shake. 'She told me I was a pathetic man who couldn't even look after his own family . . .' He broke down again.

'Oh, never mind that silly bitch,' Holly said angrily. 'You are an excellent father and a loyal husband,' she told him strongly, and realised she meant every word of it. 'Timmy and Emily love you because you're fantastic with them so don't mind what that demented woman says to you.' She wrapped her arms around him and hugged her brother while he cried. She felt so angry she wanted to go over to Meredith and punch her in the face – although she had always wanted to do that, but now she even had an excuse.

Richard's tears finally subsided and he pulled away

from her and grabbed another tissue. Holly's heart went out to him; he had always tried so hard to do the right thing and to create a perfect life and family for himself, and it hadn't worked out as he had planned. He seemed to be in a great deal of shock.

'Where are you staying?' she asked, suddenly realising that he had had no home to go to for the past few weeks.

'In a B&B down the road. Nice place. Friendly people,' he said, pouring another cup of tea. Your wife leaves you and you have a cup of tea . . .

'Richard, you can't stay there,' Holly protested. 'Why didn't you tell any of us?'

'Because I thought we could work it out, but we can't . . . She's made up her mind.'

As much as Holly wanted to invite him to stay with her she just couldn't. She had far too much to deal with on her own and she was sure Richard would appreciate that.

'What about Mum and Dad?' she asked. 'They would love to be able to help you out.'

Richard shook his head, 'No, Ciara's home now and so is Declan. I wouldn't want to dump myself on them as well. I'm a grown man now.'

'Oh, Richard, don't be silly.' Holly rolled her eyes. 'There's your old room. I'm positive you would be welcome back there,' she tried to persuade him. 'Sure, I even slept there a few nights ago.'

He looked up from staring at the table.

'There is absolutely nothing wrong with returning to the house you grew up in every now and again. It's good for the soul,' she smiled at him.

315

He looked uncertain. 'Em . . . I don't think that's such a good idea, Holly.'

'If it's Ciara you're worried about then don't. She's heading back to Australia in a few weeks with her boyfriend so the house will be . . . less hectic.'

His face relaxed a little.

Holly smiled. 'So what do you think? Come on, it's a great idea and this way you won't be throwing your money away on some smelly ol' dump. I don't care how nice you say the owners are.'

Richard smiled but it quickly faded. 'I couldn't ask Mother and Father, Holly. I . . . wouldn't know what to say.'

'I'll go with you,' she promised, 'and I'll talk to them for you. Honestly, Richard, they'll be delighted to help out. You're their son and they love you. We all do,' she added, placing her hand over his.

'OK,' he finally agreed, and she linked arms with him, as they headed out to their cars.

'Oh, by the way, Richard, thank you for my garden,' Holly smiled, then leaned over and kissed him on the cheek.

'You know?'

She nodded. 'You have such a huge talent and I'm going to pay you every single penny you deserve as soon as I find a job.'

Her brother's face relaxed into a shy smile.

They got into their cars and drove back to the house they grew up in.

Holly looked at herself in the toilet mirror of the office building where her first job interview was taking place. She had lost so much weight since she had worn all her old suits that she had had to go out and purchase a new one. It was flattering to her new slim figure. The jacket was long and went to just above her knees and it was fastened tightly by one button at the waist. The trousers were just the right fit and fell perfectly over her boots. The outfit was black with light blue lines going through it and she matched it with a light blue top underneath. She felt like a hot-shot advertising businesswoman in control of her life, and all she needed to do now was to sound like one. She applied another layer of pink lip-gloss and ran her fingers through her loose curls, which she had decided to allow to tumble onto her shoulders. She took a deep breath and headed back out to the waiting area.

She took her seat again and glanced around at all the other applicants. They looked far younger than Holly and they all seemed to have a thick folder of some kind sitting on their laps. She looked around and started to panic. Sure enough, everybody had one of these folders. She stood up from her seat again and headed over to the secretary.

'Excuse me,' Holly said, trying to get her attention.

The woman looked up and smiled. 'Can I help you?'

'Yes, I was just in the toilet there and I think I must have missed being given a folder.' Holly smiled politely at her.

The woman frowned and looked confused. 'I'm sorry, what folders were handed out?'

Holly turned and pointed to the folders perched on everyone's laps.

The woman smiled and motioned her to come closer with her finger.

Holly tucked her hair behind her ears and moved closer. 'Yes?'

'Sorry, honey, but they're actually portfolios that they brought themselves,' she whispered so that Holly wouldn't be embarrassed.

Holly's face froze. 'Oh. Should I have brought one with me?'

'Well, do you have one?' the woman asked with a friendly smile.

Holly shook her head.

'Well then, don't worry about it. It's not a requirement. People just bring these things to show off,' she said, and Holly giggled.

Holly returned to her seat but continued to worry about this portfolio business. Nobody had said anything to her about any stupid portfolios. Why was she the last to know everything? She tapped her foot and looked around the office while she waited. She got a good feeling from the place; the colours were warm and cosy, and the light poured in from the large Georgian windows. The ceilings were high and there was a lovely feeling of space. Holly could sit there all day thinking. She suddenly felt so relaxed that her heart didn't even jump as her name was called. She walked confidently towards the interview office and the secretary winked at her to wish her good luck. Holly smiled back at her; for some reason she already felt part of the team. She paused just outside the door and took a deep breath.

Shoot for the moon, she whispered to herself, shoot for the moon.

Chapter Thirty-Four

Holly knocked lightly on the door and a gruff voice told her to enter. Her heart did a little flip at the sound of it, feeling as if she had been summoned to the principal's office at school. She wiped her clammy hands on her suit and entered the room.

'Hello,' she said more confidently than she felt. She walked across the small room and held out her hand to the man who had stood up from his chair. He greeted her with a big smile and a warm handshake. The face didn't match the grumpy voice at all, thankfully. Holly relaxed a little at the sight of him; he reminded her of her father. He looked to be in his late fifties, with a big cuddly-bear physique, and she had to stop herself from leaping over the desk to hug him. His hair was neat, almost a sparkling silver colour, and she imagined he had been an extremely handsome man in his youth.

'Holly Kennedy, isn't it?' he said, taking his seat and glancing down at her CV in front of him. She sat in the seat opposite him and forced herself to stay calm. She had read every interview technique manual she could get her hands on since drawing up her CV and had tried to put it all into practice, from walking into the room, to the proper handshake to the way she positioned herself in her chair. She wanted to look as if she was experienced, intelligent and highly confident. But she would need more than a firm handshake to succeed in proving that.

'That's right,' she said, placing her handbag on the ground beside her and resting her shaking hands on her lap.

He put his glasses on the end of his nose and flicked through her CV in silence. Holly stared at him intently and tried to read his facial expressions. It wasn't an easy task as he was one of those people who had a constant frown on his face while he read. Well, it was either that or he wasn't at all impressed by what he was seeing. She glanced at his desk while she waited for him to start speaking again. Her eyes fell upon a silver-framed photo, featuring three pretty girls close to her own age, all smiling happily at the camera. She continued to stare at it with a smile on her face and when she looked up she realised he had put the CV down and was watching her. She smiled and tried to appear more businesslike.

'Before we start talking about you I'll explain exactly who I am and what the job entails,' he explained.

Holly nodded, trying to look very interested.

'My name is Chris Feeney and I'm the founder and editor of the magazine, or "the boss man", as everyone likes to call me around here,' he chuckled, and Holly was charmed by his twinkling blue eyes.

'Basically we are looking for someone to deal with the advertising aspect of the magazine. As you know, the running of a magazine or any media organisation is hugely reliant on the advertising we receive. We need the money for our magazine to be published so this job is very important. Unfortunately, our last man had to leave us in a hurry, so I would be looking for somebody who could begin work almost immediately. How would you feel about that?'

Holly nodded. 'That would be no problem at all. In fact, I'm eager to begin work as soon as possible.'

Chris nodded and looked down at her CV again. 'I see you've been out of the workforce for over a year now, am I correct in saying that?' He lowered his head and stared at her over the rim of his glasses.

'Yes, that's right,' Holly nodded, 'and I can assure you that was purely out of choice. Unfortunately my husband was ill and I had to take time off work to be with him.'

She swallowed hard; she knew that this would be an issue for every employer. Nobody wanted to employ someone who had been idle for the past year.

'I see,' he said, looking up at her. 'Well, I hope that he's fully recovered now.' He smiled warmly.

Holly wasn't sure whether that was a question or not and didn't know what to say. Did he want to hear about her personal life? He continued to look at her and she realised he was waiting for an answer.

She cleared her throat. 'Well, no actually, Mr Feeney, unfortunately he passed away in February . . . he had a brain tumour. That's why I felt it was important to leave my job.'

'Gosh.' Chris put down the CV and took his glasses off. 'Of course I can understand that. I'm very sorry

321

to hear it,' he said sincerely. 'It must be hard for you being so young and all . . .' He looked down at his desk for a while, then met her eyes again. 'My wife lost her life to breast cancer just last year so I understand how you may be feeling,' he said generously.

'I'm sorry to hear that,' Holly said sadly, her eyes meeting those of the kind man across the table.

'They say it gets easier,' he smiled.

'So they say,' Holly said grimly. 'Apparently gallons of tea do the trick.'

He started to laugh, a big guffaw of a laugh. 'Yes! I've been told that one too, and my daughters inform me that fresh air is also a healer.'

'Ah yes, the magic fresh air; it does wonders for the heart. Are they your daughters?' she smiled, indicating the photograph.

'Indeed they are,' he said proudly. 'My three little doctors who try to keep me alive,' he laughed. 'Unfortunately, the garden no longer looks like that, though.'

'Wow, is that your garden?' Holly asked wide-eyed. 'It's beautiful; I presumed it was the Botanical Gardens or somewhere like that.'

'That was Maureen's specialty. You can't get me out of the office long enough to sort through that mess.'

'Oh, don't talk to me about gardens,' Holly said, rolling her eyes. 'I'm not exactly Ms Green-fingers myself and the place is beginning to look like a jungle.' Well, it had looked like a jungle, she thought to herself.

They continued to look at each other and smile, and Holly was comforted to hear a story similar to

322

her own. Whether she got the job or not, at least it would be confirmed that she wasn't entirely alone and other people had to cope with what she did.

'Anyway, getting back to the interview,' Chris laughed, 'have you any experience in working with the media at all?'

Holly didn't like the way he said 'at all'. It meant that he had read through her CV and couldn't see any sign of experience for the job.

'Yes, I have, actually.' She returned to business mode and tried so hard to impress him. 'I once worked in an estate agents and I was responsible for dealing with the media regarding the new properties for sale. So I was on the other end of what this job requires and so I know how to deal with companies who are wishing to sell space.'

Chris nodded along. 'But you have never actually worked on a magazine or newspaper or anything like that?'

Holly nodded her head slowly and racked her brains for something to say. 'But I was responsible for printing up a weekly newsletter for a company I worked for . . .' She rambled on and on, grasping at every little straw she could and realising she was sounding rather pathetic.

Chris was too polite to interrupt her as she went through every job she'd ever worked at and exaggerated anything that was in any way advertising- or media-related. Eventually she stopped talking, having grown bored at the sound of her own voice, and she twisted her fingers around each other nervously on her lap. She was underqualified for this job and she knew it, but she also knew that she could do it if he just gave her the chance.

Chris took off his glasses. 'I see. Well, Holly, I can see that you have a great deal of experience in the workplace in various different areas, but I notice that you haven't stayed in any of your jobs for a period longer than nine months . . .'

'I was searching for the right job for me,' Holly said, her confidence now totally shattered.

'So how do I know you won't desert me after a few months?' he smiled, but she knew he was serious.

'Because this *is* the right job for me,' she said seriously. Holly took a deep breath as she felt her chances slipping away from her but she wasn't prepared to give up that easily. 'Mr Feeney,' she said, moving forward to sit on the edge of her chair, 'I'm a very hard worker. When I love something I give it one hundred per cent. I'm a very capable person and what I don't know now I am more than willing to learn so that I can do my best for myself, for you and for the company. If you put your trust in me I promise I won't let you down.' She stopped herself just short of getting down on her knees and begging for the damn job.

She blushed as she realised what she had just done.

'Well then, I think that's a good note to finish on,' Chris said, smiling at her. He stood up from his chair and held his hand out. 'Thank you very much for taking the time to come down here. I'm sure we'll be in touch.'

Holly shook his hand and thanked him quietly, picked her bag up from the ground and felt his eyes burning into her back as she headed towards the door. Just before she stepped outside she turned back to face him. 'Mr

Feeney, I'll make sure your secretary brings you in a nice hot pot of tea. It'll do you the world of good.'

She smiled and closed the door to the sound of his loud laughter. The friendly secretary raised her eyebrows at Holly as she passed her desk and the rest of the applicants held onto their portfolios tightly, wondering what the lady had said to make the interviewer laugh so loudly. Holly smiled to herself as she heard Mr Feeney continue to laugh as she made her way out into the fresh air.

Holly decided to drop in on Ciara at work so she could have a bite to eat. She rounded the corner, entered Hogan's pub and searched for a table inside. The pub was packed with people dressed smartly on their lunch breaks from work, and some were even having a few sneaky pints before heading back to the office. Holly found a small table in the corner and settled down.

'Excuse me,' she called out loudly, and clicked her fingers in the air. 'Can I get some service here, please?'

The people at the tables around her threw her the looks for being so rude to the staff, and Holly continued to click her fingers in the air.

'Oi!' she yelled.

Ciara swirled around with a scowl on her face but it broke into a smile when she spotted her sister grinning at her. 'Jesus, I was about to smack the head off you,' she laughed, approaching the table.

'I hope you don't speak to all your customers like that,' Holly teased.

'Not *all* of them,' Ciara replied seriously. 'You having lunch here today?'

Holly nodded. 'Mum told me you were working lunches; I thought you were supposed to be serving in the club upstairs?'

Ciara rolled her eyes. 'That man has got me working all the hours under the sun. He's treating me like a slave,' Ciara moaned.

'Did I hear someone mention my name?' Daniel laughed, walking up behind her.

Ciara's face froze as she realised he had overheard her. 'No, no . . . I was just talking about Mathew,' she stammered. 'He has me up all hours of the night, I'm like his sex slave . . .' she trailed off and wandered over to the bar to get a notepad and pen.

'Sorry I asked,' Daniel said, staring at Ciara, bewildered. 'Mind if I join you?' he asked Holly.

'Yes,' Holly teased, but pulled out a stool for him. 'OK, what's good to eat here?' She was looking through the menu as Ciara returned with pen in hand.

Ciara mouthed, 'Nothing' behind Daniel's back and Holly giggled.

'The toasted special is my favourite,' Daniel suggested, and Ciara shook her head wildly at Holly.

'What are you shaking your head at?' Daniel said, catching her in the act again.

'Oh, it's just that . . . Holly is allergic to onions,' Ciara stammered again. This was news to Holly.

Holly nodded her head. 'Yes . . . they, eh . . . make my head . . . eh . . . bloat.' She blew her cheeks out. 'Terrible things, those onions are. Fatal, in fact. Could kill me someday.'

Ciara rolled her eyes at her sister who once again had managed to take things way over the top.

'OK, well then, leave the onions out,' Daniel suggested, and Holly agreed.

Ciara stuck her fingers in her mouth and pretended to gag as she walked away.

'You're looking very smart today,' Daniel said, studying her outfit.

'Yes, that was the impression I was trying to give. I was just at a job interview,' Holly said, and winced at the thought of it.

'Oh yeah, that's right,' Daniel smiled. 'Didn't it go well?'

Holly shook her head. 'Well, let's just say I need to buy a smarter-looking suit. I won't be expecting a call from them anytime soon.'

'Not to worry,' Daniel said, smiling. 'There will be plenty of other opportunities. Still have that job upstairs, if you're interested.'

'I thought you gave that job to Ciara. Why is she working downstairs now?' Holly said, looking confused.

Daniel rolled his eyes. 'Holly, you know your sister, we had a bit of a *situation*.'

'Oh no!' Holly laughed. 'What did she do this time?'

'Some guy at the bar said something to her she didn't quite like so she poured him his pint, then served it to him over his head.'

'Oh no!' Holly gasped. 'I'm surprised you didn't fire her!'

'Couldn't do that to a member of the Kennedy family, could I?' he smiled. 'And besides, how would I ever be able to face you again?'

'Exactly,' Holly confirmed. 'You may be my friend but you "gotta respect the family".' Ciara frowned at her sister as she arrived with her plate of food. 'Well, that has to be the worst Godfather impression I've ever heard. Bon appetite,' she said sarcastically, slamming the plate down on the table and turning on her heel.

'Hey!' Daniel frowned, taking Holly's plate away from her, examining her sandwich.

'What are you doing?' she demanded.

'There are onions in it,' he said angrily. 'Ciara must have given the wrong order again.'

'No, no, she didn't.' Holly jumped to her sister's rescue and grabbed the plate back. 'I'm only allergic to red onions,' she blurted out.

Daniel frowned. 'How odd. I didn't think there was a huge difference.'

'Oh, there is.' Holly nodded her head and tried to sound wise. 'They may be part of the same family but the red onion . . . contains deadly toxins . . .' she trailed off.

'Toxins?' Daniel said disbelievingly.

'Well, they're toxic to me, aren't they?' she mumbled, and bit into the sandwich to shut herself up. She found if difficult to eat her sandwich under Daniel's glare without feeling like a pig so she finally gave up and left the remains on her plate.

'Not like it?' he asked worriedly.

'No, I love it, I just had a big breakfast,' she lied, patting her empty stomach.

'So have you had any luck with that leprechaun yet?' he teased.

'Well, actually I found him!' Holly laughed, wiping her greasy hands on her napkin.

'Really? Who was it?'

'Would you believe it was my brother Richard?' she laughed.

'Go away! So why didn't he tell you? Did he want it to be a surprise or something?'

'Something like that, I suppose.'

'He's a nice guy, Richard,' Daniel said, looking thoughtful.

'You think?'

'Yeah, he's a harmless kind of a guy. He has a nice nature.'

Holly nodded her head.

He cut in on her thoughts. 'Have you spoken to Denise or Sharon lately?'

'Just Denise,' she said, looking away guiltily, 'You?'

'Tom has my head done in with all this talk of weddings. Wants me to be his best man. To be honest, I didn't think they would plan it all so soon.'

'Me neither,' Holly agreed. 'How do you feel about it now?'

'Ah,' Daniel sighed, 'happy for him, in a selfish and bitter kind of way.'

'Know how you feel. You haven't spoken to your ex lately or anything?'

'Who, Laura?' he asked, surprised. 'Never want to see the woman again.'

'Is she a friend of Tom's?'

'Not as friendly as they used to be, thank God.'

'So she won't be invited to the wedding then?'

Daniel's eyes widened. 'You know I never even

329

thought of that. God, I hope not. Tom knows what I would do to him if he did invite her.' There was a silence as Daniel contemplated that thought.

'I think I'm meeting up with Tom and Denise tomorrow night to discuss the wedding plans, if you feel like coming out,' he said then.

Holly rolled her eyes. 'Gee, thanks. Well, that just sounds like the best fun ever.'

Daniel started laughing. 'I know, that's why I don't want to go on my own. Call me later if you want to go, anyway.'

Holly nodded.

'Right, here's the bill,' Ciara said, dropping a piece of paper on the table and sauntered off. Daniel watched after her and shook his head.

'Don't worry, Daniel,' Holly laughed. 'You won't have to put up with her for much longer.'

'Why not?' He looked confused.

Uh-oh, Holly thought, Ciara hadn't told him she was moving away. 'Oh, nothing,' she mumbled, rooting through her bag for her purse.

'No, really, what do you mean?' he continued.

'Oh, I mean her shift must be nearly over now,' she said, pulling her purse out of her bag and looking at her watch.

'Oh . . . listen, don't worry about the bill, I'll take care of that.'

'No, I'm not letting you do that,' she said, continuing to search through all the receipts and rubbish in her purse for some money. 'Which reminds me, I owe you twenty.' She placed the money on the table.

'Forget about that.' He waved his hand dismissively.

'Hey, are you going to let me pay for anything?' Holly joked. 'I'm leaving it here on the table anyway, so you'll have to take it.'

Ciara returned to the table and held out her hand for the money.

'It's OK, Ciara, put it on my tab,' Daniel said.

Ciara raised her eyebrows at Holly and winked at her. Then she glanced down at the table and spotted the twenty-euro note. 'Ooh, thanks, sis. I didn't know you were such a good tipper.' She pocketed the money and headed over to serve another table.

'Don't worry,' Daniel laughed, 'I'll take it out of her wages.'

Holly felt relieved finally to be home as she drove down her housing estate. She had got very little sleep the night before, due to pre-interview nerves, and the pressure of the day had worn her out. She was looking forward to opening a bottle of wine and settling down for the night to ponder her next career move.

Her heart began to pound as she spotted Sharon's car outside her house. It had been so long since Holly had spoken to her that she was embarrassed. She contemplated turning the car round and heading off in the other direction but she stopped herself. She needed to face the music sometime before she lost another best friend. If it wasn't too late already.

Chapter Thirty-Five

Holly pulled up to her driveway and took a deep breath before getting out of her car. She should have been to visit Sharon first and she knew it, now things just seemed far worse. She walked towards Sharon's car and was surprised to see John stepping out. There was no Sharon to be seen. Her throat became dry; she hoped Sharon was OK.

'Hi, Holly,' John said grimly, banging the car door behind him.

'John! Where's Sharon?'

'I just came from the hospital.' He walked towards her slowly.

Holly's hands flew to her face and tears filled her eyes. 'Oh my God! Is she OK?'

John looked confused. 'Yeah, she's just having a check-up. I'm going back to collect her after I leave here.'

Holly's hands dropped down by her side. 'Oh,' she said, feeling stupid.

'You know, if you're that concerned about her you should call her.' John held his head high and his icy blue eyes stared straight into hers. Holly could see his jaw clenching and unclenching. She held his stare until the force of his gaze caused her to look away.

'Yeah, I know,' she mumbled. 'Why don't you come inside and I'll make us a cup of tea?' At any other time she would have laughed at herself for saying that; she was turning into one of *them*.

She flicked the switch on the kettle and busied herself while John sat at the table.

'Sharon doesn't know that I'm here so I would appreciate it if you didn't say anything.'

'Oh . . . OK.' Holly felt even more disappointed. Sharon hadn't sent him. She didn't even want to see her; she must have given up on Holly altogether.

'She misses you, you know.' John continued to stare straight at her, not blinking for one moment.

Holly carried the mugs over to the table and sat down. 'I miss her too.'

'It's been two weeks, Holly.'

'It has not been two weeks!' Holly protested weakly, feeling uncomfortable under his stony stare.

'Well, almost two . . . Anyway, it doesn't matter how long it's been exactly, the two of you used to speak to each other every day.' John took the mug from her hand and placed it in front of him.

'Things used to be very different, John,' Holly said angrily. Didn't anybody understand what she was going through? Was she the only sane person in the whole world these days?

'Look, we all know what you've been through—' John started.

'I know you all *know* what I've been through, John – that's blatantly obvious – but you all don't seem to understand that I'm *still* going through it!'

There was a silence.

'That's not true at all.' John's voice was quieter and he fixed his gaze on the mug he was rotating on the table before him.

'Yes it is. I can't just move on with my life like you're all doing and pretend that nothing has happened.'

'Do you think that that's what we're doing?'

'Well, let's look at the evidence shall we?' Holly said sarcastically. 'Sharon is having a baby and Denise is getting married—'

'Holly, that's called living,' John interrupted, looking up. 'You seem to have forgotten how to do that. And I'm not saying that I think it's easy for you because I know myself that it's not. I miss Gerry too. He was my best mate. I lived right next door to him all my life. I went to playschool with the guy, for Christsake. We went to primary school together, we went to secondary school together and we played on the same football team. I was his best man at his wedding and he was at mine! Whenever I had a problem I went to Gerry, whenever I wanted to have a bit of fun I went to Gerry. I told him some things that I would never have told Sharon and he told me things he wouldn't have told you. Just because I wasn't married to him doesn't mean that I don't feel like you do. And just because he's dead doesn't mean I have to stop living too.'

Holly sat stunned. John twisted his chair round in order to face her properly. The legs of the chair squeaked loudly in the silence. He took a deep breath before he spoke again.

'Yes it's difficult. Yes it's horrible. Yes it's the worst thing that has ever happened to me in my whole life. But I can't just give up. I can't just stop going to the pub because there's two blokes laughing and joking on the stools Gerry and me used to sit on, and I can't stop going to football matches just because it's somewhere we used to go together all the time. I can remember it all right, and smile about it, but I can't just stop going there.'

Tears welled in Holly's eyes as John continued.

'Sharon knows you're hurting and she understands, but you have to understand that this is a hugely important time in her life too and she needs her best friend to help her through it. She needs your help just like you need hers.'

'I'm trying, John,' Holly sobbed, as hot tears rolled down her cheeks.

'I know you are.' He leaned forward and grabbed her hands. 'But Sharon needs you too. Avoiding the situation isn't going to help anyone or anything.'

'But I went for a job interview today,' she sobbed childishly.

John tried to hide his smile. 'That's great news, Holly. How did it go?'

'Shite,' she sniffed, and John started laughing. He allowed a silence to fall between them before he spoke again.

'She's almost five months pregnant, you know.'

'What? She didn't tell me!'

'She was afraid to,' he said gently. 'She thought you might get mad at her and never want to speak to her again.'

'Well, it was stupid of her to think that,' Holly said angrily, and wiped her eyes aggressively.

'Oh really?' he raised his eyebrows. 'So what do you call all this, then?'

Holly looked away. 'I meant to call her, I really did. I picked up the phone every day but I just couldn't do it. Then I would say to myself that I'd call the next day and the next day I would be busy . . . Oh, I'm sorry, John. I'm truly happy for the both of you.'

'Thank you, but it's not me that needs to hear any of this, you know.'

'I know, but I've been so awful! She'll never forgive me now!'

'Don't be stupid, Holly. It's Sharon we're talking about here. It will all be forgotten about by tomorrow.'

Holly raised her eyebrows at him hopefully.

'Well, maybe not *tomorrow*. Next year, perhaps . . . and you'll owe her big time, but she'll eventually forgive you . . .' His icy eyes warmed and twinkled back at her.

'Stop it!' Holly giggled, hitting him on the arm. 'Can I go with you to see her?'

Butterflies fluttered in Holly's stomach as they pulled up outside the hospital. She spotted Sharon looking around as she stood alone outside, waiting to be collected. She looked so cute Holly had to smile. Sharon was going to be a mummy. Holly couldn't believe she was nearly five months pregnant. That meant Sharon had been three months pregnant when they went away on holiday and she hadn't said a

336

word! But, more importantly, Holly couldn't believe that she stupidly hadn't noticed the changes in her friend. Of course she wouldn't have had a bump at only three months but now, as she looked at her dressed in a polo neck and jeans, she could see the swelling of a tiny bump. And it suited her. Holly stepped out of the car and Sharon's face froze.

Oh no, Sharon was going to scream at her. She was going to tell her she hated her and that she never wanted to see her again and that she was a crappy friend and that . . .

Sharon's face broke into a smile and she held her arms out to her. 'Come here to me, you fool,' she said softly.

Holly ran into her arms. There, with her best friend hugging her tight, she felt the tears begin again. 'Oh, Sharon, I'm so sorry. I'm a horrible person. I'm so so so so sorry, please forgive me. I never meant to—'

'Oh, shut up, you whiner and hug me.' Sharon cried too, her voice cracking, and they squeezed each other for a long time.

'Ahem,' John cleared his throat loudly.

'Oh, come here you,' Holly smiled, and dragged him into their huddle.

'I presume this was your idea.' Sharon looked at her husband.

'No, not at all,' he said, winking at Holly. 'I just passed Holly on the street and told her I'd give her a lift . . .'

'Yeah right,' Sharon said, linking arms with Holly as they walked towards the car. 'Well, you certainly gave me a lift, anyway.' She smiled at her friend.

'So what did they say?' Holly asked, squeezing herself forward between the two front seats from the back of the car like an excited little child. 'What is it?'

'Well, you'll never believe this, Holly.' Sharon twisted round in her chair and matched her excitement. 'The doctor told me that . . . and I believe him because apparently he's one of the best . . . anyway, he told me—'

'Come on!' Holly urged her, dying to hear.

'He says it's a baby!'

Holly rolled her eyes. 'Ha-ha. What I mean is, is it a boy or a girl?'

'It's an it for now. They're not too sure yet.'

'Would you want to know what "it" is if they could tell you?'

Sharon scrunched her nose up. 'I don't know, actually. I haven't figured that out yet.' She looked across at John and they smiled excitedly at each other. They shared a secret smile.

A familiar pang of jealousy hit Holly and she sat quietly while she let it pass and the excitement returned.

The three of them headed back to Holly's house. She and Sharon weren't quite ready to leave each other again after just making up. They had so much to talk about. Sitting around Holly's kitchen table, they made up for lost time.

'Sharon, Holly went for a job interview today,' John said when he finally managed to get a word in edgeways.

'Ooh, really? I didn't know you were job-hunting already!'

'Gerry's new mission for me,' Holly smiled.

'Oh, was that what it was this month? I was just dying to know! So how did it go?'

Holly grimaced and held her head in her hands. 'Oh, it was awful, Sharon. I made a total fool of myself.'

'Really? What was the job?'

'Selling advertising space for that magazine, X.'

'Ooh, that's cool. I read that at work all the time.'

'Don't think I know that one; what kind of magazine is it?' John asked.

'It kind of has everything in it: fashion, sports, culture, food, reviews . . . everything really.'

'And adverts,' Holly joked.

'Well, it won't have such good adverts if Holly Kennedy isn't working for them,' Sharon said kindly.

'Thanks, but I really don't think I will be.'

'Why, what was so wrong with the interview? You can't have been that bad.' Sharon looked intrigued as she reached for the pot of tea.

'Oh, I think it's bad when the interviewer asks if you have any experience working on a magazine or newspaper and you tell him you once wrote a newsletter for a shitty company.'

Sharon burst out laughing. 'Newsletter? I hope you weren't referring to that crappy little leaflet that you printed up on the computer to advertise that dive of a company?'

John and Sharon howled with laughter.

'Ah well, it was *advertising* the company . . .' Holly trailed off, feeling even more embarrassed.

'Remember you made us all go out and post them around people's houses in the pissing rain and the freezing cold? It took us days to do!'

'Hey, I remember that,' John laughed. 'Remember you sent me and Gerry out to post hundreds of them one night?'

'Yeah?' Holly was almost afraid to hear what came next.

'Well, we shoved them in the skip at the back of Bob's pub and went in for a few pints.' He chuckled at the memory of it and Holly's jaw dropped.

'You sly little bastards!' she laughed. 'Because of you two the company went bust and I lost my job!'

'Oh, I'd say it went bust the minute people took a look at those leaflets, Holly,' Sharon teased. 'Anyway, that place was a kip. You used to moan about it every day.'

'Just one of the many jobs Holly moaned about,' John joked. But he was right.

'Yeah, well, I wouldn't have moaned about this one,' she said sadly.

'There's plenty more jobs out there,' Sharon reassured her. 'You just need to brush up your interview skills.'

'Tell me about it.' Holly stabbed away at the sugar bowl with a spoon.

They sat in silence for a while.

'You published a newsletter,' John repeated a few minutes later, still laughing at the thought of it.

'Shut up, you,' Holly cringed. 'Hey, what else did you and Gerry get up to that I don't know about?' Holly suddenly demanded.

'Ah, a true friend never reveals secrets,' John teased, and his eyes danced with the memories.

But something had been unlocked. And after Holly

340

and Sharon threatened to beat some stories out of him Holly learned things about her husband that night that she never knew before. For the first time since Gerry died, the three of them laughed and talked about him all night, and Holly finally learned how to talk about her husband without being sad. It used to be the four of them together: Holly, Gerry, Sharon and John. This time only three of them gathered to remember the one they had lost. With all their talk, he came alive for them all that night. And soon they would be four again, with the arrival of Sharon and John's baby.

Life went on.

Chapter Thirty-Six

That Sunday Richard called round to visit Holly with the kids. She had told him he was welcome to bring them by whenever it was his day with them so that they could give Holly and Richard's parents some peace and quiet in their own home for the day. They played outside in the garden while Richard and Holly finished off their dinner and watched them through the patio doors.

'They seem really happy, Richard,' Holly said, watching them playing.

'Yes, they do, don't they?' he smiled. 'I want things to be as normal for them as possible. They don't quite understand what's going on and it's quite difficult to explain.'

'What have you told them?'

'Oh, that Mummy and Daddy don't love each other any more and that I moved away so that we can all be happier. Something along those lines.'

'And they're OK with that?'

Her brother nodded slowly. 'Timothy is, but Emily is worried that we might stop loving her and that she will have to move away.' He glanced at Holly, his eyes sad.

Poor Emily, Holly thought, watching her dancing around with her scary-looking doll. She couldn't believe that she was having this conversation with Richard. He seemed to be a totally different person these days. Or perhaps it was Holly who had changed; she had a higher tolerance for him now, and found it easier to ignore his annoying little comments, though there were still many of them. But then again she and Richard now had something in common. They both understood what it was like to feel lonely and unsure of themselves.

'How's everything going at Mum and Dad's house?'

Richard swallowed a forkful of mashed potato and nodded. 'Good. They're being extremely generous.'

'Ciara bothering you at all?' Holly felt as if she was questioning her child after his first day of school, wanting to know if the other kids had bullied him. But lately she felt so protective of him. It helped her to help him; it gave her strength.

'Ciara is . . . Ciara,' he smiled. 'We don't see eye to eye on a lot of things.'

'Well, I wouldn't worry about that,' Holly said, trying to stab a piece of pork with her fork. 'The majority of the world wouldn't see eye to eye with her either.' Her fork finally made contact with the pork and she sent it flying off her plate and through the air where it landed on the kitchen counter on the far side of the room.

'And they say pigs don't fly,' Richard remarked.

Holly giggled. 'Hey, Richard, you made a funny!'

He looked pleased with himself. 'I have my moments too, I suppose,' he said, shrugging his shoulders.

343

'Although I'm sure you think I don't have many of them.'

Holly speared a carrot, put down her knife and fork and chewed slowly, trying to decide how to phrase what she was going to say. 'We're all different, Richard. Ciara is slightly eccentric, Declan is a dreamer, Jack is a joker, I'm . . . well, I don't know what I am. But you were always very controlled. Straight and serious. It's not necessarily a bad thing, we're all just different.'

'You're very thoughtful,' Richard said after a long silence.

'Pardon?' Holly asked, feeling confused. To cover her embarrassment she stuffed her face with another mouthful of food.

'I've always thought you were very thoughtful,' he repeated.

'When?' Holly asked incredulously, through her mouthful.

'Well, I wouldn't be sitting here eating dinner, with the kids running around having fun outside if you weren't thoughtful now, but I was actually referring to when we were children.'

'I don't think so, Richard. Me and Jack were always so awful to you,' she said softly.

'You weren't *always* awful, Holly.' He gave her an amused smile. 'Anyway, that's what brothers and sisters are for – to make each other's lives as difficult as possible as they grow up. It forms a great basis for life, toughens you up. Anyway, I was the bossy older brother.'

'So how does that make me thoughtful?' Holly asked, feeling she had completely missed the point.

'You idolised Jack. You used to follow him around all the time and you would do exactly what he told you to do.' He started laughing. 'I used to hear him telling you to say things to me and you would run into my room, terrified, and blurt them out and run away again.'

Holly looked at her plate, embarrassed. She and Jack used to play terrible tricks on Richard.

'But you always came back,' Richard continued. 'You would creep back into my room silently and watch me working at my desk and I knew that was your way of saying sorry.' He smiled at her. 'So that makes you thoughtful. None of our siblings had a conscience in that house of ours, not even me. You were the only one, always the sensitive one.'

He continued eating his dinner and Holly sat in silence, trying to absorb all he had said. She didn't remember idolising Jack but when she thought about it she supposed Richard was right. Jack was her funny, cool, good-looking big brother, who had loads of friends, and Holly used to beg him to let her play with them. She supposed she still felt that way about him. If he called her right now and asked her to go out she would drop everything and go and she had never even realised that before. However, she was spending far more time with Richard than with Jack these days. Jack had always been her favourite brother; Gerry had always got along with Jack the best. It was Jack that Gerry would choose to go out for drinks with during the week, not Richard; it was Jack that Gerry would insist on sitting beside at a family dinner. However, Gerry was gone, and although Jack rang her every now and then he wasn't around as much as he used to be. Had Holly put Jack up on too much of a pedestal? She realised then that she had been making excuses for him every time he didn't call round or phone her when he said he would. In fact, she had been making excuses for him ever since Gerry had died. Was it only their friendship with Gerry that they now had in common?

Richard had, lately, managed to give Holly a regular intake of food for thought. She watched him remove his serviette from his collar and was interested as he folded it into a neat little square with perfect right angles. He obsessively straightened everything on the table so that they were all facing the right way in an orderly fashion. For all Richard's good qualities, which she recognised now, Holly could not live with a man like that at all.

They both jumped as they heard a thump from outside and saw little Emily lying on the ground in floods of tears while a shocked-looking Timmy looked on. Richard leaped out of his chair and hurried outside.

'But she just fell, Daddy, I didn't do anything!' Holly heard Timmy plead with his father. Poor Timmy. She rolled her eyes as she watched Richard dragging him by the arm and ordering him to stand in the corner to think about what he had done. Some people would never really change, she thought wryly.

The next day Holly jumped around the house ecstatically as she replayed the message on the answering machine for the third time.

'Hi, Holly,' came the gruff voice. 'This is Chris

Feeney here from X. I'm just calling to say that I was very impressed with your interview. Em . . .' he stalled a bit, 'well, I wouldn't normally say this on an answering machine but no doubt you'll be delighted to know that I've decided to welcome you as a new member of the team. I would love you to start as soon as possible so call me on the usual number when you get a chance and we'll discuss it further. Em . . . goodbye.'

Holly rolled around her bed in terrified delight and pressed the play button again. She had shot for the moon . . . and now she had landed!

Chapter Thirty-Seven

Holly stared up at the tall Georgian building and her body tingled with excitement. It was her first day at work and she felt good times were ahead of her. The offices of X were situated in the centre of town, on the second floor, above a small café. Holly had got very little sleep last night, due to nerves and excitement. However, she didn't feel the same dread that she usually felt before starting a new job. She had phoned Chris back immediately (after listening to his voice message another three times) and then she had shared the news with her family and friends. They had been ecstatic, and just before she left the house this morning she had received a beautiful bouquet of flowers from her parents, congratulating her and wishing her luck on her first day.

She felt as though she was starting her first day at school and had gone shopping for a briefcase that made her look extra intelligent. But although she had felt excited when she had sat down to eat her breakfast, she had also felt sad. Sad that Gerry wasn't there to share her exciting new start. They had performed a little ritual every time Holly started a new job, which was quite a regular occurrence. Gerry would wake Holly up with breakfast in bed and then he would pack her bag with ham and cheese sandwiches, an apple, a packet of crisps and a bar of chocolate. Then he would drive her into work on her first day, call her on her lunch break to see if the other kids in the office were playing nicely and later return to collect her and bring her home. Then they would sit together over dinner and he would listen and laugh as Holly explained all the different characters in her office and once again grumble about how much she hated going to work. Mind you, they only ever did that on her first day. Every other day they would tumble out of bed late, race each other to the shower and then wander around the kitchen half-asleep, grumbling while they each grabbed a quick cup of coffee to help kick-start their day. They would give each other a kiss goodbye and go their separate ways. And then they would start all over again the next day. If Holly had known their time was to be so short, she wouldn't have bothered carrying out all those tedious routines . . .

This morning, however, had been a very different scenario. She awoke to an empty house in an empty bed to no breakfast in bed. She didn't have to fight for her right to use the shower first and the kitchen was quiet without the sound of Gerry's fits of morning sneezes. She had allowed herself to imagine that when she woke up Gerry would be miraculously there to greet her because it was tradition, and such a special day that it wouldn't feel right without him. But with death there were no exceptions. Gone meant gone.

Now, poised at the entrance, Holly checked herself to see that her fly wasn't undone, her jacket wasn't tucked into her knickers and that her shirt buttons were fastened properly. Satisfied that she looked presentable she made her way up the wooden staircase to her new office. She entered the waiting room area and the secretary she recognised from the interview came from behind the desk to meet her.

'Hi, Holly,' she said, shaking her hand. 'Welcome to our humble abode.' She held her hands up to display the room. Holly had liked this woman from the moment she had met her at the interview. She looked about the same age as Holly and had long blonde hair and a face that seemed to be always smiling.

'I'm Alice, by the way, and I work out here in reception, as you know. Well, I'll bring you to the boss man now. He's waiting for you.'

'God, I'm not late, am I?' Holly asked worriedly, glancing at her watch. She had left the house early to beat the traffic.

'No, not at all,' Alice said, leading her down to Mr Feeney's office. 'Don't mind Chris and all the other lot, they're all workaholics. They need to get themselves a life, bless them. You wouldn't see me hanging around here anytime after six, that's for sure.'

Holly laughed. Alice reminded her of her former self.

'By the way, don't feel that you have to come in early and stay late just because they do. I think Chris actually lives in his office so you'll never compete with that. The man isn't normal,' she said loudly, tapping on his door and leading her in.

'Who's not normal?' Chris asked gruffly, standing up from his chair and stretching.

'You,' Alice smiled, and closed the door behind her.

'See how my staff treat me?' Chris said, holding out his hand to greet Holly. His handshake was once again warm and welcoming, and Holly felt immediately at ease by the atmosphere between the workers.

'Thank you for hiring me, Mr Feeney,' Holly said genuinely.

'You can call me Chris, and there's no need to thank me. Right, why don't you follow me and I'll show you around the place.' He led her down the hall. The walls were covered with the framed front covers of every copy of X that had been published in the last twenty years.

'There's not much to the place. In here is our office of little ants.' He pushed open the door and Holly looked into the huge office. There were about ten desks in all, and the room was packed with people all sitting in front of their computers and talking on the phone. They looked up and waved politely. Holly smiled at them all, remembering how important first impressions were. 'These are the wonderful journalists that help pay my bills,' Chris explained. 'That's John-Paul, the fashion editor, Mary, our food woman, and Brian, Sean, Gordon, Aishling and Tracey. You don't need to know what they do, they're just wasters.' He laughed and one of the men stuck his fingers up at Chris and continued talking on the phone.

'The rest of the journalists are freelancers so you won't see them hanging around these offices much,' Chris explained, leading her to the room next door.

351

'This is where all our computer nerds hide. That's Dermot and Wayne and they're in charge of layout and design so you'll be working closely with them and keeping them informed about what advertisements are going where. Lads, this is Holly.'

'Hi, Holly.' They both stood up and shook her hand, and then continued working on their computers again.

'I have them well trained,' Chris remarked, and headed back out to the hall again. 'Down here is the boardroom. We have meetings every morning at eight forty-five.'

Holly nodded to everything he was saying, trying to remember all the names.

'Down those steps are the toilets and I'll show you your office now.'

He headed back down the way they had come and Holly glanced at the walls, feeling excited. This was nothing like she had ever experienced before.

'In here is your office,' he said, pushing the door open and allowing her to walk in ahead of him.

Holly couldn't stop herself from smiling as she looked around at the small room. She had never had her own office before. It was just big enough to fit a desk and filing cabinet in but it was hers. There was a computer sitting on the desk with piles and piles of folders. Opposite the desk was a bookcase crammed with books, yet more folders and stacks of old magazines. The huge Georgian window practically covered the entire back wall behind her desk, and although it was cold and windy outside, the room had a bright and airy feel to it. She could definitely see herself working here.

'It's perfect,' she told Chris, placing her briefcase on the desk and looking around.

'Good,' Chris said. 'The last guy who was here was extremely organised, and all those folders there will explain very clearly what exactly it is you need to do. If you have any problems or any questions about anything at all just come ask me. I'm right next door.' He knocked on the wall that separated their offices.

'Now I'm not expecting miracles from you because I know you're new to this, which is why I expect you to ask lots of questions. Our next edition is due out on the first day of the month.'

Holly's eyes widened: she had a fortnight to fill an entire magazine.

'Don't worry,' he smiled again. 'I want you to concentrate on November's edition. Familiarise yourself with the layout of the magazine. We stick to the same style every month so you will know what kind of pages will need what type of advertisements. This is a lot of work for one person but if you keep yourself organised everything will run smoothly. Speak to Dermot and Wayne and they'll fill you in on the standard layout and if you need anything done just ask Alice. She's there to help everyone.' He stopped talking and looked around. 'So that's about it. Any questions?'

Holly shook her head, 'No, I think you covered just about everything.'

'Right, I'll leave you to it so.' He backed out of the room slowly but paused before closing the door. He watched her surveying the room with satisfaction. 'Holly, I hired you because you seem like a very determined young woman.'

Holly nodded confidently, assuring him he was right.

'I know a hard worker when I see one, haven't been wrong yet.' He gave a small encouraging smile and closed the door softly behind him. Holly immediately sat down at her new desk in her new office, anxious to settle in as quickly as possible. She was slightly scared of her new life. This was the most impressive job she had ever had, and by the sounds of things she was going to be extremely busy, but she was glad. She needed to keep her mind occupied. However, there was no way on earth she had remembered everyone's names so she took out her notepad and pen and wrote down the ones she knew. She opened the folders and got to work.

She was so engrossed in her reading that she realised after a while that she had worked through her lunch break. By the sounds of things, no one else from the office had budged an inch. In her other jobs, Holly would stop working at least half an hour before lunchtime just to think about what she was going to eat. Then she would leave fifteen minutes early and return fifteen minutes late due to 'traffic', even though she would walk to the shop. Holly would daydream the majority of the day, make personal phone calls, especially abroad, because she didn't have to pay the bill, and would be first in queue to collect her monthly pay cheque, which was usually spent within two weeks.

Yes, this was very different from her previous jobs, but she was looking forward to every minute of it.

* * *

'Right, Ciara, are you sure you've got your passport?' Elizabeth asked her daughter for the third time since leaving the house.

'Yes, Mum,' Ciara groaned. 'I told you a million billion times, it's right here.'

'Show me,' Elizabeth said, twisting round in the passenger seat.

'No! I'm not showing it to you. You should just take my word for it. I'm not a baby any more, you know.'

Declan snorted and Ciara elbowed him in the ribs. 'Shut up, you.'

'Ciara, just show Mum the passport so you can put her mind at rest,' Holly said tiredly.

'Fine,' she huffed, lifting her bag onto her lap. 'It's in here, look, Mum . . . no, hold on, actually it's in here . . . no, actually maybe I put it in here . . . oh fuck!'

'Jesus Christ, Ciara,' Holly's dad grumbled, slamming on the brakes and turning the car round.

'What?' she said defensively. 'I put it in here, Dad. Someone must have taken it out,' she grumbled, emptying the contents of her bag in the car.

'Bloody hell, Ciara,' Holly moaned as a pair of knickers went flying over her face.

'Ah, shut up,' Ciara grumbled again. 'You won't have to put up with me for much longer.'

Everyone in the car went silent as they realised that was true. Ciara would be in Australia for God only knew how long, and they would all miss her, loud and irritating though she was.

Holly sat squashed beside the window in the back

355

seat of the car with Declan and Ciara as their dad drove them all to the airport to say their goodbyes. Again. Richard was driving Mathew and Jack (ignoring his protestations), and they were probably already at the airport by now. This was their second time returning to the house as Ciara had forgotten her lucky nose ring and had demanded that the car be turned round.

An hour after setting off they reached the airport in what should have only been a twenty-minute drive.

'Jesus, what took you so long?' Jack moaned to Holly when they all finally trudged into the airport with long faces on them. 'I was stuck talking to Dick all on my own.'

'Oh, give it a rest, Jack,' Holly said defensively. 'He's not that bad.'

'Ooh, you've changed your tune,' he teased, his face all mock-surprise.

'No I haven't, you're just singing the wrong song,' she snapped, and walked over to Richard, who was standing alone, watching the world go by. She smiled at her elder brother.

'Pet, keep in touch with us a lot more this time, won't you?' Elizabeth pleaded with her daughter as she hugged her.

'Of course I will, Mum. Oh, please don't cry or you'll get me started too.'

A lump formed in Holly's throat and she fought back the tears. Ciara had been good company over the last few months and had always succeeded in cheering Holly up when she felt that life just couldn't be worse. She would miss her sister, but she understood

356

that she needed to be with Mathew. He was a nice guy and she was happy that they had found each other.

'Take care of my sister.' Holly stood on the tips of her toes to hug the enormous Mathew.

'Don't worry, she's in good hands,' he smiled.

'Look after her now, won't you?' Frank smacked him on the back and smiled.

Mathew was intelligent enough to know it was more of a warning than a question and gave him a very persuasive answer.

'Bye, Richard,' Ciara said, giving him a big hug. 'Stay away from that Meredith bitch now. You're far too good for her.' Ciara turned to Declan. 'You can come over anytime you like, Dec, maybe make a movie or something about me,' she said seriously, giving him a big hug.

'Jack, look after my big sis,' she said, smiling at Holly. 'Ooh, I'm gonna miss you,' she added sadly, squeezing Holly tightly.

'Me too.' Holly's voice shook. She knew it was best for her sister to go, but they had become so close in recent months that a part of Holly wished she would stay.

'OK I'm going now before all you depressing people make me cry,' she said, trying to sound happy.

'Don't go using those rope jumps again, Ciara. They're far too dangerous,' Frank said, looking worried.

'Bungee jumps, Dad!' Ciara laughed, kissing him and her mother on the cheeks again. 'Don't worry, I'm sure I'll find something new to try,' she teased.

Holly stood in silence with her family and watched

as Ciara and Mathew walked hand in hand through the boarding gate. Even Declan had a tear in his eye, but pretended his eyes were watering because he was about to sneeze.

'Just look at the lights, Declan.' Jack threw his arm around his baby brother. 'They say that helps you sneeze.'

Declan stared up at the lights and avoided watching his favourite sister walking away. Frank held his wife close to him as she waved, while tears rolled down her cheeks.

They all laughed as the alarm went off as Ciara walked through the security scanner and was ordered to empty her pockets, followed by a frisk.

'Every bloody time,' Jack laughed. 'It's a wonder they agreed to let her into the country at all.'

They all waved goodbye as Ciara and Mathew walked on and her pink hair was eventually lost among the crowd.

'OK,' Elizabeth said, wiping the tears from her face, 'why don't the rest of my babies come back to the house and we can all have lunch?'

They all agreed, seeing how upset their mother was.

'I'll let you go with Richard this time,' Jack said smartly to Holly, and wandered off with the rest of the family, leaving Richard and Holly standing there slightly taken aback.

'So how was your first week at work, darling?' Elizabeth asked Holly as they all sat around the table eating lunch.

'Oh, I love it, Mum,' Holly said, and her eyes lit

up. 'It's so much more interesting and challenging than any other job I've done, and all the staff are just so friendly. There's a great atmosphere in the place.'

'Well, that's the most important thing, isn't it?' Frank said, pleased. 'What's your boss like?'

'He's such a doll. He reminds me so much of you, Dad, I just feel like giving him a big hug and a kiss every time I see him.'

'Sounds like sexual harassment in the workplace to me,' Declan joked, and Jack sniggered.

Holly rolled her eyes at her brothers.

'Are you doing any new documentaries this year, Declan?' Jack asked.

'Yeah, on homelessness,' he said with his mouth full of food.

'Declan,' Elizabeth scrunched up her nose at him, 'don't talk with your mouth full.'

'Sorry,' Declan said, and spat the food out on the table.

Jack burst out laughing, while the rest of the family looked away in disgust.

'What did you say you were doing, son?' Frank asked, trying to avoid a family fight.

'I'm doing a documentary on homelessness this year for college.'

'Oh, very good,' he replied, retreating back to a world of his own.

'What member of the family are you using as your subject this time? Richard?' Jack said slyly.

Holly slammed down her knife and fork.

'That's not funny, man,' Declan said seriously, surprising Holly.

'God, why is everyone so touchy these days?' Jack asked, looking around. 'It was just a joke.'

'It wasn't funny, Jack,' Elizabeth said sternly.

'What did he say?' Frank asked his wife after snapping out of his trance.

Elizabeth just shook her head dismissively and he knew not to ask again.

Holly watched Richard, who sat at the end of the table eating quietly. Her heart leaped out to him. He didn't deserve this, and either Jack was being more cruel than usual, or else this was the norm and Holly must have been a fool to have found it funny.

'Sorry, Richard, I was just joking,' Jack said.

'That's OK, Jack.'

'So have you found a job yet?'

'No, not yet.'

'That's a shame,' he said drily, and Holly glared at him. What the hell was his problem?

'Oh, Jack,' Holly sighed, slicing into her chicken breast, 'you really do need to grow up, you know.'

Jack finished his beer and glared at her.

Elizabeth calmly picked up her cutlery and plate of food without a word to anyone and made her way into the living room where she turned the television on and ate her dinner in peace.

Her 'funny little elves' weren't making her laugh any more.

Chapter Thirty-Eight

Holly drummed her fingers on her desk and stared out the window. She was absolutely flying through her work this week. She didn't know it was possible to actually *enjoy* work so much. She had happily sat through lunch breaks and had even stayed late, and didn't feel like punching any of her fellow employees in the face yet. But it was only her third week, after all; give her time. The office had developed a light-hearted banter and she would often hear people screaming at each other from office to office. It was all in good humour and she loved it.

She loved feeling that she was a part of the team; as though she were actually doing something that made a huge impact on the finished product. She thought of Gerry every single day when she was at work. Every time she made a deal she thanked him, thanked him for pushing her all the way to the top. She still had her miserable days when she didn't feel worthy of getting out of bed, of course. But the excitement of her job spurred her on.

She heard the radio in Chris's office next door and she smiled. On the hour every hour without fail he turned on the news. And all the news seeped into Holly's brain subconsciously. She had never felt so intelligent in her life.

'Hey!' Holly yelled, banging on the wall. 'Turn that thing down! Some of us are trying to work!'

She heard him chuckle and she smiled. She glanced back down at her work again; a freelancer had written an article on how he had travelled around Ireland trying to find the cheapest pint and it was very amusing. There was a huge gap at the bottom of the page and it was up to Holly to fill it. She flicked through her book of contacts and an idea came to her immediately. She picked up the phone and dialled.

'Hogan's.'

'Hi, Daniel Connolly, please.'

'One moment.'

Bloody 'Greensleeves' again. She put it on speaker phone and danced around the room to the music while she waited. Chris walked in, took one look at her and closed the door again. Holly smiled.

'Hello?'

'Daniel?'

'Yes.'

'Hiya, it's Holly.'

'How are you doin', Holly?'

'I'm grand thanks, you?'

'Couldn't be better.'

'That's a nice complaint.'

He laughed. 'How's that snazzy job of yours?'

'Well, actually that's why I'm calling.' Holly sounded guilty.

'Oh no!' he laughed. 'I have made it company policy not to employ any more Kennedys here.'

Holly giggled. 'Oh damn and I was so looking forward to throwing drinks over the customers.'

He laughed. 'So what's up?'

'Do I remember hearing you say you needed to advertise Club Diva more?' Well, he had actually thought that he was saying it to Sharon, but she knew he wouldn't remember that minor detail.

'I do recall saying that, yes.'

'Good, well, how would you like to advertise it in X?'

'Is that the name of the magazine you work on?'

'No, I just thought it would be an interesting question, that's all,' she joked. 'Of course it's where I work!'

'Oh, *of course*, I'd forgotten. That's the magazine that has the offices just round the corner from me. The one that causes you to walk by my front door everyday and yet you still don't call in. Why don't I see you at lunchtime?' he teased. 'Isn't my pub good enough for you?'

'Oh, everyone here eats their lunch at their desks,' she explained. 'So what do you think?'

'I think that's very boring of you all.'

'No, I mean what do you think about the ad?'

'Yeah, sure, that's a good idea.'

'OK, well, I'll put it in the November issue. Would you like it placed monthly?'

'Would you like to tell me how much that would set me back?' he laughed.

Holly totted up the figures and told him.

363

'Hmm . . .' he said, 'I'll have to think about it, but I'll definitely go for the November edition.'

'Oh, that's great! You'll be a millionaire after this goes to print.'

'I'd better be,' he laughed. 'By the way, there's a launch party for some new drink coming up the week after next. Will I put your name down for an invite?'

'Yeah, that would be great. What new drink is it?'

'Blue Rock. It's a new alcopop that's apparently going to be huge. Tastes like shite but it's free all night so I'll buy the rounds.'

'Wow, you're such a good advertisement for it,' she laughed. 'When is it on?' She took out her diary and made a note of it. 'That's perfect. I can come straight after work.'

'Well, make sure you bring your bikini to work in that case.'

'Make sure I bring my *what?*'

'Your bikini,' he laughed. 'The launch has a beach theme.'

'But it's nearly winter, you nutter.'

'Hey, it wasn't my idea. The slogan is, "Blue Rock, the hot new drink for winter".'

'Uugghh, how tacky.'

'And messy. We're getting sand thrown all over the floor, which will be a nightmare to clean up. Anyway, listen, I'd better get back to work. We're mad busy today.'

'OK, thanks, Daniel. Have a think about what you want your ad to say and get back to me.'

'Will do.'

She stood up and went next door to Chris's office, a thought occurring to her.

'You finished dancing in there?' he chuckled.

'Yeah, I just made up a routine. Came in to show you,' she joked.

'What's the problem?' he said.

'No problem; just an idea.'

'Take a seat.' He nodded to the chair in front of him. Just three weeks ago she had sat there for an interview and now here she was putting ideas forward to her new boss. Funny how life changed so quickly – but then again she had learned that already . . .

'What's the idea?'

'Well, you know Hogan's, round the corner?'

Chris nodded.

'I was just on to the owner and he's going to place an ad in the magazine.'

'That's great, but I hope you don't tell me about every time you fill a space, we could be here all year.'

Holly rolled her eyes. 'That's not it, Chris. Anyway, he was telling me that they're having a launch party on Tuesday week for a new drink called Blue Rock. It has a beach theme, all the staff will be in bikinis and that kind of thing.'

'In autumn?' He raised his eyebrows.

'It's apparently the hot new drink for winter.'

He rolled his eyes. 'Tacky.'

Holly smiled. 'That's what I said. Anyway, I just thought it might be worth covering. I know we're supposed to raise ideas in the meetings but this is happening pretty soon.'

'I understand. That's a great idea, Holly. I'll get one of the lads on to it.'

Holly smiled and stood up from her chair. 'By the way, did you get that garden sorted yet?'

Chris frowned. 'I've had about ten different people come down to look at it. They tell me it'll cost six grand to do.'

'That's a lot of money.'

'Well, it's a big garden. A lot of work needs to be done.'

'What was the cheapest quote?'

'Five and a half grand, why?'

'Because my brother will do it for five,' she blurted out.

'Five?' his eyes nearly popped out of his head. 'Is he any good?'

'Remember I told you my garden was a jungle?'

He nodded.

'Well, no longer. He did a great job on it but the only thing is that he works alone so it takes him longer.'

'For that price I don't care how long it takes. Have you got his business card with you?'

'Eh . . . yeah, hold on and I'll get it.' She stole some impressive-looking card-like paper from Alice's desk, typed up Richard's name and mobile number in a fancy typeface and printed it out, cutting the card into a small rectangle shape.

'That's great,' Chris said, reading it. 'I'll give him a call now.'

'No, no,' Holly said quickly, 'you'll get him easier after the weekend. He's up to his eyeballs today.'

'Right so; thanks, Holly.' She started to head towards the door and stopped when he called out to her, 'Oh, by the way, how are you at writing?'

'It was one of the subjects I learned at school.'

Chris laughed. 'Are you still on that level?'

'Well, I'm sure I could purchase a thesaurus.'

'Good, because I need you to cover that launch thing.'

'Oh?'

'I can't get any of the others – they've already got events to cover that evening – and I can't go to it myself so I have to rely on you.' He shuffled some papers on his desk. 'I'll send one of the photographers down with you; get a few shots of the sand and the bikinis.'

'Oh . . . OK.' Holly's heart raced.

'How does eight hundred words sound?'

Impossible, she thought. As far as she knew she only had fifty words in her vocabulary. 'That's no problem,' she said confidently, and backed out the door.

Shit shit shit shit, she thought; how on earth was she going to pull this one off? She couldn't even spell properly.

She picked up the phone and pressed redial.

'Hogan's.'

'Daniel Connolly, please.'

'One moment.'

'Don't put me on . . . !'

'Greensleeves' started.

' . . . Hold,' she finished.

'Hello?'

'Daniel, it's me,' she said quickly.

'Would you ever leave me alone?' he teased.

'No, I need help.'

'I know you do, but I'm not qualified for that,' he laughed.

'No, seriously, I mentioned that launch to my editor and he wants to cover it.'

'Oh, brilliant. You can forget about that ad so!' he laughed.

'No, not brilliant. He wants *me* to write it.'

'That's great news, Holly.'

'No it's not. I can't write,' she panicked.

'Oh really? That was one of the main subjects in my school.'

'Oh, Daniel, please be serious for a minute . . .'

'OK, what do you want me to do?'

'I need you to tell me absolutely everything you know about this drink and the launch so I can start writing it now and have a few days to work on it.'

'Yes, just one minute, sir,' he yelled away from the phone. 'Look, Holly, I really have to get back to work now.'

'Please,' she whimpered.

'OK, listen, what time do you finish work?'

'Six.' She crossed her fingers and prayed for him to help her.

'Why don't you come around here then, and I'll take you somewhere to have a bite?'

'Oh, thank you so much, Daniel,' and she jumped around her office with relief. 'You're a star!'

She hung up the phone and breathed a sigh of relief. Maybe there was a chance she could get the article done after all, and still manage to keep her job. Then she froze as she went back over the conversation in her head.

Had she just agreed to go on a date with Daniel?

Chapter Thirty Nine

Holly couldn't concentrate during the last hour of work; she kept on watching the clock, willing the time to go more slowly. For once it was doing the exact opposite. Why didn't it go this fast when she was waiting to open her messages from Gerry? She was dreading her dinner with Daniel before then.

At six o'clock on the dot she heard Alice switch off her computer and clatter down the wooden stairs to freedom. Holly smiled, remembering how she had once felt the same. But then again everything was different when you had a beautiful husband to go home to. If she still had Gerry she would be racing Alice out the door.

She listened as a few of the others packed up their things, and prayed Chris would dump another load of work on her desk just so she would have to stay late and cancel dinner with Daniel. She and Daniel had been out together millions of times, so why was she worrying now? They were the 'two single friends', and every time somebody had a dinner party or arranged a night out the two of them had always been invited to keep each other company, as though they were unable to

369

speak to the other couples at the table. It seemed that people felt that if they invited Daniel, they must invite Holly too. And although they had spent most of the evenings monopolising each other, they had always been in others' company. But something was niggling at the back of Holly's mind. There had been something in his voice that worried her, and something had happened to her stomach earlier when they spoke that made her feel uneasy about meeting up with him. She felt so guilty and ashamed for going out with him and tried to convince herself it was just a business dinner. In fact, the more she thought about it she realised that was exactly what it was. She smiled as she thought about how she had become one of those people who discussed business over dinner. Usually the only business she discussed over food was men and life in general with Sharon and Denise – girls' business.

She shut down her computer and packed her brief-case. Everything she did was in slow motion, as though that would prevent her from having to have dinner with Daniel. She hit herself over the head . . . it was a *business* dinner.

'Hey, don't beat yourself up about it.' Alice leaned in through Holly's door.

Holly jumped with fright. 'Jesus, Alice, I didn't see you there.'

'Everything OK?'

'Yeah,' she said unconvincingly, 'I just have to do something that I really don't want to do. But I kind of want to do it, which makes me not want to do it even more because it seems so wrong even though it's right. You know?'

Alice was staring at her with wide eyes. 'I thought *I* overanalysed things.'

'Oh, don't mind me,' Holly perked up. 'I'm just going nuts.'

'It happens to the best of us.'

'What are you doing back here?' Holly asked, realising she had heard her colleague legging it out the door earlier. 'Does freedom not beckon you?'

'I know,' Alice rolled her eyes, 'but I forgot we had a meeting at six.'

'Oh.' Holly was disappointed. Nobody had told her about any meeting today, which wasn't unusual, because she wasn't required to be at all of them. But it was unusual for Alice to attend one without Holly being asked.

'Is it about anything interesting?' Holly poked around for information, trying to sound uninterested while she busied herself at her desk.

'It's the astrology meeting.'

'Astrology?'

'Yeah, we have it monthly.'

'Oh, am I supposed to be there or am I not invited to it?' She tried not to sound bitter but failed miserably, much to her embarrassment.

Alice laughed. 'Of course you're welcome to come, Holly. I was just about to ask you, which is why I'm standing outside your office.'

Holly put her briefcase down, feeling stupid, and followed Alice into the boardroom where everybody was waiting.

'Everyone, this is Holly's first astrology meeting so let's make her feel welcome,' Alice announced.

Holly took her seat while they all applauded their new member at the table.

Chris rolled his eyes at Holly. 'Holly, I just want you to know in advance that I have absolutely nothing to do with this nonsense and also to apologise to you for being dragged into it.'

'Oh, shut up, Chris,' Tracey waved a hand at her boss, taking her seat at the head of the table, clutching a notepad and pen. 'OK, who wants to go first this month?'

'Let Holly go first,' Alice said generously.

Holly looked around completely baffled. 'But I don't have a clue what's going on.'

'Well, what star sign are you?' Tracey asked.

'Taurus.'

Everyone oohed and aahed and Chris held his head in his hands and tried to look like he wasn't enjoying himself.

'Ooh, great,' Tracey said happily. 'We've never had a Taurus before. OK, so are you married or seeing anyone or single or anything?'

Holly blushed as Brian winked over at her and Chris smiled encouragingly. He was the only one at the table who knew about Gerry. Holly realised this was the first time she had had to answer this question since Gerry died, and she was confused as to how to answer. 'Em . . . no, I'm not really seeing anyone but . . .'

'OK then,' Tracey said, starting to write. 'This month Taurus shall look out for someone tall, dark and handsome and . . .' she shrugged and looked up, 'anybody?'

'Because he will have a big impact on her future,' Alice helped out.

Brian winked at Holly again, obviously finding it very amusing that he was also tall and dark, but quite obviously blind if he thought he was handsome. Holly shuddered and he looked away.

'OK, the career stuff is easy,' Tracey continued. 'So Taurus will be occupied and satisfied by a new workload that comes their way. Lucky day will be a . . .' she thought for a while, 'Tuesday, and lucky colour is . . . blue,' she decided, looking at the colour of Holly's top. 'Right, who's next?'

'Hold on a minute, is this my horoscope for next month?' Holly interrupted, shocked.

Everyone around the table laughed.

'Have we shattered your dreams?' Gordon teased.

'Completely,' she said. 'I love reading my horoscopes. Please tell me this isn't what all magazines do?' she pleaded.

Chris shook his head, 'No, not all magazines do it like this, Holly. Some of them just hire people who have the talent to make it up themselves without involving the rest of the office.' He glared at Tracey.

'Ha-ha, Chris,' she said drily.

'So, Tracey, you're not psychic?' Holly asked sadly.

Tracey shook her head. 'No, not psychic, but I'm good as an agony aunt and at making up crossword puzzles, thank you very much.' She glared at Chris, and he mouthed the word 'wow' at her.

'Ah, you've all ruined it for me now,' Holly laughed, and sat back in her chair, feeling deflated.

'OK, Chris, you're next. This month Gemini will

overwork themselves, never leave their office and eat junk food all the time. They need to find some sort of balance in their lives.'

Chris rolled his eyes. 'You write that every month, Tracey.'

'Well, until you change your lifestyle, I can't change what Gemini will do, can I?'

They went through everyone's star sign and Tracey finally gave in to Brian's demands that Leo be desired by the opposite sex all month and win the lottery. Hmm . . . wonder what star sign Brian was. Holly looked at her watch and realised she was very late for her business meeting with Daniel.

'Oh sorry, everybody, I have to rush off,' she said, excusing herself from the table.

'Your tall, dark and handsome man awaits you,' Alice giggled. 'Send him on to me if you don't want him.'

Holly headed outside and her heart beat wildly as she spotted Daniel walking down the road to meet her. The cool autumn months had arrived, so Daniel was back wearing his black leather jacket again, teamed with blue jeans. His dark hair was messy and stubble lined his chin. He had that just-out-of-bed look. Holly's stomach lurched again and she looked away.

'Ooh, I told you!' Tracey said excitedly, as she walked out the door behind Holly and hurried off down the road happily.

'I'm so sorry Daniel,' Holly apologised. 'I got tied up in a meeting and I couldn't call.'

'Don't worry about it, I'm sure it was important,' he smiled at her, and she instantly felt guilty. This was

Daniel, her friend, not someone she should be avoiding. What on earth was wrong with her?

'So where would you like to go?' he asked.

'How about in there?' Holly said, looking at the small café on the ground floor of her office building. She wanted to go to the least intimate and most casual place possible.

Daniel scrunched up his nose. 'I'm a bit hungrier than that, if you don't mind. I haven't eaten all day.'

They walked along together and Holly pointed out every single café along the way, which Daniel shook his head at every time. Eventually he settled on an Italian restaurant that Holly couldn't say no to. Not because she wanted to go in but because he had said no to every other restaurant on the road.

Inside it was quiet with just a few tables occupied by couples staring lovingly into each other's eyes in the candlelight. Daniel stood up to take his jacket off and Holly quickly blew out the candle on their table when he wasn't looking. He was dressed in a deep blue shirt, highlighting the colour of his eyes and making them seem luminous in the dim restaurant.

'They make you sick, don't they?' Daniel laughed, following Holly's gaze to a couple on the far side of the room, who were holding hands across the table.

'Actually no. They make me sad.'

Daniel hadn't heard her, as he was busy reading the menu. 'What are you having?'

'I'm going to have a Caesar salad.'

Daniel rolled his eyes, 'You women and your salads. Aren't you hungry?'

'Not really.' She shook her head, then blushed as her stomach grumbled loudly.

'I think somebody disagrees with you down there,' he laughed. 'I don't think you ever eat, Holly Kennedy.'

Just not when I'm with you, she thought. 'I just don't have a very big appetite, that's all.'

'Yeah, well, I've seen rabbits eat more than you do,' he laughed.

Holly tried to control the conversation, steering it into safe territory, and they spent the evening talking about the launch party. She wasn't in the mood for discussing their private feelings and thoughts tonight; she wasn't even sure what exactly they were right then. Daniel had kindly brought a copy of the press release so that Holly could look through it in advance and get to work on the article as soon as possible. He also gave her a list of phone numbers for the people who worked at Blue Rock so that Holly could get a few quotes. He was extremely helpful, giving her tips on what angle to take and who to talk to for more information. She was now feeling a lot less panicked about having to write an article – however, a little more panicked about why she had been so uncomfortable with a man that she was certain only wanted to be her friend. She was also still starving, having only eaten a few lettuce leaves.

She stepped outside of the restaurant for a breath of fresh air while Daniel paid the bill. He was an extremely generous man, there was no denying that, and she was glad of his friendship. It just didn't feel quite right for her to be eating in an intimate restaurant with anyone other than Gerry.

She froze and tried to hide her face as she spotted a couple walking towards her who she really did not wish to see. She bent over to pretend to tie her shoelace until she realised she had worn her zip-up boots that day and ended up embarrassingly fumbling with the ends of her trousers.

'Holly, is that you?' she heard the familiar voice. She stared at the two pairs of shoes standing in front of her and slowly looked up to meet their eyes.

'Hello, there!' She tried to sound surprised while nervously steadying herself to her feet.

'How are you?' the woman asked, giving her a hug. 'What are you doing standing out here in the cold?'

Holly prayed that Daniel stayed inside for another while longer. 'Oh, you know . . . I was just having a bite to eat,' she smiled shakily, pointing at the restaurant.

'Oh, we're just about to go in there,' the man said smiling. 'It's a shame we just missed you; we could have eaten together.'

'Yes, yes, it's a shame . . .'

'Well, good for you, anyway,' the woman said, patting her on the back. 'It's good to get out and to do things on your own.'

'Well, actually . . .' Holly glanced at the door again, praying that it wouldn't open. 'Yes, it's nice to do that . . .' she trailed off.

'There you are!' Daniel said, stepping outside. 'I thought you had run off on me.' He wrapped his arm loosely round her shoulders.

Holly smiled at him weakly and turned to face the couple.

'Oh, sorry, I didn't see you there,' Daniel smiled, turning to face them.

The couple stared back at him stonily.

'Eh . . . Daniel, this is Judith and Harold. Gerry's parents.'

Chapter Forty

Holly pressed down on her car horn heavily and cursed the driver in front of her. She was fuming. She was mad at herself for being caught in such a situation last night. She was mad at herself for feeling that she *had* been caught in a bad situation when really there was nothing to it. But she was even angrier at herself for feeling like there was more to it because she had really enjoyed Daniel's company all evening. And she shouldn't be enjoying herself because it didn't feel right, but it had felt so right at the time . . .

She held her hand up to her head and massaged her temples. She had a headache and she was over-analysing things again, and the stupid traffic all the way home was driving her insane. Poor Daniel, she thought sadly. Gerry's parents had been so rude to him and had ended the conversation abruptly and charged into the restaurant, refusing to make eye contact with Holly. Oh, why did they have to see her the one time she was happy? They could have come round to the house any day of the week to see her feeling so miserable and living the perfect grieving widow life. But they hadn't and now they probably thought she was having a great life without their son. Well, screw them, she thought angrily, pushing down on the horn again. Why did it always take people five minutes to move from the traffic lights when they went green?

She had to wait at every single set of traffic lights she came across when all she wanted to do was to go home and throw a tantrum. She picked up her mobile while she waited and called Sharon, knowing she would understand.

'Hello?'

'Hi, John, it's Holly. Can I speak to Sharon?'

'Sorry, Holly, she's asleep. I would wake her for you but she's been absolutely exhausted—'

'No, don't worry,' she interrupted. 'I'll call her tomorrow.'

'Is it important?' he asked, worried.

'No,' she said quietly, 'it's not important at all.' She hung up and immediately dialled Denise's number.

'Hello?' Denise giggled.

'Hiya,' Holly said.

'Are you OK?' Denise giggled again. 'Tom, stop!' she whispered, and Holly realised she had called at a bad time.

'Yeah, I'm fine. I just called for a chat but I can hear you're busy there.' She forced a laugh.

'OK then, I'll call tomorrow, Hol,' Denise replied.

'OK, b—' Holly didn't even get to finish her sentence as Denise had hung up.

She sat at the traffic lights, lost in thought until loud beeps behind her caused her to jump.

She decided to go to her parents' house and talk to Ciara. She would cheer her up. Just as she pulled up outside the house, she remembered Ciara was no longer there and her eyes filled with tears. Once again she had nobody.

She rang the doorbell anyway and Declan answered.

'What's wrong with you?'

'Nothing,' she said, feeling sorry for herself. 'Where's Mum?'

'In the kitchen with Dad talking to Richard. I'd leave them alone for a bit.'

'Oh . . . OK . . .' she felt lost. 'What are you up to?'

'I'm just watching what I filmed today.'

'Is this for the documentary on homelessness?'

'Yeah, do you wanna watch it?'

'Yeah.' She smiled gratefully and settled herself down on the couch. A few minutes into the video and Holly was in tears, but for once they weren't for herself. Declan had done the most amazing interview with an incredible guy who was living on the streets of Dublin. She realised there were people far worse off than she, and the fact that Gerry's parents had bumped into her and Daniel walking out of a restaurant suddenly seemed such a stupid thing to worry about.

'Oh, Declan, that was excellent,' she said, drying her eyes when it had finished.

'Thanks,' he said quietly, taking the video out of the player and packing it in his bag.

'Are you not happy with it?'

He shrugged his shoulders. 'When you end up spending the day with people like that it's kind of hard to be happy about the fact that what he has to say is *so* bad that it makes a great documentary. The worse off he is the better off I am.'

Holly listened with interest. 'No, I don't agree with that, Declan. I think that you filming this will make a difference to him. People will see it and want to help.'

Declan just shrugged, 'Maybe. Anyway, I'm going to bed now, I'm absolutely knackered.' He picked up his bag and kissed her on the top of her head as he passed, which really touched Holly. Her baby brother was finally growing up.

Holly glanced at the clock on the mantelpiece and noticed it was almost twelve. She reached for her bag and took out the October envelope from Gerry. She dreaded the days when there would be no more letters. There were only two left after this. She ran her fingers over the writing once again before tearing the seal open. Holly slid the card out of the envelope and a dried flower which had been pressed between two cards, fell on to her lap. Her favourite, a fragile little sunflower. Along with it, a small pouch had landed on her lap. She studied it with curiosity and realised it was a packet of sunflower seeds. Her hands shook as she touched the delicate petals of the flower, not wanting them to snap between her fingers. Gerry's message read:

A sunflower for my sunflower, to brighten the dark October days you hate so much. Plant

some more, safe in the knowledge that a
warm and bright summer awaits.
PS. I love you . . .
PPS. Could you please pass this card on to
John?

Holly lifted the second card that had fallen onto her lap and read the words through her tears and her laughter.

To John,
Happy 32nd Birthday,
You're getting old, my friend, but I hope
you have many, many more birthdays. Take
care, enjoy life, take care of my wife and
Sharon. You're the man now! Lots of love,
Your friend,
Gerry
Told you I'd keep my promise . . .

Holly read and reread every single word Gerry had written. She sat on that couch for what seemed like hours and thought about how happy John would be to hear from his friend. She thought about how much her life had changed over the past few months. Her working life had definitely improved and she was proud of herself for sticking at it. She loved the feeling of satisfaction she got each day when she switched off her computer and left the office. Gerry had pushed her to be brave; he had encouraged her to want a job that meant more to her in life than just a pay cheque. She wouldn't have needed to search for those extra things if Gerry were still with her. Life without him was emptier but left more room for herself. She'd exchange it all to have Gerry back, though.

That wasn't an option. She needed to start thinking about herself and her own future. Because there was no one else to share the responsibilities with her any more.

She wiped her eyes and stood up from the couch. She felt a new bounce in her step. She tapped lightly on the kitchen door.

'Come in,' Elizabeth called.

Holly stepped in and looked around at her parents and Richard sitting at the table, holding cups of tea.

'Oh, hello, love,' her mum said happily, getting up to give her a hug and a kiss. 'I didn't hear you come in.'

'I've been here about an hour. I was just watching Declan's documentary.' Holly beamed at her family and felt like giving them all a hug.

'It's great, isn't it?' Frank said, standing up to greet his elder daughter.

Holly nodded and joined them at the table. 'Have you found a job yet?' she asked Richard.

He shook his head sadly and looked as though he were going to cry.

'Well, I did.'

He looked at her disgusted that she could say such a thing. 'Well, I know *you* did.'

'No, Richard,' she smiled, 'I mean I got *you* a job.'

'You what?'

'You heard me,' she grinned. 'My boss will be calling you on Monday.'

His face fell. 'Oh, Holly, that's very nice of you indeed but I have no interest in advertising. My interest is in science.'

'And gardening.'

'Yes, I like gardening.' He looked confused.

'So that's why my boss will be calling you. To ask you to work on his garden. I told him you'll do it for five thousand, I hope that's OK.' She smiled as his jaw dropped.

He was completely speechless so Holly kept on talking.

'And here are your business cards,' she said, handing him a large pile of cards that she had printed up.

Richard and her parents picked up the cards and read them in silence.

Suddenly Richard started laughing, jumped out of his chair, pulled Holly with him and danced her around the kitchen while her parents looked on and cheered.

'Oh, by the way,' Richard said, calming down and glancing at the card again, 'you spelled gardener wrong.' He spoke slowly. 'It's not gardner, it is garden er. See the difference?'

Holly stopped dancing and sighed with frustration.

Chapter Forty-One

'OK, this is the last one, I promise, girls!' Denise called as her bra was sent flying over the changing-room door.

Sharon and Holly groaned and collapsed in their chairs again.

'You said that an hour ago,' Sharon complained, kicking off her shoes and massaging her swollen ankles.

'Yeah, but I mean it this time. I have a really good feeling about this dress,' Denise said, full of excitement.

'You said *that* an hour ago too,' Holly grumbled, resting her head back on the chair and closing her eyes.

'Don't you go falling asleep on me now,' Sharon warned Holly and her eyes immediately shot open.

They had been dragged to every single wedding gown boutique in the city and Sharon and Holly were exhausted, irritated and extremely fed up. Whatever excitement they had felt for Denise and her wedding had been drained from their systems as Denise tried on dress after dress. And if Holly heard Denise's irritating squeals one more time she would . . .

'Oooh, I love it!' Denise shrieked.

'OK, here's the plan,' Sharon whispered to Holly.

'If she walks out of there looking like a meringue that has sat on a bicycle pump we are going to tell her she looks beautiful.'

Holly giggled. 'Oh, Sharon, we can't do that!'

'Oooh, wait till you see!' Denise shrieked again.

'On second thoughts . . .' Holly looked at Sharon miserably.

'OK, are you ready?'

'Yes,' Sharon groaned unenthusiastically.

'Ta-da!' Denise stepped out of the dressing room and Holly's eyes widened.

'That's so beautiful on you,' the sales assistant, who had been hovering, gushed.

'Oh, stop it!' Denise cried. 'You're no help to me at all! You've loved every single one of them.'

Holly gazed at Sharon uncertainly and tried not to laugh at the look on her face; she looked as if there was a bad smell in the air.

Sharon rolled her eyes and whispered, 'Hasn't Denise ever heard of a thing called commission?'

'What are you two whispering about?' Denise asked.

'Oh, just about how pretty you look.'

Holly frowned at Sharon.

'Oh, do you like it?' Denise squealed again, and Holly winced.

'Yes,' Sharon said unenthusiastically.

'Are you sure?'

'Yes.'

'Do you think Tom will be happy when he looks down the aisle and sees me walking towards him?' Denise even practised her walk just so the girls could imagine it.

'Yes,' Sharon repeated.

'But are you sure?'

'Yes.'

'Do you think it's worth the money?'

'Yes.'

'Really?'

'Yes.'

'It'll be nicer with a tan, won't it?'

'Yes.'

'Oh, but does it make my bum look enormous?'

'Yes.'

Holly looked at Sharon, startled, realising she wasn't even listening to the questions any more.

'Oh, but are you sure?' Denise carried on, obviously not even listening to the answers.

'Yes.'

'So will I get it?'

Holly expected the sales assistant to start jumping up and down with excitement screaming 'Yessss!' but she managed to contain herself.

'No!' Holly interrupted before Sharon said yes again.

'No?' Denise asked.

'No,' Holly confirmed.

'Do you not like it?'

'No.'

'Is it because it makes me look fat?'

'No.'

'Do you not think Tom will like it?'

'No.'

'Do you think it's worth the money, though?'

'No.'

'Oh.' She turned to face Sharon. 'Do you agree with Holly?'

'Yes.'

The sales assistant rolled her eyes and approached another customer, hoping for better luck with her.

'OK then, I trust you two,' Denise said sadly, taking one last look at herself in the mirror. 'To be honest, I wasn't really that keen on it myself.'

Sharon rolled her eyes and put her shoes back on. 'Denise, you said that was the last one. Let's go get something to eat before I drop dead.'

'No, I meant it was the last dress I would try on in *this* shop. There's loads more shops to go to yet.'

'No way!' Holly protested. 'Denise, I am starving to death and at this stage all the dresses are beginning to look the same to me. I need a break.'

'Oh, but this is my wedding day, Holly!'

'Yes, and . . .' Holly tried to think of an excuse, 'and Sharon's pregnant.'

'Oh, OK then, we'll get something to eat,' Denise said, disappointed, and headed back to the changing room.

Sharon elbowed Holly in the ribs. 'Hey, I'm not diseased, you know, just pregnant.'

'It's the only thing that I could think of,' Holly said tiredly.

The three of them trudged into Bewley's café and managed to grab their usual spot by the window overlooking Grafton Street.

'Oh, I hate shopping on Saturdays,' Holly moaned, watching as people bumped and crushed each other on the busy street below.

'Gone are the days of shopping mid-week now you're no longer a lady of leisure,' Sharon teased as she picked up a club sandwich and began stuffing her face.

'I know, and I'm *so* tired, but I feel like I've earned the tiredness this time. Unlike before when I just used to stay up late watching insomniac TV,' Holly said happily.

'Tell us about the little episode with Gerry's parents,' Sharon said with a mouthful of food.

Holly rolled her eyes. 'They were just so rude to poor Daniel.'

'I'm sorry I was asleep. I'm sure if John had known that's what it was about he would have woken me,' Sharon apologised.

'Oh, don't be silly, it wasn't a really big deal. It just felt like it at the time.'

'Too right. They can't tell you who to see and who not to see,' Sharon gave out.

'Sharon, I'm not seeing him.' Holly tried to get the record straight. 'I have no intentions of seeing anyone for at least twenty years. We were just having a business dinner.'

'Oooh, a *business* dinner!' Sharon and Denise giggled.

'Well, that's what it was, but it was also nice to have a bit of company,' Holly admitted. 'And I'm not bitching about you two,' she said quickly before they had a chance to defend themselves. 'All I'm saying is that when everyone else is busy it's nice to have someone else to chat to. Especially male company, you know? And he's easy to get along with and he makes me feel very comfortable. That's all.'

'Yeah, I understand,' Sharon nodded. 'It's good for you to get out and meet new people.'

'So did you find out anything else about him?' Denise leaned forward, her eyes sparkling as she dug for gossip. 'He's a bit of a dark horse, that Daniel.'

'I don't find him secretive at all,' Holly said. 'He told me about that girl he was engaged to. Laura was her name. He said he used to be in the army but left after four years . . .'

'Oooh, I love yummy army men,' Denise drooled.

'And DJs,' Sharon added.

'Oh, and DJs, of course,' Denise replied, laughing.

'Well, I told him my view about the army, anyway,' Holly smiled.

'Oh no, you didn't!' Sharon laughed.

'What's this?' Denise asked.

'So what did he say?' Sharon ignored Denise.

'He just laughed.'

'What's this?' Denise asked again.

'Holly's theory about the army,' Sharon explained.

'And what is it?' Denise asked, irritated.

'Oh, that fighting for peace is like screwing for virginity.'

The girls burst out laughing.

'Yeah, but you can have hours of endless fun trying,' Denise quipped.

'So you haven't mastered it yet?' Sharon asked.

'No, but at every available chance, we try, you know?' Denise replied, and the girls all giggled. 'Well, I'm glad you get along with him, Holly, because you're going to have to dance with him at the wedding.'

'Why?'

'Because it's tradition for the best man to dance with the maid of honour at the wedding.' Her eyes sparkled.

Holly gasped. 'You want me to be your maid of honour?'

Denise nodded excitedly. 'Don't worry, I already asked Sharon and she doesn't mind.'

'Oh, I would love to!' Holly said happily. 'But, Sharon, are you sure you don't mind?'

'Oh, don't worry about me, I'm happy just being a blown-up bridesmaid.'

'You won't be blown up!' Holly laughed.

'Yes I will. I'll be eight months pregnant. I'll need to borrow Denise's marquee to wear as a dress!'

'Oh, I hope you don't go into labour at the wedding,' Denise said, horrified.

'Don't worry, Denise, I won't steal the limelight from you on your day,' Sharon smiled. 'I'm not due till the end of January so that'll be weeks later.'

Denise looked relieved.

'Oh, by the way, I forgot to show you the photograph of the baby!' Sharon said, excitedly rooting through her bag. Finally she pulled out a small photograph of the scan.

'Where is it?' Denise asked, frowning.

'There,' Sharon pointed out the area.

'Whoa! That's one big boy,' Denise exclaimed, moving the picture closer to her face.

Sharon rolled her eyes. 'Denise that's a leg, you fool. We still don't know the sex yet.'

'Oh,' Denise blushed, 'well, congratulations, Sharon. It looks like you're having a little alien.'

'Oh, stop it, Denise,' Holly laughed. 'I think it's a beautiful picture.'

'Good,' Sharon smiled, and looked at Denise, and Denise nodded at her. 'Because I wanted to ask you something.'

'What?' Holly looked worried.

'Well, John and I would love it if you would be our baby's godmother.'

Holly gasped with shock for the second time that day, and tears filled her eyes.

'Hey, you didn't cry when I asked you to be maid of honour,' Denise huffed.

'Oh, Sharon, I would be honoured!' Holly said, giving her friend a big hug. 'Thank you for asking!'

'Thank you for saying yes! John will be so delighted!'

'Oh, don't you two start crying,' Denise moaned, but Sharon and Holly ignored her and continued hugging.

'Hey!' Denise yelled, causing them to jump from their embrace.

'What?'

Denise pointed out the window. 'I can't believe I never noticed that wedding shop over there! Drink up quick and we'll go there next,' she said excitedly as her eyes darted enthusiastically from dress to dress.

Sharon sighed and pretended to pass out. 'I can't, Denise, I'm pregnant . . .'

Chapter Forty-Two

'Hey, Holly, I was just thinking,' Alice said to Holly as they were reapplying their make-up in the toilets at work before leaving for the day.

'Oh, no, did it hurt?' Holly teased.

'Ha-ha,' she said drily. 'No, honestly, I was thinking about the horoscope in this month's magazine and I think Tracey may have got it eerily right.'

Holly rolled her eyes. 'How?'

Alice put down her lipstick and turned away from the mirror to face Holly. 'Well, first there was the thing about the tall, dark handsome man who you are now seeing . . .'

'I'm not seeing him, we're just friends,' Holly explained for what felt like the millionth time.

'Whatever you say. Anyway, then there was the thing—'

'I'm not,' Holly repeated.

'Yeah, yeah,' Alice said, disbelieving her. 'Well, then there's the—'

Holly slammed down her make-up bag. 'Alice, I am *not* seeing Daniel.'

'OK, OK,' she held up her hands defensively, 'I get

it! You're *not* seeing him, but please stop interrupting me and listen!' She waited for Holly to calm down. 'OK, so the other thing she said was that your lucky day is Tuesday, which is today . . .'

'Wow, Alice, I think you're on to something here,' Holly said sarcastically, applying her lip liner.

'Listen!' Alice said impatiently, and Holly shut up. 'So she also said that blue was your lucky colour. So today, being *Tuesday,* you have been invited by a *tall, dark handsome* man to the launch of *Blue* Rock.' Alice looked pleased with herself as she summed it all up.

'So what?' Holly said, unimpressed.

'So it's a sign.'

'A sign that the colour shirt I happened to be wearing that day was blue, which was why Tracey chose that particular colour, which I happened to be wearing because everything else I owned was dirty. And she just picked the day off the top of her head. It means *nothing*, Alice.'

Alice sighed. 'Oh, ye of little faith.'

'Well, if I am to believe your little theory, as screwed up as it is, then that also means that Brian is going to win the lotto and become the object of every woman's affections,' Holly laughed.

Alice bit her lip and looked sheepish.

'What?'

'Well, Brian won four euro on a scratch card today.'

'Whoopdeedoo,' Holly chortled. 'Well, there's still the problem of at least one human being finding him attractive.'

Alice remained silent.

'What now?' Holly demanded.

'Nothing,' Alice shrugged, and smiled.

'You don't!'

'I don't what?' Alice's face lit up.

'You don't fancy him, do you? You couldn't possibly!'

Alice shrugged. 'He's nice, that's all.'

'Oh, no!' Holly covered her face with her hands. 'You're taking this way too far just to try to prove a point to me.'

'I'm not trying to prove anything to you,' Alice laughed.

'Well, then I can't believe you fancy him!'

'Who fancies who?' Tracey asked, walking into the toilet.

Alice shook her head wildly at Holly, begging her not to tell.

'Oh, nobody,' Holly muttered, staring at Alice in shock. How could Alice fancy the slime ball of all slime balls?

'Hey, did you hear Brian won money on a lotto scratch card today?' Tracey asked them from the cubicle.

'We were just talking about that,' Alice laughed.

'I just might have psychic powers after all, Holly,' Tracey smirked and flushed the toilet.

Alice winked at Holly in the mirror as Holly headed out of the bathroom, saying, 'Come on, Alice, we'd better get going or the photographer will go mad.'

'The photographer's already here,' Alice explained, applying some mascara.

'Where is he?'

'She.'

'Well then, where is she?'

'Ta-da!' Alice took a camera out of her bag.

'You're the photographer?' Holly laughed. 'Well, at least we can both lose our jobs together when this article is published.'

Holly and Alice pushed through the crowds in Hogan's and made their way upstairs to Club Diva. Holly gasped as they approached the door. A group of young muscular males dressed in swimwear were banging out some Hawaiian drum beats to welcome all the guests. Some very skinny female models, dressed in skimpy bikinis, greeted the girls at the door by wrapping beautiful multi-coloured lei around their necks.

'I feel like I'm in Hawaii,' Alice giggled, snapping away with her camera. 'Oh my God!' she exclaimed as they entered the club.

Holly barely recognised the place. It had been completely transformed. A huge water feature dominated the room, aqua-blue water cascading down it from some rocks.

'Oh, look, Blue Rock!' Alice laughed. 'Very clever.'

Holly smiled; so much for her wonderful powers of journalistic observation. She hadn't even copped that the water was actually the drink itself. Daniel hadn't told her anything about this, which meant she would have to adjust the article so she could hand it in to Chris tomorrow. She looked around the club for Denise and Tom, and saw her being photographed holding her hand up to the camera to show off her sparkly engagement ring. Holly was amused at the big celebrity couple.

The bar staff were also dressed in bikinis and swimwear, and lined the entrance, bearing trays of blue drinks. Holly lifted a drink from the tray and took a sip, trying not to make a face at its overly sweet taste as a photographer snapped her. As Daniel had said, the floors were scattered with sand, making it appear as if they were at a beach party, and each table was sheltered by a huge bamboo umbrella. The bar stools were all big kettle drums and there was a beautiful barbecue smell in the air. Holly's mouth watered as she spotted the waiters carrying trays of barbecued food to the tables. She darted to the nearest table, helped herself to a kebab, and took a big bite.

'Oh, so you do eat.'

Holly found herself facing Daniel. Chewing valiantly, she swallowed her food.

'Em, hello. I haven't had a thing to eat all day so I am absolutely starving. The place looks great,' she said, looking around, keen to distract him from the sight of her with a mouthful of kebab.

'Yeah, it worked well all right.' He looked pleased. Daniel was slightly more dressed than his staff members: he wore faded blue jeans and a blue Hawaiian shirt with big pink and yellow flowers. He still hadn't shaved and Holly wondered how painful it would be to kiss him with that sharp stubble. Not for her to kiss him, of course. Somebody else . . . Why was she even wondering about it?

'Hey, Holly! Let me get a photo of you and the tall, dark handsome man,' Alice yelled, rushing over with her camera.

Holly was mortified.

Daniel laughed. 'You should bring your friends here more often.'

'She's not my friend,' Holly said through gritted teeth, and posed beside Daniel for the photo.

'Hold on a second,' Daniel said, covering the camera lens with his hand. He took a napkin from the table and wiped the grease and barbecue sauce from Holly's face. Holly's skin tingled at his touch and warmth rushed through her body. She convinced herself it was from blushing so much.

'Now it's gone,' he said, smiling at her, wrapping an arm round her and facing the camera.

Alice skipped away again and continued to snap all around her. Holly turned to Daniel. 'I'm really sorry about the other night. Gerry's parents were so rude to you, and I'm sorry if you felt uncomfortable.'

'Oh, there's no need to apologise again, Holly – in fact there's no need to apologise *at all*. I only felt uncomfortable for you. They shouldn't be able to tell you who to see and who not to see. Anyway, if you're worried about me then there's no need,' he smiled, and placed his hands on her shoulders as though he was going to say something more, but then somebody called him from the bar and he rushed over to sort the problem out.

'But I am *not* seeing you,' Holly muttered to herself. If she had to convince even Daniel of that then they certainly had a problem. She hoped he didn't think there was more to the dinner than there really was. He had called her almost every day since that episode. She realised that she looked forward to his calls. There was that niggling thing at the back of her mind again. Holly wandered over to Denise and joined her on the sun bed where she was sipping on the blue concoction.

'Hey, Holly, I saved this for you.' She pointed to the Lilo in the corner of the room and the two girls giggled, remembering their adventure while on holidays.

'So what do you think of the hot new drink for winter?'

Denise rolled her eyes. 'Tacky. I've only had a few and my head is spinning already.'

Alice ran over to Holly, dragging an enormously muscular man dressed in tiny little shorts. One of his biceps was the size of Alice's waist. She handed the camera to Holly. 'Take a picture of the two of us, will you?'

Holly didn't think that these were the kind of photographs Chris was hoping for but she obliged Alice.

'It's for the screen saver on my computer at work,' Alice explained to Denise.

Holly enjoyed herself that evening, laughing and chatting with Denise and Tom while Alice ran around taking photographs of all the half-naked male models. Holly felt guilty for ever being annoyed by Tom all those months ago at the karaoke competition. He was a sweet guy and he and Denise made a lovely couple. Holly barely got to speak to Daniel as he was too busy being the responsible manager. She watched as he gave orders to his staff and they immediately got to work. It was obvious that they had great respect for him. He got things done. Every time she spotted him heading over to her group, somebody stopped him in his tracks for a chat. Most of the time, he was stopped by skinny young girls in bikinis. They annoyed Holly so she looked away.

'I don't know how I'm going to write this article,'

Holly moaned to Alice as they made their way outside into the cold air.

'Don't worry, Holly, you'll be fine. It's only eight hundred words, isn't it?'

'Yeah, *only*,' she said sarcastically. 'You see, I already wrote a draft a few days ago because Daniel gave me all the information. But after seeing all that I'll have to change it extensively. It already almost killed me trying to get this version done in the first place.'

'You're really worried about this, aren't you?'

Holly sighed. 'I just can't write, Alice. I was never any good at putting things into words and describing exactly how things are.'

Alice looked thoughtful. 'Have you got the article in the office?'

Holly nodded.

'Why don't we go there now? I'll look over it, and maybe I'll make a few changes if it needs it.'

'Oh, Alice, thank you so much!' Holly said, hugging her with relief.

The following day Holly sat nervously before Chris and watched him read the article. His face remained grumpy as he turned the page. Alice hadn't just made a few changes to the article, she had completely rewritten it, and Holly thought it was incredible. It was funny yet informative, and she explained the night exactly as it had been. Alice was an extremely talented writer and Holly couldn't understand why she was still working on reception instead of writing for the magazine.

Finally, Chris finished reading and he slowly took

off his glasses. He looked up at Holly. Holly's hands fidgeted on her lap; she felt as if she had just cheated on a school exam.

'Holly, I don't know what you're doing in advertising,' Chris finally said. 'You are a fantastic writer. I love it! It's cheeky and funny, yet it gets the point across. It's fabulous.'

Holly smiled weakly. 'Eh . . . thanks.'

'You have such a wonderful talent; I can't believe you tried to hide it from me.'

Holly's smile stayed glued on her face.

'How would you feel about writing every now and again?'

Holly's face froze. 'Well, Chris, I'm really much more interested in the advertising side of things.'

'Oh, of course, and I will pay you more for this too. But if we are ever stuck again at least I know I have another talented writer on the team. Well done, Holly.' He grinned at her and held out his hand.

'Eh . . . thanks,' Holly repeated, shaking his hand weakly. 'I better get back to work now.' She stood up from her chair and walked stiffly out of the office.

'Well, did he like it?' Alice asked loudly, walking down the hall.

'Eh . . . yeah, he loved it. He wants me to write more.' Holly felt guilty for taking all the credit.

'Oh.' Alice looked away. 'Well, aren't you the lucky one?' She continued on to her desk.

Chapter Forty-Three

Denise banged the till closed with her hip and handed the receipt to the customer. 'Thanks,' she smiled, but the smile quickly faded as soon as the customer turned away from the counter. She sighed loudly, staring at the long queue forming in front of the cash register. She would have to stand at the till all day and she was just dying for a cigarette break. But there was no way she could slip away so she grumpily grabbed the item of clothing from the next customer, de-tagged it, scanned it, and wrapped it.

'Excuse me, are you Denise Hennessey?' she heard a deep voice ask, and she looked up to see where the sexy voice came from. She frowned as she saw a garda before her.

She hesitated while trying to think if she had done anything illegal in the past few days. When she was satisfied that she was crime free she smiled and replied, 'Yes I am.'

'I'm Garda Ryan and I was wondering if you would accompany me to the station, please.'

It was more of a statement than a question and Denise's mouth dropped open in shock. He was no

403

longer sexy garda, he was the evil-lock-her-up-forever-in-a-tiny-cell-with-a-luminous-orange-jumpsuit-and-noisy-flipflops-and-no-hot-water-or-make-up-type garda. Denise gulped and had an image of herself being beaten up by a gang of tough angry women who didn't care about mascara, in the exercise yard at the prison, while the guards looked on and made bets over who would win.

She gulped. 'What for?'

'If you just comply with what I've said, everything will be explained to you down at the station.' He walked round the counter and Denise backed away slowly, looking at the long line of customers helplessly. Everybody just stared back at her, amused by the scene that was unfolding before them.

'Check his ID, love,' one of the customers shouted from the end of the queue.

Denise's voice shook as she demanded to see his ID, which was pointless, as she had never seen a garda ID before, nor knew what a real one would look like. Her hand trembled as she held the ID and studied it closely but didn't read a thing. She was too self-conscious of the crowd of customers and staff that had gathered to stare at her with looks of disgust on their faces. They were all thinking the same thing: she was a criminal.

Denise hardened, refusing to go without a fight. 'I won't go with you until you tell me what this is about.'

He continued towards her again. 'Ms Hennessey, if you just work with me here then there will be no need to use these.' He took out a pair of handcuffs from his trousers pocket.

'But I didn't do anything!' she protested, starting to panic.

'Well, we can discuss that down at the station, can't we?' he began to get irate.

Denise crossed her arms across her chest to show how tough she was. 'I said I will *not* go with you until you tell me what this is about.'

'OK then,' he shrugged, 'if you insist.' He opened his mouth to speak and she yelled as she felt the cold handcuffs being snapped around her wrists. It wasn't exactly the first time she had ever worn a pair of handcuffs so she wasn't surprised at how they felt, but she was in so much shock she couldn't speak.

'Good luck, love,' the customer shouted again as she was led by the queue. 'If they send you to Mount Joy tell my Orla I said hi and that I'll be there to visit her at Christmas.'

Denise's eyes widened and images of her pacing a cell, shared with a psycho murderer, jumped into her mind. Maybe she would find a little bird with a broken wing and nurse it and teach it to fly to pass the years inside, just like in the movie . . .

Her face reddened as they stepped out onto Grafton Street and the crowds immediately scattered as soon as they saw the garda and a hardened criminal. Denise kept her eyes peeled to the ground, hoping nobody she knew would spot her. Her heart beat wildly and she briefly thought of escape. She looked around quickly and tried to figure out an escape route but she was already being led toward a mini-bus, the well-known colour blue of the gardaí with blackened-out windows. Denise sat in the front, and although she could sense people behind her, she sat rigidly in her seat, too terrified to turn round and meet her future fellow inmates. She leaned her head against the window and said goodbye to freedom.

'Where are we going?' she asked. The female police officer driving the bus and garda Ryan ignored her and continued to stare ahead of them.

'Hey!' she shouted. 'We're going in the wrong direction! I thought you said you were taking me to the station?'

They continued to stare straight ahead.

'HEY! WHERE ARE WE GOING?'

No answer.

'I HAVEN'T DONE ANYTHING WRONG!'

Still no answer.

'I'M INNOCENT, GODDAMMIT! INNOCENT, I TELL YOU!'

Denise started kicking the chair in front of her, trying to get their attention. Her blood started to boil when the female garda pushed a cassette into the player and turned the music up. Denise's eyes widened at the choice of song.

Garda Ryan turned round in his seat with a big grin on his face. 'Denise, you have been a very naughty girl.' He stood up and made his way in front of her. She gulped as he started to gyrate his hips to the song 'Hot Stuff'.

She was about to give him a great big kick between his legs when she heard whooping and laughing from the back of the bus. She twisted round and spotted her sisters, Holly, Sharon, and about five other friends, picking themselves up from the floor of the mini bus.

She finally figured out what was really happening when her sisters placed a veil on her head while screaming, 'Happy hen party!'

'Oh, you bitches!' Denise spat at them, effing and blinding them until she had used every single curse word invented and even made up a few of her own.

The girls continued to hold their stomachs, doubled up with laughter.

'You are so lucky I didn't kick you in the balls!' Denise screamed at the gyrating garda.

'Denise, this is Ken,' her sister Fiona giggled, 'and he's your stripper for the day.'

Denise narrowed her eyes and continued to curse them, 'I almost had a heart attack, I hope you know! I thought I was going to prison! Oh my God, what will my customers think? And my staff!' Denise closed her eyes as though she was in pain.

'We told the staff about it last week,' Sharon giggled. 'They were all just playing along.'

'Oh, the little bitches,' Denise repeated. 'When I go back to work I'm going to fire the lot of them. But what about the customers?' Denise asked, panicking.

'Don't worry,' her sister giggled, 'we told your staff to inform the customers it was your hen party after you left the shop.'

Denise rolled her eyes, 'Well, knowing *them* they deliberately won't, and if they *don't,* then there will be complaints and if there are complaints I will be *so* fired.'

'Denise! Stop *worrying*! You don't think we would have done this without running it by your boss, do you? It's OK!' Fiona explained. 'They thought it was funny. Now *relax* and enjoy the weekend.'

'Weekend? What the hell are you girls going to do to me next? Where are we going?' Denise looked around at her friends, startled.

'We're going to Galway and that's all you need to know,' Sharon said mysteriously.

'If I wasn't bloody handcuffed I'd slap you all in the face,' Denise threatened.

The girls all cheered as Ken stripped out of his uniform and poured baby oil all over his body for Denise to massage into his skin.

'Men in uniform are so much nicer out of them . . .' Denise mumbled as she watched him flex his muscles before her.

'Lucky she's handcuffed, Ken, or you would be in big trouble!' the girls teased.

'*Big* trouble is right,' Denise mumbled again, staring in shock as the rest of the clothes came off. 'Oh, girls! Thank you so much!' she giggled, her voice taking a very different tone than before.

'Are you OK, Holly?' Sharon asked, handing her a glass of champagne and keeping a glass of orange juice for herself. 'You've barely said a word since we got into the van.'

Holly turned to look out of the window and stared at the green fields as they flew by. The hills were dotted with little white specks as the sheep bravely climbed to new heights, oblivious to the wonderful views. Neat stone walls separated each field and you could see the grey lines, jagged like jigsaw puzzles, for miles, connecting each piece of land together.

Holly had yet to find a few pieces for her own puzzled mind.

'Yeah,' she sighed, 'I'm OK.'

'Oh, I really have to ring Tom!' Denise groaned, collapsing onto the double bed she and Holly were sharing in the hotel room. Sharon was fast asleep on the single bed beside them. She had gone to bed much earlier than the girls after eventually becoming bored of their drunken behaviour.

'I'm under strict orders not to let you ring Tom,' Holly yawned. 'This is a girls-only weekend.'

'Oh, please,' Denise whimpered.

'No. I am confiscating your phone.' She grabbed the mobile from Denise's hand and hid it in the press beside the bed.

Denise looked as if she was going to cry. She watched as Holly lay back on the bed and closed her eyes, and she began to formulate a plan. She would wait until Holly was asleep and then she would call Tom. Holly had been so quiet all day it was really starting to irritate Denise. Every time Denise had asked her a question she kept on getting yes/no answers back, and every attempt to strike up a conversation had failed. It was obvious that Holly wasn't enjoying herself, but what really annoyed Denise was to see that Holly wasn't even *trying*, or even *pretending* to be. She could understand that Holly was upset and that she had a lot to deal with at the moment but it was her hen party and she couldn't help feeling that Holly was bringing the atmosphere down.

* * *

The room was still spinning. Having closed her eyes, Holly was now unable to sleep. It was five o'clock in the morning, which meant that she had been drinking for almost twelve hours and her head was pounding. Her stomach became queasy as the walls around her spun around and around and around . . . She sat up on the bed and tried to keep her eyes open to avoid the feeling of seasickness.

She turned to face Denise on the bed so that they could talk but the sound of her snores ended all thought of communication between them. Holly sighed and looked around the room. She wanted nothing more than to go home and sleep in her own bed. She felt her way across the bedcovers in the dark for the remote control and flicked on the television. Commercial presentations adorned the screen. Holly watched as they demonstrated a new knife to slice oranges without spraying yourself in the face with the juice; the amazing socks that never got lost in the wash.

Denise snored loudly beside her and kicked Holly in the shins as she changed position. Holly winced and rubbed her leg as she watched with sympathy at Sharon's extremely frustrated struggle to lie on her stomach. Eventually she settled on her side.

Holly rushed to the toilet and hung her head over the pan, prepared for what was inevitably to come. She wished she hadn't drunk so much but with all the talk of weddings and husbands and happiness she had needed all the wine in the bar to prevent her from screaming at everyone to shut up. She dreaded to think what the next two days would be like. Denise's friends were twice as bad as Denise. They were loud and hyper – exactly how girls should be on a hen week-end – but Holly just didn't have the energy to keep up with them. At least Sharon had the excuse of being pregnant; she could pretend she wasn't feeling well or that she was tired. Holly had no excuse apart from the fact that she had turned into a complete bore, and she was saving that excuse for a time when she really needed it.

It felt as if it was only yesterday that Holly had had her own hen party, but in fact it was over seven years ago. She had flown to London with a group of girls for the weekend to party hard but she had ended up missing Gerry so much she had to speak to him on the phone every hour. Back then she had been so excited about what was to come. The future had looked so bright.

She was to marry the man of her dreams and live with him for the rest of their lives. For the entire week-end she was away she had counted the hours until she could return home. She was so excited on the flight back to Dublin. Although they had only been apart for a few days, it had felt like an eternity. He had been waiting for her at arrivals with a huge board in his hand saying 'My future wife'. She had dropped her bags when she saw him and had run into his arms and hugged him *so* tight. She had never wanted to let go; what a luxury it was for people to be able to hold their loved ones whenever they wanted, she thought now bitterly. The scene at the airport had been like a part of a movie, but it was real: real feelings, real emotions, and real love because it was real life. Real life which had now become a nightmare for her.

411

Yes, she had finally managed to drag herself out of bed every morning; yes, she had even managed to get dressed most of the time. Yes, she had succeeded in finding a new job where she met new people and yes, she had finally started buying food again and feeding herself. But no, she didn't feel ecstatic about any of these things. They were just formalities, something else to check off on the 'things that normal people do' list. None of them filled the hole in her heart; it was like her body had become one great jigsaw just like the green fields with their pretty grey-stone walls connecting the whole of Ireland. She had started working on the corners and the edges of her jigsaw because they were the easy bits but now that they were all in place she needed to do all the bits in between, the hard parts. But nothing she had done so far had managed to fill that hole in her heart; that piece of the jigsaw had yet to be found.

Holly cleared her throat loudly and pretended to have a coughing fit just so the girls would wake up and talk to her. She needed to talk, she needed to cry, she needed to vent all her frustrations and disappointments. But what more could she say to Sharon and Denise that she hadn't said already? What more advice could they give her that they hadn't given her before? Ever since the holiday Holly had opened up to Sharon and Denise a lot more, but now she felt that she was repeating the same old worries over and over again. Sometimes they would succeed in getting through to her and she would feel positive and confident, only to be thrown back into despair days later.

After a while Holly, tired of staring at the four walls, threw on a tracksuit and made her way back downstairs to the hotel bar.

Charlie rolled his eyes as the table down the back of the bar began to roar with laughter again. He wiped down the counter and glanced at his watch: five thirty and he couldn't wait to go home. He had thought he was so lucky when the girls from the hen party had gone to bed earlier than expected, and had been about to tidy up and go home when another gang arrived. And they were still here. In fact he would have preferred if the girls had stayed up instead of this arrogant crowd. They weren't even residents of the hotel but he had to serve them because they included the hotel owner's daughter and her friends.

'Don't tell me you're back for more!' the barman laughed as one of the women from the hen party walked into the room. She walked towards the bar, bumping into the wall as she tried to make her way on to the high stool. Charlie tried not to laugh.

'I just came down for a glass of water,' she hiccuped. 'Oh my God,' she wailed, catching sight of herself in the mirror over the bar. Charlie had to admit that she did look shocking: a bit like the scarecrow on his dad's farm. Her hair was like straw, and sticking out in all directions, her eyes had black circles around them from smudging her mascara and her teeth were stained from red wine.

'There you go,' Charlie said, placing a glass of water on a beer mat in front of her.

'Thanks.' She dipped her finger into her glass and

wiped the mascara from her eyes and rubbed the wine stains from her lips.

Charlie began to laugh and she squinted at his nametag.

'What are you laughing at, Charlie?'

'I thought you were thirsty but I would have given you a face cloth if you had asked for one,' he chuckled.

The woman smiled and her features softened. 'I find the ice and lemon helps my skin.'

'Well, that's a new one.' Charlie continued to wipe down the counter. 'Did you girls have fun tonight?'

Holly sighed. 'I suppose.' Fun wasn't a word she used often any more. She had laughed along with the jokes all night, had been excited for Denise, but she hadn't felt as if she was *completely* there. She had felt like the shy girl at school who was always *just there,* but who never spoke and was never spoken to. She didn't recognise the person she had become; she wanted to be able to stop staring at the clock whenever she went out, hoping the night would soon be over so she could go home and crawl into bed. She wanted to stop wishing time would pass and enjoy the moment instead.

'Are you OK?' Charlie stopped wiping the counter and watched her. He had a horrible feeling she was going to cry but he was used to it. A lot of people became emotional when they drank.

'I miss my husband,' she whispered, and her shoulders trembled.

The corners of Charlie's lips turned up into a smile.

'What's so funny?' She looked at him angrily.

'How long are you here for?' he asked.

414

'The weekend,' she told him, twisting a used tissue around her finger.

He laughed. 'Have you never gone the weekend without seeing him?'

She frowned. 'Only once before,' she finally replied, 'and that was at my own hen party.'

'How long ago was that?'

'Seven years ago.' A tear spilled down her face.

Charlie shook his head. 'That's a long time ago. Well, if you did it once you can do it again,' he smiled. 'Seven years lucky, isn't that what they say?'

Holly snorted into her drink. Lucky her arse.

'Don't worry,' Charlie said gently, 'your husband's probably miserable without you too.'

'Oh God, I hope not,' Holly replied.

'Well then, see? I'm sure he hopes you're not miserable without him either. You're supposed to be enjoying your life.'

'You're right,' Holly said, perking up. 'He wouldn't want me to be unhappy.'

'That's the spirit,' Charlie smiled, and jumped as he saw his boss's daughter coming towards the bar with one of those looks on her face.

'Hey, Charlie,' she yelled, 'I've been trying to get your attention for ages. Maybe if you stopped chatting to the customers at the bar and did a bit of work, me and my friends wouldn't be so thirsty.'

Holly's mouth dropped open with shock. That woman had a nerve, speaking to Charlie like that, and her perfume was so strong it made Holly cough.

'I'm sorry, do you have a problem?' the woman demanded, looking Holly up and down.

415

'Yes, actually,' Holly slurred, taking a sip of her water. 'Your perfume is disgusting and it's making me want to throw up.'

Charlie started laughing and dropped to his knees behind the counter to pretend to look for a lemon. He tried to block out the sounds of the two women snapping at each other so he would stop.

'What's the delay here?' a deep voice enquired. Charlie shot to his feet at the sound of the woman's fiancé's voice. He was even worse. 'Why don't you sit down, honey, and I'll bring the drinks over?' said the man.

'Fine. At least *someone* is polite around here,' she snapped, looking Holly up and down once more before storming off back to her table. Holly watched her hips working furiously – boom, boom, boom – from side to side as she walked. She must be a model or something, Holly decided. That would explain the tantrums.

'So how are you?' the man beside Holly asked, staring at her chest.

Charlie had to bite his tongue to stop himself from saying anything as he poured a pint of Guinness from the tap and then allowed it to sit on the counter for a while. He had a feeling the woman at the bar wouldn't succumb to Stevie's charms anyway, especially as she seemed to be so head over heels about her husband. Charlie was looking forward to seeing Stevie being ceremoniously dumped.

'I'm fine,' Holly replied shortly, staring straight ahead and deliberately avoiding eye contact.

'I'm Steve,' he said, holding out his hand to her.

'I'm Holly,' she mumbled, and took his hand lightly, not wanting to be overly rude.

'Holly, that's a lovely name.' He held her hand for much too long and Holly was forced to look up. He had big blue sparkly eyes.

'Eh . . . thanks,' she said, embarrassed by his compliment, and her face flushed.

Charlie sighed to himself. Even she had fallen for it, his only hope of satisfaction for the night gone.

'Can I buy you a drink, Holly?' Steve asked smoothly.

'No thanks, I have one here.' She sipped on her water again.

'OK, well, I'm just going to bring these drinks down to my table and then I'll be back to buy the lovely Holly a drink.' He smiled at her creepily as he walked away.

Charlie rolled his eyes as soon as he had turned his back.

'Who the hell is that eejit?' Holly asked, looking bewildered, and Charlie laughed, delighted that she hadn't fallen for him. She was a lady with sense, even if she was crying because she missed her husband after only one day of separation.

Charlie lowered his voice. 'That's Stevie, fiancé of Laura, that blonde bitch who was here a minute ago. Her dad owns this hotel, which means I can't exactly tell her where to go although I would love to. Not worth losing my job over.'

'Definitely worth losing your job over, I should think,' Holly said, staring at the beautiful Laura and thinking nasty thoughts. 'Anyway, good night, Charlie.'

'You off to bed?'

She nodded. 'It's about time; it's after six.' She tapped on her watch. 'I hope you get home soon,' she smiled.

'I wouldn't bet on it,' he replied, and watched her leave the bar. Steve followed after her and Charlie made his way closer to the door just to make sure she was OK. Laura, noticing her fiancé's sudden departure, left the table and arrived at the door at the same time as Charlie. They both stared down the corridor in the direction Holly and Steve had headed.

Laura gasped and her hand flew to her mouth.

'Hey!' Charlie called out angrily as he witnessed a distressed Holly pushing a drunken Steve away from her.

Holly angrily wiped her mouth, disgusted at Steve's attempt to kiss her. She backed away from him. 'I think you've got the wrong idea here, Steve. Go back to the bar to your *fiancée*.'

Steve wobbled slightly on his feet and slowly turned to face Laura and an angry Charlie who was charging towards them.

'Stevie!' Laura shrieked. 'How could you?' She ran from the hotel with tears streaming down her face, closely followed by a protesting Steve.

'Uuggghh!' Holly said with disgust. 'I did not want to do that *at all*!'

'Don't worry, I believe you,' Charlie said, placing his hand comfortingly on her shoulder. 'I saw what happened through the door.'

'Ah well, thanks very much for coming to my rescue!' Holly complained.

418

'Got here too late, sorry. But I must admit, I did enjoy her witnessing that,' he laughed, referring to Laura.

Holly smiled as she stared down the corridor at Steve and Laura screaming at each other.

'Oops,' she said.

Holly knocked into everything in the bedroom as she tried to make her way back to her bed in the darkness. 'Ouch!' she yelped, stubbing her toe on the bedpost.

'Sshhh!' Sharon said sleepily.

Holly tapped Denise on the shoulder continuously until she woke up.

'What? What?' Denise moaned sleepily.

'Here,' Holly forced a mobile phone in Denise's face, 'phone your future husband, tell him you love him and don't let the girls know.'

The next day Holly and Sharon went for a long walk on the beach just outside Galway city. Although it was October the air had warmth in it and Holly didn't need her coat. She stood and listened to the water gently lapping. The rest of the girls had decided to go for a liquid lunch but Holly's stomach wasn't quite ready for that today.

'Are you OK, Holly?' Sharon wrapped her arm around her friend's shoulders.

Holly sighed. 'Every time someone asks me that question, Sharon, I say, "I'm fine, thank you," but to be honest I'm not. Do people *really* want to know how you feel when they ask, "How are you?"? Or are they just trying to be polite?' Holly smiled. 'The next time the woman across the road from my house says to me, "How are you?" I'm going to say to her;

well, actually, I'm not very well at all, thank you. I'm feeling a bit depressed and lonely. Pissed off at the world. Envious of you and your perfect little family but not particularly envious of your husband at having to live with you. And then I'll tell her about how I started a new job and met lots of new people and how I'm trying hard to pick myself up but that I'm now at a loss about what else to do. Then I'll tell her how it pisses me off when everyone says time is a healer when at the same time they also say absence makes the heart grow fonder, which really confuses me, because that means that the longer he's gone the more I want him. I'll tell her that nothing is healing at all and that every morning I wake up in my empty bed it feels like salt is being rubbed into those unhealing wounds.' Holly took a deep breath. 'And then I'll tell her about how much I miss my husband and about how worthless my life seems without him. How uninterested I am in getting on with things without him and I'll explain how I feel like I'm just waiting for my world to end so that I can join him. She'll probably just say, "Oh that's good," like she always does, kiss her husband goodbye, hop into her car and drop her kids to school, go to work, make the dinner and go to bed with her husband and she'll have done it all while I'm still trying to decide what colour shirt to wear to work. What do you think?' Holly finally finished and turned to Sharon.

'Oooh!' Sharon jumped, and her arm flew away from Holly's shoulders.

'Oooh?' Holly frowned. 'I say all that and all you can say is "Oooh"?'

Sharon placed her hand over her bump and laughed. 'No, silly, the baby kicked!'

Holly's jaw dropped.

'Feel it!' Sharon giggled.

Holly placed her hand over Sharon's swollen belly and felt the tiny little movement. Their eyes filled with tears.

'Oh, Sharon, if only every minute of my life was filled with perfect little moments like this I would never moan again.'

'But, Holly, nobody's life is filled with perfect little moments. And if they were, they wouldn't be perfect little moments. They would just be normal. How would you ever know happiness if you'd never experienced downs?'

'Oooh!' they both shrieked as the baby kicked for a third time.

'I think this little boy is going to be a footballer like his daddy!' Sharon laughed.

'Boy?' Holly gasped. 'You're having a boy?'

Sharon nodded happily and her eyes glistened. 'Holly, meet baby Gerry. Gerry, meet your godmother, Holly.'

Chapter Forty-Four

'Hi, Alice,' Holly said, hovering in front of her desk. Holly had been standing there for a few minutes now and Alice hadn't said a word yet.

'Hi,' Alice said shortly, refusing to look up at her.

Holly took a deep breath. 'Alice, are you mad at me?'

'No,' she said abruptly again. 'Chris wants to see you in his office again. He wants you to write another article.'

'*Another* article?' Holly gasped.

'That's what I said.'

'Alice, why don't you do it?' Holly said softly. 'You're a fantastic writer. I'm sure if Chris knew you could write he would def—'

'He knows,' she interrupted.

'What?' Holly was confused. 'He knows you can write?'

'Five years ago I applied for a job as a writer but this was the only job going. Chris said if I hung on then maybe something would come up.' Alice sounded so angry and Holly wasn't used to seeing the usually chirpy girl looking so . . . upset wasn't even the word. She was just *angry*.

Holly sighed and made her way into Chris's office. She had a sneaking suspicion she would be writing this one all on her own.

Holly smiled as she flicked through the pages of the November magazine she had worked on. It would be out in the shops tomorrow, the first of November and she felt so excited. Her first magazine would be on the shelves and she could also open Gerry's next letter. Tomorrow would be a good day.

Although she had organised only the advertisements, she felt great pride in being a member of a team that had managed to produce something so professional-looking. It was a far cry from that pathetic leaflet she had printed up years ago and she giggled at the memory of mentioning it at her interview. As if it would have impressed Chris at all. But despite all that she felt she had really proved herself. She had taken her job by the reins and guided it through to success.

'It's nice to see you're looking so happy,' Alice snapped, strolling tartly into Holly's office and throwing two little scraps of paper on to her desk. 'You got two calls while you were out. One from Sharon and one from Denise. Please tell your friends to call you on your lunch break in future.'

'OK, thanks,' Holly said, glancing at the messages. Alice had scrawled something completely illegible, most likely on purpose. 'Hey, Alice!' Holly called after her.

'What?' she asked coldly.

423

'Did you read the article on the launch? The photos and everything turned out great! I'm really proud,' Holly grinned broadly.

'No I have not!' Alice retorted, looking disgusted, and slammed the door behind her.

Holly chased her out of the office with the magazine in her hand. 'But look at it, Alice! It's so good! Daniel will be so happy!'

'Well, whoopdeedoo for you and Daniel.' Alice busied herself with random bits of paper on her desk.

Holly rolled her eyes. 'Look, stop being such a baby and read the damn thing!'

'No!' Alice huffed.

'Fine then, you won't see the photo of you with that gorgeous half-naked man . . .' Holly turned and walked away slowly.

'Give me that!' Alice grabbed the magazine from Holly's hand and flicked through the pages. Her jaw dropped as she reached the page featuring the Blue Rock launch.

At the top of the page it read 'Alice in Wonderland', with the photograph Holly had taken of her and the muscular model.

'Read it out loud,' Holly ordered.

Alice's voice shook as she began to read. 'A new alcopop has hit the shelves and our *party correspondent* Alice Goodyear went to find out if the hot new drink for winter was as it claimed to be . . .' She trailed off and her hands flew to her mouth in shock. 'Party correspondent?' she squealed.

Holly called Chris out of his office and he came to join them, a broad grin on his face.

'Well done, Alice; that was a fantastic article you wrote. It was very amusing,' he told her, with a pat on the shoulder. 'So I've created a new page called "Alice in Wonderland", where you will go to all the weird and wonderful things you love to go to and write about them every month.'

Alice gasped at them and then stuttered, 'But Holly—'

'Holly can't spell,' Chris laughed. 'You, on the other hand, are a great writer. One I should have used before now. I'm very sorry, Alice.'

'Oh my God!' she gasped, ignoring him. 'Thank you so much, Holly!' She threw her arms around her and squeezed her so hard Holly couldn't breathe.

Holly tried to pull Alice's arms away from around her neck and gasped for air. 'Alice, this was the hardest secret to keep from anyone ever!'

'It must have been! How on earth did you manage it?' Alice looked at Holly, startled, before turning to Chris. 'Five years, Chris,' she said accusingly.

Chris winced and nodded.

'I waited five years for this,' she continued.

'I know, I know.' Chris looked like a chastised schoolboy and he scratched his eyebrow awkwardly. 'Why don't you step into my office now and we can talk about that.'

'I suppose I could do that,' Alice replied sternly, but she couldn't hide the glint of happiness in her eyes. As Chris headed towards his office, Alice turned to Holly and winked before doing a quickskip behind him.

Holly made her way back to her office. Time to get working on the December edition.

'Oops!' she said, tripping over a pile of handbags lying outside her door. 'What's all this?'

Chris rolled his eyes as he stepped out of his office to make Alice a cup of tea for a change, 'Oh, they're John-Paul's handbags.'

'John-Paul's handbags?' Holly giggled.

'It's for the article he's doing on this season's handbags or something stupid like that,' Chris pretended not to be interested.

'Oh, they're gorgeous,' Holly said, bending down to pick one up.

'Nice, isn't it?' John-Paul said, leaning against the door frame of his office.

'Yeah, I love it,' Holly said, sliding it over her shoulder. 'Does it suit me?'

Chris rolled his eyes again. 'How can a handbag not suit someone – it's a handbag, for Christsake!'

'You'll have to read the article I'm writing for next month, won't you?' John-Paul wagged a finger at his boss. 'Not all handbags suit everyone, you know.' He turned to Holly. 'You can have it if you want.'

'For keeps?' she gasped. 'This must cost hundreds.'

'Yeah, but I've got loads of them. You should see the amount of stuff the designer gave me. Trying to sweeten me up with freebies; the cheek of him!' John-Paul pretended to be outraged.

'I bet it works, though,' Holly suggested.

'Absolutely. The first line of my article will be: "Everybody go out and buy one, they're fab!"' he laughed.

'What else have you got?' Holly tried to peek behind him into the office.

426

'I'm doing an article on what to wear for all the Christmas parties coming up. A few dresses arrived today. In fact,' he looked her up and down and Holly sucked in her belly, 'there's one that would look fab on you. Come in and try it on.'

'Oh, goody,' Holly giggled. 'I'll just have a look, though, John-Paul. I have no need for a party dress at all this year. I intend to sit home and *relax* in peace and quiet.'

Chris shook his head and yelled from his office, 'Does anybody in this bloody office ever do any work?'

'Yes!' Tracey yelled back. 'Now shut up and don't be distracting us.'

Everyone in the office laughed and Holly could swear she saw Chris smile before he slammed his office door shut for dramatic effect.

After rummaging through John-Paul's collection, Holly returned to work and eventually called Denise back.

'Hello? Disgusting, stuffy and ridiculously expensive clothes shop. Pissed off manager speaking, how can I help you?'

'Denise!' Holly gasped. 'You can't answer the phone like that!'

Denise giggled. 'Oh, don't worry, I have caller ID so I knew it was you.'

'Hmm,' Holly was suspicious; she didn't think Denise *did* have caller ID on her work phone. 'I got a message you called earlier.'

'Oh yeah, I was just ringing you to confirm you were going to the ball. Tom is going to buy a table this year.'

'What ball?'

'The Christmas ball we go to every year, you dope.'

'Oh yeah, the Christmas ball they always hold in the middle of November?' Holly laughed. 'Sorry, but I can't make it this year.'

'But you don't even know what date it's on yet!' Denise protested.

'Well, I assume it's being held on the same date as it has been every other year, which means I can't make it.'

'No, no, it's on the thirtieth of November this year, so you can make it!' Denise said excitedly.

'Oh, the thirtieth . . .' Holly paused and pretended to flick through some pages on her desk very loudly. 'No, Denise, I can't. Sorry. I'm busy on the thirtieth. I have a deadline,' she lied.

'But we don't have to be there till at least eight o'clock,' Denise tried to convince her. 'You could even come at nine if it was easier. You would just miss the drinks reception first.'

'Look, Denise, I'm sorry,' Holly said firmly. 'I'm just far too busy.'

'Well, that makes a change,' she muttered under her breath.

'What did you say?' Holly asked, getting angry.

'Nothing,' Denise replied shortly.

'I heard you; you said that makes a change, didn't you? Well, it just so happens that I take my work seriously, Denise, and I have no plans to lose my job over a stupid ball.'

'Fine then,' Denise huffed. 'Don't go.'

'I won't!'

'Fine!'

'Good. Well, I'm glad that's fine with you, Denise.' Holly couldn't help but smile at the ridiculousness of the conversation.

'I'm glad you're glad,' Denise huffed.

'Oh, don't be so childish, Denise.' Holly rolled her eyes. 'I have to work, simple as that.'

'Well, that's no surprise, that's all you ever do these days,' Denise blurted out. 'You never come out any more. Every time I ask you out you're busy doing something apparently much more important, like *work*. At my hen weekend you looked like you were having the worst time of your life and you didn't even bother coming out the second night. In fact, I don't know why you bothered to come at all. If you have a problem with me, Holly, I wish you would just say it to my face instead of being such a miserable bore!'

Holly sat back in shock and stared at the phone. She couldn't believe Denise had said those things. She couldn't believe Denise could be so stupid and selfish to think that this whole thing was about her. No wonder she felt she was going insane, when one of her best friends couldn't even understand her.

'That is the most selfish thing I have ever heard anyone say.' Holly tried to control her voice but she knew her anger was spilling out into her words.

'I'm selfish?' Denise squealed. 'You're the one who hid in the hotel room on my hen weekend! *My* hen weekend! You're supposed to be my maid of honour!'

'I was in the room with Sharon, you know that!' Holly defended herself.

'Oh, bullshit! Sharon would have been fine on her

429

own. She's pregnant, not bloody dying. You don't need to be by her side twenty-four seven!' Denise went quiet as she realised what she had said.

Holly's blood boiled and as she spoke her voice trembled with rage. 'And you wonder why I don't go out with you – when you say stupid insensitive remarks like that. Did you ever think for one moment that it might be hard for me? The fact that all you talk about are your bloody wedding arrangements and how happy and excited you are and how you can't wait to spend the rest of your life with Tom in wedded bliss. In case you hadn't noticed, Denise, I didn't get that chance because my husband *died*. But I am very happy for you, really I am. I'm delighted you're happy and I'm not asking for any special treatment at all, I'm just asking for a bit of patience and for you to understand that *I will not get over this in a few months*! As for the ball, I have no intention of going to a place that Gerry and I have been going to together for the past ten years. You might not understand this, Denise, but funnily enough I would find it A BIT DIFFICULT. So don't book a ticket for me, I am perfectly happy staying at home,' she yelled and slammed the phone down.

She burst into tears and lay her head down on the desk as she sobbed. She felt lost. Her best friend couldn't even understand her. Maybe she was going mad. Maybe she *should* be over Gerry already. Maybe that's what normal people did when their loved ones died. She should have bought the rule book for widows to see what the recommended time for grieving was so she wouldn't have to keep on inconveniencing her family and friends.

Her weeping eventually died down into little sobs and she listened to the silence around her. She realised that everyone must have heard everything she had said and she felt so embarrassed that she was afraid to go to the bathroom for a tissue. Her face was hot and her eyes felt swollen from all her tears. She wiped them on the sleeve of her shirt.

'Shit!' she swore, swiping some papers off her desk as she realised she had smudged foundation, mascara and lipstick all along the sleeve of her spensive white shirt. She sat up to attention quickly as she heard a light knock on her door.

'Come in.' Her voice shook.

Chris entered her office, clutching two cups of tea.

'Tea?' he offered, raising his eyebrows at her, and she smiled weakly, remembering the joke they had shared on the day of her interview. He placed the mug down in front of her and relaxed in the chair opposite.

'Having a bad day?' he asked as gently as his gruff voice allowed.

She nodded as tears rolled down her face again. 'I'm sorry, Chris.' She tried to compose herself. 'It won't affect my work,' she said shakily.

He waved his hand dismissively. 'Holly, I'm not worried about that. You're a great worker.'

She smiled, grateful for the compliment. At least she was doing something right.

'Would you like to go home early?'

'No, thanks. Work will keep my mind off things.'

He shook his head sadly. 'That's not the way to go about it, Holly. I, of all people, should know that. I've buried myself inside these walls for the last couple of years and it doesn't help things. Not in the long run, anyway.'

'But you seem happy.' Her voice trembled.

'Seeming and being are not one and the same. I *know* you know that.'

She nodded sadly.

'You don't have to put on a brave face all the time, you know.' He handed her a tissue.

'Oh, I'm not brave at all.' She blew her nose.

'Ever hear the saying that you need to be scared to be brave?'

Holly thought about that. 'But I don't feel brave, I just feel scared.'

'Oh, we all feel scared at times – there's nothing wrong with that – but there will come a day when you will stop feeling scared. Look at all you've done!' He held his hands up, indicating her office. 'And look at all this.' He flicked through the pages of the magazine. 'That's the work of a very brave person.'

Holly smiled. 'I love the job.'

'And that's great news! But you need to learn to love more than your job.'

Holly frowned. She hoped this wasn't one of those get-over-one-man-by-sleeping-under-another-type chats.

'I mean learn to love yourself,' Chris continued. 'Learn to love your new life. Don't let your entire life revolve around your job. There's more to it than that.'

Holly raised her eyebrows at him. Talk about the pot calling the kettle black.

'I know I'm not the greatest example of that,' he

conceded, 'but I'm learning too . . .' He placed his hand on the table and started to brush away imaginary crumbs while he thought about what to say next. 'I heard you don't want to go to this ball.'

Holly cringed. He had definitely heard all of her phone conversation.

'There were a million places I refused to go to when Maureen died,' he said sadly. 'We used to go for walks in the Botanical Gardens every Sunday and I just couldn't go there any more after I lost her. There were a million little memories contained in every flower and tree that grew in there. The bench we used to sit on, her favourite tree, her favourite rose garden – just everything about it reminded me of her.'

'Did you go back?' Holly asked, sipping the hot tea, feeling it warm her insides.

'A few months ago,' he replied. 'It was a difficult thing to do but I did it and now I go every Sunday again. You have to confront things, Holly, and think of things positively. I say to myself, this is a place we used to laugh in, cry in, fight in, and when you go there and remember all those beautiful times you feel closer to them. You can celebrate the love you had instead of hiding from it.'

He leaned forward in his chair and stared directly into her eyes. 'Some people go through life searching and *never* find their soul mates. They *never* do. You and I did, we just happened to have them for a shorter period of time than we hoped for. It's sad, but it's life! So you go to this ball, Holly, and you embrace the fact that you had someone whom you loved and who loved you back.'

433

Tears trickled down Holly's face as she realised he was right. She needed to remember Gerry and be happy about the love they shared and the love she still continued to feel; but not to cry about them, not to yearn for the many more years with him that would never come. She thought of the line he had written to her, 'Remember our wonderful memories, but please don't be afraid to make some more.' She needed to put the ghost of Gerry that haunted her to rest but to keep his memory alive.

There was still life for her after his death.

Chapter Forty-Five

'I'm so sorry, Denise,' Holly apologised to her friend. They were sitting in the staffroom of Denise's workplace surrounded by boxes of hangers, rails of clothes, bags and accessories untidily strewn around the room. There was a musty smell in the air from the dust that had landed on the rails of clothes that had been sitting out for so long. A security camera attached to the wall stared at them and recorded their conversation.

Holly watched Denise's face for a reaction and saw her friend purse her lips in an attempt to stop them trembling and nod her head as if to let Holly know it was OK.

'No, it's not OK.' Holly sat forward in her chair. 'I didn't mean to lose my temper on the phone. Just because I'm feeling extra sensitive these days, it doesn't give me the right to take it out on you.'

Denise looked brave enough finally to speak. 'No, you were right, Holly . . .'

Holly shook her head and tried to disagree but Denise kept on talking.

'I've been so excited about this wedding that I didn't

stop to think about how you might be feeling.' Her eyes rested on her friend, whose face looked so pale against her dark jacket. Holly was doing so well it was easy for them all to forget that she still had ghosts to be rid of.

'But you're right to be excited,' Holly insisted.

'And you're right to be upset,' Denise said firmly. 'I didn't think, I just didn't think.' She held her hands to her cheeks as she shook her head. 'Don't go to the ball if you don't feel comfortable. We will all understand.' She reached out to hold her friend's hands.

Holly felt confused. Chris had succeeded in convincing her to go to the ball but now her best friend was saying it was OK not to go. And she had a headache and headaches scared her. She hugged Denise goodbye in the shop, promising to call her later to give her a decision about the ball.

She headed back to the office, feeling even more unsure than before. Maybe Denise was right: it was only a stupid ball and she didn't have to go if she didn't want to. However, it was a stupid ball that was hugely representative of Holly and Gerry's time together. It was a night they had both enjoyed, a night they shared with their friends and danced to their favourite songs. If she went without him she would be destroying that tradition, replacing old, happy memories with entirely different ones. She didn't want to do that. She wanted to hang on to every single shred of memory of her and Gerry together. It was scaring her that she was forgetting his face. When she dreamed about him he was always somebody else; a person she made up in her mind with a different face and a different voice.

Now and again she rang his mobile phone just to hear his voice on his answering machine. She had even been paying the mobile company every month just to keep his account open. His smell had faded from the house; his clothes long gone under his own orders. He was fading from her mind and so she clung desperately on to every little bit of him that she could. She deliberately thought about him every night just before she went to sleep just so that she would dream about him. She even bought his favourite aftershave and splashed it around the house. Sometimes she would be out and a familiar smell or song would transport her back to another time and another place. A happier time.

She would catch a glimpse of him walking down the street or driving by in a car and would chase that person for miles, only to discover it wasn't him; merely a lookalike. She just couldn't seem to let go.

Just before heading back to the office she poked her head into Hogan's. She was feeling much more at ease with Daniel. Since that dinner where Holly had felt so uncomfortable in his company, she had realised that she was being ridiculous. She understood now why she had felt that way. Before, the only close friendship she had ever had with a man was with Gerry, and that was a romantic relationship. The idea of becoming so close to Daniel seemed strange and unusual. Holly had since convinced herself that there didn't need to be a romantic link for her to share a friendship with a man. Even if he was good-looking.

And the ease she felt had become a feeling of companionship. She had felt that from the moment she met him. They could talk for hours, discussing her feelings, her life, his feelings, his life, and she knew that they shared a common enemy: loneliness. She knew that he was suffering from a different kind of grief but they were helping one another through the difficult days when all they needed was a caring ear or someone to make them laugh. And there were many of those days.

'Well?' he said, walking round from behind the bar. 'Will Cinderella go to the ball?'

Holly smiled and scrunched up her nose about to tell him that she wouldn't be going when she stopped herself. 'Are you going?'

He smiled and scrunched up his nose and she laughed. 'Well, it's definitely going to be a case of Couples-R-Us. I don't think I could cope with another night of Sam and Samantha or Robert and Roberta.' He pulled out a high stool for her at the bar and she sat down.

Holly giggled. 'Well, we could just be terribly rude and ignore them all.'

'Then what would be the point in going?' Daniel sat beside her and rested his leather boot on the foot rest of her chair. 'You don't expect me to talk to you all night, do you? We've talked the ears off each other by now; maybe I'm bored with you.'

'Fine then!' Holly pretended to be insulted. 'I was planning on ignoring you anyway.'

'Phew!' Daniel wiped his brow and pretended to look relieved. 'I'm definitely going then.'

Holly became serious. 'I think I really need to be there.'

Daniel stopped laughing. 'Well then, we shall go.'

Holly smiled at him. 'I think it would be good for you too, Daniel,' she said softly.

His foot dropped from her chair and he turned his head away from her, pretending to survey the lounge. 'Holly, I'm fine,' he said unconvincingly.

Holly hopped off her chair, grabbed his face and kissed him roughly on the forehead. 'Daniel Connolly, stop trying to be all macho and strong. It doesn't wash with me.'

They hugged each other goodbye, and Holly marched back to her office, determined not to change her mind. She banged loudly up the stairs and marched straight by Alice, who was still staring dreamily at her article. 'John-Paul!' Holly yelled. 'I need a dress, quick!'

Chris smiled to himself in his office as he heard everyone across the hall making a fuss over Holly. He slid open his desk drawer and peeked at the photograph of himself and his wife. He vowed to visit the Botanical Gardens someday. If Holly could do it, then so could he.

Chapter Forty-Six

Holly was running late as she rushed around her bedroom, trying to get ready for the ball. She had spent the past two hours applying her make-up, crying and smudging it and then reapplying it. She rolled the mascara brush over her eyelashes for the fourth time, praying the tear reservoir had run dry for the night. An unlikely prospect, but a girl could always hope.

'Cinderella, your prince has arrived!' Sharon yelled upstairs to her.

Holly's heart raced; she needed more time. She needed to sit down and rethink the idea of going to the ball all over again as she had completely forgotten her reasons for going. Now she was faced with only the negatives.

Reasons not to go: she didn't want to go at all; she would spend all night crying; she would be stuck at a table full of so-called friends who hadn't talked to her since Gerry had died; she felt like shit; she looked like shit and Gerry wouldn't be there.

Reasons to go: she had an overwhelming feeling that she needed to go and, most importantly, an overriding reason preventing her from backing out . . .

She breathed slowly, trying to prevent a whole new batch of tears from appearing.

'Holly, be strong. You can do this,' she whispered at her reflection in the mirror. 'You need to do this, it will help you, it will make you stronger.' She repeated this over and over again until a creak at the door made her jump.

'Sorry,' Sharon apologised, appearing from round the door. 'Oh, Holly, you look fabulous!' she said excitedly.

'I look like shit,' Holly grumbled.

'Oh, stop saying that,' Sharon said angrily. 'I look like a blimp and do you hear me complaining? Accept the fact that you're a babe!' She smiled at her in the mirror. 'You'll be fine.'

'I just want to stay home tonight, Sharon. I have to open Gerry's last message.' Holly couldn't believe the time had come to open the last one. After tomorrow there would be no more kind words from Gerry and she still felt that she needed them. In all her excitement back in April, she couldn't wait for the months to pass so that she could rip the envelopes open and read his words but she had wished the months away all too quickly and now it was nearly the end. She wanted to stay in that night and savour their last special moment.

'I know,' Sharon said understanding. 'But that can wait for a few hours, can't it?'

Holly was just about to say no when John shouted up the stairs. 'Come on, girls! The taxi's waiting! We have to collect Tom and Denise!'

Before Holly followed Sharon downstairs she slid open the drawer of her dressing table and took out the

November letter from Gerry that she had opened weeks ago. She needed his words of encouragement to help her out now. She ran her fingers over the ink and pictured him writing it. She imagined the face he made when he wrote, which she always used to tease him about. He used to have a look of pure concentration and his tongue licked his lips as he moved the pen. She loved that face. She missed that face. She slid the card from the envelope. She needed strength from this letter and she knew she would find it. Everyday, she read:

> *Cinderella must go to the ball this month.*
> *And she will look glamorous and beautiful*
> *<u>and</u> have the time of her life just like always*
> *. . . But no white dresses this year . . .*
> > *PS. I love you . . .*

The day after Holly had rowed with Denise over whether to go to the ball or not, Holly opened her November letter. Despite pep talks from Chris and Daniel, she had tortured herself all day over what her decision would be. She needn't have worried, as Gerry had chosen for her and his words reinforced the idea that she should go to the ball. This was her new task. She took a deep breath and followed Sharon downstairs.

'Wow!' Daniel said, his mouth dropping open. 'You look fabulous, Holly.'

'I look like—,' Holly started to grumble and Sharon shot her a look. 'But thanks,' she quickly added. John-Paul had helped her choose a simple black halter-neck dress, with a split to the thigh up the middle. No white dresses this year.

They all piled into the taxi and as they approached each set of traffic lights Holly prayed that they would turn red to delay the moment they arrived. No such luck. For once the traffic on the streets of Dublin was nonexistent, and they made it to the hotel in record time. Despite her prayers, a mudslide didn't cascade down the Dublin mountains and no volcano erupted. Hell refused to freeze over too.

They stepped up to the table just inside the door of the function room and Holly looked at the ground as she felt all eyes in their direction from the women eager to see how the newcomers were dressed. When they were satisfied that they were still the most beautiful people there, they looked away and continued their conversations. The woman sitting behind the desk smiled as they approached her. 'Hello, Sharon; hello, John; hi, Denise . . . oh gosh!' Her face might actually have gone whiter under her streaky fake tanned face, but Holly couldn't be sure. 'Oh, hello, Holly. It's so good of you to come considering . . .' she trailed off and quickly flicked through the guest list to tick off their names.

'Let's go to the bar,' Denise said, linking Holly's arm and dragging her away.

As they walked across the room a woman Holly hadn't spoken to for months approached her. 'Holly, I was sorry to hear about Gerry. He was a lovely man.'

'Thank you,' Holly smiled, and was led away again by Denise. They finally reached the bar.

'Hi there, Holly,' a familiar voice behind her said.

'Oh, hello, Patrick,' she said, turning to face the

large businessman who sponsored the charity. He was tall and overweight, with a bright red face, probably due to the stress of running one of Ireland's most successful businesses. That and the fact that he drank too much. He looked like he was choking with the tightness of his bow tie, and he pulled at it, looking uncomfortable. The buttons on his tuxedo looked as if they were about to pop at any moment. Holly didn't know him very well; he was just one of the people she knew from being at the ball every year.

'You're looking as lovely as always.' He gave her a kiss on the cheek. 'Can I get you a drink?' he asked, holding his hand up to attract the barman's attention.

'Oh no, thanks,' she smiled.

'Ah, let me,' he said, taking his bulging wallet out of his pocket. 'What'll you have?'

Holly gave in. 'A white wine then, please, if you insist,' she smiled.

'I might as well get a drink for that miserable husband of yours,' he laughed. 'What's he having?' He searched the room for Gerry.

'Oh, he's not here, Patrick,' Holly said, feeling uncomfortable.

'Why not? The dryshite. That's two years now he's gone missing. What's he up to?' Paul asked loudly, at the same time mouthing his order to the barman.

'Em, he passed away early in the year, Patrick,' Holly said gently, hoping not to embarrass him.

'Oh . . .' Patrick reddened even more and cleared his throat nervously. He stared down at the bar. 'I'm very sorry to hear that,' he stuttered, and looked away. He pulled at his bow tie again.

'Thank you,' Holly said, counting the seconds in her head till he made an excuse to leave the conversation. He escaped after three seconds, mumbling that he had to bring his wife her drink. Holly was left standing at the bar alone as Denise had already made her way back to the group with their drinks. She picked up her glass of wine and she headed over.

'Hi, Holly.'

She turned to see who had called her name.

'Oh, hello, Jennifer.' She was faced with another woman she knew only from attending the ball. She was dressed in an over-the-top ball gown, dripping in expensive jewellery and she held a glass of champagne between the thumb and forefinger of her gloved hand. Her blonde hair was almost white and her skin dark and leathery as a result of too much sun.

'How are you? You look fab, the dress is fab!' She sipped on her champagne and looked Holly up and down.

'I'm fine, thank you. You?'

'I'm just fab, thanks. Gerry not with you tonight?' She looked around the room for him.

'No, he passed away in February,' Holly repeated gently.

'Oh gosh, I'm so sorry to hear that.' She placed her glass of champagne down on the table next to them and her hands flew to her face, her forehead creasing with worry. 'I had no idea. How are you keeping, you poor love?' She reached out and placed her hand on Holly's arm.

'I'm fine, thank you,' Holly repeated, smiling to keep the atmosphere light.

'Oh, you poor thing.' Jennifer's voice was hushed and looked at her pityingly. 'You must be devastated.'

'Well, yes, it is hard but I'm dealing with it. Trying to be positive, you know?' she perked up.

'Gosh, I don't know how you can be. That's awful news.' Her eyes continued to bore into Holly. She seemed to look at her differently now. Holly nodded along and wished this woman would stop telling her what she already knew.

'And was he ill?' she probed.

'Yes, he had a brain tumour.'

'Oh dear, that's *awful*. And he was so *young*.' Every word she emphasised became a high-pitched screech.

'Yes, he was . . . but we had a happy life together, Jennifer,' Holly said, trying to be as cheery as she could.

'Yes, you did, but it's such a shame it wasn't a longer life. That's devastating for you. Absolutely *awful* and *so* unfair. You must feel miserable. And how on earth did you come here tonight? With all these couples around?' She looked around at all the couples as though there was suddenly a bad smell in the air.

'Well, you just have to learn to move on,' Holly smiled.

'Of course you do. But it must be so difficult. Oh, how *awful*.' She held her gloved hands up to her face, looking appalled.

Holly smiled and spoke through gritted teeth. 'Yes it's difficult, but like I said you just have to stay positive and move on. Anyway, speaking of moving on, I'd better go and join my friends,' she added politely and dashed off.

'You all right?' Daniel asked as she appeared beside him.

'Yes, I'm fine, thank you,' Holly repeated for the tenth time that night. She glanced over at Jennifer, who was in a huddle with her female friends, talking and staring over at her and Daniel.

'I have arrived!' a loud voice announced at the door. Holly turned round to see the legendary party animal Jamie standing at the door with his arms held high in the air. 'I am once again dressed in my penguin suit and ready to partaaay!' He did a little dance before joining the group, attracting stares from around the room. Just what he wanted. He made his way around their circle, greeting the men with a handshake and a kiss on the cheek for the women, sometimes 'hilariously' switching the gesture. He paused when he got to Holly and glanced back and forth from Holly to Daniel a couple of times. He shook Daniel's hand stiffly, pecked Holly on the cheek quickly as though she was diseased and rushed off. Holly tried to swallow the lump in her throat angrily. That had been very rude.

His wife, Helen, smiled timidly over at Holly from across the other side of their circle but didn't come over. Holly wasn't surprised. It had obviously been too difficult for them to drive ten minutes down the road to visit Holly after Gerry died, so she would hardly expect Helen to take ten steps towards her to say hello. She ignored them and turned to talk to her real friends, the people who had supported her for the past year.

Holly was laughing at one of Sharon's stories when she felt a light tapping on her shoulder. She turned round mid-laughter to face a very sad-looking Helen.

447

'Hi, Helen,' she said happily.

'How *are* you?' Helen said quietly, touching Holly gently on the arm.

'Oh, I'm fine,' Holly nodded. 'You should listen to this story, it's very funny,' she smiled, and continued to listen to Sharon.

Helen left her hand on Holly's arm and eventually tapped her again after a few seconds. 'I mean, how are you since Gerry . . .'

Holly gave up listening to Sharon.

'Since Gerry died, you mean?' Holly understood that people sometimes felt awkward about these situations. Holly often did too, but she felt that if someone had brought the subject up themselves they could at least be adult enough to carry the conversation through properly.

Helen appeared to wince at Holly's question. 'Well, yes, but I didn't want to say . . .'

'It's OK, Helen; I've accepted that that's what happened.'

'Have you?'

'Of course I have,' Holly frowned.

'It's just that I haven't seen you for a very long time so I was beginning to get worried . . .'

Holly laughed. 'Helen, I still live round the corner from you in the same house as before, my home phone number is still the same, as is my mobile number. If you were ever that worried about me I was never that difficult for you to find.'

'Oh yes, but I didn't want to intrude . . .' she trailed off.

'Friends don't intrude, Helen,' Holly said politely,

but hoped she had got her message across.

Helen blushed slightly and Holly turned away to talk to Sharon.

'Keep me a seat beside you, will you? I just need to run to the ladies again,' Sharon asked, doing a little dance on the spot.

'Again?' Denise blurted out. 'You were just there five minutes ago!'

'Yes, well, this tends to happen when you have a seven-month-old baby pushing down on your bladder,' she explained, before waddling off to the toilet.

'It's not actually seven months old, though, is it?' Denise said, scrunching her face up. 'Technically, it's minus two months because otherwise that would mean that the baby would be nine months old when he was born and then they would be celebrating his first birthday after only three months. And usually babies are walking by the time they're one.'

Holly frowned at her. 'Denise, why do you torment yourself with thoughts like that?'

Denise frowned and turned to Tom, 'I'm right, though, aren't I, Tom?'

'Yes, love.' He smiled sweetly at her.

'Chicken,' Holly teased Tom.

The bell was rung to signal that it was time to take their places for dinner, and the crowds began to swarm in. Holly took her seat and placed her new handbag down on the chair beside her to reserve it for Sharon. Helen wandered over and pulled out the chair to sit down.

'Sorry, Helen, but Sharon asked me to save this seat for her,' Holly explained politely.

Helen waved her hand dismissively. 'Oh, Sharon won't mind,' she said, plonking herself down on the chair and squashing Holly's handbag. Sharon made her way over to the table and stuck out her bottom lip in disappointment. Holly apologised and motioned over to Helen as her excuse. Sharon rolled her eyes and stuck her fingers in her mouth, pretending to gag. Holly giggled.

'Well, you're in high spirits,' Jamie announced to Holly, sounding very unimpressed.

'Is there any reason why I shouldn't be?' Holly replied tartly.

Jamie replied with some smart retort that a few people laughed at because he was 'so funny' and Holly ignored him. She didn't find him funny any more, though she and Gerry had always been amongst those people who had hung on his every word. Now he was just being stupid.

'Are you OK?' Daniel asked quietly from beside her.

'Yes, I'm fine, thank you,' she replied, taking a sip of wine.

'Oh, you don't have to give me that bullshit answer, Holly. It's me,' he laughed.

Holly smiled and groaned. 'People are being very nice and all by offering me their sympathies but I feel like I'm back at his funeral again. Having to pretend to be all strong and Superwoman-like, even though all some of them want is for me to be devastated because it's so *awful*.' She mimicked Jennifer and rolled her eyes. 'And then there's the people who don't know about Gerry and this is *so* not the place to have to tell them.'

Daniel listened to her patiently. He nodded when she finally stopped talking. 'I understand what you're saying. When Laura and I broke up I felt that for months everywhere I went I was always having to tell people that we broke up. But the good thing is that eventually word goes around so you can stop having those awkward conversations with people all the time.'

'Any word on Laura, by the way?' Holly asked. She enjoyed having bitching sessions about Laura, even though she had never met her. She loved to hear stories about her from Daniel, and then the two of them would spend the evening talking about how much they hated her. It passed the time and right now Holly really needed something to avoid having to talk to Helen.

Daniel's eyes lit up. 'Yes, actually, I do have a bit of gossip about her.'

'Oooh good, I love a bit of gossip,' Holly said, rubbing her hands together with delight.

'Well, a friend of mine named Charlie, who works as a barman in Laura's dad's hotel, told me that her fiancé tried to come on to some other woman who was a guest there and Laura caught him so they split up.' He laughed evilly with a twinkle in his eye. He was delighted to hear of her heartbreak.

Holly froze because that story sounded rather familiar. 'Eh . . . Daniel, what hotel does her father own?'

'Oh, the Galway Inn. It's a real kip of a place but it's in a nice area, across the road from the beach.'

'Oh.' Holly didn't know what to say and her eyes widened.

'I know,' Daniel laughed. 'It's brilliant, isn't it? I can

451

tell you, if I ever met the woman who split them up I would buy her the most expensive bottle of champagne.'

Holly smiled weakly. 'Would you now . . . ?' Holly stared at Daniel curiously, interested to know why on earth he had once been interested in Laura. Holly would have bet all her money against those two ever being together. She didn't seem his type, whatever his 'type' was. Daniel was so easy-going and friendly, and Laura was . . . well, Laura was a bitch. Holly couldn't think of any other word to describe her.

'Em, Daniel?' Holly nervously tucked her hair behind her ears, preparing herself to question him on his choice of women.

He smiled at her, eyes still twinkling from the news of his ex-girlfriend and ex-best friend's break-up. 'Yes, Holly.'

'Well, I was just wondering. Laura seems to sound like a bit of a . . . em . . . a . . . bitch, to be honest.' She bit her lip and studied his face to see if she had insulted him. His face was blank as he stared at the candlesticks in the centre of the table and listened. 'Well,' she continued, feeling she had to tiptoe carefully around this subject, knowing how badly Laura had broken Daniel's heart, 'well, my question is really, whatever did you see in her? How could you two *ever* have been in love? You're both so different – at least you *sound* like you're so different,' she back-pedalled fast, remembering she wasn't supposed ever to have met Laura.

Daniel was silent for a moment and Holly feared she had stepped in the wrong territory. He dragged his eyes away from the flame dancing around on the candlestick to face Holly. His lips broke into a sad smile. 'Laura isn't really a bitch, Holly. Well, for leaving me for my best friend she is . . . but as a person, when we were together, she was never a bitch. Dramatic, yes. A bitch, no.' He smiled and turned to face Holly properly. 'You see, I loved the drama of our relationship. I found it exciting, she *enthralled* me.' His face became animated as he explained their relationship and his speech quickened with the excitement of the memory of his lost love. 'I loved waking up in the morning and wondering what kind of mood she would be in that day, I loved our fights, I loved the passion of them and I loved how we would make love after them.' His eyes sparkled. 'She would make a song and dance about most things but I suppose that's what I found different and attractive about her. I used to always tell myself that as long as she kept making a fuss about our own relationship then I knew she cared. If she hadn't then it wouldn't have been worth it really. I loved the drama,' he repeated, believing himself even more this time. 'Our temperaments contrasted but we made a good team. You know what they say about opposites attracting . . .' He looked into the face of his new friend and saw her concern. 'She didn't treat me badly, Holly. She wasn't a bitch in that way.' He smiled to himself. 'She was just . . .'

'Dramatic,' Holly finished for him, finally understanding. He nodded. Although she did cheat on him, Holly thought angrily, but decided not to say it aloud.

Holly watched his face as he became lost in another memory. She supposed it was possible for anybody to love anybody. That was the great thing about love: it came in all different shapes, sizes and temperaments.

'You miss her,' Holly said gently, putting her hand on his arm.

Daniel snapped out of his daydream and stared deeply into Holly's eyes. A shiver went down her spine and she felt the hairs on her arms stand up.

He snorted loudly and twisted back round in his chair, 'Wrong again, Holly Kennedy,' he said, and frowned as though she had said the most bizarre thing ever. 'Completely and *utterly* wrong.' He picked up his knife and fork and began to eat his salmon starter.

Holly gulped back some cool water and turned her attention to the plate that was being set before her.

After dinner and a few bottles of wine, Helen stumbled over to Holly, who had escaped over to Sharon and Denise's side of the table. She gave her a big hug and tearily apologised for not keeping in touch.

'That's OK, Helen. Sharon, Denise and John have been very supportive friends so I wasn't alone.'

'Oh, but I feel so awful,' Helen slurred.

'Don't,' Holly said, anxious to continue her enjoyable conversation with the girls.

But Helen insisted on talking about the good old times when Gerry was alive and everything was rosy. She talked about all the times that she and Gerry shared together, which were memories that Holly wasn't particularly interested in. Eventually Holly had had enough of Helen's tearful whinging and realised that all her friends were up having fun on the dance floor.

'Helen, please stop,' Holly interrupted. 'I don't know why you feel you have to discuss this with me

454

tonight when I am trying to enjoy myself, but you obviously feel guilty for not keeping in touch with me. To be honest, I think that if I hadn't come to this ball tonight I still wouldn't have heard from you for another ten months or more. And that's not the kind of friend I need in my life. So please stop crying on my shoulder and let me enjoy myself.'

Holly felt that she had phrased it reasonably, but Helen looked like she had been slapped in the face. A small dose of what Holly had felt like for the past year. Daniel appeared out of nowhere, took Holly by the hand and led her to the dance floor to join all her friends. As soon as they reached the dance floor the song ended and Eric Clapton's 'Wonderful Tonight' began. The dance floor began to empty out bar a few couples, and Holly was left facing Daniel. She gulped. She hadn't planned on this. She had only ever danced with Gerry to this song.

Daniel placed his hand lightly on her waist and gently took her hand and they began to circle round. Holly was stiff. Dancing with another man felt wrong. A tingle went down her spine and she shuddered. Daniel must have thought she was cold because he pulled her closer as if to keep her warm. She was led round the floor in a trance until the song ended and she made the excuse of having to go to the toilet. She locked herself in the cubicle and leaned against the door, taking deep breaths. She had been doing so well up until now. Even with everyone asking her about Gerry she had remained calm. But the dance had shaken her. Perhaps it was time to go home, while the going was good. She was about to unlock the door when she heard a voice outside say her name. She froze and listened to the women chatting outside.

'Did you see Holly Kennedy dancing with that man tonight?' a voice asked. The unmistakable whine of Jennifer.

'I know!' another voice spoke with a tone of disgust. 'And her husband not yet cold in his grave!'

'Ah, leave her alone,' another woman said light-heartedly. 'They could just be friends.'

Thank you, Holly thought.

'But I doubt it,' she continued, and the women giggled.

'Did you see the way they were wrapped around each other? I don't dance with any of my friends like that,' Jennifer said.

'That's disgraceful,' another woman said. 'Imagine flaunting your new man in a place you used to come to with your husband in front of all his friends. It's disgusting.'

The women tutted and a toilet flushed in the cubicle beside Holly. She stood frozen in her position, shocked by what she was hearing and embarrassed they were saying it where others could hear.

The toilet door opened beside her and the women were silenced. 'Would you bickering old bitches ever go and get yourselves lives?' Sharon's voice yelled. 'It is absolutely no business of yours what *my best friend* does or does not do! Jennifer, if your life was so bloody perfect then what are you doing sneaking around with Pauline's husband?'

Holly heard someone gasp. Probably Pauline. She covered her mouth to stop herself laughing.

'Right, so keep your noses in your own business and piss off the lot of you!' Sharon yelled.

When Holly had heard everyone leave she unlocked the door and stepped outside. Sharon looked up at her from the sink in shock.

'Thanks, Sharon.'

'Oh Holly, I'm sorry you had to hear that,' she said, giving her friend a hug.

'It doesn't matter. I couldn't give a crap what they think,' Holly said bravely. 'But I can't believe Jennifer is having an affair with Pauline's husband!'

Sharon shrugged. 'She's not but it'll give them something to bitch about for the next few months.'

The girls chuckled.

'I reckon I'll go home now, though,' Holly said, glancing at her watch and thinking about the final message from Gerry. Her heart sank.

'Good idea,' Sharon agreed. 'I didn't realise how shite this ball was when you're sober.'

Holly smiled.

'Anyway, you were great tonight, Holly. You came, you conquered, now go home and open Gerry's message. Ring me and let me know what it says.' She hugged her friend again.

'It's the last one,' Holly said sadly.

'I know, so enjoy it,' Sharon smiled. 'Memories last a lifetime, remember that.'

Holly made her way back to the table to say goodbye to everyone, and Daniel stood up to go with her. 'You're not leaving me here on my own,' he laughed. 'We can share a cab.'

Holly was slightly irritated when Daniel hopped out

of the taxi and followed her to her house. It was a quarter to twelve, which gave her fifteen minutes. With luck he would have drunk his tea and gone by then. She had even called another taxi to arrive at her house in a half an hour, just to let him know he couldn't stay too long.

'Ah, so this is the famous envelope,' Daniel said, picking it up from the table.

Holly's eyes widened; she felt protective over that envelope and wasn't happy with him touching it, removing Gerry's touch from it.

'December,' he said, reading the outside and running his fingers along the lettering. Holly wanted to tell him to put it down but didn't want to sound psychotic. Eventually he placed it back on the table and she breathed a sigh of relief and continued to fill the kettle.

'How many more envelopes are left?' Daniel asked, taking his overcoat off and walking over to join her at the kitchen counter.

'That's the last one.' Holly's voice was husky and she cleared her throat.

'So what are you going to do after that?'

'What do you mean?' she asked, feeling confused.

'Well, as far as I can see, that list is like your Bible, your Ten Commandments. What the list says goes, as far as your life is concerned. So what will you do when there aren't any more?'

Holly looked up at his face to see if he was being smart but his blue eyes twinkled kindly back at her.

'I'll just live my life,' she replied, turning her back and flicking the switch on the kettle.

'Will you be able to do that?' He walked closer to

her and she could smell his aftershave. It was a real Daniel smell.

'I suppose so,' she replied, uncomfortable with his questions.

'Because you will have to make your own decisions then,' he said softly.

'I know that,' she replied defensively, avoiding eye contact with him.

'And do you think you'll be able to do that?'

Holly rubbed her face tiredly. 'Daniel, what's this about?'

He swallowed hard and adjusted his stance before her, trying to make himself comfortable. 'I'm asking you this because I'm going to say something to you now, and you are going to have to make your own decision.' He looked her straight in the eye and her heart beat wildly. 'There will be no list, no guidelines; you will just have to follow your own heart.'

Holly backed away from him a little. A feeling of dread pulled at her and she hoped he wasn't going to say what she thought he was.

'Em . . . Daniel . . . I d-don't think that this is . . . the right time to . . . um . . . we shouldn't talk about . . .'

'This is a perfect time,' he said seriously. 'You already know what I'm going to say to you Holly and I *know* you already know how I feel about you.'

Holly's jaw dropped as she glanced at the clock.

It was twelve o'clock.

Chapter Forty-Seven

Gerry touched Holly's nose and smiled to himself as she wrinkled it up in her sleep. He loved watching her while she was sleeping; she looked like a princess, so beautiful and peaceful.

He tickled her nose again and smiled as her eyes slowly opened. 'Good morning, sleepy-head.'

She smiled at him. 'Good morning, beautiful.' She cuddled closer to him and rested her head on his chest. 'How are you feeling today?'

'Like I could run the London marathon,' he joked.

'Now that's what I call a quick recovery,' she smiled, lifting her head and kissing him on the lips. 'What do you want for breakfast?'

'You,' he said, biting her nose.

Holly giggled. 'I'm not on the menu today, unfortunately. How about a fry?'

'No,' he frowned, 'that's too heavy for me,' and his heart melted as he saw Holly's face fall. He tried to perk himself up. 'But I would love a big, huge bowl of vanilla ice cream!'

'Ice cream!' she laughed. 'For breakfast?'

'Yes,' he grinned, 'I always wanted that for breakfast

when I was a kid but my darling mother would never allow me to have it. But now I don't care any more,' he smiled bravely.

'Then ice cream you shall have,' Holly hopped happily out of bed. 'Do you mind if I wear this?' she asked, putting his dressing gown on.

'My dear, you can wear it all you like,' Gerry smiled, watching her modelling the oversized robe up and down the bedroom for him.

'Mmm, it smells of you,' she said, sniffing it. 'I'm never going to take it off. OK, I'll be back in a minute,' and he heard her racing down the stairs and clattering around in the kitchen.

Lately he had noticed her racing around every time she left his side. It was as though she was afraid to leave him for too long on his own, and he knew what that meant. Bad news for him. He had finished his radiation therapy, which they had prayed would target the residual tumour. It had failed, and now all he could do was lie around all day, too weak to get up most of the time. It just seemed so pointless to him to be wasting time like that because it wasn't even as if he was waiting to recover. His heart beat wildly at the thought. He was afraid; afraid of where he was going, afraid of what was happening to him and afraid for Holly. She was the only person who knew exactly what to say to him to calm him down and ease his pain. She was so strong, his rock, and he couldn't imagine his life without her. But he needn't worry about that scenario, because it was her that would be without him. He felt angry, sad, jealous and scared for her. He wanted to stay with her and carry out every wish and promise that they had ever made to one another, and he was fighting for that right. But he knew he was fighting a losing battle. After two operations the tumour had returned, and it was growing rapidly inside him. He wanted to reach into his head and tear out the disease that was destroying his life but that was just another thing he had no control over. He feared that after this month Holly would be alone . . .

They had become even closer over the past few months, which was something he knew was a bad idea, for Holly's sake, but he couldn't bear to distance himself from her. He was living for their chats that carried on till the early hours of the morning and left them giggling, just like when they were teenagers. But that was only on their good days.

They had their bad days too.

He wouldn't think about that now. His therapist kept telling him to 'give your body a positive environment – socially, emotionally, nutritionally and spiritually.'

And his new little project was doing just that. It was keeping him busy and making him feel as if he was doing something other than lie in bed all day. His mind was kept occupied as he mapped out his plan to remain with Holly even when he was gone. He was also fulfilling a promise he had made to her years ago. At least there was one promise he could follow through on for her. Shame it had to be this particular one.

He heard Holly thudding up the stairs and he smiled; his plan was working.

'Babe, there's no ice cream left,' she said sadly. 'Is there anything else you would prefer?'

462

'Nope,' he shook his head. 'Just the ice cream, please.'

'Oh, but now I have to go to the shop to get it,' she complained.

'Don't worry, hon, I'll be fine for a few minutes,' he assured her.

She looked at him uncertainly. 'I really would rather stay.'

'Don't be silly,' he smiled, and lifted his mobile off the bedside table, placing it on his chest. 'If there's a problem, which there won't be, I'll call you.'

'OK,' Holly bit her lip, 'I'll only be five minutes down the road. Are you sure you'll be all right?'

'Positive,' he smiled.

She slowly took off his robe and threw on a track-suit. He could see she still wasn't happy about the arrangement.

'Holly, I'll be fine,' he said firmly.

'OK.' She gave him a long kiss and he heard her race down the stairs, rush out to the car, and speed off down the road.

As soon as Gerry knew it was safe, he pulled back the covers and slowly climbed out of bed. He sat on the edge of the mattress for a while, waiting for the dizziness to pass, then slowly made his way to the wardrobe. He took out an old shoebox from the top shelf that contained junk he had collected over the past few years and that now also contained nine sealed envelopes. He took out a tenth empty envelope and neatly wrote 'December' on the front. Today was the first of December and he moved himself forward one year from now when he knew he wouldn't be around. He imagined Holly to be a karaoke genius, relaxed from her holiday in Spain, bruise-free as a result of the bedside lamp and, he hoped, happy in a new job that she loved.

He imagined her on this very day in one year's time, possibly sitting on the bed right where he was now and reading the final instalment to the list. He thought long and hard about what to write for this last message. Tears filled his eyes as he placed the full stop beside the sentence; he kissed the page, wrapped it in the envelope and hid it back in the shoebox. He would post the envelopes to Holly's parents' house in Portmarnock where he knew the package would be in safe hands until she was prepared to open it. He wiped the tears from his eyes and slowly made his way back to bed where his phone was ringing on the mattress.

'Hello?' he said, trying to control his voice, and he smiled when he heard the sweetest voice on the other end. 'I love you too, Holly . . .'

Chapter Forty-Eight

'No, Daniel, this isn't right,' Holly said, upset, and pulled her hand away from his grip.

'But why isn't it right?' he pleaded with her.

'It's too soon,' she said, rubbing her face tiredly. Things for her just seemed to get more and more complicated.

'Too soon because that's what people have been telling you, or too soon because that's what your heart's telling you?'

'Oh, Daniel, I don't know,' she said, pacing the kitchen floor. 'I'm so confused. *Please* stop asking me so many questions!'

Her heart beat wildly and her head spun, even her body was telling her this wasn't a good situation to be in. It was panicking on her behalf, indicating that danger was ahead. This felt wrong – it all felt so wrong, 'I can't, Daniel. I'm married! I love Gerry!' she said in a panic.

'Gerry?' he asked, his eyes widening as he went over to the kitchen table and grabbed the envelope roughly. 'This is Gerry! This is what I'm competing with! It's a piece of paper, Holly. It's a *list*. A list you have

465

allowed to run your life for the past year without having to think for yourself or live your own life. Now you have to think for yourself, right now. Gerry's gone,' he said gently, walking back over to her. 'Gerry's gone and I'm here. I'm not saying that I could ever take his place but at least give us a chance to be together.'

She took the envelope from his hand and hugged it close to her heart as tears rolled down her cheeks. 'Gerry's not gone,' she sobbed. 'He's here, every time I open these, he's here.'

There was a silence as Daniel watched her crying. She looked so lost and helpless he just wanted to hold her. 'It's a piece of paper,' he said softly, stepping closer to her again.

'Gerry is *not* a piece of paper,' she said angrily through her tears. 'He was a living breathing human being that I loved. Gerry is a man that consumed my life for fifteen years. He is a million billion happy memories. He is *not* a piece of paper,' she repeated.

'So what am I?' Daniel asked quietly.

Holly prayed that he wouldn't cry. She didn't think she could bear it if he cried.

'You,' she took a deep breath, 'are a kind, caring and incredibly thoughtful friend who I respect and appreciate—'

'But I'm not Gerry,' he interrupted her.

'I *don't want* you to be Gerry,' she insisted. 'I want you to be Daniel.'

'How do you feel about me?' His voice shook slightly.

'I just told you how I feel about you,' she sniffed.

'No, how do you *feel* about me?'

She stared at the ground. 'I feel strongly about you, Daniel, but I need time . . .' she paused, '. . . lots and lots of time.'

'Then I will wait.' He smiled sadly and wrapped his strong arms around her.

The doorbell rang and Holly silently breathed a sigh of relief. 'That's your taxi.' Her voice shook.

'I'll call you tomorrow, Holly,' he said softly, kissing her on the top of her head and making his way to the front door. Holly continued to stand in the middle of the kitchen after he'd gone, running over and over in her mind the scene that had just occurred. She stood there for some time, tightly gripping the crumpled envelope close to her heart.

Still in shock she eventually made her way slowly up the stairs to bed. She slipped out of her dress and wrapped herself in Gerry's warm oversized robe. His smell had disappeared. She slowly climbed into bed like a child, tucked herself under the covers and flicked on the bedside lamp. She stared at the envelope for a long time, thinking about what Daniel had said.

The list *had* become some sort of Bible to her. She obeyed the rules, lived by the rules and never broke any of them. When Gerry said jump, she jumped. But the list had helped her. It had helped her get out of bed in the morning and start a new life at a time when all she wanted to do was curl into a ball and die. Gerry had helped her and she didn't regret one thing she had done in the past year. She didn't regret her new job or her new friends or any new thought or feeling she had developed all by herself without Gerry's opinion. But this was the final instalment to the list.

This was her tenth Commandment, as Daniel had phrased it. There would be no more. He was right: she would have to start making decisions for herself, live a life that she felt happy with without holding back and wondering whether or not Gerry would agree with it. Well, she could always wonder, but she needn't let it stop her.

When he was alive she had lived through him, and now he was dead she was still living through him. She could see that now. It made her feel safe, but now she was out on her own and she needed to be brave.

She took the phone off the hook and switched off her mobile. She didn't want to be disturbed. She needed to savour this special and final moment without interruptions. She needed to say goodbye to Gerry. She was alone now and she needed to think for herself.

She slowly tore open the envelope, carefully trying not to rip the paper as she slid the card out.

Don't be afraid to fall in love again. Open your heart and follow where it leads you . . . and remember, shoot for the moon . . .
    PS. I will always love you . . .

'Oh, Gerry,' she sobbed, and her shoulders shook as her body heaved.

She got very little sleep that night and the times she did nod off, her dreams were obscure images of Daniel and Gerry's faces and bodies being mingled together. She awoke in a sweat at 6 a.m. and decided to get up and go for a walk to clear the jumbled thoughts from her head. Her heart felt heavy as she walked along the path of her local park. She had bundled herself up well to protect herself from the stinging cold that whipped at her ears and numbed her face. Yet her head felt hot. Hot from the tears, hot from her headache, hot from her brain working overtime.

The trees were bare and looked like skeletons lining the pathway. Leaves danced in circles around her feet like wicked little elves threatening to trip her up. The park was deserted; people had once again gone into hibernation, too cowardly to brave the winter elements. Holly wasn't brave, nor was she enjoying her stroll. It felt like punishment to be out in the icy cold weather.

How on earth had she found herself in this situation? Just as soon as she was getting round to picking up the pieces of her shattered life, she dropped them all again and sent them scattering. She thought she had found a friend, someone she could confide in. She wasn't looking to become entangled in some ridiculous love triangle. And it was ridiculous because the third person wasn't even around. He wasn't even a possible candidate for the job. Of course she thought of Daniel a lot, but she also thought about Sharon and Denise, and surely she wasn't in love with them? What she felt for Daniel wasn't the love she felt for Gerry, it was an entirely different feeling. So perhaps she wasn't in love with Daniel. And, anyway, if she was, wouldn't she be the first person to realise it, instead of being given a few days to 'think about it'? But then why was she even thinking about it? If she didn't love him, then she should come right out and say it . . . but she was thinking about it. It was a simple yes/no question, wasn't it? How odd life was.

And why was Gerry urging her to find a new love? What had he been *thinking* when he wrote that message? Had he already let go of her before he died? Had it been *so* easy for him to just give her up and resign himself to the fact that she would meet someone else? Questions, questions, questions. And she would never know the answers.

After hours of tormenting herself with further interrogations and the freezing cold nipping at her skin, she headed back in the direction of her house. As she walked down her road, the sound of laughter caused her to lift her gaze from the ground. Her neighbours were decorating the tree in their garden with tiny Christmas lights.

'Hi, Holly,' her neighbour said, stepping out from behind the tree with bulbs wrapped around her wrists.

'I'm decorating Jessica,' her partner laughed, wrapping the tangled cords around her legs. 'I think she'll make a beautiful garden gnome.'

Holly smiled sadly as she watched them laughing together. 'Christmas already.'

'I know,' Jessica stopped laughing long enough to answer. 'Hasn't the year just flown?'

'Too fast,' Holly said quietly. 'It went far too fast.'

Holly crossed the road and continued on her way to her house. A scream caused her to swirl round and see Jessica lose her balance and collapse onto the grass, wrapped in a pile of lights. Laughter echoed down the street as Holly stepped into her house.

'OK Gerry,' Holly announced as she closed the front door, 'I've been for a walk and I've thought deeply about what you said and I have come to the conclusion that you had lost your mind when you wrote that message. If you really *really* mean it then give me some sort of sign, and if not I'll completely understand that it was all a big mistake and that you have changed your mind,' she said matter-of-factly into the air.

She looked around the living room, waiting to see if anything happened. Nothing happened.

'OK then,' she said happily, 'you made a mistake, I understand. I will just disregard that final message.' She looked around the room again and wandered over towards the window. 'OK, Gerry, this is your last chance . . .'

The lights on the tree across the road flew on and Jessica and Tony danced about their garden, giggling. Suddenly the lights flickered and went out again. They stopped dancing and their faces fell.

Holly rolled her eyes. 'I'll take that as an "I don't know".'

She sat down at the kitchen table and sipped on a hot mug of tea to thaw out her frozen body. Friend tells you he loves you and dead husband tells you to fall in love again so you make a cup of tea.

She had three weeks left at work until she could take her Christmas holidays, which meant that, if she had to, she would only have to avoid Daniel for fifteen working days. That seemed possible. Hopefully by the time of Denise's wedding at the end of December she would have made a decision about what to do. But first she had to get through her first Christmas alone and she was dreading it.

Chapter Forty-Nine

'OK, where do you want me to put it?' Richard panted, dragging the Christmas tree into her living room. A trail of pine needles led all the way out of the living-room door, down the hall, out the front door and into her car. Holly sighed. She would have to vacuum the house again today to get rid of the mess and she stared at the tree with disgust. They smelled so fresh but, damn, were they messy.

'Holly!' Richard repeated, and she jumped from her thoughts to face him.

She giggled. 'You look like a talking tree, Richard.' All she could see were his little brown shoes sticking out from underneath the tree.

'Holly,' he grunted, losing his balance slightly under the weight.

'Oh, sorry,' she said, suddenly realising that he was about to fall over. 'Just by the window.'

She bit her lip and winced as he sent lamps, photo frames and candles from the fireplace crashing around him while he made his way over to the window.

'There now,' he said, wiping his hands and stepping back to take a look at his work.

Holly frowned. 'It looks a little bit bare, don't you think?'

'Well, you will have to decorate it, of course.'

'I know that, Richard, but I was referring to the fact that it only has about five branches left. It's got bald patches,' she moaned.

'I told you to buy a tree earlier, Holly, not leave it until Christmas Eve. Anyway that was the best of a bad lot; I sold the best ones weeks ago.'

'I suppose,' Holly frowned.

She hadn't wanted to get a Christmas tree at all this year. She wasn't in the mood to celebrate and it wasn't as if she had any children in the house to please by putting up decorations. Richard had insisted, though, and Holly felt that she had to help him out with his new Christmas tree selling venture in addition to his flourishing landscaping business. But the tree was awful and no amount of tinsel could hide that. Looking at it made her wish she had just bought one from Richard earlier. At least then maybe it would have looked like a real tree instead of a pole with a few pine needles hanging off.

She couldn't believe it was Christmas Eve already. She had spent the past few weeks working overtime, trying to get the January issue of the magazine ready early before they all took their Christmas break. They had eventually finished the day before, and when Alice had suggested they all go for Christmas drinks at Hogan's, Holly had politely declined. She still hadn't spoken to Daniel; she had ignored all of his calls, had avoided Hogan's like the plague, and had ordered Alice to tell him she was in a meeting if ever he called the office. He called the office nearly every day.

She didn't intend to be rude but she needed more time to think things through. OK, so it wasn't as if he had just proposed to her but it almost felt like it.

Richard's voice snapped her back to reality.

'Sorry, what?'

'I said would you like me to help you decorate it?'

Holly's heart fell. That was her and Gerry's job, nobody else's. Every year without fail they would put the Christmas CD on, open a bottle of wine and decorate the tree . . .

'Eh . . . no, it's OK Richard, I'll do it. I'm sure you've better things to be doing now.'

'Well, actually I would quite like to do it,' he said eagerly. 'Usually myself, Meredith and the children do it together but I missed out on that this year . . .' he trailed off.

'Oh.' Holly hadn't even thought about Richard's Christmas as being difficult as well; she was too self-ishly caught up in her own worries.

'OK, then, why not?' she smiled.

Richard beamed and he looked like a child.

'But the only thing is, I'm not too sure where the decorations are. Gerry always used to store them away in the attic somewhere . . .' she murmured.

'No problem,' he smiled encouragingly. 'That used to be my job too. I'll find them.' He bounded up the stairs to the attic.

Holly opened a bottle of red wine and pressed play on the CD player. Bing Crosby's 'White Christmas' played softly in the background. Richard returned with a black sack slung over his shoulder and a dusty Santa hat on. 'Ho ho ho!'

Holly giggled and handed him his glass of wine.

'No no,' he waved his hand, 'I'm driving.'

'You can have one glass, Richard,' she said, feeling disappointed.

'No no,' he repeated, 'I don't drink and drive.'

Holly threw her eyes up to heaven and knocked back his glass of wine before beginning her own. By the time Richard left she had finished the bottle and was opening another. She noticed then the red light flashing on the answering machine. She had switched it on for some peace and quiet that day, and was hoping the message wasn't from who she thought it was. She hit the play button.

'Hi, Sharon, it's Daniel Connolly here. Sorry to bother you but I had your phone number from when you called the club months ago about entering Holly into the karaoke. Em . . . well, I was really just hoping you could pass on a message for me. Denise has been so busy with the wedding arrangements that I knew I couldn't rely on her to remember . . .' He laughed slightly and cleared his throat. 'Anyway, I was wondering if you could just tell Holly that I'm going down to my family in Galway for Christmas. I'm heading down there tomorrow. I haven't been able to get through to her on her mobile, I know she's on holiday from work now, and I don't have her home number . . . so if you . . .'

He got cut off and Holly waited for the next message to be played.

'Eh, sorry, Sharon, it's me again. Eh . . . Daniel,

that is. I just got cut off there. Yeah, so anyway, if you could just tell Holly that I'll be in Galway for the next few days and that I'll have my mobile with me if she wants to reach me. I know she has some things to think about so . . .' he paused. 'Anyway, I'd better go before I get cut off again. I'll see you all at the wedding next week. OK thanks . . . bye.'

The next message was from Denise, telling her that Daniel was looking for her, the fourth message was from her brother Declan, also telling her that Daniel was looking for her and the fifth message was from an old school friend whom Holly hadn't seen in years, telling her that she bumped into a friend of hers called Daniel in a pub the previous night, oh yeah, and Daniel was looking for Holly and he wanted her to call him back. The sixth message was from Daniel again.

'Hi, Holly, it's Daniel here. Your brother Declan gave me your number. I can't believe we've been friends so long and you never gave me your home number, yet I have the sneaking suspicion I've had it all along without realising . . .' There was a silence as he exhaled. 'Anyway, I really need to talk to you, Holly. I think it should be in person, and it should be before we see each other at the wedding. Please, Holly, please take my calls. I don't know how else to get to you.' Silence, another deep breath and exhalation. 'OK, well, that's all. Bye.'

Holly pressed play again, lost in thought.

She sat in the living room staring at the tree and listening to Christmas songs. She cried. Cried for her Gerry and for her baldy Christmas tree.

Chapter Fifty

'Happy Christmas, love!' Frank opened the door to a shivering Holly standing on the doorstep.

'Happy Christmas, Dad,' she smiled, and gave him a big bear hug. She inhaled as she walked round the house. The beautiful smell of pine mixed with wine and Christmas dinner cooking in the kitchen filled her nostrils, and she was hit with a pang of loneliness. Christmas reminded her of Gerry. Gerry was Christmas. It was their special time together where they would hide from the stresses of work and just relax in between entertaining their friends and family and enjoy their time alone. She missed him so much it gave her a sick feeling in the pit of her stomach.

She had visited the graveyard that morning to wish him a happy Christmas. It was the first time she had been there since the funeral; she had avoided visiting the grave since then as she found it too painful. It had been an upsetting morning. No parcel under the tree for her, no breakfast in bed, no noise, no nothing. Gerry had wanted to be cremated, which meant that she had to stand in front of a wall that had his name engraved on it. And she really did feel that she was talking to a wall. However, she had told him about her year and what her plans were for the day, had told him Sharon and John were expecting a baby boy and they were planning on calling him Gerry. She told him that she was to be his godmother; that she was to be maid of honour at Denise's wedding. She explained what Tom was like because Gerry had never met him, and she talked about her new job. She didn't mention Daniel. She had felt peculiar standing there talking to herself. She wanted to get some deep spiritual feeling that he was there with her and listening to her voice, but she really just felt like she was talking to a drab grey wall.

Her situation was no extraordinary sight on Christmas day. The graveyard had been packed with visitors, families bringing their aged mothers and fathers to visit their departed spouses, young women like Holly wandering alone, young men . . . She had watched as a young mother broke down over a gravestone while her two startled children watched, not knowing what to do. The younger child could only have been three years old. The woman had quickly dried her eyes to protect her children. Holly was thankful that she could afford to be selfish and only have to worry about herself. How on earth that woman could find the strength to carry on through the day with two infants to worry about had cropped up in Holly's head regularly since then.

All in all it hadn't been a good day.

'Oh, happy Christmas, dear!' Elizabeth announced, walking out of the kitchen with her arms held open to embrace her child. Holly started to cry. She felt

478

like the young child at the graveyard. She still needed her mammy too. Elizabeth's face was flushed from the heat of the kitchen, and the warmth of her body warmed Holly's heart.

'I'm sorry,' she wiped her face, 'I didn't want to do that.'

'Hush,' Elizabeth said soothingly, hugging her even tighter. She didn't even need to say anything more; her just being there was enough.

Holly had called round to visit her mother the previous week in a panic about what to do about the Daniel situation. Elizabeth, not usually the baking kind of mother, was in the middle of making the Christmas cake for the following week. Her face was powdered with patches of flour, the sleeves of her sweater rolled up to her elbows, bits of flour gathered in her hair. The kitchen counter was covered in stray raisins, sultanas and cherries. Flour, pastry, baking trays and tin foil cluttered the surfaces. The kitchen was decorated in colourful glittery decorations and that wonderful festive smell filled the air.

The moment Elizabeth had laid eyes on her daughter, Holly knew that she could sense there was something wrong. They had sat at the kitchen table that was overflowing with red and green Christmas serviettes with picture prints of Santa, reindeers and Christmas trees. There were boxes and boxes of Christmas crackers for the family to get competitive over, chocolate biscuits, beer and wine, the whole lot . . . Holly's parents had stocked up well for the Kennedy family.

'What's on your mind, love?' Holly's mother had asked, pushing a plate of chocolate biscuits towards her.

Holly's stomach had rumbled but she couldn't stomach any food. Once again she had lost her appetite. She had taken a deep breath and explained to her mother what had happened between her and Daniel and the decision she was faced with. Her mother had listened patiently.

'So how do you feel about him?' Elizabeth had asked, studying her daughter's face.

Holly had shrugged helplessly. 'I like him, Mum, I really do, but . . .' She had shrugged again and trailed off.

'Is it because you don't feel ready just yet for another relationship?' her mother had asked gently.

Holly had rubbed her forehead roughly. 'Oh, I don't know, Mum. I don't feel like I know anything any more.' She had thought for a while. 'Daniel is a brilliant friend. He is always there for me, always makes me laugh; he makes me feel good about myself . . .' She had picked up a biscuit and began to pick away at the crumbs. 'But I don't know if I'll *ever* feel ready for another relationship, Mum. Maybe I will, maybe I won't; maybe this is as ready as I'll ever feel. He's not Gerry but I'm not expecting him to be. What I feel now is a different kind of feeling; but a nice one too.' She had paused to think about that feeling. 'I don't know if I'll ever love the same way again, I find it hard to believe that will happen, but it's a nice thought to have that maybe someday I could.' She had smiled sadly at her mother.

'Well, you don't know if you can if you don't try,' Elizabeth had said encouragingly. 'It's important not to rush into things, Holly. I know you know that, but all I want is for you to be happy. You deserve it. Whether being happy is with Daniel, the man on the moon, or alone, I just want you happy.'

'Thanks, Mum,' Holly had smiled weakly and rested her head on her mother's shoulder. 'I just don't know which of those things will do that for me.'

As comforting as her mother had been to her that day, Holly was no closer to making her decision. First she had to get through Christmas Day without Gerry.

The rest of Holly's family – minus Ciara, who was still in Australia – joined them in the living room, and one by one they greeted her with warm hugs and kisses. They gathered around the tree and exchanged gifts, and Holly allowed the tears to flow throughout. She hadn't the energy to hide them; she hadn't the energy to care. But the tears were a strange mixture of happiness and sadness. A peculiar sensation of feeling alone yet loved.

Holly sneaked away from the family so she could have a moment to herself to think, her head was a jumble of thoughts that needed to be sorted and filed. She found herself in her old bedroom, staring out the window into the dark blustery day. The sea was fierce and threatening and Holly shuddered at its power.

'So this is where you were hiding.'

Holly turned to see Jack watching her from the bedroom door. She smiled weakly and turned to face the sea again, uninterested in her brother and his recent lack of support. She listened to the waves and watched the black water swallow the sleet that had begun to fall. She heard Jack sigh loudly and felt his arm round her shoulder.

'Sorry,' he said softly.

Holly raised her eyebrows, unimpressed, and continued to stare ahead.

He nodded to himself slowly. 'You're right to treat me like this, Holly. I've been acting like a complete idiot lately. And I'm so sorry.'

Holly turned to face him and her eyes glistened. 'You let me down, Jack.'

He closed his eyes slowly as though the very thought of that pained him. 'I know, I'm so sorry,' he said even more softly than before. 'I just didn't handle the whole situation well, Holly. I found it so hard to deal with Gerry . . . you know . . .'

'Dying,' Holly finished for him.

'Yeah.' He clenched and unclenched his jaw and looked as though he had finally accepted it.

'It wasn't exactly easy for me, you know, Jack.' A silence fell between them. 'But you helped me pack away all his things. You went through his belongings with me and made the whole thing so much easier,' Holly said, feeling confused. 'You were there with me for that, why did you just suddenly disappear?'

'God, that was so tough to do.' He shook his head sadly. 'You were so strong, Holly . . . you *are* strong,' he corrected himself. 'Getting rid of his things just tore me up, being in the house and him not being there just . . . *got* to me. And then I noticed you were getting closer to Richard so I just figured it would be OK for me to take a step back because you had him . . .' He blushed at the ridiculousness of finally explaining his feelings.

'You fool, Jack,' Holly said, thumping him playfully

in the stomach. 'As if Richard could ever take your place.'

He smiled. 'Oh, I don't know, you two seem very pally-pally these days.'

Holly became serious again. 'Richard has been very supportive over the past year – and, believe me, people haven't failed to surprise me at all during this whole experience,' she added pointedly. 'Give him a chance, Jack.'

He stared out to the sea and nodded slowly, digesting this. 'I'm sorry, Holly.'

Holly wrapped her arms around him and felt the familiar comforting hug of her brother. 'I know. So am I. I'm sorry that all of this had to happen. But I need you, you know.'

'I know,' he said, hugging her even tighter. 'And I'm here for you now. I'm going to stop being so selfish and take care of my little sister.'

'Hey, your little sister is doing just fine on her own, thank you very much,' she said sadly as she watched the sea crash violently against the rocks, its spray kissing the moon.

They sat down for their meal and Holly's mouth watered at the spread of food before her.

'I got an email from Ciara today,' Declan announced.

Everyone oohed and aahed.

'She sent this picture of her.' He passed around the photograph he had printed off.

Holly smiled at the sight of her sister lying on the beach eating barbecued Christmas dinner with Mathew. Her hair was blonde and her skin was tanned, and she and Mathew looked so happy. Holly stared at the picture for a while, feeling proud that her sister had found her place in the world. After travelling around the world searching and searching, she reckoned Ciara had finally found contentment. Holly hoped that would happen to her eventually. She passed the photo on to Jack, and he smiled as he studied it.

'They're saying it might snow today,' Holly announced, taking a second helping of dinner. She had already undone the top button on her trousers, but it was Christmas after all; the time of giving and er . . . eating.

'No, it won't snow,' Richard said, sucking on a bone. 'It's too cold for that.'

Holly frowned. 'Richard, how could it be too cold to snow?'

He licked his fingers and wiped them on his napkin that was tucked into his shirt, and Holly tried not to laugh at his black woolly jumper with a big picture of a Christmas tree emblazoned across the front. 'It needs to get milder before it can snow,' he explained.

'Richard, it's about minus a million in the Antarctic and it snows there. That's hardly mild,' Holly said.

'That's the way it works,' he said matter-of-factly.

'Whatever you say.' Holly rolled her eyes.

'He's right, actually,' Jack added after a while, and everyone stopped chewing to stare at him. That was not a phrase they often heard from Jack. He went on to explain how snow worked and Richard helped him out on the scientific parts. They both smiled at each other and seemed satisfied they were Mr Know-it-alls.

Abbey raised her eyebrows at Holly and they shared a look of shock.

'You want some vegetables with your gravy, Dad?' Declan asked seriously, offering him a bowl of broccoli.

Everyone looked at Frank's plate and laughed. Once again it was a sea of gravy.

'Ha-ha,' Frank said, taking the bowl from his son. 'Anyway, we live too close to the sea to get any,' he added.

'To get what? Gravy?' Holly teased, and they all laughed again.

'Snow, silly,' he said, grabbing her nose like he used to do when she was a child.

'Well, I bet you all a million quid that it snows today,' Declan said eagerly, glancing around at his brothers and sister.

'Then you'd better start saving, Declan, because if your brainiac brothers say it ain't so, it ain't so!' Holly joked.

'You better pay up then, boys.' Declan rubbed his hands together greedily, nodding towards the window.

'Oh my God!' Holly exclaimed, excitedly jumping out of her chair. 'It's snowing!'

'So much for that theory, then,' Jack said to Richard, and they both laughed as they watched the white flakes sparkling down from the sky.

Everyone deserted the dinner table and threw on their coats to run outside like excited children. Holly glanced down into the gardens lining the street and spotted the families of every household standing outside staring up into the sky.

Elizabeth wrapped her arms around her daughter and squeezed her tight. 'Well, it looks like Denise will have a white Christmas for her white wedding,' she smiled.

Holly's heart beat wildly at the thought of Denise's wedding. In just a few days she would have to confront Daniel.

As though her mother had been reading her mind she asked Holly quietly so no one else would hear, 'Have you thought about what to say to Daniel yet?'

Holly glanced up at the snowflakes glistening down from the black star-filled sky in the moonlight. The moment felt so magical; there and then she made her final decision.

'Yes I have,' she smiled, and took a deep breath.

'Good.' Elizabeth kissed her on the cheek. 'And remember, God leads you to it and takes you through it.'

Holly smiled at the phrase. 'He'd better because I'm going to need Him a lot over the next while.'

'Sharon, don't carry that case, it's too heavy!' John yelled at his wife, and Sharon dropped the bag angrily.

'John, I am not an invalid. I am *pregnant*!' she shouted back at him.

'I know that, but the doctor said not to lift heavy things!' he said firmly, walking round to her side of the car and grabbing the bag.

'Well, screw the doctor, he's never been bloody pregnant,' Sharon yelled, watching John storm off.

Holly banged down the boot of the car loudly. She had had enough of John and Sharon's tantrums;

she had been stuck listening to them bicker all the way down to Wicklow in the car. Now all she wanted to do was to go to the hotel and relax. She was growing quite afraid of Sharon as well. Her voice had risen three octaves in the past two hours and she looked as if she was going to explode. Actually, by the size of her bump, Holly was afraid she really would explode, and she didn't want to be around for that happening.

Holly grabbed her bag and glanced up at the hotel. It was more like a castle. Tom and Denise couldn't have picked a more beautiful place as the venue for their New Year's Eve wedding. The building was covered in dark green ivy, and a huge fountain adorned the front courtyard. Acres and acres of beautifully kept lush green gardens surrounded the hotel. Denise hadn't had her white Christmas wedding after all: the snow had melted minutes after it had arrived. Still, it had been a beautiful moment for Holly to share with her family on Christmas Day, and it had succeeded in lifting her spirits for a short time. Now all she wanted to do was find her room and pamper herself. She wasn't even sure if her bridesmaid dress would still fit her after piling on the pounds over Christmas. It was a fear she wasn't willing to share with Denise, who would probably have a heart attack. Perhaps some minor alterations wouldn't be too difficult . . . She also regretted telling Sharon she was worried about the fit, as Sharon had screamed that she couldn't even fit into the clothes she had worn the day before, never mind a dress she was fitted for months ago.

She dragged her bag behind her over the cobblestones

and was suddenly jerked forward and sent flying as someone tripped over her luggage.

'Sorry,' she heard a singsong voice say, and looked back angrily to see who had almost caused her to break her neck. She watched the tall blonde as her hips swung boom, boom, boom, heading towards the hotel. Holly frowned: that walk was familiar. She knew she knew it from somewhere but . . . uh-oh!

Laura.

Oh no, she thought, panicking. Tom and Denise had invited Laura after all! She had to find Daniel quickly so that she could warn him. He would be disgusted to find out his ex had received an invite. And then if the moment was right Holly would finish off that chat with him – if he still wanted to hear from her. After all, it had been almost a month since she had last spoken to him. She crossed her fingers tightly behind her back and rushed towards the reception area.

She was greeted with mayhem.

The place was crowded with angry people and luggage. Denise's voice was instantly recognisable above all the noise.

'Look, I don't *care* if you've made a mistake! *Fix it!* I booked fifty rooms *months* ago for my wedding guests! Did you hear me? *My wedding!* Now I am not sending ten of them to some crappy B&B down the road. Sort it out!'

A very startled-looking receptionist gulped and nodded wildly, trying to explain the situation.

Denise held her hand up in his face. 'I don't want to hear any more excuses! Just get ten more rooms for my guests!'

Holly spotted Tom looking perplexed, and she beat her way through the crowd to him.

'Tom!'

'Hi, Holly,' he said, looking very distracted.

'What room is Daniel in?' she asked quickly.

'Daniel?' He looked confused.

'Yes, Daniel! The best man . . . I mean *your* best man,' she corrected herself.

'Oh, I don't know, Holly,' he said, turning away to grab a member of the hotel staff.

Holly jumped to face him, blocking his view of the staff member. 'Tom, I really need to know!' she panicked.

'Look, Holly, I really don't know. Ask Denise,' he mumbled, and ran off down the corridor, chasing the staff member.

Holly looked at Denise and gulped. Denise seemed like someone possessed, and Holly had no intention of asking her in that mood. She queued in line behind all the other guests, and twenty minutes and a few sneaky moves to skip the queue later, she reached the front.

'Hi, I was wondering if you could tell me what room number Daniel Connolly is in, please?' she asked quickly.

The receptionist shook his head. 'I'm sorry we can't give out guests' room numbers.'

Holly rolled her eyes, 'Look, I'm a friend of his,' she explained, and smiled sweetly.

The man smiled politely and shook his head again, 'I'm sorry, but it's against hotel policy to—'

'Listen!' she yelled, and even Denise, beside her, shut up screaming. 'It's very important that you tell me!'

489

The man shook his head slowly, apparently too afraid to open his mouth. Finally he said, 'I'm sorry but—'

'Aaaaaggghhh!' Holly screamed with frustration, interrupting him again.

'Holly,' Denise said gently, placing her hand on Holly's arm, 'what's wrong?'

'I need to know what room Daniel is staying in,' she yelled, and Denise looked startled.

'It's room three four two,' she stuttered.

'Thank you!' Holly yelled angrily, not knowing why she was still screaming, and stormed off in the direction of the elevators.

Upstairs, Holly rushed down the corridor, dragging her bag behind her and checking the door numbers. When she reached his room she knocked furiously on the door and as she heard footsteps approaching the door she realised she hadn't even thought about what she was going to say. She took a deep breath as the door was opened.

She stopped breathing.

It was Laura.

'Honey, who is it?' she heard Daniel's voice call, and saw him step out of the bathroom.

'You!' Laura screeched.

Chapter Fifty-One

Holly stood outside Daniel's bedroom door and glanced from Laura to Daniel and back again. She gathered from their semi-nakedness that Daniel had already known Laura was coming to the wedding. She also assumed that he hadn't informed Denise and Tom that she was here as they hadn't warned Holly. But even if they had known they wouldn't have considered it important to tell her. Holly hadn't shared what Daniel had told her before Christmas with any of her friends. As Holly stared into the hotel room, she realised this meant that she had absolutely no reason to be standing where she was right then.

Daniel hung on to his tiny towel tightly, glued to the spot, his face a picture of shock. Laura's face was stormy. Holly's jaw had dropped. Nobody spoke for a while. Holly could almost hear everybody's brains ticking. Then eventually someone spoke and Holly wished it hadn't been that particular person.

'What are *you* doing here?' Laura hissed.

Holly's mouth opened and closed like a goldfish's. Daniel's forehead wrinkled in confusion as he stared from one girl to the other. 'Do you two . . .' He stopped as if the idea was totally ridiculous, but then thought about it and decided to ask anyway, 'Do you two know each other?'

Holly gulped.

'Ha!' Laura's face twisted in contempt. 'She is *no* friend of mine! I caught this little bitch kissing my fiancé!' Laura yelled, and then stopped herself as she realised what she had said.

'Your *fiancé*?'

'Sorry . . . ex-fiancé,' Laura mumbled, staring at the floor.

A small smile crept across Holly's face, glad that Laura had dumped herself in it. 'Yeah, Stevie, wasn't it? A good friend of Daniel's, if I remember correctly.'

Daniel's face reddened as he looked at them both. Laura stared back at Daniel, angrily wondering how this woman knew her boyfriend . . . her current boyfriend, that was.

'Daniel's a good friend of mine,' Holly explained, crossing her arms over her chest.

'So have you come to steal him from me too?' Laura said bitterly.

'Oh, please, like you're one to talk,' Holly fired at Laura, and she blushed.

'You kissed Stevie?' Daniel asked Holly, slowly getting the gist of the story. He looked angry.

'No I did *not* kiss Stevie.' Holly rolled her eyes.

'You did too!' Laura yelled childishly.

'Oh, would you ever shut up?' She looked at Laura. 'What does it matter to you, anyway? I take it you're back with Daniel, so it looks like everything worked out for you in the end!' Holly then turned to Daniel.

'No, Daniel,' she continued, 'I did not kiss Stevie. We were down in Galway for Denise's hen weekend and Stevie was drunk and tried to kiss me,' she explained calmly.

'Oh, you're such a liar,' Laura said bitterly. 'I saw what happened.'

'And so did Charlie,' Holly continued to face Daniel. 'So ask him if you don't believe me but if you don't believe me I really don't care either,' she added. 'Anyway, I came to have that chat with you but you're obviously busy.' She glanced down at the skimpy towel wrapped around his waist. 'So I'll see you both later at the wedding.' And with that she turned on her heel and marched off down the corridor. She glanced back at Daniel, who was still staring at her from his door, and looked away as she turned the corner. She froze when she realised she had reached a dead end. The elevators were the other way. She kept on walking to the end of the corridor so she wouldn't look completely stupid by going past their door again, then waited at the end of the corridor for a while until she heard the door close. Tiptoeing back up the hall, she rounded the corner, sneaked past Daniel's bedroom door and rushed down to the elevator.

She pressed the button and breathed a sigh of relief, closing her tired eyes. She didn't even feel angry with Daniel; in fact in a really childish way she was glad he had done something to stop them having their little chat. So she had been dumped and not the other way round, like she was expecting. But Daniel can't have been that much in love with Holly if he was able to get over her and go back to Laura so quickly. Ah well, at least she hadn't hurt his feelings . . . but she did think he was a complete fool for taking Laura back . . .

'Are you getting in or what?'

Holly's eyes flew open; she hadn't even heard the elevator doors open. 'Leo!' she smiled, stepping in and hugging him. 'I didn't know you were coming down!'

'I'm doing hair for the queen bee today,' he laughed, referring to Denise.

'Is she that bad?' Holly winced.

'Oh, she was just in a tizzy because Tom saw her on the day of her wedding. She thinks it'll be bad luck.'

'Well, it will only be bad luck if she thinks it's bad luck,' Holly smiled.

'I haven't seen you for ages,' Leo said, glancing at Holly's hair, making it *very* obvious.

'Oh, I know,' Holly moaned, covering her roots with her hand. 'I've been so busy at work this month I just haven't had time.'

Leo raised his eyebrows and looked amused. 'Never did I think I would ever hear you say those words about work. You're a changed woman.'

Holly was thoughtful. 'Yes. Yes, I really think I am.'

'Come on then,' Leo said, stepping out on his floor, 'the wedding isn't for another few hours; I'll tie your hair up so we can cover those awful roots.'

'Oh, are you sure you don't mind?' Holly asked guiltily.

'No, I don't mind at all.' Leo waved his hand dismissively. 'We can't have you ruining Denise's wedding photos with that head on you, can we?'

Holly smiled and dragged her suitcase out of the

elevator after him. That was more like it. For a minute there he was just being too nice.

Denise looked at Holly excitedly at the head table of the hotel's function room as someone rapped a spoon against a glass and the speeches began. Holly fumbled nervously with her hands in her lap, going over and over her speech in her head and not even listening to what the other speakers were saying.

She should have written it down because now she was so nervous she couldn't remember the start of it. Her heart beat wildly as Daniel sat down and everyone applauded. She was next and there was to be no running into the toilets this time. Sharon grabbed her trembling hand and assured her she would be fine. Holly smiled back at her shakily, not feeling at all fine. Denise's father announced that Holly was going to speak and the room turned to face her. All she could see was a sea of faces. She stood up slowly from her chair and glanced over at Daniel, for encouragement. He winked at her. She smiled back at him and her heartbeat slowed. Her friends were all there. She spotted John sitting at a table with his and Gerry's friends. John gave her the thumbs-up and Holly's speech went out the window as a new one formed in her head. She cleared her throat.

'Please forgive me if I get a little emotional while I speak but I am just so happy for Denise today. She is my best friend . . .' She paused and glanced down at Sharon beside her, ' . . . well, one of them.'

The room laughed.

'And I am so proud of her today and delighted that she has found love with a wonderful man like Tom.'

Holly smiled as she saw tears fill Denise's eyes. The woman who never cried.

'Finding someone you love and who loves you back is a wonderful, wonderful feeling. But finding a true soul mate is an even *better* feeling. A soul mate is someone who understands you like no other, loves you like no other, will be there for you *for ever,* no matter what. They say that nothing lasts for ever, but I am a firm believer in the fact that for some, love lives on even after they're gone. I know a thing or two about having someone like that and I know that Denise has found a soul mate in Tom. Denise, I'm glad to tell you that a bond like that will never die.' A lump formed in Holly's throat and she took a moment to compose herself before continuing. 'I am both honoured and petrified that Denise asked me to speak today.'

Everyone laughed.

'But I am delighted to have been asked to share this beautiful day with them and here's to them having many more beautiful days like this together.'

Everyone cheered and reached for their glasses.

'However!' Holly raised her voice over the crowd and held her hand up to silence them. The noise died down and once again all eyes were on her.

'However, some guests here today will be aware of the list that a marvellous man thought up,' Holly smiled as John's table, as well as Sharon and Denise, cheered. 'And among one of those rules was to *never ever* wear a spensive white dress.'

Holly giggled as John's table went wild and Denise broke down into hysterics, remembering the fateful night when the new rule was added to the list.

'So on behalf of Gerry,' Holly giggled, 'I will forgive you for breaking that rule only because you look so amazing and I will ask you all to join me in a toast to Tom and Denise and her very, very spensive white dress – and I should know because I was dragged around every bridal shop in Ireland!'

The guests in the room all held up their glasses and repeated, 'To Tom and Denise and her very, very spensive white dress!'

Holly took her seat and Sharon hugged her with tears in her eyes. 'That was perfect, Holly.'

Holly beamed as John's table held their glasses up to her and cheered. And then the party began.

Tears formed in Holly's eyes as she watched Tom and Denise dancing together for the first time as husband and wife, and she remembered that feeling. That feeling of excitement, of hope, of pure happiness and pride, a feeling of not knowing what the future held but being so ready to face it all. And that thought made her happy; she wouldn't cry about it, she would embrace it. She had enjoyed every second of her life with Gerry, but now it was time to move on. Move on to the next chapter of her life, bringing wonderful memories with her, and experiences that would teach her and help mould her future. Sure, it would be difficult; she had learned that nothing was ever easy. But it didn't feel as difficult as it had been a few months ago, and in another few months it would be even less difficult.

She had been given a wonderful gift: life. Sometimes it was cruelly taken away too soon, but it's what you did with it that counted, not how long it lasted.

'Could I have this dance?' A hand appeared before her and she looked up to see Daniel smiling down at her.

'Sure,' she replied happily, and took his hand.

'May I say that you're looking very beautiful tonight?'

'You may,' Holly smiled. She was happy with how she looked. Denise had chosen a beautiful lilac-coloured dress for her with a corset top that hid her Christmas belly, and there was a large slit up the side of the skirt. Leo had done an inspired job with her hair, pinning it up and allowing some curls to tumble down on to her shoulders. She felt beautiful. She felt like Princess Holly, and she giggled to herself at the thought.

'That was a lovely speech you made,' Daniel smiled. 'I realise that what I said to you was selfish of me. You said you weren't ready and I didn't listen,' he apologised.

'That's OK, Daniel; I don't think I'll be ready for a long, long time. But thank you for getting over me so fast.' She raised her eyebrows and nodded over at Laura, who was sitting moodily on her own at the table.

Daniel bit his lip. 'I know it must seem crazy fast to you, but when you didn't return any of my calls, even I got the hint that you weren't ready for a relationship. And when I went home for the holidays and met up with Laura, that old flame just sparked again. You were right, I never got over her. Believe me if I hadn't known with all my heart that you weren't in love with me I never would have brought her to the wedding.'

Holly smiled at Daniel. 'Sorry about not getting back to you, Daniel. I was having a bit of "me" time.

But I still think you're a fool.' She shook her head as she watched Laura scowl back at her.

Daniel sighed. 'I know me and her have a lot to discuss over the next while, but, like you said, for some people love just lives on.'

Holly threw her eyes up to heaven. 'Oh, don't start quoting me on that one,' she laughed. 'Ah well, as long as you're happy, I suppose. Although I don't see how you ever will be.' She sighed dramatically and Daniel laughed.

'I am happy, Holly. I guess I just can't live without the drama.' He glanced over at Laura, and his eyes softened. 'I need someone who is passionate about me and, for better or for worse, Laura is passionate. What about you? Are you happy?' He studied Holly's face.

Holly thought about it. 'Tonight I'm happy. I will worry about tomorrow when tomorrow comes. But I'm getting there . . .'

Holly gathered in a huddle with Sharon, John, Denise and Tom, and awaited the countdown.

'Five . . . four . . . three . . . two . . . one! HAPPY NEW YEAR!' Everyone cheered and balloons of all colours of the rainbow fell from the ceiling and bounced around on the heads of the crowd.

Holly hugged her friends, with tears in her eyes.

'Happy new year.' Sharon squeezed her tightly and kissed her on the cheek.

Holly placed her hand over Sharon's bump and held Denise's hand tightly. 'Happy *new* year for all of us!'

Epilogue

Holly flicked through the newspapers to see which one contained a photo of Denise and Tom on their wedding day. It wasn't every day that Ireland's top radio DJ and a girl from *Girls and the City* got married. That's what Denise liked to think, anyway.

'Hey!' the grumpy newsagent yelled at her, 'this is not a library. You either buy it or put it down.'

Holly sighed and began to gather every newspaper from the newsstand once again. She had to take two trips to the counter, due to the weight of the papers, and the man didn't even think to help her. Not that she would have wanted his help anyway. Once again a queue had formed behind the till. Holly smiled to herself and took her time. It was his own fault: if he would just let her flick through the papers she wouldn't have to hold him up. She made her way to the top of the queue with the last of the papers and began to add bars of chocolate and packets of sweets to the pile.

'Oh, and can I have a bag too, please?' She batted her eyelashes and smiled sweetly.

The old man stared down at her over the rim of

his glasses as though she was a naughty schoolgirl. 'Mark!' he yelled angrily.

The spotty teenager appeared from the shopping aisles with a pricing gun in his hand.

'Open the other till, son,' he was ordered, and Mark dragged his body over to the till.

Half the queue behind Holly moved over to the other side.

'Thank you,' Holly smiled and made her way towards the door. Just as she was about to pull the door open it was pushed from the other side, causing her purchases to spill out all over the floor once again.

'I'm so sorry,' the man said, bending down to help her.

'Oh, it's OK,' Holly replied politely, not wanting to turn round to see the smug look on the old man's face that was burning into her back.

'Ah, it's you! The chocoholic!' the voice said, and Holly looked up startled.

It was the friendly customer with the unusual green eyes, who had helped her before. 'We meet again.'

'Holly, isn't it?' he smiled, handing her, the king-size chocolate bars.

'That's right. Rob, isn't it?' she smiled.

'You've a good memory,' he laughed.

'As do you.' She piled everything back into her bag, lost in thought, and got back onto her feet.

'Well, I'm sure I'll bump into you again soon,' Rob smiled, and made his way over to the queue.

Holly stared after him, still in a daze. Finally she walked over to him. 'Rob, is there any chance you would like to go for that coffee today? If you can't, that's fine . . .' She bit her lip.

He smiled and glanced down nervously at the ring on her finger.

'Oh, don't worry about that,' she held her hand out, 'it only represents a life-time of happy memories these days.'

He nodded his head understandingly. 'Well, in that case I would love to.'

They crossed the road and headed over to The Greasy Spoon. 'By the way, I'm sorry for running off on you the last time,' he apologised, looking into her eyes.

'Don't worry; I usually escape out the toilet window after the first drink.' Holly teased.

He laughed.

Holly smiled to herself as she sat at the table waiting for him to bring back the drinks. He seemed nice. She relaxed back in her chair and gazed out of the window to the cold January day that caused the trees to dance wildly in the wind. She thought about what she had learned, who she once was and who she had now become. She was a woman who had been given advice from a man she loved, who had taken it and tried her hardest to help heal herself. She now had a job that she loved and felt confident within herself to reach for what she wanted.

She was a woman who made mistakes, who sometimes cried on a Monday morning or at night alone in bed. She was a woman who often became bored with her life and found it hard to get up for work in the morning. She was a woman who more often than not had a bad hair day, who looked in the mirror and wondered why she couldn't just drag herself to the gym more often; she was a woman who sometimes questioned what reason had she to live on this planet. She was a woman who sometimes just got things wrong.

On the other hand, she was a woman with a million happy memories, who knew what it was like to experience true love and who was ready to experience more life, more love and make new memories. Whether it happened in ten months or ten years, Holly would obey Gerry's final message. Whatever lay ahead, she knew she would open her heart and follow where it led her.

In the meantime, she would just live.

THE END

If You Could See
Me Now

For Georgina, who believes ...

Infinite thank yous to my family, Mimmie, Dad, Georgina and Nicky for everything – I couldn't narrow that down if I tried. To David, the best coffee-maker around – thanks for checking on me every few hours and for believing so passionately in this book. Huge thanks to the endlessly encouraging you-know-what agent Marianne for the buns, tea and advice, and thank you Pat and Vicki at the you-know-what agency for taking care of you-know-what.

Thank you Lynne and Maxine and all at HarperCollins for your faith in me and for all your hard work.

To my readers, old and new, I hope this is as good for you as it was for me – an absolute joy to work on.

Most importantly thanks to Ivan for keeping me company in my office until all hours. Do you think they will ever believe our story?

Chapter 1

It was a Friday morning in June when I first became best friends with Luke. It was 9.15 a.m., to be precise and I happen to know exactly what time it was because I looked at my watch. I don't know why I did, because I didn't need to be anywhere by any specific time. But I believe there's a reason for everything so perhaps I checked my watch at that time just so I could tell you my story properly. Details are important in storytelling, aren't they?

I was glad I met Luke that morning because I was a bit down after having to leave my old best friend, Barry. He couldn't see me any more. But it doesn't really matter because he's happier now and that's what's important, I suppose. Having to leave my best friends is all part of my job. It's not a very nice part, but I believe in finding a positive side in everything, so the way I see it is, if I didn't have to leave my best friends then I wouldn't be able to make new ones. And making new friends is my favourite part by far. That's probably why I was offered the job.

1

We'll get on to what my job is in just a moment but first I want to tell you about the morning I first met my best friend Luke.

I closed the gate to Barry's front garden behind me and I started walking, and for absolutely no reason at all I took the first left, then a right, then a left, went straight on for a while, took another right and I ended up beside a housing estate called Fuchsia Lane. It must have been called that because of the fuchsias growing all around the place. They grow wild here. Sorry, when I say 'here' I mean a town called Baile na gCroíthe which is in County Kerry. That's in Ireland.

Baile na gCroíthe somewhere along the line ended up being known in English as Hartstown, but as a direct translation from Irish it means the Town of Hearts. Which I think sounds nicer.

I was glad I ended up back here again; I had done a few jobs here when I was starting out but hadn't returned for years. My work takes me all over the country, sometimes even overseas when my friends take me away on holidays which just goes to show, no matter where you are, you always need a best friend.

Fuchsia Lane had twelve houses, six on each side, and all were different. The cul-de-sac was really busy with lots of people buzzing about. It was a Friday morning, remember, and June too, so it was really sunny and bright and everyone was in a good mood. Well, not *everyone*.

There were lots of children playing on the road, cycling, chasing, enjoying hopscotch, tip the can and loads of other stuff. You could hear the sounds of delighted screams and laughter coming from them. I suppose they were happy to be on their school holidays too. As much as they seemed really nice and all, I just wasn't drawn to them. You see, I can't just make friends with anyone. That's not what my job is about.

A man was cutting the grass in his front garden, and a woman tending to the flowerbed with big mucky gloves on her hands. There was a lovely smell of freshly cut grass and the sound of the lady snipping, clipping, cropping and pruning was like music in the air. In the next garden a man whistled a tune I wasn't familiar with while he pointed the garden hose towards his car and watched as the soapy suds slithered down the side, revealing a new sparkle. Every now and again he whipped round and sprayed water on two little girls who were dressed in yellow and black striped swimsuits. They looked like big bumble bees. I loved hearing them giggling so much.

In the next driveway a boy and girl were playing hopscotch. I observed them for a spell but none of them responded to my interest so I kept on moving. I walked by children playing in every garden yet none of them saw me or invited me to play. People on bicycles and skateboards, and remote controlled cars were whizzing by, oblivious to me. I was beginning to think that coming to

Fuchsia Lane was a bit of a mistake, which was rather confusing because usually I was so good at choosing places and there were so many children here. I sat down on the garden wall of the last house and began to think about where I could have taken a wrong turn.

After a few minutes, I came to the conclusion that I was in the right area after all. I very rarely take wrong turns. I spun on my backside to face the house behind the garden wall. There was no action in this garden so I sat and studied the house. It had two storeys and a garage with an expensive car parked outside that glistened in the sun. A plaque on the garden wall beneath me said 'Fuchsia House', and the house had blooming fuchsia climbing up the wall, clinging to the brown bricks over the front door and reaching all the way up to the roof. It looked pretty. Fractions of the house had brown bricks and other sections had been painted a honey colour. Some of the windows were square and others were circles. It was really unusual. It had a fuchsia-coloured front door with two long windows with frosted glass in the top two panels, a huge brass knocker and letter box beneath; it looked like two eyes, a nose and a mouth smiling at me. I waved and smiled back just in case. Well, you can never be too sure these days.

Just as I was studying the face of the front door, it opened and was slammed shut rather loudly and angrily by a boy who came running outside. He had a big red fire engine in his right hand and a

4

police car in his left hand. I love red fire engines; they're my favourite. The boy jumped off the front step of the porch and ran to the grass where he skidded to his knees. He got grass stains all down his black tracksuit bottoms, which made me laugh. Grass stains are so much fun because they never come out. My old friend Barry and I used to slide all of the time. Anyway, the little boy started crashing his fire engine against his police car and making all these noises with his mouth. He was good at the noises. Barry and I always used to do that too. It's fun pretending to do things that don't usually happen in real life.

The boy rammed the police car into the red fire engine and the head fireman, who was clinging to the ladder at the side of the truck, slid off. I laughed out loud and the boy looked up.

He actually looked at me. Right into my eyes.

'Hi,' I said, nervously clearing my throat and shifting from one foot to the other. I was wearing my favourite blue Converse runners and they still had grass stains on the white rubber tips from when Barry and I went sliding. I started to run the rubber tip against the brick garden wall to try to scrape it off and thought about what to say next. As much as making friends is my favourite thing to do I still get a bit nervous about it. There's always that scary chance that people won't like me and it gives me the collywobbles. I've been lucky so far but it would be silly to presume that the same thing will happen every time.

'Hi,' the boy replied, fixing the fireman back onto the ladder.

'What's your name?' I asked, kicking my foot against the wall on front of me and scraping the rubber tip. The grass stains still wouldn't come off.

The boy studied me for a while, looked me up and down as though trying to decide whether to tell me his name or not. This is the part of my job I absolutely loathe. It's tough wanting to be friends with someone and them not wanting the same back. That happens sometimes but in the end they always come round because, whether they know it or not, they want me to be there.

The boy had white-blond hair and big blue eyes. I knew his face from somewhere but couldn't quite think where.

Finally he spoke. 'My name's Luke. What's yours?'

I shoved my hands deep into my pockets and concentrated on kicking my right foot against the garden wall. I was making parts of the bricks crumble and fall to the ground. Without looking at him I said, 'Ivan.'

'Hi, Ivan,' he smiled. He had no front teeth.

'Hi, Luke,' I smiled back.

I have all mine.

'I like your fire engine. My bes— my old best friend Barry used to have one just like it and we used to play with it all the time. It's got a stupid name, though, because it can't drive through fire because it melts,' I explained, still keeping my

6

hands shoved into my pockets, causing my shoulders to hunch up past my ears. It made things a little quieter so I took my hands out of my pocket just so I could hear what Luke was saying.

Luke rolled on the grass laughing. 'You put your fire engine through *fire*?' he screeched.

'Well, it is called a *fire* engine, isn't it?' I replied defensively.

Luke rolled onto his back, kicked his feet in the air and hooted. 'No, you dummy! Fire engines are for putting *out* fires!'

I thought about that one for a while. 'Hmm. Well, I'll tell you what puts out fire engines, Luke,' I explained matter-of-factly. 'Water does.'

Luke hit himself lightly on the side of the head, screamed 'Doh!', made his eyes go cockeyed and then fell over on the grass.

I started laughing. Luke was really funny.

'Do you want to come and play?' He raised his eyebrows questioningly.

I grinned. 'Of course, Luke. Playing is my favourite!' and I jumped over the garden wall and joined him on the grass.

'What age are you?' He looked at me suspiciously. 'You look like you're the same age as my aunt,' he frowned, 'and my aunt doesn't like to play with my fire engine.'

I shrugged. 'Well, then your aunt is a boring old gnirob!'

'A *gnirob*!' Luke screamed with mirth. 'What's a gnirob?'

'Someone who's *boring*,' I said, scrunching my nose up and saying the word like it was a disease. I liked saying words backwards; it was like inventing my own language.

'Boring,' Luke repeated after me and scrunched up his nose, 'uugh.'

'What age are you anyway?' I asked Luke as I crashed the police car into the fire engine. The fireman fell off the ladder again. 'You look like *my* aunt,' I accused him, and Luke fell about the place. He had a loud laugh.

'I'm only six, Ivan! And I'm not a *girl*!'

'Oh.' I don't really have an aunt but I just said it to make him laugh. 'Well, there's nothing *only* about being six.'

Just as I was about to ask him what his favourite cartoon was, the front door opened and I heard screaming. Luke went white and I looked up to where he was faced.

'SAOIRSE, GIVE ME BACK MY KEYS!' a voice yelled desperately. A flustered-looking woman, red in the cheeks, frantic eyes, with long unwashed red hair swinging in strands around her face, came running out of the house alone. Another shriek from the voice in the house behind caused her to stumble in her platforms on the step of the front porch. She cursed loudly and reached out to the wall of the house for balance. Looking up, she stared in the direction of where Luke and I were sitting at the end of the garden. Her mouth widened into a smile to reveal a set of crooked yellow teeth.

8

I crawled back a few more inches. I noticed Luke did too. She gave Luke the thumbs-up and croaked, 'See ya, kiddo.' She let go of the wall, wavered slightly and walked quickly to the car parked in the driveway.

'SAOIRSE!' The voice of the person inside the house screamed again. 'I'M CALLING THE GARDAÍ IF YOU SET ONE FOOT IN THAT CAR!'

The red-haired woman snorted, pressed the car keys and the lights flashed and beeped. She opened the door, climbed in, banged her head on the side, cursed loudly again and slammed the door shut behind her. I could hear the doors locking from where I was at the end of the garden. A few kids on the road stopped playing and stared at the scene unfolding before them.

Finally the owner of the mystery voice came running outside with a phone in her hand. She looked very different from the other lady. Her hair was tied back neatly and tightly at the back of her head. She wore a smart grey trouser suit, which didn't match the high-pitched, uncontrolled voice she currently had. She too was red in the face and out of breath. Her chest heaved up and down rapidly as she tried to run as quickly as she could in her high heels to the car. She danced around beside the car, first trying the door handle and, when finding it locked, threatened to dial 999.

'I'm calling the gardaí, Saoirse,' she warned, waving the phone at the window on the driver's side.

Saoirse just grinned from inside the car and started up the engine. The lady with the phone's voice cracked as she pleaded with her to get out of the car. Jumping from foot to foot, she looked like there was somebody else bubbling under her own flesh, trying to get out, like the Incredible Hulk.

Saoirse sped off down the long cobble-stoned driveway. Halfway down, she slowed the car. The woman with the phone relaxed her shoulders and looked relieved. Instead of stopping completely, the car crawled along as the window of the driver's side was lowered and two fingers appeared out of it, held up proud and high for all to see.

'Ah, she'll be back in two minutes, so,' I said to Luke, and he looked at me oddly.

The woman with the phone watched in fright as the car sped off again down the road, narrowly missing hitting a child on the road. A few hairs escaped from the tight bun on her head, as though attempting to chase the car themselves.

Luke lowered his head and quietly put the fireman back on his ladder. The woman let out an exasperated screech, threw her hands in the air and turned on her heel. There was a crack as the heel of her shoe became lodged between the cobbles of the drive. The woman shook her leg wildly, growing more frustrated by the second, and eventually the shoe flew out, but the heel remained lodged between the crack.

'FUUUUCCCK!' she yelled. Hobbling on one

10

high heel and what was now one flat pump, she made her way back up the front porch. The fuchsia door was slammed shut and she was swallowed back up by the house. The windows, door knob and the letter box smiled at me again and I smiled back.

'Who are you smiling at?' Luke asked with a frown on his face.

'The door,' I replied, thinking it an obvious answer.

He just stared at me with the same frown, his mind evidently lost in the thoughts of what he had just seen, and the oddity of smiling at a door.

We could see the woman with the phone through the glass of the front door, pacing the hall.

'Who is she?' I asked, turning to Luke.

He was clearly shaken.

'That's my aunt,' he almost whispered. 'She looks after me.'

'Oh,' I said. 'Who was the one in the car?'

Luke slowly pushed the fire engine through the grass, flattening the blades as he went along. 'Oh, her. That's Saoirse,' he said quietly. 'She's my mom.'

'Oh.' There was a silence and I could tell he was sad. 'Seer-sha,' I repeated the name, liking how it felt when I said it; like the wind blowing out of my mouth in one big gust or how the trees sounded when they talked to one another on windy days. 'Seeeeer-ssshaaaa . . .' I eventually stopped when Luke looked at me oddly.

I picked a buttercup out of the ground and held

it under Luke's chin. A yellow glow appeared on his pale skin. 'You like butter,' I stated. 'So Saorise's not your girlfriend then?'

Luke's face immediately lit up and he giggled. Not as much as before, though.

'Who's your friend Barry that you mentioned?' Luke asked, smashing into my car much harder than before.

'Barry McDonald is his name,' I smiled, remembering the games me and Barry used to play.

Luke's eyes lit up. 'Barry McDonald is in my class in school!'

Then it clicked. 'I knew I knew your face from somewhere, Luke. I used to see you everyday when I went to school with Barry.'

'You went to school with Barry?' he said, surprised.

'Yeah, school was fun with Barry,' I laughed.

Luke narrowed his eyes, 'Well, I didn't see you there.'

I started laughing. 'Well, *of course* you didn't *see* me, you silly sod,' I said matter-of-factly.

Chapter 2

Elizabeth's heart hammered loudly against her chest, as, having slipped on another pair of shoes, she paced the long maple-floored hall of her home. With the phone pressed hard between her ear and shoulder, her mind was a blizzard of thoughts as she listened to the shrill ring tone in her ear.

She stopped pacing long enough to stare at her reflection in the mirror. Her brown eyes widened with horror. Rarely did she allow herself to look so bedraggled. *So out of control.* Strands of her chocolate-brown hair were fleeing from the tight French pleat, causing her to appear as though she had placed her fingers in an electric socket. Mascara nestled in the lines under her eyes; her lipstick had faded, leaving only her plum-coloured lipliner as a frame, and her foundation clung to the dry patches of her olive skin. Gone was the usual pristine look. This caused her heart to beat faster, the panic to accelerate.

Breathe, Elizabeth, just breathe, she told herself. She ran a trembling hand over her tousled hair, forcing the wild hairs back down. She wiped the mascara away with a wet finger, pursed her lips together, smoothed down her suit jacket and cleared her throat. It was simply a momentary lapse of concentration on her part, that was all. Not to happen again. She transferred the phone to her left ear and noticed the impression of her Claddagh earring against her neck. Such was the pressure of her shoulder's grip on the phone against her skin.

Finally someone answered and Elizabeth turned her back on the mirror to stand to attention. Back to business.

'Hello, Baile na gCroíthe Garda Station.'

Elizabeth winced as she recognised the voice on the phone. 'Hi, Marie, Elizabeth here . . . again. Saoirse's gone off with the car,' she paused, 'again.'

There was a gentle sigh on the other end of the phone. 'How long ago, Elizabeth?'

Elizabeth sat down on the bottom stair and settled in for the usual line of questioning. She closed her eyes, only meaning to rest them briefly, but at the relief of blocking everything out she kept them closed. 'Just five minutes ago.'

'Right. Did she say where she was going?'

'The moon,' she replied matter-of-factly.

'Excuse me?' Marie asked.

'You heard me. She said she was going to the moon,' Elizabeth said firmly. 'Apparently people will understand her there.'

'The moon,' Marie repeated.

'Yes,' Elizabeth replied, feeling irritated. 'You

could perhaps start looking for her on the motorway. I would imagine that if you were heading to the moon that would be the quickest way to get there, wouldn't you? Although I'm not entirely sure which exit she would take. Whichever is more northerly, I suppose. She could be headed north-east to Dublin, or, who knows, she could be making her way to Cork; perhaps they've a plane that can take her off this planet. Either way, I'd check the motor—'

'Relax, Elizabeth; you know I have to ask.'

'I know.' Elizabeth tried to calm herself again. She was missing an important meeting right now. Important for her, important for her interior design business. Luke's babysitter was standing in as a replacement for his nanny, Edith. Edith had left a few weeks ago for the three months of travelling the world she had threatened Elizabeth with for the past six years, leaving the young babysitter inexperienced to the ways of Saoirse. She had rung her at work in a panic . . . again . . . and Elizabeth had to drop everything . . . again . . . and rush home . . . again. But she shouldn't be surprised that this had happened . . . again. She was, however, surprised that Edith, apart from the current trip to Australia, was still turning up to work every day. Six years she had been helping Elizabeth with Luke, six years of drama, and still after all her years of loyalty, Elizabeth expected a phone call or her letter of resignation practically every day. Being Luke's nanny came with a lot of baggage. Then again, so did being Luke's adoptive parent.

'Elizabeth, are you still there?'

'Yes.' Her eyes shot open. She was losing concentration. 'Sorry, what did you say?'

'I asked you what car she took.'

Elizabeth rolled her eyes and made a face at the phone. 'The same one, Marie. The same bloody car as last week, and the week before and the week before that,' she snapped.

Marie remained firm, 'Which is the—'

'BMW,' she interrupted. 'The same damn black BMW 330 Cabriolet. Four wheels, two doors, one steering wheel, two wing mirrors, lights and—'

'A partridge in a pear tree,' Marie interrupted. 'What condition was she in?'

'Very shiny. I'd just washed her,' Elizabeth replied cheekily.

'Great, and what condition was Saoirse in?'

'The usual one.'

'Intoxicated.'

'That's the one.' Elizabeth stood up and walked down the hall to the kitchen. Her sun trap. Her heels against the marble floor echoed loudly in the empty high-ceilinged room. Everything was in its place. The room was hot from the sun's glare through the glass of the conservatory. Elizabeth's tired eyes squinted in the brightness. The spotless kitchen gleamed, the black granite counter tops sparkled, the chrome fittings mirrored the bright day. A stainless steel and walnut heaven. She headed straight to the espresso machine. Her saviour. Needing an injection of life into her exhausted body, she opened the kitchen cabinet and took out a small beige coffee cup. Before closing the press she turned a cup round so that the handle was on the right side like all the others. She slid open the long steel cutlery drawer, noticed a knife in the fork's compartment, put it back in its rightful place, retrieved a spoon and slid it shut.

From the corner of her eye she saw the hand towel messily strewn over the handle of the cooker. She threw the crumpled cloth into the utility room, retrieved a fresh towel from the neat pile in the press, folded it exactly in half and draped it over the cooker handle. Everything had its place.

'Well, I haven't changed my licence plate in the past week so yes, it's still the same,' she replied with boredom to another of Marie's pointless questions. She placed the steaming espresso cup on a marble coaster to protect the glass kitchen table. She smoothed out her trousers, removed a piece of fluff from her jacket, sat down in the conservatory and looked out at her long garden and the rolling green hills beyond that seemed to stretch on for ever. Forty shades of green, golds and browns.

She breathed in the rich aroma of her steaming espresso and immediately felt revived. She pictured her sister racing over the hills with the top down on Elizabeth's convertible, arms in the air, eyes closed, flame-red hair blowing in the wind, believing she was free. Saoirse meant freedom in Irish. The name had been chosen by their mother in her last desperate attempt to make the duties of motherhood she despised so much seem less like a punishment. Her wish was for her second daughter to bring her freedom from the shackles of marriage, motherhood, responsibility . . . reality.

Her mother had met her father when she was sixteen. She was travelling through the town with a group of poets, musicians and dreamers, and got talking to Brendan Egan, a farmer in the local pub. He was twelve years her senior and was enthralled by her mysterious wild ways and carefree nature. She was flattered. And so they married. At eighteen they had their first child, Elizabeth. As it turned out, her mother couldn't be tamed and found it increasingly frustrating being held in the sleepy town nestled in the hills she had only ever intended to pass through. A crying baby and sleepless nights drove her further and further away in her head. Dreams of her own personal freedom became confused with her reality and she started to go missing for days at a time. She went exploring, discovering places and other people.

Elizabeth, at twelve years of age, looked after herself and her silent, brooding father and didn't ask when her mother would be home because she knew in her heart that she would eventually return, cheeks flushed, eyes bright, and speaking breathlessly of the world and all it had to offer. She would waft into their lives like a fresh summer breeze, bringing excitement and hope. The feel of their bungalow farmhouse always changed when she returned; the four walls absorbed her enthusiasm.

Elizabeth would sit at the end of her mother's bed, listening to stories, giddy with delight. This ambience would last for only a few days until her mother quickly tired of sharing stories rather than making new ones.

Often she brought back mementoes such as shells, stones, leaves. Elizabeth could recall a vase of long fresh grasses that sat in the centre of the dining-room table as though they were the most exotic plants ever created. When asked about the field they were pulled from, her mother just winked and tipped her nose, promising Elizabeth that she would understand some day. Her father would sit silently in his chair by the fireplace, reading his paper but never turning the page. He was as lost in her world of words as she was.

When Elizabeth was twelve years old her mother became pregnant again and, despite the new-born baby being named Saoirse, this child didn't offer the freedom her mother craved, and so she set off on another expedition. And didn't return. Her father, Brendan, had no interest in the young life that had driven his wife away so he waited in silence for her in his chair by the fire. Reading his paper but never turning the page. For years. For ever. Soon Elizabeth's heart grew weary of awaiting her mother's return and Saoirse became Elizabeth's responsibility.

Saoirse had inherited her father's Celtic looks of strawberry-blonde hair and fair skin, while Elizabeth was the image of her mother. Olive skin, chocolate hair, almost black eyes; in their blood from the Spanish influence thousands of years before. Elizabeth resembled her mother more and more with every passing day and she knew her father found that difficult. She grew to hate herself for it, and along with making the effort of trying to have conversations with her father, she tried even harder to prove to her father and to herself that she was nothing like her mother – that she was capable of loyalty.

When Elizabeth finished school at eighteen she was faced with the dilemma of having to move to Cork to attend university. A decision that took all her courage to make. Her father regarded her acceptance of the course as abandonment; he saw any friendship she created with anyone as abandonment. He craved attention, always demanding to be the only person in his daughters' lives, as though that would prevent them from moving away from him. Well, he almost succeeded and certainly was part of the reason for Elizabeth's lack of a social life or circle of friends. She had been conditioned to walk away when polite conversation was started, knowing she would pay for any unnecessary time spent away from the farm with sullen words and disapproving glares. In any case, looking after Saoirse as well as going to school was a full-time job. Brendan accused her of being like her mother, of thinking she was above him and superior to Baile na gCroíthe. She found the small town claustrophobic and felt the dull farmhouse was dipped in darkness, with no sense of time. It was as though even the grandfather clock in the hall was waiting for her mother to return.

'And, Luke, where is he?' Marie asked over the phone, bringing Elizabeth swiftly back to the present.

Elizabeth replied bitterly. 'Do you really think Saoirse would take him with her?'

Silence.

Elizabeth sighed. 'He's here.'

The name Saoirse had brought more than something to call Elizabeth's sister by. It had given her an identity, a way of life. Everything the name represented was passed into her blood. She was fiery, independent, wild and free. She followed the pattern of the mother she could not remember, so much that Elizabeth almost felt as though she were watching her mother. But she kept losing sight of her. Saoirse became pregnant at sixteen and no one knew who the father was, not least Saoirse. Once she had the baby she didn't care much for naming him but eventually took to calling him Lucky. Another wish. So Elizabeth named him Luke. And once again, at the age of twenty-eight, Elizabeth took responsibility for a child.

There was never as much as a flicker of recognition in Saoirse's eyes when she looked at Luke. It startled Elizabeth to see that there was no bond, no connection at all. Elizabeth had never planned on having children – in fact she had made a pact with herself *never* to have children. She had raised herself and raised her sister; she had no desires to raise anybody else. It was time to look after herself. But at twenty-eight years old, after having slaved away at school and college, she had been successful in starting up her own interior design business. Her hard work meant that she was the only member of the family capable of providing a good life for Luke. She had reached her goals by being in control, maintaining order, not losing sight of herself, always being realistic, believing in fact and not dreams, and above all applying herself and working hard. Her mother and sister had taught her that she wouldn't get anywhere by following wistful dreams and having unrealistic hopes.

So now she was thirty-four years old and living alone with Luke in a house that she loved. A house she had bought, and was paying for, all by herself. A house she had made her haven, the place she could retreat to and feel safe. Alone because love was one of those feelings that you could never control. And she needed to be in control. She had loved before, had been loved, had tasted what it was to dream and had felt what it was to dance on air. She had also learned what it was to land back on the earth with a cruel thud. Having to take care of her sister's child had sent her love away and there had been no one since. She had learned not to lose control of her feelings again.

The front door banged shut and she heard the patter of little feet running down the hall.

'Luke!' she called, putting her hand over the receiver.

'Yeah?' he asked innocently, blue eyes and blond hair appearing round the doorpost.

'*Yes,* not yeah,' Elizabeth corrected him sternly. Her voice was full of the authority she had become a pro at over the years.

'*Yes,*' he repeated.

'What are you doing?'

Luke stepped into the hall and Elizabeth's eyes immediately went to his grass-stained knees.

'Me and Ivan are just playing the computer,' he explained.

'Ivan and I,' she corrected him, and continued listening to Marie at the other end of the phone arranging to send a garda car out. Luke looked at his aunt and returned to the playroom.

'Hold on a minute,' Elizabeth shouted down the phone, finally registering what Luke had just told her. She jumped up from her chair, bumping the table leg and spilling her espresso onto the glass. She swore. The black wrought-iron legs of the chair screeched against the marble. Holding the phone to her chest, she raced down the long hall to the playroom. She tucked her head round the corner and saw Luke sitting on the floor, eyes glued to the TV screen. Here and his bedroom were the only rooms in the house she allowed his toys. Taking care of a child had not succeeded in changing her as many thought it would; he hadn't softened her views in any way. She had visited many of Luke's friends' houses, picking him up or dropping him off, so full of toys lying around, they tripped up everyone who dared walk in their path. She reluctantly had cups of coffee with the mothers while sitting on teddies, surrounded by bottles, formula and nappies. But not in her home. Edith had been told the rules at the beginning of their working relationship and she had followed them. As Luke grew up and understood his aunt's ways, he obediently respected her wishes and contained his playing to the one room she had dedicated to his needs.

'Luke, who's Ivan?' Elizabeth asked, eyes darting around the room. 'You know you can't be bringing strangers home,' she said, worried.

'He's my new friend,' he replied, zombie-like, not moving his eyes from the beefed-up wrestler body-slamming his opponent on the screen.

'You know I insist on meeting your friends first before you bring them home. Where is he?' Elizabeth questioned, pushing open the door and stepping into Luke's space. She hoped to God that this friend would be better than the last little terror who had decided to draw a picture of his happy family in magic marker on her wall, which had since been painted over.

'Over there.' Luke nodded his head in the direction of the window, still not budging his eyes.

Elizabeth walked towards the window and looked out at the front garden. She crossed her arms. 'Is he hiding?'

Luke pressed Pause on his computer keypad and finally moved his eyes away from the two wrestlers on the screen. His face crinkled in confusion. 'He's right there!' He pointed at the beanbag at Elizabeth's feet.

Elizabeth's eyes widened as she stared at the beanbag. 'Where?'

'Right there,' he repeated.

Elizabeth blinked back at him. She raised her arms questioningly.

'Beside you, on the beanbag.' Luke's voice became louder with anxiety. He stared at the yellow corduroy beanbag as though willing his friend to appear.

Elizabeth followed his gaze.

'See him?' He dropped the control pad and stood up quickly.

This was followed by a tense silence in which Elizabeth could feel Luke's hatred for her emanating from his body. She could tell what he was thinking: why couldn't she just see him, why couldn't she just play along just this once, why couldn't she ever pretend? She swallowed the lump in her throat and looked around the room to see if she really was missing his friend in some way. Nothing.

She leaned down to be on an even level with him and her knees cracked. 'There's no one else but you and me in this room,' she whispered softly. Somehow saying it quietly made it easier. Easier for herself or Luke, she didn't know.

Luke's cheeks flushed and his chest heaved faster. He stood in the centre of the room, surrounded by computer keypad wires, with his little hands down by his side, looking helpless. Elizabeth's heart hammered in her chest as she silently begged, *please do not be like your mother, please do not be like your mother*. She knew only too well how the world of fantasy could steal you away.

Finally Luke exploded and, staring into space, demanded, 'Ivan, say something to her!'

There was a silence as he looked into space and then giggled hysterically. He looked back at Elizabeth and his smile quickly faded when he noticed her lack of response. 'Do you not see him?' he squealed nervously. Then, more angrily, repeated, 'Why don't you see him?'

'OK, OK!' Elizabeth tried not to panic. She stood back up to her own level. A level where she had control. She couldn't see him and her brain refused to let her pretend. She wanted to get out of the room quickly. She lifted her leg to step over the beanbag and stopped herself, instead choosing to walk round it. Once at the door, she glanced around one last time to see if she could spot the mystery Ivan. No sign.

Luke shrugged, sat down and continued playing his wrestling game.

'I'm putting some pizza on now, Luke.'

Silence. What else should she say? It was at moments like this she realised that reading all the parenting manuals in the world never helped. Good parenting came from the heart, was instinctive, and not for the first time she worried she was letting Luke down.

26

'It will be ready in twenty minutes,' she finished awkwardly.

'What?' Luke pressed Pause again and faced the window.

'I said it will be ready in twen—'

'No, not you,' Luke said, once again being sucked into the world of video games. 'Ivan would like some too. He said pizza is his favourite.'

'Oh.' Elizabeth swallowed helplessly.

'With olives,' Luke continued.

'But, Luke, you hate olives.'

'Yeah, but Ivan loves them. He says they're his favourite.'

'Oh . . .'

'Thanks,' Luke said to his aunt, looked to the beanbag, gave the thumbs-up, smiled, then looked away again.

Elizabeth slowly backed out of the playroom. She realised she was still holding the phone to her chest. 'Marie, are you still there?' She chewed on her nail and stared at the closed playroom door, wondering what to do.

'I thought you'd gone off to the moon as well. I was about to send a car over to your house too,' Marie chuckled.

Marie mistook Elizabeth's silence for anger and apologised quickly. 'Anyway, you were right, Saoirse *was* headed to the moon but luckily she decided to stop off on the way to refuel. Refuelling herself, more like. Your car was found blocking the main street with the engine still running and the driver's door wide open. You're lucky Paddy found it when he did before someone took off with it.'

'Let me guess. The car was outside the pub.'

'Correct.' Marie paused. 'Do you want to press charges?'

Elizabeth sighed. 'No. Thanks, Marie.'

'Not a problem. We'll have someone bring the car home to you.'

'What about Saoirse?' Elizabeth paced the hall. 'Where is she?'

'We'll just keep her here for a while, Elizabeth.'

'I'll come get her,' Elizabeth said quickly.

'No,' Marie insisted. 'Let me get back to you about that. She needs to calm down before she goes anywhere yet.'

From inside the playroom Elizabeth heard Luke laughing and talking away to himself.

'Actually, Marie,' she added with a weak smile, 'while we're on the phone, tell whoever's bringing the car to bring a shrink with them. It seems Luke is imagining friends now . . .'

Inside the playroom Ivan rolled his eyes and wiggled his body down further into the beanbag. He had heard her on the phone. Ever since he had started this job, parents had been calling him that and it was really beginning to bother him. There was nothing imaginary about him whatsoever.

They just couldn't see him.

28

Chapter 3

It was really nice of Luke to invite me to lunch that day. When I said that pizza was my favourite I hadn't actually intended being asked to stay to eat it. But how can you say no to the treat of *pizza* on a *Friday*? That's a cause for double celebration. However, I got the impression from the incident in the playroom that his aunt didn't like me very much, but I'm not at all surprised because that's usually the way it goes. The parents always think that making food for me is a waste because they always just end up throwing it out. But it's tricky for me – I mean, you try eating your dinner squashed in a tiny place at the table while everyone looks at you and wonders whether the food is going to disappear or not. I eventually get so paranoid that I can't eat and just have to leave the food on the plate.

Not that I'm complaining – being invited to dinner is nice but the grown-ups never quite put the same amount of food on my plate as everyone else's. It's never even half as much food as the rest and they always say things like, 'Oh, I'm sure Ivan's not that hungry today anyway.' I mean, how would they know? They never even ask. I'm usually sandwiched between whoever my best friend is at the time and some annoying older brother or sister who steals my food when no one's looking.

They forget to give me things like serviettes, cutlery, and they sure aren't generous with the wine. (Sometimes they just give me an empty plate and tell my best friends that invisible people eat invisible food. I mean, *please*, does the invisible wind blow invisible trees?) I usually get a glass of water and that's only when I ask my friends politely. The grown-ups think it's weird that I need a glass of water with my food, but they make an even bigger deal about it when I want ice. I mean, the ice is free anyway and who doesn't like a cool drink on a hot day?

It's usually the moms who have conversations with me. Only they ask questions and don't listen to the answers, or pretend to everyone else that I've said something else just to make them all laugh. They even look at my chest when they're talking to me as if they expect me to be three feet tall. It's such a stereotype. For the record, I'm six foot tall and we don't really do the 'age' thing where I'm from; we come into existence as we are and grow spiritually rather than physically. It's our brains that do the growing. Let's just say my brain is pretty big by now, but there's always room for more growth. I've been doing this job for a long, long time and I'm good at it. I've never failed a friend.

The dads always say things under their breath to me when they think no one else is listening. For example, me and Barry went to Waterford on our summer holidays and we were lying on the beach on Brittas Bay and a lady walked by in a bikini. Barry's dad said under his breath, 'Getta loada that, Ivan.' The dads always think that I agree with them. They always tell my best friends that I told them things like, 'It's good to eat vegetables. Ivan told me to tell you to eat your broccoli,' and stupid things like that. My best friends know full well that's not what I would say.

But that's grown-ups for you.

Nineteen minutes and thirty-eight seconds later, Elizabeth called Luke for dinner. My tummy was grumbling and I was really looking forward to the pizza. I followed Luke down the long hall to the kitchen, looking in every room as we passed. The house was really quiet and our footsteps echoed. Every room was all white or beige, and so spotless that I began to get nervous about eating my pizza because I didn't want to make a mess. As far as I could see, not only was there no sign of a child living in the house, there was no sign of *anyone* living in the house. It didn't have what you'd call a homely feel.

I liked the kitchen, though. It was warm from the sun and because it was surrounded by glass, it felt like we were sitting in the garden. Kind of like a picnic. I noticed the table was set for two people so I waited until told where to sit. The plates were big, black and shiny, the sun through the window made the cutlery sparkle and the two crystal glasses reflect rainbow colours on the table. There was a bowl of salad and a glass jug of water with ice and lemon in the centre of the table. Everything was resting on black marble place mats. Looking at how everything glistened, I was afraid even to get the napkins dirty.

Elizabeth's chair legs squeaked against the tiles as she sat down. She put her serviette on her lap. I noticed she'd changed into a chocolate-brown tracksuit to match her hair and complement her skin. Luke's chair squeaked and he sat down. Elizabeth picked up the giant salad fork and spoon and began to gather leaves and baby tomatoes onto her plate. Luke watched her and frowned. Luke had a slice of margherita pizza on his plate. No olives. I shoved my hands deep into my pockets and shuffled nervously from foot to foot.

'Is something wrong, Luke?' Elizabeth asked, pouring dressing over her lettuce.

'Where's Ivan's place?'

Elizabeth paused, screwed the lid on tightly and put the jar back in the centre of the table. 'Now, Luke, let's not be silly,' she said light-heartedly, not looking at him. I knew she was afraid to look.

'I'm not being silly,' Luke frowned. 'You said Ivan could stay for dinner.'

'Yes, but where *is* Ivan?' She tried to keep the soft tone in her voice while sprinkling grated cheese over her salad. I could tell she didn't want this to become an issue. She would knock it on the head straight away and there would be no more talk of invisible friends.

'He's standing right beside you.'

Elizabeth slammed her knife and fork down and Luke jumped in his seat. She opened her mouth to silence him but was interrupted by the doorbell ringing. As soon as she left the room, Luke got up from his chair and took out a plate from the kitchen press. A big black one just the same as the other two. He placed a slice of pizza on the plate, took out the cutlery and a napkin and placed it on a third place mat beside him.

'That's your seat, Ivan,' he said happily, and took a bite out of his pizza. A piece of melted cheese dribbled down his chin, looking like yellow string.

To be truthful I wouldn't have sat down at the table if it wasn't for my grumbling stomach shouting at me to eat. I knew Elizabeth would be mad, but if I gobbled the food up real fast before she returned to the kitchen then she wouldn't even know.

'Want some olives on that?' Luke asked, wiping his tomatoey face on his sleeve.

I laughed and nodded. My mouth was watering.

Elizabeth hurried back into the kitchen just as Luke was reaching up to the shelf.

'What are you doing?' she asked, rummaging through a drawer for something.

'Getting the olives for Ivan,' Luke explained. 'He likes olives on his pizza, remember?'

She looked across to the kitchen table and saw that it had been set for three. She rubbed her eyes tiredly. 'Look, Luke, don't you think it's a waste of food, putting the olives on the pizza? You hate them and I'll only have to throw it out.'

'Well, it won't be a waste because Ivan will eat them, won't you, Ivan?'

'I sure will,' I said, licking my lips and rubbing my aching tummy.

'Well?' Elizabeth cocked an eyebrow. 'What did he say?'

Luke frowned. 'You mean you can't *hear* him either?' He looked at me and circled his forefinger around his temple, signalling to me that his aunt was crazy. 'He said he sure will eat them all.'

'How polite of him,' Elizabeth mumbled, continuing to rummage through the drawer. 'But you better make sure every last crumb is gone because it'll be the last time Ivan eats with us if not.'

'Don't worry, Elizabeth, I'll gobble it all right up,' I told her, taking a bite. I couldn't face not being able to eat with Luke and his aunt again. She had sad eyes, sad brown eyes, and I was convinced that I was going to make her happy by eating every last crumb. I ate quickly.

'Thanks, Colm,' Elizabeth said tiredly, taking the car keys from the garda. She circled the car slowly, inspecting the paintwork closely.

'There's no damage done,' Colm said, watching her.

'Not to the car, anyway,' she attempted a joke, patting the bonnet. She always felt embarrassed. At least once a week there was some sort of incident involving the gardaí and although they were never anything but professional and polite about the situation, she couldn't help feeling ashamed. She would work even harder in their presence to appear 'normal' just to prove that it wasn't her fault, and that it wasn't the *entire* family that was nuts. She wiped down the splashes of dried mud with a tissue.

Colm smiled at her sadly. 'She was arrested, Elizabeth.'

Elizabeth's head shot up, now fully alert. 'Colm,' she said, shocked, 'why?' They had never done that before. They had always just warned Saoirse off and then dropped her back to wherever she was staying. Unprofessional, Elizabeth knew, but in such a small town where everyone knew everyone, they had always just kept their eye on Saoirse, stopping her before she did anything incredibly stupid. But Elizabeth feared Saoirse had been warned once too often.

Colm fidgeted with the navy-blue cap in his hands. 'She was drink driving, Elizabeth, in a stolen car, and she doesn't even have a licence.'

Hearing those words, Elizabeth shivered. Saoirse was a danger. Why did she keep protecting her sister? When would the words finally sink in and she'd accept that they were right: that her sister would never be the angel she wished her to be?

'But the car wasn't stolen,' Elizabeth stammered, 'I told her that she c—'

'Don't, Elizabeth.' Colm's voice was firm.

She had to hold her hand across her mouth to stop herself. She took a deep breath and tried to regain control. 'She has to go to court?' Her voice was a whisper.

Colm looked down at the ground and moved a stone with his foot. 'Yes. It's not just about her harming herself now. She's a danger to others.'

Elizabeth swallowed hard and nodded. 'One more chance, Colm,' she gulped, feeling her pride disintegrating. 'Just give her one more chance . . . please.' The last word pained her to have to say. Every bone in her body pleaded with him. Elizabeth never asked for help. 'I'll keep an eye on her. I promise she won't be out of my sight for a minute. She's going to get better, you know. She just needs time to work things out.' Elizabeth could feel her voice shaking. Her knees trembled as she begged on behalf of her sister.

There was a sad tone in Colm's voice. 'It's already been done. We can't change it now.'

'What will the punishment be?' She felt sick.

'It depends on the judge on the day. It's her first offence – well, her first *known* offence. He may go lightly on her, then again he may not.' He shrugged then looked at his hands. 'And it also depends on what the garda who arrested her says.'

'Why?'

'Because if she was co-operative and gave no

36

trouble it could make a difference, but then again . . .'

'It might not,' Elizabeth said worriedly. 'Well? Did she co-operate?'

Colm laughed lightly. 'Took two people to hold her down.'

'Damn it!' Elizabeth swore. 'Who arrested her?' She nibbled on her nails.

There was a silence before Colm spoke. 'I did.'

Her mouth dropped open. Colm had always had a soft spot for Saoirse. He was the one who was always on her side so the fact that he had arrested her rendered Elizabeth speechless. She chewed nervously on the inside of her mouth and the taste of blood slid down her throat. She didn't want people to start giving up on Saoirse.

'I'll do the best I can for her,' he said softly. 'Just try and keep her out of trouble until the hearing in a few weeks.'

Elizabeth, who realised she hadn't been breathing for the last few seconds, suddenly let her breath out. 'Thank you.' She couldn't say any more. Although she felt huge relief, she knew it was no victory. No one could protect her sister this time; she would have to face the consequences of her actions. But how was she expected to keep her eye on Saoirse when she didn't know where to begin looking for her? Saoirse couldn't stay with her and Luke – she was far too out of control to be around him – and her father had long since told her to move out and stay out.

'I'd better leave you at it so,' Colm said gently, fixed his cap back on his head, and he made his way down the cobbled drive.

Elizabeth sat on the porch, trying to rest her knocking knees, and looked at her mud-stained car. Why did Saoirse have to taint everything? Why was everything . . . every*one* Elizabeth loved chased away by her younger sister? She felt the clouds above push all that was between them and her onto her shoulders and she worried about what her father was going to do when they would undoubtedly bring Saoirse to his farm. She would give him five minutes before he rang Elizabeth complaining.

Inside the house, the phone started ringing and Elizabeth's heart sank even deeper. She rose from the porch, turned slowly on her heel and headed inside. When she got to the door the ringing had stopped and she spotted Luke sitting on the stairs with the phone pressed to his ear. She leaned against the wooden doorframe, arms folded, and watched him. A small smile crept onto her face. He was growing up so fast and she felt such a disconnection from the whole process, as though he was doing everything without her help, without the nurturing she knew she should be providing but that she felt awkward summoning. She knew she lacked that emotion – sometimes lacked emotion full stop – and everyday she wished the maternal instincts had come with the paperwork she signed. When Luke fell and cut his knee, her immediate response was to clean it and plaster his cut. To her that felt like enough, not dancing him around the room to stop his tears and slapping the ground like she'd watched Edith do.

'Hi, Granddad,' Luke was saying politely.

He paused to listen to his granddad on the other end.

'I'm just having lunch with Elizabeth and my new best friend, Ivan.'

Pause.

'A cheese and tomato pizza but Ivan likes olives on his.'

Pause.

'Olives, Granddad.'

Pause.

'No, I don't think you can grow them on the farm.'

Pause.

'O-L-I-V-E-S.' He spelled it out slowly.

Pause.

'Hold on, Granddad, my friend Ivan is telling me something.' Luke held the phone to his chest and looked into thin air, concentrating hard. Finally he lifted the phone back to his ear. 'Ivan said that the olive is a small, oily fruit that contains a pit. It's grown for its fruit and oil in subtropical zones.' He looked away and appeared to be listening. 'There are lots of types of olives.' He stopped talking, looked into the distance and then back to the phone. 'Underripe olives are always green but ripe olives are either green or black.' He looked away and listened to the silence again. 'Most tree-ripened olives are used for oil, the rest are brine- or salt-cured and are packed in olive oil or a brine or vinegar solution.' He looked into the distance. 'Ivan, what's brine?' There was silence then he nodded. 'Oh.'

Elizabeth raised her eyebrows and laughed nervously to herself. Since when had Luke become an expert on olives? He must have learned about them at school; he had a good memory for things like that. Luke paused and listened to the other end. 'Well, Ivan can't wait to meet you too.'

Elizabeth rolled her eyes and dashed towards Luke for the phone in case he said any more. Her father was confused enough as it was, at times, without having to explain the existence, or lack thereof, of an invisible boy.

'Hello,' Elizabeth said, grabbing the phone. Luke dragged his feet back to the kitchen. Irritation at the noise reared itself within Elizabeth again.

'Elizabeth,' said the stern formal voice, thick with a Kerry lilt, 'I just returned to find your sister lying on my kitchen floor. I gave her a boot but I can't figure out whether she's dead or not.'

Elizabeth sighed. 'That's not funny, and my sister is *your* daughter, you know.'

'Oh, don't give me that,' he said dismissively. 'I want to know what you're going to do about her. She can't stay here. The last time she did, she released the chickens from the coop and I spent all day getting them back in. And with my back and my hip, I can't be doing that any more.'

'I know, but she can't stay here either. She upsets Luke.'

'That child doesn't know enough about her to be upset. Half the time she forgets she's given birth to him. You can't have him all to yourself, you know.'

Elizabeth bit her tongue in rage. 'Half the time' was being overly generous. 'She can't come here,' she said more patiently than she felt. 'She was around earlier and took the car again. Colm just brought it back a few minutes ago. It's really serious this time.' She took a deep breath. 'They arrested her.'

Her father was silent for a moment and then he tutted. 'And rightly so. The experience will do her the world of good.' He quickly changed subject. 'Why weren't you at work today? Our Lord only intended us to rest on a Sunday.'

'That's the whole point. Today was a really important day for me at wor—'

'Well, your sister's come back to the land of the living and is outside trying to push the cows over again. Tell young Luke to come around with this new friend on Monday. We'll show him the farm.'

There was a click and the line went dead. Hello and goodbye were not her father's speciality; he still thought that mobile phones were some sort of futuristic alien-like technology designed to confuse the human race.

Elizabeth hung up the phone and made her way

back to the kitchen. Luke sat alone at the table, holding his stomach and laughing hysterically. She took her seat and continued eating her salad. She wasn't one of those people who was interested in eating food; she only did it because she had to. Evenings spent over long dinners bored her and she never had much of an appetite – she was always too busy worrying about something or too hyper to be able to sit still and eat. She glanced at the plate directly ahead of her and to her surprise saw that it was empty.

'Luke?'

Luke stopped talking to himself and faced her. 'Yeah?'

'Yes,' she corrected him. 'What happened to the slice of pizza that was on that plate?'

Luke looked at the empty plate, looked back at Elizabeth like she was crazy and took a bite of his own pizza. 'Ivan ate it.'

'Don't speak with your mouth full,' she admonished him.

He spat the food out onto the plate. 'Ivan ate it.' He began laughing hysterically again at the mush on his plate that had been in his mouth.

Elizabeth's head began to ache. What had gotten into him? 'What about the olives?'

Sensing her anger, he waited until he swallowed the rest of his food before speaking. 'He ate them too. I told you olives were his favourite. Granddad wanted to know if he could grow olives on the farm,' Luke smiled and revealed his gums.

Elizabeth smiled back. Her father wouldn't even know what an olive was if it walked up to him and introduced itself. He wasn't into any of those 'fancy' foods; rice was about as exotic as he would get and even then he complained that the pieces were too small and that he'd be better off eating 'a crumblin' spud'

Elizabeth sighed as she scraped the remainder of her food from her plate into the bin but not before checking through the rubbish to see if Luke had thrown the pizza and olives in. No sign. Luke usually had such a small appetite and would struggle to finish one large slice of pizza, never mind two. She presumed she would find it weeks later, mouldy and hiding at the back of a cabinet somewhere. But if he had eaten the entire thing, he would be sick all night and Elizabeth would have to clean up the mess. Again.

'Thank you, Elizabeth.'

'You're very welcome, Luke.'

'Huh?' Luke said, poking his head around the corner of the kitchen.

'Luke, I told you before, it's pardon, not huh.'

'Pardon?'

'I said you're very welcome.'

'But I haven't said thank you yet.'

Elizabeth slid the dishes into the dishwasher and stretched her back. She rubbed the base of her aching spine. 'Yes you did. You said, "Thank you, Elizabeth."'

'No I didn't,' Luke frowned.

Elizabeth felt her temper rising. 'Luke, stop playing games now, OK? We've had our fun at lunchtime, now you can stop pretending. OK?'

'No. That was Ivan who said thank you,' he said angrily.

A shiver ran through her body. She didn't think this was funny. She banged the dishwasher door shut, too fed up even to reply to her nephew. Why couldn't he, just this once, not give her a hard time?

Elizabeth rushed by Ivan with a cup of espresso in her hand, and the smell of perfume and coffee beans filled his nostrils. She sat down at the kitchen table, her shoulders sagged and she held her head in her hands.

'Ivan, come on!' Luke called impatiently from the playroom. 'I'll let you be The Rock this time!'

Elizabeth groaned quietly to herself.

But Ivan couldn't move. His blue Converse runners were rooted to the marble kitchen floor.

Elizabeth had heard him say thank you. He knew it.

He circled her slowly for a few minutes, studying her for signs of a reaction to his presence. He snapped his fingers next to her eardrums, jumped back and watched her. Nothing. He clapped his hands and stamped his feet. The sound echoed loudly in the large kitchen but Elizabeth remained at the table with her head in her hands. No reaction at all.

But she had said, 'You're very welcome.' After all his efforts of making noise around her, he was confused to discover his deep disappointment that she couldn't sense him. After all, she was a parent and who cared what parents thought? He stood behind her and stared down at the top of her head, wondering what noise he could make next. He sighed loudly, exhaling a deep breath.

Suddenly Elizabeth sat up straight, shuddered and pulled the zip on her tracksuit top higher.

And then he *knew* she had felt his breath.

Chapter 4

Elizabeth pulled her dressing gown tighter around her body and secured it at the waist. She tucked her long legs up underneath her body and snuggled down into the oversized armchair in the living room. Her wet hair sat tower-like on the top of her head, twisted in a towel; her skin smelled fruity from her passion fruit bubble bath. She cradled a fresh cup of coffee, complete with dollop of cream, in her hands and stared at the television. She was literally watching paint dry. Her favourite house makeover show was on and she loved to see how they could transform the most run-down rooms into sophisticated, elegant homes.

Ever since she was a child she had loved giving everything she touched a makeover. She had passed the time, spent waiting for her mother to return, by decorating the kitchen table with scattered daisies, sprinkling glitter on the welcome mat by the door, causing a trail of glitter to garnish the dull stone floors of the bungalow, decorating the photo frames with fresh flowers and sprinkling the bed linen with petals. She supposed it was her fix-it nature, always wanting something better than she had, never settling, never satisfied.

She also supposed it was her own childish way of trying to convince her mother to stay. She remembered thinking that perhaps the prettier the house, the longer her mother would remain home. But the daisies on the table were celebrated for no more than five minutes, the glitter on the doormat quickly trampled on, the flowers by the photo frames could not survive without water and the petals on the bed would be tossed and float to the floor during her mother's fitful night's sleep. As soon as these were tired of, Elizabeth would immediately start thinking of something that would really grab and take hold of her mother's attention, something that she would be drawn to for longer than five minutes, something that she would love so much she would be unable to leave it. Elizabeth never considered that as her mother's daughter, she should have been that something.

As she got older she grew to love bringing the beauty out in things. She had had much practice with that at her father's old farmhouse. Now she loved the days at work when she could restore old fireplaces and rip up ancient carpets to reveal beautiful original floors. Even in her own home she was always changing things, rearranging and trying to improve. She strived for perfection. She loved setting herself tasks, sometimes impossible ones, to prove to her heart that underneath every seemingly ugly thing there was something beautiful inside.

She loved her job, loved the satisfaction it brought, and with all the new housing developments in Baile na gCroíthe and the surrounding nearby towns, she had made a very good living out of it. If anything new was happening, Elizabeth's company was the one the developers all called. She was a firm believer that good design enhanced life. Beautiful, comfortable and functional spaces were what she endorsed.

Her own living room was about soft colours and textures. Suede cushions and fluffy carpets; she loved to touch and feel everything. There were light colours of coffees and creams and just like the mug in her hand they helped clear her mind. In a world where most things were a clutter, having a peaceful home was vital to her sanity. It was her hideaway, her nest, where she could hide from the problems outside her door. At least in her home she was in control. Unlike the rest of her life, she could allow whoever she wanted in, she could decide how long they should stay and where in her home they could be. Not like a heart that invites people in without permission, holds them in a special place she never had any say in and then yearns for them to remain there longer than they plan. No, the guests in Elizabeth's home could come and go on her command. And she chose for them to stay away.

Friday's meeting had been vital. She had spent weeks planning for it, updating her portfolio, creating a slide show, gathering magazine cuttings and newspaper write-ups of the places she had designed. Her whole life's work had been condensed into a folder book in order to convince these people to hire her. An old tower standing high on the mountainside overlooking Baile na gCroíthe was to be knocked down to make space for a hotel. It had once protected the small town from approaching attackers during the Viking times, but Elizabeth couldn't see the point of it remaining there today as it was neither pretty nor of any historical interest. When the tour buses, packed full with eager eyes from all over the world, passed through Baile na gCroíthe, the tower wasn't even mentioned. No one was proud of it nor interested in it. It was an ugly pile of stones that had been allowed to crumble and decay, that by day housed the village teenagers and by night housed the village drunks, Saoirse having been among both groups.

But many of the townspeople had put up a fight to prevent the hotel from being built, claiming the tower had some sort of mythical and romantic story behind it. A story began to circulate that if the building was knocked down, all love would be lost. It grabbed the attention of the tabloids and soft news programmes, and eventually the developers saw the opportunity for an even bigger goldmine than expected. They decided to restore the tower to a version of its former glory and build around it, leaving the tower as a historical piece for their courtyard, that way keeping the love alive in the Town of Hearts. There was suddenly a huge rush of interest from believers all around the country wanting to stay in the hotel to be near the tower blessed by love.

Elizabeth would have driven the JCB through it herself. She thought it was a ridiculous story, one created by a town afraid of change and intent on keeping the tower on the mountain. It was a story kept alive for tourists and dreamers, but she couldn't deny that the job of designing the hotel's interiors would be perfect for her. It would be a small place, but one that would provide employment for the people of Hartstown. Better yet, it was only a few minutes from her home and she wouldn't have to worry about being away from Luke for long periods of time while working on the project.

Before Luke was born Elizabeth used to travel all the time. She would never spend more than a few weeks in Baile na gCroíthe and loved having the freedom to move around and work in different counties on various projects. Her last big project took her to New York, but as soon as Luke was born that had all ended. When Luke was younger, Elizabeth couldn't continue with her work around the country, never mind around the world. It had been a very difficult time, trying to set up her business in Baile na gCroíthe and trying to get used to raising a child again. She had no other choice but to hire Edith, as her father wouldn't help out and Saoirse certainly hadn't any interest. Now Luke was older and settled at school, Elizabeth was discovering that finding work within commuting distance was becoming increasingly difficult. The development boom in Baile na gCroíthe would eventually settle and she constantly worried whether the work would then dry up completely.

Her walking out of the meeting on Friday should not have happened. Nobody in her office could sell her abilities as an interior decorator better than she could. Her employees consisted of receptionist Becca, and Poppy. Becca was a timid and extremely shy seventeen-year-old, who had joined Elizabeth in her transition year while on work experience and decided not to go back to school. She was a hard worker who kept to herself, and was quiet around the office, which Elizabeth liked. Elizabeth had hired her quickly after Saoirse, who had been hired by Elizabeth to work there part time, had let her down. She had *more* than let her down and Elizabeth had been desperate to get someone in quickly. To tidy up the mess. Again. Keeping Saoirse near her during the day as an attempt to help her on her feet had only succeeded in driving her further away and knocking her right back down.

Then there was twenty-five-year-old Poppy, a recent graduate from art college, full of lots of wonderfully impossible creative ideas and ready to paint the world a colour she had yet to invent. There were just the three of them in the office but Elizabeth often called on the services of Mrs

Bracken, a sixty-eight-year-old genius with a needle and thread, who ran her own upholstery shop in the town. She was also an incredible grump and insisted on being called *Mrs Bracken* and not Gwen, out of respect for her dearly departed *Mr Bracken*, whom Elizabeth didn't think had been born with a first name. And finally there was Harry, fifty-two years old and an all-round handyman, who could do anything from hanging paintings to rewiring buildings but who couldn't understand the concept of an unmarried woman with a career, not to say an unmarried woman with a career and a child not her own. Depending on people's budgets, Elizabeth would do anything from instructing painters and decorators to doing it all herself, but mostly she liked to be hands-on. She liked to see the transformation before her very eyes and it was part of her nature to want to fix everything herself.

It wasn't unusual for Saoirse to have shown up at Elizabeth's house that morning. She would often arrive drunk and abusive, and willing to take any-thing that she could get her hands on – anything worth selling, of course, which automatically excluded Luke. Elizabeth didn't even know if it was just the drink she was addicted to any more; it was a long time since she'd had a conversation with her sister. She had been trying to help her since she was fourteen. It was as if a switch had been flicked in her head and they had lost her to another world. She tried sending her to counselling, rehab, doctors, she gave her money, found her jobs, hired her herself, allowed her to move in with her, rented her flats. She had tried being her friend, had tried being her enemy, had laughed with her and shouted at her, but nothing would work. Saoirse was lost to her, lost in a world where nobody else mattered.

Elizabeth couldn't help thinking of the irony of her name. Saoirse wasn't free. She may have felt that she was, coming and going as she pleased, not being tied down to anyone, anything, any place, but she was a slave to her addictions. She couldn't see it, though, and Elizabeth couldn't help her see it. She couldn't turn her back completely on her sister but she had run out of energy, ideas and faith in ever believing Saoirse could be changed, and had lost lovers and friends with her persistence. Their frustration would grow as they stood by and watched Elizabeth being taken advantage of time and time again till they could no longer be in her life. But contrary to their beliefs, Elizabeth didn't feel like the victim. She was always in control. She knew what and why she was doing what she was doing, and she refused to desert a family member. She would not be like her mother. She had worked too hard all her life at trying not to be.

Elizabeth suddenly pressed Mute on the television remote control and the room was silenced. She cocked her head to one side. She thought she'd heard something again. After looking around the room and seeing that everything was as it should be, she turned the volume back up again.

There it was again.

She silenced the TV once more and stood up from the armchair.

It was 10.15 and not yet fully dark. She looked out to the back garden and in the dusk she could only see black shadows and shapes. She pulled the curtains closed quickly and immediately felt safer in her cream and beige cocoon. She tightened her dressing gown again and sat back down in her armchair, tucking her legs even closer to her body and wrapping her arms protectively around her knees. The vacant cream leather couch stared back at her. She shuddered again, turned the volume up even higher than before and took a gulp of coffee. The velvety liquid slid down her throat and warmed her insides and she tried once again to be sucked back into the world of television.

All day she had felt odd. Her father always said that when you got a chill up your spine it meant that someone was walking over your grave. Elizabeth didn't believe that but as she stared at the television, she turned her head away from the three-seater leather couch and tried to shake off the feeling that a pair of eyes was watching her.

Ivan watched her mute the television once again, quickly put her coffee cup on the table next to her and jump out of her chair as though she had been sitting on pins. Here she goes again, he thought.

Her eyes were wide and terrified as they darted around the room. Once again Ivan prepared himself and pushed his body to the edge of the couch. The denim of his jeans squeaked against the leather.

Elizabeth jumped to face the couch.

She grabbed a black iron poker from the large marble fireplace and spun round on her heels. Her knuckles turned white as they tightened around it. She slowly tiptoed about the room, eyes wild with fear. The leather squeaked again underneath him and Elizabeth charged towards the couch. Ivan leaped from his seat and dived into the corner.

He hid behind the curtains for protection and watched as she pulled the cushions out of the chair while grumbling to herself about mice. After ten minutes of searching through the couch, Elizabeth put all the cushions back in place to restore its immaculate form.

She picked up her coffee cup self-consciously and made her way into the kitchen. Ivan followed closely on her heel; he was so close that strands of her soft hair tickled his face. Her hair smelled of coconut and her skin of rich fruits.

He couldn't understand his fascination with her. He had been watching her since after lunch on Friday. Luke had kept calling him to play game after game and all Ivan had wanted was to be around Elizabeth. At first it was just to see if she could hear him or sense him again, but then after a few hours he found her compelling. She was obsessively neat. He noticed she couldn't leave the room to answer the phone or front door until everything had been tidied away and wiped clean. She drank a lot of coffee, stared out to her garden, picked imaginary pieces of fluff from almost everything. And she thought. He could see it in her face. Her brow would furrow in concentration and she would make facial expressions as though she was having conversations with people in her head. They seemed to turn into debates more often than not, judging by the activity on her forehead.

He noticed she was always surrounded by silence. There was never any music or sounds in the background like most people had, a radio blaring, the window open to allow in the sounds of summer – the birdsong and the lawn mowers. Luke and she spoke little and when they did it was mostly her giving him orders, him asking permission, nothing fun. The phone rarely rang, nobody called by. It was almost as if the conversations in her head were loud enough to fill her silence.

He spent most of Friday and Saturday following her around, sitting on the cream leather couch in the evenings and watching her watching the only programme she seemed to like on TV. They both laughed in the same places, groaned in the same places and they seemed to be completely in sync, yet she didn't know he was there. He had watched her sleeping the previous night. She was restless – she slept only three hours at the most; the rest of the time she spent reading a book, putting it down after five minutes, staring into space, picking the book up again, reading a few pages, reading back over the same pages, putting it down again, closing her eyes, opening them again, turning the light on, doodling sketches of furniture and rooms, playing with colours and shades and scraps of material, turning the light off again.

She had made Ivan tired just watching her from the straw chair in the corner of the room. The trips to the kitchen for coffee couldn't have helped her either. On Sunday morning she was up early, tidying, vacuuming, polishing and cleaning an already spotless home. She spent all morning at it while Ivan played chasing with Luke out in the back garden. He recalled Elizabeth being particularly upset by the sight of Luke running around the garden laughing and screaming to himself. She had joined them at the kitchen table and watched Luke playing cards, shaking her head and looking worried when he explained the rules of patience in extreme detail to thin air.

But when Luke went to bed at nine o'clock, Ivan read him the story of Tom Thumb quicker than he usually would, and then hurried to continue watching Elizabeth. But he could sense her getting jitterier as the days wore on.

She washed her coffee cup out, ensuring it was already spotless before putting it in the dishwasher. She dried the wet sink with a cloth and put the cloth in the wash basket in the utility room. She picked imaginary fluff from a few items in her path, picked crumbs from the floor, switched off all the lights and began the same process in the living room. She had done the exact same thing the last two nights.

But before leaving the living room this time, she stopped abruptly, almost sending Ivan into the back of her. His heart beat wildly. Had she sensed him?

She turned round slowly.

He fixed his shirt to look presentable.

Once facing him he smiled. 'Hi,' he said, feeling very self-conscious.

She rubbed her eyes tiredly and opened them again. 'Oh, Elizabeth, you are going mad,' she whispered. She bit her lip and charged towards Ivan.

Chapter 5

Elizabeth knew she was losing her mind right at that moment. It had happened to her sister and mother, and now it was her turn. For the last few days she had felt incredibly insecure, as if someone was watching her. She had locked all the doors, drawn all the curtains, set the alarm. That probably should have been enough but now she was going to go that one step further.

She charged through the living room straight towards the fireplace, grabbed the iron poker, marched out of the room, locked the door and made her way upstairs. She looked at the poker lying on her bedside locker, rolled her eyes and turned her lamp off. She *was* losing her mind.

Ivan emerged from behind the couch and looked around. He had dived behind it thinking Elizabeth was charging towards him. He had heard the door lock after she stormed out. He slumped with a disappointment he had never experienced before. She still hadn't seen him.

* * *

I'm not magic, you know. I can't cross my arms, nod my head, blink and disappear and reappear on the top of a bookshelf or anything. I don't live in a lamp, don't have funny little ears, big hairy feet or wings. I don't replace loose teeth with money, leave presents under a tree or hide chocolate eggs. I can't fly, climb up the walls of buildings or run faster than the speed of light.

And I can't open doors.

That has to be done for me. The grown-ups find that part the funniest but also the most embarrassing when their children do it in public. I don't laugh at grown-ups when they can't climb trees or can't say the alphabet backwards because it's just not physically possible for them. It doesn't make them freaks of nature.

So Elizabeth needn't have locked the living-room door when she went to bed that night because I couldn't turn the handle anyway. Like I said, I'm not a superhero; my special power is friendship. I listen to people and I hear what they say. I hear their tones, the words they use to express themselves and, most importantly, I hear what they *don't* say.

So all I could do that night was think about my new friend, Luke. I need to do that occasionally. I make notes in my head so that I can file a report for admin. They like to keep it all on record for training purposes. We've new people joining up all the time. In fact, when I'm between friends, I lecture.

I needed to think about why I was here. What made Luke want to see me? How could he benefit from my friendship? The business is run extremely professionally and we must always provide the company with a brief history of our friends and then list our aims and objectives. I could always identify the problem straight away but this scenario was slightly baffling. You see, I'd never been friends with an adult before. Anyone who has ever met one would understand why. There's no sense of fun with them. They stick rigidly to schedules and times, they focus on the most unimportant things imaginable, like mortgages and bank statements, when everyone knows that the majority of the time it's the people around them that put the smiles on their faces. It's all work and no play, and I work hard, I really do, but playing is by far my favourite.

Take, for example, Elizabeth; she lies in bed worrying about car tax and phone bills, babysitters and paint colours. If you can't put magnolia on a wall then there are always a million other colours you can use; if you can't pay your phone bill then just write letters telling them. People forget they have options. And they forget that those things really don't matter. They should concentrate on what they have and not what they don't have. But I'm veering away from the story again.

I worried about my job a little the night I was locked in the living room. It's the first time that had ever happened. I worried because I couldn't figure out why I was there. Luke had a difficult family scenario but that was normal and I could tell he felt loved. He was happy and loved playing, he slept well at night, ate all his food, had a nice friend called Sam and when he spoke I listened and listened and tried to hear the words he wasn't saying but there was nothing. He liked living with his aunt, was scared of his mom and liked talking about vegetables with his granddad. But Luke seeing me every day and wanting to play with me every day meant that I definitely needed to be here for him.

On the other hand, his aunt never slept, ate very little, was constantly surrounded by silence so loud that it was deafening, she had nobody close to her to talk to, that I had seen yet anyway, and she *didn't* say *far more* than she did actually say. She had heard me say thank you once, felt my breath a few times, heard me squeak on the leather couch but yet she couldn't see me nor could stand me being in her house.

Elizabeth did not want to play.

Plus she was a grown-up, she gave me butterflies and wouldn't know fun if it hit her in the face, and believe me I'd tried to throw it at her plenty of times over the weekend. So I couldn't possibly be here to help her. It was unheard of.

People refer to me as an invisible or an imaginary friend. Like there's some big mystery surrounding me. I've read the books that grown-ups have written asking why kids see me, why do they

believe in me so much for so long and then suddenly stop and go back to being the way they were
before? I've seen the television shows that try to
debate why it is that children invent people like
me.

So just for the record for all you people, I'm
not invisible or imaginary. I'm always here walking
around just like you all are. And people like Luke
don't *choose* to see me, they just see me. It's people
like you and Elizabeth that choose not to.

Chapter 6

Elizabeth was woken up at 6.08 a.m. by the sun streaming through the bedroom window and onto her face. She always slept with the curtains open. It had stemmed from growing up on a farm. Lying in her bed she could see through the bungalow window, down the garden path and out of the front gate. Beyond that was a country road that led straight from the farm, stretching on for a mile. Elizabeth could see her mother returning from her adventures, walking down the road for at least twenty minutes before she reached home. She could recognise the half-hop, half-skip from miles away. Those twenty minutes always felt like an eternity to Elizabeth. The long road had its own way of building up Elizabeth's excitement, almost teasing her.

And finally she would hear that familiar sound, the squeak of the front gate. The rusting hinges acted as a welcoming band to the free spirit. Elizabeth had a love/hate relationship with that gate. Like the long stretch of road, it would tease her, and some days on hearing the creak she would run to see who was at the door and her heart would sink that it was only the postman.

Elizabeth had annoyed college room-mates and lovers with her insistence on keeping the curtains open. She didn't know why she remained firm on this; it certainly wasn't as though she was still waiting. But now in her adulthood, the open curtains acted as her alarm clock; with them open she knew the light would never allow her to fall back into a deep sleep. Even in her sleep she felt alert, and in control. She went to bed to rest, not to dream.

She squinted in the bright room and her head throbbed. She needed coffee, fast. Outside the window a bird's song echoed loudly in the quiet of the countryside. Somewhere far away a cow answered its call. But despite the idyllic morning, there was nothing about this Monday that Elizabeth was looking forward to. She had to try to reschedule a meeting with the hotel developers, which was going to prove difficult because after the little stunt in the press about the new love nest at the top of the mountain, they had people flying in from all parts of the world willing to share their design ideas. This annoyed Elizabeth; this was her territory. But that wasn't her only problem.

Luke had been invited to spend the day with his grandfather on the farm. That bit, Elizabeth was happy with. It was the part about him expecting another six-year-old by the name of Ivan that worried her. She would have to have a discussion with Luke this morning about it because she dreaded to think of what would happen if there was a mention of an imaginary friend to her father.

Brendan was sixty-five years old, big, broad, silent and brooding. Age had not mellowed him; instead it had brought bitterness, resentment, and even more confusion. He was small-minded and unwilling to open up or change. Elizabeth could at least try to understand his difficult nature if being that way made him happy, but as far as she could see, his views frustrated him and only made his life more miserable. He was stern, rarely spoke except to the cows or vegetables, never laughed, and whenever he did decide someone was worthy of his words, he lectured. There was no need to respond to him. He didn't speak for conversation. He spoke to make statements. He rarely spent time with Luke as he didn't have time for the airy-fairy ways of children, for their silly games and nonsense. The only thing that Elizabeth could see that her father liked about Luke was that he was an empty book, ready to be filled with information and not enough knowledge to question or criticise. Fairy tales and fantasy stories had no place with her father. She supposed that was the only belief they actually shared.

She yawned and stretched and, still unable to open her eyes against the bright light, she felt around her bedside locker for her alarm clock. Although she woke up every morning at the same time, she never forgot to set her alarm. Her arm knocked against something cold and hard and it fell with a loud bang to the floor. Her sleepy heart jumped with fright.

Hanging her head over the side of the bed she caught sight of the iron poker lying on her white carpet. Her 'weapon' also reminded her that she had to call Rentokil to get rid of the mice. She had sensed them in the house all weekend and she had felt so paranoid that they were in her bedroom the past few nights she could hardly sleep, although that wasn't particularly unusual for her.

Washed and dressed, after waking Luke she made her way downstairs to the kitchen. Minutes later, with espresso in hand, she dialled the number of Rentokil. Luke wandered into the kitchen sleepily, blond hair tossed, dressed in an orange T-shirt half tucked into red shorts. The outfit was completed with odd socks and a pair of runners that lit up with every step he took.

'Where's Ivan?' he asked groggily, looking around the kitchen as though he'd never been in the room before in his life. He was like that every morning; it took him at least an hour to wake up even once he was up and dressed. During the dark winter mornings it took even longer. Elizabeth supposed that at some point in his morning classes as school he finally realised what he was doing.

'Where's Ivan?' he repeated.

Elizabeth silenced him by holding her finger to her lips, and giving him the glare, as she listened to the lady from Rentokil. He knew not to interrupt her when she was on the phone. 'Well, I only noticed it this weekend. Since Friday lunchtime actually, so I was wond—'

'IVAN?' Luke yelled, and began looking under the kitchen table, behind the curtains, behind the doors. Elizabeth rolled her eyes. This carry-on again.

'No, I haven't actually seen . . .'

'IVAAAAN?'

'. . . one yet but I definitely feel that they're here.' Elizabeth finished, and tried to catch Luke's eye so that she could give him the glare again.

'IVAN, WHERE ARE YOOOUUU?' Luke called.

'Droppings? No, no droppings,' Elizabeth said, getting frustrated.

Luke stopped shouting and his ears perked up. 'WHAT? I CAN'T HEAR YOU PROPERLY.'

'No, I don't have any mousetraps. Look, I'm very busy, I don't have time for twenty questions. Can't someone just come out and check for themselves?' Elizabeth snapped.

Luke suddenly ran from the kitchen and out into the hall. She heard him banging at the living-room door. 'WHAT ARE YOU DOING IN THERE, IVAN?' He pulled at the handle.

Finally Elizabeth's conversation ended and she slammed down the phone. Luke was shouting through the living-room door at full volume. Her blood boiled.

'LUKE! GET IN HERE NOW!'

The banging at the living-room door stopped immediately. He shuffled slowly into the kitchen.

'DON'T DRAG YOUR FEET!' she yelled.

He lifted his feet and the lights on the soles of his runners flashed with every step. He stood before her and spoke quietly and as innocently as he possibly could in his high-pitched voice. 'Why did you lock Ivan in the living room last night?'

Silence.

She had to put an end to this now. She would choose this moment to sit down and discuss the issue with Luke and by the end of it he would respect her wishes. She would help him see sense and there would be no more talk of invisible friends.

'And Ivan wants to know why you brought the fire poker to bed with you?' he added, feeling more confident by her failure to scream at him again.

Elizabeth exploded. 'There will be no more talk of this Ivan, do you hear me?'

Luke's face went white.

'DO YOU HEAR ME?' she shouted. She didn't even give him a chance to answer. 'You know as well as I do that there is *no such thing* as Ivan. He does *not* play chasing, he does *not* eat pizza, he is *not* in the living room and he is *not* your friend because he *does not exist.*'

Luke's face crumpled up as though he were about to cry.

Elizabeth continued, 'Today you are going to your granddad's and if I hear from him that there was one mention of Ivan, you will be in *big trouble*. Do you understand?'

Luke began to cry softly.

'Do you understand?' she repeated.

He nodded his head slowly as tears rushed down his face.

Elizabeth's blood stopped boiling and her throat began to ache from shouting. 'Now sit at the table and I'll bring you your cereal,' she said softly. She fetched the Coco Pops. Usually she didn't allow him to eat such sugary breakfasts but she hadn't exactly discussed the Ivan situation with him as planned. She knew she had a problem keeping her temper. She sat at the table and watched him pour Coco Pops into his cereal bowl and then his little hands wobbled with the weight of the milk carton. Milk splashed onto the table. She held back from shouting at him again although she had cleaned that only yesterday evening until it sparkled. Something Luke had said was bothering her and she couldn't quite remember what it was. She rested her chin on her hand and watched him eating.

He munched slowly. Sadly. There was silence apart from his crunching. Finally, after a few minutes, he spoke. 'Where's the key to the living room?' he asked, refusing to catch her eye.

'Luke, not with your mouth full,' she said softly. She took the key to the living room out of her pocket, went to the doorway in the hall and twisted the key. 'There now, Ivan is free to *leave* the house,' she joked, and immediately regretted saying it.

'He's not,' Luke said sadly from the kitchen table. 'He can't open doors himself.'

Silence.

'He can't?' Elizabeth repeated.

Luke shook his head as if what he had said was the most normal thing in the world. It was the most ridiculous thing Elizabeth had ever heard. What kind of an imaginary friend was he if he couldn't walk through walls and doors? Well, she wasn't opening the door, she had unlocked it and that was silly enough. She went back to the kitchen to gather her belongings for work. Luke finished his cereal, placed the bowl in the dishwasher, washed his hands, dried them and made his way to the living-room door. He turned the handle, pushed open the door, stepped out of the way, smiled broadly at nothing, placed a finger over his lips, pointed at Elizabeth with his other hand and giggled quietly to himself. Elizabeth watched with horror. She walked down the hall and stood beside Luke at the doorway. She looked into the living room.

Empty.

The girl from Rentokil had said that it would be unusual for mice to be in the house in June and as Elizabeth eyed the living room suspiciously, she wondered what on earth could be making all those noises.

Luke's giggling snapped her out of her trance and, glancing down the hall, she spotted him sitting at the table, swinging his legs happily and making faces into thin air. There was an extra place set and a freshly poured bowl of Coco Pops across from him.

*　　*　　*

'Boy, is she strict,' I whispered to Luke at the table, trying to grab spoonfuls of Coco Pops without her noticing. I wouldn't usually whisper around parents but as she had heard me a couple of times already over the past few days, I wasn't about to take any risks.

Luke giggled and nodded.

'Is she like this all the time?'

He nodded again.

'Does she never play games and give you hugs?' I asked, watching as Elizabeth cleaned every inch of the already sparkling kitchen countertops, moving things half an inch to the right and a half an inch to the left.

Luke thought for a while and then shrugged. 'Not much.'

'But that's horrible! Don't you mind?'

'Edith says that there are some people in the world that don't hug you all the time or play games but they still love you. They just don't know how to say it,' he whispered back.

Elizabeth eyed him nervously.

'Who's Edith?'

'My nanny.'

'Where is she?'

'On her holidays.'

'So who's going to mind you while she's on her holidays?'

'You,' Luke smiled.

'Let's shake on it,' I said, holding out my hand. Luke grabbed it. 'We do it like this,' I explained,

72

shaking my head and my whole body, like I was having a convulsion. Luke started laughing and copied me. We laughed even harder when Elizabeth stopped cleaning to stare. Her eyes widened.

'You ask a lot of questions,' Luke whispered.

'You answer a lot,' I fired back, and we both laughed again.

Elizabeth's BMW rattled along the bumpy track leading to her father's farm. She clenched her hands around the steering wheel in exasperation as the dust flew up from the ground and clung to the side of her newly washed car. How she had lived on this farm for eighteen years was beyond her. Nothing could be kept clean. The wild fuchsias danced in the light breeze, waving their welcome from the side of the road. They lined the mile-long road like landing lights and rubbed against the windows of the car, pressing their faces to see who was inside. Luke lowered his window and allowed his hand to be tickled by their kisses.

She prayed that no traffic would come towards her as the road just about allowed her car through, leaving no room for two-way traffic. In order to let someone pass she would have to reverse half a mile back the way she'd come just to make room. At times it felt like the longest road in the world. She could see where she was trying to get to yet she would have to keep reversing in order to get there.

Two steps forward and one step back.

It was like when she was a child seeing her mother from a mile away but being forced to wait the twenty minutes it took her to dance down the road, till Elizabeth heard the familiar sound of the gate creak.

But thankfully, because they were already delayed as it was, no traffic came this time. Elizabeth's words had obviously fallen on deaf ears because Luke refused to leave the house until Ivan had finished his cereal. He then insisted on pushing forward the passenger seat in the car in order to let Ivan into the back seat.

She glanced quickly at Luke. He sat buckled up in the front seat, arm out the window, humming the same song he had been singing all weekend. He looked happy. She hoped he wouldn't keep his play-acting up for much longer, at least while he was at his granddad's.

She could see her father at the gate, waiting. A familiar sight. A familiar action. Waiting was his forte. He wore the same brown cords Elizabeth could have sworn he was wearing when she was a child. They were tucked into muddy green Wellington boots that he wore in the house. His grey cotton jumper was stitched with a faded green and blue diamond pattern, there was a hole in the centre, and the green of his polo shirt peeked through from underneath. A tweed cap sat firmly on his head, a blackthorn cane in his right hand kept him steady, and silver grey stubble decorated his face and chin. His eyebrows were grey and wild, and when he frowned they seemed to cover his grey eyes completely. His nose commanded his face with large nostrils filled with grey hairs. Deep wrinkles cracked his face, his hands as big as shovels, shoulders as wide as the Gap of Dungloe. He dwarfed the bungalow that stood behind him.

Luke stopped humming as soon as he saw his grandfather and brought his arm back into the car. Elizabeth pulled up, turned the engine off and jumped out. She had a plan. As soon as Luke climbed out of the car she shut the door and locked it before he had a chance to push the seat forward and make way for Ivan. Luke's face crumpled again as he looked from Elizabeth and back to the car.

The gate outside the bungalow creaked.

Elizabeth's stomach churned.

'Morning,' a deep voice boomed. It wasn't a greeting. It was a statement.

Luke's lower lip trembled and he pressed his face and hands up against the glass of the back seat of the car. Elizabeth hoped he wouldn't throw a tantrum now.

'Aren't you going to say good morning to your granddad, Luke?' Elizabeth asked sternly, fully aware that she herself had yet to acknowledge him.

'Hi, Granddad.' Luke's voice wobbled. His face remained pressed against the glass.

Elizabeth contemplated opening the car door

for him just to avoid a scene but thought better of it. He needed to get over this phase.

'Where's th'other one?' Brendan's voice boomed.

'The other what?' She took Luke's hand and tried to turn him away from the car. His blue eyes looked pleadingly into hers. Her heart sank. He knew better than to cause a scene.

'The young lad who knew about them foreign veg.'

'Ivan,' Luke said sadly, tears welling up.

Elizabeth jumped in, 'Ivan couldn't come today, isn't that right, Luke? Maybe another day,' she said quickly, and before it could be discussed any further, 'Right, I'd better go to work or I'll be late. Luke, have a good day with your granddad, OK?'

Luke looked at her uncertainly and nodded.

Elizabeth hated herself but she knew she was right to control this ludicrous behaviour.

'Off you go so.' Brendan swung his blackthorn cane at her as if to dismiss her and he turned his back to face the bungalow. The last thing she heard was the gate creaking before she slammed her car door shut. She had to reverse twice down the road in order to let two tractors pass. From her mirror she could see Luke and her father in the front garden, her father towering over him. She couldn't get away from the house fast enough; it was as though the flow of traffic kept pulling her back to it, like the tide.

Elizabeth remembered the moment when she was

76

eighteen when she thrived on the freedom of such a view. For the first time in her life, she was leaving the bungalow with her bags packed and with the intention of not coming back until Christmas. She was going to Cork University, after winning the battle with her father but in turn losing all respect he had ever had for her. Instead of sharing in her excitement, he had refused to see her off on her big day. The only figure standing outside the bungalow Elizabeth could see that bright August morning as they drove away was that of six-year-old Saoirse, her red hair in messy pigtails, her smile toothless in places yet broad and wide, with her arm waving frantically goodbye, full of pride for her big sister.

Instead of the relief and excitement she always dreamed of feeling when the taxi finally pulled away from her home, breaking the umbilical cord that held her there, she felt dread and worry. Not for what lay ahead but for what she was leaving behind. She couldn't mother Saoirse for ever, she was a young woman who needed to be set free, who needed to find her own place in the world. Her father needed to step into his rightful place of fatherhood, a title he had discarded many years ago and refused to recognise. She only hoped now that as the two of them were alone, he would realise his duties and show as much love as he could for what he had left.

But what if he didn't? She continued watching her sister out the back window, feeling as if she was never going to see her again, waving as fast and as furiously as she could as tears filled her eyes for the little life and bundle of energy she was leaving behind. The red hair jumping up and down was visible from a mile away and so they both kept on waving. What would her little sister do now that the fun of waving her off had ended and the realisation set in that she was alone with the man who never spoke, never helped and never loved. Elizabeth almost asked the driver to stop the car right there and then, but quickly told herself to stay strong. She needed to live.

You do the same as me someday, little Saoirse, her eyes kept telling the little figure as they drove away. Promise me you'll do the same. Fly away from there.

With eyes full of tears, Elizabeth watched as the bungalow got smaller and smaller in her mirror until finally it disappeared when she reached the end of the mile-long road. At once her shoulders relaxed and she realised she had been holding her breath the entire time.

'Right, Ivan,' she said, looking in the mirror at the empty back seat, 'I guess you're coming to work with me so.' Then she did a funny thing.

She giggled childishly.

Chapter 7

Baile na gCroíthe was stirring as Elizabeth drove over the grey-stone bridge that served as its gateway. Two huge coaches full of tourists were currently trying to inch past each other on the narrow street. Inside, Elizabeth could see faces pressed against the windows, oohing and aahing, smiling and pointing, cameras being held up to the glass to snap the doll-like town on film. The coach driver facing Elizabeth licked his lips in concentration and she could see the sweat glistening on his brow as he slowly manoeuvred the oversized vehicle along the narrow road originally designed for horses and carts. The sides of the coaches were almost touching. Beside him, the tour guide, with microphone in hand, did his best to entertain his one-hundred-strong audience so early in the morning.

Elizabeth lifted the handbrake and sighed loudly. This wasn't a rare occurrence in the town and she knew it could take a while. She doubted the coaches would stop. They rarely did unless it was for a toilet break. Traffic always seemed to be moving through Baile na gCroíthe but never stopping. She didn't blame them; it was a great place to help you get to where you're going but not one for sticking around in. Traffic would slow down and visitors would take a good look alright, but then the drivers would put a foot down and accelerate off out the other end.

It's not that Baile na gCroíthe wasn't beautiful – it was certainly that. Its proudest moment was winning the Tidy Town competition for the third year running, and as you entered the village, over the bridge, a display of bright blooming flowers spelled out a welcome. The flower display continued through the town. Window boxes adorned the shop fronts, hanging baskets hung from black lampposts, trees grew tall along the main street. Each building was painted a different colour, and the main street, the only street, was a rainbow of pastels and bold colours of mint greens, salmon pinks, lilacs, lemons and blues. The pavements were litter free and gleaming, and as soon as you averted your gaze above the grey slate roofs you found yourself surrounded by majestic green mountains. It was as though Baile na gCroíthe was cocooned, safely nestled in the bosom of Mother Nature.

Cosy or suffocating.

Elizabeth's office was located beside a green post office and a yellow supermarket. Her building was a pale blue, and sat above Mrs Bracken's curtain, fabric and upholstery shop. The shop had previously been a hardware shop run by Mr Bracken, but when he died ten years ago, Gwen had decided to turn it into her own store. She seemed to make decisions based purely on what her deceased husband would think. She opened the shop 'because it's what Mr Bracken would have wanted'. However, Gwen refused to go out at the weekends or involve herself in any social outings as 'it's not what Mr Bracken would have wanted'. As far as Elizabeth could see, what made Mr Bracken happy or unhappy seemed to tie in nicely with Gwen's philosophy on life.

The coaches moved past each other inch by inch. Baile na gCroíthe in rush-hour traffic; the result of two oversized buses trying to share the narrow road. Finally they were successful in their passing and Elizabeth looked on, not amused as the tour guide jumped from his seat in excitement, microphone in hand, succeeding in turning what was essentially a boring halt into an eventful bus journey on Ireland's country roads. Cue clapping and cheering on board the bus. A nation in celebration. More flashes out the window and the occupants on both buses waved goodbye to each other after sharing the morning's excitement.

Elizabeth drove on, looked in her rear-view mirror to see the excitement on the celebrating coach die down as they came face to face with another on the small bridge that led out of the town. Arms slowly went down and the flashes died as the tourists settled down for another lengthy struggle to continue.

The town had a tendency to do that. Almost as if it did it purposely. It welcomed you into its heart with open arms, showed you all it had to offer with its gleaming multicoloured florally decorated shop fronts. It was like bringing a child into a sweet shop and showing them the shelves of luminous sugar-coated, mouth-watering delights. And then while they stand there looking around with wide eyes and a racing pulse, the lids were put back on the jars and sealed tightly. Once its beauty was realised, so was the fact that it had nothing else to offer.

The bridge, oddly, was easier to drive over from outside the town. It curved in an unusual shape, making driving out of the village difficult. It disturbed Elizabeth every time.

It was just like the road leading from Elizabeth's childhood home; she found it impossible to leave in a hurry. But something about the town kept dragging her back and she had spent years trying to fight it. She had successfully moved to New York at one time. She had followed her boyfriend, and the opportunity to design a nightclub, over. She had loved it there. Loved that no one knew her name, her face or family history. She could buy a coffee, a thousand different types of coffee, and not receive a look of sympathy for whatever recent family drama had occurred. Nobody knew that her mother had left her when she was a child, that her sister was wildly out of control and that her father barely spoke to her. She had loved being in love there. In New York she could be whoever she wanted to be. In Baile na gCroíthe she couldn't hide from who she was.

She realised she had been humming to herself the entire time, that silly song that Luke was trying to convince her that 'Ivan' had made up. Luke called it 'the humming song', and it was annoyingly catchy, chirpy and repetitive. She stopped herself singing and spun her car into the empty space along the road. She pushed back the driver's seat and reached in to grab her briefcase from the back seat of the car. First things first: coffee. Baile na gCroíthe had yet to be educated on the wonders of Starbucks – in fact, it was only last month Joe's had finally allowed Elizabeth to take away her coffee, but the owner was growing increasingly tired of having to ask for his mugs back.

Sometimes Elizabeth thought that the entire town needed an injection of caffeine; it was as though some winter days the place still had its eyes closed and was sleepwalking. It needed a good shake. But summer days like today were always busy with people passing through. She entered the purple painted Joe's, which was virtually empty all the same. The concept of eating breakfast outside their own homes had yet to be grasped by the townspeople.

'Ah, there she is, the very woman herself,' boomed the singsong voice of Joe. 'No doubt spittin' feathers for her coffee.'

'Morning, Joe.'

He made a show of checking his watch and tapping the clock face. 'Bit behind time this morning, aren't we?' He raised his eyebrows at her. 'Thought maybe you were in bed sick with a bout of the summer flu. Seems like everyone's got it this week.' He tried to lower his voice but only succeeded in lowering his head and raising his voice. 'Sure didn't Sandy O'Flynn come down with it right after disappearing the other night from the pub with P. J. Flanagan, who had it the other week. She's been in bed all weekend.' He snorted. 'Walking her home me arse. I've never heard such nonsense before in my life.'

Irritation rose within Elizabeth. She didn't care for tittle-tattle about people she didn't know, especially as she was aware for so many years that her own family had been the root of all the gossip.

'A coffee, please, Joe,' Elizabeth said crisply, ignoring his rambling. 'To take away. Cream not milk,' she said sternly, even though she had the same every day, while rooting in her bag for her wallet, trying to hint to Joe that she hadn't time for yapping.

He moved slowly towards the coffee pot. To Elizabeth's utter annoyance Joe's sold only one kind of coffee. And that was the instant kind. Elizabeth missed the variety of flavours that she used to get in other towns; she missed the smooth, sweet-tasting French vanilla in a Paris café, the creamy full-bodied flavour of hazelnut cream in a bustling café in New York, the rich velvety masterpiece of the macadamia nut in Milan and her favourite, the Coco Mocha-Nut, the mixture of chocolate and coconut that transported her from a Central Park bench to a sunbed in the Caribbean. Here in Baile na gCroíthe, Joe filled the kettle with water and flicked the switch. One measly little kettle in a café and he hadn't even boiled the water. Elizabeth rolled her eyes.

Joe stared at her. He looked like he was going to say –

'So what has you so late then?'

– that.

'I'm *five minutes* later than usual, Joe,' Elizabeth said incredulously.

'I know, I know, and five minutes could be five hours for you. Sure don't the bears plan their hibernation on your time?'

That made Elizabeth smile, despite herself.

Joe chuckled and winked. 'That's better.' The kettle clicked as it boiled and he turned his back to make the coffee.

'The coaches delayed me,' Elizabeth said softly, taking the warm mug from Joe's hands.

'Ah, I saw that.' He nodded towards the window. 'Jaimsie did well to get himself out of that one.'

'Jaimsie?' Elizabeth frowned, adding a dollop of cream. It quickly melted and filled the cup to the top. Joe looked on with disgust.

'Jaimsie O'Connor. Jack's son,' he explained.

85

'Jack, whose other daughter, Mary, just got engaged to the Dublin boy last weekend. Lives down in Mayfair. Five kids. The youngest was arrested there last week for throwing a wine bottle at Joseph.'

Elizabeth froze and stared back at him blankly.

'Joseph McCann,' he repeated, as though she were crazy for not knowing. 'Son of Paddy. Lives up in Newtown. Wife died last year when she drowned in the bog. His daughter Maggie said it was an accident but sure weren't the family suspicious on account of the row they'd being having about not letting her run off with that trouble-maker from Cahirciveen.'

Elizabeth placed her money on the counter and smiled, no longer wanting to be a part of his bizarre conversations. 'Thanks, Joe,' she said as she made her way to the door.

'Well, anyway,' he concluded his rambling, 'Jaimsie was the one driving the coach. Don't forget to bring that mug back,' he called to her, and grumbled to himself, 'Takeaway coffee, have you ever heard something so ludicrous in your life?'

Before Elizabeth stepped outside she called from the door, 'Joe, would you not think of getting a coffee machine? So you can make lattes and cap-puccinos and espressos instead of all this instant stuff?' She held up her mug.

Joe crossed his arms, leaned against the counter and replied in a bored voice, 'Elizabeth, you don't like my coffee, you don't drink it. I drink tea.

86

There's only one kind of tea I like. It's called Tea. No fancy names for it.'

Elizabeth smiled. 'Actually, there are lots of different types of tea. The Chinese—'

'Ah, be off with you.' He waved his hand at her dismissively. 'We'd all be drinking tea with chopsticks and putting chocolate and cream in our coffees like they're desserts, if you have your way. But, if you're at it, why don't I make a suggestion too then: how's about you buy yourself a kettle over there for your office and put me out of my misery?'

'And out of business,' Elizabeth smiled, and stepped outside.

The village had taken a big stretch and a yawn and was wandering sleepily from its bed to the bathroom. Soon it would be showered, dressed and wide awake. As usual she was one step ahead of it, even if she was running late today.

Elizabeth was always the first in; she loved the silence, the stillness that her office brought at that time of day. It helped her focus on what lay ahead before her noisy colleagues rattled around and before the major traffic hit the road. Elizabeth wasn't the chatty giggly type. Just as she ate to keep herself alive, she spoke to say only what she had to say. She wasn't the type of woman that she overheard in restaurants and cafés, chuckling and gossiping over what someone said someday about something. Conversations about nothing just didn't interest her.

She didn't break down or analyse conversations, glares, looks or situations. There were no double meanings with her; she meant what she said at all times. She didn't enjoy debates or heated discussions. But sitting in the silence of her small office she supposed that was why she didn't have a group of friends. She had tried to be involved before, especially during her college days with her attempts to settle in, but, just as she did then, she would quickly tune out of the mindless nattering.

Since childhood she hadn't pined for friendship. She liked her own company and liked her own thoughts, and then later, in her teens, she had Saoirse as a distraction. She liked the orderly way in which she could depend on herself and manage her time more effectively without friends. When she returned from New York she had tried to host a dinner party in her new home with the neighbours. She thought she would try a fresh beginning, try to make friendships, like most people did, but Saoirse as usual burst into the house and in one fell swoop managed to offend every single person at the table. She accused Ray Collins of having an affair, Bernie Conway of having a boob job and sixty-year-old Kevin Smith of looking at her in a sexual way. The result of Saoirse's ranting and raving was a crying nine-month-old Luke, a few red faces at the table and a burned rack of lamb.

Of course her neighbours wouldn't be as close-minded as to think that Elizabeth was responsible for her family's behaviour, but she gave up after that. She didn't desire company enough to be able to cope with the embarrassment of having to explain and apologise all the time.

Her silence was worth more to her than a thousand words. In that silence she had peace and clarity. Apart from during the night, when her own jumbled thoughts would keep her awake, sounding like a thousand voices jumping in, out and interrupting each other so much that she could barely close her eyes.

She was worried about Luke's behaviour right now. This Ivan character had been hanging around her nephew's head for too long. She had watched Luke all weekend walking, talking and playing games by himself. Laughing and giggling as though he were having the time of his life. Maybe there was something she should be doing. And Edith wasn't there to witness his odd behaviour and deal with it in the wonderful way she always succeeded in doing. Perhaps Elizabeth was supposed to know automatically what to do. Once again the mysteries of motherhood reared their ugly head and she had no one to ask for advice. Nor had she any example to learn from. Well, that wasn't strictly true – she had learned what *not* to do, a lesson just as good as any. So far she had followed her gut instinct, had made a few mistakes along the way, but overall thought Luke had turned out to be a polite and stable child. Or maybe she was doing it all wrong. What if Luke ended up like

Saoirse? What had she done so wrong with Saoirse as a child that had caused her to turn out the way she was? Elizabeth groaned with frustration and rested her head on her desk.

She turned on her computer and sipped on her coffee while it loaded. Then she went to Google, typed in the words 'imaginary friend', and hit Search. Hundreds of sites came up on her screen. Thirty minutes later she felt much better about the Ivan situation.

To her surprise she learned that imaginary friends were very common and not a problem as long as they didn't interfere with normal life. Although the very fact that having an imaginary friend was a direct interference with normal life, it didn't seem to be an issue with the online doctors. Site after site told her to ask Luke what Ivan was thinking and doing as it would be a positive way of giving Elizabeth an understanding into what Luke was thinking. They encouraged Elizabeth actually to set a place for their phantom dinner guest and that there was no need to point out that Luke's 'friend' existed only in his imagination. She was relieved to learn that imaginary friends were a sign of creativity and not of loneliness or stress.

But even so, this was going to be difficult for Elizabeth to grasp. It went against everything she believed. Her world and the land of make-believe existed on two very different plains and she found it difficult to play-act. She couldn't make baby noises to an infant, she couldn't pretend to hide behind her hands or give life or a voice to a teddy, she couldn't even role-play at college. She had grown up knowing not to do that, not to sound like her mother for fear of her father getting mad. It was instilled in her from an early age but now the experts were telling her to change all that.

She finished the last of her cold coffee and read the final line on the screen.

Imaginary friends disappear within three months, whether or not you encourage them.

After three months she would be more than glad to see the back of Ivan and return to normal life again. She flicked through her calendar and circled August with a red marker. If Ivan wasn't out of her house by then, she'd open the door and show him the way herself.

Chapter 8

Ivan laughed as he spun around in the black leather chair at the reception desk outside Elizabeth's office. He could hear her in the other room on the phone, organising a meeting using her boring grown-up voice. But as soon as she hung up the phone he heard her humming his song again. He laughed to himself. It definitely was addictive; once you got the tune in your head there was very little you could do to stop.

He swirled himself round in the chair faster and faster, doing pirouettes on wheels until his stomach danced and his head began to throb. He decided that chair spinning was his absolute favourite. Ivan knew that Luke would have loved to play the spin-the-chair game and, on picturing his sad little face pressed up against the car window from earlier that morning, his mind drifted and the chair slowed. Ivan wanted so much to visit the farm, and Luke's granddad looked like he could do with a bit of fun. He was similar to Elizabeth in that way. Two boring old gnirobs.

Anyway, at least this separation gave Ivan time to monitor Elizabeth so he could write a report on her. He had a meeting in a few days and would have to give a presentation to the rest of the team about who he was working with at the moment. They did it all the time. A few more days with her to prove that she couldn't see him would be enough and then he could get back to concentrating on Luke. Maybe there was something he was missing with him, despite his years of experience.

As Ivan's head began to get dizzy he put his foot down on the floor to stop. He decided to leap from the whirling chair so he could pretend he was jumping from a moving car. He rolled dramatically across the floor just like they did in the movies and looked up from where he was crouched in a ball to see a teenage girl standing before him open-mouthed, watching her office chair spin out of control.

Ivan saw her look around the office to see if anyone else was present. She frowned, approached the desk as if she were walking on landmines and placed her bag on the desk ever so quietly as if afraid to disturb the chair. She looked to see if anyone was watching and then tiptoed over to study it. She held out her hands as though trying to tame a wild horse.

Ivan chuckled.

Seeing that nothing was wrong Becca scratched her head in wonder. Perhaps Elizabeth had been sitting in the chair before she came in. She smirked at the thought of Elizabeth swinging around like a child, hair tied back tightly, dressed in one of her sharp black suits with her sensible shoes dangling in the air. No, the picture didn't fit. In Elizabeth's world chairs were made to be sat on. So that's exactly what Becca did and got to work immediately.

'Good morning, everyone,' a high-pitched voice sang from the door later that morning. A plum-haired Poppy danced into the room, dressed in denim flares embroidered with flowers, platform shoes and a tie-dyed T-shirt. As usual, every inch of her body was splashed with paint. 'Everyone have a nice weekend?' She was always singing her sentences and dancing about the room, flinging her arms around with all the grace of an elephant.

Becca nodded.

'Great.' Poppy stood in front of Becca with her hands on her hips. 'What did you do, Becca, join a debating team? Go out on a date and talk the ear off some bloke? Huh?'

Becca turned the page of the book she was reading and ignored her.

'Wow, that's fabulous, sounds like a blast. You know, I really do love the banter we have in this office.'

Becca turned a page.

'Oh, really? Well, that's enough information for now, if you don't mind. What the . . . ?' She whipped her body away from Becca's desk and was silent.

Becca didn't look up from the book she was reading. 'It's been doing that all morning,' she said in a quiet bored tone.

It was Poppy's turn to remain quiet.

There was silence in the office for a few minutes while Becca read her book and Poppy stared at the sight ahead of her. In her office, Elizabeth heard the long silence between the two and stuck her head out of her door.

'Everything alright, girls?' she asked.

A mystery squeaking sound was all the reply.

'Poppy?'

She didn't move her head as she spoke. 'The chair.'

Elizabeth stepped out of her office. She turned her head in the same direction. The paint-splattered chair behind Poppy's desk, which Elizabeth had been trying to convince Poppy to get rid of for months, was flying around all by itself, the screws squeaking loudly. Poppy let out a nervous laugh. They both moved closer to examine it. Becca was still reading her book in silence as if it was the most normal thing in the world.

'Becca,' Elizabeth half laughed, 'have you seen this?'

Becca still didn't lift her eyes from the page. 'It's been doing that for the past hour,' she said softly. 'It just stops and starts all the time.'

Elizabeth frowned. 'Is it some sort of new artistic creation of yours, Poppy?'

'I wish it was,' Poppy replied, still in awe.

They all watched it spin in silence. Squeak, squeak, squeak.

'Maybe I should call Harry. It's probably something to do with the screws,' Elizabeth reasoned.

Poppy raised her eyebrows uncertainly. 'Yeah, I'm sure the *screws* are making it spin out of control,' she said sarcastically, gazing in wonder at the whirling multicoloured chair.

Elizabeth picked an imaginary piece of fluff from her jacket and cleared her throat. 'You know, Poppy, you really need to get your chair reupholstered; it's not a very positive sight for when customers come to see us. I'm sure Gwen will do it quickly for you.'

Poppy's eyes widened. 'But it's supposed to be like that. It's an expression of personality, an extension of myself. It's the only item I can project myself onto in this room.' She looked around in disgust. 'This fucking *beige* room.' She said the word like it was a disease. 'And *Mrs Bracken* spends more time gossiping with those pals of hers that have nothing else to do but drop by everyday, than actual work.'

'You know that's not true, and remember that not everyone appreciates your taste. Besides, as an interior design company we should be reflecting less . . . alternative designs and more of what people can apply to their own homes.' She studied the chair some more. 'It looks like a bird with a very bad stomach has gone to the toilet on it.'

Poppy looked at her proudly. 'I'm glad *someone* got the idea.'

'Anyway, I've already allowed you to put up that screen,' Elizabeth nodded her head at the partition Poppy had decorated with every colour and material known to man, to act as a dividing wall between Becca and herself.

'Yes, and people *love* that screen,' Poppy said. 'I've already had three requests from customers.'

'Requesting what? To take it down?' Elizabeth smiled.

They both studied the divider thoughtfully, arms folded, heads cocked to one side as though studying a piece of art in a museum, while the chair continued to spin in front of them.

Suddenly the chair leaped and the screen beside Poppy's desk went crashing to the floor. The three women jumped and each took a step back. The chair began to slow down and came to a stop.

Poppy held her hand over her mouth. 'It's a sign.' Her voice was muffled.

On the other side of the room the usually silent Becca began laughing loudly.

Elizabeth and Poppy looked at each other, stunned.

'Hmm,' was all Elizabeth could say before she turned slowly and returned to her office.

Lying on the floor of the office from where he had leaped from the chair to on top of he couldn't tell what, Ivan held his head in his hands until the room stopped spinning. He had a headache and had come to the conclusion that maybe chair spinning wasn't his favourite any more. He watched groggily as Elizabeth entered her office and pushed the door closed behind her with her foot. He leaped from the floor and dived towards it, managing to squeeze his body between the gap before it shut. She wouldn't be locking any doors on him today.

He sat in the (non-swivel) chair on front of Elizabeth's desk and looked around the room. He felt like he was in a principal's office waiting to be given out to. It had the atmosphere of a principal's office, quiet and tense, and it smelled like one too, apart from the scent of Elizabeth's perfume, which he loved so much. Ivan had been in a few headmasters' offices with previous best friends so he knew well what that feeling was like. In training they were generally taught not to go to school with their best friends. There was really no need for them to be there and the rule was introduced because children were getting into trouble and parents were being called in. Instead they hung around outside and waited in the yard until break time. And even if the children chose not to play with them in the yard, they knew they were around, which gave them more confidence to play with the other kids. This was all a result of years of research but Ivan tended to ignore all those facts and statistics. If his best friend needed him at school, he'd be there and he sure wasn't afraid of breaking any rules.

Elizabeth sat behind a large glass desk in an oversized black leather chair, dressed in a severe black suit. As far as he could see, that was all she seemed to wear. Black, brown and grey. So restrained and so very boring, boring, boring. The desk was immaculate, glistening and sparkling as though it had just been polished. All that was on it was a computer and keypad, a thick black diary and the work Elizabeth was huddled over, which looked to Ivan like some boring pieces of material cut into small squares. Everything else had been tidied away in black cabinets. There was absolutely nothing on display apart from framed photographs of rooms that Elizabeth had obviously decorated. As with the house there was no sign of a personality in the room. Just black, white and glass. He felt like he was in a spaceship. The principal's office of a space ship.

Ivan yawned. She definitely was a gnirob. There were no photographs of family or friends, no cuddly toys sitting on the computer, and Ivan couldn't see any sign of the picture Luke had drawn for her over the weekend. She had told him she would put it in her office. The only thing of interest was a collection of coffee mugs from Joe's sitting on the windowsill. He bet Joe wouldn't be happy about that.

He leaned forward in his chair, rested his elbows on the desk and stuck his face near hers. Her face was fixed in pure concentration, her forehead was smooth and no frown lines creased her skin like they usually did. Her glossy lips, which smelled to Ivan like strawberries, pursed and unpursed themselves gently. She hummed quietly to herself.

His opinion of her changed once again right then. She was no longer the headmistress he saw her as when she was among others; she had become peaceful, calm and untroubled, and unlike the way she normally was when she was thinking alone. He guessed it was because for once she wasn't worrying. After watching her for a while, Ivan's eyes drifted down to the piece of paper she was working on. Between her fingers she held a brown colouring pencil and was shading in a drawing of a bedroom.

Ivan's eyes lit up. Colouring was by far his favourite. He stood up from the chair and made his way behind her so he could get a better look at what she was doing and to see if she was any good at staying between the lines. She was left-handed. He leaned over her shoulder and placed his arm on the desk beside her to steady himself. He was so close he could smell the coconut from her hair. He breathed in deeply and felt her hair tickle his nose.

Elizabeth stopped shading for a moment, closed her eyes, leaned her head back, relaxed her shoulders, took a deep breath and smiled softly to herself. Ivan did the same and felt her skin brush against his cheek. His body tingled. For a moment he felt odd, a nice kind of odd. Like the feeling he got when embraced in a warm hug and that was good because hugging was by far his favourite. He felt light-headed and a bit dizzy but nothing like the chair-spinning dizzy. This feeling was so much better. He held onto the feeling for a few minutes until eventually they opened their eyes at the same time and stared down at her drawing of a bedroom. Her hand moved over to the brown pencil as she decided whether or not to pick it up.

Ivan groaned softly. 'Elizabeth, not brown again. Come on, go for some colour, like that lime green,' he whispered into her ear, fully aware she couldn't hear him.

Her fingers hovered over the pencil as though a magnetic force was stopping her from touching it. She moved slowly away from the chocolate-brown pencil and moved to the lime green. She smiled slightly as though amused by her choice and gingerly held the implement between her fingers as if it was for the first time. She moved it around in her fingers as though holding it felt alien to her. Slowly she began to shade in the scatter cushions on the bed, and the tassels on the curtain tiebacks, moving on to bigger pieces like the throw at the end of the bed and eventually the lounger in the corner of the room.

'Much better,' Ivan whispered, feeling proud.

Elizabeth smiled and closed her eyes again, breathing slowly and deeply.

There was suddenly a knock at the door. 'Can I come in?' Poppy sang.

Elizabeth's eyes sprang open and dropped the offending pencil from her hand as though it were a dangerous weapon. 'Yes,' she called out, sitting back in the chair, her shoulder briefly brushing off Ivan's chest. Elizabeth looked around behind her, touched her shoulder lightly with her hand and turned back to face Poppy, who was skipping into the room, eyes glistening with excitement.

'OK, so Becca just told me you've got another meeting with the love hotel people.' Her words skipped together as though she were singing a song.

Ivan sat down on the windowsill behind Elizabeth's desk and stretched out his legs. They both folded their arms across their chests at the same time. Ivan smiled.

'Poppy, please do *not* call it "the love hotel",' Elizabeth rubbed her eyes wearily. Ivan was disappointed. That gnirob voice was back.

'OK, so the "hotel", then,' Poppy exaggerated the word. 'I have some ideas. I'm thinking waterbeds in the shape of hearts, hot tubs, champagne flutes that rise from the bedside lockers.' She lowered her voice to an excited whisper. 'I'm thinking the *Romantic era* meets *art deco*. *Caspar David Friedrich* meets *Jean Dunand*. It will be an *explosion* of rich reds, burgundys and wines that make you feel like you're being embraced in a velvet-lined *womb*. Candles *everywhere*. French boudoir meets—'

'Las Vegas,' Elizabeth finished drily.

Poppy snapped out of her trance and her face fell in disappointment.

'Poppy,' Elizabeth sighed, 'we've been through

102

this before. I really think you should stick to the profile for this one.'

'Ah,' she fell back as though she'd been shot in the chest, 'but the profile is so *boring*.'

'Hear, hear!' Ivan stood and applauded. 'Gnirob,' he said loudly into Elizabeth's ear.

Elizabeth flinched and scratched at her ear. 'I'm sorry you feel that way, Poppy, but unfortunately what you consider boring is how other people choose to decorate their homes. In liveable, comfortable, and calming environments. People don't want to return home after a hard day's work to a house that shouts dramatic statements from every beam or colours that give them a headache. With work environments so full of stress, people just want manageable, relaxing and peaceful homes.' It was a speech she delivered to all of her customers. 'And this is a *hotel*, Poppy. We need to appeal to all kinds of people and not just the few, the *very* few, in fact, that would like to reside in a velvet-lined womb,' she added, deadpan.

'Well, I don't know many people that *haven't* once resided in velvet-lined wombs, do you? I don't think it rules out anyone, on *this* planet at least.' She kept trying. 'It might spark off some comforting memories for people.'

Elizabeth looked disgusted.

'Elizabeth.' Poppy groaned her name and dissolved dramatically into the chair in front of her. 'There has to be something that you will let me put my stamp on. I just feel so constrained here, like my creative juices aren't being allowed to flow and – oooh, that's nice,' she said chirpily, leaning over to look at the page in front of Elizabeth. 'Chocolate and lime are really gorgeous together. What made *you* of all people go for that?'

Ivan returned to Elizabeth's side and crouched down beside her, studying her face. Elizabeth stared at the sketch before her as if seeing it for the first time. She frowned but then her face softened. 'I don't know, actually. It just,' she closed her eyes briefly, breathed deeply and remembered the feeling, 'it just kind of . . . floated into my head suddenly.'

Poppy smiled and nodded excitedly. 'You see, now you understand how it is for me. I can't suppress my creativeness, you know? I know *exactly* what you mean. It's such a natural instinctive thing,' her eyes glistened and her voice lowered to a whisper, 'like *love*.'

'Hear, hear!' Ivan repeated, watching Elizabeth, so close to her now his nose was almost touching her cheek, but this time it was a light whisper that blew Elizabeth's loose hair softly around her ear.

Chapter 9

'Poppy, did you call me?' Elizabeth asked from under the mound of carpet samples piled on her desk later that day.

'No, *again*,' came the dull, bored reply. 'And please refrain from disturbing me as I'm about to order two thousand pots of magnolia paint for our future projects. May as well be organised and plan ahead for the next twenty years,' she muttered, then grumbled loud enough for Elizabeth to hear, 'because it's not as if we're about to change our ideas any time soon.'

'Oh, OK,' Elizabeth smiled, giving in. 'You can order another colour in too.'

Poppy almost fell off her chair with excitement.

'Order a few hundred pots of beige as well, while you're at it. "Barley" it's called.'

'Ha ha,' Poppy said drily.

Ivan raised his eyebrows at Elizabeth. 'Elizabeth, Elizabeth,' he sang, 'did you just make a funny? I think you did.' He stared directly at her, elbows on the desk. He sighed, blowing the loose strands of her hair as he did so.

Elizabeth froze, moved her eye sockets from left to right suspiciously and then continued working.

'Oh, see how she treats me?' Ivan said dramatically, holding his hand to his forehead and pretending to faint onto a black leather chaise longue in the corner of the room. 'It's like I'm not even here,' he declared. He put his feet up and stared at the ceiling. 'Forget about being at a principal's office, this is like being at a shrink's.' He stared at the cracks in the ceiling and put an American accent on. 'You see, Doc, it all started when Elizabeth kept ignoring me,' he said loudly in the room. 'It just made me feel so *unloved*, so *alone*, so *very, very alone*. It's like I don't exist. Like I'm *nothing*,' he exaggerated. 'My life is a mess.' He pretended to cry. 'It's all Elizabeth's fault.' He stopped and watched her for a while, matching carpets with fabrics and paint charts, and when he spoke again, his voice had returned to normal and he said softly, 'But it is her fault that she can't see me because she's just too afraid to believe. Isn't that right, Elizabeth?'

'What?' Elizabeth shouted again.

'What do you mean, "what"?' shouted back an irritated Poppy. 'I didn't say anything!'

'You called me.'

'No I didn't, you're hearing voices again, and please stop humming that bloody song!' Poppy shrieked.

'What song?' Elizabeth frowned.

'Whatever that *thing* is that you've been humming all morning. It's driving me *insane*.'

'Thank you very much!' Ivan announced, standing up and taking a dramatic bow before plonking his body back down on the chaise longue. 'I *invented* that song. Andrew Lloyd Webber, eat your heart out.'

Elizabeth continued working. She started humming again, then immediately stopped herself.

'You see, Poppy,' Ivan called into the other room, 'I think Elizabeth can hear me.' He crossed his hands over his chest and twiddled his thumbs. 'I think she can hear me very well. Isn't that right, Elizabeth?'

'Christ Almighty.' Elizabeth dropped the samples onto her desk. 'Becca, is that you saying my name?'

'No.' Becca's voice was barely audible.

Elizabeth's face turned red and flustered-looking, embarrassed at appearing a fool in front of her employees. Trying to assert control again, she called out sternly, 'Becca, can you get me a coffee from Joe's?'

'Oh, by the way,' Ivan sang, enjoying himself, 'don't forget to tell her to take one of the mugs over with her. Joe will be pleased.'

'Oh,' Elizabeth snapped her fingers as though she'd just remembered something, 'you might as well bring one of these with you.' She handed Becca a coffee mug. 'Joe will be,' she paused and looked confused, 'pleased.'

'Oh, she can hear me alright,' laughed Ivan. 'She just won't admit it to herself. That self-commanding mind of hers just won't allow her to. Everything is black and white to her,' then he added, 'and beige. But I'm going to shake things up a bit around here and we are going to have some *fun*. Ever done that before, Elizabeth? Had fun?' His eyes danced with mischief.

He swung his legs off the chaise longue and jumped upright. He sat on the edge of Elizabeth's desk and glanced at the printouts of the online information about imaginary friends. He tutted and shook his head. 'No, you don't believe all that gobbledegook, do you, Lizzie? Can I call you Lizzie?'

Elizabeth's face flinched.

'Oh,' Ivan said gently, 'you don't like being called Lizzie, do you?'

Elizabeth swallowed softly.

He lay across the desk on top of all the carpet samples and rested his head on his hand. 'Well, I've got news for you,' he lowered his voice to a whisper, 'I'm real. And I'm not going anywhere until you open those eyes properly and see me.'

Elizabeth stopped fiddling with the paint charts and raised her eyes slowly. She looked around her office and then settled on staring straight ahead of her. For some reason she felt calm, calmer than she had felt in a very long time. She was stuck in a trance, staring at nothing but unable to blink or look away, feeling surrounded by warmth and security.

Suddenly the door to her office sprung open, so quickly and forcefully that the handle crashed against the wall. Elizabeth and Ivan jolted in fright.

'Oooh, well excuse me for interrupting the love-birds,' Saoirse cackled from the door.

Ivan jumped off the desk.

Elizabeth, mystified, immediately started to tidy her desk, a natural panicked reflex to her at the unannounced arrival of her younger sister. She smoothed down her jacket and pushed her palms over her hair.

'Oh, don't tidy up on my account.' Saoirse waved her hand dismissively, chewing quickly on a piece of gum. 'You're such a fusspot, you know. Just *chill*.' Her eyes moved up and down as she examined the area beside Elizabeth's desk suspiciously. 'So aren't you going to introduce me?'

Elizabeth examined her sister through narrow eyes. Saoirse made her nervous with her neurotic behaviour and sporadic tantrums. Alcohol or no alcohol, Saoirse had always been the same – difficult. In fact Elizabeth could hardly tell when she was drunk or sober. Saoirse had never found herself; she had never grown into a personality or learned about who she was, what she wanted, what made her happy or where she wanted to go in life. She still didn't know. She was a concoction of personalities never allowed to develop. Elizabeth wondered who her sister could be if she ever managed to stop drinking. She feared it would only be one problem less on a list of many.

109

It was so rare that Elizabeth could get Saoirse on her own in a room to talk to her – like, as a child alone in the fields, trying to catch a butterfly in a jar. They were so beautiful to look at, brightened up a room but never settled on anything for long enough to be caught. Elizabeth was forever chasing and when she did manage to catch her sister, Saoirse would all the time be fluttering her wings in panic, wanting to get away.

When she did have Saoirse's company she tried so hard to be understanding, to treat Saoirse with the sympathy and empathy she deserved. She had learned all about it when she had sought professional help. She wanted advice from as many places as possible in order to help her sister. She needed to know the elusive magical words to say to Saoirse on the rare times that she visited. So even when Saoirse mistreated Elizabeth, she remained supportive and kind because she was afraid to lose her for good, afraid of how much further out of control Saoirse might spiral. Besides, she felt she had a duty to look out for her. But mostly it was because she was tired of seeing all the beautiful butterflies in her life fly away.

'Introduce you to whom?' Elizabeth replied gently.

'Oh, stop with that patronising tone. If you don't want to introduce me then that's fine.' She turned to the empty seat. 'She's ashamed of me, you see. She thinks I let her "good name" down. You know how the neighbours like to talk,' she laughed bitterly. 'Or maybe she's afraid I'll chase you away. Happened to the other one, you see. He—'

'OK, OK, Saoirse,' Elizabeth interrupted her play-acting. 'Look, I'm glad you dropped by because there's something I wanted to talk to you about.'

Saoirse's knee bounced up and down. Her jaw chomped on the gum.

'Colm brought the car back to me on Friday and he told me they'd arrested you. This is serious, Saoirse. You have to be really careful between now and the hearing. It's on in a few weeks and if you do anything . . . else, well, it will effect your punishment.'

Saoirse rolled her eyes, 'Elizabeth, *relax*! What are they going to do? Lock me up for years for driving two minutes down the road in my own sister's car? They can't take away my licence because I don't have one and if they prevent me from ever getting one I don't care because I don't want one. All they'll do is give me a few weeks of some community service bullshit, probably helping a few old ladies cross the road or something. It'll be fine.' She blew a bubble and it smacked against her chapped lips.

Elizabeth's eyes widened with disbelief. 'Saoirse, you didn't *borrow* my car. You took it without my permission and you don't have a licence. Come on,' her voice cracked, 'you're not stupid, you know well that's wrong.'

Elizabeth paused and tried to compose herself. This time she would succeed in talking her round. But even though it was the same situation every time, Saoirse continued to be in denial. She swallowed hard.

'Look,' Saoirse said, getting angry, 'I'm twenty-two years old and I'm doing exactly the same thing that everyone else my age is doing – going out and having fun.' Her tone turned nasty. 'Well, just because you had no life at my age it doesn't mean that I can't have one.' Her wings were fluttering wildly as if she was trapped in a jar and was running out of air.

That's because I was busy raising you, Elizabeth thought angrily. And obviously doing a terrible job of it too.

'Are you going to sit here and listen to our entire conversation or what?' Saoirse said rudely to the chaise longue.

Elizabeth frowned and cleared her throat. 'But what about what Paddy said? Whether *you* think you did nothing wrong is not important. The gardaí think that you have.'

Saoirse chewed her gum and her cold blue eyes stared back. 'Paddy couldn't organise a piss-up in a brewery. He has no reason to charge me for *anything*. Unless having fun is suddenly illegal.' Flutter, flutter.

'Please, Saoirse,' Elizabeth said softly, 'please listen to me. They really mean it this time. Just . . . just relax a bit with the, eh,' she paused, 'with the drinking, OK?'

'Oh, shut up about that,' Saoirse's face twisted. 'Shut up, shut up, shut up, I'm fed up listening to you.' She stood up. 'My drinking's fine. It's you who's got the problem, thinking you're fucking perfect.' She opened the door and shouted so that everyone could hear, 'Oh, and you,' she nodded at the chaise longue, 'I don't think you'll be hanging around for long. They all leave eventually, isn't that right, *Lizzie*?' She spat out the name.

Elizabeth's eyes glistened with angry tears.

Saoirse banged the door loudly behind her. She had forced the jar lid open and was free to fly away once again. The noise of the bang shuddered through Elizabeth's body. The office was so silent even the fly that had been buzzing around stopped to settle on the light fitting. A moment later there was a feeble knock on the door.

'What?' she snapped.

'It's, eh, Becca,' came the quiet reply, 'with your coffee?'

Elizabeth smoothed back her hair and dabbed her eyes. 'Come in.'

As Becca was leaving the room, Elizabeth spotted Saoirse marching back through the reception area.

'Oh, by the way, I forgot to ask you for a loan of a few euros.' Her voice was gentler. It always was when she wanted something.

Elizabeth's heart sank. 'How much?'

Saoirse shrugged her shoulders. 'Fifty.'

Elizabeth rooted in her bag. 'You still staying at the B&B?'

Saoirse nodded.

She pulled out fifty euro and paused before handing it over. 'What's it for?'

'Drugs, Elizabeth, lots and lots of drugs,' Saoirse said smartly.

Elizabeth's shoulders dropped, 'I just meant—'

'Groceries – you know, bread, milk, toilet paper. That kind of thing.' She swiped the crisp note out of Elizabeth's hand. 'Not all of us wipe our arses on silk, you know.' She lifted a swatch of material from the desk and tossed it at her.

The door banged shut behind her as Elizabeth stood alone in the centre of her office and watched the black piece of silk effortlessly drift to the white carpet.

She knew what it felt like to fall.

Chapter 10

A few hours later, Elizabeth shut down her computer, tidied her desk for the twentieth time and left her office for the day. Becca and Poppy stood together staring into space. Elizabeth turned to see what kept their attention.

'It's doing it again,' Poppy sang nervously.

They all watched the chair spinning around unaided.

'You think it's Mr Bracken?' Becca asked quietly.

Poppy imitated Mrs Bracken's voice. 'Chair-spinning isn't what Mr Bracken would have wanted.'

'Don't worry, girls,' Elizabeth said, trying not to laugh. 'I'll get Harry in tomorrow to fix it. You two head off home.'

After saying their goodbyes Elizabeth continued to stare at the chair spinning in silence. She neared it slowly, inch by inch. As she got very close to it, it stopped spinning.

'Chicken,' Elizabeth muttered.

She looked about to ensure she was alone and

slowly she grabbed the handles of the chair and lowered herself into it. Nothing happened. She bounced up and down a few times, looked to the sides and under the seat and still nothing happened. Just as she was about to get up and leave, the chair began to move. Slowly at first, then gradually it began to pick up speed. Feeling nervous, she contemplated leaping off but as it spun faster and faster she began to giggle. Louder and louder she laughed, the faster it went. Her sides ached. She couldn't remember the last time she had felt so young, legs up, feet out, hair blowing in the breeze. Eventually, after a few moments, it slowed to a stop and Elizabeth caught her breath.

Her smile slowly faded and the childish laughing in her head began to die down. All she was left with was complete silence in the abandoned office. She began to hum and her eye scanned across Poppy's disorganised desk of books of material, paint sample tubs, sketches and house interior magazines. Her eye fell upon a gold photo frame. In it was a photograph of Poppy, her two sisters, three brothers and parents, all squeezed together on a couch like a football team. The resemblance between them was obvious. They had little button noses and green eyes that narrowed to slits when they laughed. In the corner of the frame was a strip of passport photos of Poppy and her boyfriend, both of them making faces to the camera in the first three of them. But the fourth was of them staring lovingly into each other's eyes. A

116

moment between them eternally caught on camera.

Elizabeth stopped humming and swallowed. She had known that look once.

She continued to stare at the frame, trying not to remember those times but, again, she lost the battle, drowning in the sea of memories that flooded her mind.

She began to sob. Quiet whimpers at first that soon exited her mouth as pain-filled wails from the depths of her heart. She could hear her own hurt. Each tear was a call for help that had never been answered before, and that she didn't expect to be answered now. And that made her cry even more.

Elizabeth marked off another day on her calendar with a red pen. Her mother had been gone for exactly three weeks this time. Not the longest amount of time so far but long enough for Elizabeth. She hid the calendar under her bed and got into bed. She had been sent to her room by her father three hours ago as he had grown tired of her excited pacing in front of the living-room window. Since then she had been battling to keep her eyes open. She needed to fight sleep so that she wouldn't miss her mother returning. Those were the best times because her mother would be in one of her happy moods, delighted to be home, telling Elizabeth how much she'd missed her, smothering her with hugs and kisses so much that Elizabeth couldn't remember ever feeling sad.

Her mother would float through the rooms of the house almost as if her feet weren't touching the ground. Her words were big whispers of excitement, her voice so hushed making Elizabeth feel that every word her mother breathed was their big secret. Her eyes glistened and danced with delight as she told her daughter of her adventures and who she'd met along the way. Elizabeth certainly did not want to miss all that while she was sleeping.

Elizabeth jumped out of bed again and splashed ice-cold water over her face from the sink in her room. Stay awake, Elizabeth, stay awake, she told herself. She propped her pillows up against the wall and sat up straight on her bed, staring out through the open curtains and out to the dark road that led into blackness. She had no doubt that her mother would be back tonight because she had promised her. And she just had to keep that promise because it was Elizabeth's tenth birthday the next day and she wouldn't miss that. Only weeks ago she had promised her that they would eat cakes, buns and all the sweets they wanted. And they'd have balloons of all Elizabeth's favourite colours that they'd bring out into the field, let them go and watch fly away up to the clouds. Elizabeth hadn't stopped thinking of it since her mother had left. Her mouth watered for fairy cakes with pretty pink icing, and she dreamed of pink balloons attached to white ribbons floating up to the blue sky above. And the day was almost here, no more waiting!

She picked up *Charlotte's Web*, a book she had been reading at night to keep herself awake and she turned on her torch as her father wouldn't let her keep the lights on past eight. A few pages in and her eyelids grew heavy and started to droop. She slowly closed her eyes, only intending to rest them for a little while. Every night she fought sleep because it was always sleep that allowed her mother to slip away into the night and it was sleep that missed her big arrivals. Even when her mother was home she fought it, instead choosing to stay outside her door, sometimes watching her sleep, other times protecting her and guarding her from leaving. Even the rare times that she did sleep, her dreams shouted at her to wake up as though she was doing wrong. People were always commenting to her father that she was too young for the dark circles under her eyes.

The book fell away from Elizabeth's hands and she was lost to the world of sleep.

The front gate creaked.

Elizabeth's eyes shot open to the brightness of the early morning and her heart beat wildly. She heard the crunching of footsteps over gravel as they approached the front door. Elizabeth's heart did cartwheels across her chest with delight. Her mother hadn't forgotten her; she knew she wouldn't have missed her birthday.

She leaped out of bed and did a little dance around her room, not knowing whether or not to open the door for her mother or to allow her to make the grand entrance she loved doing so much. She ran out into the hall in her nightdress. She could see the blurry image of a body through the rippled glass of the front door. She hopped from foot to foot with nervousness and excitement.

Elizabeth's father's bedroom door opened. She turned to face him with a grin. He gave her a small smile and leaned against the doorframe, watching the door. Elizabeth turned her head back to the door, twisting her hem of her nightdress in her little hands. The letter box opened. Two white envelopes slid through and landed on the stone floor. The figure at the door began to fade again. The gate creaked and closed.

Elizabeth dropped the hem of her nightdress from her hands and stopped hopping. She suddenly felt the cold of the stone floor.

She slowly picked up the envelopes. Both were addressed to her and her heart quickened again. Maybe her mother hadn't forgotten, after all. Maybe she had got so caught up in one of her adventures that she couldn't make it home in time and had to explain it all in a letter. She opened the envelopes, careful not to rip the paper that could contain precious words from her mother.

Both were birthday cards from distant, dutiful relatives.

Her shoulders slumped and her heart fell. She turned to face her father and shook her head slowly. His face darkened and he stared angrily into the distance. They caught eyes again and for a moment, a rare moment, Elizabeth and he shared the same knowing feeling and Elizabeth didn't feel so alone any more. She took a step forward to give him a hug.

But he turned away and closed his door behind him.

Elizabeth's bottom lip trembled. There were no fairy cakes or buns that day. The pink balloons floating up towards the clouds remained nothing but dreams. And Elizabeth learned that imagining and fantasising did nothing but break her heart.

Chapter 11

The hissing of the water boiling over onto the cooker brought Elizabeth sharply back to the present. She raced across the kitchen to lift the pot off the hob and lowered the heat. She poked at the steamed chicken and vegetables, wondering where her head was today.

'Luke, dinner,' she called.

She had collected Luke from her father's after work, although she had been in absolutely no mood to drive down that road after sobbing in her office. She hadn't cried in years. She didn't know what was happening to her over the last few days. Her mind just kept drifting, and she never drifted. She always stayed the same, had stable, controlled thoughts and was always constant, never stopped. Nothing at all like her behaviour today at the office.

Luke shuffled into the kitchen, already dressed in his Spiderman pyjamas. He stared sadly at the table. 'You didn't set a place for Ivan again.'

Elizabeth opened her mouth to protest but

stopped herself in time, remembering the advice the websites had given. 'Oh, didn't I?'

Luke looked at her in surprise.

'Sorry, Ivan,' she said, taking out a third plate. What a waste of food, she thought spooning broccoli, cauliflower and potatoes onto his plate. 'I'm sure he doesn't like chicken so this will have to do.' She placed the plate of leftover vegetables down opposite her.

Luke shook his head. 'No, he said he really does like chicken.'

'Let me guess,' Elizabeth said, cutting a corner off her own, 'chicken's his favourite.'

Luke smiled. 'He says it's his favourite kind of *poultry*.'

'Right.' Elizabeth rolled her eyes. She watched Ivan's plate, wondering how on earth Luke was going to manage to eat a second plate of vegetables. It was difficult enough trying to get him to eat his own.

'Ivan said he had fun in your office today,' Luke said, forking broccoli into his mouth, chewing quickly and making a face in disgust. He swallowed quickly and gulped back some milk.

'Did he?' Elizabeth smiled. 'What was so fun about my office?'

'He liked the chair-spinning,' he replied as he speared a baby potato.

Elizabeth stopped chewing and stared at Luke. 'What do you mean?'

Luke popped the potato into his mouth and

munched. 'He says spinning around in Poppy's chair is his favourite.'

Elizabeth for once ignored the fact that he was speaking with his mouth full. 'Did you speak to Poppy today?' Luke loved Poppy and sometimes chatted to her when Edith called the office to check a detail with Elizabeth. He knew Elizabeth's office number by heart – she had insisted he learn it as soon as he learned his numbers – so it was quite possible he might have called, missing his little chats with her while Edith was away. That must have been it, she thought, relieved.

'Nope.'

'Did you speak to Becca?'

'Nope.'

The chicken suddenly tasted like cardboard in her mouth. She swallowed it quickly and put down her knife and fork. She watched Luke eat, lost in thought. Ivan's plate went untouched unsurprisingly.

'Did you speak to Saoirse today?' She studied his face. She wondered if Saoirse's little role-play in her office earlier had anything to do with Luke's new obsession with Ivan. Knowing her sister as well as she did, she would have continued to taunt her had she found out about an invisible friend.

'Nope.'

Perhaps it was just a coincidence. Perhaps Luke was just guessing about the chair-spinning. Perhaps, perhaps, perhaps. Where had all her certainties suddenly gone?

'Don't play with your vegetables, Luke. Ivan told me to tell you that they are good for you.' She may as well use the Ivan situation to her advantage.

Luke started laughing.

'What's so funny?'

'Ivan says that all mums use him to make their kids eat vegetables.'

Elizabeth raised her eyebrows and smiled. 'Well, you can tell Ivan that's because mums know best.' Her smile faded – well, *some* mums, at least.

'Tell him yourself,' Luke giggled.

'Right then.' Elizabeth faced the empty chair ahead of her. 'Where do you come from Ivan?' She leaned forward and spoke as if addressing a child.

Luke started laughing at her and she felt silly. 'He's from Ekam Eveileb.'

It was Elizabeth's turn to laugh. 'Oh, really? And where's that?'

'Far, far away,' Luke said.

'How far? Like Donegal-far?' she smiled.

Luke shrugged, already bored with the conversation.

'Hey,' Elizabeth looked at Luke and laughed, 'how did you do that?'

'Do what?'

'Take a potato from Ivan's plate?'

'I didn't,' Luke frowned. 'Ivan ate it.'

'Don't be sil—' she stopped herself.

Later that evening Luke lay on the floor of the living room, humming *that* song, while Elizabeth drank a cup of coffee and stared at the television. It was a long time since they had done that. Usually they went their own separate ways after dinner. Usually they didn't talk so much during the meal, but then *usually* Elizabeth didn't humour Luke by playing silly games. She began to regret what she had done. She watched Luke colouring with his crayons on the floor. She had put down a mat so that he wouldn't dirty the carpet and although she hated when he played with his toys outside the playroom, she was glad that he was playing with some toys that she could at least see. Every cloud and all that. She turned her attention back to her house makeover show.

'Elizabeth.' She felt the tap of a little finger on her shoulder.

'Yes, Luke?'

'Drew this for you.' He handed her a brightly coloured picture. 'It's of me and Ivan playing in the garden.'

Elizabeth smiled and studied the drawing. Luke had written their names over two matchstick men but what came to her as a surprise was the height of Ivan. He was over twice the size of Luke and was dressed in a blue T-shirt, blue jeans, blue shoes and had black hair and great big blue eyes. What looked like black stubble lined his jawline, and he held hands with Ivan with a big smile on his face. She froze, not quite knowing what to say. Shouldn't his imaginary friend be the same age as he?

'Eh, Ivan is very tall for only being six, isn't

he?' Maybe he had drawn him larger than life because he was so important to him, she reasoned.

Luke rolled around the floor giggling. 'Ivan always says there's nothing *only* about being six and, anyway, *he's* not six.' He laughed loudly again. 'He's old like you!'

Elizabeth's eyes widened in horror. *Old like her?* What kind of imaginary friend had her nephew created?

Chapter 12

Friends come in all different shapes and sizes, we all know that, so why should 'imaginary' friends be any different? Elizabeth had it all wrong. In fact Elizabeth had it *completely* wrong because as far as I could see she didn't have *any* friends. Maybe it's because she was only looking for thirty-four-year-old women that looked, dressed and acted like her. You could tell by the look on her face, she thought Luke should have found someone exactly like himself when she looked at Luke's picture of me and him. And that's no way to make friends.

The important thing is not what we *look* like but the role we play in our best friend's life. Friends choose certain friends because that's the kind of company they are looking for at that specific time, not because they're the correct height, age or have the right hair colour. It's not always the case but often there's a reason why, for example, Luke will see me and not my colleague Tommy, who looks six years old and constantly has a runny nose. I mean, I don't see any other older males interacting with Luke, do you? Just because you see 'imaginary' friends, it doesn't mean you see them all. You have the *ability* to see them all but as humans only use ten per cent of the brain, you wouldn't believe the other abilities there are. There are so many other wonderful things that eyes could see if they really focused. Life's kind of like a painting. A really bizarre abstract painting. You could look at it and think that all it is is a blur. And you can continue living your life thinking that all it is is a blur. But if you really look at it, really see it, focus on it and use your imagination, life can become so much more. That painting could be of the sea, the sky, people, buildings, a butterfly on a flower or *anything* except the blur you were once convinced it was.

After the events in Elizabeth's office I needed to call an emergency 'What IF' meeting. I've been in this job for years and I thought I'd seen it all but I obviously hadn't. Saoirse seeing me and talking to me had really stumped me. I mean, that's completely unheard of. OK, so Luke could see me – that was normal. Elizabeth had some sort of a sense of me, which was weird enough, but I was beginning to get used to it. But Saoirse seeing me? Of course it's common to be seen by more than one person on a job, but never by an *adult*, and never by *two* adults. The only friend in the company who dealt with adults was Olivia and it wasn't any kind of a rule, just what seemed to be happening all the time. I was confused, I can tell you that, so I got 'the boss' to round up all the usual suspects for an unscheduled 'What IF' meeting.

Our 'What IF' meetings were set up to discuss everyone's current situations and to knock around some ideas and suggestions for people who are slightly stuck. I've never had to call one on my behalf, so I could tell the boss was shocked when I did. The name of the meeting has a double meaning. We were all tired of being labelled as 'imaginary friends' among people and the media, so we decided to call the meeting the What Imaginary Friends meeting. I thought up that idea myself.

The six people that meet are the most senior people in the company. I arrived at the What IF room to the sound of everyone laughing and playing. I greeted them all and we sat and waited for the boss. We don't meet around long confer-ence tables with smelly leather chairs in a board-room with no windows. We have a more relaxed approach to it and it really has a much more pos-itive effect because the more comfortable we all feel, the more we can contribute. We sit in a circle on comfortable seats. Mine's a beanbag. Olivia's is a rocking chair. She says it's easier for her to do her knitting that way.

The boss's not really bossy, we just call her that. She's really one of the nicest people you'll ever meet in your whole entire life. Now she's *really* seen it all: she knows everything there is to know about being a best friend. She's patient and caring, listens and hears what people don't say more than anyone I know. Opal is her name and she's beautiful. She floated into the room just then in a purple robe, her dreadlocks tied back in a half-ponytail away from her face, and they hung down past her shoulders. She had tiny sparkling beads throughout that glistened when she moved. She had daisies nestled into her dreadlocks like a tiara, a daisy chain around her neck and around her wrists. Round purple-tinted glasses sat on her nose, and when she smiled the beam was enough to guide ships into shore on a black night.

'Nice daisies, Opal,' Calendula said softly from beside me.

'Thank you, Calendula,' she smiled. 'Me and little Tara made them today in her garden. You're looking very dressed up today. What a lovely colour.'

Calendula beamed. She's been a best friend for absolute donkey's years, like me, but she only looks the same age as Luke. She is small with blonde hair that was today styled into bouncing curls, softly spoken, with big blue eyes, and was dressed in a yellow summer dress with matching yellow ribbons in her hair. She had gleaming new white shoes that swung from her hand-crafted wooden chair. The chair always reminded me of a Hansel and Gretel chair, yellow with painted hearts and candy sticks.

'Thank you, Opal.' Calendula's cheeks turned rosy. 'I'm going to a tea party after this meeting with my new best friend.'

'Oh?' Opal raised her eyebrows, impressed. 'Very nice. Where is it?'

'In the back garden. She got a new tea set for her birthday yesterday,' she replied.

'Well, that's lovely. How are things with little Maeve?'

'Well, thank you.' Calendula looked down in her lap.

The noise from the others in the room died down and all the focus was on Opal and Calendula. Opal wasn't the type of person to ask everyone to be quiet in order to start the meeting. She always began it quietly herself, knowing that the others would soon finish their conversations and settle down in their own time. She always said that all people needed was time and then they could figure most things out for themselves.

Opal was still watching Calendula fidgeting with a ribbon on her dress.

'Is Maeve still bossing you around, Calendula?'

Calendula nodded and looked sad. 'She's still telling me what to do all the time and when she breaks things and her parents get mad, she blames it on me.'

Olivia, an old-looking best friend, who was rocking in her chair while knitting, tutted loudly.

'You know why Maeve is doing that, don't you, Calendula?' Opal said softly.

Calendula nodded. 'I know that me being around provides her with the opportunity to be in charge and she is mirroring the behaviour of her parents. I understand why she is doing it and the importance of her doing it, but that kind of treatment day in day out becomes a little disheartening at times.'

Everybody nodded in agreement. We had all been in her shoes at some stage. Most young children liked to boss us around as it was their only chance to do it without getting into trouble.

'Well, you know she won't be doing it for very much longer, Calendula,' Opal said encouragingly, and Calendula nodded, her curls bouncing up and down.

'Bobby.' Opal turned to face a little boy sitting on a skateboard with his cap turned backwards. He had been rolling back and forth while listening to the conversation. On hearing his name he stopped rolling. 'You must stop playing computer games with little Anthony. You know why, don't you?'

The little boy with the face of an angel nodded and when he spoke his voice sounded much older than his apparent six years. 'Well, because Anthony is only three and he shouldn't be forced to conform to gender roles. He needs to play with toys that allow him to take control, that are flexible and that do more than one thing. Too many of the other toys will stunt his early development.'

'What kind of things do you think you should be playing with?' Opal asked.

'Well, I'm going to concentrate on playing with, well, mostly nothing, actually, so we can do role-playing, or else use boxes, cooking utensils or empty toilet paper rolls.'

We all laughed at the last one. Toilet paper rolls are my absolute favourite. You can do so many things with them.

'Very good, Bobby. Just try to keep it in mind when Anthony tries to get you to play the computer again. Like Tommy does . . .' She trailed off, looking around. 'Actually, where is Tommy?'

'Sorry I'm late,' a loud voice called from the door. Tommy charged in with his shoulders back and arms swinging like a man fifty years older than he. There was muck all over his face, grass stains all down his knees and shins, cuts, scabs and mud on his elbows. He dived onto the beanbag, making a crashing noise with his mouth.

Opal laughed. 'Welcome, Tommy. Busy, were you?'

'Yeah,' Tommy replied cockily. 'Me and Johnno were down in the park, digging up grubs.' He wiped his snotty nose across his bare arm.

'Uugh!' Calendula wrinkled her nose in disgust and moved her chair closer to Ivan.

'Alright, princess.' Tommy winked at Calendula, resting his feet on the table in front of him. The table had been laid out with fizzy drinks and chocolate biscuits.

Calendula looked away from him with wide eyes and concentrated on Opal.

'So John is the same as usual,' Opal stated with amusement.

'Yep, still sees me,' he replied as though that were some kind of victory. 'He's got a problem with bullies at the moment, Opal, and as he's been intimidated into secrecy, he won't tell his parents.' He shook his head sadly. 'He's afraid they'll criticise him or intervene, which will make it worse, and he's also ashamed that he allowed it to happen. All the typical emotions that goes with bullying.' He popped a sweet into his mouth.

'So what are you doing about it?' Opal asked with concern.

'Unfortunately what was happening before I came along is that John was experiencing chronic intimidation. He developed a pattern of compliance with the unfair demands of those he perceived as stronger and he was beginning to identify with the bully and become one himself. But I wouldn't let him push me around,' Tommy said toughly. 'We've been working on his posture, voice and eye contact – as you know, these communicate a lot about whether you're vulnerable. I'm teaching him to be vigilant for suspicious individuals and everyday we run over a list of possible attributes.' He sat back and rested his arms behind his head. 'We're working on him developing a mature sense of justice.'

'And you've been digging for grubs,' Opal added with a smile.

'There's always time for grub-digging, isn't there, Ivan?' Tommy winked at me.

'Jamie-Lynn.' Opal turned to a little girl in denim dungarees and dirty runners. Her hair was cut short and she balanced her behind on a football. 'How's little Samantha getting along? I hope you're both not still digging up her mother's flower garden.'

Jamie-Lynn was a tomboy and kept getting her friends into trouble, whereas Calendula mostly went to tea-parties in pretty dresses and played with Barbie and My Little Pony. Jamie-Lynn opened her mouth and began blabbering away in a mystery language.

Opal raised her eyebrows. 'So I see you and Samantha are still speaking your own language.'

Jamie-Lynn nodded.

'OK, but be careful. It's not a good idea to keep speaking like that for much longer.'

'Don't worry, I know Samantha is learning to talk in sentences and develop her memory so I won't keep it up,' Jamie-Lynn said, returning to normal language. Her voice saddened. 'Samantha didn't see me this morning when she woke up. But then she did again at lunchtime today.'

Everyone felt sad for Jamie-Lynn and we gave her our condolences because we all knew how that felt. It was the beginning of the end.

'Olivia, how's Mrs Cromwell?' Opal's voice was gentler.

Olivia stopped knitting and rocking and shook her head sadly. 'Not long for her to go now. We had a great chat last night about a day trip she had with her family seventy years ago to

Sandymount beach. That put her in a great mood. But as soon as she told her family this morning that she'd been talking to me about it they all left. They think she's talking about her great-aunt Olivia that died forty years ago and are convinced she's going mad. Anyway, I'll stay with her till the end. Like I said, there isn't long for her to go and the family have only visited twice in the past month. She's not hanging on for anyone.'

Olivia always made friends in hospitals, hospices and homes for the elderly. She was good at that kind of thing, helping people reminisce to fill the time if they couldn't sleep.

'Thanks, Olivia,' Opal smiled, and then she turned to me. 'So, Ivan, how's it all going in Fuchsia Lane? What's the big emergency? Little Luke seems to be doing OK.'

I made myself comfortable on the beanbag. 'Yeah, he is OK. There are a few things we need to work on, like how he feels about his family setup, but nothing earth-shattering.'

'Good.' Opal looked pleased.

'But that's not what the problem is.' I looked around the circle at everyone. 'His *aunt*, who adopted him, is *thirty-four* and sometimes she can feel my *presence*.'

Everyone gasped and looked at each other in horror. I knew they'd react like that.

'But that's not even the half of it,' I continued, trying not to enjoy the drama too much because, after all, it was my problem. 'Luke's *mom*, who's *twenty-two*, came into Elizabeth's office today and *saw* me and *spoke* to me!'

Double gasp – apart from Opal, whose eyes twinkled back at me knowingly. I felt better when I saw that because I knew that Opal would know what to do. She always did and I wouldn't have to feel so confused any more.

'Where was Luke when you were in Elizabeth's office?' Opal asked, a smile forming at the corner of her lips.

'On his granddad's farm,' I explained. 'Elizabeth wouldn't let me out of the car to go with him because she was afraid her dad would get mad that Luke had a friend that he couldn't see.' I was out of breath after that.

'So why didn't you walk back to Luke when you got to the office?' Tommy asked, sprawled across the beanbag with his arms behind his head.

Opal's eyes glinted again. What was up with her?

'Because,' I replied.

'Because why?' Calendula asked.

Not her too, I thought.

'How far is the farm from the office?' Bobby asked.

Why were they asking all these questions? Shouldn't the important thing be why on earth all these people were sensing me?

'It's about a two-minute drive but twenty minutes' walking,' I explained, confused. 'What's with all the questions?'

'Ivan,' Olivia laughed, 'don't act the fool. You know that when you get separated from a friend you find them. A twenty-minute walk is nothing compared to what you did to get to that last friend of yours.' She chuckled.

'Ah, come on, everyone.' I threw my hands up helplessly. 'I was trying to figure out whether Elizabeth could see me or not. I was confused, you know. This has never happened before.'

'Don't worry, Ivan,' Opal smiled, and when she spoke again her voice was like honey. 'It's rare. But it's happened before.'

Everyone gasped once more.

Opal stood up, gathered her files together and prepared to leave the meeting.

'Where are you going?' I asked in surprise. 'You haven't told me what to do yet.'

Opal took off her purple-tinted shades and her chocolate-brown eyes gazed at me. 'This is not an emergency at all, Ivan. There is no advice that I can give you. You will just have to trust yourself that when the time comes, you'll make the right decision.'

'What decision? About what?' I asked, feeling even more confused now.

Opal grinned at me. 'When the time comes, you will know. Good luck.' And with that she left the meeting, with everyone staring at me in confusion. The blank faces were enough to prevent me from asking any of them for advice.

'Sorry, Ivan, I would be just as confused as you

are,' Calendula said, standing up and smoothing out the wrinkles in her summer dress. She gave me a big hug and a kiss on the cheek. 'I'd better go now too or I'll be late.'

I watched her skipping towards the door, her blonde curls bouncing with every step. 'Enjoy your tea party!' I called.

'Make the right decision,' I grumbled to myself, thinking about what Opal had said. 'The right decision about what?' And then a chilling thought occurred to me. What if I didn't make the right decision? Would someone get hurt?

Chapter 13

Elizabeth pushed herself forward gently on the swinging bench in her back garden. She cradled a warm coffee cup in her hands, wrapping her slender fingers round the limestone-coloured mug. The sun was slowly setting and a slight chill was creeping out from hiding to take its place. She stared up into the sky, a perfect vision of candy-floss clouds, pink, red and orange, like an oil painting. An amber glow rose from behind a mountain before her, like the kind of secret glow that rose from Luke's bedcovers when he was reading with a torch. She breathed in the cooling air deeply.

Red sky at night, she heard a voice inside her head say.

'Shepherd's delight,' she whispered softly.

A soft breeze blew, as if the air, like her, was sighing. She had been sitting outside now for the past hour. Luke was upstairs playing with his friend Sam, after spending the day at his grandfather's. She was awaiting the arrival of Sam's father, whom she'd never met before, to come and collect him.

Usually Edith dealt with the friends' parents and so Elizabeth wasn't at all looking forward to children chitchat.

It was 9.45 p.m. and light, it seemed, was calling it a day. She had been rocking herself back and forth, fighting the tears that threatened to fall, swallowing the lump that threatened to rise in her throat, forcing back the thoughts that threatened to drown her mind. She felt that she was fighting the world that threatened to jeopardise her plans. She fought the people that invited themselves into her world without her permission; she fought Luke and his head of childish ways, her sister and her problems, Poppy and her ideas at work, Joe and his coffee shop, competitors in her business. She felt she was always fighting, fighting, fighting. And now here she sat fighting her very own emotions.

She felt as if she'd been through a hundred rounds in the ring, as if she'd taken every punch, thump and kick her opponents could throw at her. Now she was tired. Her muscles ached, her defence was falling and her wounds weren't healing so quickly. A cat leaped from the high wall that separated Elizabeth from her neighbours and landed in her garden. It glanced at Elizabeth; chin held high, eyes glowing in the darkness. It walked slowly across the grass without a care in the world. So sure of itself, so confident, so full of its own self-importance. It jumped onto the opposite wall and disappeared into the night. She envied its ability to come and go as it pleased without owing anybody anything, not even those closest, who loved and cared for it.

Elizabeth used her foot to push herself back again. The swing squeaked slightly. In the distance the mountain appeared to be burning as the sun slipped down and out of sight. On the other side the full moon awaited its final call to centre stage. The crickets continued to chatter loudly to each other, the last of the children ran to their homes for the night. Car engines stopped, car doors slammed, front doors closed, windows shut and curtains were drawn. And then there was silence and Elizabeth was once again alone, feeling like a visitor in her own back garden that had taken on a new life in the falling darkness.

Her mind began to rewind over the events of the day. It stopped and played Saoirse's visit. Played it over and over again, the volume rising at every repetition. *They all leave eventually, isn't that right, Lizzie?* The sentence repeated itself like a broken record. It kept on at her like a finger prodding her chest. Harder and harder, first grazing the skin, then breaking it, prodding and prodding until eventually it tore right through and reached her heart. The place where it hurt most. The breeze blew and stung her open flesh wound.

She shut her eyes tightly. For the second time that day Elizabeth cried. *They all leave eventually, isn't that right, Lizzie?*

It played continuously, waiting for an answer from her. Her mind exploded. *YES!* it shouted.

Yes, they all eventually leave. Every single one of them, every single time. Every person that ever succeeded in brightening her day and cheering her heart disappeared as quickly as a cat in the night. As though happiness was only supposed to be some kind of weekend treat, like ice cream. Her mother had done, just as this evening's sun had done: had left her, had taken away the light and warmth and replaced it with a chill and dark.

Uncles and aunts that visited and helped moved or passed on. Friendly school teachers could only care for a school year; school friends developed and tried to find themselves too. It was always the good people that left, the people that weren't afraid to smile or to love.

Elizabeth hugged her knees and cried and cried, like a little girl who had fallen and cut her knee. She wished for her mother to come and pick her up, to carry her and rest her on the kitchen counter while she applied a plaster to her cut. And then just like she always did, she would carry her around the room, dancing and singing until the pain was forgotten and her tears had dried.

She wished for Mark, her only love, to take her in his arms, in arms so big she was dwarfed in his embrace. She wished to be surrounded by his love while he rocked her slowly and softly as he used to do, whispering hushes of assurance in her ears and running his fingers through her hair. She believed him when he said them. He made her believe that everything would be OK and, lying in

144

his arms, she knew that it would, *felt* that it would.

And the more she wished the more she cried because she realised she was surrounded by a father who could barely look her in the eye for fear of remembering his wife, a sister who had forgotten her own son, and a nephew who looked to her everyday with big hopeful blue eyes, just *asking* to be loved and cuddled. Emotions that she felt she was never given enough of to be able to share.

And as Elizabeth sat there crying and rocking, shivering in the breeze, she wondered why it was that she allowed one sentence that had passed the lips of a girl who had never received enough kisses of love, felt warm embraces or who had never herself allowed words of love to drift over her own lips to be the one whose thump and kick sent her falling to the ground. Just as she had done with the piece of black silk in her office.

Damn Saoirse. Damn her and her hatred of life, damn her for her disregard for others and disrespect for her sister. Damn her for not trying when all Elizabeth did was try with her whole heart. What gave her the power to speak with such churlishness? How could she be so flippant with her insults? And the voice inside Elizabeth's head reminded her that it wasn't the drink talking, it was never the drink talking. It was the hurt.

Elizabeth's hurt was screaming at her tonight. 'Oh, help,' she cried softly, covering her face in her hands. 'Help, help, help . . .' she whispered through her sobs.

A light creaking at the sliding door of the kitchen caused her head to jerk up from where it was cradled in her knees. At the door stood a man, lit like an angel by the kitchen light behind him.

'Oh.' Elizabeth swallowed hard, her heart pounding at being caught. She wiped her eyes roughly and smoothed down her wild hair. She rose to her feet. 'You must be Sam's dad.' Her voice still shook from the emotion bubbling inside her. 'I'm Elizabeth.'

There was a silence. He was probably wondering what on earth he was thinking of to let his six-year-old son be minded by this woman, a woman who let her young nephew open the front door by himself at ten o'clock at night.

'I'm sorry, I didn't hear the doorbell ring.' She pulled her cardigan tighter round her waist and crossed her arms. She didn't want to step into the light. She didn't want him to see that she had been crying. 'I'm sure Luke has told Sam you're here but . . .' *But what, Elizabeth?* '. . . but I'll just give him a quick call anyway,' she mumbled. She walked across the grass towards the house with her head down, rubbing her forehead with her hand to hide her eyes.

When she reached the kitchen door, she squinted against the bright light but kept her head lowered, not wanting to make eye contact with the man. All she could see of him were a pair of blue Converse runners at the end of faded blue jeans.

146

Chapter 14

'Sam, your dad is here to collect you!' Elizabeth called weakly upstairs. There was no answer, just the sound of a pair of little feet running along the landing. She sighed and looked at her reflection in the mirror. She didn't recognise the woman she saw. Her face was swollen and puffy, her hair messed from being blown in the breeze and damp from rubbing her teary hands through it.

Luke appeared at the top of the stairs, sleepy-eyed and dressed in his Spiderman pyjamas that he refused to allow her to wash, instead hiding them behind his favourite teddy, George, for protection. He rubbed his eyes tiredly with his fists and looked at her confused.

'Huh?'

'Luke, it's pardon, not huh,' Elizabeth corrected him, then wondered in her current mood why the hell it mattered. 'Sam's father is still waiting so could you please tell him to hurry down?'

Luke scratched his head in a daze. 'But,' he stopped and rubbed his face tiredly.

'But what?'

'Sam's dad collected him when you were in the gar—' He stopped as his gaze was averted to over Elizabeth's shoulder.

Luke's face broke into a toothless smile. 'Oh, hello Sam's dad.' He giggled uncontrollably. 'Sam will be down in a minute,' he laughed, and ran off back down the landing.

Elizabeth had no choice but to turn slowly and face Sam's father. She couldn't continue to avoid him while he waited in her home for his son. On first glance she noticed he had a look of bewilderment as he watched Luke run back down the landing, giggling. He turned to face her, evidently worried. He was leaning against the doorframe, hands tucked into the back pockets of a pair of faded blue jeans below a blue T-shirt, and wisps of jet-black hair escaped from under his blue cap. Despite his youthful attire she presumed he was her age.

'Don't worry about Luke,' Elizabeth said, slightly embarrassed at her nephew's behaviour. 'He's just a little hyper tonight and,' she rushed her words, 'I'm sorry you caught me at a bad time in the garden.' She wrapped her arms around her body protectively. 'I'm not usually like this.' She wiped her eyes with a trembling hand and quickly clasped her hands together to hide her shaking. Her overflow of emotion had disoriented her.

'That's OK,' the soft deep voice replied. 'We all have our bad days.'

Elizabeth chewed on the inside of her mouth and tried in vain to remember her last good one. 'Edith is away at the moment. I'm sure you've had dealings with her, which is why we've never met.'

'Oh, Edith—' he smiled – 'Luke's mentioned her lots of times. He's very fond of her.'

'Yes,' she smiled weakly and wondered if Luke had ever mentioned her. 'Would you like to sit down?' She motioned towards the living room. After offering him a drink she returned from the kitchen with a glass of milk for him and an espresso for herself. She paused at the door of the living room in surprise to catch him spinning around in the leather swivel chair. The sight of him made her smile.

On seeing her at the door he smiled back, stopped spinning, took the glass from her and then moved to the leather couch. Elizabeth sat in her usual chair, so oversized it almost swallowed her up, and hated herself for hoping his runners wouldn't dirty her cream carpet.

'I'm sorry, I don't know your name,' she said, trying to brighten up the dull tone in her voice.

'My name's Ivan.'

She spluttered coffee down her top as it caught in her throat.

Ivan rushed over to pat her on the back. His concerned eyes stared right into hers. His forehead creased with worry.

Elizabeth coughed, feeling stupid, quickly broke eye contact and cleared her throat. 'Don't worry,

I'm fine,' she murmured. 'It's just funny that your name is Ivan because—' She stopped. What was she going to say? Tell a stranger that her nephew was delusional? Regardless of the internet advice she still wasn't sure his behaviour could be considered normal. 'Oh, it's a long story.' She waved her hand dismissively and looked away to take another sip. 'So what is it that you do, Ivan, if you don't mind me asking?' The warm coffee ran through her body, filling her with a familiar, comfortable feeling. She felt herself coming back, slipping out of the coma of sadness.

'I guess you could say I'm in the business of making friends, Elizabeth.'

She nodded understandingly. 'Aren't we all, Ivan.'

He contemplated that idea.

'So what's your company called?'

His eyes lit up. 'It's a good company. I really love my job.'

'Good Company?' she frowned. 'I'm not familiar with it. Is it based here in Kerry?'

Ivan blinked. 'It's based everywhere, Elizabeth.'

Elizabeth raised her eyebrows. 'It's international?'

Ivan nodded and gulped down some milk.

'What is the company involved in?'

'Children,' he said quickly. 'Apart from Olivia, who works with the elderly, but I work with children. I help them, you see. Well, it used to be children but now it seems we're branching out . . . I

150

think . . .' He trailed off, tapped his glass with his fingernail and frowned into the distance.

'Ah, that's nice,' Elizabeth smiled. That explained the youthful clothes and playful nature. 'I suppose if you see room in another market you need to get in there, don't you? Expand the company, increase the profit. I'm always looking at ways to do that.'

'What market?'

'The elderly.'

'They have a market? Great, I wonder when it's on. Sundays, I suppose? You can always pick up a few good knick-knacks here and there, can't you? My old friend Barry's dad used to get second-hand cars and fix them up. His mom used to buy curtains and make them into clothes. She looked like something from *The Sound of Music*, good thing she lives here too because every Sunday she wanted to "climb every mountain", and because Barry was my best friend I had to do it, you see. When is it on, do you think? Not the film, I mean the market.'

Elizabeth barely heard him; her mind had slipped back into thinking mode. She couldn't stop herself.

'Are you alright?' the kind voice asked.

She stopped staring into the bottom of her coffee cup to face him. Why did he look like he cared so much? Who was this softly spoken stranger who made her feel so comfortable in his presence? Each twinkle in his blue eyes added another goose

151

bump to her skin, his gaze was hypnotic and the tone of his voice was like a favourite song she wanted to blare and put on repeat. Who was this man who came into her house and asked her a question not even her own family could ask? *Are you alright?* Well? Was she alright? She swirled the coffee around in the cup and watched it hitting the sides and spraying up like the sea against the cliffs of Slea Head. She thought about it and came to the conclusion that if the last time she had heard those words uttered by anyone was more than a few years ago then she supposed the answer was no. She was not alright.

She was tired of hugging pillows, counting on blankets for warmth and of reliving romantic moments only in her dreams. She was tired of hoping that every day would hurry so she could get on to the next. Hoping that it would be a better day, an easier day. But it never was. Worked, paid the bills and went to bed but never slept. Each morning the weight on her shoulders got heavier and heavier and each morning she wished for night to fall quickly so she could return to her bed to hug her pillows and wrap herself in the warmth of her blankets.

She looked at the kind stranger with the blue eyes watching her and saw more care in those eyes than she had in anyone she knew. She wanted to tell him how she felt, she wanted to hear him say it would be OK, that she wasn't alone and that they would all live happily ever after and that— She stopped herself. Dreams, wishes and hopes

152

were not realistic. She needed to stop her mind from wandering onto those paths. She had a good job and she and Luke were healthy. That was all she needed. She looked up at Ivan and thought about how to respond to his question. Was she alright?

He took a sip of his milk.

Her face broke into a smile and she started laughing, for above his lip was a milk moustache so big it reached the end of his nostrils. 'Yes, thank you, Ivan, I'm alright.'

He looked unsure as he wiped his mouth and, after a while of studying her, spoke. 'So, you're an interior designer?'

Elizabeth frowned. 'Yes, how do you know?'

Ivan's eyes danced. 'I know everything.'

Elizabeth smiled. 'Don't all men?' She looked at her watch. 'I don't know what Sam's up to. Your wife will probably think I've abducted the two of you.'

'Oh, I'm not married,' Ivan replied quickly. 'Girls, uugh!' He made a face.

Elizabeth laughed. 'I'm sorry, I didn't realise you and Fiona weren't together.'

'Fiona?' Ivan looked confused.

'Sam's mother?' Elizabeth asked, feeling foolish.

'Oh, *her*?' Ivan made another face. 'No *way*.' He leaned forward on the leather couch and it squeaked beneath his jeans. A familiar sound to Elizabeth. 'You know she makes this *awful* chicken dish. Sauce really ruins the chicken.'

Elizabeth found herself laughing again. 'That's an unusual reason not to like someone,' but funnily enough Luke had complained about it to her also, after eating dinner at Sam's over the weekend.

'Not if you like chicken, it's not,' Ivan replied honestly. 'Chicken is by far my favourite,' he smiled.

Elizabeth nodded, trying to suppress a giggle.

'Well, my favourite kind of *poultry* really.'

That did it. She started laughing again. Luke must have picked up some of his phrases.

'What?' Ivan smiled widely, revealing a set of sparkling white teeth.

'You,' Elizabeth said, trying to calm herself and control her laughter. She couldn't believe she was acting like this with a total stranger.

'What about me?'

'You're funny,' she smiled.

'You're beautiful,' he said calmly and she looked up at him in surprise.

Her face flushed. What kind of a thing was that to say? There was another silence, uncomfortable on her part as she wondered whether to be insulted or not. Rarely did people make such comments to Elizabeth. She didn't know how she was supposed to feel.

On sneaking a peak at Ivan she was intrigued to see he didn't look at all perplexed or embarrassed. As though he said it all the time. A man like him probably did, she thought cynically. A charmer, that's all he was. Although, as much as she stared at him with forced disdain, she couldn't really bring herself to believe that. This man did not know her, had met her less than ten minutes ago, had told her she was beautiful and yet remained seated in her living room as if he were her best friend, looking around the room as if it were the most interesting place he had ever seen. He had such a friendly nature, was easy to talk to, easy to listen to, and despite telling her she was beautiful while she sat in old tattered clothes with red-rimmed eyes and greasy hair, he didn't make her feel uncomfortable. The more they sat in silence the more she realised he had simply paid her a compliment.

'Thank you, Ivan,' she said politely.

'And thank you too.'

'For what?'

'You said I was funny.'

'Oh, yes. Well, em . . . you're welcome.'

'You don't get many compliments, do you?'

Elizabeth should have stood up right there and then, and ordered him out of her living room for being so intrusive, but she didn't, because as much as she thought she should *technically*, according to her own rules, be bothered by this, she wasn't. She sighed, 'No, Ivan, I don't.'

He smiled at her. 'Well, let that be the first of many.'

He stared at her and her face began to twitch from holding his stare for so long. 'Is Sam staying with you tonight?'

Ivan rolled his eyes. 'I hope not. For a boy of only six years of age, he snores awfully loud.'

Elizabeth smiled. 'There's nothing *only* about being si—' She stopped herself and gulped back some coffee.

He raised his eyebrows. 'What was that?'

'Nothing,' she mumbled. While Ivan was looking around the room Elizabeth stole another glance at him. She couldn't figure out how old he was. He was tall and muscular, manly but yet had a boyish charm. He confused her. She decided to cut to the chase.

'Ivan, I'm confused about something.' She took a breath to ask her question.

'Don't be. Never be confused.'

Elizabeth felt herself frown and smile at the same time. Even her face was confused by his statement. 'OK,' she said slowly, 'do you mind me asking what age you are?'

'No,' he said happily. 'I don't mind at all.'

Silence.

'Well?'

'Well what?'

'What age are you?'

Ivan smiled. 'Let's just say I've been told by one person in particular that I'm old like you.'

Elizabeth laughed. She had thought as much. Obviously Ivan hadn't been spared any of Luke's unsubtle comments.

'Children keep you young, though, Elizabeth.' His voice turned serious, his eyes deep and thoughtful. 'My job is to care for children, help them along and just be there for them.'

'You're a care worker?' Elizabeth asked.

Ivan thought about that. 'You could call me a care worker, professional best friend, guide . . .' He held out his hands and shrugged. 'Children are the ones that know exactly what's going on in the world, you know. They *see* more than adults, *believe* in more, are honest and will always, *always* let you know where you stand.'

Elizabeth nodded along with him. He obviously loved his job – as a father and as a care worker.

'You know, it's interesting,' he leaned forward again, 'children learn much more, far more quickly than adults. Do you know why that is?'

Elizabeth assumed there was some scientific explanation for it but shook her head.

'Because they're open-minded. Because they *want* to know and they *want* to learn. Adults,' he shook his head sadly, 'think they know it all. They grow up and forget so easily and instead of opening their minds and developing it they *choose* what to believe and what not to believe. You can't make a choice on things like that: you either believe or you don't. That's why their learning is slower. They are more cynical, they lose faith and they only demand to know things that will help them get by day by day. They've no interest in the extras. But, Elizabeth,' he said, his voice a loud whisper, eyes wide and sparkling, and Elizabeth shivered as goose pimples rose on her arms. She felt as if he was sharing the world's greatest secret with her. She moved her head closer. 'It's the *extras* that make life.'

'That make life what?' she whispered.

He smiled. 'That make *life*.'

Elizabeth swallowed the lump in her throat. 'That's it?'

Ivan smiled. 'What do you mean, that's it? How much more can you get than life, how much more can you ask for than life? That's the gift. Life is *everything*, and you haven't lived it properly until you believe.'

'Believe in what?'

Ivan rolled his eyes and smiled. 'Oh, Elizabeth, you'll figure it out.'

Elizabeth wanted the extras he spoke about. She wanted the sparkle and the excitement of life, she wanted to release balloons in a barley field and fill a room with pink fairy cakes. Her eyes filled again and her heart thudded in her chest at the thought of crying in front of him. She needn't have worried because he stood up slowly.

'Elizabeth,' he said gently, 'on that note, I shall leave you. It was my pleasure to spend this time with you.' He held out his hand.

When Elizabeth held out her own to touch his soft skin, he grasped it gently and pumped it hypnotically. She couldn't speak for the lump in her throat that had taken over.

'Good luck with your meeting tomorrow,' he smiled encouragingly, and with that he exited the living room. The door was closed behind him by Luke who shouted, 'Bye, Sam!' at the top of his voice, laughed loudly, and then pounded up the stairs.

Later that night Elizabeth lay in bed, her head hot, her nose blocked and her eyes sore from crying. She hugged her pillow and snuggled down into her duvet. The open curtains allowed the moon to shine a path of silver-blue light across her room. She gazed out the window at the same moon she had watched as a child, at the same stars she had wished upon, and a thought struck her.

She hadn't mentioned anything at all to Ivan about her meeting tomorrow.

Chapter 15

Elizabeth hauled her luggage out of the boot of the taxi and trailed it along behind her into the departure and arrival area of Farranfore Airport. She breathed a sigh of relief. Now she really felt that she was going home. After spending only a month living in New York she felt she fitted in there more than she ever had in Baile na gCroíthe. She was beginning to make friends; more importantly, she was beginning to *want* to make friends.

'The plane is on time at least,' Mark said, joining the small check-in queue.

Elizabeth smiled at him and rested her forehead against his chest. 'I'll need another holiday to recover from this one,' she joked wearily.

Mark chuckled, kissed the top of her head and ran his hands through her dark hair. 'You call coming home to visit our families a holiday?' he laughed. 'Let's go to Hawaii when we get back.'

Elizabeth lifted her head and raised an eyebrow, 'Of course, Mark, I'll just let you tell my boss that.

You know I need to get back to that project urgently.'

Mark studied her determined face. 'You should go it alone.'

Elizabeth rolled her eyes and leaned her forehead against his chest again. 'Not this again.' Her voice was muffled in his duffel coat.

'Just listen.' He lifted her chin with his forefinger. 'You work all the hours under the sun, rarely take time off and stress yourself out. For what?'

She opened her mouth to reply.

'For what?' he repeated, stopping her.

Again she opened her mouth to answer and he jumped in. 'Well, seeing as you're so reluctant to answer,' he smiled, 'I'll tell you what for. For *other people*. So that they get all the glory. *You* do all the work, *they* get all the glory.'

'Excuse me,' Elizabeth half laughed, 'that job pays me extremely well as you *well* know, and at the rate I'm going, by this time next year – if we decide to stay in New York, that is – I'll be able to afford that house we saw—'

'My dear Elizabeth,' Mark interrupted, 'the rate you're going, this time next year that house will be *sold* and in its place will be a skyscraper or terribly trendy bar that doesn't sell alcohol or a restaurant that doesn't serve food "*just to be different*",' he made quotation marks with his fingers, making Elizabeth laugh, 'which you will no doubt paint white, put fluorescent lights in the floors and refuse to purchase furniture for, in case it clutters the place,' he teased. 'And other people will get the credit for that.' He looked at her in pretend disgust. 'Imagine. That's *your* blank canvas, nobody else's, and they shouldn't take that away from you. I want to be able to bring our friends in there and say, "Look, everyone, Elizabeth did this. Took her three months to do, all it is is white walls and no chairs but I'm proud of her. Didn't she do well?"'

Elizabeth held her stomach from laughing so hard. 'I would *never* let them knock down that house. Anyway, this job pays me *lots* of money,' she explained.

'That's the second time you've mentioned money. We're doing fine. What do you need all this money for?' Mark asked.

'A rainy day,' Elizabeth said, her laughter dying down and her smile fading as her thoughts drifted to Saoirse and her father. A very rainy day, indeed.

'Just as well we're not living here any more then,' Mark said, not noticing her face and looking out the window, 'or you'd be broke.'

Elizabeth looked out the window to the wet day and couldn't help feeling that the week had been a complete waste of time. She hadn't exactly been expecting a welcoming committee and bunting to be hung from the shops but neither Saoirse nor her father seemed to be in the least bit interested in whether she was home or not, and what she has been up to in her time away. But she hadn't returned to share stories about her new life in New York; she had returned to check up on them.

Her father still wasn't talking to her on account of her leaving home and deserting him. Working for a few months at a time in different counties had seemed at the time the ultimate sin, but leaving the country altogether was now the mightiest sin of all. Before Elizabeth had left she had made arrangements to ensure they would both be looked after. Much to her great disappointment, Saoirse had dropped out of school the previous year and Elizabeth had had to set her up with her eighth job in two months, stocking shelves in the local supermarket. She had also arranged with a neighbour to drive her into Killarney twice a month to see her counsellor. To Elizabeth, that part was far more important than the job and she knew that Saoirse had only agreed to it as it gave her the opportunity to escape from her cage twice a month. In the unlikely event that Saoirse ever decided to talk about how she was feeling, at least there would be someone there to listen.

There had been no sign of the housekeeper Elizabeth had organised for her father, though. The farmhouse was a dusty, smelly, damp mess and after spending two days scrubbing the place Elizabeth gave up, realising there was no amount of cleaning products that would bring back the shine to the farmhouse. When her mother left, she had taken the sparkle with her.

Saoirse had moved out of the bungalow and

into a house with a group of strangers she had met while camping out at a music festival. All they seemed to do was sit in a circle by the old tower near the town, lying on the grass, with long hair and beards, strumming on a guitar and singing songs about suicide.

Elizabeth had only managed to catch her sister twice during her stay. The first meeting was very brief. On the day of Elizabeth's arrival she received a phone call from the only ladies' clothes store in Baile na gCroíthe. They were holding Saoirse as they had caught her shoplifting some T-shirts. Elizabeth had gone down, apologised profusely, paid the women for the T-shirts and as soon as they had stepped outside Saoirse had headed for the hills. The second time they met was only long enough for Elizabeth to loan Saoirse some money and then organise to meet for lunch the next day, a lunch Elizabeth ended up eating alone. At least she was glad to see Saoirse had put on some weight at last. Her face was fuller and her clothes didn't seem to hang off her as they once had. Perhaps living alone was good for her.

November in Baile na gCroíthe was lonely. The young population was away at school and college, the tourists were at home or visiting hotter countries, businesses were quiet and empty, some closed, the others struggling. The village was drab, cold and dreary, the flowers not yet out to brighten the streets. It was like a ghost town. But Elizabeth was glad she had returned.

Her small family may not have given two flutes whether she was home or not, but she knew with a certainty now that she couldn't live her life worrying about them.

Mark and Elizabeth moved up the queue. There was only one person ahead of them and then they would be free. Free to catch their flight to Dublin so they could go on to New York from there.

Elizabeth's phone rang and her stomach lurched instinctively.

Mark whipped around. 'Don't answer that.'

Elizabeth took the phone out of her bag and looked at the number.

'Don't answer it, Elizabeth.' His voice was steady and stern.

'It's an Irish number.' Elizabeth bit down on her lip.

'Don't,' he said gently.

'But something could be wro—' The ringing stopped.

Mark smiled, looked relieved. 'Well done.'

Elizabeth smiled weakly and Mark turned back to face the check-in desk. He took a step forward to approach the desk and as he did so her phone began ringing again.

It was the same number.

Mark was talking to the woman behind the desk, laughing and as charming as usual. Elizabeth clutched the phone tightly in her hand and stared at the number on her screen until it disappeared and the ringing stopped again.

It beeped, signalling a voicemail.

'Elizabeth, she needs your passport.' Mark swirled round. His face fell.

'I'm just checking my messages,' Elizabeth said quickly, and began rooting in her bag for her passport, phone pressed to her ear.

'Hello, Elizabeth, this is Mary Flaherty calling from the maternity ward in Killarney Hospital. Your sister, Saoirse, has been taken in with labour pains. It's a month earlier than expected, as you know, so Saoirse wanted us to call you to let you know in case you wanted to be here with her . . .' Elizabeth didn't hear the rest. She stood frozen to the spot. Labour pains? Saoirse? She wasn't even pregnant. She replayed the message, thinking maybe it was the wrong number, ignoring Mark's pleas for her to hand over her passport.

'Elizabeth,' Mark said loudly, interrupting her thoughts, 'your passport. You're holding everyone up.'

Elizabeth turned round and was greeted by a line of angry faces.

'Sorry,' she whispered, her whole body shaking, feeling stunned.

'What's wrong?' Mark said, his anger fading and concern spreading across his face.

'Excuse me,' the check-in assistant called. 'Are you getting on this flight?' she asked as politely as she could.

'Em,' Elizabeth rubbed her eyes in confusion, looked from Mark's issued ticket on the counter, to his face and back again. 'No, no, I can't.' She stepped backwards out of the queue. 'Sorry.' She turned to the few people in the queue who looked at her with softened faces. 'So sorry.' She looked at Mark standing in the queue, looking so . . . so disappointed. Not disappointed she wasn't coming but disappointed *in* her.

'Sir,' the lady called, handing him his ticket.

He took it distractedly and slowly stepped out of the queue. 'What happened?'

'It's Saoirse,' Elizabeth said weakly, a lump forming in her throat. 'She's been taken into hospital.'

'Did she drink too much again?' The concern had instantly disappeared from Mark's voice.

Elizabeth thought about that answer long and hard, and the shame and embarrassment of not having known about Saoirse's pregnancy took charge and shouted at her to lie. 'Yes, I think so. I'm not too sure.' She shook her head – trying to shake her thoughts away.

Mark's shoulders relaxed. 'Look, she probably just has to get her stomach pumped again. It's nothing new, Elizabeth. Let's just get you checked in and we can talk about it in the café.'

Elizabeth shook her head. 'No, no, Mark, I have to go.' Her voice trembled.

'Elizabeth, it's probably *nothing*,' he smiled. 'How many of these phone calls do you get a year and it's always the same thing.'

'It could be *something*, Mark.' Something that

167

a sister in her right mind should have known, should have spotted.

Mark's hands dropped from her face. 'Don't let her do this to you.'

'Do what?'

'Don't let her make you choose her life over your own.'

'Don't be so ludicrous, Mark, she's my sister, she *is* my life. I have to look out for her.'

'Even though she never looks out for you. Even though she couldn't care less whether you were here for her or not.'

It was like a thump in the stomach.

'No, I've got you to look out for me.' She tried to lighten the mood, tried to make everyone happy as usual.

'But I can't if you won't let me.' His eyes were dark with hurt and anger.

'Mark,' Elizabeth tried to laugh but failed, 'I promise I'll be on the earliest flight possible. I just need to find out what's happened. Think about it. If this was your sister you'd be out of this airport long before now, you'd be by her side as we speak and you wouldn't have given a bit of thought to having this stupid conversation.'

'Then what are you still standing here for?' he said coldly.

Anger and tears welled in Elizabeth all at once. She lifted her case and walked away from him. Walked out of the airport and rushed to the hospital.

She did return to New York, just as she promised him. She flew over two days after him, collected her belongings from their apartment, handed in her notice at work and returned to Baile na gCroíthe with a pain in her heart so sore she almost couldn't breathe.

Chapter 16

Elizabeth was thirteen years old and had settled into her first few weeks of secondary school. This meant she had to travel further out of town to go to school so she was up and out earlier than everyone else in the morning and, because classes finished later, she returned home in the dark in the evening. She was spending very little time with eleven-month-old Saoirse. Unlike her primary school bus, the school bus dropped her at the end of the long road that led from the bungalow, leaving her to her lonely walk to the front door where nobody stood to greet her. It was winter and the dark mornings and evenings draped black velvet over the country. Elizabeth, for the third time that week, had walked down the road in the harsh wind and rain, her school skirt lifting and dancing around her legs while her school bag, laden with books, stooped her back.

Now she sat by the fire, in her pyjamas, trying to warm her body, with one eye on her home-work, the other eye on Saoirse, who was crawling along the floor, putting everything she could lay her chubby hands on in her drooling mouth. Her father was in the kitchen heating up his home-made vegetable stew again. It's what they ate everyday. Porridge for breakfast, stew for dinner. Occasionally they would have a thick piece of beef or some fresh fish her father had caught that day. Elizabeth loved those days.

Saoirse gurgled and dribbled to herself, waving her hands around and watching Elizabeth, happy to see her big sister home. Elizabeth smiled at her and made encouraging noises before turning back to her homework. Using the couch as security, Saoirse pulled herself up onto her feet as she had been doing for the past few weeks. She slowly stepped sideways, going back and forth, back and forth before turning round to Elizabeth.

'Come on, Saoirse, you can do it.' Elizabeth put down her pencil and fixed her attention on her little sister. Every day now, Saoirse had attempted the walk across the room to her sister, but had ended on her padded behind. Elizabeth was deter-mined to be there when she finally made that leap. She wanted to make a song and dance about it like her mother would if she'd been still here.

Saoirse blew air out of her mouth, bubbles forming on her lips, and spoke in her own mys-terious language.

'Yes,' Elizabeth nodded, 'come to Elizabeth.' She held her arms out.

Slowly Saoirse let go and with a determined look

on her face she began to take those steps. Further and further she walked while Elizabeth held her breath, trying not to shout in excitement for fear of throwing her off. Saoirse held Elizabeth's stare all the way. Elizabeth would never forget that look in her baby sister's eyes, such determination. Finally she reached Elizabeth and she took her in her arms and danced her around, smothering her in kisses while Saoirse giggled and blew more bubbles.

'Dad, Dad!' Elizabeth called out.

'What?' he shouted crankily.

'Come here, quick!' Elizabeth called, helping Saoirse applaud herself.

Brendan appeared at the door, concern written across his face.

'Saoirse walked, Dad! Look, do it again, Saoirse; walk for Daddy!' She placed her sister on the floor and encouraged her to repeat the feat.

Brendan huffed, 'Jaysus, I thought it was something important. I thought there was somethin' wrong with ya. Don't be botherin' me like that.' He turned his back and returned to the kitchen.

When Saoirse looked up in her second attempt to show her family how clever she was and saw that her daddy was gone, her face fell, and so did she, landing on her bum again.

Elizabeth had been at work the day Luke learned to walk. Edith had called her in the middle of a meeting and she couldn't talk so had heard about it when she got home. Thinking about it now, she realised she had reacted very similarly to her dad and, once again, she hated herself for it. As an adult she could now understand her father's reaction. It wasn't that he wasn't proud or that he didn't care, it was just that he cared too much. First they walk, then they fly away.

The encouraging thought was, if Elizabeth had managed to help her sister to walk once, surely she could help her back on her feet a second time.

Elizabeth awoke with a jump, feeling cold and frozen in fear after a nightmare. The moon had finished its shift on her side of the world and had moved on, making way for the sun. The sun kept a paternal gaze on Elizabeth, keeping a close eye on her as she slept. The silver-blue light thrown across her bedclothes had been replaced by a yellow trail. It was 4.35 a.m., and Elizabeth immediately felt awake. She propped herself up on her elbows. Her duvet lay half on the floor, the other half caught up in her legs. She'd had a fitful sleep where dreams began and were unfinished before jumping into new ones, overlapping into each other to create a bizarre blur of faces, places and random words. She felt exhausted.

Looking around the room, she felt irritation seeping into her body. Although she had cleaned the house from top to bottom till it glistened two days ago, she felt the urge to do it all over again. Items were out of place and kept catching the corner of her eye. She rubbed her nose, which was

173

beginning to itch out of frustration, and she threw off the bedclothes.

Immediately she began tidying. She had a total of twelve pillows to display on her bed, six rows of two consisting of regular pillows, with oblong-shaped and circular at the front. All had different textures, ranging from rabbit fur to suede, and were various shades of cream, beige and coffee. Once satisfied with the bed, she ensured her clothes were hanging in the correct order, from dark colours on the left to bright, although she had very little colour in her wardrobe. Wearing the slightest bit of colour felt to her as though she were walking down the street in flashing neon. She vacuumed the floor, dusted and polished the mirrors, straight-ened the three small hand towels in the bathroom, taking a few minutes to perfectly align the stripes through them. The taps glistened and she kept on scrubbing furiously until she could see her reflec-tion in the tiles. By 6.30 she had completed the living room and kitchen and, feeling less restless, she sat outside in the garden with a cup of coffee while looking over her designs in preparation for that morning's meeting. She had had a total of three hours sleep that night.

Benjamin West rolled his eyes and ground his teeth in frustration while his boss paced the floor of the Portakabin and ranted in his thick New York accent.

'You see, Benji, I'm just—'

'Benjamin,' he interrupted.

'– sick and tired,' he continued, not acknowledging him, 'of hearing all the same shit from everyone. All these designers are the same. They want contemporary this, minimalist that. Well, art deco my balls, Benji!'

'It's—'

'I mean, how many of these companies have we met with over here so far?' He stopped pacing and looked at Benjamin.

Benjamin flicked through his diary, 'Em, eight, not including the woman who had to leave early on Friday, Elizabeth—'

'It doesn't matter,' he cut him off, 'she's the same as the rest.' He waved his hand dismissively and spun round to look out the window at the construction site. His thin grey plait swung with his head.

'Well, we have another meeting with her in a half-hour,' Benjamin said, checking his watch.

'Cancel it. Whatever she has to say I don't care. She's as strait-laced as they come. How many hotels have you and I worked on together, Benji?'

Benjamin sighed. 'It's Benjamin and we've worked together a lot, Vincent.'

'A lot.' He nodded to himself. 'That's what I thought. And how many of them have had as good a view as this?' He held out his hand to display the scenery out the window. Benjamin spun round in his chair, uninterested, and could barely bring himself to look past the noise and mess of the site. They were behind time. Sure it was pretty, but he'd prefer to look out that window and see a hotel standing there, not rolling hills and lakes. He'd been in Ireland for two months now and the hotel was scheduled to be finished by August, three months away. Born in Haxton, Colorado but living in New York, he thought he'd long escaped the claustrophobic feeling that only a small town could bring. Apparently not.

'Well?' Vincent had lit a cigar and was sucking on the end.

'It's a great view,' Benjamin said in a bored tone.

'It's a fucking fantastic view and I'm not gonna let some fancy shmancy interior designer come in here and make it look like some city hotel we've done a million times before.'

'What have you got in mind, Vincent?' All Benjamin had been hearing for the past two months was what he didn't want.

Vincent, dressed in a shiny grey suit, marched towards his briefcase, took out a folder and slid it down the table to Benjamin. 'Look at those newspaper articles. The place is a goddamn goldmine. I want what they want. People don't want some average hotel – it needs to be romantic, fun, artistic, none of all this clinical modern stuff. If the next person walks in here with the same shitty ideas I'll design the damn thing myself.' He turned his reddening face to the window and puffed on his cigar.

Benjamin rolled his eyes at Vincent's dramatics.

'I want a real artist,' he continued, 'a raving damn lunatic. Someone creative with a bit of flair.

176

I'm sick of these corporate suits talking about paint colours like they're pie charts, who've never picked up a paint brush in their life. I want the Van Gogh of interior design—'

A knock on the door interrupted him.

'Who's that?' Vincent said gruffily, still red in the face from his rant.

'It's probably Elizabeth Egan, here for the meeting.'

'I thought I told you to cancel that.'

Benjamin ignored him and walked over to the door to let Elizabeth in.

'Hello,' she said, entering the room, followed by a plum-haired Poppy, spattered with paint and weighed down with folders spilling with carpet samples and fabrics.

'Hi, I'm Benjamin West, project manager. We met on Friday.' He shook Elizabeth's hand.

'Yes, I'm sorry about having to leave early,' she replied crisply, not looking him in the eye. 'It's not a regular occurrence, I can assure you.' She turned to face the struggling lady behind her. 'This is Poppy, my assistant. I hope you don't mind her sitting in with us,' she said curtly.

Poppy battled with the folders in order to shake Benjamin's hand, resulting in a few folders crashing to the ground.

'Oh shit,' she said loudly, and Elizabeth spun round with a face like thunder.

Benjamin laughed. 'That's OK. Let me help you.'

'Mr Taylor,' Elizabeth said loudly, walking across the room with an extended hand, 'good to meet you again. Sorry about the last meeting.'

Vincent turned from the window, looked her black suit up and down and puffed on his cigar. He didn't shake her hand, but instead turned to face out the window again.

Benjamin helped Poppy carry the folders to the table and spoke to clear the awkwardness from the room. 'Why don't we all take a seat?'

Elizabeth, flushed in the face, slowly lowered her hand and turned to face the table. Her voice went up an octave. 'Ivan!'

Poppy's face crumpled into a frown and she looked about the room.

'It's OK,' Benjamin said to her, 'people get my name wrong all the time. The name's Benjamin, Ms Egan.'

'Oh, not you,' Elizabeth laughed. 'I'm talking about the man in the chair beside you.' She walked towards the table. 'What are you doing here? I didn't know you were involved in the hotel. I thought you worked with children.'

Vincent raised his eyebrows and watched her nodding and smiling politely in the silence. He began to laugh, a hearty guffaw that ended in hacking coughs.

'Are you OK, Mr Taylor?' Elizabeth asked with concern.

'Yes, Ms Egan, I'm fine. Absolutely fine. It's a pleasure to meet you.' He held out his hand.

While Poppy and Elizabeth were arranging their

files, Vincent spoke under his breath to Benjamin. 'This one mightn't be too far from cutting her ear off after all.'

The door to the cabin opened and in walked the receptionist with a tray of coffee cups.

'Well, it was lovely to meet you again. Bye, Ivan,' Elizabeth called out as the door closed behind the woman.

'Gone now, is he?' Poppy asked drily.

'Don't worry,' Benjamin laughed under his breath to Poppy while watching Elizabeth in admiration, 'she's fitting the profile perfectly. You guys were listening outside the door, right?'

Poppy looked at him confused.

'Don't worry, you're not gonna get into trouble or anything,' he laughed. 'But you heard us talking, right?'

Poppy thought for a while then nodded her head slowly up and down, still looking rather confused.

Benjamin chuckled and looked away. 'I knew it. Clever woman,' he thought aloud, watching Elizabeth engrossed in conversation with Vincent.

They both tuned into the conversation.

'I like you, Elizabeth, I really do,' Vincent was saying genuinely. 'I like your eccentricity.'

Elizabeth frowned.

'You know, your quirkiness. That's when you know someone's a genius and I like geniuses on my team.'

Elizabeth nodded slowly, utterly bewildered at what he was going on about.

'But,' Vincent continued, 'I'm not too convinced on your ideas. In fact, I'm not convinced at all. I don't like 'em.'

There was silence.

Elizabeth moved uncomfortably in her seat. 'OK,' she tried to remain businesslike, 'what is it exactly that you have in mind?'

'Love.'

'Love,' Elizabeth repeated dully.

'Yes. Love.' He leaned back in the chair, fingers interlocked across his stomach.

'You have love in mind,' Elizabeth said stonily, looking at Benjamin for assurance.

Benjamin rolled his eyes and shrugged.

'Hey, *I* don't give a shit about love,' Vincent said. 'I've been married twenty-five years,' he added by way of explanation. 'It's the Irish public that wants it. Where is that thing?' He looked around the table, then slid the folder of newspaper articles towards Elizabeth.

After a moment of flicking through the pages, Elizabeth spoke. In her voice Benjamin sensed disappointment. 'Ah, I see. You want a *themed* hotel.'

'You make it sound tacky when you say that.' He waved his hand dismissively.

'I believe themed hotels *are* tacky,' Elizabeth said firmly. She couldn't forsake her principles, even for a plum job like this.

Benjamin and Poppy looked to Vincent for his response. It was like watching a tennis match.

'Elizabeth,' Vincent said with a smile twitching

at the corner of his lips, 'you're a beautiful young woman, surely you should know this. Love is not a theme. It's an atmosphere, a mood.'

'I see,' Elizabeth said, sounding and looking as if she didn't see at all. 'You want to create a feeling of love in a hotel.'

'Exactly!' Vincent said, looking pleased. 'But it's not what I want, it's what *they* want.' He stabbed the newspaper with his finger.

Elizabeth cleared her throat and spoke as if addressing a child. 'Mr Taylor, it's June, what we call silly season, when there's nothing else to write about. The media simply represents a distorted image of the public's opinion – it's not accurate, you know. It doesn't represent the hopes and wishes of the Irish people. To strive for something to meet the needs of the media would be to make a huge mistake.'

Vincent looked unimpressed.

'Look, the hotel is in a wonderful location with stunning views, bordering a beautiful town with an endless amount of outdoor amenities available. My designs are about bringing the outside in, making the landscapes part of the interior. With the use of natural earthy tones like the dark greens, browns and with the use of stone we can—'

'I've heard all this before,' Vincent puffed. 'I don't want the hotel to blend in with the mountains, I want it to stand out. I don't want the guests to feel like damn hobbits sleeping in a mound of grass and mud.' He stabbed his cigar out angrily in the ashtray.

She's lost him, Benjamin thought. Too bad: this one really tried. He watched her face melt as the job slipped away from her.

'Mr Taylor,' she said quickly, 'you haven't heard *all* my ideas yet.' She was grasping at straws.

Vincent grunted and looked at his diamond-studded Rolex. 'You've thirty seconds.'

She froze for twenty of them and eventually her face fell and she looked to be in a great deal of pain as she spoke her next few words. 'Poppy,' she sighed, 'tell him your ideas.'

'Yes!' Poppy jumped up in excitement and danced around the other side of the table to Vincent. 'OK, so I'm thinking waterbeds in the shape of hearts, hot tubs, champagne flutes that rise from the bedside lockers. I'm thinking the *Romantic era* meets *art deco*. An *explosion*,' she made explosion signs with her hands, 'of rich reds, burgundy and wine that make you feel like you're being embraced in a velvet-lined *womb*. Candles *everywhere*. French boudoir meets . . .'

As Poppy rambled on and Vincent nodded his head animatedly while hanging on her every word, Benjamin turned to look at Elizabeth, who in turn had her head in her hand, wincing at every one of Poppy's ideas. Their eyes met and they both shared an exasperated look over their respective colleagues.

Then they shared a smile.

Chapter 17

'Oh, my goodness, oh, my goodness,' Poppy squealed with delight, dancing towards Elizabeth's car. 'I'd like to thank Damien Hirst for inspiring me, Egon Schiele,' she wiped an imaginary tear from her eye, 'Banksy and Robert Rauschenberg for providing me with such incredible art that helped my creative mind develop, opening delicately like a bud and for—'

'Stop it,' Elizabeth hissed through gritted teeth. 'They're still watching us.'

'Oh, they are not, don't be so paranoid.' Poppy's tune changed from elation to frustration. She turned to face the cabin on the site.

'Don't turn round, Poppy!' Elizabeth spoke as if giving out to a child.

'Oh, why not? They're not watchi— Oh, they are. BYEEE! THA-ANKSSS,' she waved her hands wildly.

'Do you *want* to lose your job?' Elizabeth threatened, refusing to turn round. Her words had the same effect as they would on Luke when she threatened to take away his PlayStation. Poppy stopped skipping immediately and they both walked in silence back to the car, Elizabeth feeling two pairs of eyes burning into her back.

'I can't believe we got the job,' Poppy said breathily once inside, hand on her heart.

'Nor can I,' Elizabeth grumbled, securing her seat belt around her body and starting up the engine.

'What's wrong with you, grumpy? You'd swear we didn't *get* this job or something,' Poppy accused, settling down in the passenger seat and drifting off to her own world.

Elizabeth thought about that. In fact she *hadn't* got the job, Poppy had. It was the kind of victory that didn't feel like a victory at all. And why had Ivan been there? He had told Elizabeth he worked with children – what had the hotel got to do with children? He hadn't even stuck around long enough for her to find out, instead leaving the room as soon as the drinks were brought without a goodbye to anyone apart from Elizabeth. She pondered this. Perhaps he was involved in business with Vincent and she'd walked in during an important meeting, which would make sense as to why Vincent had seemed so rudely preoccupied. Well, whatever it was, she needed to be informed and she was angry that Ivan hadn't mentioned it last night. She had plans to make and despised disruptions.

Separating from an overexcited Poppy, she headed over to Joe's for a coffee and to think.

'Good afternoon, Elizabeth,' Joe shouted. The three other customers jumped in their seats at his sudden outburst.

'Coffee, please, Joe.'

'For a change?'

She smiled tightly. She chose a table by the window looking onto the main street. She sat with her back to the window. She wasn't a gazer, she needed to think.

'Excuse me, Ms Egan.' The male American voice startled her.

'Mr West,' she said, looking up in surprise.

'Please call me Benjamin.' He smiled and indicated to the chair beside her. 'Mind if I join you?'

Elizabeth moved her papers out of his way. 'Would you like a drink?'

'Coffee would be great.'

Elizabeth took her mug and held it out towards Joe, 'Joe, two tall slim mango Frappaccinos, please.'

Benjamin's eyes lit up. 'You're kidding, I thought they didn't sell that he—' He was cut short by Joe dumping two mugs of milky coffee on the table. It spilled over the sides of the mugs. 'Oh,' he finished, looking disappointed.

She turned her attention to the extremely dishevelled-looking Benjamin. His thick black hair was in wavy curls around his head, and he had jet-black stubble growing from the top of his hairy chest to his cheekbones. He wore scruffy jeans streaked with muck, an identically soiled denim jacket, turf-clad sandy Caterpillar boots that had left a trail from the front door to the table, under which a small mountain of dry mud was gathering. A line of black dirt collected underneath his fingernails and as he rested his hands on the table on front of Elizabeth, she felt herself having to look away.

'Congratulations on today,' Benjamin said, seeming genuinely happy. 'It was a very successful meeting for you. You really pulled it off. You guys say *sláinte*, right?' He held up his coffee mug.

'Excuse me?' Elizabeth asked coldly.

'*Sláinte*? Isn't that right?' He looked worried.

'No,' she said with frustration, 'I mean yes, but I'm not talking about that.' She shook her head. 'I didn't "pull it off", as you say, Mr West. Getting this contract was no stroke of luck.'

Benjamin's sun-kissed skin pinked slightly. 'Oh, that's not what I meant at all and please call me Benjamin. Mr West seems so formal.' He moved uncomfortably in his chair. 'Your assistant, Poppy . . .' he looked away, trying to find the words, 'she's very talented, has lots of "out there" ideas and Vincent pretty much has the same philosophy but sometimes he gets carried away and it's up to us to talk him down from the window ledge. Look, it's my job to make sure we get this thing built on time and under budget so I plan to do what I usually do and just convince Vincent that we haven't the money to put Poppy's ideas from paper to practice.'

Elizabeth's heart quickened. 'Then he'll want a designer he can afford. Mr West, have you come here to try to talk me out of this job?' she asked coldly.

'No,' Benjamin sighed. 'It's *Benjamin*,' he stressed, 'and no, I'm not trying to talk you out of this job.' He said it in a way that made her feel foolish. 'Look, I'm trying to help you out here. I can see that you're not happy with the whole idea and truthfully I don't think the locals would be too delighted by it either.' He gestured around at the people in the room and Elizabeth tried to picture Joe going for Sunday lunch in a 'velvet womb'. No, it definitely wouldn't work, definitely not in this town.

Benjamin continued, 'I care about the projects I work on, and I think this hotel has a huge amount of potential. I don't want it to end up looking like a Las Vegas shrine to Moulin Rouge.'

Elizabeth had slid down ever so slightly in her seat.

'Now,' he said assertively, 'I came here to meet you because I like your ideas. They're sophisticated yet comfortable, modern without being too modern, and the look will appeal to a broad range of people. Vincent and Poppy's idea is too themed and will alienate three-quarters of the country immediately. However, maybe you could punch them with a bit more colour? I do agree with Vincent that your whole concept needs to look less like The Shire and more like a hotel. We don't want people feeling like they have to travel bare-foot to Macgillycuddy's Reeks to drop a ring down the centre.'

Feeling offended, Elizabeth dropped her mouth open.

'Do you think,' he continued, ignoring her reaction, 'that you could work with Poppy? You know, water down her ideas . . . a lot?'

Elizabeth had been prepared once again for a stealth attack but he was here to help her. She cleared her throat that didn't need clearing and pulled at the end of her suit jacket, feeling awkward. Once she had composed herself she said, 'Well, I'm glad we're on the same page here, but.' She signalled to Joe for another coffee and thought about fusing her natural colours with Poppy's rich tones.

Benjamin shook his head wildly to Joe's offer of another coffee, still with a full untouched mug in front of him. 'You drink a lot of coffee,' he commented as Joe placed her third mug on the table before her.

'It helps me think,' she said, taking a sip.

There was a silence for a moment.

Elizabeth snapped out of her trance. 'OK, I've an idea.'

'Wow, that worked fast,' Benjamin smiled.

'What?' Elizabeth frowned.

'I said it—'

'OK,' Elizabeth interrupted, not hearing him in her rush of ideas. 'Let's say Mr Taylor is right and the legend lives on and people see this place as a place of love, blah dee blah.' She made a face, clearly not impressed by that belief. 'So there's a market there we need to cater for, which is where Poppy's ideas will work, but we'll keep them just to a minimum. Maybe a honeymoon suite and a snug thrown in here and there, the rest can be my designs,' she said happily. 'With a bit more colour,' she added with less enthusiasm.

Benjamin smiled when she'd finished. 'I'll run it by Vincent. Look, when I said earlier about you pulling it off in the meeting I didn't mean you hadn't the talent to back it up. I meant doing that whole *crazy* thing.' He circled his dirty fingers beside his temples.

Elizabeth's good mood vanished. 'Excuse me?'

'You know,' Benjamin smiled broadly, 'the whole I-see-dead-people-thing.'

Elizabeth stared at him blankly.

'You know, the *guy* at the table. The one you were talking to? Is this ringing any bells with you?'

'Ivan?' Elizabeth asked uncertainly.

'That's the name!' Benjamin snapped his fingers and bounced back in his chair, laughing. 'That's it, Ivan the very, very silent partner,' he laughed.

Elizabeth's eyebrows almost lifted off her forehead. 'Partner?'

Benjamin laughed even harder. 'Yeah, that's it, but don't tell him I said so, will you? I'd be so embarrassed if he ever found out.'

'Don't worry,' Elizabeth said drily, shocked by

this information. 'I'll be seeing him later and I won't mention a word.'

'Neither will he,' Benjamin chuckled.

'Well, we'll see about that,' Elizabeth huffed. 'Although I was with him last night and he didn't say a word then either.'

Benjamin looked shocked by her. 'I don't think that kind of thing is allowed in Taylor Constructions. Office dating is strictly frowned upon. I mean, you never know, Ivan could be the reason you got the job in the first place.' He wiped his eyes wearily and his laughter calmed. 'When you think about it, isn't it amazing what we do to get jobs these days?'

Her mouth dropped.

'But it shows how much you love your job to be able to do a thing like that.' He looked at her in admiration. 'I don't think I could.' His shoulders shook again.

Elizabeth's mouth gaped even wider. Was he accusing her of sleeping with Ivan to get the job? She was rendered speechless.

'Anyway,' Benjamin said, standing up, 'it's been great meeting you. I'm glad we got the Moulin Rouge thing fixed up. I'll run it by Vincent and give you a call as soon as I know more. Do you have my number?' he asked, padding down his pockets. He reached into his front breast pocket and pulled out a leaking biro that had left a blob of ink at the bottom of his pocket. He grabbed a napkin from the dispenser and messily scrawled his name and number across the tissue.

'That's my cell number and the office number.' He handed it to her and pushed forward his leaking pen and a ripped napkin damp from his spilled coffee. 'Can I have yours? Saves me having to go through the files.'

Elizabeth was still angry and offended but reached into her bag, retrieved her leather-bound card holder and held out one of her gold-trimmed business cards. She would refrain from hitting him just this once; she needed this job. For Luke and her business's sakes, she would hold her tongue.

Benjamin flushed slightly. 'Oh right,' he retracted his torn napkin and leaking biro and took her card. 'That's a better idea, I guess.' He held out his hand to her.

She took one look at his hand stained with blue ink and with dirty fingernails, and she instantly sat on her hands.

After he had left, Elizabeth looked around in confusion, wondering if anyone else had witnessed what she had. Joe met her eyes, winked and tapped his nose as though they were sharing some sort of secret. After work she planned to collect Luke from Sam's house and although she knew Ivan and Sam's mother were no longer together she was hoping among all hopes that she would see him there.

To give him a piece of her mind, naturally.

Chapter 18

Mistake number one: going to Elizabeth's meeting. I shouldn't have done it. It's the same rule as not being allowed to go into school with our younger friends, and I should have had the sense to realise that Luke's school is the equivalent to Elizabeth's workplace. I could have kicked myself. Actually I did, but Luke thought it looked so funny that he started doing it to himself and now both his shins are bruised. So I stopped.

After I left the meeting I walked back to Sam's house, where Luke was being minded. I sat on the grass in the back garden, keeping an eye on them wrestling each other, hoping it wouldn't end in tears and also doing my favourite mental sport. Thinking.

It was constructive thinking too because I realised a few things. One of the things I learned was that I went to the meeting that morning because my gut feelings were telling me to. I couldn't figure out how my being there would possibly help Elizabeth but I had to go with my instincts and I just presumed she wouldn't see me.

My meeting her the previous night had been so dreamlike and unexpected that I started the day feeling as if it was all in my imagination. And yes, I am aware of the irony there.

I was so happy she saw me. When I saw her swinging on that garden bench looking so lost, I knew that if she was ever going to see me that would be the time. I felt it in the air. I knew she needed to see me and I had prepared myself for the fact that one day she would, but I hadn't prepared myself for the shiver that ran up my spine when our eyes first locked together. It was odd because I'd been looking at Elizabeth for the past four days and I was used to her face, knew it inside out, could see it clearly even when I shut my eyes, knew that there was a tiny mole on her left temple, that one cheekbone was slightly higher than the other, that her bottom lip was larger than her top, that she had fine baby hair at the edge of her hairline. I knew it so well, but isn't it strange how different people can look when you actually look them in the eyes? They suddenly appear to be someone else. If you ask me, it's true what they say about eyes being the windows to your soul.

I had never felt that feeling before, but I put that down to not having been in the position before. I had never had a friendship with someone of Elizabeth's age and I supposed it was nerves. It was all a new experience for me but one I was immediately willing and able to take on.

There are two things that I am rarely. The first

is confused and the second is worried, but while I waited in Sam's back garden on that sunny day, I was worried. And that confused me and because I was confused, that worried me even more. I was hoping I hadn't caused trouble for Elizabeth at work, but later that evening, as the sun and I were playing hide and seek, I soon found out.

The sun was trying to hide behind Sam's house, covering me in a blanket of shadow. I was moving around the garden, sitting in the very last patches of sun before they disappeared completely. Sam's mom was having a bath after doing a dance work-out video in her back room, which had been hugely entertaining, so when the doorbell rang Sam answered it. He was under strict instructions not to answer to anyone except Elizabeth.

'Hello, Sam,' I heard her say, stepping into the hall. 'Is your dad here?'

'No,' Sam replied, 'He's at work. Me and Luke are playing in the garden.'

I heard footsteps coming down the hall, the sound of heels on wood and then an angry voice as she stepped out into the garden.

'Oh, he's at work, is he?' Elizabeth said standing at the top of the garden with her hands on her hips looking down at me.

'Yeah, he is,' Sam said, confused, and ran off to play with Luke.

There was something so endearing about the sight of Elizabeth looking so bossy that it made me smile.

'Is something funny, Ivan?'

'Lots of things are,' I replied, sitting down on the only part of the grass that still had sun on it. I guess I won the hide-and-seek game. 'People getting splashed with puddles by passing cars, being tickled right here,' I gestured to my side, 'Chris Rock, Eddie Murphy in the second *Beverly Hills Cop* an—'

'What are you talking about?' She frowned, moving closer.

'Things that are funny.'

'What are you doing?' She stepped closer still.

'Trying to remember how to make a daisy chain. Opal's looked nice,' I looked up at her. 'Opal's my boss and she had them in her hair,' I explained. 'The grass is dry if you want to sit down.' I continued pulling daisies from the ground.

It took Elizabeth a moment to settle herself on the grass. She looked uncomfortable and made faces as though she was sitting on pins. After brushing invisible dirt off her slacks and attempting to sit on her hands so her bum wouldn't get grass stains, she resumed glaring at me.

'Is something the matter, Elizabeth? I sense that there is.'

'How acutely aware of you.'

'Thank you. It's part of my job but nice of you to compliment me.' I sensed her sarcasm.

'I've a bone to pick with you, Ivan.'

'A funny one, I hope.' I threaded one stalk through the other. 'There's another thing that's funny – funny bones. They hurt but they also make you laugh. Like lots of things in life, I suppose, or even life itself. Life is like a funny bone. Hmm.'

She looked at me in confusion. 'Ivan, I've come to give you a piece of my mind. I spoke to Benjamin today after you left and he told me you were a partner in the company. He also accused me of something else but I won't even get into that,' she fumed.

'You've come to give me a piece of your mind,' I repeated, looking at her. 'That phrase is really beautiful. The mind is the most powerful thing in the body, you know. Whatever the mind believes, the body can achieve. So to give someone a piece of it . . . well, thank you, Elizabeth. Funny how people are always intent on giving it to the people they dislike when it really should be for the ones they love. There's another funny thing. But a piece of your mind . . . what a gift that would be.' I looped the last stalk and formed a chain. 'I'll give you a daisy chain in return for a piece of your mind.' I slid the bracelet onto her arm.

She sat on the grass. Didn't move, didn't say anything, just looked at her daisy chain. Then she smiled and when she spoke her voice was soft. 'Has anyone ever been mad at you for more than five minutes?'

I looked at my watch, 'Yes. You, from ten o'clock this morning until now.'

She laughed. 'Why didn't you tell me that you work with Vincent Taylor?'

'Because I don't.'

'But Benjamin said that you did.'

'Who's Benjamin?'

'The project manager. He said you were a silent partner.'

I smiled. 'I suppose I am. He was being ironic, Elizabeth. I've nothing to do with the company. I'm so silent that I don't say anything at all.'

'Well, that's one side of you I've never met,' she smiled. 'So you're not actively involved with this project?'

'My work is with people, Elizabeth, not buildings.'

'Well then, what on earth was Benjamin talking about?' She was confused. 'He's an odd one, that Benjamin West. What business were you talking to Vincent about? What have children got to do with the hotel?'

'You're very nosy,' I laughed. 'Vincent Taylor and I weren't talking about any business.' Anyway, that's a good question – what do you think children *should* have to do with the hotel?'

'Absolutely nothing,' Elizabeth laughed, and then stopped abruptly, afraid she had offended me. 'You think the hotel should be child-friendly.'

I smiled. 'Don't you think everything and every*one* should be child-friendly?'

'I can think of a few exceptions,' Elizabeth said smartly, looking out to Luke.

I knew she was thinking of Saoirse and her father, possibly even herself.

197

'I'll talk to Vincent tomorrow about a play-room/play area kind of thing . . .' She trailed off. 'I've never designed a children's room before. What the hell do children want?'

'It will come easily to you, Elizabeth. You were a child once – what did you want?'

Her brown eyes darkened and she looked away. 'It's different now. Children don't want what I wanted then. Times have changed.'

'Not that much they haven't. Children always want the same things because they all need the same basic things.'

'Like what?'

'Well, why don't you tell me what you wanted and I'll let you know if they're the same things?'

Elizabeth laughed lightly. 'Do you always play games, Ivan?'

'Always,' I smiled. 'Tell me.'

She studied my eyes, battling with herself about whether to speak or not and after a few moments she took a deep breath. 'When I was a child, my mother and I would sit down at the kitchen table every Saturday night with our crayons and fancy paper and we'd write out a full plan of what we were going to do the next day.' Her eyes shone with the fondness of remembering. 'Every Saturday night I got so excited about how we were going to spend the next day, I'd pin the schedule up on the wall of my bedroom and force myself to go to sleep so that morning would come.' Her smile faded and she snapped out of her trance. 'But you can't incorporate those things into a playroom; children want PlayStations and Xboxes and that kind of thing.'

'Why don't you tell me what sorts of things were on the Sunday schedule?'

She looked away into the distance, 'They were collections of hopelessly impossible dreams. My mother promised me we would lie on our backs in the field at night, catch as many falling stars as we could and then make all the wishes our hearts desired. We talked about lying in great big baths filled up to our chins with cherry blossoms, tasting sun showers, twirling around in the village sprinklers that watered the grass in the summer, having a moon-lit dinner on the beach and then doing the soft-shoe shuffle in the sand.' Elizabeth laughed at the memory. 'It's all so silly, really when I say it aloud, but that's the way she was. She was playful and adventurous, wild and carefree, if not a bit eccentric. She always wanted to think of new things to see, taste and discover.'

'All those things must have been so much fun,' I said, in awe of her mother. Tasting sun showers beat a toilet roll telescope any day.

'Oh, I don't know.' Elizabeth looked away and swallowed hard. 'We never actually did any of them.'

'But I bet you did them all a million times in your head,' I said.

'Well, there was one thing we did together. Just

199

after she had Saoirse, she brought me out to the field, lay down a blanket and set down a picnic basket. We ate freshly-baked brown bread, still piping hot from the oven, with homemade strawberry jam.' Elizabeth closed her eyes and breathed in. 'I can still remember the smell and the taste.' She shook her head in wonder. 'But she chose to have the picnic in our cow field. There we were, in the middle of the field, having a picnic surrounded by curious cows.'

We both laughed.

'But that's when she told me she was going away. She was too big a person for this small town. It's not what she said but I know it must have been how she felt.' Elizabeth's voice trembled and she stopped talking. She watched Luke and Sam chasing each other around the garden but didn't see them, listened to their childish squeals of joy but didn't hear them. She shut it all out.

'Anyway,' her voice became serious again and she cleared her throat, 'that's irrelevant. It's got nothing to do with the hotel; I don't even know why I brought it up.'

She was embarrassed. I bet Elizabeth had never said all that aloud, ever in her life, and so I let the long silence sit between us as she worked it all out in her head.

'Do you and Fiona have a good relationship?' she asked, still not looking me in the eye after what she told me.

'Fiona?'

'Yes, the woman you're not married to.' She smiled for the first time and seemed to settle.

'Fiona doesn't talk to me,' I replied, still confused as to why she thought I was Sam's dad. I would have to have a chat with Luke about that one. I wasn't comfortable with this case of mistaken identity.

'Did things end badly between you both?'

'They never began to be able to end,' I answered honestly.

'I know that feeling.' She rolled her eyes and laughed. 'At least one good thing came out of it, though.' She looked away and watched Sam and Luke playing. She had been referring to Sam but I got the feeling she was looking at Luke and I was pleased at that.

Before we left Sam's house, Elizabeth turned to me. 'Ivan, I've never spoken to anyone about what I said before,' she swallowed, 'ever. I don't know what made me blurt it out.'

'I know,' I smiled, 'so thank you for giving me a very big piece of your mind, I think that deserves another daisy chain,' I held out another bracelet I'd made.

Mistake number two: when sliding it onto her wrist, I felt myself give her a little piece of my heart.

Chapter 19

After the day I gave Elizabeth the daisy chains . . .
and my heart, I learned far more about her than just
what she and her mother did on Saturday evenings.
I realised she's like one of those cockles that you see
clinging to the rocks down on Fermoy beach. You
know by looking at it that it's loose but as soon as
you touch it or get close to it, it seizes up and clings
onto the rock's surface for life. That's what Elizabeth
was like: open until someone came near and then
she'd tense up, and cling on for dear life. Sure, she
opened up to me on that day in the back garden,
but then the next day when I dropped by it was as
though she was mad at me because she'd talked
about it. But that was Elizabeth all round – mad
at everyone including herself – and she was probably embarrassed. It wasn't often Elizabeth told
anybody anything about herself unless she was
talking to customers about her company.

It was difficult to spend time with Luke now
that Elizabeth could see me and, frankly she would
have been worried if I'd knocked on her fuchsia

door to ask her if Luke was coming out to play. She has a thing about friends being a certain age. The important thing, though, was that Luke didn't seem to mind. He was always so busy playing with Sam and whenever Luke decided to include me, it would make Sam frustrated because he couldn't see me, of course. I think I was getting in Luke's way of playing with Sam and I don't think Luke was bothered if I showed up or not because it wasn't him I was there for, you see, and I think he knew it. I told you kids always know what's going on, even before you know yourself sometimes.

As for Elizabeth, I think she'd go crazy if I just strolled into her living room at twelve o'clock at night. A new kind of friendship meant that there had to be new boundaries. I had to be subtle, call round less yet still be there for her at the right moments. Like an adult friendship.

One thing I definitely didn't like was the fact that Elizabeth thought that I was Sam's dad. I don't know how that started and without me even saying anything it just kept going. I never lie to my friends, ever, so I tried many times to tell her that I wasn't Sam's dad. One of the times, the conversation went like this.

'So where are you from, Ivan?'

It was one evening after Elizabeth had been at work. She had just finished a meeting with Vincent Taylor about the hotel and apparently, according to her, she just walked right up to him and told him she had been speaking with Ivan and we both felt the hotel needed a children's area to give the parents even more relaxing romantic time together. Well, Vincent laughed so much that he just gave in and agreed. She's still confused as to why he thought it was so funny. I told her it was because Vincent hadn't a clue who I was and she just rolled her eyes at me and accused me of being secretive. Anyway, because of that, she was in a good mood so she was ready to talk, for a change. I was wondering when she'd start asking me questions (other than the ones about my job, how many staff we had, what was the turnover every year. She bored me to tears with all that kind of stuff).

But she'd finally asked me where I was from so happily I answered, 'Ekam Eveileb.'

She frowned. 'That name is familiar; I've heard of it somewhere before. Where is it?'

'A million miles from here.'

'Baile na gCroíthe is a million miles from everywhere. Ekam Eveileb . . .' she allowed the words to roll off her tongue, 'what does that mean? That's not Irish *or* English, is it?'

'It's draw kcab-ish.'

'Draw Cab?' she repeated, raising an eyebrow. 'Honestly, Ivan, sometimes you're as bad as Luke. I think he gets most of his sayings from you.'

I chuckled.

'In fact,' Elizabeth leaned forward, 'I didn't want to say this to you before but I think he looks up to you.'

'Really?' I was flattered.

'Well, yes, because . . . well,' she searched for the correct words, 'please don't think my nephew is insane or anything but last week he invented this friend.' She laughed nervously. 'We had him over in the house for dinner for a few days, they chased each other around outside, played everything from football, to the computer to *cards*, can you believe it? But the funny thing is that his name was *Ivan*.'

My blank reaction started her back-tracking and she blushed wildly. 'Well, actually it's not funny at all, it's completely preposterous, *of course*, but I thought that maybe it meant that he looked up to you and saw you as some sort of male role model . . .' she trailed off. 'Anyway, Ivan's gone now. He left us. All alone. It was devastating as you can imagine. I was told that they could stay around for as long as *three* months.' She made a face. 'Thank God he left. I had the date marked off on the calendar and everything,' she said, her face still red. 'Actually, funnily enough, he left when you arrived. I think you scared Ivan off . . . Ivan.' She laughed but my blank face caused her to stop and sigh. 'Ivan, why am I the only one talking?'

'Because I'm listening.'

'Well, I'm finished now so you can say something,' she snapped.

I laughed. She always got mad when she felt stupid. 'I have a theory.'

'Good, share it with me for once. Unless it's to

put me and my nephew in a grey concrete building run by nuns with bars on the windows.'

I looked at her in horror.

'Go on,' she laughed.

'Well, who's to say that Ivan disappeared?'

Elizabeth looked horrified. 'No one says he disappeared because he never appeared in the first place.'

'He did to Luke.'

'Luke made him up.'

'Maybe he didn't.'

'Well, I didn't see him.'

'You see me.'

'What have you got to do with Luke's *invisible* friend?'

'Maybe I *am* Luke's friend, only I don't like being called invisible. It's not very PC.'

'But I can see you.'

'Exactly, so I don't know why people insist on saying "invisible". If *someone* can see me then surely that's visible. Think about it – has Ivan, Luke's friend, and me ever been in the same room at the same time?'

'Well, he could be here right now, for all we know, eating olives or something,' she laughed, then suddenly stopped, realising Ivan was no longer smiling. 'What are you talking about, Ivan?'

'It's very simple, Elizabeth. You said that Ivan disappeared when I arrived.'

'Yes.'

'Don't you think that means that I'm Ivan and you just suddenly started seeing me?'

Elizabeth looked angry. 'No, because you are a real person with a real life and you have a wife and a child and you—'

'I'm not married to Fiona, Elizabeth.'

'Ex-wife then, it's not the point.'

'I was never married to her.'

'Well, far be it for me to judge.'

'No, I mean Sam isn't my son.' My voice sounded more forceful than I intended. Children understand these things far better. Adults always make things so complicated.

Elizabeth's face softened and she reached out to put her hand on mine. Her hands were delicate, with baby-soft skin and long slender fingers.

'Ivan,' she spoke gently, 'we have something in common. Luke isn't my son either,' she smiled. 'But I think it's great that you still want to see Sam.'

'No, no, you don't understand, Elizabeth. I'm *nothing* to Fiona, and I'm *nothing* to Sam. They don't see me like you do, they don't even *know* me, that's what I'm trying to tell you. I'm invisible to them. I'm invisible to everybody else but you and Luke.'

Elizabeth's eyes filled with tears and her grip tightened. 'I understand,' her voice shook. She placed her other hand on mine and clung to it tightly. She struggled with her thoughts. I could tell she wanted to say something but couldn't. Her

207

brown eyes searched mine and after a moment's silence, looking as though she had found what she was looking for, her face finally softened. 'Ivan, you have no idea how similar you and I are, and it's such a *relief* to hear you talking like this because I sometimes feel invisible to everybody too, you know?' Her voice sounded lonely. 'I feel like nobody knows me, that nobody sees me how I really am . . . except you.'

She looked so upset that I put my arms around her. Still I couldn't help feeling so disappointed that she'd completely misunderstood me, which was odd, because my friendships aren't supposed to be about me, or what I want. And it had never been about me before.

But as I lay down alone that night and processed all the information of the day, I realised that for the first time in my life, Elizabeth was the only friend I had ever met who had completely understood me after all.

And for anyone who's ever had that connection with someone, even if it only lasted for five minutes, it's important. For once I didn't feel that I was living in a different world from everyone else, but that, in fact, there was a person, a person I *liked* and *respected*, who had a piece of my heart, who felt the same way.

You all know exactly how I was feeling that night.

I didn't feel so alone. Even better than that, I felt as if I was floating on air.

Chapter 20

The weather had changed overnight. The past week of June sunshine had burned the grass, dried the soil and brought wasps in their thousands to swarm around and annoy everyone. Saturday evening it all changed. The sky darkened and the clouds had moved in. But that was typical Irish weather: one moment a heat wave and the next, gale-force winds. It was predictably unpredictable.

Elizabeth shivered in her bed and pulled her duvet up to her chin. She didn't have the heating on and even though she needed it she refused to put it on during the summer months as a principle. Outside the trees shivered, their leaves tossed in the wind. They cast wild shadows across her bedroom walls. The fierce gusts blowing sounded like giant waves crashing against the cliffs. Inside, the doors rattled and shuddered. The bench in the garden swung back and forth, squeaking. Everything moved violently and sporadically; there was no rhythm and no sense of consistency.

Elizabeth wondered about Ivan. She wondered

why she was feeling a pull towards him, and why every time she opened her mouth the world's best-kept secrets flowed out. She wondered why she welcomed him into her home and into her head. Elizabeth loved to be alone – she didn't crave companionship – but she craved Ivan's companionship. She wondered if she should take a few steps back because of Fiona living only down the road. Wouldn't her closeness to Ivan, albeit only a friendship, be disturbing for Sam *and* Fiona? She relied so much on Fiona to mind Luke at last-minute notice.

As usual, Elizabeth tried to ignore such thoughts. She tried to pretend that everything was the same as always, that there hadn't been a shift within her, that her walls weren't crumbling down and allowing in unwelcome guests. She didn't want that to happen, she couldn't deal with change.

Eventually she focused on the only thing that remained constant and unmoving in the determined gusts. And in return, the moon kept its watchful eye on her as she eventually fell into an uneasy sleep.

'Cock-a-doodle-doo!'

Elizabeth opened one eye, confused at the sound. The room was bright. She slowly opened the other eye and saw that the sun had returned and was perched low in the cloudless blue sky, yet the trees were still dancing wildly, having a disco in the back garden.

'Cock-a-doodle-doo!'

There it was again. Feeling groggy from her sleep, she dragged herself out of bed and to the window. Out on the grass in the garden stood Ivan, hands cupped to his mouth shouting, 'Cock-a-doodle-doo!'

Elizabeth covered her mouth, laughing, and pushed open the window. The wind rushed in.

'Ivan, what are you doing?'

'This is your wake-up call!' he shouted, the wind stealing the end of his words and taking them north.

'You are crazy!' she yelled.

Luke appeared at her bedroom door, looking afraid. 'What's happening?'

Elizabeth motioned for Luke to come to the window and he relaxed as he saw Ivan standing outside.

'Hi, Ivan!' Luke yelled.

Ivan looked up and smiled, removed his hand from holding down his cap to wave at Luke. His cap disappeared from his head as a sudden great big gust of wind lifted it off. They laughed as they watched him chase it across the garden, dashing to and fro as the wind's direction changed. Eventually he used a fallen branch to knock it down from a tree where it was caught.

'Ivan, what are you doing out there?' Luke yelled.

'It's Jinny Joe day!' Ivan announced, holding his arms out to display his surroundings.

211

'What's that?' Luke looked at Elizabeth, confused.

'I have no idea,' she shrugged.

'What's Jinny Joe day, Ivan?' Luke yelled.

'Come on down and I'll show you both!' Ivan replied, his loose clothes flapping around his body.

'We're not dressed, we're in our pyjamas!' Luke giggled.

'Well then, get dressed! Just throw anything on, it's six a.m., no one's going to see us!'

'Come on!' Luke said excitedly to Elizabeth, clambering off the windowsill, running out of her room and returning minutes later with one leg in his tracksuit bottoms, an inside-out sweater on and his runners on the wrong feet.

Elizabeth laughed.

'Come on, hurry!' he said, gasping for breath.

'Calm down, Luke.'

'No.' Luke threw open Elizabeth's wardrobe. 'Get dressed, IT'S JINNY JOE DAY!' he shouted with a toothless grin.

'But, Luke,' Elizabeth said uneasily, 'where are we supposed to be going?' She was looking for reassurance from a six-year-old.

Luke shrugged. 'Somewhere fun?'

Elizabeth thought about it, saw the excitement in Luke's eyes, felt the curiosity welling within her, went against her better judgement, threw on a tracksuit and ran outside with Luke.

The warm wind hit her as she stepped outside, taking her breath away.

'To the Bat Mobile!' Ivan announced, meeting them at the front door.

Luke giggled with excitement.

Elizabeth froze. 'Where?'

'The car,' Luke explained.

'Where are we going?'

'Just drive and I'll tell you when to stop. It's a surprise.'

'No,' Elizabeth said as if it were the most ridiculous thing she had ever heard. 'I never get into the car unless I know exactly where I'm going,' she huffed.

'You do it every morning,' Ivan said softly.

She ignored him.

Luke held the door open for Ivan and once they were all in, Elizabeth very uncomfortably set out on her journey with an unknown destination, feeling that she wanted to turn the car round at every turn and then wondering why she wasn't.

After driving for twenty minutes through winding roads, an agitated Elizabeth followed Ivan's directions for the last time and pulled up outside a field that, to her, looked the same as all the others they had passed. Except this one had a view over the glistening Atlantic Ocean. She ignored the scenery and fumed in her wing mirror at the mud splashed along the side of her shining car.

'Wow, what are they?' Luke leaped forward between the two front seats and pointed out the front window.

'Luke, my friend,' Ivan announced happily, 'they are what you call Jinny Joes.'

Elizabeth looked up. Ahead of her were hundreds of dandelion seeds, blowing in the wind, catching the light of the sun with their white fluffy threads and floating towards the three in the car like dreams.

'They look like fairies,' Luke said in amazement.

Elizabeth rolled her eyes. 'Fairies,' she tutted. 'What books have you been reading? They're dandelion seeds, Luke.'

Ivan looked at her in frustration. 'How did I know you'd say that? Well, I got you here, at least. I suppose *that's* something.'

Elizabeth looked at him in surprise. He had never snapped at her like that before.

'Luke,' Ivan turned to him, 'they're also known as the Irish Daisy but they're not only dandelion seeds, they are what most *normal* people,' he threw Elizabeth a nasty look, 'call Jinny Joes. They carry wishes in the wind and you're supposed to catch them in your hand, make your wish and then let them go so they can deliver them.'

Elizabeth snorted.

'Wow,' Luke whispered. 'But why do people do that?'

Elizabeth laughed. 'That's my boy.'

Ivan ignored her. 'Hundreds of years ago people used to eat the green leaves of the dandelion plant because they are extremely high in vitamins,' he explained, 'which gave it its Latin name, which translates as the "official cure of all ills". So people see them as good luck and now make their wishes on the seeds.'

'Do the wishes come true?' he asked hopefully.

Elizabeth looked at Ivan angrily for filling her nephew's head with false hopes.

'Only the ones that are delivered properly, so who knows? Remember, even the post gets lost sometimes, Luke.'

Luke nodded his head, understanding. 'OK then, let's go catch them!'

'You two go on, I'll wait here in the car,' Elizabeth said, staring straight ahead.

Ivan sighed. 'Eliza—'

'I'll wait here,' she said firmly, turning on the radio and settling down to show them she wasn't budging.

Luke climbed out of the car and she turned to Ivan. 'I think it's ridiculous that you fill his head with these lies,' she fumed. 'What are you going to tell him when absolutely nothing he wishes for comes true?'

'How do you know it won't come true?'

'I have *common sense*. Something which you seem to be lacking.'

'You're right, I don't have common sense. I don't want to believe what every one else believes. I have my *own* thoughts, things that weren't taught to me or things that I didn't read in a book. I learn from experience – you, you are afraid to

215

experience anything and so you will always have your common sense and only your common sense.'

Elizabeth looked out the window, counting to ten so that she wouldn't explode. She hated all this new-age crap; contrary to what he said, she believed it was *exactly* the kind of thing that could be learned only from books. Written and read by people who spent their life searching for something, *anything*, to take them away from the boredom that was their real life. People who had to believe that there was always more than the very obvious reason, for everything.

'You know, Elizabeth, a dandelion is also known as a love herb. Some say that to blow the seeds upon the winds will carry your love to your lover. If you blow the puff ball while making a wish and succeed in blowing off all the seeds, your wish will come true.'

Elizabeth frowned in confusion. 'Stop your gobbledy-gook, Ivan.'

'Very well. For today, Luke and I will settle for catching Jinny Joes. I thought you always wanted to catch a wish?' Ivan asked.

Elizabeth looked away. 'I know what you're doing, Ivan and it won't work. I told you about my childhood in the strictest of confidence. It took a lot for me to say the things I said. It wasn't so you could turn it into some game,' she hissed.

'This is not a game,' Ivan said quietly. He clambered out of the car.

'Everything is a game to you,' Elizabeth snapped.

'Tell me, how is it you know so much about dandelion seeds? What exactly is the point of all your silly information?'

Ivan leaned forward through the open door and spoke softly. 'Well, I think it's quite obvious that if you're going to rely on something to carry your wishes in the wind, you might as well know where exactly it has come from and where it intends on going.'

The door slammed shut.

Elizabeth watched them both run to the field. 'Then if that's so, where exactly are you from, Ivan?' she asked aloud. 'And where and when do you intend going?'

Chapter 21

Elizabeth watched as Ivan and Luke darted around the long grass in the field, jumping and diving to catch the dandelion seeds that floated in the air like balls of feathers.

'I got one!' she heard Luke yell.

'Make a wish,' Ivan whooped.

Luke pressed it between his hand and squeezed his eyes shut. 'I wish that Elizabeth would get out of the car and play Jinny Joes!' he roared. He lifted his podgy hand to the air, opened his tiny fingers slowly and released the ball to the wind, which carried it away.

Ivan raised his eyebrows at Elizabeth.

Luke watched the car to see if his wish came true.

As much as Elizabeth watched his hopeful little face she couldn't bring herself to do it – to get out of the car and make Luke believe in fairy tales, just a fancy word for lies. She wouldn't do it. But again she watched as Luke raced around the field, holding his arms out. He caught the seed, grasped it tightly and shouted the same wish.

218

Her chest tightened and her breathing quickened. They both watched her with such hope in their eyes and she felt the pressure of being relied upon. It was only a game, she tried to convince herself; all she had to do was get out of the car. But it meant more to her than that. It meant filling a child's head with thoughts and ideas that would never happen. It meant sacrificing a moment of fun for a lifetime of disappointment. She gripped the steering wheel so tightly her knuckles were white.

Again a joyful Luke jumped up and down, trying to catch another. He repeated his wish at the top of his lungs this time adding, 'Please, please, please, Jinny Joe!' Holding up his arm he looked like the Statue of Liberty and then he released the ball of seeds.

Ivan didn't do anything. He just stood still in the field observing it all with a look and presence Elizabeth felt so drawn to. She saw the frustration and disappointment growing in Luke's face as he caught another, squashed it angrily between his hands and let it go with an attempt to kick it into the air.

Already he was losing faith and she hated to be the one to be the cause of that. She took a deep breath and reached for the door handle. Luke's face lit up and immediately began chasing more. As she walked onto the field, the fuchsias danced wildly, like spectators waving their red and purple flags to welcome a player on to the field.

*   *   *

Driving slowly by in his tractor, Brendan Egan almost drove into a ditch at the sight he saw in a faraway field. With the sparkling sea and the sun in the background he could see two dark figures dancing around in the field. One was a woman whose long black hair was being caught by the wind and wildly draped around her face and neck. She was whooping and hollering with joy as she leaped about with a young child, trying to catch the dandelion seeds that were parachuting in the wind.

Brendan stopped the tractor and stopped breathing in shock at the familiar sight. It was as though he was seeing a ghost. His body shook as he watched in wonder and fright until a beeping behind him startled him and urged him on.

Benjamin was driving back from Killarney at 6.30 on Sunday morning, enjoying the sea view, when a tractor in the middle of the road caused him to step on the brakes. Inside the cab was an old man with a face as white as a sheet, looking into the distance. Benjamin followed his gaze. His face broke into a smile as he spotted Elizabeth Egan dancing with a young boy in a field filled with dandelions. She was laughing and cheering, bounding about. She was dressed in a tracksuit, her hair was down, loose and blowing freely instead of being tied back severely. He hadn't thought she had a son but he watched her lifting him up into the air, helping him to reach something and swinging him back down again. The little blond boy giggled with delight and Benjamin smiled, enjoying the sight. He could have watched her all morning but a beeping from behind startled him and as the tractor's engine started up and moved on, they both crawled down the road slowly, still watching Elizabeth.

Inventing imaginary men and dancing around fields at 6.30 on a Sunday morning . . . Benjamin couldn't help but laugh and admire her for her fun and energy for life. She never seemed to be afraid of what anyone thought. As he continued down the winding road his view of her became clearer. On Elizabeth's face was an expression of pure happiness. She looked like a completely different woman.

Chapter 22

Elizabeth felt giddy with delight as she drove back to town with Luke and Ivan. They had spent the past two hours chasing and catching what Ivan insisted she called Jinny Joes. Then when they were tired and out of breath they had collapsed in a heap in the long grass, breathing in the fresh early morning sea air. Elizabeth couldn't remember the last time she had laughed so much. In fact, she didn't think she had *ever* laughed so much in her life.

Ivan seemed to have boundless energy, with an appetite for all things new and exciting. Elizabeth hadn't felt excited in a very long time; it wasn't a feeling she associated with her adult life. She hadn't felt the tingle of anticipation in her stomach since she was a child; she hadn't looked forward to anything so much she felt she would burst if it didn't happen right here, right now. But being with Ivan brought all those feelings back. Time went so fast when she was with him, whether they were leaping in fields or simply sitting in each other's company in silence, as they so often did. She always wished for time to slow down when he was there, and when he left her she always felt she wanted more. She had caught many dandelion seeds that morning and among her many wishes had been for their time spent together that day to be longer and for the wind to keep up so she could hold on to the moment, with Luke too.

She likened it to a childhood crush, such strong, almost obsessive, feelings – but *more*, it had depth. She felt attracted to everything about Ivan – the way he talked, the way he dressed, the words he used, his apparent innocence yet he was filled with a deep knowledge of wise insights. He always said the right things, even when she didn't want to hear them. The darkness lifted from the end of her tunnels and she could suddenly see *beyond*. When he breezed into the room he brought clarity and brightness with him. He was walking hope, and she could tell that things for her could be, not fantastic or wonderful or happily-ever-after, but that they could be OK. And that was enough for Elizabeth.

He filled her head every moment; she recounted conversations over and over. She asked him question after question and he was always so open and honest in his answers, but then later, while lying in bed, she would realise she knew no more about him than before, despite his replies to every question. But she sensed that they were very similar beings. Two solitary people blowing around in the breeze like dandelion seeds, carrying each other's wishes.

Of course she felt frightened by her feelings. Of course it went against the grain of her every belief, but as much as she tried, she couldn't stop her heartbeat from quickening when his skin brushed against hers, she couldn't stop herself from seeking him out when she thought he might be nearby. She couldn't prevent him from invading her thoughts. He was welcoming himself into her arms even when they weren't open; he was dropping by her home uninvited yet she couldn't stop herself from opening her door time and time again.

She was attracted to his presence, to how he made her feel, to his silences and his words. She was falling in love with him.

On Monday morning Elizabeth found herself walking into Joe's with a spring in her step, humming the same song she'd been humming for the last week and couldn't seem to get out of her head. It was 8.30 and the café was crowded with tourists who had stopped for their breakfast before heading back to their coach, which would take hours to deliver them to the next stopping place. The café was noisy with chatter in German. Joe was rushing around collecting used crockery, bringing it to the kitchen and returning with plates full of Irish breakfasts that his wife had prepared.

Elizabeth signalled to him for a coffee and he quickly nodded his head in acknowledgement, having no time for gossip today. She looked for a seat and her heart quickened at the sight of Ivan in the far corner of the room. She couldn't control the smile that broke over her face. She felt the excitement rushing around her body as she wound her way between the tables to get to him. Elizabeth was overwhelmed by the sight of him.

'Hello,' she breathed, noticing the change in her voice, and hating herself for it.

'Morning, Elizabeth,' he smiled. His voice was different too.

They both sensed it, sensed *something*, and just stared at one another.

'Kept you a table.'

'Thanks.'

Smiles.

'Can I take a breakfast order?' Joe asked her, pen and pad in hand.

Elizabeth usually didn't eat breakfast, but by the way Ivan was looking through the menu she thought she could just be a few minutes late to the office for a change.

'Can I have a second menu, please, Joe?'

Joe glared at her. 'Why do you want a second menu?'

'So I can read it,' she stated.

'What's wrong with the one on the table?' he said moodily.

'OK, OK,' she backed off, leaning closer to Ivan to share the menu.

Joe eyed her suspiciously.

'I think I'll have the Irish breakfast,' Ivan said, licking his lips.

'I'll have the same,' Elizabeth said to Joe.

'The same as what?'

'The Irish breakfast.'

'OK, so one Irish breakfast and a coffee.'

'No,' Elizabeth's forehead wrinkled, '*two* Irish breakfasts and *two* coffees.'

'Eatin' for two, are ye?' Joe asked, looking her up and down.

'No!' Elizabeth exclaimed, and turned to Ivan with an apologetic look on her face when Joe had walked away. 'Sorry about him; he acts oddly sometimes.'

Joe placed the two coffees on the table, eyed her suspiciously and hurried off to serve another table.

'Busy in here today.' Elizabeth barely even looked away from him.

'Is it?' he asked, not moving his eyes from hers.

A tingle ran through Elizabeth's body. 'I like it when the town's like this. It brings it to life. I don't know what Ekam Eveileb is like, but here you get sick of seeing the same people all the time. Tourists change the scenery, give you something to hide behind.'

'Why would you want to hide?'

'Ivan, the whole town knows about me. They practically know more about my family history than I do.'

'I don't listen to the town, I listen to you.'

226

'I know. During the summer, the place is like a big tree, strong and beautiful,' she tried to explain, 'but in winter, it's robbed of its leaves, standing bare, with nothing to cover you or give you privacy. I always feel like I'm on display.'

'You don't like living here?'

'It's not that. It's just it needs some livening up sometimes, a real kick in the behind. I sit in here every morning and dream of pouring my coffee all over the streets, to give it the buzz it needs to waken the place up.'

'Well then, why don't you?'

'What do you mean?'

Ivan stood up. 'Elizabeth Egan, come with me and bring your coffee cup.'

'Bu—'

'No buts, just come.' With that he walked out of the café.

She followed him in confusion, carrying her cup outside.

'Well?' she asked, taking a sip.

'Well, I think it's high time you gave this town a caffeine high,' Ivan announced, looking up and down the empty street.

Elizabeth stared at him blankly.

'Go on.' He tapped her cup slightly and milky coffee sploshed over the side and onto the pavement. 'Oops,' he said drily.

Elizabeth laughed at him. 'You're so silly, Ivan.'

'Why am I silly? You're the one that suggested it.' He hit her cup again, harder this time, sending

227

more coffee dripping to the ground. Elizabeth let out a shout and jumped back to avoid it staining her shoes.

She attracted a few stares from inside the café.

'Go on, Elizabeth!'

It was ludicrous, preposterous, ridiculous and completely juvenile. It didn't make sense to do it, but remembering the fun in the field yesterday, how she laughed and how she floated for the remainder of the day, she craved more of that feeling. She toppled the cup to the side, allowing the coffee to fall to the ground. It first formed a pool, then she watched it flow down the cracks in the slabs of stones and run slowly down the street.

'Come on, that won't even have woken the insects up,' Ivan teased.

'Well then, stand back.' She raised an eyebrow. Ivan stepped away as Elizabeth held out her arm and spun around on the spot. The coffee shot out as though in a fountain.

Joe stuck his head out the door. 'What are you upta, Elizabeth? Did I make a bad cuppa?' He looked worried. 'You're not making me look good in front of these folk.' He nodded towards the tourists gathered at the window, watching her.

Ivan laughed. 'I think this calls for another cup of coffee,' he announced.

'Another cup?' Elizabeth asked startled.

'OK so,' Joe said, slowly backing up.

'Excuse me, what is she doing?' a tourist asked Joe as he headed back inside.

'Ah, 'tis a, eh,' Joe floundered, ''tis a custom we have here in Baile na gCroíthe. Every Monday morning we just, eh,' he looked back at Elizabeth, standing alone, laughing and twirling as she splattered coffee on the pavement, 'we like to splatter the coffee around, you see. It's good for the, eh,' he watched as it splashed over his window boxes, 'flowers,' he gulped.

The man's eyebrows rose with interest and he smiled in amusement. 'In that case, five more cups of coffee for my dear friends.'

Joe looked uncertain, then his face broke into a great big smile as the money was thrust towards him. 'Five cups on the way.'

Moments later Elizabeth was joined by five strangers who danced around beside her, whooping and hollering as they spilled coffee down the pavement. This made her and Ivan laugh even more until eventually they escaped the crowd, who were giving each other secret looks of confusion over the silly Irish custom of spilling coffee on the ground, but who were finding amusement in it all the same.

Elizabeth looked around the village in astonishment. Shopkeepers stood at their front doors watching the commotion outside Joe's. Windows opened and heads peaked out. Cars slowed down to have a look, causing the traffic behind to beep in frustration. In a matter of moments a sleepy town had woken.

'What's wrong?' Ivan asked, wiping the tears of

laughter from his eyes. 'Why have you stopped laughing?'

'Are there no such things as dreams to you, Ivan? Can't some things remain only in your head?' As far as she could see he could make everything happen. Well, almost everything. She looked up into his blue eyes and her heart beat wildly.

He gazed down at her and took a step closer. He looked so serious, and older than he had previously appeared, as if he had seen and learned something new in the last few seconds. He placed a soft hand on her cheek and moved his head slowly towards her face. 'No,' he whispered, and kissed her so gently on the lips her knees almost buckled beneath her, '*everything* must come true.'

Joe looked out the window and laughed at the tourists dancing and splattering coffee outside his shop. Catching a glimpse of Elizabeth across the road, Joe moved closer to the window to get a better look. She held her head high in the air with her eyes closed in perfect bliss. Her hair, which was usually tied back, was down and blowing in the light morning breeze and she looked to be revelling in the sun shining down on her face.

Joe could have sworn he saw her mother in that face.

Chapter 23

It took Ivan and Elizabeth's mouths a while to pull away from one another but when they finally did, with tingling lips Elizabeth half skipped, half walked along the path to her office. She felt if she lifted her feet any higher from the ground she would float away. Humming as she tried to control her non-flight, she bumped straight into Mrs Bracken, who stood in her doorway, eyeing up the tourists across the road.

'Jesus!' Elizabeth jumped back in fright.

'Is the son of God, who sacrificed his life and died on the cross to spread the Lord's word and to give you a better life, so don't take his name in vain,' Mrs Bracken rattled off. She nodded in the direction of the café. 'What are those foreigners up to at all, at all?'

Elizabeth bit her lip and tried not to laugh. 'I have no idea. Why don't you join them?'

'Mr Bracken wouldn't be pleased about that carry-on at all.' She must have sensed something in Elizabeth's voice because her head shot up, her

231

eyes narrowed and she studied Elizabeth's face intently. 'You look different.'

Elizabeth ignored her and laughed as Joe guiltily mopped up the coffee on the pavement.

'You've been spending time up at that tower?' Mrs Bracken accused her.

'Of course I have Mrs Bracken. I'm designing the place, remember? And by the way, I've ordered the fabric; it should be arriving in three weeks, which gives us two months to get everything ready. Do you think you can get some extra help here?'

Mrs Bracken's eyes narrowed suspiciously. 'Your hair's down.'

'And?' Elizabeth asked, moving into the fabric shop to see if her order had arrived.

'And Mr Bracken used to say beware of a woman who drastically changes her hair.'

'I would hardly call letting my hair down a drastic change.'

'Elizabeth Egan, for you of all people, I would call letting your hair down a drastic change. By the way,' she moved on quickly, not allowing Elizabeth to get a word in, 'there's a problem with the order that came in today.'

'What's wrong with it?'

'It's *colourful*.' She said the word as if it were a disease and, widening her eyes, she emphasised it even more: '*Red*.'

Elizabeth smiled. 'It's raspberry, not red, and what's wrong with a bit of colour?'

'What's wrong with a bit of colour, she says.'

232

Mrs Bracken raised her voice an octave. 'Up until last week your world was brown. It's the tower that's doing it to you. The American fella, isn't it?'

'Oh, don't you start with that tower talk as well,' Elizabeth dismissed her. 'I've been up there all week, and all it is is a crumbling wall.'

'A crumbling wall is right,' Mrs Bracken said, eyeing her, 'and it's the American fella that's knocking it.'

Elizabeth rolled her eyes. 'Goodbye, Mrs Bracken.' She ran upstairs to her office.

On her entry a pair of legs sticking out from underneath Poppy's desk greeted her. They were men's legs – brown cords with brown shoes moving and squiggling around.

'Is that you, Elizabeth?' a voice shouted out.

'Yes, Harry,' Elizabeth smiled. Oddly, she was finding the two people who usually irritated her on a daily basis strangely lovable. Ivan was certainly passing the silly smile test.

'I'm just tightening up this chair. Poppy told me it was acting up on ya last week.'

'It was, Harry, thanks.'

'No problem.' His legs slithered up under the desk and disappeared as he struggled to his feet. Banging his head against the desk he finally appeared, his bald head covered by spaghetti-strings of hair brushed over from one side to the other.

'Ah, there you are,' he said, popping his head up, spanner in hand. 'It shouldn't spin on its own any more. Funny that it did that.' He gave it one last check, then looked at Elizabeth with the same expression as the one he had when examining the chair. 'You look different.'

'No, I'm still the same,' she said, walking through to her office.

'It's the hair. The hair's down. I always say it's better for a woman's hair to be down and—'

'Thank you, Harry. Will that be all?' Elizabeth said firmly, ending the conversation.

'Oh, right so.' His cheeks flushed as he waved her off and made his way downstairs, no doubt to gossip to Mrs Bracken about Elizabeth's hair being down.

Elizabeth settled at her desk and tried to concentrate on her work but found herself gently placing her fingers on her lips, reliving the kiss with Ivan.

'OK,' Poppy said, entering Elizabeth's office and placing a money box on her desk. 'See this here?'

Elizabeth nodded at the little pig. Becca stood at the door in the background.

'Well, I've come up with a plan.' Poppy gritted her teeth. 'Every time you start to hum that bloody song of yours, you have to put money in the pig.'

Elizabeth raised her eyebrows in amusement. 'Poppy, did you *make* this pig?' she stared at the papier-mâché pig sitting on her desk.

Poppy tried to hide her smile. 'It was a quiet night last night. But, seriously, it's getting beyond irritating now, Elizabeth, you've got to believe me,' Poppy pleaded. 'Even Becca is sick of it.'

'Is that right, Becca?'

Becca's cheeks pinked and she walked away quickly, not wanting to be dragged into the conversation.

'Great backup,' Poppy grumbled.

'So who gets the money?' Elizabeth asked.

'The pig. He's raising funds for a new sty. Hum a song and support a pig,' she said, quickly thrusting the pig in Elizabeth's face.

Elizabeth tried not to laugh. 'Out.'

Moments later, after they had settled down and gone back to work, Becca came charging into the office, placed the pig on the table and said with wide eyes, 'Pay!'

'Was I humming it again?' Elizabeth asked in surprise.

'Yes,' she hissed, her patience frayed, and turned on her heel.

Later that afternoon Becca brought a visitor into Elizabeth's office.

'Hello, Mrs Collins,' Elizabeth said politely, nerves forming in the pit of her stomach. Mrs Collins ran the B&B Saoirse had been staying in for the past few weeks. 'Please, sit down.' She indicated the chair before her.

'Thank you.' Mrs Collins took a seat. 'And call me Margaret.' She looked around the room like a frightened child who had been called to the principal's office. She kept her hands clasped on her lap as though afraid to touch anything. Her blouse was buttoned up to her chin.

'I've come to you about Saoirse. I'm afraid I haven't been able to pass on any of your notes and phone messages to her over the past few days,' Margaret said uncomfortably, fiddling with the hem of her blouse. 'She hasn't been back to the B&B for three days now.'

'Oh,' Elizabeth said, feeling embarrassed. 'Thank you for informing me, Margaret, but there's no need to worry. I expect she'll be calling me soon.' She was tired of being the last to know everything, of being informed of her own family's activities by complete strangers. Despite being distracted by Ivan, Elizabeth had tried to keep her eye on Saoirse as much as she could. Her hearing was on in a few weeks, but Elizabeth hadn't been able to find her anywhere. Anywhere being the pub, her dad's or the B&B.

'Well, actually it's not that. It's just that, well, it's a very busy period for us. There are a lot of tourists coming through and looking for boarding, and we need to use Saoirse's room.'

'Yes.' She sprang back in her chair, feeling foolish. *Of course.* 'That's completely understandable,' Elizabeth said awkwardly. 'I can call round after work to collect her things, if you like.'

'That won't be necessary,' Margaret smiled sweetly, then shouted, 'BOYS!'

In walked Margaret's two young teenage sons, each with a suitcase in his hand.

'I took the liberty of gathering her things together,' Margaret continued, her smile still plastered across her face. 'Now all I need is the three days' rent and that will be everything settled.'

Elizabeth froze. 'Margaret, I'm sure you'll understand that Saoirse's bills are her own. Just because I'm her sister it doesn't mean I can be expected to pay. She will return soon, I'm sure.'

'Oh, I know that, Elizabeth,' Margaret smiled, revealing a pink lipstick stain on her front tooth. 'But seeing as mine is currently the only B&B that will allow Saoirse to stay I'm sure you'll make an allow—'

'How much?' Elizabeth snapped.

'Fifteen per night,' Margaret said sweetly.

Elizabeth rooted through her wallet. She sighed. 'Look, Margaret, I don't seem to have any ca—'

'A cheque will do fine,' she sang.

After handing over the cheque to Margaret, for the first time in a while Elizabeth stopped thinking about Ivan and started worrying about Saoirse. Just like old times.

At 10 p.m. in downtown Manhattan, Elizabeth and Mark stared out of the huge black windows of the hundred-and-fourteenth-floor bar that Elizabeth had finished designing. Tonight was the opening night of Club Zoo, an entire floor dedicated to animal prints, fur couches and cushions with greenery and bamboo sporadically placed. It was everything she loathed in a design, but she had been given a brief and she had to stick to it. It was a huge success, everyone was enjoying the night, and a live performance of drummers performing jungle beats and the constant sound of happy conversation added to the party atmosphere. Elizabeth and Mark clinked their champagne glasses together and looked outside to the sea of skyscrapers, the random lights dotting the buildings like chequers and the tide of yellow cabs below them.

'To another of your successes,' Mark toasted, sipping on the bubble-filled glass.

Elizabeth smiled, feeling proud. 'We're a long way from home now, aren't we?' she pondered, looking out at the view and seeing the reflection of the party going on behind her. She saw the owner, Henry Hakala, making his way through the crowd.

'Elizabeth, there you are.' He held out his arms and greeted her. 'What is the star of the night doing in the corner away from everyone?' he asked.

'Henry, this is Mark Leeson, my boyfriend; Mark, this is Henry Hakala, owner of Club Zoo,' she introduced the two.

'So you're the person that's kept my girlfriend out late every night,' Mark joked, taking Henry's hand.

Henry laughed. 'She's saved my life. Three weeks to do all this?' He motioned at the room decorated vibrantly in zebra print on the walls, bear skins draped on the couches, leopard print lying across the timber floors, enormous plants sitting in chrome pots and bamboo lining the bar area. 'It was a tough deadline and I knew she'd do it, but I didn't think she'd do it this well.' He looked grateful. 'Anyway, the speeches are about to begin. I just want to say a few words, mention a few investors' names,' he muttered under his breath, 'thank all you glorious people that worked so hard. So don't go anywhere, Elizabeth, because I'll have all eyes on you in a minute.'

'Oh,' Elizabeth blushed, 'please don't.'

'Believe me, you'll have a few hundred more offers after I do,' he said before he made his way towards the microphone, decorated with a vine of leaves.

'Excuse me, Ms Egan.' A member of the bar staff approached her. 'You have a phone call just outside at the main desk.'

Elizabeth frowned, 'Me? A phone call? Are you sure?'

'You are Ms Egan, yes?'

She nodded, confused. Who would be ringing her here?

'It's a young woman, says she's your sister?' he explained quietly.

'Oh.' Her heart beat wildly. 'Saoirse?' she asked, shocked.

'Yes, that's it,' the young man said, sounding relieved. 'I wasn't sure I'd remembered right.'

At that moment it felt as if the music got louder, the drumming beats were pounding her head, the fur prints were all coming together in a blur. Saoirse

239

never called her; something had to be seriously wrong.

'Leave it, Elizabeth,' Mark said rather forcefully. 'Tell the woman on the phone that Ms Egan is busy at the moment,' Mark said to the barman. 'This is your night, enjoy it,' he added softly to Elizabeth.

'No, no, don't tell her that,' Elizabeth stammered. It must be 3 a.m. in Ireland – why was Saoirse calling so late? 'I'll take the call, thank you,' she said to the young man.

'Elizabeth, the speech is about to begin,' Mark warned her as the room began to quieten down and gather before the microphone. 'You can't miss it,' he hissed. 'This is *your* moment.'

'No, no, I can't,' she trembled, and she left him, heading in the direction of the phone.

'Hello?' she said a few moments later, the concern evident in her voice.

'Elizabeth?' Saoirse's voice sobbed.

'It's me, Saoirse. What's wrong?' Elizabeth's heart thudded in her chest.

There was silence in the club as Henry made his speech.

'I just wanted to . . .' Saoirse trailed off and was silent.

'You wanted to what? Is everything OK?' Elizabeth asked hurriedly.

Henry's voice boomed, '. . . And last but not least I'd like to thank the wonderful Elizabeth Egan from Morgan Designs for designing this place so wonderfully in such a short time. She's created something that's completely different to what's out there right now, making Club Zoo the most popular, trendy and newest club on the scene, guaranteed to have people queuing down the block to get in. She's down the back there somewhere. Elizabeth, give us all a wave, let them know who you are so they can steal you away from me.'

Everyone turned around in silence, searching for the designer.

'Oh,' Henry's voice echoed, 'well, she was there a second ago. Maybe someone's snapped her up already to do a job.'

Everyone laughed.

Elizabeth looked inside and saw Mark standing alone with two champagne glasses in his hand, shrugging at everyone who had turned to him and laughing. Pretending to laugh.

'Saoirse,' Elizabeth's voice broke, 'please tell me if there's something wrong. Have you gotten into trouble again?'

Silence. Instead of the weak sobbing voice Elizabeth had heard previously, Saoirse's voice had become strong again. 'No,' she snapped. 'No, I'm fine. Everything's fine. Enjoy your party,' and she hung up.

Elizabeth sighed and slowly hung up the phone.

Inside the speech had finished and the drums had started up again; the conversation and drinks continued to flow.

Neither she nor Mark was in the mood to party.

*   *   *

241

Elizabeth could see a giant figure looming in the distance as she drove down the road that led to her father's bungalow. She had left work early and was searching for Saoirse. Nobody had seen her for days, not even the local publican, which made a change.

It had always been difficult to direct people to the bungalow as it was so cut off from the rest of the town. The road didn't even have a name, which Elizabeth thought was appropriate; it was the road that people forgot. Postmen and milkmen new to the job always took a few days to find the address, politicians never canvassed to their door, there were no trick-or-treaters. As a child Elizabeth had tried to convince herself that her mother had simply become lost and couldn't find her way home. She remembered sharing her theory with her father, who gave a smile so small it was hardly a smile at all and replied, 'You know, you're not far wrong there, Elizabeth.'

That was the only explanation, if you could even call it that, which she got. They never discussed her mother's disappearance; neighbours and visiting family hushed when Elizabeth was near. Nobody would tell her what had happened and she didn't ask. She didn't want that uncomfortable quiet to descend on them or for her father to storm out of the house when her mother's name was mentioned. If not mentioning her mother ensured that everyone was happy, then Elizabeth was happy to oblige, as usual.

She didn't think she really wanted to know, anyway. The mystery of not knowing was more enjoyable. She would create scenarios in her head, painting her mother in exotic and exciting worlds and she would fall asleep imagining her mother on a desert island, eating bananas and coconuts and sending messages in a bottle to Elizabeth. She would check the coastline every morning with her father's binoculars for sign of a bobbing bottle.

Another theory was that she had become a Hollywood movie star. Elizabeth sat with her nose almost up against the TV screen for every Sunday matinée, searching for her mother's grand debut. But she grew tired of searching, hoping, imagining, and not asking, and eventually she no longer even wondered.

The figure didn't move from the window of Elizabeth's old bedroom. Usually her father would be waiting in the garden for her. Elizabeth hadn't been inside the bungalow for years. She waited outside for a few minutes, and when there was no sign of her father or of Saoirse she got out of the car, slowly pushed open the gate, goose pimples rising on her skin from the noise of the gate's hinges, and wobbled up the uneven stone slabs in her high heels. Weeds popped up from the cracks to study the stranger trespassing on their territory.

Elizabeth knocked twice on the green paint-flecked door and quickly pulled her fist away, cradling it as though it had been burned. There was no answer yet she knew there was someone in the bedroom to the right. She held out her hand and pushed open the door. There was a stillness inside and the familiar musty smell of what she once considered home hit her and stopped her in her tracks for a few moments. Once she had adjusted to the emotions the scent had woken inside her, she stepped inside.

She cleared her throat. 'Hello?'

No answer.

'Hello?' she called more loudly. Her grown-up voice sounded wrong in her childhood home.

She began to walk towards the kitchen, hoping her father would hear her and come out to her. She had no desire to revisit her old bedroom. Her high heels echoed on the stone floor, another sound unfamiliar to the house. She held her breath as she stepped into the kitchen and dining area. Everything and nothing was the same. The smells, the clock on the mantel, the lace tablecloth, the rug, the chair by the fireplace, the red teapot on the green Aga, the curtains. Everything still had its place, had aged and was faded with time, but still belonged. It was as though no one had lived there since Elizabeth had left. Maybe no one *had* truly lived there.

She stayed standing in the centre of the room for a while, eyeing the ornaments, reaching out to touch them but allowing her fingers only to linger. Nothing had been disturbed. She felt as though she were in a museum; even the sounds of tears, laughter, fights and love had been preserved and hung in the air like cigarette smoke.

244

Eventually she couldn't take it any more; she needed to talk to her father, to find out where Saoirse was, and in order to do that she needed to go to her bedroom. She slowly turned the brass door knob that was still hanging loose as it had been in her childhood. She pushed the door open, didn't step in, and didn't look around. She just looked straight at her father, who sat in an armchair in front of the window, not moving.

Chapter 24

She didn't move her eyes from the back of his head, couldn't move her eyes anywhere else. She tried not to breathe in the smell but it gathered in her throat, blocking her wind pipe.

'Hello?' she croaked.

He didn't move, just kept his head straight ahead.

Her heart skipped a beat. 'Hello?' She detected an air of panic in her voice.

Without thinking, she stepped into the room and rushed towards him. She fell to her knees and examined his face. He still didn't move and kept his eyes straight ahead. Her heart quickened. 'Daddy?' rushed out of her mouth in a panic, sounding childlike. It felt real to her then. The word meant something. She held out to touch him, placed one hand on his face and another on his shoulder. 'Dad, it's me – are you OK? Talk to me.' Her voice shook. His skin was warm.

He blinked and she breathed a sigh of relief.

He slowly turned to look at her. 'Ah, Elizabeth,

I didn't hear you come in.' His voice sounded like it was coming from another room. It was gentle; gone were his gravelly tones.

'I was calling you,' she said softly. 'I drove down the road – didn't you see me?'

'No,' he said in surprise, turning back to face the window.

'Then what were you looking at?' She too turned to the window and the view took her breath away. The scene – the path, the garden gate and the long stretch of road – momentarily threw her into the same trance as her father. The same hopes and wishes of the past came back in that instant. On the windowsill sat a photograph of her mother, which had never been there before. In fact, Elizabeth thought her father had got rid of all the photographs after her mother left.

But the image of her silenced Elizabeth. It was so long since she had seen her mother; she no longer had a face in Elizabeth's mind. All she was was a fuzzy memory, more like a feeling than a picture. Seeing her was a shock. It was like looking at herself, a perfect mirror image. When she found her voice again she spoke quietly, shaken. 'What are you doing, Dad?'

He didn't move his head, didn't blink, just had a faraway look in his eye and an unfamiliar voice that came deep from within him. 'I saw her, Elizabeth.'

Palpitations. 'Saw who?' But she knew who.

'Gráinne, your mother. I saw her. At least I

247

think I did. It's been so long since I've seen her that I wasn't sure. So I got the photo just so I can remember. So that when she walks down the road I'll remember.'

Elizabeth gulped. 'Where did you see her, Dad?'

His voice was higher pitched and slightly bewildered. 'In a field.'

'A field? What field?'

'A field of magic.' His eyes glistened, seeing it all over again. 'A field of dreams, as they say. She looked so happy, dancing and laughing just like she always did. She hasn't aged a day.' He looked confused. 'But she should have, shouldn't she? She should be older, like me.'

'Are you sure it was her, Dad?' Her whole body was shaking.

'Oh aye, 'twas her, moving in the wind like the dandelions, sun shining on her like she was an angel. 'Twas her, alright.' He was sitting upright in the chair, two hands lying on the armrests, looking more relaxed than ever.

'She had a child with her, though, and it wasn't Saoirse. No, Saoirse's grown up now,' he reminded himself. 'It was a boy, I think. Little blond fella, like Saoirse's boy . . .' His thick caterpillar-like eyebrows furrowed for the first time.

'When did you see her?' Elizabeth asked, dread and relief both filling her body, realising it was she her father had seen in the field.

'Yesterday,' he smiled, remembering. 'Yesterday morning. She'll be coming to me soon.'

Tears filled Elizabeth's eyes. 'Have you been sitting here since yesterday, Dad?'

'Aye, I don't mind. She'll be here soon but I need to remember her face. I sometimes don't remember, you see.'

'Dad,' Elizabeth's voice was a whisper, 'wasn't there someone else in the field with her?'

'No,' Brendan smiled, 'just her and the boy. He looked so happy too.'

'What I mean is,' Elizabeth held his hand; hers was childlike next to his tough-skinned fingers, 'I was in the field yesterday. It was me, Dad, catching dandelion seeds with Luke and a man.'

'No.' He shook his head and scowled. 'There was no man. Gráinne was with no man. She's coming home soon.'

'Dad, I promise you it was me, Luke and Ivan. Perhaps you were mistaken,' she said as gently as she could.

'No!' he yelled, causing Elizabeth to jump. He faced her with a look of disgust. 'She's coming home to me!' He glared at her. 'Get out!' he finally yelled, waving his hand and knocking her small hand off his.

'What?' Her heart beat wildly. 'Why, Dad?'

'You're a liar,' he spat. 'I saw no man in the field. You know she's here and you're keeping her from me,' he hissed. 'You wear suits and sit behind desks, you know nothing of dancing in fields. You're a liar, pollutin' the place. Get out,' he repeated quietly.

She looked at him in shock. 'I've met a man, Dad, a beautiful, wonderful man who's been teaching me of all these things,' she started to explain.

He moved his face in front of hers until they were almost touching nose to nose. 'GET OUT!' he yelled.

Tears spilled from her eyes and her body shook as she rushed to her feet. Her room became a whirl as she saw everything she didn't want to see in her disoriented state – old teddies, dolls, books, a writing desk, the same duvet cover. She charged for the door, not wanting to see any more, not being able to see any more. Her trembling hands fumbled with the latch as her father's yells for her to leave got louder and louder.

She pulled the door open and ran outside into the garden, breathing the fresh air into her lungs. A knocking on the window spun her round. She faced her father, waving angrily at her to get out of his garden. She gasped for breath, her tears raced down her face and she pulled open the gate and left it open, not wanting to hear the closing creak of its hinges.

She sped down the road in her car as fast as she could, not looking in the rear-view window, not wanting ever to see the place again, not wanting ever to have to drive down the road of disappointment again.

There would be no more looking back.

Chapter 25

'What's wrong?' a voice called from the back patio door. Elizabeth was sitting at the kitchen table, head in her hands, as still as Muckross Lake on a calm day.

'Jesus,' Elizabeth said under her breath, not looking up but wondering how it was that Ivan always managed to appear at the moments when she least expected him but needed him most.

'Jesus? Has he been giving you a hard time?' He stepped into the kitchen.

Elizabeth looked up from her hands. 'It's actually his father I'm having an issue with right now.'

Ivan took another step towards her; he had the ability to overstep the boundaries but never in a threatening or intrusive way. 'I hear that a lot.'

Elizabeth wiped her eyes with a mascara-stained and crumpled tissue. 'Don't you ever work?'

'I work all the time. May I?' He gestured to the chair opposite her.

She nodded. 'All the time? So is this work for you? Am I just another hopeless case for you to deal with today?' she asked sarcastically, catching a tear halfway down her cheek with the tissue.

'There's nothing hopeless about you, Elizabeth. However, you are a case; I've already told you that,' he said seriously.

She laughed. 'A headcase.'

Ivan looked sad. Misunderstood again.

'So is that your uniform?' She indicated his attire.

Ivan looked down at himself in surprise.

'You've been wearing that outfit everyday I've seen you,' she smiled, 'so it's either a uniform or you're completely unhygienic and lack imagination.'

Ivan's eyes widened. 'Oh, Elizabeth, I don't lack imagination at all.' Not realising what he had implied, Ivan continued, 'Do you want to talk about why you are so sad?'

'No, we're always talking about me and my problems,' Elizabeth replied. 'Let's talk about you for a change. What did you do today?' she asked, trying to perk herself up. It had seemed like such a long time ago since she had kissed Ivan on the main street that morning. She had thought about it all day and had worried about who had seen her, but amazingly, for a town that learned of everything quicker than Sky News, nobody had mentioned a thing to her about the mystery man.

She had longed to kiss Ivan again, had felt scared about that longing and tried to numb herself of feeling for him but she couldn't. There was something about him so pure and untarnished, yet he was powerful and well-versed in life. He was like the drug she knew she shouldn't take but which kept coming back to feed her addiction. As her weariness set in later in the day, the memory of the kiss had become a comfort to her and the uneasiness vanished. All she wanted now was a repeat of that moment where her troubles fizzled away.

'What did I do today?' Ivan twiddled his thumbs and thought aloud. 'Well, today I gave Baile na gCroíthe a big wake-up call, kissed a very beautiful woman and then spent the rest of the day being unable to do anything but think of her.'

Elizabeth's face brightened and his piercing blue eyes warmed her heart.

'And then I couldn't stop thinking,' Ivan continued, 'so I sat down and spent the day thinking.'

'About what?'

'Apart from the beautiful woman?'

'Apart from her,' Elizabeth grinned.

'You don't want to know.'

'I can take it.'

Ivan looked uncertain. 'OK, if you really want to know,' he took a deep breath, 'I thought about the Borrowers.'

Elizabeth frowned. 'What?'

'The Borrowers,' Ivan repeated, looking thoughtful.

'The television programme?' Elizabeth said, feeling irate. She had prepared herself for whispers of sweet nothing like they did in the movies, not this unscripted loveless conversation.

'Yes.' Ivan rolled his eyes, not noticing her tone, 'if you want to refer to *that* commercial side of them.' He sounded angry. 'But I thought long and hard about them and I've come to the conclusion that they didn't borrow. They *stole*. They downright stole and everybody knows it but nobody ever talks about it. To borrow means to take and use something belonging to someone else and then eventually return it. I mean, when did they ever give anything back? I don't recall Peagreen Clock ever giving anything back to the Lenders at all, do you? Especially the food – how can you borrow *food*? You eat it and it's gone; there's no giving it back. At least when I eat your dinner you know where it's going.' He sat back and folded his arms, looking cross. 'And they get a film made about them, a bunch of thieves, while us? We do nothing but good but we get labelled a figment of people's imaginations and are still,' he made a face and made inverted commas with his fingers, '*invisible*. Please . . .' He rolled his eyes.

Elizabeth stared at him open-mouthed.

There was a long silence as Ivan looked around the kitchen, shaking his head in anger, and then returned his attention to Elizabeth. 'What?'

Silence.

'Oh, it doesn't matter.' He waved his hand dismissively. 'I told you, you wouldn't want to know.

So enough about my problems. Please tell me, what's happened?'

Elizabeth took a deep breath, the question of Saoirse distracting her from the confusing talk of the Borrowers. 'Saoirse has disappeared. Joe, the man with his finger on the pulse of Baile na gCroíthe, told me she headed off with the group of people she was hanging out with. He heard it from a family member of a guy from the group she's with but she's been gone for three days and no one seems to know where they've gone.'

'Oh,' Ivan said in surprise, 'and here I am rattling off my problems. Did you tell the gardaí?'

'I had to,' she said sadly. 'I felt like a snitch but they had to know she was gone just in case she didn't turn up for her hearing in a few weeks, which I'm almost sure she won't be at. I'll have to get a solicitor to go on her behalf, which won't look very good.' She rubbed her face tiredly.

He took her hands and cradled them in his own. 'She'll be back,' he said confidently. 'Maybe not for the hearing but she'll come back. Believe me. There's no need to worry.' His soft voice was firm.

Elizabeth stared deep into his eyes, searching for the truth. 'I believe you,' she said. But deep down Elizabeth was afraid. She was afraid of believing Ivan, afraid of believing full stop, because when that happened, her hopes were raised up the flagpole, waving and blowing in the breeze for all to see. There they would weather the storms and winds, only to be lowered, tattered and ruined.

And she didn't think she could spend any more years with her bedroom curtains open, with one eye on the road, waiting for a second person to return. She was weary and she needed to close her eyes.

Chapter 26

As soon as I left Elizabeth's house the next morning, I decided to head straight to Opal. Actually, I had decided I was going to do that long before I left Elizabeth's house. Something she said had hit a nerve – actually, everything she said hit a nerve with me. When I was with her I was like a hedgehog, all prickly and sensitive, as if all of my senses were alert. The funny thing is I thought all my senses had been alert already – as a professional best friend they should have been   but there was one emotion I hadn't experienced before and that was love. Sure, I loved all my friends but not in this way, not in the way that made my heart thud when I looked at Elizabeth, not in a way that made me want to be with her the whole time. And I didn't want to be with her for *her*, I realised it was for me. This love thing awakened a group of slumbering senses in my body that I never even knew existed.

I cleared my throat, checked my appearance and made my way into Opal's office. In Ekam

Eveileb there were no doors, because nobody here could open them, but there was another reason: doors acted as barriers; they were thick, unwelcoming things that you could control to shut people in or out and we didn't agree with that. We chose open-plan offices for a more open and friendly atmosphere. Although that's what we were always taught, lately I had found Elizabeth's fuchsia front door with the smiling letter box to be the friendliest door I had ever seen, so that shot that particular theory to hell. She was making me question all sorts of things.

Without even looking up, Opal called out, 'Welcome, Ivan.' She was sitting behind a desk, dressed in purple, as usual, her dreadlocks were tied up and scattered in glitter so that with every movement she sparkled. On each of her walls were framed photos of hundreds of children, all smiling happily. They were even covering her shelves, coffee table, sideboard, mantelpiece and windowsill. Everywhere I looked were rows and rows of photographs of people Opal had worked with and become friends with in the past. Her desk was the only surface that was clear and on it sat one single photo frame. The frame had sat there for years facing Opal so that nobody ever really got a chance to see who or what was in it. We knew that if we asked she would tell us, but nobody was ever rude enough to ask. What we didn't need to know, we didn't need to ask. Some people just don't quite get the gist of that. You can have plenty of conversations with people, *meaningful* conversations without getting too personal. There's a line, you know, like an invisible field around people that you just know not to enter or cross, and I had never crossed it with Opal, or anyone else for that matter. Some people just can't even see that.

Elizabeth would have hated the room, I thought as I looked around. She would have removed everything in an instant, dusted it and polished it until it gleamed with the clinical glow of a hospital. Even at the coffee shop she had arranged the salt and pepper shakers and the bowl of sugar into an equilateral triangle in the centre of the table. She always moved things an inch to the left or an inch to the right, back and forward until it stopped nagging and she could concentrate again. Funny thing was, she sometimes ended up moving things back to exactly how they were in the first place and then convincing herself she was happy with them. That said a lot about Elizabeth.

But why did I start thinking of Elizabeth just then? I kept on doing that. In situations that were totally unrelated to her, I would think of her and she would become part of the scenario. I would suddenly wonder, what would she think, how would she feel, what would she do or say if she was with me? That was all part of giving someone a piece of your heart; they ended up taking a whole chunk of your mind and reserving it all for themselves.

Anyway, I realised I had been standing in front of the desk not saying anything since I walked in.

'How did you know it was me?' I finally spoke.

Opal looked up and smiled one of those smiles that made her look as if she knew it all. 'I was expecting you.' Her lips looked like two big cushions, and were purple to match her robe. I thought of what it felt like to kiss Elizabeth's lips.

'But I didn't make an appointment,' I protested. I knew I was intuitive but Opal was in a whole league of her own.

She just smiled again. 'What can I do for you?'

'I thought you'd know that without having to ask me,' I teased, sitting down in her spinning chair and thinking about the spinning chair in Elizabeth's office, then thinking of Elizabeth, what it was like to hold her, hug her, laugh with her and hear the little breaths she took while she slept last night.

'You know the dress Calendula was wearing at last week's meeting?'

'Yes.'

'Do you know how she got that?'

'Why, do you want one too?' Opal asked with a glint in her eyes.

'Yes,' I replied, fidgeting with my hands. 'I mean no,' I said quickly. I took a breath. 'What I mean is, I was wondering where I could get a change of clothes for myself.' There I'd done it.

'The wardrobe department, two floors down,' Opal explained.

'I didn't know there was a wardrobe department,' I said in surprise.

'It's always been there,' Opal said, narrowing her eyes. 'May I ask what you need it for?'

'I don't know.' I shrugged. 'It's just that, Elizabeth, you see, is, um, she's *different* from all my other friends. She notices these things, you know?'

She nodded slowly.

I felt I should explain a bit more. The silence was making me uncomfortable. 'You see, Elizabeth said to me today that the reason I wore these clothes was because it was either a uniform, I was unhygienic or because I lacked imagination.' I sighed, thinking about it. 'The last thing I am is lacking in imagination.'

Opal smiled.

'And I know I'm not unhygienic,' I continued. 'And then I was thinking about the uniform part,' I looked myself up and down, 'and maybe she was right, you know?'

Opal pursed her lips.

'One of the things about Elizabeth is that she too is dressed in uniform. She wears black – the same stuffy suits all the time – her make-up is a mask, her hair is always tied back, *nothing* is free. She works all the time and takes it so seriously,' I looked up at Opal in shock, just realising something. 'That's exactly like me, Opal.'

Opal was silent.

'All this time I was calling her a gnirob.'

Opal laughed lightly.

'I wanted to teach her to have fun, to change

261

her clothes, stop wearing a mask, change her life so she can find happiness and how can I do that when I'm the very same as her?'

Opal nodded her head lightly. 'I understand, Ivan. You're learning a lot from Elizabeth too, I can see that. She is bringing something out in you and you are showing her a whole new way of life.'

'We caught Jinny Joes on Sunday,' I said softly, agreeing with her.

Opal opened a cabinet behind her and grinned. 'I know.'

'Oh, good, they arrived,' I said happily, watching the Jinny Joes floating in a jar in the cabinet.

'One of yours arrived too, Ivan,' Opal said seriously.

I felt my face redden. I changed the subject. 'You know she got six hours of undisturbed sleep last night. That's the first time that's ever happened.'

Opal's expression didn't soften. 'Did she tell you that, Ivan?'

'No, I saw her . . .' I trailed off. 'Look, Opal, I stayed the night, I only held her in my arms till she fell asleep, it's no big deal. She asked me to.' I tried to sound convincing. 'And when you think about it, I do it all the time with other friends. I read them bedtime stories, stay with them till they sleep and sometimes even sleep on their floor. This is no different.'

'Isn't it?'

I didn't answer.

Opal picked up her fountain pen with a great big purple feather on the top, looked down and continued with her calligraphy writing. 'How much longer do you think you'll need to work with her?'

That got me. My heart did a little dance. Opal had never asked me that before. It was never a matter of time for anyone, it was always a natural progression. Sometimes you only had to spend a day with someone, other times you could be there months. When our friends were ready, they were ready, and we had never before had to put a time on it. 'Why do you ask?'

'Oh,' she was nervous, fidgety, 'I'm just wondering. As a matter of interest . . . you're the best I have here, Ivan, and I just want you to remember that there are lots more people that need you.'

'I know that,' I said rather forcefully. Opal's voice had all sorts of tones I had never heard before, negative ones that sent blue and black colours into the air and I didn't like it one bit.

'Great,' she said, a bit too perky for her, and she knew it. 'Can you drop these by the analysis lab on your way to wardrobe?' She handed me the jar of Jinny Joes.

'Sure.' I took the jar from her. There were three Jinny Joes inside, one from Luke, one from Elizabeth and the third was mine. They sat on the floor of the jar, resting from their journey in the wind. 'Bye,' I said rather awkwardly to Opal, backing out of the office. I felt as though we'd just had an argument even though we hadn't.

I made my way down the hall to the analysis lab, holding the lid of the jar closed tightly so they wouldn't escape. Oscar was running around the lab with a look of panic on his face when I reached the entrance.

'Open the hatch!' he yelled to me while passing the door, arms out in front of him, white coat flapping like a cartoon character.

I placed the jar away from danger and hurried to the hatch. Oscar ran towards me and, at the last minute, jumped to the side, fooling what was chasing him so that it raced straight into the cage.

'Ha!' he exploded, turning the key and waving it at the cage. His forehead was glittered with perspiration.

'What on earth is that?' I asked, moving closer to the cage.

'Be careful!' Oscar shouted, and I jumped back. 'You are incorrect in asking what on earth it is because it's not.' He dabbed his forehead with a handkerchief.

'It's not what?'

'On earth,' he replied. 'Never seen a shooting star before, Ivan?'

'Of course I have.' I circled the cage. 'But not up close.'

'Of course,' he added, an overly sweet tone to his voice, 'you just see them from afar, looking so pretty and bright, dancing across the sky, and you make your wishes on them but,' his tone turned nasty, 'you forget about Oscar, who has to gather your wishes from the star.'

'I'm sorry, Oscar, I really did forget. I didn't think stars were so dangerous.'

'Why?' Oscar snapped, 'Did you think a burning asteroid millions of miles away, which is visible from earth, is going to shoot down to me and kiss me on the cheek? Anyway, it doesn't matter. What have you brought to me? Oh great, a Jinny Joe jar. Just what I needed after that ball of fire,' he shouted loudly at the cage, 'something with a bit of respect.'

The ball of fire bounced around angrily in response.

I stepped further away from the cage. 'What kind of wish was it carrying?' I found it hard to believe that this burning ball of light could be of any help to anyone.

'Funny you ask,' Oscar said, showing it wasn't funny at all. 'This particular one was carrying the wish to chase me around the lab.'

'Was that Tommy?' I tried not to laugh.

'I can only assume so,' he said angrily. 'But I can't really complain to him because that was twenty years ago when Tommy didn't know any better and was just starting out.'

'Twenty years ago?' I asked in surprise.

'It took that long to get here,' Oscar explained, opening the jar and lifting out a Jinny Joe with an odd-looking implement. 'It is, after all, millions of light years away. I thought twenty years was doing rather well.'

I left Oscar studying the Jinny Joes and made my way to wardrobe. Olivia was in there being measured.

'Hello, Ivan,' she said in surprise.

'Hi, Olivia, what are you doing?' I asked, watching as a woman measured her tiny waist.

'Being measured for a dress, Ivan. Poor Mrs Cromwell passed away last night,' she said sadly. 'The funeral's tomorrow. I've been to so many funerals my only black dress is worn out.'

'I'm sorry to hear that,' I said, knowing how fond Olivia was of Mrs Cromwell.

'Thank you, Ivan, but we must keep going. A lady arrived at the hospice this morning, who needs my help and now I must focus on her.'

I nodded, understanding.

'So what brings you here?'

'My new friend, Elizabeth, is a woman. She notices my clothes.'

Olivia chuckled.

'You want a T-shirt in another colour?' the woman who was measuring asked. She took a red T-shirt from a drawer.

'Em, no.' I shifted from foot to foot and looked around at the shelves reaching from floor to ceiling. Each of them was labelled with a name and I saw Calendula's name underneath a row of pretty dresses. 'I was looking for something a lot . . . smarter.'

Olivia raised her eyebrows. 'Well then, you'll have to be measured for a suit, Ivan.'

We agreed to make me a black suit to go with a blue shirt and tie because they were my favourite colours.

'Anything else, or will that be all?' Olivia asked me with a twinkle in her eye.

'Actually,' I lowered my voice and looked around to make sure the woman was out of earshot. Olivia moved her head closer to mine.

'I was wondering if you could teach me the soft-shoe shuffle.'

Chapter 27

Elizabeth stared at the sparse wall, dirty with dried and patchy plaster. She already felt at a loss. The wall wasn't saying anything to her. It was 9.00 a.m. on the building site, and it was already overrun by men in hard hats, drooping jeans, check shirts and Caterpillar boots. They looked like an army of ants as they rushed around carrying all sorts of materials on their backs. In the emptiness of the hotel their cheers, laughter, songs and whistling echoed around the cemented shell on top of the hill that had yet to be filled by the ideas in Elizabeth's head. Their sounds rolled down the corridors like thunder and into what was to be the children's playroom.

All it was now was a blanched and pallid canvas that would in a matter of only weeks have children frolicking in the recreation room, while outside would be a cocoon of calm. Perhaps she should have sound-proofed the walls. She had no idea what she could add to these walls to bring a smile to the children's little faces when they walked in feeling nervous and upset at being taken from their parents. She knew about chaise longues, plasma screens, marble floors and wood of every kind. She could do chic, funky, sophisticated and rooms of splendour and grandeur. But none of these things would excite a child, and she knew she could do better than a few building blocks, jigsaw puzzles and beanbags.

She knew it would be perfectly within her rights to hire a muralist, ask the on-site painters to do the job or even ask Poppy for some guidance, but Elizabeth liked to be hands-on. She liked to get lost in her work and she didn't want to have to ask for help. Handing the brush over to someone else would be a sign of defeat in her eyes.

She laid ten tubs of primary colours in a line on the floor, opened the lids and placed the brushes next to them. She spread a white sheet on the floor and, making sure her jeans, which she wore only as work wear, wouldn't touch the dirty floor in any way, she sat crosslegged in the centre of the room and stared at the wall. But all she could think of was the fact she couldn't think of anything but Saoirse. Saoirse, who was on her mind every second of every day.

In time she wondered how long she had been sitting there. She had a vague recollection of builders entering and exiting the room, collecting their tools, watching her in puzzlement as she stared at a blank wall. She had a feeling she was suffering an interior designer's version of writer's block. No ideas would come, no pictures could be formed and, just as the ink would dry in a pen, the paint would not flow from her brush. Her head was filled with . . . nothing. It was as though her thoughts were being reflected onto that drab plastered wall and it was probably thinking the very same thing as her.

She felt someone's presence behind her and she turned round. Benjamin was standing at the door.

'I'm sorry, I would have knocked but,' he held his hands up, 'there's no door.'

Elizabeth gave him a welcoming grin.

'Admiring my handiwork?'

'You did this?' She turned back to face the wall.

'My best work, I think,' he replied, and they both looked at it in silence.

Elizabeth sighed. 'It's not saying anything to me.'

'Ah.' He took a step into the room. 'You have no idea how difficult it is to create a piece of art that doesn't say anything at all. Someone always has some kind of interpretation but with this . . .' he shrugged, 'nothing. No statements.'

'A sign of a true genius, Mr West.'

'Benjamin,' he winced. 'I keep telling you, please call me Benjamin; you make me sound like my math teacher.'

'OK, you can keep calling me Ms Egan.'

He caught the sides of her cheeks lifting into a smile as she turned back to face the wall.

'Do you think there's any chance at all that the kids will like this room just as it is?' she asked hopefully.

'Hmm,' Benjamin thought aloud, 'the nails protruding from the skirting board would be particularly fun for them to play with. I don't know,' he admitted. 'You're asking the wrong guy about kids. They're another species to me. We don't have a real close relationship.'

'Me neither,' Elizabeth muttered guiltily, thinking of her inability to connect with Luke like Edith did. Although after meeting Ivan she found herself spending more time with him. That morning in the field with Ivan and Luke had been a real milestone for her, yet when she was alone with Luke she still couldn't let herself go with him. It was Ivan that released the child in her.

Benjamin went down on his haunches, placing his hand on the dusty floor to steady himself. 'Well, I don't believe that for a second. You've got a son, don't you?'

'Oh, no, I haven't . . .' she started, then stopped. 'He's my nephew. I adopted him but the last thing in this world I understand is children.' Everything was blurting out of her mouth today. She missed the Elizabeth who could have a conversation without revealing the tiniest part of herself but it seemed that lately the floodgates to her heart had been opened and things rushed out of it of their own accord.

'Well, you seem to have a pretty good idea what he wanted on Sunday morning,' Benjamin said softly, looking at her differently. 'I drove past you when you were dancing around that field.'

271

Elizabeth rolled her eyes and her dark skin pinked. 'You and the rest of the town, apparently. But that was Ivan's idea,' she said quickly.

Benjamin laughed. 'You give Ivan the credit for everything?'

Elizabeth thought about that but Benjamin didn't wait for the answer. 'I suppose in this case you just gotta sit here like you're doin' and put yourself in the position of the kids. Put that wild imagination of yours to use. If you were a kid what would you want to do in this room?'

'Other than get out and grow up quickly?'

Benjamin moved to get up.

'So how long do you plan on staying in the big smoke of Baile na gCroíthe?' Elizabeth asked quickly. She figured the longer he stayed, the more she could put off admitting to herself that for the first time in her life she had absolutely no idea of what to do with a room.

Benjamin, sensing her desire for a conversation, lowered himself to the dusty floor and Elizabeth had to ignore what she could imagine were millions of dust mites crawling all over him.

'I plan on leaving as soon as the last lick of paint is on the walls and the last nail has been hammered in.'

'You've obviously fallen head over heels in love with this place,' Elizabeth said sarcastically. 'Don't the stunning panoramic views of Kerry impress you?'

'Yeah, the views are nice but I've had six months

of good views and now I could do with a decent cup of coffee, a choice of more than one shop to buy my clothes and to be able to walk around without everyone staring at me like I've escaped from a zoo.'

Elizabeth laughed.

Benjamin held his hands up. 'I don't mean to be offensive or anything – Ireland's great – but I'm just not a fan of small towns.'

'Me neither . . .' Elizabeth's smile faded at the thought. 'So where did you escape from then?'

'New York.'

Elizabeth shook her head. 'That is not a New York accent I hear.'

'No, you got me; I'm from a place called Haxtun in Colorado, which I'm sure you've probably heard of. It's well known for a great number of things.'

'Such as?'

He raised his eyebrows. 'Absolutely nothing. It's a small town in a big dust bowl, a good strong farming town with a population of one thousand.'

'You didn't like it there?'

'No I didn't like it,' he said firmly. 'You could say I suffered from claustrophobia,' he added with a smile.

'I know how that feels,' Elizabeth nodded. 'Sounds like here.'

'It's a bit like here.' Benjamin looked out the window. He relaxed then. 'Everyone waves at you as you pass. They haven't a damn clue who you are but they wave.'

273

Elizabeth hadn't realised it until now. She pictured her father in the field, cap on, covering his face, holding his arm up in an L shape to passing cars.

'They wave in fields and on the streets,' Benjamin continued, 'farmers, old ladies, kids, teens, newly born and serial killers. And I've studied this to a fine art.' His eyes twinkled at her. 'You even get the one-finger wave with the index finger raised off the steering wheel as you pass traffic. Man, you'd leave the place waving at cows if you're not careful.'

'And the cows would probably wave back.'

Benjamin laughed loudly. 'You ever think of leaving?'

'I did more than think about it.' Her smile faded. 'I went to New York too but I've commitments here,' she said, quickly looking away.

'Your nephew, right?'

'Yes,' she said softly.

'Well, there's one good thing about leaving a small town. They all miss you when you're gone. They all notice it.'

Their eyes locked on one another. 'I suppose you're right,' she said. 'It's ironic, though, that we both moved to a big city where we were surrounded by more people and more buildings than we'd ever known, just so we could feel more isolated.'

'Huh.' Benjamin stared at her, not blinking. She knew he wasn't seeing her face; he was lost in his own world. And he did look lost for a moment.

'Anyway,' he snapped out of his trance, 'it was a pleasure talking to you again, Ms Egan.'

She smiled at his address.

'I'd better go and let you stare at the wall some more.' He stopped and turned at the doorway. 'Oh, by the way,' she felt her stomach turn, 'without running the risk of making you uncomfortable, I mean this in the most innocent way possible, maybe you'd like to meet up outside of work sometime? It would be nice to have a conversation with a like-minded person for a change.'

'Sure.' She liked this casual invitation. No expectations.

'Maybe you'll know some of the good places to go. Six months ago, when I just arrived, I made the mistake of asking Joe where the nearest sushi bar was. I had to tell him it was raw fish before he directed me to a lake about an hour's drive away and told me to ask for a guy called Tom.'

Elizabeth burst out laughing, the sound, which was becoming more familiar to her these days, echoing around the room. 'That's his brother, the fisherman.'

'Anyway, I'll see you again.'

The room was empty once more and Elizabeth was faced with the same dilemma. She thought of what Benjamin had said about using her imagination and putting herself in the place of a child. She closed her eyes and imagined the sounds of children hollering, laughing, crying and fighting. The noisy clatter of toys, feet pounding on the floor as they ran around, the sound of bodies falling, a shocked silence and then wails. She pictured herself as a child sitting alone in a room, not knowing anyone, and it suddenly occurred to her what she would have wanted.

A friend.

She opened her eyes and spotted a card on the floor beside her, though the room was still empty and quiet. Someone must have crept in when she had her eyes closed and left it there. She picked up the card, which had a black thumb print on the side. She didn't even need to read it to know it was Benjamin's new business card.

Maybe imagining had worked after all. It looked like she'd just made a friend in the playroom.

Sliding the card into her back pocket, she forgot about Benjamin and continued staring at the four walls.

Nope. Still nothing.

Chapter 28

Elizabeth sat at the glass table in the spotless kitchen surrounded by gleaming granite worktops, polished walnut cupboards and shining marble tiles. She had just had a cleaning frenzy and her mind still wasn't clear. Every time the phone rang, she leaped at it, thinking it was Saoirse, but it was Edith checking up on Luke. Elizabeth still hadn't heard from her sister, her father was still waiting in her old bedroom for her mother; sitting, eating and sleeping in the same chair for almost two weeks now. He wouldn't speak to Elizabeth, wouldn't even let her come as far as the front door so she had arranged for a housekeeper to call round to cook him a meal a day, and tidy up now and then. Some days he let her in, others he didn't. The young man who worked with her father on his farm had taken over all the duties. This was costing Elizabeth money she couldn't afford, but there was nothing else she could do. She couldn't help the other two members of her family if they didn't want to be helped. And she wondered for the first time if she had something in common with them after all.

They had all lived together – the girls had grown up together – but separately, and still they stayed together in the same town. They hadn't much communication with one another but when somebody left . . . well, it mattered. They were tied by an old and fraying rope that ended up being the object of tug of war.

Elizabeth couldn't bring herself to tell Luke what was going on and, of course, he knew there was something. Ivan was right, children had a sixth sense for that kind of thing, but Luke was such a good child and as soon as he sensed Elizabeth's sadness he retreated into the playroom. Then she would hear the quiet clatter of building blocks. She couldn't bring herself to say more to him than to tell him to wash his hands, fix his speech and order him to stop dragging his feet.

She wasn't capable of holding her arms out to him, her lips couldn't form the words 'I love you', but she tried in her own ways to make him feel safe and wanted. But she knew what he really wanted. She had been in his position, knew what it was like to want to be held, cuddled, kissed on the forehead and rocked. To be made to feel safe for just a few minutes at least, to know that someone else is there looking out for you and that life just isn't in your own hands and you're stuck living it all alone in your head.

Ivan had provided her with a few of those

moments over the past few weeks. He had kissed her on the forehead and rocked her to sleep, and she had fallen asleep not feeling alone, not feeling the urge to look out the window and search beyond for someone else. Ivan, sweet, sweet Ivan was shrouded in mystery. She had never known anyone have the ability to help her realise just exactly who she was, to help her find her feet, but she was struck by the irony that this man who jokingly spoke of invisibility actually did wear a cloak of invisibility. He was putting her on a map, showing her the way, yet he had no idea where he was going himself, where he came from, *who* he was. He liked to speak of her problems, help heal her, help fix her, and he never once spoke of his own. It was as though she was a distraction to him and she wondered what would happen when the distraction ended and the realisation dawned.

She got a sense that their time together was valuable, as though she needed to hold on to every minute as if it was their last. He was too good to be true, every moment spent with him magical, so much so that she presumed this couldn't last for ever. None of her good feelings had lasted; none of the people who lightened her life managed to stay. Going by her previous luck, from pure *fear* of not wanting to lose something so special, she was just waiting for the day he would leave. Whoever he was, he was healing her, he was teaching her to smile, teaching her to laugh, and she wondered what she could teach him. With Ivan, she feared that the sweet man with the soft eyes would reach a day when he would realise she had nothing to offer. That she had simply drained him of his resources and had none to give.

It had happened with Mark. She just couldn't give him any more of herself without taking away the care she had for her family. That's what he wanted her to do, of course – cut the strings that connected her to her family – but she couldn't do it, she would never do it. Saoirse and her father knew how to pull those strings and so she remained their puppet. As a result she was alone, raising a child she never wanted, with the love of her life living in America, a married man and a father of one. She hadn't heard from him or seen him for five years. A few months after Elizabeth had moved back to Ireland he visited her while on a trip home to see his family.

Those beginning months were the hardest. Elizabeth was intent on making Saoirse bring up the baby herself and as much as Saoirse protested and claimed she didn't care, Elizabeth wasn't about to let her sister throw away the opportunity of raising her son.

Elizabeth's dad couldn't hack it any more; he couldn't take the baby's screaming all night while Saoirse was out partying. Elizabeth supposed it reminded him too much of the years before when he was left holding the baby, the baby he subsequently passed on to his twelve-year-old daughter. Well, he did the same again. He threw Saoirse out of the bungalow, forcing her to arrive on Elizabeth's doorstep, cradle and all. The day that all happened was the day Mark decided to take the trip over to visit Elizabeth.

One look at the state of her life and she knew he was gone for ever. It wasn't long before Saoirse disappeared from Elizabeth's home, leaving the baby with her. She thought about giving Luke up for adoption, she really did. Every sleepless night and every stressful day she promised herself she would make that phone call. But she couldn't do it. Maybe it had something to do with her fear of giving in. She was obsessive in her strive for perfection and she couldn't give up on trying to help Saoirse. Also there was a part of her that was intent on proving she could raise a child, that it wasn't her fault for the way Saoirse turned out. She didn't want to get it all wrong with Luke. He deserved far better.

She cursed as she picked up another of her sketches, scrunched it in a ball and threw it across the room to the bin. It landed short of it and, not being able to cope with something out of place, Elizabeth walked across the room and delivered it to its rightful position.

The kitchen table was covered in paper, colouring pencils, children's books, cartoon characters. All she had succeeded in doing was drawing doodles all over the page. It wasn't enough for the playroom and it certainly wasn't the whole new world that she aspired to create.

As usual, the same thing happened that always happened when she thought of Ivan: the doorbell rang and she knew it was him. She rushed to her feet, fixing her hair, her clothes, checking her reflection in the mirror. Gathering her colouring pencils and paper, she jogged on the spot in panic, trying to decide where to dump them. They slid from her hand; swearing, she dived down to pick them up. Her papers flew out of her hands and floated to the floor like leaves in an autumn breeze.

While on the floor, her eyes fell upon red Converse runners casually crossed one another at the doorway. Her body slumped, her cheeks pinked.

'Hi, Ivan,' she said, refusing to look at him.

'Hello, Elizabeth. Have you ants in your pants?' his amused voice asked.

'How good of Luke to let you in,' Elizabeth said sarcastically. 'Funny he never actually does that when I need him to.' She reached for the sheets of paper on the floor and got to her feet. 'You're wearing red,' she stated, studying his red cap, red T-shirt and red shoes.

'Yes I am,' he agreed. 'Wearing different colours is my favourite thing now. It makes me feel even happier.'

Elizabeth looked down at her black outfit and thought about that.

'So what have you got there?' he asked, breaking into her thoughts.

282

'Oh, nothing,' Elizabeth mumbled, folding the pages together.

'Let me see it.' He grabbed the sheets. 'What have we got here? Donald Duck, Mickey Mouse,' he flicked through the pages, 'Winnie-the-Pooh, a racing car – and what's this?' He twirled the page round to get a better view.

'It's nothing,' Elizabeth snapped, snatching the page from his hand.

'That's not nothing – nothing looks like this.' He stared at her blankly.

'What are you doing?' she asked after a few moments' silence.

'Nothing, see?' He held out his hands.

Elizabeth stepped away from him, rolling her eyes. 'Sometimes you are worse than Luke. I'm going to have a glass of wine, would you like anything? Beer, wine, brandy?'

'A ssalg of klim, please.'

'I wish you'd stop speaking backwards,' she snapped, handing him a glass of milk. 'For a change?' she asked irritatedly, throwing her pages into the bin.

'No, that's what I always have,' he said rather perkily, eyeing her suspiciously. 'Why is that cabinet locked?'

'Em . . .' she faltered, 'so Luke can't get at the alcohol.' She couldn't say it was to keep Saoirse out. Luke had taken to hiding the key in his room whenever he heard his mother coming.

'Oh. What are you doing on the twenty-ninth?'

Ivan swung himself around on the tall bar stool at the breakfast table and watched Elizabeth rooting through the wine bottles, face twisted in concentration.

'When is the twenty-ninth?' She locked the cabinet and searched through the drawer for a corkscrew.

'It's on Saturday.'

Her cheeks pinked and she looked away, giving her full concentration to opening the wine bottle. 'I'm going out on Saturday.'

'Where to?'

'A restaurant.'

'With who?'

She felt like it was Luke firing questions at her. 'I'm meeting Benjamin West,' she said, still keeping her back turned. She just couldn't face turning round right at that moment but she didn't know why she felt so uncomfortable.

'Why are you meeting him on Saturday? You don't work on Saturdays,' Ivan stated.

'It's not about work, Ivan. He doesn't know anybody here and we're going to get something to eat.' She poured the red wine into a crystal glass.

'Eat?' he asked incredulously. 'You're going to eat with Benjamin?' His voice went up a few octaves.

Elizabeth's eyes widened and she spun round, glass in hand. 'Is that a problem?'

'He's dirty and he smells,' Ivan stated.

Elizabeth's mouth dropped open; she didn't know how to reply to that.

'He probably eats with his hands. Like an animal,' Ivan continued, 'or a caveman, half man half animal. He probably hunts for—'

'Stop it, Ivan,' Elizabeth started laughing.

He stopped.

'What's really wrong?' She raised an eyebrow at him and sipped her wine.

He stopped spinning on his chair and stared at her. She stared back. She saw him swallow, his Adam's apple moving down his throat. His childishness disappeared and he appeared to her as a man, big, strong, with such a presence. Her heartbeat quickened. His eyes didn't move from her face and she couldn't look away, couldn't move.

'Nothing's *wrong*.'

'Ivan, if you've got anything to say to me, you should say it,' Elizabeth said firmly. 'We're big boys and girls now.' The corner of her lips twitched at that.

'Elizabeth, would you come out with me on Saturday?'

'Ivan, it would be rude of me to cancel the appointment at such short notice – can't we go out another night?'

'No,' he said firmly, stepping off the stool. 'It has to be July the twenty-ninth. You'll see why.'

'I can't—'

'You can,' he interrupted her firmly. He took her by her elbows. 'You can do whatever you want. Meet me at Cobh Cúin at 10 p.m. on Saturday.'

'Cobh Cúin? And why so late?'

'You'll see why,' he repeated, tipped his cap and disappeared as quickly as he had arrived.

Before I left the house I called in to Luke in the playroom.

'Hey there, stranger,' I said, collapsing on the beanbag.

'Hi, Ivan,' Luke said, watching TV.

'Have you missed me?'

'Nope,' Luke smiled.

'Wanna know where I've been?'

'Smooching with my aunt.' Luke closed his eyes and did fake kisses in the air before collapsing into hysterical laughter.

My mouth dropped open. 'Hey! What makes you say that?'

'You *love* her,' Luke laughed, and continued watching cartoons.

I thought about that for a while. 'Are you still my friend?'

'Yep,' Luke replied, 'but Sam is my *best* friend.'

I pretended to be shot in the heart.

Luke looked away from the television to face me with hopeful big blue eyes. 'Is my aunt your best friend now?'

I thought about that carefully. 'Do you want her to be?'

Luke nodded emphatically.

'Why?'

'She's much better fun, she doesn't give out to

me as much and she lets me colour in the white room.'

'Jinny Joe day was fun, wasn't it?'

Luke nodded again. 'I've never seen her laugh so much.'

'Does she give you big hugs and play lots of games with you?'

Luke looked at me as if that was a ridiculous idea and I sighed, worried about the small part of me that felt relieved.

'Ivan?'

'Yes, Luke.'

'Remember you told me that you can't stay around all the time, that you have to go to help other friends and so I shouldn't feel sad.'

'Yes.' I swallowed hard. I dreaded that day.

'What will happen to you and Aunt Elizabeth when that happens?'

And then I worried about the part in the centre of my chest that pained when I thought about that.

I stepped into Opal's office, hands in my pockets and wearing my new red T-shirt and a new pair of black jeans. Red felt good on me today. I was angry. I didn't like the tone in Opal's voice when she called me.

'Ivan,' she said, putting down her feather pen and looking up at me. Gone was her beaming smile that once used to greet me. She looked tired, bags hung under her eyes and her dreadlocks were down around her face and not in one of her usual styles.

'Opal,' I imitated her tone, throwing one leg over the other as I sat before her.

'What are the things you teach your students about becoming a part of your new friend's life?'

'Assist don't hinder, support don't oppose, help and listen don't—'

'You can stop right there.' She raised her voice and cut in on my bored tones. 'Assist and don't hinder, Ivan.' She allowed those words to hang in the air. 'You made her cancel a dinner reservation with Benjamin West. She could have made a friend, Ivan.' She stared at me, her black eyes like coal. Any more anger and they would have gone on fire.

'Can I remind you that the last time Elizabeth Egan made any reservations with anyone for non-business purposes was five years ago. *Five* years ago, Ivan,' she stressed. 'Can you tell me why you undid all that?'

'Because he's dirty and he smells,' I laughed.

'Because he's dirty and he smells,' she repeated, making me feel stupid. 'Then let her figure that out for herself. Don't overstep your mark, Ivan.' With that she looked back down at her work and continued writing, the feather blowing as she scribbled furiously.

'What's going on, Opal?' I asked her. 'Tell me what's really going on.'

She looked up, anger and sadness in her eyes. 'We are incredibly busy, Ivan, and we need you to work as quickly as you can and move on instead of hanging around and undoing the good work you've already done. That's what's going on.'

Stunned by her chastising I silently left her office. I didn't believe her for one minute but whatever was happening in her life was her own business. She'd change her mind about Elizabeth cancelling her dinner with Benjamin as soon as she saw what I had planned for the twenty-ninth.

'Oh, and, Ivan,' Opal called out.

I stopped at her doorway and turned. She was still looking down and writing as she spoke. 'I'll need you to come in here next Monday to take over for a while.'

'Why?' I asked with disbelief.

'I'm not going to be here for a few days. I need you to cover for me.'

That had never happened before. 'But I'm still in the middle of a job.'

'Good to hear you're still calling it that,' she snapped. Then she sighed, put down her feathered pen and looked up. She looked as if she was going to cry. 'I'm sure Saturday will be such a success you won't need to be there next week, Ivan.'

Her voice was so soft and genuine that I forgot that I was angry at her and realised for the first time that if it was any other situation, she would be right.

Chapter 29

Ivan placed the finishing touches to the dinner table, snipped a stem of fuchsia that was growing wild and placed it in the small vase in the centre. He lit a candle and watched as the flame darted in the breeze, like a dog running around the garden yet chained to his kennel. Cobh Cúin was silent, just as the name, which literally meant silent cave, suggested, christened hundreds of years ago by the locals and untouched since then. The only sound was the water gently lapping, swishing back and forth, and tickling the sand. Ivan closed his eyes and swayed to the music. A small fishing boat tied to the pier bobbed up and down on the sea, occasionally bumping the side of the pier and adding a soft drumbeat.

The sky was blue and beginning to darken with a few stray wisps of teenage clouds lagging behind the older clouds of hours ago. The stars twinkled brightly and Ivan winked back at them; they too knew what was coming. Ivan had asked the head chef at the work canteen to help him out tonight.

He was the same chef responsible for catering the tea parties in the back gardens of best friends but this time he went all out. He had created the most luscious spread Ivan could have imagined. For starter was foie gras and toast cut into neat little squares, followed by wild Irish salmon and asparagus cooked in garlic, followed by a white chocolate mousse with dribbles of raspberry sauce for dessert. The aromas were being lifted by the warm gulf wind and being carried past his nose, tickling his taste buds.

He played around with the cutlery nervously, fixing all that didn't need to be fixed, tightened his new blue silk tie, loosened it again, opened the button of his navy-blue suit jacket and decided to close it again. He had been so busy all day arranging the setup that he had barely taken time to think about the feelings that were stirring inside him. Glancing at his watch and at the darkening sky, he hoped Elizabeth would come.

Elizabeth drove down the narrow winding road slowly, barely able to see past the end of her nose in the thick blackness of the countryside. Wild flowers and hedge growth reached out to brush the sides of her car as she passed. Her full headlights startled moths, mosquitoes and bats as she drove in the direction of the sea. Suddenly the inky veil lifted as she reached a clearing and the whole world was spread out before her.

Ahead were thousands of miles of ebony sea glistening under the moonlight. Inside the small cove was a tiny fishing boat tied up beside the steps, the sand was a velvety brown, the edges being licked and teased by the approaching tide. But it wasn't the sea that took her breath away; it was the sight of Ivan standing in the sand, dressed in a smart new suit, beside a small beautifully set table for two, a candle flickering in the centre, casting shadows across his smiling face.

The sight was enough to bring a tear from a stone. It was an image her mother had stamped in her mind, an image she had whispered excitedly into her ear about moonlit dinners on the beach, so much so that her mother's dreams had become her own. And there Ivan was, standing in the picture Elizabeth and her mother had painted so vividly and that had remained etched in Elizabeth's mind. She understood the phrase of not knowing whether to laugh or cry and so she unashamedly did both.

Ivan stood proudly, blue eyes glistening in the moonlight. He ignored her tears, or rather, accepted them.

'My dear,' he bowed theatrically, 'your moonlit dinner awaits you.'

Wiping her eyes and smiling a smile so big Elizabeth felt she could light the entire world, she took his extended hand and stepped out of the car.

Ivan took a sharp intake of breath. 'Wow, Elizabeth, you look stunning.'

'Wearing red is my favourite thing to do now,' she imitated him, taking his arm and allowing him to lead her to the dinner table.

After much humming and hawing Elizabeth had purchased a red dress that accentuated her slender figure, giving her curves she never even knew she had. She had taken it on and off at least five times before she left the house, feeling too exposed in such a bright colour. To prevent herself from feeling like a traffic light she had brought a black pashmina to drape over her shoulders.

The white Irish table linen flapped in the light warm breeze and Elizabeth's hair tickled her cheek. The sand was cool and soft beneath her feet, like fluffy carpet, and was protected in the cove from the sharp wind. Ivan pulled out her chair for her and she sat. Then he reached for her serviette, which had been wrapped in a stem of fuchsia, and he laid it on her lap.

'Ivan, this is beautiful, thank you,' she whispered, not feeling able to lift her voice over the peaceful lapping water.

'Thank you for coming,' he smiled, pouring her a glass of red wine. 'Now for starters we have foie gras.' He reached under the table and retrieved two plates covered in silverware. 'I hope you like foie gras,' he said, frown lines appearing on his forehead.

'I love it,' Elizabeth smiled.

'Phew.' The muscles in his face relaxed. 'It doesn't really look like grass,' he said, examining his plate closely.

'It's goose liver, Ivan,' Elizabeth laughed, spreading some on her toast. 'What made you choose this cove?' she asked, wrapping the shawl tighter around her shoulders as the breeze began to chill.

'Because it's quiet and because it's a perfect location away from streetlights,' he explained, munching on his food.

Elizabeth thought it better not to ask any questions, knowing Ivan had his own peculiar way.

After dinner Ivan turned to look at Elizabeth, who had her hands wrapped around her wine glass and was staring wistfully out to the sea. 'Elizabeth,' his voice was soft, 'will you lie with me on the sand?'

Elizabeth's heartbeat quickened. 'Yes.' Her voice was husky. She couldn't think of a better way to end the evening with him. She was longing to touch him, for him to hold her. Elizabeth made her way to the water's edge and sat down on the cool sand. She felt Ivan padding behind her.

'You're going to have to lie on your back for this to work,' he said loudly, looking down at her.

Elizabeth's mouth dropped open. 'Excuse me?' She wrapped the shawl protectively around her shoulders.

'If you don't lie back, this just won't work,' he repeated, putting his hands on his hips. 'Look, like this.' He sat down beside her and lay back on the sand. 'You have to be flat on your back, Elizabeth. It's best this way.'

'Is it now?' Elizabeth stiffened and clambered to get to her feet. 'Was all this,' she gestured around the cove, 'just to get me flat on my back, as you so beautifully phrased it?' she asked, hurt.

Ivan stared up at her from the sand, eyes wide with a flabbergasted look on his face. 'Well . . .' he stalled, trying to think of an answer, 'actually, yes,' he squeaked. 'It's just that, it's better when it peaks, for you to be flat on your back,' he stuttered.

'Ha!' Elizabeth spat and, putting her shoes back on, she struggled through the sand to get back to her car.

'Elizabeth, look!' Ivan shouted with excitement. 'It's peaked! Look!'

'Uugh,' Elizabeth grunted, climbing the small sand dune to her car. 'You really are disgusting!'

'It's not disgusting!' Ivan said, panic in his voice.

'That's what they all say,' Elizabeth grumbled, fumbling in her bag for her car keys. Unable to see into her bag in the dark, she leaned it towards the moonlight and as she glanced up, her mouth dropped open. Above her, in the black cloudless sky, was a hive of activity. Stars glowed brighter than she had ever seen before, some darting across the sky.

Ivan lay on his back, staring up to the night sky.

'Oh,' Elizabeth said quietly, feeling foolish, glad that the darkness was hiding her skin absorbing the colour of her dress. She stumbled back down the sand dune, removed her shoes, allowed her feet to curl into the sand and took a few steps closer to Ivan. 'It's beautiful,' she whispered.

'Well, it would be a lot more beautiful if you lay flat on your back like I told you to,' Ivan huffed, crossing his arms across his chest and staring up to the sky.

Elizabeth covered her mouth with her hand and tried not to laugh out loud.

'I don't know what you're laughing at. No one accused you of being disgusting,' he said smartly.

'I thought you were talking about something else,' Elizabeth giggled, sitting down on the sand beside him.

'Why else would I be asking you to lie flat on your back?' Ivan asked in a dull tone and then he turned to her, his voice rising a few octaves, his eyes mocking. 'Oh,' he sang.

'Shut up,' Elizabeth said harshly, throwing her purse at him but letting her smile show. 'Oh, look,' she was distracted by a shooting star, 'what's going on up there tonight, I wonder.'

'It's the Delta Aquarids,' Ivan said as though that explained everything. Elizabeth's silence made him continue. 'They're meteors that come from the constellation Aquarius. The normal dates are the fifteenth of July to the twentieth of August but they peak on the twenty-ninth of July. That's why I had to take you out tonight, away from street-lights.' He turned to look at her. 'So yes, all of this was just to get you on your back.'

They studied each other's faces in comfortable silence until more action above diverted their attention.

'Why don't you make a wish?' Ivan asked her.

'No,' Elizabeth said softly, 'I'm still waiting for my Jinny Joes wish to come true.'

'Oh, I wouldn't worry about that,' Ivan said seriously. 'They just take a while to process. You won't be waiting long.'

Elizabeth laughed and stared hopefully up into the sky.

A few minutes later, sensing her sister would be on her mind, Ivan asked, 'Any word from Saoirse?'

Elizabeth gave a single shake of her head.

'She'll be home,' Ivan said positively.

'Yes, but in what condition?' Elizabeth said uncertainly. 'How is it other families manage to hold it together? And even when they've problems, how do they manage to keep it from the rest of the people in their neighbourhoods?' she asked in confusion, thinking about all the whispers she had been hearing over the past few days about her father's behaviour and her sister's disappearance. 'What's their secret?'

'See that cluster of stars right there?' Ivan asked, pointing upwards.

Elizabeth followed his hand, embarrassed to have bored him with talk of her family so much that he'd changed the subject. She nodded.

'Most meteors from a common meteor shower are parallel to one another. They appear to emerge from the same point in the sky called "the radiant" and they travel in all directions from this point.'

'Oh, I see,' Elizabeth said.

'No, you don't see.' Ivan turned on his side to face her. 'Stars are like people, Elizabeth. Just because they *appear* to emerge from the same point doesn't mean that they do. This is an illusion of perspective created by distance.' And as if Elizabeth hadn't quite understood the meaning he added, 'Not all families manage to hold it together, Elizabeth. Everyone moves in different directions. That we all emerge from the same point is a misconception; to travel in different directions is the very nature of every being and every existing thing.'

Elizabeth turned her head and faced the sky again, trying to see if what he said was true. 'Well, they could have fooled me,' she said quietly, watching more appear from the blackness every second.

She shivered and wrapped her shawl around her tighter; the sand was getting cooler with each passing hour.

'Are you cold?' Ivan asked with concern.

'A little,' she admitted.

'Right, well, the night isn't over yet,' he said, jumping to his feet. 'Time to warm up. Mind if I borrow the keys to your car?'

'Not unless you intend driving away,' she joked, handing them over.

He retrieved something from under the table once again and brought it to the car. Moments later music was softly drifting through its open door.

Ivan began to dance.

Elizabeth giggled nervously. 'Ivan, what are you doing?'

'Dancing!' he said, offended.

'What kind of dancing?' She took his extended hand and allowed herself to be pulled to her feet.

'It's the soft-shoe shuffle,' Ivan announced, dancing expertly in circles around her on the sand. 'Also called the sand dance, you'll be interested to know, which means that your mother wasn't so mad wanting to do the shuffle in the sand after all!'

Elizabeth's hands flew to her mouth, tears filled her eyes with happiness as she realised he was fulfilling yet another of her and her mother's intended activities.

'Why are you fulfilling all of my mother's dreams?' she asked, studying his face and searching for answers.

'So you don't run away like she did in search of them,' he replied, taking her hand. 'Come on, join in!'

'I don't know how!'

'Just copy me.' He turned his back and danced away from her, swinging his hips exaggeratedly.

Lifting her dress to above her knees, Elizabeth threw caution to the wind and joined in dancing the soft-shoe shuffle on the sand in the moonlight, laughing until her stomach was sore and she was out of breath.

'Oh, you make me smile so much, Ivan,' she gasped, collapsing on the sand later that evening.

'Just doin' my job,' he grinned back. As soon as the words had left his mouth his smile faded and Elizabeth detected a hint of sadness in those blue eyes.

Chapter 30

Elizabeth allowed her red dress to slide down her legs, gather at her ankles and then stepped out of it. She wrapped a warm bathrobe around her body, pinned her hair up and climbed onto her bed with a cup of coffee she had brought upstairs. She had wanted Ivan to come to bed with her tonight; despite her earlier protests she had wanted him to take her in his arms on the sand in the cove right there, but it seemed the more she felt drawn to him, the further he pulled himself away.

After they had watched the stars dancing in the sky, and then they had danced on the sand, Ivan had withdrawn into himself in the car on the journey home. He had asked her to let him out in the small town, from where he would make his own way home, wherever home was. He had yet to bring her there or introduce her to his friends and family. Elizabeth had never before been interested in meeting the others in her partners' lives. She felt as long as she enjoyed their company, whether or not she liked the company of those who surrounded him was irrelevant. But with Ivan she felt she needed to see another side to him. She needed to witness his relationships with other people so he could become a three-dimensional character to her. That was always the argument old partners had with Elizabeth and now she finally understood what it was they were searching for.

Elizabeth had watched Ivan in her mirror as she drove away; intrigued to know what direction he would walk in. He had looked left and right down the deserted streets that were empty at the late night hour, began to walk left in the direction of the mountains and the hotel. After a few steps he stopped, turned round and walked in the other direction. He crossed the road and strode confidently toward Killarney but halted suddenly, eventually folded his arms across his chest and sat down on the stone windowsill of the butcher's.

She didn't think he knew where home was, or if he did, he didn't know his way there. She knew how he felt.

On Monday afternoon Ivan stood at the doorway to Opal's office and chuckled as he listened to Oscar ranting to Opal for a steady ten minutes. As amusing as he was to listen to, they'd have to hurry their meeting along because Ivan was due to meet Elizabeth at 6 p.m. He had twenty minutes. He hadn't seen her since the Delta Aquarids viewing on Saturday night, the greatest night of his long, long life. He had tried to walk away from her after that. He had tried to leave Baile na gCroíthe, tried to move on to someone else who needed his help, but he couldn't. He didn't feel drawn to any other direction other than Elizabeth and it was stronger than any other pull he had experienced before. This time it wasn't just his mind that was pulling him, it was his heart too.

'Opal,' Oscar's serious tones floated out to the hallway, 'I desperately need more staff for next week.'

'Yes, I understand, Oscar, and we've already arranged for Suki to help you in the lab,' Opal explained gently yet firmly. 'There's nothing more we can do for now.'

'That's simply not good enough,' he fumed. 'On Saturday night millions of people viewed the Delta Aquarids, do you know how many wishes will come shooting in here over the next few weeks?' He didn't wait for an answer and Opal didn't offer one. 'It's a dangerous procedure, Opal, and I need more hands. While Suki is extremely efficient in the administration area, she is not qualified in wish analysis. Either I'm helped out by more staff or you'll have to find a new wish analyst,' he puffed. With that he stormed out of the office, past Ivan and down the hallway mumbling, 'After years of studying to be a meteorologist I get stuck doing *this*!'

'Ivan,' Opal called.

'How do you do that?' Ivan asked, entering the

office. He was beginning to think she could see through walls.

She glanced up from the desk, smiled weakly, and Ivan took a quick intake of breath. She looked very tired, with dark circles under her bloodshot eyes. She looked as if she hadn't slept for weeks.

'You're late,' she said gently. 'You were supposed to be here at 9 a.m.'

'I was?' Ivan asked, confused. 'I only called in to ask you a quick question. I have to rush off in a minute,' he added quickly. *Elizabeth, Elizabeth, Elizabeth*, he sang in his head.

'We agreed you would cover for me today, remember?' Opal said firmly, standing up from her desk and walking round to the other side.

'Oh, no, no, no,' Ivan said quickly, backing towards the door. 'I'd love to help you, Opal, really I would. Helping is one of my favourite things to do but I can't now. I've made plans to meet my client. I can't miss it, you know how it is.'

Opal leaned against the desk, folded her arms and cocked her head to one side. She blinked and her eyes closed slowly and tiredly, taking an age to open again. 'So she's your *client* now, is she?' she said wearily. Dark colours surrounded her today. Ivan could see them spreading out from all around her body.

'Yes, she's my client,' he replied less confidently. 'And I really can't miss her this evening.'

'Sooner or later you're going to have to say goodbye to her, Ivan.'

She said it so coldly, without padding or frills, that it chilled him. He gulped and shifted his weight to his other foot.

'How do you feel about that?' she asked, when he didn't answer.

Ivan thought about it. His heart thudded in his chest and he felt as if it was going to move up through his throat and out of his mouth. His eyes filled. 'I don't want to,' he said quietly.

Opal's arms lowered slowly to her sides. 'Pardon?' she asked, a little gentler.

Ivan thought about his life without Elizabeth and he raised his voice more confidently. 'I don't want to say goodbye to her. I want to stay with her for ever, Opal. She makes me feel happier than I've ever felt before in my life and she tells me that I do the same for her. Surely it would be wrong to walk away from that?' He smiled widely, recalling the feeling of being with her.

Opal's hardened face softened. 'Oh, Ivan, I knew this would happen.' There was pity in her voice and he didn't like it. He would have preferred anger. 'But I thought you of all people would have made the right decision a long time ago.'

'What decision?' Ivan's face crumpled at the thought of his having made the wrong one. 'I asked you what I should do and you wouldn't tell me.' He began to panic.

'You should have left her a long time ago, Ivan,' she said sadly, 'but I couldn't tell you to do that. You had to realise it for yourself.'

305

'But I couldn't leave her.' Ivan sat down on the chair before her desk slowly as the sadness and shock crept through his body. 'She kept seeing me.' His voice was almost a whisper. 'I couldn't leave until she stopped seeing me.'

'You made her keep seeing you, Ivan,' Opal explained.

'No, I didn't.' He stood up and walked away from the desk, angry at the suggestion that anything about their relationship had been forced.

'You followed her, you watched her for days, you allowed the small connection you both had to blossom. You tapped into something extraordinary and made her realise it too.'

'You don't know what you're talking about,' he spat, pacing the room. 'You have no idea how either of us is feeling.' He stopped pacing, marched up to her and looked her directly in the eye, his chin lifted, his head steady. 'Today,' he spoke with perfect clarity, 'I am going to tell Elizabeth Egan that I love her and that I want to spend my days with her. I can still help people while I'm with her.'

Opal's hands went to her face. 'Oh, Ivan, you can't!'

'You taught me that there was nothing that I couldn't do,' he snarled between gritted teeth.

'No one else will see you but her!' Opal exclaimed. 'Elizabeth won't understand. It just won't work.' She was clearly distraught by this revelation.

'If what you said is true and I made Elizabeth

see me, then I can make everyone else see me too. Elizabeth will understand. She understands me like nobody else has ever done. Do you have any idea what that feels like?' He was excited now by the prospect. Before it had only been a thought, but now, now it was a possibility. He could make it happen. He looked at his watch: 6.50 p.m. He had ten minutes. 'I have to go,' he said urgently. 'I have to tell her I love her.' He strode towards the doorway with confidence and determination.

Suddenly Opal's voice broke the silence. 'I do know how you feel, Ivan.'

He stopped in his tracks, turned and shook his head. 'You can't know how this feels, Opal, not unless you've lived through this. You can't even begin to imagine.'

'I have,' she said quietly and uncertainly.

'What?' He viewed her warily with narrowed eyes.

'I have,' she said with strength in her voice this time, and crossed her hands across her stomach, clasping her fingers together. 'I fell in love with a man who saw me more than I had ever been seen in my whole entire life.'

There was a silence in the room while Ivan tried to come to terms with this. 'So that should mean that you understand me all the more.' He stepped towards her, clearly thrilled by the revelation. 'Maybe it didn't end well for you, Opal, but for me,' he smiled widely, 'who knows?' He threw his hands up and shrugged. 'This could be it!'

Opal's tired eyes stared back at him sadly. 'No.' She shook her head and his smiled faded. 'Let me show you something, Ivan. Come with me this evening. Forget the office,' she waved her hand around the room dismissively. 'Come with me and let me give you your final lesson.' She tapped his chin fondly.

Ivan looked at his watch, 'But Eliz—'

'Forget Elizabeth for now,' she said softly. 'If you choose not to take my advice you'll have Elizabeth tomorrow, the next day and everyday for the rest of her life. Nothing ventured, nothing gained.' She held out her hand to him.

Reluctantly Ivan reached out to take it. Her skin was cold.

Chapter 31

Elizabeth sat on the end of the staircase and looked out the window to the front garden. The clock on the wall said 6.50 p.m. Ivan had never been late before and she hoped he was OK. However, her sense of anger was rather more active at that moment than her worry for him. His behaviour on Saturday night gave her reason to think that his absence was due more to cold feet rather than foul play. She had thought about Ivan all day yesterday, about not meeting his friends, his family or his work colleagues, the lack of sexual contact and, in the dead of the night, as she battled to find sleep, she had realised what it was that she had being trying to hide from herself. She felt she knew what the problem was: Ivan was either in a relationship already or unwilling to enter into one.

Any niggling feeling she had along the way she had ignored. It was unusual for Elizabeth not to plan, not to know exactly where a relationship was going. She wasn't comfortable with this big change. She liked stability and routine, everything Ivan lacked. Well, she was sure that now it could never work, as she sat on the stair waiting for a free spirit, just as her father was. And she never discussed her fears with Ivan – why? Because when she was with him, every little fear dissipated. He would just show up, take her by the hand and lead her into another exciting chapter in her life, and while she was reluctant to go with him at times, often apprehensive, *with* him she was never nervous. It was when she was without him, moments like now, that she questioned everything.

She decided immediately that she was going to distance herself from him. Tonight would be the night she would discuss it with him once and for all. They were like chalk and cheese; her life was full of conflict and, as far as she could see, Ivan ran so far so fast just to avoid it. As the seconds ticked on and it moved into his fifty-first minute of being late it looked as if she didn't need to have the conversation with him after all. She sat on the stair in her new cream casual trousers and shirt, colours she would never had worn before, and she felt foolish. Foolish for listening to him, believing him, for not reading the signs properly and, even worse, for falling for him.

Her anger was hiding her pain but the last thing she wanted to do was to stay home alone and allow it to surface. She was good at doing that.

She picked up the phone and dialled.

'Benjamin, it's Elizabeth,' she said rather quickly,

speaking before she had a chance to backtrack. 'How would you like to get that sushi tonight?'

'Where are we?' Ivan asked, strolling down a darkly lit cobbled street in inner city Dublin. Puddles gathered in the uneven surfaces of an area that consisted mainly of warehouses and industrial estates. One red-brick house stood alone between them all.

'That house looks funny there, sitting all on its own,' Ivan remarked. 'A bit lonely and out of place,' he decided.

'That's where we're going,' Opal said. 'The owner of this house refused to sell his property to the surrounding businesses. He stayed here while they sprung up around him.'

Ivan eyed the small house. 'I bet they offered him a fair bit. He could probably have bought a mansion in the Hollywood Hills with what they would have paid him.' He looked down at the ground as his red Converse runner splashed into a puddle, 'I've decided cobblestones are my favourite.'

Opal smiled and laughed lightly. 'Oh, Ivan, you are so easy to love, you know that?' She walked on, not expecting an answer. Just as well, because Ivan wasn't sure.

'What are we doing?' he asked for the tenth time since they had left the office. They stood directly across the road from the house and Ivan watched Opal viewing it.

'Waiting,' Opal replied calmly. 'What time is it?'

Ivan checked his watch. 'Elizabeth will be so mad at me,' he sighed. 'It's just gone seven.'

Right on cue, the front door to the red-brick house opened. An old man leaned against the doorway, which appeared to act as a crutch. He stared outside and looked so far into the distance he appeared to be seeing the past.

'Come with me,' Opal said to Ivan, and she crossed the road and entered the house.

'Opal,' Ivan hissed, 'I can't just enter a stranger's house.' But Opal had already disappeared inside.

Ivan quickly skipped across the road and paused at the doorway, 'Em, hello, I'm Ivan.' He held out his hand.

The old man's hands remained clinging to the doorway; his watery eyes stared straight ahead.

'Right,' Ivan said awkwardly, moving his hand away. 'I'll just slide past you so, to Opal.' The man didn't blink and Ivan stepped inside. The house smelled old. It smelled as if an old person lived there with old furniture, a wireless and a grandfather clock. The clock's ticking was the loudest thing in the silent building. Time sounded and smelled to be the essence of the house, a long life lived listening to those ticks.

Ivan found Opal in the living room, looking around at all the framed photographs cluttering every surface of the room.

'This is almost as bad as your office,' he teased. 'Come on then, tell me what's going on.'

Opal turned to him and she smiled sadly. 'I told you earlier that I understand how you feel.'

'Yes.'

'I told you I knew how it felt to fall in love.'

Ivan nodded.

Opal sighed and clasped her hands together once again, almost like she was bracing herself for the news. 'Well, this is the home of the man I fell in love with.'

'Oh,' Ivan said softly.

'I still come here every day,' she explained, looking around the room.

'The old man doesn't mind us just barging in like this?'

Opal gave a small smile. 'He is the man I fell in love with, Ivan.'

Ivan's mouth dropped open. The front door closed. Footsteps slowly made their way towards them over creaking floorboards. 'No way!' Ivan hissed. 'The old man? But he's ancient – he must be at least eighty!' he whispered in shock.

The old man wandered into the room. A hacking cough stopped him in his tracks and his small frame shuddered. He winced from the pain and slowly, leaning his hands on the arms of the chair, he lowered himself into the seat.

Ivan looked from the old man to Opal and back, with a disgusted look that he tried unsuccessfully to hide from his face.

'He can't hear you or see you. We are invisible to him,' Opal said loudly. Her next sentence changed Ivan's life for good. Nineteen simple words he heard her say everyday but never in that order. She cleared her throat and there was a slight tremor in her voice as she said against the ticking of the clock, 'Remember, Ivan, forty years ago when he and I met, he wasn't ancient. He was as I am now.'

Opal watched as Ivan's face displayed many different emotions in a matter of seconds. He went from confusion, to shock, to disbelief, to pity, and then as soon as he had applied Opal's words to his own situation, to despair. His face crumpled, he paled and Opal rushed towards him to steady his swaying body. He held on to her tightly.

'That's what I was trying to tell you, Ivan,' she whispered. 'You and Elizabeth can live together perfectly happy in your own cocoon without anyone knowing but what you forget is that she will have a birthday every year and you won't.'

Ivan's body began to shake and Opal held on to him tighter. 'Oh, Ivan, I'm sorry,' she said, 'I'm so, so sorry.'

She rocked him as he cried. And cried.

'I met him in very similar circumstances to how you met Elizabeth,' Opal explained later that evening after his tears had subsided.

They both sat in armchairs in the living room of Opal's love, Geoffrey. He continued to sit in his

314

chair by the window in silence, looking around the room and occasionally breaking into horrendous coughs that made Opal rush to his side protectively.

She twisted a tissue around in her hands, her eyes and cheeks were wet as she told her story and her dreadlocks fell around her face.

'I made every single mistake that you made,' she sniffed, and forced herself to smile, 'and I even made the one you were about to make tonight.'

Ivan swallowed hard.

'He was forty when I met him, Ivan, and we stayed together for twenty years until it became too difficult.'

Ivan's eyes widened and hope returned to his heart.

'No, Ivan,' Opal shook her head sadly and it was the weakness in her voice that convinced him. Had she spoken firmly he would have retaliated in the same manner but her voice displayed her pain. 'It couldn't work for you.' She didn't need to say any more.

'He seems to have travelled a lot,' Ivan remarked, looking around at the photos. Geoffrey in front of the Eiffel Tower, Geoffrey in front of the Leaning Tower of Pisa, Geoffrey lying on the golden sand on the shores of a faraway country, smiling and looking the picture of health, happiness at varying ages in every photo. 'At least he could move on in some way and manage to do those things alone,' he smiled encouragingly.

Opal looked at him in confusion. 'But I was there with him, Ivan.' Her forehead wrinkled.

'Oh, that's nice.' He was surprised. 'Did you take the photos?'

'No.' Her face fell. 'I'm in the photographs too, can't you see me?'

Ivan shook his head slowly.

'Oh . . .' She said studying them and seeing a different picture from Ivan.

'Why can't he see you any more?' Ivan asked, watching Geoffrey take a handful of prescribed pills and wash them down with water.

'Because I'm not who I once was, which is probably why you can't see me in the photographs. He's looking out for a different person; the connection we once had is gone,' she replied.

Geoffrey stood up from his chair, this time grabbing his cane, and made his way to the front door. He opened it and stood at the doorway.

'Come on, time to go,' Opal said, standing up from her chair and moving out to the hallway.

Ivan looked at her quizzically

'When we first started seeing each other I visited him from seven to nine every evening,' she explained, 'and seeing as I can't open doors, he used to be there waiting for me. He's been doing this every evening since we met. That's why he wouldn't sell the house. He thinks it's the only way I'll find him.'

Ivan watched his old frame wobbling on his feet as he stared out once again into the distance, perhaps thinking of that day when they had frolicked on the beach or the visit to the Eiffel Tower. Ivan didn't want that to be Elizabeth.

'Goodbye, my Opal,' his gravelly voice spoke quietly.

'Good night, my love.' Opal kissed him on the cheek and he closed his eyes softly. 'I'll see you tomorrow.'

Chapter 32

So it was clear in my mind. I knew what I had to do next. I needed to do what I was sent here to do – make Elizabeth's life as comfortable for her as possible. But now I had got so involved with her I would have to help heal old wounds *and* the new wounds that I'd foolishly caused. I was angry at myself for making a mess of everything, for getting caught up and taking my eye off the ball. My anger was overpowering the pain I felt and I was glad because, in order for me to help Elizabeth, I needed to ignore my own feelings and do what was best for her. Which was what I should have done from the start. But that's the thing about lessons: you always learn them when you don't expect them or want them. I'd have plenty of time in my life to deal with the pain of losing her.

I'd walked all night, thinking about the past few weeks and about my life. I'd never done that before – thought about *my* life. It never seemed relevant to my aim but it should always have been. I found myself back at Fuchsia Lane the next morning, sitting on the garden wall where I had first met Luke over a month ago. The fuchsia door still smiled at me and I waved back. At least that wasn't angry at me; I knew Elizabeth sure would be. She doesn't like people being late for business meetings, never mind dinner dates. I'd stood her up. Not intentionally. Not out of any malice but out of love. Imagine not meeting someone because you loved them so much. Imagine hurting someone, making them feel lonely, angry and unloved because you think it's the *best* for them. All these new rules – they were making me doubt my abilities as a best friend. They were beyond me, laws that I wasn't comfortable with at all. How could I teach Elizabeth about hope, happiness, laughter and love when I didn't know if I believed in any of those things any more? Oh, I knew they were possible, alright, but with possibility comes impossibility. A new word in my vocabulary.

At 6.00 a.m., the fuchsia door opened and I stood to attention as though a teacher had entered the classroom. Elizabeth stepped out, closed the door behind her, locked it and walked down the cobblestoned drive. She was wearing her chocolate-brown tracksuit again, her only informal outfit in her wardrobe. Her hair was tied back messily, she had no make-up on and I don't think I'd ever seen her look so beautiful in my life. A hand reached into my heart and twisted it momentarily. It hurt.

She looked up and saw me and stalled. Her face didn't break into a smile like it usually did. The hand around my heart squeezed tighter. But at least she saw me and that was the main thing. Don't ever take for granted when people look in your eyes – you've no idea how lucky you are. Actually, forget about luck, you've no idea how *important* it is to be acknowledged, even if it is with an angry glare. It's when they ignore you, when they look right through you, that you should start worrying. Elizabeth usually ignores her problems; she usually looks right past them and never in the eye. But I was obviously a problem worth solving.

She walked towards me with her arms folded across her chest, her head held high, her eyes tired but determined.

'Are you alright, Ivan?'

Her question threw me. I expected her to be angry, to shout at me and not listen or believe my side of the story, like they do in the movies, but she didn't. She was calm, but with a temper bubbling beneath the surface, ready to erupt depending on my answer. She studied my face, searching for answers she would never believe.

I don't think I've ever been asked that question before. I was thinking about that as she was studying my face. No, it was as clear as day to me that I did not feel alright. I felt brittle, tired, angry, hungry, and there was a pain – not a hunger pain, but an ache that started in my chest and worked its way through my body and head. I felt that my views and philosophies had been changed overnight. The philosophies that I had gladly carved in stone, recited and danced upon. I felt as though the magician of life had cruelly revealed his hidden cards and it wasn't magic at all, just a mere trick of the mind. Or a lie.

'Ivan?' She looked concerned. Her face softened, her arms dropped from their folded position and she stepped forward and reached out to touch me.

I couldn't answer.

'Come on, walk with me.' She linked arms with me and we walked out of Fuchsia Lane.

They walked in silence deep into the heart of the countryside. The birds sang loudly in the early morning, the crisp air filled their lungs, rabbits bounded daringly across their path and butterflies danced through the air, waving through them as they strode along the woodlands. The sun shone down through the leaves of the dominant oaks, sprinkling light on their faces like gold dust. The sound of water trickled alongside them while the scent of eucalyptus refreshed the air. Eventually they reached an opening, where the trees held their branches out, making a grand and proud presentation of the lake. They crossed a wooden bridge, sat on a hard, carved bench and sat in silence, watching as the salmon jumped to the surface of the water to catch the flies in the warming sun.

Elizabeth was the first to speak. 'Ivan, in a complicated life, I try my best to make things as simple

321

as possible. I know what to expect, I know what I'm going to do, where I'm going, who I'm going to meet *every single day*. In a life that is surrounded by complicated, unpredictable people, I need *stability*.' She looked away from the lake and met Ivan's eyes for the first time since they'd sat down. 'You,' she took a breath, 'you take the simplicity out of my life. You shake things around and turn them upside down. And sometimes I like it, Ivan. You make me laugh, you make me dance around streets and beaches like a lunatic and make me feel like someone I'm not.' Her smile faded. 'But last night you made me feel like someone I don't want to be. I *need* things to be simple, Ivan,' she repeated.

There was a silence between them.

Eventually Ivan spoke. 'I'm very sorry about last night, Elizabeth. You know me: it wasn't done out of any malice.' He stopped to try and figure out if and how he should explain the events of last night. He decided against it for now. 'You know, the more you try to simplify things, Elizabeth, the more you complicate them. You create rules, build walls, push people away, lie to yourself, and ignore true feelings. That is not simplifying things.'

Elizabeth ran a hand through her hair. 'I have a sister who is missing, a six-year-old nephew to mother, whom I know nothing about, a father that has not moved away from a window for weeks because he is waiting for his wife, who disap-

322

peared over twenty years ago, to return. I realised last night that I was just like him as I sat on the stairs staring out the window, waiting for a man with no surname who tells me he's from a place called Ekam Eveileb, a place that has been Googled, and searched in the damn atlas at least once a day and that I now know doesn't exist.' She took a breath. 'I care for you, Ivan, I really do, but one minute you're kissing me and the next you're standing me up. I don't know what is going on with us. I have enough worries and I have enough pain as it is and I am not volunteering myself for any more.' She rubbed her eyes tiredly.

They both watched the activities in the lake as the leaping salmon brought ripples to the surface, making soothing splashing sounds in the water. Across the lake a heron moved silently and skilfully on his stilt-like legs along the water's edge. He was a fisherman at work, watching and waiting patiently for the right moment to break the glassy surface of the water with his beak.

Ivan couldn't help but see the similarities in both their jobs at that moment.

When you drop a glass or a plate to the ground it makes a loud crashing sound. When a window shatters, a table leg breaks, or when a picture falls off the wall it makes a noise. But as for your heart, when that breaks, it's completely silent. You would think as it's so important it would make the loudest noise in the whole world, or even have some sort

323

some sort of ceremonious sound like the gong of a cymbal or the ringing of a bell. But it's silent and you almost wish there was a noise to distract you from the pain.

If there is a noise, it's internal. It screams and no one can hear it but you. It screams so loud your ears ring and your head aches. It thrashes around in your chest like a great white shark caught in the sea; it roars like a mother bear whose cub has been taken. That's what it looks like and that's what it sounds like, a thrashing, panicking, trapped great big beast, roaring like a prisoner to its own emotions. But that's the thing about love – no one is untouchable. It's as wild as that, as raw as an open flesh wound exposed to salty sea water, but when it actually breaks, it's silent. You're just screaming on the inside and no one can hear it.

But Elizabeth, she saw the heartbreak in me and I saw it in her, and without having to talk about it we both knew. It was time to stop walking with our heads in the clouds, and instead, keep our feet on the harder soil of ground level we should always have been rooted to.

Chapter 33

'We should get back to the house now,' Elizabeth said, jumping up from the bench.

'Why?'

'Because it's starting to rain.' She looked at him as though he had ten heads, and flinched as another droplet of rain landed on her face.

'What is it with you?' Ivan laughed, settling down into the bench as a sign he wasn't budging. 'Why is it you're always dashing in and out of cars and buildings when it rains?'

'Because I don't want to get wet. Come on!' She looked to the safety of the trees longingly.

'Why don't you like getting wet? All it does is dries.'

'Because.' She grabbed him by the hand and attempted to pull him off the bench. She stamped her foot in frustration when she couldn't move him, like a child who couldn't get her way.

'Because why?'

'I don't know.' She swallowed hard. 'I've just never liked rain. Do you have to know all the reasons for all my little problems?' She held her hands over her head to stop the feeling of the rain falling on her.

'There's a reason for everything, Elizabeth,' he said, holding out his hands and catching the raindrops in his palms.

'Well, my reason is simple. In keeping with our earlier conversation, rain complicates things. It makes your clothes wet, is uncomfortable and ultimately gives you a cold.'

Ivan made a game-show noise signalling a wrong answer. 'The rain doesn't give you a cold. The *cold* gives you a cold. This is a sun shower and it's warm.' He held back his head, opened his mouth and allowed the raindrops to fall in. 'Yep, warm and tasty. And you weren't telling me the truth, by the way.'

'What?' she shrilled.

'I read between the lines, hear between the words and know when a full stop is not a full stop but more like a but,' he sang.

Elizabeth groaned and stood with her arms wrapped round herself protectively and with her shoulders hunched as though gunge were being thrown over her.

'It's only rain, Elizabeth. Look around.' He waved his hands wildly. 'Do you see anybody else here running?'

'There *is* nobody else!'

'*Au contraire!* The lake, the trees, the heron and the salmon, all getting soaked.' He threw

326

his head back and continued tasting the rain.

Before Elizabeth headed to the trees she gave one last lecture. 'Be careful of that rain, Ivan. It's not a good idea to drink it.'

'Why?'

'Because it could be dangerous. Do you know what effect carbon monoxide has on the air and the rain? It could be acidic.'

Ivan slid off the bench while holding his throat and pretended to choke. He crawled to the edge of the lake. Elizabeth's eyes followed him but she continued lecturing him.

He dipped his hand into the lake. 'Well, there's no fatal contaminations in this, is there?' He scooped out a handful of water and threw it at her.

Her mouth fell open and her eyes widened with shock as she stood there with water dripping from her nose. She held her arm out and pushed him roughly into the lake, laughing as he disappeared under the water.

She stopped laughing when he didn't reappear.

She began to get worried and stepped towards the edge. The only movement were the ripples caused by the heavy raindrops landing on the calm lake. The cold drops on her face no longer bothered her. A minute went by.

'Ivan?' Her voice was shaky. 'Ivan, stop playing. Come out now.' She leaned over further to see if she could see him.

She sang nervously to herself and counted to

ten. Nobody could hold their breath for that long.

The glassy surface broke and a rocket shot out of the water. 'Water fight!' exploded from the water creature. It grabbed her by the hands and pulled her head-first into the lake. Elizabeth was so relieved not to have killed him she didn't even mind when the cool water hit her face and buried her.

'Good morning, Mr O'Callaghan; morning, Maureen; hello, Fidelma; hi, Connor; Father Murphy . . .' She nodded sternly to her neighbours as she walked through the sleepy town. Silent, stunned stares followed her as her runners squelched beneath her and her clothes dripped.

'That's a good look for you,' Benjamin laughed, holding up a cup of coffee to her while he stood beside a small crowd of tourists, who were dancing, laughing and sprinkling coffee on the pavement outside Joe's.

'Thank you, Benjamin,' she answered seriously, continuing on through the town, her eyes sparkling.

The sun shone over the town, which hadn't yet received any rain that morning, and its inhabitants watched, whispered and laughed as Elizabeth Egan walked with her head held high and her arms swinging by her side as a piece of seaweed clung to her tangled hair.

Elizabeth threw another colouring pencil down; crumpled up the sheet she had been working on

328

and tossed it across the room. It missed the bin but she didn't care. It could stay there with the other ten crumpled balls. She made a face at her calendar. A red X, which had originally signalled the end date for Ivan, Luke's invisible friend, who had long since gone, now signalled the end of her career. Well, she was being melodramatic – September was the opening date for the hotel and everything was going according to plan. All the materials had arrived on time with only the minor disasters of a few wrong orders. Mrs Bracken had her team working long hours, making cushions, curtains and duvet covers, but unusually, it was Elizabeth who was slowing things down. She just couldn't find a design for the children's playroom and was beginning to detest herself for even men-tioning the idea to Vincent. She was too distracted lately.

She sat at her favourite place at the kitchen table and laughed to herself at the memory of her earlier 'swim'.

Things between her and Ivan were more unusual than ever. Today she had effectively ended their relationship and it broke her heart to do it, yet here he was, still with her in her home, making her laugh as though nothing had happened. But something had happened, something huge, and she could feel the effect of it right under her chest. As the day wore on she realised that she had never backtracked so much in a relationship with a man and yet still felt satisfied to be in his company.

Neither of them was ready for more, not yet anyway, but she wished so much that he was.

Dinner with Benjamin the previous night had been pleasant. She had battled with her dislike of going out to eat, her dislike of food and her dislike of unnecessary conversations, and while she managed to put up with those things with Ivan, sometimes even enjoy them, she still found it a task. Socialising wasn't enjoyable for her, however they had much in common. They had a nice chat and a nice meal, but Elizabeth wasn't upset when it was all over and time to go home. Her mind was hugely distracted, wondering about her future with Ivan. Not like when Ivan left her.

Luke's giggles brought her out of her daydream.

Ivan spoke. '*Bonjour, madame.*'

Elizabeth looked up to see both Ivan and Luke entering the conservatory from the garden. Each had a magnifying glass held up to his right eye, causing their eyes to appear gigantic. Across each of their upper lips a moustache had been drawn in black marker. She couldn't help but laugh.

'Ah, but zis is no laffing matter, madame. Zere 'az been a mur-dare,' Ivan said gravely, approaching the table.

'A murder,' Luke translated.

'What?' Elizabeth's eyes widened.

'We're looking for clues, madame,' Luke explained, his uneven moustache wobbling up and down as he spoke.

'A ghastly mur-dare 'az taken place in your

jardin,' Ivan explained, running the magnifying glass along the surface of the kitchen table in search for clues.

'That's French for garden,' Luke explained.

Elizabeth nodded, trying not to laugh.

'Forgive us for just barging into your 'ome. Allow us to introduce ourselves. I am Mister Monsieur and zis iz my foolish sidekick, Monsieur Rotalsnart.'

Luke giggled. 'It's backwards for translator.'

'Oh,' Elizabeth nodded. 'Well, it's very nice to meet you both but I'm afraid I'm very busy here, so if you don't mind . . .' She widened her eyes at Ivan.

'Mind? Of course we mind. We are in ze middle of a very serious mur-dare investigay-c-on and you are what?' He looked around, his eyes fell upon the crumpled balls of paper by the bin. He picked one up and studied it with his magnifying glass. 'You are making snowballs, as far as I can see.'

Elizabeth made a face at him and Luke giggled.

'We must interrogate you. Have you any harsh lights we can shine in your face?' Ivan looked around the room and withdrew the question on glancing at Elizabeth's face. 'Very well, madame.'

'Who has been murdered?' Elizabeth asked.

'Ah, just as I suspected, Monsieur Rotalsnart.' They paced the floor in opposite directions with the magnifying glasses still over their eyes. 'She pretends to not know so we don't suspect her. Clever.'

331

'Do you think she did it?' Luke asked.

'We shall see. Madame, a worm was found squished to death earlier today on the path leading from your conservatory to the clothes line. His devastated family tell us he left home when the rain had stopped in order to cross the path to the other side of the garden. His reasons for wanting to go there are not known but it's what worms do.'

Luke and Elizabeth looked at one another and laughed.

'The rain stopped at 6.30 p.m., which is when the worm left his home to cross the path. Could you tell me your whereabouts, madame?'

'Am I a suspect?' Elizabeth laughed.

'At zis stage of the investigay-c-on, everyone is a suspect.'

'Well, I returned from work at 6.15 and put the dinner on. Then I went to the utility room and emptied the damp clothes from the washing machine into the basket.'

'Then what did you do?' Ivan thrust the magnifying glass in her face and moved it around, studying her. 'I am checking for clues,' he whispered to Luke.

'After that I waited for the rain to stop and then I hung the washing on the line.'

Ivan gasped dramatically. 'Monsieur Rotalsnart, did you hear that?'

Luke's giggling revealed his gums, from where yet another tooth had fallen.

'Well then, this means you are the mur-dare-air!'

'The murderer,' Luke translated.

They both turned to her with their magnifying glasses over their eyes.

Ivan spoke. 'As you tried to keep your birthday of next week a secret from me, your punishment will be to have a party in the back *jardin* in the memory of the recently deceased Monsieur Wriggles, the worm.'

Elizabeth groaned. 'No way.'

'I know, Elizabeth,' he changed to an upper-class British accent, 'having to socialise with the village folk is so terribly frightful.'

'What folk?' Elizabeth's eyes narrowed.

'Oh, just a few people we invited,' Ivan shrugged. 'Luke posted the invites this morning, isn't he great?' He nodded to a proud and beaming Luke. 'Next week you will be the host of a garden party. People you don't know very well will be stomping through your home, possibly making it dirty. Think you can handle that?'

Chapter 34

Elizabeth sat cross-legged on the white sheet covering the dusty cement floor of the building site, with her eyes closed.

'So this is where you disappear to every day.'

Elizabeth's eyes remained closed. 'How do you do it, Ivan?'

'Do what?'

'Just appear out of nowhere exactly when I'm thinking of you?'

She heard him laugh lightly but he didn't answer the question. 'Why is this room the only room that hasn't been finished? Or started, by the looks of it.' He stood behind her.

'Because I need help. I'm stuck.'

'Well, what do you know, Elizabeth Egan is asking for help.' There was a silence until Ivan started humming a familiar song, the song she hadn't been able to get out of her head for the past two months and the song that was making her almost broke, thanks to Poppy and Becca's pig in the office.

Her eyelids flew open. 'What are you humming?'

'The humming song.'

'Did Luke teach you that?'

'No, *I* taught *him*, thank you very much.'

'Oh, really,' Elizabeth grumbled. 'I thought his *invisible* friend made it up.' She laughed to herself and then looked up to him. He wasn't laughing.

Eventually he spoke. 'Why do you sound like you're speaking with socks in your mouth? What is that on your face? A muzzle?' he chortled.

Elizabeth flushed. 'It's not a muzzle,' she spat. 'You have no idea how much dust and bacteria this building has. Anyway, you should be wearing a hard hat,' she knocked on her own. 'God forbid this place should come down on us.'

'What else are you wearing?' He ignored her moodiness and looked her up and down. 'Gloves?'

'So my hands don't get dirty,' she pouted like a child.

'Oh, Elizabeth,' Ivan shook his head and strolled comically around her, 'all the things I've taught you and you're still worrying about being clean and tidy.' He picked up a paintbrush, which was sitting beside an open pot of paint and dipped it in.

'Ivan,' Elizabeth said nervously watching him, 'what are you going to do?'

'You said you wanted help,' he grinned.

Elizabeth rose slowly to her feet. 'Ye-es, help with painting the *wall*,' her voice warned.

'Well, unfortunately you didn't quite specify that

335

when you asked, so I'm afraid that doesn't count.' He dipped the paintbrush into the red paint, held the bristles back in his hand and released them towards Elizabeth like a catapult. Paint splattered across her face. 'Ooh, too bad you weren't wearing protective clothing on the rest of your face,' he teased, watching her eyes widen in anger and shock. 'But it just goes to show, no matter how hard you try to wrap yourself in cotton wool, you can still hurt yourself.'

'Ivan,' there was venom in her voice, 'throwing me in the lake is *one* thing but this is *ludicrous*,' she squealed. 'This is my *work*. I'm serious, I want absolutely *nothing* more to do with you, Ivan, Ivan . . . I don't even know your surname,' she spluttered.

'It's Elbisivni,' he explained calmly.

'What are you, *Russian*?' she shouted almost hyperventilating. 'Is Ekam Eveileb Russian too or does it even *exist*?' She was screaming now, and breathless.

'I'm very sorry,' Ivan said seriously, his smile disappearing. 'I can sense that you're upset. I'll just put this back down.' He slowly lowered the paintbrush back to the pot and left it back at the perfect angle it had been placed, mirroring the others. 'That was over the top. I apologise.'

Elizabeth's anger began to subside.

'The red is perhaps too much of an angry colour for you,' he continued. 'I should have been more subtle.' Suddenly another paintbrush appeared before Elizabeth's face. Her eyes widened.

336

'White maybe?' he grinned, and splashed the paint down her top.

'Ivan!' Elizabeth half laughed and half shouted. 'Fine,' she dived towards the pots of paint, 'you wanna play? I can play. Wearing colours is your favourite thing to do now, you say?' she grumbled to herself. She dipped a paintbrush in the pot and chased Ivan round the room. 'Blue's your favourite colour, Mr Elbisivni?' She painted a strip of blue down his face and hair, and began laughing evilly.

'You thought that was funny?'

She nodded in hysterics.

'Good,' Ivan laughed, grabbing her by the waist and pushing her to the floor, pinning her down masterfully and painting her face while she squealed and struggled to get free. 'If you don't stop shouting, Elizabeth, you'll have a green tongue,' Ivan warned.

After they had both been covered head to toe in paint and Elizabeth was laughing so much she could no longer put up a fight, Ivan turned his attention to the wall. 'What this wall needs now is some paint.'

Elizabeth removed her mouth cover and tried to regain her breathing, revealing the only normal skin colour on her face.

'Well, at least that came in handy,' Ivan noted, and turned back to face the wall. 'A little birdie told me that you went on a date with Benjamin West,' Ivan said, dipping a fresh brush into the red paint pot.

'Dinner, yes. A date, no. And may I add that I went out with him the night you stood me up.'

He didn't reply. 'You like him?' he asked.

'He's a nice man.' She still didn't turn round.

'You want to spend more time with him?'

Elizabeth began to roll up the paint-splattered sheet from the floor. 'I'd like to spend more time with you.'

'What if you couldn't?'

Elizabeth froze. 'Then I'd ask you why.'

He avoided the question. 'What if I didn't exist and you'd never met me, would you want to spend more time with Benjamin then?'

Elizabeth swallowed hard, put her paper and pens into her bag and zipped it shut. She was tired of playing games with him and his talk was making her nervous. They needed to discuss this properly. She stood up and faced him. On the wall, Ivan had written 'Elizabeth ♥s Benjamin' in big red letters.

'Ivan!' Elizabeth giggled nervously. 'Don't be such a child. What if someone was to see that!' She went to grab the brush from him.

He wouldn't let go and their eyes locked. 'I can't give you what you want, Elizabeth,' he said softly.

A coughing from the doorway caused them both to jump.

'Hi, Elizabeth,' Benjamin looked at her with curious amusement. He glanced at the wall behind her and grinned. 'That's an interesting theme.'

There was a pregnant pause. Elizabeth looked to her right. 'It was Ivan.' Her voice came out childlike.

Benjamin chuckled slightly. 'Him again.'

She nodded and he looked to the paintbrush in her hand, dripping red onto her jeans. A red, blue, purple, green and white splashed face now turned crimson.

'Looks like it's *you* who's been caught painting the roses red,' Benjamin said, and went to take a step into the room.

'Benjamin!'

He paused mid-step, with a pained expression at the sound of Vincent's demanding voice. 'I'd better go,' he smiled. 'I'll talk to you later,' and he headed off in the direction of Vincent's shouts. 'Oh, by the way,' he called out, 'thanks for the party invitation.'

A fuming Elizabeth ignored Ivan, doubled over laughing and occasional snorting. She dipped her brush in the white pot and erased Ivan's words, trying to erase this embarrassing moment from her memory.

'Good afternoon, Mr O'Callaghan; hello, Maureen; hello, Fidelma; hi, Connor, Father Murphy,' she greeted her neighbours as she walked through the town to get to her office. Red paint dribbled down her arms, blue paint clung in strands around her hair and her jeans looked like Monet's palette. Silent, stunned stares followed her as her clothes continued to drip with paint, leaving a multi-coloured trail behind her.

'Why do you always do that?' Ivan asked, running alongside her to keep up as she marched through the town.

'Do what? Good afternoon, Sheila.'

'You always cross the road before you get to Flanagan's pub, walk on the opposite path and then cross again once you get to Joe's.'

'No I don't.' She smiled at another gawker.

'Talk about painting the town red, Elizabeth,' Joe called out to her, laughing as she left red footprints behind her as she ran across the road.

'Look, you just did it!' Ivan pointed out.

Elizabeth stopped and looked back on her track, visible by her footprints. True enough, she had crossed the road at Flanagan's, walked on the opposite path and crossed over once again to get to her office, instead of staying on the same path. She hadn't noticed that before. She looked back at Flanagan's pub. Mr Flanagan stood at the door having a cigarette. He nodded at her strangely, appearing surprised she held his stare. She frowned and swallowed the lump that had formed in her throat as she stared at the building.

'Everything OK, Elizabeth?' Ivan asked, cutting into her thoughts.

'Yes.' Her voice came out as a whisper. She cleared her throat, looked at Ivan in confusion and unconvincingly repeated, 'Yes, I'm fine.'

Chapter 35

Elizabeth passed a gobsmacked and disapproving Mrs Bracken, who was standing at the door with two other elderly women, all with pieces of fabric in their hands. They tutted as she trudged by, with paint in clumps in the ends of her hair, which was rubbing against her back and causing a beautiful multicoloured effect.

'Is she losing her marbles or what?' one of the women whispered loudly.

'No, quite the opposite.' Elizabeth could hear the smile in Mrs Bracken's voice. 'I'd say she's been on her hands and knees looking for them.'

The other women tutted and wandered away, muttering about Elizabeth not being the only one losing her marbles.

Elizabeth ignored the stare from Becca and the shout from Poppy, 'That's more like it!' and marched into her office, closing the door softly behind her. Shutting everything out. She leaned her back against the door and tried to figure out why her body was shaking so much. What had been stirred inside her? What monsters had awoken from their slumber and were bubbling away under her skin? She breathed in deeply through her nostrils and exhaled slowly, counting one, two, three times until her weak knees stopped trembling.

Everything had been fine, if not mildly embarrassing, as she walked through the town looking like she had dipped herself in a pot of rainbow-coloured paint. It had all been fine until Ivan said something. What did he say . . . ? He said . . . and then she remembered and a chill ran through her body.

Flanagan's pub. She always avoided Flanagan's pub, he said. She hadn't noticed until he brought it to her attention. Why did she do it? Because of Saoirse? No, Saoirse drank in the Camel's Hump, on the hill, down the road. She remained leaning against the door, thinking until her head was dizzy. The room spun her and she decided she needed to get home. Home to where she could control what went on, who could enter, who could leave, where things had their own place and where every memory was clear. She needed order.

'Where's your beanbag, Ivan?' Calendula asked, looking up at me from her yellow-painted wooden chair.

'Oh, I got tired of that,' I replied. 'Spinning is my new favourite thing now.'

'Nice,' she nodded with approval.

'Opal's really late,' Tommy said, wiping his runny nose along his arm.

Calendula looked away in disgust, straightened her pretty yellow dress, crossed her ankles and swung her white patent shoes and frilly socks while she hummed the humming song.

Olivia knitted in her rocking chair. 'She'll be here,' she rasped.

Jamie-Lynn reached out to the centre table to grab a chocolate Rice Krispie bun and a glass of milk, and as she coughed and spluttered, her glass of milk spilled all over her arm. She licked it off.

'Have you been playing in the doctor's waiting room again, Jamie-Lynn?' Olivia asked, glaring at her over the rim of her glasses.

Jamie-Lynn nodded, coughed again on her bun and took another bite.

Calendula wrinkled her nose in disgust and continued combing her Barbie's hair with a small comb.

'You know what Opal told you, Jamie-Lynn. Those places are full of bacteria. Those toys you like to play with are the cause of you being ill.'

'I know,' Jamie-Lynn said with food in her mouth, 'but someone's got to keep the kids company when they're waiting for the doc.'

Twenty minutes passed and eventually Opal showed. Everyone looked at each other with worry. It looked as though Opal's shadow had taken her place. She didn't float into the room like a fresh morning breeze as she usually did; it was as though every step she took she was laden down with heavy buckets of cement. The others all quietened down immediately, seeing the deep blue, almost black, colour that followed her in.

'Good afternoon, my friends.' Even Opal's voice was different, as though she was being muffled and held back in another dimension.

'Hello, Opal.' The replies were soft and hushed, as though more than a whisper would knock her to rubble.

She gave them a gentle smile, acknowledgeing their support. 'Somebody who has been a friend of mine for a great deal of time is sick. Very sick. He's going to die and I'm very sad to lose him,' she explained.

Everyone made soothing noises. Olivia stopped rocking in her chair, Bobby stopped rolling back and forth on his skateboard, Calendula's legs stopped kicking, Tommy even stopped sniffing the snot back up his nose and I stopped swinging on my chair. This was serious stuff, and the group talked about what it's like to lose people they love. Everyone understood. It happened to best friends all the time and each time it happened, the sadness was never less.

I couldn't contribute to the conversation. Every emotion I have ever felt for Elizabeth gathered and swelled in my throat like a pumping heart receiving more and more love every moment and growing bigger and prouder as a result. The lump in my throat prevented me from speaking just as my growing heart prevented me from stopping loving Elizabeth.

As the meeting was ending, Opal looked to me. 'Ivan, how are things with Elizabeth?'

Everyone looked at me and I found a tiny hole in that lump for my sound to seep through. 'I've left her until tomorrow to figure something out.' I thought of her face and my heart pumped quicker and grew, and that tiny hole in the lump in my throat closed.

And without anyone knowing my situation, they all understood it to mean 'not long now'. By the way Opal quickly picked up her files and fled the adjourned meeting, I figured it was the same case for her.

Elizabeth's feet pounded on the treadmill that faced the back garden in her home. She looked out at the hills, the lakes and mountains spread before her and ran even faster. Her hair blew behind her as she ran, her brow glistened, her arms moved with her legs and she imagined as she did every day that she was running over those hills, across the seas, far, far away. After thirty minutes of running and running yet staying in the same place she stopped, left the small gym panting and weak, and immediately began to clean, scrubbing furiously on surfaces that already sparkled.

As soon as she had cleaned the house from top to bottom, had wiped away all the cobwebs, cleared every darkened hidden corner, she began to do the same with her mind. All her life she had run from shedding light on those darkened corners of her mind. The cobwebs and dust had settled and now she was ready to start clearing them. Something was trying to crawl out of that darkness and now she was ready to help it. Enough running.

She sat at the kitchen table and stared out at the country spread before her, tumbling hills, valleys and lakes with fuchsia and montbretia lacing them all. The sky was darkening earlier now that August had arrived.

She thought long and hard about nothing and everything, allowing whatever was niggling her mind to have a chance to step out of the shadows and show itself. It was the same niggling feeling she ran from while she lay in bed trying to sleep, the feeling she fought while furiously cleaning. But now she sat at the table a surrendered woman, with her hands held high, stepping away from her weapon and allowing her thoughts to hold her under arrest. She had been like an escaped criminal on the run for so long.

'Why are you sitting in the dark?' a sweet voice called out to her.

She smiled lightly. 'I'm just thinking, Luke.'

'Can I sit with you?' he asked, and she hated herself for wanting to say no. 'I won't say anything or touch anything, I promise,' he added.

That twisted her heart – was she really that bad? Yes, she knew she was.

'Come over and sit down,' she smiled, pulling out the chair beside her.

They both sat in the darkened kitchen in silence

until Elizabeth spoke. 'Luke, there are some things that I should talk to you about. Things I should have spoken to you before but . . .' She twisted her fingers, trying very carefully to decide how to word what she was saying. When she was a child, all she wanted was for people to explain what had happened, where her mother had gone and why. A simple explanation would have helped years and years of tortuous wondering.

He looked at her with big blue eyes from under long lashes, chubby cheeks that were rosy and a glistening upper lip from a runny nose. She laughed and ran a hand through his snow-white hair and left it resting on the back of his hot little neck.

'But,' she continued, 'I didn't know how to say them to you.'

'Is it about my mom?' Luke asked, his legs swinging below the glass table.

'Yes. She hasn't visited us in a while, as you've probably noticed.'

'She's gone on an adventure,' Luke said happily.

'Well, I don't know if you could call it that, Luke,' Elizabeth sighed. 'I don't know where she's gone, sweetheart. She didn't tell anyone before she left.'

'She told me,' he chirped.

'What?' Elizabeth's eyes widened, her heart quickened.

'She came to the house before she went away. She told me she was going away but she didn't

347

know for how long. And I said that's kind of like an adventure and she laughed and said yes.'

'Did she say why?' Elizabeth whispered, surprised that Saoirse had the compassion to say goodbye to her son.

'Mm-hmm,' he nodded, kicking his feet faster now. 'She said because it was best for her and you and Granddad and me because she kept doing the wrong things and making everyone mad. She said she was doing what you always told her to do. She said she was flying away.'

Elizabeth held her breath lightly and remembered how she used to tell her baby sister to fly away when things were tough at home. She remembered how she watched her little six-year-old sister as she drove away to college and told her over and over again to fly away. All her emotions caught in her throat.

'What did you say?' Elizabeth managed to force out, running her hand through Luke's baby-soft hair and feeling and overwhelming urge to protect him more than anything for the first time in her life.

'I told her she was probably right,' Luke replied matter-of-factly. 'She said that I was a big boy now and it was my job to look after you and Granddad.'

Tears fell from her eyes. 'She did?' she sniffed.

Luke lifted his hand and delicately wiped her tear.

'Well, don't you worry,' she kissed his hand and

reached out to hug him, 'because it's my job to look after you, OK?'

His reply was muffled as his head was pushed against her chest. She let go of him quickly to allow him to breathe.

'Edith will be home soon,' he said excitedly after he had taken a deep breath. 'Can't wait to see what she got me.'

Elizabeth smiled, tried quickly to compose herself and cleared her throat. 'We can introduce her to Ivan. Do you think she'll like him?'

Luke wrinkled up his face. 'I don't think she'll be able to see him.'

'We can't keep him to ourselves, you know, Luke,' Elizabeth laughed.

'Anyway, Ivan might not even be here when she gets back,' he added.

Elizabeth's heart thudded, 'What do you mean? Did he say something?'

Luke shook his head.

Elizabeth sighed. 'Oh, Luke, just because you're close to Ivan it doesn't mean he'll leave you, you know. I don't want you to be afraid of that happening. I used to be afraid like that. I used to think that everyone I loved would always go away.'

'*I* won't go away.' Luke looked at her caringly.

'And I promise you I won't go anywhere either.' She kissed him on the head, then cleared her throat. 'You know the things that you and Edith do together, like going to the zoo and the cinema, things like that?'

Luke nodded.

'Would you mind if I came along sometimes?'

Luke smiled happily. 'Yeah, that'd be cool.' He thought for a while. 'We're kind of the same now, aren't we? My mom leaving is kinda like what your mom did, isn't it?' he asked, breathing on the glass table and writing his name in the fog with his finger.

Elizabeth's body grew cold. 'No,' she snapped, 'it's nothing like that at all.' She stood up from the table, switched on the light and started wiping down the counter. 'They are totally different people, it's not the same at all.' Her voice trembled as she scrubbed furiously. Looking up to check on Luke she caught sight of her reflection in the glass of the conservatory and froze. Gone was the composure, gone were her emotions, she looked like a possessed woman hiding from the truth, running from the world.

And then she knew.

And the memories that lurked in the dark corners of her mind began to creep ever so slowly into the light.

Chapter 36

'Opal,' I called gently from her office doorway. She seemed so brittle and I was afraid that the slightest noise would shatter her.

'Ivan.' She smiled tiredly, pinning her dreadlocks back from her face.

I could see myself in her shining eyes as I entered the room. 'We're all worried about you – is there anything we, I can do to help?'

'Thank you, Ivan, but apart from keeping an eye on things around here, there's really nothing anyone can do to help. I'm just so tired. I've been spending the past few nights at the hospital and I haven't allowed myself to sleep. He's got only days left now; I don't want to miss it when he . . .' She looked away from Ivan and to the picture frame on her desk, and when she spoke again her voice was trembling. 'I just wish there was some way I could say goodbye to him, to let him know he's not alone, that I'm by his side.' Her tears fell.

I went to her side and comforted her, feeling helpless and knowing that for once there was absolutely nothing I could do to help this friend. Or was there?

'Hold on a minute, Opal. Maybe there is a way you can. I have an idea.' And with that I ran.

Elizabeth had made last-minute arrangements for Luke to sleep over at Sam's house. She knew she needed to be alone that night. She could feel a change within her; a chill had entered her body and wouldn't leave. She sat huddled up in her bed, wearing an oversized jumper covered by a blanket, desperate to keep warm.

The moon outside her window noticed something was wrong and guarded her protectively from the darkness. Her stomach cramped with anticipation. The things that Ivan and Luke had said today had turned a key in her mind and had unlocked a chest of memories so terrifying that Elizabeth was afraid to close her eyes.

She gazed out the window through the open curtains at the moon, then allowed herself to drift . . .

She was twelve years old. It was two weeks since her mother had brought her for a picnic in the field, two weeks since she had told her she was going away, two weeks of waiting for her to come back. Outside Elizabeth's bedroom a screeching one-month-old Saoirse was held, hushed and comforted by her father.

'Hush now, baby, hush . . .' She could hear his gentle tones getting louder and then quietening as he paced the floor of the bungalow in the late night hour. Outside, the wind howled, squeezing itself through the windows and door locks with a whistling sound. It raced in and danced around the rooms, taunting, teasing and tickling Elizabeth as she lay in her bed, hands over her ears, tears falling down her cheeks.

Saoirse's cries got louder, Brendan's pleas got louder and Elizabeth covered her head with her pillow.

'Please, Saoirse, please stop crying,' her father begged, and attempted a song, a lullaby that Elizabeth's mother always sang to them. She clamped her hands over her ears harder but still could hear Saoirse's cries and her father's tuneless song. Elizabeth sat up in her bed, her eyes stinging from yet another night of tears and lack of sleep.

'You want your bottle?' her father asked gently over the roars. 'No? Ah, love, what is it?' he asked in a pained voice. 'I miss her too, love, I miss her too,' and he too began to cry. Saoirse, Brendan and Elizabeth all cried for Gráinne together, but all feeling alone, in their bungalow blown by the wind.

Suddenly headlights appeared at the end of the long road. Elizabeth leaped out of her covers and sat at the end of her bed with her stomach twisted in excitement. It was her mother – it had to be. Who else would be calling all the way down here at ten o'clock at night? Elizabeth bounced up and down at the end of her bed in delight.

The car pulled up outside the house, the car door opened and out stepped Kathleen, Gráinne's sister. Leaving the door open with the headlights still on and the wipers moving violently across the windscreen, she marched to the gate, pushed it open causing it to creak, and banged on the door.

With a screaming Saoirse in his arms Brendan opened the door. Elizabeth rushed to the keyhole of her bedroom door and looked out into the hall at the action.

'Is she here?' Kathleen demanded, without a hello or a kind word.

'Sshh,' Brendan said, 'I don't want you waking Elizabeth.'

'As if she's not already awake with all that screaming. What have you done to the poor child?' she asked incredulously.

'The child wants her mother,' he raised his voice. 'Like us all,' he added in softer tones.

'Give her to me,' Kathleen said.

'You're wet,' Brendan stepped away from her and his arms tightened around the tiny bundle.

'Is she here?' Kathleen asked again, her voice still angry. She was still standing outside the front door. She hadn't asked to come in and she hadn't been invited.

'Of course she's not here.' Brendan bounced Saoirse around, trying to calm her. 'I thought you'd taken her to that magical place that would cure her for ever,' he said angrily.

'It was supposed to be the best place, Brendan

– better than the other ones, anyhow. Anyway,' she mumbled the next few words, 'she's gone.'

'Gone? What do you mean, gone?'

'She was missing this morning from her room. Nobody's seen her.'

'Has a habit of disappearing in the night, does your mother,' Brendan said angrily, rocking Saoirse. 'Well, if she's not where you sent her, you don't need to look far from here. Sure won't she be in Flanagan's?'

Elizabeth's eyes widened and she gasped. Her mother was here in Baile na gCroíthe; she hadn't left her after all.

In between their bitter exchanges, Saoirse wailed.

'For Christsake, Brendan, can you not quieten her?' Kathleen complained. 'You know I can take the children. They can live with me and Alan in—'

'They're *my* children and you won't take them from me like you did Gráinne,' he bellowed. Saoirse's wails quietened.

There was a long silence.

'Be off with you.' Brendan spoke weakly as though his earlier boom had broken his voice.

The front door closed and Elizabeth watched from the window as Kathleen banged the gate shut and got into her car. It sped off, the lights disappearing into the distance along with Elizabeth's hopes of going with her to see her mother.

A glimmer of hope remained. Her father had

mentioned Flanagan's. Elizabeth knew where that was – she passed it everyday going to school. She would pack her bag, find her mother and live with her away from her screaming little sister and father, and they would go on adventures every day.

The handle on the door shook and she dived into bed and pretended to be asleep. Squeezing her eyes tightly shut, she decided that as soon as her father had gone to bed, she would make her own way to Flanagan's.

She would sneak out into the night, just like her mother.

'Are you sure this is going to work?' Opal stood against the wall of the hospital ward, her hands trembling as they clasped and unclasped themselves against her anxiety-filled stomach.

Ivan looked at her with uncertain eyes. 'It's worth a try.'

Through the glass in the corridor they could see Geoffrey in his private room. He was hooked up to a ventilator, his mouth covered by the oxygen mask, and around him contraptions beeped while wires ran from his body into machines. In the centre of all this action, his body lay still and calm, his chest rising and falling rhythmically. They were surrounded by that eerie sound that only hospitals provided, the sound of everyone waiting, of being in between one timeless place and another.

As soon as the nurses who were tending to

Geoffrey opened the door to leave, Opal and Ivan entered.

'Here she is,' Olivia spoke from beside Geoffrey's bed, as Opal entered.

His eyes shot open quickly and he began to look around wildly, searching the room.

'She's on your left-hand side, dear, she's holding your hand,' Olivia said gently.

Geoffrey attempted to speak, his sound coming out muffled from under the mask. Opal's hand flew to her mouth, her eyes filled and the lump in her throat was visible. It was a language that only Olivia could understand; the words of a dying man.

Olivia nodded as he made sounds; her eyes filled and when she spoke Ivan could no longer stay in the room.

'He said to tell you, that his heart has ached every moment you were apart, dear Opal.'

Ivan stepped out of the room through the open door and walked as quickly as he could down the hall and out of the hospital.

Chapter 37

Outside Elizabeth's bedroom window on Fuchsia Lane, the rain fell, hitting off the bedroom window like pebbles. The wind began warming its vocal chords for the night and Elizabeth, tucked up in bed, was transported back to the time she journeyed out in the late winter night to find her mother.

She had packed her schoolbag with only a few things – underwear, two jumpers and skirts, the book her mother gave her and her teddy. Her money box had revealed £4.42, and after wrapping her raincoat around her favourite floral dress and stepping into her red Wellington boots, she set out into the cold night. She climbed the small garden wall to avoid the sound of the gate alerting her father, who these days slept like the farmyard dog, with one ear pricked. She kept alongside the bushes so as not to be spotted walking up the straight road. The wind pushed and pulled the branches, scraping them against her face and legs, and wet kisses from soggy leaves brushed against her skin. The wind was vicious that night. It whipped her legs and stung her ears and cheeks, blowing against her face so hard it took her breath away. Within minutes of walking up the road, her fingers, nose and lips were numb and her body was freezing to the bone but the thought of seeing her mother that night kept her going. And on she journeyed.

Twenty minutes later she arrived at the bridge to Baile na gCroíthe. She had never seen the town at eleven o'clock at night; it was like a ghost town, dark, empty and silent, as if it were about to bear witness to something and never speak a word of it.

She walked towards Flanagan's with butterflies in her tummy, no longer feeling the lash of the cold, just pure excitement at the thrill of being reunited with her mother. She heard Flanagan's before she saw it; there, and the Camel's Hump, were the only buildings in the village with lights on. From an open window, out floated the sounds of a piano, fiddle, badhrán, and loud singing and laughter, occasional cheers and whoops. Elizabeth giggled to herself; it sounded like everyone was having such fun.

Outside, Aunt Kathleen's car was parked and Elizabeth's legs automatically moved faster. The front door was open and inside there was a small hallway, but the door to the pub, complete with stained glass, was closed. Elizabeth stood in the porch and shook the rain from her coat; hung it up alongside the umbrellas on the rack on the wall. Her black hair was soaking wet and her nose was red and running. The rain had found its way into the top of her boots, and her legs shook from the cold and her feet squelched in the ice-cold pools of water.

The piano stopped suddenly, and there was a loud roar from a crowd of men that made Elizabeth jump.

'Come on, Gráinne, sing us another one,' one man slurred, and they all cheered.

Elizabeth's heart leaped at the sound of her mother's name. She was inside! She was such a beautiful singer. She sang around the house all the time, composing lullabies and nursery rhymes all by herself, and in the mornings Elizabeth loved to lie in her bed and listen to her mother as she hummed around the rooms of the bungalow. But the voice that began in the silence, followed by the rowdy cheers of drunken men, was not the sweet voice of her mother that she knew so well.

In Fuchsia Lane, Elizabeth's eyes darted open and she sat upright in her bed. Outside, the wind howled like a wounded animal. Her heart was hammering in her chest; her mouth was dry and her body clammy. Throwing the covers off her, she grabbed her car keys from the bedside table, ran down the stairs, threw her raincoat around her shoulders and escaped the house to her car. The cold drops of rain hit her, and she remembered why she hated to feel the rain against her face: it reminded her of that night. She hurried to her car, shivering as the wind tossed her hair across her eyes and cheeks, and by the time she sat behind the wheel she was already drenched.

The windscreen wipers lashed across the window furiously as she drove down the dark roads to the town. Driving over the bridge she was faced with the ghost town. Everyone was locked safely inside, in the warmth of their houses and hostels. Apart from the Camel's Hump and Flanagan's there was no nightlife. Elizabeth parked her car and stood across the road from Flanagan's, standing in the cold rain staring across at the building, remembering. Remembering that night.

Elizabeth's ears hurt from the words of the song being sung by the woman. It was crude, the words disgusting, being sung in such crass and dirty tones. Every rude word Elizabeth was taught not to say by her father was winning the plaudits of a boozy, sozzled pack of beasts.

She stood on tiptoes to look through the red of the stained-glass windows to see what awful woman was croaking the awful tune. She was sure her mother would be sitting beside Kathleen, absolutely disgusted.

Elizabeth's heart jumped into her throat and for a moment she fought hard to breathe, for on top of the wooden piano sat her mother, opening her mouth and releasing all those awful words. A skirt she had never seen before was hitched up to her thighs and around her a handful of men taunted, teased and laughed as she threw shapes with her body Elizabeth had never seen any woman do before.

'Now, now, lads, calm down over there,' the young Mr Flanagan called from behind the bar.

The men ignored him, continuing to leer at Elizabeth's mother.

'Mummy,' Elizabeth whimpered.

Elizabeth walked slowly across the road towards Flanagan's pub, her heart beating at the memory so alive in her head. She held out her hand and pushed open the bar door. Mr Flanagan looked up from behind the counter and gave her a small smile, as though he expected to see her.

Young Elizabeth held out a trembling hand and pushed open the door to the bar. Her hair was wet and dripping around her face, her bottom lip out and trembling. Her big brown eyes looked around the room in panic as she saw a man reach out to touch her mother.

'Leave her alone!' Elizabeth shouted so loud the room was quietened. Her mother stopped singing and all heads turned to the little girl standing at the door.

Her mother's corner of the room erupted in such a loud laughter. Tears spilled from Elizabeth's terrified eyes.

'Boo hoo hoo,' her mother sang the loudest of them all. 'Let's all try to save Mummy, shall we?' she slurred. She set her eyes upon Elizabeth. They were bloodshot and dark, not the eyes Elizabeth remembered so well; they belonged to someone else.

'Shit,' Kathleen cursed, jumping up from the other side of the bar and rushing over to Elizabeth, 'What are you doing here?'

'I c-c-c-came t-t-t-to,' Elizabeth stammered in the quietened room, looking at her mother in bewilderment, 'I came to find my mum so I could live with her.'

'Well, she's not here,' her mother shrieked. 'Get out!' She pointed a finger at her accusingly. 'Drowned little rats aren't allowed in pubs,' she cackled, knocking back her glass, but she missed her mouth, causing most of the drink to land down her chest, where it glistened on her neck and replaced the smell of her sweet perfume with whiskey.

'But, Mummy . . .' Elizabeth whimpered.

'But Mummy,' Gráinne imitated and a few of the men laughed. 'I'm not your mummy,' she said harshly, stepping down onto the piano keys and causing a disturbing sound. 'Little drowned Lizzies don't deserve mummies. They should be poisoned, the whole lot of you,' she spat.

'Kathleen,' Mr Flanagan shouted, 'what are you doing? Get her out of here. She shouldn't be seeing this.'

'I can't,' Kathleen stayed rooted to the spot. 'I have to keep an eye on Gráinne, I have to bring her back with me.'

Mr Flanagan's mouth dropped open in shock at her. 'Would you look at the child?'

Elizabeth's brown skin had paled. Her lips were blue from the cold and her teeth were chattering, a soaking wet floral dress clung to her body and her legs shook in her Wellington boots.

Kathleen looked from Elizabeth to Gráinne, caught between the two. 'I can't, Tom,' she hissed.

Tom looked angry. 'I'll have the decency to bring her home myself.' He grabbed a set of keys from under the bar and started to come round the other side to Elizabeth.

'NO!' Elizabeth screamed. She took one look at her mother, who had already become bored by this scene and was lost in the arms of a strange man, turned to face the door and ran back out to the cold night.

Elizabeth stood at the door of the bar, her hair dripping, rain rolling down her forehead and off her nose, her teeth chattering and her fingers numb. The sounds of the room weren't the same. Inside there was no music, no cheers or whoops, no singing, just the sound of an occasional clinking glass and quiet chatter. There were no more than five people in the bar on the quiet Tuesday night.

An aged Tom continued to stare at her.

'My mother –' Elizabeth called out from the door.

The sound of her childlike voice surprised her – 'she was an alcoholic.'

Tom nodded.

'She came in here a lot?'

He nodded again.

'But there were weeks,' she swallowed hard, 'weeks at a time when she wouldn't leave us.'

Tom's voice was soft. 'She was what you'd call a binge drinker.'

'And my father,' she paused, thinking of her poor father who waited and waited at home every night, 'he knew this.'

'The patience of a saint,' he replied.

She looked around the small bar, at the same old piano that stood in the corner. The only thing that had changed in the room was the age of all that was in it.

'That night,' Elizabeth said, her eyes filling with tears, 'thank you.'

Tom just nodded at her sadly.

'Have you seen her since?'

He shook his head.

'Do you . . . do you expect to?' she asked, her voice catching in her throat.

'Not in this lifetime, Elizabeth.' He confirmed for her what she had always felt deep down.

'Daddy . . .' Elizabeth whispered to herself and took off out of the bar back into the cold night.

Little Elizabeth ran from the pub, feeling every drop of rain lash against her body, feeling her chest hurt as she breathed in the cold air and the water splash up her legs as she pounded in the puddles. She was running home.

Elizabeth jumped into her car and sped off out of the town towards the mile-long road that led to her father's bungalow. Approaching headlights meant she had to reverse back the way she had come and wait for the car to pass before she could continue her journey.

Her father had known all this time and he had never told her. He had never wanted her to shatter her illusions of her mother and she had always held her up on a pedestal. She had thought her a free spirit and of her father as a suffocating force, as the butterfly catcher. She needed to get to him quickly, to apologise, to make things right.

She set off again down the road only to see a tractor slowly chugging before her, unusually at this late hour. She reversed the car back to the entrance of the road again. With her impatience rising she abandoned her car and began to run. She ran as fast as she could down the mile-long road that brought her home.

'Daddy,' little Elizabeth sobbed as she ran down the road towards the bungalow. She screamed his name louder, the wind helping her for the first time that night by lifting her words and carrying them for her towards the bungalow. A light went on, followed by another, and she could see the front door open.

'Daddy!' she cried even louder, and ran even faster.

Brendan sat at the window of the bedroom, looking out to the dark night, sipping a cup of tea, hoping among all hopes that the vision he was waiting for would appear. He had chased them all away, he had done exactly the opposite to what he wanted and it was all his fault. All he could do was wait. Wait for one of his three women to appear. One, he knew for certain, would and could never return.

A movement in the distance caught his eye and he sat to attention like a guard dog. A woman ran towards him, long black hair floating behind her, her image blurring as the rain hit against the window and streamed down the glass.

It was her.

He dropped his cup and saucer to the floor and stood up, knocking his chair backward.

'Gráinne,' he whispered.

He grabbed his cane and moved as quickly as his legs would take him to the front door. Pulling the door open, he strained his eyes in the stormy night to see his wife.

He heard the sound of distant panting as the woman ran.

'Daddy,' he heard her say. No she couldn't be saying that, his Gráinne wouldn't say that.

'Daddy,' he heard her sob again.

He was taken back over twenty years by the familiar sounds. It was his little girl, his little girl

367

was running home in the rain again and she needed him.

'Daddy!' she called again.

'I'm here,' he called, quietly at first, and then he shouted louder, 'I'm here!'

He heard her crying, saw her opening the creaking gate, dripping wet, and just as he did over twenty years ago he held out his arms to her and welcomed her into his embrace.

'I'm here, don't you worry,' he soothed her, patting her head and rocking her from side to side. 'Daddy's here.'

Chapter 38

Elizabeth's garden on the day of her birthday was like the scene of the Mad Hatter's tea party in Wonderland. She had one long table set out in the middle of the garden decorated with a red and white tablecloth. Covering every inch of the table was a huge array of plates piled high with cocktail sausages, crisps, chips and dips, sandwiches, salads, cold meats and sweets. The garden had been pruned to within an inch of its life, new flowers had been planted and the air smelled of freshly cut grass mixed with the aroma of the barbecue in the corner. It was a hot day, the sky was an indigo colour with not a cloud in sight, the surrounding hills were a rich emerald green, the sheep upon them like snowflakes, and Ivan felt the pain of having to leave such a beautiful place and the people in it.

'Ivan, I'm so glad you're here.' Elizabeth came charging out of the kitchen.

'Thank you,' Ivan smiled, swirling round to greet her. 'Wow, look at you!' His mouth dropped open. Elizabeth was wearing a simple white linen summer dress that contrasted with her dark skin beautifully; her long hair was lightly curled and hung down past her shoulders. 'Give me a twirl,' Ivan said, still taken aback by her appearance. Her features had softened and everything about her seemed gentler.

'I gave up twirling for men when I was eight. Now stop gawking at me, there's work to be done,' she snapped.

Well, not *everything* about her was gentler.

She looked around the garden, hands on her hips as though she was on patrol.

'OK, let me show you what's happening here.' She grabbed Ivan by the arm and dragged him towards the table.

'When people arrive through the side gate, they come over here first. This is where they collect their napkins, knives, forks and plates, and then they go along here.' She moved on, still clutching his arm and speaking quickly. 'When they get here, *you* will be standing behind this barbecue where you will prepare whatever they choose from *this* selection.' She displayed a side table of meats. 'On the left is soya meat, on the right is regular. *Do not* confuse the two.'

Ivan opened his mouth to protest but she held a finger up and continued, 'Then after they take their burger buns, they move on to the salad *here*. Please note that the sauces for the burgers are *here*.'

Ivan picked up an olive and she slapped his

hand, causing him to drop it back into the bowl. She continued, 'Desserts are over *here*, tea and coffee *here*, organic milk in the left jug, regular milk on the right, toilets through the door on the left *only*; I don't want them traipsing through the house, OK?'

Ivan nodded.

'Any questions?'

'Just one.' He grabbed an olive and popped it into his mouth before she had a chance to steal it from his grasp. 'Why are you telling me all this?'

Elizabeth rolled her eyes. 'Because,' she wiped her clammy hands in a napkin, 'I've never done this whole *hosting* thing before, and seeing as you got me into this mess, I need you to help me.'

Ivan laughed. 'Elizabeth, you will be fine but my barbecuing food will *clearly* not help.'

'Why, don't you have barbecues in Ekam Eveileb?' she asked sarcastically.

Ivan ignored her comment. 'Look, you don't need rules and schedules today. Just let people do what they like, roam the garden, mingle with everyone and choose their food themselves. Who cares if they start at the apple pie?'

Elizabeth looked horrified. 'Start at the apple pie?' she spluttered. 'But that's the wrong end of the table. No, Ivan, you need to tell them where the queue starts and ends. I won't have time.' She rushed towards the kitchen. 'Dad, I hope you're not eating all those cocktail sausages in there,' she called.

'Dad?' Ivan's eyes widened, 'He's here?'

'Yes.' She rolled her eyes but Ivan could tell she didn't mean it. 'It's just as well you weren't here the past few days because I've been up to my eyes in family secrets, tears, break-ups and make-ups. But we're getting there,' she relaxed for a moment and smiled at Ivan. The doorbell rang and she jumped, her face contorting into panic.

'Relax, Elizabeth!' Ivan laughed.

'Come around the side!' she called to the visitor.

'Before they get here I just want to give you a present,' Ivan said, removing his arm from where it had been hiding behind his back. He held out a large red umbrella towards her and her forehead crumpled in confusion.

'It's to protect you from the rain,' Ivan explained softly. 'You could have done with this the other night, I suppose.'

Elizabeth's forehead cleared as the realisation set in. 'That's so thoughtful of you, thank you.' She hugged him. Her head shot up suddenly. 'But how did you know about the other night?'

Benjamin appeared at the gate with a bouquet of flowers and a bottle of wine.

'Happy birthday, Elizabeth.'

She spun round and her cheeks pinked. She hadn't seen him since that day in the building site when Ivan had splattered her alleged love for him in large red letters across the wall.

'Thank you,' she replied, making her way to him.

372

He held the gifts towards her and she struggled to find a way to take them with the umbrella in her hand. Benjamin spotted the umbrella and laughed. 'I don't think you'll need that today.'

'Oh, this?' Elizabeth reddened even more. 'This was a gift from Ivan.'

Benjamin raised his eyebrows. 'Really? You give him a hard time, don't you? I'm beginning to think there's something going on with you two.'

Elizabeth didn't allow her smile to waver. She wished. 'Actually, he's somewhere around here – maybe I can finally get to introduce the two of you properly.' She scanned the garden, wondering why it was Benjamin found her so funny all the time.

'Ivan?' I could hear Elizabeth calling my name.

'Yes,' I replied, not looking up from helping Luke put on his party hat.

'Ivan?' she called again.

'Ye-es,' I said impatiently, standing to my feet and looking at her. Her eyes passed over me and she continued scanning the garden.

My heart stopped beating; I swear I felt it stop.

I took deep breaths and tried not to panic. 'Elizabeth,' I called, my voice so shaky and distant I barely recognised myself.

She didn't turn round. 'I don't know where he's disappeared to. He was here just a minute ago.' She sounded angry. 'He was supposed to get the barbecue ready.'

Benjamin laughed again. 'How appropriate. Well, that's a subtle way of asking me but I can do it, no problem.'

Elizabeth looked at him in confusion, lost in thought. 'OK, great, thanks.' She continued looking around. I watched as Benjamin put the apron on over his head and Elizabeth explained everything to him. I watched from the outside, no longer a part of the picture. People began to arrive and I felt dizzy as the garden filled, as the volume went up, voices and laughter grew louder, the smell of food became stronger. I watched as Elizabeth tried to force Joe to taste some of her flavoured coffee as everyone else looked on and laughed; I watched Elizabeth and Benjamin's heads close together as they shared a secret and then laughed; I watched as Elizabeth's father stood at the end of the garden, blackthorn cane in one hand, cup and saucer in the other as he stared out wistfully to the rolling hills and waited for another of his daughters to return; I watched as Mrs Bracken and her lady friends stood by the dessert table, sneakily taking another slice of cake when they thought that no one was looking.

But I saw them. I saw it all.

I was like a visitor in an art museum, standing in front of a busy painting, trying to make sense of it, loving it so much and wanting to jump in and become a part of it. I was pushed further and further to the back of the garden. My head spun and my knees were weak.

I watched as Luke carried out Elizabeth's

birthday cake, helped by Poppy, and led everyone in singing 'Happy Birthday to You' as Elizabeth's face pinked in surprise and embarrassment. I watched as she looked around for me and couldn't find me, as she closed her eyes, made a wish and blew out the candles like the little girl that never had her twelfth birthday party and who was living it all now. It brought back to me what Opal had said about me never having a birthday, never ageing while Elizabeth did and would this day, every year. The local crowd smiled and cheered as she blew out the candles, but for me they represented the passing of time, and as she extinguished those dancing flames, she extinguished a tiny bit of hope that was left inside me. They represented why we couldn't be together, and that stabbed my heart. The cheery mass celebrated while I commiserated and I couldn't help but be more aware than ever that with every minute that ticked by she was getting older. Me, I just felt it.

'Ivan!' Elizabeth grabbed me from behind. 'Where have you been for the past hour? I've been looking all over for you!'

I was so shocked she acknowledged me I could barely speak. 'I've been here all day,' I said weakly, savouring every second her brown eyes were locked onto mine.

'No you haven't. I've been by this way at least five times and you weren't here. Are you OK?' she looked worried. 'You're very pale.' She felt my forehead. 'Have you eaten?'

I shook my head.

'I've just heated some pizza; let me get you some, OK? What kind do you want?'

'One with olives, please. Olives are by far my favourite.'

She narrowed her eyes and studied me curiously, looking me up and down. Slowly she said, 'OK, I'll go get it but don't go disappearing on me again. There are some people I want to introduce you to, OK?'

I nodded.

Moments later she came rushing out with a huge slice of pizza. It smelled so good, my tummy screamed out with joy and I hadn't even thought I was hungry. I held my hands up to take the luscious slice from her, but her brown eyes darkened, her face hardened and she pulled the plate away. 'Damn it, Ivan, where have you gone now?' she muttered, searching the garden with her eyes.

My knees were so weak now I couldn't keep my body up any more; I just collapsed onto the grass, back up against the wall of the house, leaning my elbows on my knees.

I heard a little whisper in my ear, felt the warm breath and smelled sweets on Luke's breath. 'It's happening, isn't it?'

All I could do was nod.

This is the part where the fun stops. This part is, by far, not my favourite.

Chapter 39

Feeling every mile with every step, every stone and pebble beneath the sole of my foot, and every second that ticked by, I eventually arrived at the hospital, exhausted and totally drained. There was still one friend that needed me.

Olivia and Opal must have seen it in my face when I entered the room; they must have seen the dark colours emanating from my body, the way my shoulders were slumped, the way the entire weight of everything in the atmosphere had suddenly decided to balance itself on my shoulders. I knew from the look in their tired eyes that they knew. Of course they knew – it was all a part of our job. At least twice a year we all met special people who consumed our days and nights and all of our thoughts, and each time with each person, we had to go through the process of losing them. Opal liked to teach us that it wasn't us *losing* them; it was a matter of them moving on. But I couldn't see how I wasn't losing Elizabeth. Without having any control, any ability to make

377

her hold on to me, to still see me, she was slipping through my fingers. What did I win? What did I gain? Every time I left a friend I was as lonely as the day before I met them, and in Elizabeth's case, lonelier, because I knew that I was missing out on the possibility of so much more. And here's the sixty-four-million-dollar question, what do our friends get out of it?

A happy ending?

Would I call Elizabeth's current situation a happy ending? Mothering a six-year-old boy she never wanted, worrying about a missing sister, a mother who had deserted her and a complex father? Wasn't her life the exact same as when I arrived?

But I guess this wasn't Elizabeth's ending. *Remember the detail*, Opal always tells me. I suppose what had changed in Elizabeth's life was her mind, the way she was thinking. All I had done was plant the seed of hope; she alone could help it to grow. And because she was starting to lose sight of me, perhaps that seed was being cultivated.

I sat in the corner of the hospital room watching Opal clinging to Geoffrey's hands as if she was hanging off the edge of the cliff. Perhaps she was. You could see in her face that she was willing for everything to be as it once was; I bet she would have done a deal with a devil right then and there if it would have brought him back. She would have gone to hell and back, she would have faced every single one of her fears just for him, right then.

The things we do to go back in time.

The things we don't do the first time round.

Opal's words were being spoken through Olivia's lips; Geoffrey could no longer speak. Tears were falling from Opal's eyes and landing on his lifeless hands, her bottom lip was trembling. She wasn't ready to let go. She had never let go of him and now it was too late, he was leaving before she had a chance.

She was losing him.

Life seemed dreary to me right then. As depressing as the cracked blue paint on the walls built to hold up a building intended to heal.

Geoffrey slowly raised a hand; you could tell he was mustering all his strength. The movement surprised everyone as he hadn't spoken in days, hadn't reacted to anything at all. No one was more surprised than Opal, who suddenly felt the touch of his hand across her face, as he wiped away her tears. Contact after twenty years. He could finally see her. Opal kissed his large hand and allowed it to cradle her small face and comfort her through her shock, relief and regret.

Geoffrey gave one last gasp, his chest rose one final time and fell, his hand dropping to the bed.

She had lost him and I wondered if Opal was still telling herself that he had merely moved on.

I decided then and there that I needed to have control of my final moment. I needed to say goodbye to Elizabeth properly, tell her the truth about me one final time so she wouldn't think I had run off and deserted her. I didn't want her to spend years being bitter about the man she once loved who broke her heart. No, that would have been too easy for her; that would have given her an excuse to never love again. And she wanted to love again. I didn't want her, like Geoffrey, to wait for ever for my return and finally die a lonely old woman.

Olivia nodded to me encouragingly as I stood up, kissed Opal on the top of her head from where she sat face down on the bed, still grasping his hand and wailing so loudly I knew it was the sound of her heart breaking. I didn't notice until I got out into the chilly air that tears were streaming down my face.

I began to run.

Elizabeth was dreaming. She was in an empty white room and she was dancing around, sprinkling and splashing colours of paint all around her. She was singing the song she hadn't been able to get out of her head for the past two months and she was so happy and free as she leaped around the room, watching the thick pulpous paint land on the walls with a splish-splosh.

'Elizabeth,' a voice was whispering.

She continued to swirl around the room. No one else was there.

'Elizabeth,' the voice whispered, and her body started to rock slightly as she danced.

'Mmm?' she responded happily.

'Wake up, Elizabeth. I need to talk to you,' came the sweet voice.

She opened her eyes slightly, spotted Ivan's worried handsome face beside her, rubbed her hand over his face and for a moment they stared deeply into each other's eyes. She revelled in the look he gave her, tried to return it but lost the battle with sleep and allowed her eyelids to flutter closed again. She was dreaming, she knew that, but she couldn't keep her eyes open.

'Can you hear me?'

'Mmm,' she responded, twirling and twirling and twirling.

'Elizabeth, I came to tell you that I have to go.'

'Why?' she murmured sleepily. 'You just got here. Sleep.'

'I can't. I'd love to but I can't. I've got to go. Remember I told you this would happen?'

She felt his warm breath on her neck, smelled his skin; fresh and sweet as though he had bathed in blueberries.

'Mmm,' she replied, 'Ekam Eveileb,' she stated, painting blueberries across the wall, reaching her hand to the paint and tasting it as though it was freshly squeezed.

'Something like that. You don't need me any more, Elizabeth,' he said softly. 'You're going to stop seeing me now. Someone else will need me.'

She ran a hand across his jawline, felt his soft stubble-free skin. She ran the length of the room, running her hand along the red paint. This tasted like strawberries. She looked down to the can of

381

paint in her hand and spotted them – fresh strawberries piled high.

'I've figured something out, Elizabeth. I've figured out what my life is all about and it's not that different to yours.'

'Mmm,' she smiled.

'Life is made up of meetings and partings. People come into your life everyday, you say good morning, you say good evening, some stay for a few minutes, some stay for a few months, some a year, others a whole lifetime. No matter who it is, you meet and then you part. I'm so glad I met you, Elizabeth Egan; I'll thank my lucky stars for that. I think I wished for you all of my life,' he whispered. 'But now it's time for us to part.'

'Mmm,' she murmured sleepily. 'Don't go.' He was with her now in the room, they were chasing each other, splashing each other, teasing one another. She didn't want him to go; she was having so much fun.

'I have to go,' his voice cracked. 'Please understand.'

The tone of his voice made her stop running. She dropped the paint brush. It fell to the floor, leaving a red smudge on the brand-new white carpet. She looked up at him; his face was crumpled in sadness.

'I loved you the moment I saw you and I will always love you, Elizabeth.'

She felt him kiss her below her left ear, so soft and sensual she didn't want him to stop.

'I love you too,' she said sleepily.

But he did stop. She looked around the paint-splattered room and he was gone.

Her eyes flew open at the sound of her voice. Had she just said 'I love you?' She leaned up on one elbow and groggily looked around the bedroom.

But the room was empty. She was alone. The sun was rising over the tips of the mountains, night had ended and it was the start of a new day. She closed her eyes and continued dreaming.

Chapter 40

One week on from that morning and Elizabeth found herself moping around the house in her pyjamas, dragging her slipper-clad feet from room to room early on a Sunday morning. She stood at the doorway of each room, gazed inside and searched for . . . something, although she didn't quite know what for. None of these rooms offered her any solution and so she wandered on. Warming her hands on a mug of coffee, she stood still in the hallway, trying to decide what to do. She didn't usually move so slowly and her mind had never felt so clouded before, but she was a lot of things now that she never used to be.

It wasn't as though she didn't have things to do; the house was due its bi-weekly scrub from top to bottom and there was still the problem of the children's room in the hotel to be completed. Never mind completing it, it wasn't even started. Vincent and Benjamin had been on her back all week, she was losing even more sleep than usual because she had simply no idea what to do and, being the perfectionist, she couldn't begin it unless it was completely clear in her mind. To pass this on to Poppy would be a failure on her part. She was a talented professional woman, but this month she had felt like a schoolgirl again, ignoring her pencils and pens and avoiding her laptop so she didn't have to do her homework. She was looking for a distraction, a decent excuse to drag her away for once from the mindless block she found herself in.

She hadn't seen Ivan since her party last week; she hadn't received a phone call, a letter, nothing. It was as though he had disappeared off the face of the earth, and as well as being angry, she felt lonely. She missed him.

It was seven o'clock in the morning and the playroom was alive with the sounds of cartoons. Elizabeth made her way down the hall and popped her head into the room.

'Mind if I join you?' *I promise I won't say anything,* she felt like adding.

Luke look surprised but shook his head. He sat on the floor, straining his neck up to see the television. It looked uncomfortable but she chose silence instead of criticising him. She collapsed on the beanbag beside him and tucked her legs close to her body.

'What are you watching?'

'*SpongeBob Squarepants.*'

'*Sponge* what?' she laughed.

'*SpongeBob Squarepants,*' he repeated, not taking his eyes away from the television.

'What's it about?'

'A sponge called Bob who wears square pants,' he giggled.

'Any good?'

'Mm-hmm,' he nodded. 'Seen it before twice, though.' He spooned Rice Krispies into his mouth messily, spilling milk down his chin.

'Why are you watching it again? Why don't you go out into the fresh air and play with Sam? You've been inside all weekend.'

She was greeted with silence.

'Actually, where is Sam? Is he away?'

'We're not friends any more,' Luke said sadly.

'Why not?' she asked in surprise, sitting up and placing her coffee cup on the floor.

Luke shrugged.

'Did you have a fight?' Elizabeth asked gently.

Luke shook his head.

'Did he say something to make you sad?' she probed.

He shook his head again.

'Did you make him mad?'

Another shake of the head.

'Well, what happened?'

'Nothing,' Luke explained. 'He just told me one day he didn't want to be my friend any more.'

'Well, that's not very nice,' Elizabeth said gently. 'Do you want me to talk to him for you, see what's wrong?'

Luke shrugged. There was a silence between them as he continued staring at the screen, lost in thought.

'You know, I know what it's like to miss a friend, Luke. You know my friend Ivan?'

'He was my friend too.'

'Yes,' she smiled. 'Well, I miss him. I haven't seen him all week either.'

'Yeah, he's gone now. He told me so; he has to help someone else now.'

Elizabeth's eyes widened and anger welled inside her. He hadn't even the decency to say goodbye to her. 'When did he say goodbye to you? What did he say?' From the startled look on Luke's face she immediately stopped firing questions so aggressively. She needed to keep reminding herself that he was only six.

'He said goodbye to me the same day as he said goodbye to you.' His voice went up a pitch as though she was crazy. His face crumpled up and he looked at her as though she'd ten heads, and if she hadn't been so confused she would have laughed at the sight of him.

But inside she wasn't laughing. She paused and thought for a moment and then exploded. 'What! What are you talking about?'

'After the party in the garden, he came to the house and he told me that his job with us was finished, that he was going to be invisible again like he used to be but he would still be around and that meant that we were OK.' He spoke chirpily turning his attention back to the television.

'Invisible,' Elizabeth said the word like it had a bad taste.

'Yep,' Luke chirped. 'Well, people don't call him imaginary for no reason, doh!' He hit himself on the head and fell over onto the ground.

'What is he putting into your head?' she grumbled angrily, wondering if she was wrong to introduce a person like Ivan into Luke's life. 'When is he coming back?'

Luke lowered the volume on the TV and turned to her with that crazy look on his face again. 'He's not. He told you that already.'

'He didn't . . .' Her voice failed her.

'He did, in your bedroom. I saw him go in; I heard him talking.'

Elizabeth cast her mind back to that night and to the dream she had, the dream she had been thinking about all week, the dream that had been *bothering* her and suddenly realised with a sinking feeling in her heart that it hadn't been a dream at all.

She had lost him. In her dreams and in real life, she had lost Ivan.

Chapter 41

'Hello, Elizabeth.' Sam's mother opened her front door wider and welcomed her in.

'Hi, Fiona,' Elizabeth said, stepping in. Fiona had been taking Elizabeth's relationship with Ivan so well during the past few weeks. They hadn't discussed it directly but Fiona was being as polite as she always was. Elizabeth was thankful there was no awkwardness between them. Unfortunately, she was worried Sam hadn't taken it as well. 'I came round to have a chat with Sam, if that's OK. Luke is so upset without him.'

Fiona looked at her sadly. 'I know, I've been trying to talk to him all week about it. Maybe you can do a better job than me.'

'Has he told you what their falling-out is about?'

Fiona tried to hide a smile and nodded.

'Is it about Ivan?' Elizabeth asked, worried. She had always been anxious that Sam would be jealous of the amount of time Ivan was spending with her and Luke, and so she had invited him over to the house and included him in Ivan's activities as much as possible.

'Yes,' Fiona confirmed with a broad smile. 'Children can be funny at that age, can't they?' Elizabeth relaxed at finally learning Fiona hadn't a problem with the time she and Luke spent with Ivan, and was putting it down to Sam's behaviour.

'I'll let him tell you in his own words,' she continued, leading Elizabeth through her home.

Elizabeth had to fight the urge to look round to see if Ivan was there. As much as she was here to help Luke she was also trying to help herself. Finding and returning two best friends was better than one and she ached to be with Ivan so much.

Fiona pushed open the playroom door and Elizabeth entered. 'Sam, honey, Luke's mom is here to talk to you,' Fiona said gently, and for the first time, Elizabeth experienced a warm glow when she heard those words.

Sam paused the PlayStation and looked up at her with sad brown eyes. Elizabeth bit on her lip and fought the urge to smile. Fiona left them alone to talk.

'Hi, Sam,' she said gently. 'Mind if I sit down?'

He shook his head and she balanced herself on the edge of the couch.

'Luke tells me you don't want to be his friend any more, is that right?'

Unashamedly, he nodded his head.

'Do you want to tell me why?'

He took a moment to ponder that and then nodded. 'I don't like to play the same games as him.'

'Did you tell him this?'

He nodded.

'And what did he say?'

Sam looked confused and shrugged his shoulders. 'He is weird.'

A lump formed in Elizabeth's throat and she was immediately defensive. 'What do you mean, weird?'

'At first it was funny but then it just got boring and I didn't want to play any more but Luke wouldn't stop.'

'What game is that?'

'The games with his *invisible friend*.' He put on a bored voice and made a face.

Elizabeth's hands grew clammy. 'But his invisible friend was only around for a few days, and that was months ago, Sam.'

Sam gave her a funny look. 'But you played with him too.'

Elizabeth's eyes widened. 'Excuse me?'

'Ivan whatshisface,' he grumbled, 'boring old Ivan who just wants to spin on chairs all day, or have mud fights or play chasing. Every single day it was Ivan, Ivan, Ivan and,' his already squeaky voice raised a pitch, 'I couldn't even see him!'

'What?' Elizabeth was confused. 'You couldn't see him? What do you mean?'

Sam thought hard about how he could explain

that. 'I mean, I couldn't see him,' he said simply, shrugging his shoulders.

'But you played with him all the time.' She ran her clammy fingers through her hair.

'Yeah, because Luke was, but I got sick of pretending and Luke wouldn't stop. He kept saying he was *real*.' He rolled his eyes.

Elizabeth placed her fingers on the bridge of her nose. 'I don't know what you mean, Sam. Ivan is your mum's friend, is he not?'

Sam's eyes widened. He had a startled expression. 'Eh, nope.'

'No?'

'No,' he confirmed.

'But Ivan minded you and Luke. He collected you and brought you home,' Elizabeth stammered.

Sam looked worried. 'I'm allowed to walk home by myself, Ms Egan.'

'But the, eh, the, em . . .' Elizabeth suddenly snapped to attention, remembering something. She clicked her fingers, making Sam jump. 'The water fight – what about the water fight in the back garden? It was you, me, Luke and Ivan, remember that?' she probed. 'Remember, Sam?'

His face paled. 'There was only three of us.'

'What?' she shouted louder than she meant to.

Sam's face crumpled up and he began to cry silently.

'Oh, no,' she panicked, 'please don't cry, Sam, I didn't mean to.' She held her hands out to him but he ran towards the door, shouting for his mother. 'Oh, I'm sorry, Sam. Please stop. Ssshhh,' she said quietly. 'Oh God,' she groaned, listening as Fiona hushed him.

Fiona entered the room.

'I'm sorry, Fiona,' Elizabeth apologised.

'It's OK.' Fiona looked a little worried. 'He's a bit sensitive about it.'

'I understand,' Elizabeth gulped. 'About Ivan,' she swallowed again and stood to her feet, 'you know him, don't you?'

Fiona's brow wrinkled. 'What do you mean by "know him"?'

Elizabeth's heart raced. 'I mean, he's been around here before?'

'Oh, yes,' Fiona smiled, 'he was here many times with Luke. We even had him over for dinner,' she winked.

Elizabeth relaxed but was unsure of how to interpret the wink. She placed her hand on her heart and it began to slow down. 'Phew, Fiona, thank God,' she laughed with relief. 'For a minute there, I thought *I* was going mad.'

'Oh, don't be silly,' Fiona placed a hand on her arm. 'We all do it, you know. When Sam was two years old, he went through the exact same thing. Rooster, he called his little friend,' she beamed. 'So, believe me, I know exactly what you're going through, opening car doors, cooking extra dinners and setting an extra place at the table. Don't worry, I understand. You were right to play along.'

Elizabeth's head was beginning to spin but Fiona's voice kept going on and on.

'When you think about it, it's *such* a waste of food really, isn't it? It just sits there through the entire meal completely untouched and, *believe* me, I know, I was keeping an eye on it. I'll have no spooky invisible men in this house, thank you very much!'

Moisture was rising to Elizabeth's throat. She grabbed the corner of the chair to steady herself.

'But like I said earlier, that's six-year-olds for you. I'm sure this so-called Ivan will disappear in time; they say they don't last for more than two months really. He should be gone soon, don't you worry.' She finally stopped talking but moved her face quizzically towards Elizabeth, 'Are you OK?'

'Air,' Elizabeth gasped. 'I just need to get some air.'

'Of course,' Fiona said hurriedly, leading her towards the front door.

Elizabeth charged outside, taking in big gulps of air.

'Can I get you a glass of water?' Fiona asked worriedly, rubbing her back as Elizabeth leaned over facing the ground, with her hands resting on her knees.

'No, thanks,' she said quietly, standing up. 'I'll be OK.' She wandered unsteadily down the path without a goodbye, leaving Fiona staring after her nervously.

Once back in her own house, Elizabeth slammed

the front door behind her and slid down to the floor with her head in her hands.

'Elizabeth, what's wrong?' Luke asked worriedly, still in his pyjamas and barefoot as he stood before her.

She couldn't answer. She could do nothing but go through the past few months over and over in her mind – all her special memories and moments with Ivan, all their conversations together. Who was there with them, who had seen them, spoken to him. They had been in crowded places, people had seen them together, Benjamin had seen them, and Joe had seen them. She kept on thinking back over everything, trying to remember moments when Ivan had conversations with all of these people. She couldn't be imagining all this. She was a sane, responsible woman.

Her face was pale as she finally looked up to face Luke.

'Ekam Eveileb,' was all she could say.

'Yep,' Luke giggled. 'It's backwards language. Cool, isn't it?'

It took Elizabeth seconds to work it out.

Make Believe.

Chapter 42

'Come *on*,' Elizabeth shouted, pounding on her horn, to the two coaches inching by each other slowly on the main street of Baile na gCroíthe. It was September and the last of the tourists were passing through the town. After this the busy place would return to its usual silence, like a banquet hall the morning after a party, leaving the locals to tidy up and remember the events and people that came through. The students would be heading back to college in the neighbouring counties and towns and the locals would once again be alone to struggle with their businesses.

Elizabeth held her hand down on her horn and blasted it at the coach before her. A sea of foreign faces turned around in the back of the bus to glare at her. Beside her, the locals spilled out of the church after attending morning Mass. Taking advantage of the glorious sunny day they gathered around in groups on the street, chatting and catching up on the week's events. They too turned to stare at the source of the angry beeping but Elizabeth didn't care. She was following no rules today; she was desperate to get to Joe's as she knew Joe at least could admit to seeing Ivan and her together, putting an end to this cruel and bizarre joke.

Too impatient to wait for the coaches to pass one other, leaving the car in traffic, she jumped out and ran across the road to the café.

'Joe!' she called, charging in through the door. She couldn't keep the panic out of her voice.

'Ah, there ye are, just the woman I was lookin' for.' Joe stepped out from the kitchen. 'I want to show ye my new fancy machine. It's—'

'I don't care,' she butted in, breathlessly, 'I've no time. Just please answer me this question. You remember me being in here with a man a few times, don't you?'

Joe looked up to the ceiling in thought, feeling important.

Elizabeth held her breath.

'Aye, I do.'

Elizabeth breathed a sigh of relief. 'Thank *God*,' she laughed, a little too hysterically.

'Now could you pay attention to me new device,' he said proudly. 'It's a brand-new coffee-makin' machine. Makes these espressos and cap'chinos and all.' He picked up an espresso cup. 'Sure that would only hold a drip. Brings a whole new meanin' to the phrase "hot drop".'

Elizabeth laughed, so happy about the news about Ivan and the coffee she could have jumped over the counter and kissed him.

'So where is this man?' Joe asked, trying to figure out how to make Elizabeth an espresso.

Elizabeth's smile faded. 'Oh, I don't know.'

'Gone back to America, is he? Sure, doesn't he live there in New York? The Big Apple, don't they call it? I've seen it on the telly and if you ask me it looks nothin' like an apple at all.'

Elizabeth's heart pounded in her chest. 'No, Joe, *not Benjamin*. You're thinking of Benjamin.'

'The fella you had drinks with in here a few times,' Joe confirmed.

'No,' Elizabeth's anger rose. 'Well, yes, I did. But I'm talking about the other man who was with me here. *Ivan* is his name. I-v-a-n,' she repeated slowly.

Joe made a face and shook his head. 'Don't know an Ivan.'

'Yes you do,' she said rather forcefully.

'Listen here,' Joe took off his reading glasses and put down the manual, 'I know just about everyone in this town and I don't know an Ivan nor have I ever heard of one.'

'But, Joe,' Elizabeth pleaded, 'please think back.' Then she remembered. 'The day we splashed coffee all around outside – that was Ivan.'

'Oh.' Joe understood now. 'Part of the German crowd, was he?'

'No!' Elizabeth shouted in frustration.

'Well, where's he from?' Joe asked, trying to calm her.

'I don't know,' she said angrily.

'Well, what's his surname then?'

Elizabeth swallowed hard. 'I-I-I don't know that either.'

'Sure then how can I help you at all if you don't know his surname or where he's from? It doesn't sound much like you know him either. As far as I remember you were dancin' around out there on your own like a mad woman. Don't know what got into you that day, at all.'

Elizabeth suddenly had an idea, grabbed her car keys from the counter and ran out the door.

'But what about your hot drop?' he called as she banged the door behind her.

'Benjamin,' Elizabeth called out, banging her car door shut and running across the gravel to him. He was standing among a group of builders hunched over documents, which were spread across a table. They all looked up at her.

'Can I talk to you for a minute?' She was breathless and her hair danced around her face from the strength of the wind at the top of the hill.

'Sure,' he said, stepping away from the silent group and leading her to a quieter area. 'Is everything OK?'

'Yes,' she nodded uncertainly, 'I just want to ask you a question, is that OK?'

He braced himself.

'You've met my friend Ivan, right?' She cracked her knuckles and shuffled from foot to foot, in anticipation of his answer.

He adjusted his hard hat, studied her face and

waited for her to laugh or tell him she was joking but no smile hid behind those dark and worried eyes. 'Is this a joke?'

She shook her head and chewed nervously on the inside of her cheek, brow furrowed.

He cleared his throat. 'Elizabeth, I don't really know what you want me to say.'

'The truth,' she said quickly, 'I want you to tell me the truth. Well, I want you to tell me you've seen him, but I want that to be the truth, you see.' She swallowed.

Benjamin studied her face some more and eventually shook his head slowly.

'No?' she asked quietly.

He shook his head again.

Her eyes filled and she looked away quickly.

'Are you OK?' He reached out to touch her arm but she swayed her body away. 'I assumed you were joking about him,' Benjamin said gently, slightly confused.

'You didn't see him at the meeting with Vincent?'

He shook his head.

'At the barbecue last week?'

Another shake.

'Walking through the town with me? In the playroom that day when that, that . . . *thing* was written on the wall?' she asked hopefully, her voice full of emotion.

'No, I'm sorry,' Benjamin said kindly, trying to hide his confusion as best he could.

She looked away again, turned her back on him

to face out towards the view. From this point she could see the sea, the mountains and the neat little village tucked away in the bosom of the hills.

Finally she spoke. 'He was so real, Benjamin.'

He didn't know what to say so he remained silent.

'You know when you can feel someone with you? And even though not everyone believes in that person, you know they're there?'

Benjamin thought about it and nodded understandingly even though she couldn't see him. 'My granddad died and we were close.' He kicked at the gravel self-consciously. 'My family never agreed on much – they never believed much in anything – but I knew he was there with me at times. You knew Ivan well?'

'He knew me better,' she laughed lightly.

Benjamin heard her sniff and she wiped her eyes.

'So was he a real person? Did he pass away?' Benjamin asked, feeling confused.

'I just believed so much . . .' she trailed off. 'He's really helped me over the past few months.' She looked around at the view for another moment in silence. 'I used to hate this town, Benjamin,' a tear rolled down her cheek. 'I used to hate every single blade of grass on every hill, but he taught me so much. He taught me that it's not the job of this town to make me feel happy. It's not Baile na gCroíthe's fault that I don't feel I fit in. It doesn't matter where you are in the world because it's about where you are up here,' she touched the side of her head lightly. 'It's about the other world I inhabit. The world of dreams, hope, imagination and memories. I'm happy up here,' she tapped her temple again and smiled, 'and because of that I'm happy up here too.' She held out her arms and displayed the countryside around her. She closed her eyes and allowed the wind to dry her tears. Her face was softer when she turned to Benjamin. 'I just thought it was important for you of all people to know that.' Quietly and slowly she headed back to her car.

Leaning against the old tower Benjamin watched her walk away. He hadn't known Elizabeth as well as he'd have liked but he had an idea she'd let him in her life more than she'd let others. Likewise, he had done the same. They'd had enough conversations for him to see how similar they really were. He'd seen her grow and change and now his unsettled friend had settled. He stared out to the view Elizabeth had been looking at for so long, and for the first time in the year he'd been here he opened his eyes and saw it.

In the early hours of the morning Elizabeth sat up in her bed, wide awake. She looked around the room – saw the time, 3.45 – and when she spoke aloud to herself, her voice was firm and confident.

'To hell with you all. I *do* believe.'

She threw off the covers and jumped out of bed, imagining the sound of Ivan howling with laughter in celebration.

Chapter 43

'Where's Elizabeth?' Vincent Taylor hissed angrily at Benjamin, out of earshot of the crowd that had gathered for the opening of the new hotel.

'She's still in the kids' room,' Benjamin sighed, feeling the cement of the building wall of pressure from the last week finally dry and lay heavy on his aching shoulders.

'*Still?*' Vincent shouted, and a few people turned round from paying attention to the speech being made at the top of the room. The local politician from Baile na gCroíthe had come to open the hotel officially, and a few speeches were being made beside the original tower in the hotel grounds that had stood at the top of the mountain for thousands of years. Soon the crowd would be trampling through the hotel, looking in each room to admire the work, and the two men still didn't know what Elizabeth was up to in the playroom. The last time either of them had seen it was four days ago and it had still been a blank canvas.

Elizabeth literally hadn't come out of that room

for the past few days. Benjamin had brought her some drinks and food from a vending machine and she had hastily grabbed it from him at the door and slammed it shut again. He had no idea what the interior was like and his life had been hellish all week, trying to deal with a panicking Vincent. The novelty of Elizabeth speaking to an invisible person had long since worn off on Vincent. He had never had rooms being worked on during the very moment the building was being opened, it was a ridiculous and extremely unprofessional situation.

The speeches finally finished, there was polite clapping and the crowd filed inside where they inspected the new furniture, everyone inhaling the smell of fresh paint as they were led round.

Vincent swore loudly over and over again, receiving angry glances from parents. Room by room, they got closer to the playroom. Benjamin could barely take the suspense and paced the floor behind the crowd. He recognised Elizabeth's father, looking bored while leaning on his blackthorn cane, and her nephew with his nanny, among the crowd and he hoped to God she wouldn't let them all down. Judging by their last conversation on top of the hill, he believed she would come through for them. At least he hoped so. He was due to fly back to his hometown in Colorado next week and he couldn't take having to deal with any delays on site. For once, his personal life would come before his work.

'OK, boys and girls,' the guide spoke as if she were in an episode of *Barney*, 'this next room is especially for *you* so, moms and dads, you'll have to take a few steps back to allow them through because this is a very *special* room.'

There were oohs and aahs, excited giggles and whispers as the children let go of their parents' hands, some shyly, some daringly racing to the front. The guide turned the handle on the door. It didn't open.

'Jesus Christ,' Vincent muttered, placing his hand over his eyes, 'we're ruined.'

'Eh, just a minute, girls and boys.' The guide looked questioningly at Benjamin.

He just shrugged and shook his head hopelessly.

The guide tried the door again but to no avail.

'Maybe you should knock,' one child shouted out, and the parents laughed.

'You know what, that's a very good idea.' The guide played along, not knowing what else to do.

She knocked once on the door and suddenly it was pulled open from the other side. The children slowly shuffled forward.

There was complete silence and Benjamin covered his face in his hands. They were in big trouble.

Suddenly one child let out a 'Wow!' and one by one, the hushed and stunned children gradually began calling excitedly to one another: 'Look at that!', 'Look over there!'

The children looked around the room in awe. The parents followed them in and Vincent and

Benjamin looked at each other in surprise as they heard similar whispers of approval. Poppy stood at the doorway, her eyes darting about, her mouth open wide in total shock.

'Let me see this,' Vincent said rudely, pushing his way through the crowd. Benjamin followed and what he saw inside took his breath away.

The walls of the large room were covered with enormous murals of splendid bursts of colour, each wall with a different scene. One wall in particular was a familiar sight to him: three people happily jumping in a field of long grass, their arms held upward, bright smiles on their face, their hair blowing in the wind as they reached up to catch –

'Jinny Joes!' Luke exploded with excitement, his eyes popping along with those of the other children in the room. They were mostly silent as they all stood alone, looking at the detail on each wall. 'Look, it's *Ivan* in the picture!' he shouted to Elizabeth.

Stunned, Benjamin looked at Elizabeth, who was standing in the corner in scruffy denim overalls, splattered in paint, with dark circles under her eyes. But despite her apparent tiredness, she was beaming, her face alight from the visitors' reaction to the room. The pride in her shining eyes was evident as everyone pointed to each painting.

'Elizabeth!' Edith whispered, her hands flying to her mouth in shock. '*You* did all this?' She looked at her employer with both confusion and pride.

Another scene was of a little girl in a field

watching a pink balloon floating up to the sky; in another a crowd of children were having a water fight, splattering paint and dancing on the sand on a beach, a little girl sat in a green field having a picnic with a cow who wore a straw hat, a group of young boys and girls climbed trees and hung from its branches, and on the ceiling Elizabeth had painted it a deep blue with shooting stars, comets and distant planets. On the far wall she had painted a man and a boy with magnifying glasses held up to their eyes and black moustaches, leaning over and studying a set of black footprints that led from the wall, all the way across the floor and up the wall on the other side. She had created a new world, a wonderland of escapism, fun and adventure but it was the attention to detail, the looks of glee on the characters' faces, the happy smiles of pure childish enjoyment, that jumped out at Benjamin. Such a face he had seen on Elizabeth when he had caught her dancing in the field and traipsing through the village with seaweed in her hair. It was the face of someone who had let go and was truly happy.

Elizabeth looked down at the floor, to a toddler who was playing with one of the many toys scattered throughout the room. She was about to bend down to talk to the little girl when she noticed that the girl was speaking to herself. Carrying out a very serious conversation, in fact, she was introducing herself to mid-air.

Elizabeth looked around the room, breathed in deeply, and tried to smell that familiar Ivan smell. 'Thank you,' she whispered, closing her eyes and imagining him with her.

The little girl continued babbling away all by herself, looking to her right as she spoke and listening before speaking again. And then she began to hum, that familiar song that Elizabeth hadn't been able to get out of her head.

Elizabeth threw her head back and laughed.

I stood at the back wall of the playroom in the new hotel with tears in my eyes and a lump so huge in my throat I didn't think I'd ever be able to speak again. I couldn't stop looking around at the walls, at the photo album of all I had done with Elizabeth and Luke over the past few months. It was as though someone had sat in the distance and painted a perfect vision of us.

Looking at the walls, at the colour and at the eyes of the characters, I knew that she had realised and I knew that I would be remembered. Beside me, standing in a line at the back of the room, my friends joined me for moral support on this special day.

Opal placed a hand on my arm and gave me an encouraging squeeze.

'I'm very proud of you, Ivan,' she whispered, and planted a kiss on my cheek, no doubt leaving a purple lipstick stain on my skin. 'We're all here for you, you know. We will always have each other.'

408

'Thank you, Opal. I know that,' I said, feeling very emotional and looking to Calendula, who was on my right, Olivia, who was beside her, Tommy, who was looking around the walls in fascination, Jamie-Lynn, who had bent down to play with a toddler on the ground and Bobby, who pointed and giggled at each of the scenes before him. They all gave me the thumbs-up and I knew that I would never be truly alone as I was in the company of real friends.

Imaginary friend, invisible friend – call us what you like. Maybe you believe in us, maybe you don't. The point is, it's not important. Like most people who do truly great work, we don't exist to be talked about and praised; we exist only to serve the needs of those who need us. Maybe we don't exist at all; maybe we're just a figment of people's imaginations; maybe it's just pure coincidence that children of two, who can barely speak, all decide to start making friends with people only adults can't see. Maybe all those doctors and psychotherapists are right to suggest that they are merely developing their imagination.

Or humour me for a second. Is there possibly another explanation that you haven't thought about for the entirety of my story?

The possibility that we do exist. That we're here to help and assist those who need us, who believe in believing and who can therefore see us.

I always look on the positive side of things. I always say that with every cloud there's a silver lining but, the truth be told – and I'm a firm believer of the truth – for a while I was struggling with my experience with Elizabeth. I couldn't figure out what I had won, all I could see was that my losing her was one big black stormy cloud. But then I realised that, as every day went by and I thought about her every second and smiled, I knew that meeting her, knowing her and above all loving her, was the biggest silver lining of all.

She was better than pizza, better than olives, better than Fridays and better than spinning and even these days when she is no longer with us – and I'm not supposed to say this – of all my friends, Elizabeth Egan was *by far* my favourite.